Finding
Perfect

Also by Colleen Hoover

SLAMMED SERIES
Slammed
Point of Retreat
This Girl

HOPELESS SERIES
Hopeless
Losing Hope
Finding Cinderella
Finding Perfect

MAYBE SOMEDAY SERIES
Maybe Someday
Maybe Not
Maybe Now

IT ENDS WITH US SERIES
It Ends with Us
It Starts with Us

STAND-ALONES
Ugly Love
Confess
November 9
Without Merit
All Your Perfects
Too Late
Regretting You
Heart Bones
Layla
Verity
Reminders of Him

Also by Colleen Hoover and Tarryn Fisher
Never Never: The Complete Series

Finding Perfect

A Novella

Colleen Hoover

ATRIA PAPERBACK

NEW YORK LONDON TORONTO SYDNEY NEW DELHI

ATRIA
PAPERBACK

An Imprint of Simon & Schuster, Inc.
1230 Avenue of the Americas
New York, NY 10020

This Atria Paperback edition June 2022

ATRIA PAPERBACK and colophon are trademarks of Simon & Schuster, Inc.

For information about special discounts for bulk purchases, please contact Simon & Schuster Special Sales at 1-866-506-1949 or business@simonandschuster.com.

The Simon & Schuster Speakers Bureau can bring authors to your live event. For more information or to book an event, contact the Simon & Schuster Speakers Bureau at 1-866-248-3049 or visit our website at www.simonspeakers.com.

Manufactured in China

1 3 5 7 9 10 8 6 4 2

Library of Congress Control Number: 2022941208

ISBN 978-1-6680-1338-0
ISBN 978-1-6680-1339-7 (ebook)

This is dedicated to Maggie.
You know what you did.

Note to the Reader

This novella focuses on characters in both *Finding Cinderella* and *All Your Perfects*. This will make more sense once you've read both of the novels that this novella ties together. For the best reading experience, the correct order is *Hopeless*, *Losing Hope*, *Finding Cinderella*, *All Your Perfects*, and then *Finding Perfect*. Please note that *All Your Perfects* can also be read as a standalone. Thank you and happy reading!

Finding
Perfect

Chapter One

"That's three for me," Breckin says, dropping his Xbox controller. "I really need to go home now."

I pick up the controller and try to hand it back to him. "Just one more," I say. Or *beg*, really. But Breckin already has on his ridiculous puffy jacket and is making his way to my bedroom door.

"Call Holder if you're this bored," he says.

"He and Sky had Thanksgiving dinner at his dad's house yesterday. They won't be back until tonight."

"Then ask Six to come over. I've hung out with you enough today to last me until Christmas break. I have family shit tonight."

That makes me laugh. "You said *shit*."

Breckin shrugs. "Yeah. It's Thanksgiving. I have family shit."

"I thought Mormons couldn't swear."

Breckin rolls his eyes and opens my bedroom door. "Bye, Daniel."

"Wait. You coming Saturday?" On our drive home from school a couple days ago, Holder suggested we do a Friendsgiving while we're home on Thanksgiving break. Sky and Six are going to cook. *Which means we'll probably end up ordering pizza.*

"Yeah, I'll be there. But only if you stop pointing out my religious flaws."

"Deal. And I'll never call you Powder Puff again if you stay and play one more game with me."

Breckin looks bored with me. I don't blame him. I'm bored with myself.

"You need to go somewhere," he says. "You've been playing video games for twelve hours. It's starting to smell like a waffle cone in here."

"Why do you say that like it's a bad thing?"

"I meant it in a bad way." Breckin closes my bedroom door and I'm alone again.

So alone.

I fall back onto my bedroom floor and stare up at the ceiling for a while. Then I look at my phone and there's nothing. Six hasn't texted me at all today. I haven't texted her either, but I'm waiting for her to text me first. Things have been weird between us for the past couple months now. I was hoping it was because we were in a new setting, both in our first semesters of college, but she was quiet on the drive home, too.

She had family shit yesterday and hasn't even invited me over today.

I feel like she's about to break up with me.

I don't know why. I've never had a girl break up with me. I'm the one who broke up with Val, but I would think this is what it's like just before a breakup. Less communication. Less making time for each other. Less making out.

Maybe she does want to break up with me, but she knows it would hurt the awesome foursome we've got going on. We do everything with Sky and Holder now that we're all in college together. Breaking up with me would make it awkward for all three of them.

Maybe I'm overthinking things. Maybe it's college that's stressing her out.

My bedroom door opens and Chunk leans against the doorframe, arms folded. "Why are you on the floor?"

"Why are you in my room?"

She takes a step back so that she's technically in the hallway. "It's your turn to do the dishes."

"I don't even live here anymore."

"But you're home for Thanksgiving," she says. "Which means you're eating our food and using our dishes and sleeping under our roof, so go do the chores."

"You haven't changed at all."

"You moved out three months ago, Daniel. No one changes in the span of three months." Chunk walks back down the hallway without closing my door.

I have the urge to run after her and argue about people

not changing in just three months because Six has changed in that short of a time span. But if I disagree with her, I'll have to back it up with an example, and I'm not talking to Chunk about my girlfriend.

I check my phone one more time for a text from Six and then push myself off the floor. On my way to the kitchen, I pause at the doorway to Hannah's bedroom. She doesn't come home as often as I do because she goes to college in South Texas and is in med school.

I haven't even declared a major yet, nor have I found a job. That's not surprising, though. I haven't filled out a single application.

Hannah is sitting up in bed with her laptop. Probably doing homework for med school or something equally responsible. "Do they still make you do dishes when you come home?" I ask her.

She glances up at me before looking back down at her computer screen. "No. I don't live here anymore."

I knew she was the favorite. "Then why do *I* have to do chores?"

"Mom and Dad still support you financially. You owe them."

That's a fair point. I remain in her doorway, stalling the inevitable. "What are you doing?"

"Homework," she says.

"Want to take a break and play video games with me?"

Hannah looks up at me like I've suggested she murder someone. "Have I *ever* wanted to play video games with you?"

I groan. "Ugh." *This is going to be a long week.*

Holder and Sky get back tonight, but they're busy until Saturday. Breckin has family shit. I can already feel the unavoidable heartbreak coming from Six, which is why I've avoided her all day. I really don't want to be dumped over Thanksgiving break. Or at all. Maybe if I never text or call or speak to Six again, she'll never be able to break up with me and then I can continue to live in my blissful ignorance.

I push off Hannah's door and head toward the kitchen when she calls for me to come back. I turn around in the hallway, my whole body floppy and defeated when I reappear in her doorway.

"What's wrong with you?" she asks.

My shoulders are sagging and I'm in the midst of feeling really sorry for myself, so I sigh dramatically. "Everything."

Hannah motions toward the beanbag chair across the bedroom. I walk over to it and plop down. I don't know why I'm allowing her to summon me into her room, because she's just going to ask questions I don't want to answer. But it makes me a little less bored than I've been all day. And, also, it beats doing the dishes.

"Why are you moping? Did you and Six break up?" she asks.

"Not yet, but it feels imminent."

"Why? What'd you do wrong?"

"Nothing," I say defensively. "At least I don't remember doing anything. I don't know, it's complicated. Our whole relationship is complicated."

Hannah laughs and closes her laptop. "Med school is complicated. Relationships are easy. You love a person; they love you back. If that's not how your relationship is, you end it. Simple."

I shake my head in disagreement. "But I do love Six and she does love me and it's still very, very complicated."

Sometimes Hannah gets this look of excitement in her eyes, but it seems to happen at the worst moments. Like right now, as I tell her my relationship may be doomed.

That shouldn't excite her. "Maybe I can help," she says.

"You can't help."

Hannah hops off her bed and walks to her bedroom door and shuts it. She turns around and faces me, her eyebrows narrowed, the excitement in her expression gone. "You haven't made me laugh since I got home. Something is changing you, and as your big sister, I want to know what it is. And if you don't tell me, I'll call a Wesley family meeting."

"You wouldn't." I hate those meetings. They always seem to be an intervention for me and my behavior when they're supposed to be about the entire family.

"Try me," Hannah says.

I groan and cover my face with both hands as I bury myself deeper into the beanbag. In all honesty, Hannah is the best voice of reason in our whole family. She might even be the *only* voice of reason. Chunk is too young to understand these issues. My father is too immature, like me. And my mother would flip out if I told her about Six and my truth.

I do want to talk about it, and Hannah is probably the only person in the world besides Sky and Holder who I would trust with this. But Sky and Holder don't talk about it because we made them pinky swear they'd never bring it up.

I'm scared if I don't talk to someone about it, Six and I will be over. And I can't imagine a life without Six in it now that I've had a life with Six in it.

I blow out a conceding breath. "Okay. But sit down first."

The excitement in her expression returns. She doesn't just sit down on her bed. She hops onto her bed, next to a lump of covers, and sits cross-legged, eager to hear what I'm about to tell her. She rests her chin in her hand, waiting.

I take a moment to figure out how to start the conversation. How to summarize it without going into too much detail.

"This sounds crazy," I say, "but I had sex with a girl in the maintenance closet during junior year of high school. I didn't know who she was or what she looked like because it was dark."

"That doesn't sound crazy," Hannah interjects. "That sounds exactly like something you would do."

"No, that's not the crazy part. The crazy part is that after I got with Six, I found out that *she* was the girl I had sex with in the closet. And . . . well . . . I got her pregnant. And because she didn't know who I was, she put the baby up for adoption. A closed adoption. So, I'm a dad, but I'm not.

And Six is a mom, but she's not. And we thought it would be okay and we'd be able to move past it, but we can't. She's sad all the time. And because *she's* sad all the time, *I'm* sad all the time. And when we're together, we're double sad, so we don't even really hang out all that much anymore. Now I think she's about to break up with me."

I feel protected by the beanbag right now because my gaze is on the ceiling and not on Hannah. I don't want to look at her after vomiting all that. But an entire minute goes by and neither of us says anything, so I finally lower my head.

Hannah is sitting as still as a statue, staring at me in shock, like I've just told her I got someone pregnant. Because I did. And that's apparently very shocking, which is why she's looking at me like this.

I give her another moment to let it sink in. I know she wasn't expecting to find out she's sort of an aunt with a nephew she'll never meet during a conversation she probably expected to be about something a lot more trivial, like miscommunication with my girlfriend.

"Wow," she says. "That's . . . *wow*. That's really complicated, Daniel."

"Told you so."

The room is silent. Hannah shakes her head in disbelief. She opens her mouth a couple of times to speak, but then shuts it.

"So, what do I do?" I ask.

"I have no idea."

I throw my hands up in defeat. "I thought you were going to *help* me. That's why I told you all that."

"Well, I was wrong. This is like . . . *severe* adult shit. I'm not there yet."

I drop my head back against the beanbag. "You suck as a big sister."

"Not as much as you suck at being a boyfriend."

Why does any of that make me suck? I sit up straight now and scoot to the edge of the beanbag. "Why? What did I do wrong?"

She waves her hand at me. "*This.* You're avoiding her."

"I'm giving her space. That's different."

"How long have things been weird between you?"

I think back on the months we've been together. "It was great when we first got together. But when I found out what had happened, it got weird for like a day, but we moved past it. Or I *thought* we did. But she always has this sadness about her. I see it a lot. Like she's forcing herself to pretend to be happy. It's just getting worse, though, and I don't know if it's college or me or everything she went through. But I noticed in October she started making more and more excuses not to hang out. She had a test, or a paper, or she was tired. So, then *I* started making excuses because I thought that if she doesn't want to hang out with me, I don't want to force her to."

Hannah is listening intently to every word I say. "When was the last time you kissed her?" she asks.

"Yesterday. I still kiss her and treat her the same when we're together. It's just . . . different. We're hardly together."

She lifts a shoulder. "Maybe she feels guilty."

"I know she does, and I've tried to tell her she made the right choice."

"Then maybe she just wants to forget it ever happened, but you ask her too many questions about it."

"I don't ask her *any*. I never ask her. She doesn't seem to want to talk about it, so we don't."

Hannah tilts her head. "She carried your child for nine months and then put it up for adoption and you haven't asked her questions about it?"

I shrug. "I *want* to. I just . . . don't want her to feel pressured to relive it."

Hannah makes a groaning sound like I just said something that disappoints her.

"What?"

She looks at me pointedly. "I have never liked a single girl you've dated until Six. Please go fix this."

"How?"

"*Talk* to her. Be there for her. Ask her questions. Ask her what you can do to make it better for her. Ask her if it would help her to talk about it with you."

I chew on that suggestion. It's good advice. I don't know why I haven't just straight-up asked her how I can help make it better for her. "I don't know why I haven't done that yet," I admit.

"Because you're a guy and that's not your fault. It's Dad's fault."

Hannah might actually be right. Maybe the only problem between Six and me right now is that I'm a guy and guys are dumb. I push myself out of the beanbag. "I'm gonna go over there."

"Don't get her fucking pregnant again, you idiot."

I nod, but I don't go into detail with Hannah about the fact that Six and I haven't had sex since we've officially been a couple. That's no one's business but ours.

The one time we had sex was honestly the greatest sex I've ever had. If she breaks up with me, we won't get to experience that again. I've thought about what it'll be like so much, in such extensive detail, I'm confident it would be damn near perfect. Now I'm even more bummed by our prospective breakup. Not only will I have to spend my life without Six, I'll also have to spend the rest of my life never being interested in sex again, since it won't be with Six. Sex with Six is the only sex I'm willing to entertain. She's ruined me forever.

I open Hannah's door to leave.

"Do the dishes first," Chunk says with a muffled voice. *Chunk?*

I turn around, inspecting Hannah's room, looking for where Chunk might be hiding. I walk over to the pile of covers on Hannah's bed and pull them back. Chunk is lying there with a pillow over her head.

What in the hell? I point to Chunk while looking at Hannah. "She's been here this whole time?"

"Yeah," Hannah says with a careless shrug. "I thought you knew."

I run my hands over my face. "Christ. Mom and Dad are gonna *kill* me."

Chunk tosses the pillow aside and rolls over to look up at me. "I can keep a secret, you know. I've matured since you moved out."

"You literally just told me ten minutes ago that no one can change in a span of three months."

"That was ten minutes ago," she says. "People can change in a span of three months and ten minutes."

There's no way she's going to be able to keep this quiet. I should never have said anything to either of them. I throw the covers back over Chunk and make my way to the door. "If either of you tell Mom and Dad about this, I'll never speak to you again."

"That's an incentive, not a threat," Chunk says.

"Then I'll move back home if you tell them!"

"My lips are sealed," she says.

Chapter Two

It's been a long time since I've knocked on Six's bedroom window.

She and Sky share a dorm on campus now, but it's on the fifth floor of a building and I can't climb that high. I tried a few weeks ago because our dorm curfew is ten o'clock, but it was almost midnight and I really wanted to see Six. I got scared halfway up to the first floor and climbed back down.

I glance at Sky's bedroom window, but the lights are out. I guess she and Holder haven't made it back from Austin yet. When I look at Six's window, her lights are out, too. I hope she's home. She didn't mention she was going anywhere.

But then again, I haven't asked her. I never ask her anything. I hope Hannah is right and I can somehow fix whatever is weird between us.

I knock quietly on the windowpane, hoping she's in her

room. I immediately hear movement and then her curtains are pushed aside.

She looks like a fucking angel. Still.

I wave at her and she smiles at me. She actually looks happy to see me. That smile eliminates the majority of my nerves.

This always happens. I get paranoid and worried when I'm away from her, but when I'm with her, I can still see how she feels about me. Even when she looks sad.

Six opens the window so I can climb inside. Her bedroom is dark, like she's been sleeping, but it's only nine o'clock.

I turn to face her and take her in. She's wearing a T-shirt and pajama bottoms plastered with pizza slices. It reminds me that I haven't eaten dinner today. I don't even remember eating lunch. I haven't had much of an appetite.

"What's up?" she asks.

"Nothing."

She stares at me for a moment and then gets this look in her eyes like she's uncomfortable. She walks to her bed and sits down. She pats the spot next to her, so I lie down and stare up at her.

"I lied," I say. "It isn't nothing."

Six sighs heavily and then scoots down so that she's lying down next to me. She doesn't turn toward me, though. She stares up at the ceiling. "I know."

"You do?"

She nods. "I was expecting you to show up tonight."

I'm suddenly regretting coming over here and confronting it, because confronting it means action will be taken, and it might not be an action I want. *Shit. Now I'm scared.* "Are you breaking up with me?" I ask her.

She rolls her head and looks at me sincerely. "No, Daniel. Don't be a dumbass. Why? Are you breaking up with me?"

"No," I say immediately. Convincingly. "Dumbass."

She laughs a little. That's a good sign, but she looks away again, back to the ceiling, and offers up nothing else.

"Why are things weird between us?" I ask her.

"I don't know," she answers quietly. "I've been wondering the same thing."

"What am I doing wrong?"

"I don't know."

"But *am* I doing something wrong?" I ask.

"I don't know."

"What can I do to be better?"

"I don't even know if you can *be* any better."

"Well, if I'm not the issue, what is?"

"Everything else? Nothing else? I don't know."

"This conversation isn't going anywhere," I say.

She smiles. "Yeah, we've never been the best at deep conversation."

We aren't. We're shallow. Both of us. Our conversations are mostly shallow. We like to keep things fun and light because everything under the surface is so damn heavy. "That doesn't seem to be working out for us too well, so tell me what you're thinking. Let's dig a little and figure this out."

Six turns her head and eyes me. "I'm thinking about how much I hate the holidays," she says.

"Why? They're the best. No classes, lots of food; we get to sit around and be fat and lazy."

She doesn't laugh. She just looks sad. And then it hits me why she hates the holidays, and I feel like an idiot. I want to apologize but I don't know how. So instead, I slip my fingers through hers and squeeze her hand. "Do holidays make you think about him?"

She nods. "Always."

I don't know what to say to that. While I'm trying to think of a way to make her feel better, she rolls onto her side and faces me.

I let go of her hand and reach up to her cheek, stroking it with my thumb. Her eyes are so sad, and I want to kiss her eyelids, as if it'll make that look go away. It won't. It's always there, hidden behind fake smiles.

"Do you ever think about him?" she asks.

"Yes," I admit. "Not in the way you do, I'm sure. You carried him for nine months. Loved him. Held him. I didn't know about him until I already knew the outcome, so I don't think it left as big of a hole in me as it did in you."

A single tear rolls down her cheek, and while I'm glad we're talking about this, I'm also very, very sad for her. I think this has affected her a lot more than I realized.

"I wish I could make it better for you," I say, pulling her against my chest. I always try to use humor to fix the sad things, but humor can't fix this and it's all I know. "It scares me because I don't know how to make you happy."

"I'm scared I'll always be sad."

I'm scared she'll always be sad, too. And, of course, I would take whatever version of Six I can get, whether that's happy or sad or mad, but for her sake, I want her to be happy. I want her to forgive herself. I want her to stop worrying.

It's a while before she starts talking again. And when she does, her voice is shaking. "It feels like . . ." She sighs heavily before she continues. "It's like someone took a huge chunk out of my chest and there are two parts of me now that don't connect. I feel so disconnected, Daniel."

Her painful admission makes me wince. I kiss the top of her head and just hold her. I don't know what to say that'll make her feel better. I never know what to say. Maybe that's why I don't ask her about him, because I feel like she carries all the burden and I don't know how to lift it off of her.

"Does it help you to talk about it?" I ask her. "Because you never do."

"I didn't think you wanted to know."

"I do. I just didn't think you wanted to talk about it. But I do want to know. I want to know everything if you feel like telling me."

"I don't know. It might make me feel worse, but I do sometimes want to tell you about it all."

"Then tell me. What was it like? The pregnancy?"

"Scary. I hardly left my host family's house. I think

I was depressed, now that I look back on it. I didn't want anyone to know, not even Sky, because I had already made up my mind that I would put him up for adoption before I came back. So, I kept it all to myself and didn't tell anyone back home because I thought it would make the decision more bearable if no one else knew about it. I thought it was a brave choice at the time, but now I wonder if it was a scared choice."

I pull back and look her in the eyes. "It was both. You were scared *and* you were brave. But most of all, you were selfless."

That makes her smile. Maybe I'm actually doing something right here. I think of more questions to ask her. "How did you find out you were pregnant? Who was the first person you told?"

"I was late for my period, but I thought it might have been the travel and being in an entirely foreign situation. But when I didn't get it the second time, I bought a test. I took it and it wasn't one of those plus or minus sign tests. It was the kind that said "pregnant" or "not pregnant," but it was in Italian. It said "*incinta.*" I had no idea what that meant, and I had taken the test at school, so I couldn't use my phone to google it because it was in my locker. So, after my last class, I asked the American teacher at my school what *incinta* meant, and when she said, "pregnant," I started crying. So . . . I guess Ava was technically the first person I told."

"How did she react?"

"She was amazing. I really liked her, and for the first month, she was the only one I told. She went over all my options with me. She even came with me when I told my host family. And she never made me feel pressured, so it was nice to have her to talk to. When I decided on adoption, she said she knew a couple who was looking to adopt, but they wanted a closed adoption because they were scared I would change my mind in the future. But Ava vouched for them and I trusted her, so she helped us get a lawyer and was by my side through the whole process. And even though she knew the host family, she never tried to get them to persuade her decision."

I don't want to interrupt her, because I've been wanting to know all of this since the day I found out she'd had a baby, but I can't get past the tidbit of information Six just shared. "Wait," I say. "This teacher. She knows who adopted the baby? Can't we reach out to her?"

Six looks deflated when I ask that. She shakes her head. "I agreed to the closed adoption. We all signed legal paperwork. And despite all that, I've called her twice since I've been back, begging her for information. Her hands are tied. Legally and ethically. It's a dead end, Daniel. I'm sorry."

I deflate at that news but try not to show it. I nod and kiss her forehead reassuringly. I feel stupid even assuming she hadn't tried that avenue already. I feel stupid that I haven't tried any avenue *at all*. I haven't even offered. Now that I'm looking at this situation as a whole, I'm surprised she still puts up with me.

I keep her talking so she can't focus on the same thing I'm focused on—how much I suck.

"What was the delivery like?"

"Hurt like hell, but it went pretty quick. They let me keep him in my room for an hour. It was just me and him. I cried the whole time. And I almost changed my mind, Daniel. I almost did. But it wasn't because I thought he'd be better off with me. It was because I didn't want to hurt. I didn't want to miss him. I didn't want to feel the emptiness I knew I was going to feel. But I knew if I kept him, it would just be for selfish reasons. I was worried how it would affect *me*." She wipes at her eyes before continuing. "Before they came and got him, I looked down at him and said, '*I'm not doing this because I don't love you. I'm doing it because I do.*' That was the only thing I said to him out loud before they came for him. I wish I would have said more."

I can feel tears stinging my own eyes. I just pull her closer to me. I can't imagine what that was like for her. I can't imagine how much pain she's been in this whole time. I can't believe I thought it was because of me. I'm not significant enough to cause someone the kind of pain having to say goodbye to your own child causes.

"After the nurse took him away, she came back to my room and sat with me while I cried. She said, '*I know this is the worst day of your life. But thanks to you, it just became the best day of two other people's lives.*'" Six inhales a shaky breath. "It made me feel a little better in that moment. Like maybe she saw adoptions happen a lot and she knew it was hard for me. It helped me realize I wasn't the only mother giving up her child."

I shake my head adamantly. "You didn't *give him up*, Six. I hate that phrase. You gave him a life. And you gave his new parents a life. The last thing you did was give up. You *stood up*."

That makes her cry. Hard. She curls into me and I just hold her, running my hand gently over her head. "I know it's scary because we don't know what kind of life he has, but you don't know what kind of life he would have had if you had kept him. And you'd have the same kind of doubts if you had made that choice, too—wondering if you should have given him to someone in a position to care for him. There's so much unknown to swim around in and that'll probably always be there. You might always feel disconnected. But you have me. I know I can't change what you went through in the past, but I *can* make you promises. And I can keep them."

She lifts her face from my chest and looks up at me with red eyes and a little bit of hope. "What kind of promises?"

I brush hair away from her face. "I promise that I will never doubt your decision," I say. "I promise I will never talk about it unless you feel like talking about it. I promise I'll keep trying to make you smile, even when I know it's the kind of sadness that a joke can't fix. I promise to always love you, no matter what." I press my lips against hers and kiss her, then pull back. "No matter *what*, Six. *No. Matter. What.*"

Her eyes are still full of tears and I know her heart is still full of sadness, but through it all, she smiles at me. "I don't deserve you, Daniel."

"I know," I say in complete agreement. "You deserve someone way better."

She laughs, and the sound of it makes my heart swell.

"I guess I'm stuck with you until someone better comes along, then."

I smile back at her, and finally, *finally*, things feel normal again. As normal as things can be between people like Six and me.

"I love you, Cinderella," I whisper.

"I love you, too. No matter what."

Chapter Three

When I got home from Six's house last night, I slept through the night for the first time in a month. I went to bed relieved that we were okay.

But I woke up this morning feeling *not* okay.

Sure, our relationship finally seems stable. But Six is hurting. A lot. And I keep telling myself there's nothing I can do, but when I woke up feeling unsettled, I realized it's because I haven't even been trying. Sure, it was a closed adoption. Sure, I'll probably keep getting doors slammed in my face. But what kind of boyfriend would I be if I didn't at least try to make Six's world better?

This is why I've been on the phone for two hours. I called seven adoption agencies and was told the same thing from each of them. They aren't allowed to release any information. I keep trying, though, because what if I get the one person who is a little bit unethical in my favor?

I was on the eighth phone call when Hannah walked in. I told her all about my conversation with Six and how I feel like I should be doing more to try to find out information about who might have our son, or if someone can just tell us he's okay.

I told Chunk, too, because she's Hannah's shadow every time Hannah's home from med school.

I debated not updating them, because I really don't want them to talk about it at all, ever, but it's also nice to have people who know the truth. And besides, three brains are better than one, even if they're all Wesley brains.

Hannah has called three lawyers in Italy so far. Two immediately told her no, there's nothing they can do to help. She's on the phone with the third one now.

"Adoption," she says, googling something. "Um. Italian. *Adozione*?" She waits for a moment, and then looks down at the phone with a defeated expression. "He hung up on me."

Every phone call leaves me a little more disappointed than the last.

"Someone has to be able to help," Hannah says. She falls back onto my bed, just as frustrated as I am.

Chunk is seated in my desk chair, spinning in a circle. "What if you're kicking a hornet's nest?" she says. "I mean, there was a reason they wanted a closed adoption. They don't want you guys involved."

"Yeah, because they were scared Six would come back to take her baby," I say. "But she won't. She just wants to know he's okay."

"I think you need to leave it be," Chunk says.

I look at Hannah, hoping she doesn't feel the same way.

"I'm usually on Chunk's side, but I'm actually on your side this time," Hannah says to me. "Keep pushing. Maybe ask Six more questions. Someone has to know something. Italy isn't that big, is it?"

"Sixty million people live in Italy," I say. "Even if we contacted forty people a day, it would take us over four thousand years to make it through everyone in Italy."

Hannah laughs. "You actually did the math?"

I nod pathetically.

"Well, shit," she mutters. "I don't know. You just have to keep trying. Maybe the host family knows who it was."

I shake my head. "Six said they weren't really involved. There was an American teacher who worked at the school who helped Six with the adoption. I asked Six if there was a way to get in touch with her, but Six has already tried to get information from her on more than one occasion. The woman refuses to share anything based on legal grounds."

Hannah looks hopeful. "But this woman knows? Does anyone know where she might be?"

I shrug. "I don't know *what* she knows, exactly. I just know she helped Six."

"Call her," Hannah says.

"No."

"Why not?"

"Because Six said she's tried that already. More than once. The woman is a brick wall."

"But you're annoying. It might work for you."

Should I be offended by that? "What does me being annoying have to do with it?"

Hannah picks up my phone and puts it back in my hand. "You have to be persistent to be annoying. Be persistent with her."

I look at my phone. "I don't even know who to call. I don't know what school it was."

Hannah asks for the name of the city where Six did her foreign exchange, and then writes down three numbers as she searches the internet. I can't remember the name of the woman Six said she knew, but I do remember she said she was American. I call the first two schools and ask if they have an American teacher on the faculty and both say no.

I dial the third number with little hope left.

A woman answers in Italian.

"Do you speak English?" I ask her.

"Yes. How can I help you?"

"I'm looking for a teacher. An American teacher. I can't remember her name, but I need to speak to her."

"We have one American teacher on staff. Ava Roberts."

"Ava!" I yell. *That's it!* That's the name Six mentioned last night. "Yes," I say, trying to calm myself. I'm standing now and I don't even remember standing up. I clear my throat. "May I please speak to Ava Roberts?"

"One moment." I'm placed on hold and my heart is pounding. I use my T-shirt to wipe sweat from my forehead.

"What's happening?" Chunk asks, appearing a little more interested.

"I'm on hold. But I think this is the right school."

Hannah brings her hands to her mouth right when someone picks up on the other end. "Ava Roberts, how can I help you?"

My voice is shaking when I start to speak. "Hi. Hello." I clear my throat again. "My name is Daniel Wesley."

"Ah, a fellow American," she says. *She sounds friendly.* "Are you wanting to sign up as an exchange student?"

"No. No, I'm in college. I'm calling about something else. It might be weird, I don't know."

There's a pause. "Okay," she says, drawing the word out. I hear the sound of a door close, as if she's giving this conversation privacy. "What can I help you with?"

"Um. Do you remember a student by the name of Six Jacobs? Or maybe she went by Seven Jacobs?"

The lack of reply on her end gives me my answer. She definitely knows who I'm talking about. It doesn't mean I'll get any answers, but it feels good to know I'm on the right track.

"Daniel, you said?"

"Yes, ma'am."

"Daniel, I hope you understand that I'm not allowed to discuss students in any capacity. Is there anything else I can help you with?"

She knows. She knows why I'm calling. I can hear the fear in her voice.

"Don't hang up," I beg. "Please. I just. Okay, so I'm going to go out on a limb here and assume you're the teacher who helped Six with the adoption. She mentioned you knew a couple who was looking to adopt, which means you might still know the couple. Which means you're the only living person I've been in touch with who can tell us where our baby is."

More heart-pounding silence. "Why are you calling me? I'm not allowed to discuss this."

"We just want to know that he's okay."

"It was a closed adoption, Daniel. I'm sorry. I can't legally discuss this with anyone."

"I know." My voice is desperate. I'm scared she's about to hang up, so I just start talking faster, hoping to get it all out before she does. "We know you can't discuss it. We aren't asking for contact. And I'm not calling because we want him back. I mean, if he's not in a good situation, we do, but if he's happy and his parents are happy, that'll make *us* happy. We just . . ." I feel out of my element. Nervous. Like I don't know how to ask this woman for a morsel of information. But then I think about what Hannah said. She's right. I *am* annoying. I'm persistent. I blow out a breath and continue. "She cries, you know. Every night. It's the not knowing that kills her. I don't know if you have a way of contacting the people who adopted him, but if you do, maybe they wouldn't mind just sending her an email. An update. Even if *you* just respond with one sentence saying he's fine, I'm sure that would mean the world to Six. That's all I'm asking for. Just . . . it's hard, you know? Not knowing. It's really hard on her."

There's a long silence. *Such* a long silence. I'm worried

she hung up, so I look down at the phone, but it still says the call is connected. I put it on speaker and wait. Then I hear something that sounds like a sniffle come from the phone.

Is she crying?

Hannah and I lock eyes, and I know my expression must match the shock on her face.

"I can't make any promises," Ava says. "I can reach out to the adoption agency with your message. Email me your contact information, but . . . don't get your hopes up, Daniel. Please. All I can do is try to get a message to them. I can't promise they'll receive it or that they'll even feel comfortable answering it if they do."

I frantically point at my desk, motioning for Chunk to get me a pen and paper. "Okay." I sound so desperate, I know. "Thank you. *Thank you.* You have no idea what this means to me. To us."

"You already sound excited," the woman says. "I told you not to get your hopes up."

I grip the back of my neck. "Sorry. I'm not excited. I mean, I am. But a realistic excited."

"Do you have a pen?" she asks. She already sounds full of regret for even agreeing to do this, but I don't care how much regret she feels. I feel no shame.

I take down her email address and thank her two more times. When I hang up, Hannah and Chunk and I stare at each other.

I think I might be in shock. I can't form any words, or even much of a thought.

This is the first time I've ever been grateful for being called annoying.

"Wow," Chunk says. "What if it works?"

Hannah presses her hands to the sides of her head. "Oh my God. I honestly didn't think we'd get anywhere."

I let it all out by punching the air with my fists. I want to scream, but Mom and Dad are here in the house somewhere. I pull Hannah and Chunk in for a hug and we start jumping up and down. Hannah starts squealing because that's what she does when she's excited, but it actually doesn't annoy me this time.

"What the hell is going on?"

We all separate immediately. My father is standing in the doorway, looking at us suspiciously.

"Nothing," we all say in unison.

He cocks an eyebrow. "Bullshit."

I put one arm around Hannah's shoulders and one arm around Chunk's. "I just missed my sisters, Dad."

He points at us. "Bullshit," he says again.

My mother is behind him now. "What's wrong?"

"They were happy," my father says, accusatory.

My mother looks at him like he's lost his mind. "What do you mean?"

He motions toward us. "They were hugging and squealing. Something is up."

My mother is looking at us suspiciously now. "You were hugging? Like all three of you?" She folds her arms across her chest. "You three never hug. What the hell is going on?"

Hannah walks toward the door and smiles at my parents. "With all due respect," she says, "this is none of your business." Then she closes the door in their faces.

I can't believe she just did that.

She locks the door, and when she looks back at Chunk and me, we all just start laughing, and then we hug again and resume our celebratory moment.

My parents don't knock. I think we've thoroughly confused them.

Hannah falls onto the bed. "Are you telling Six?"

"No," I say immediately. "I don't want to get her hopes up. We may never hear from them."

"I bet you do," Chunk says.

"I hope so. But like you said, there's a reason they chose a closed adoption."

"Yeah," she says. "The waiting is going to suck."

It really is going to suck. I sit down on my bed and think about how much it's going to suck. Especially if I never hear back from anyone.

I hope she knows I'll be calling her again next week. And the week after that. And the week after that. I'll call her until she changes her number or her name.

But if either of those things happen, I'll be back to square one.

Now that the energy is leaving the room, the reality of it all begins to sink in. The three of us grow quiet in the midst of our declining hope.

"Well," Hannah says. "If you never hear from them,

you could always do one of those online DNA tests and hope your child does one when they're older, too. There's always that."

"Yeah, but then Daniel would never be able to commit a murder," Chunk says. "His DNA would always be in the system." Hannah and I both look at her. Chunk shrugs off our wary looks. "I just wouldn't take that chance."

Hannah and I continue to stare at her. "You scare me," I say.

"Not as much as the idea of you being a dad scares *me*," Chunk retorts. Loudly.

I cover her mouth with my hand, staring at the door to my bedroom. "Shh. They could still be at the door," I whisper. I slowly release my hand from her mouth.

Hannah pipes up from her position on the bed. "Oh, man. I didn't think about that. If this works out, you're gonna *have* to tell Mom and Dad."

I didn't think about that, either. But finding out even the most insignificant information for Six would be worth my parents' anger.

Chunk starts giggling. "Dude, you're gonna be in *so* much trouble."

Hannah laughs, too. I glare at her because I thought we were on the same team, but that cruel excitement is back in her eyes.

"You know," I say, "for a moment there, I felt like the three of us bonded. But now I see that the two of you still find pleasure in the idea of my failure."

I open the door and motion for them to leave my room. "You can go now. You two are no longer needed here."

Hannah hops off the bed and grabs Chunk's hand, pulling her out of the chair. "We want this to work out for you, Daniel," Hannah says on her way out the door. "But we also look forward to shit hitting the fan when Mom and Dad find out."

"Yes," Chunk agrees. "Looking very forward to that."

I close the door and lock them out of my bedroom.

Chapter Four

We decided on Sky's house for our Friendsgiving because Karen and Jack will be gone most of the day. Six recruited me to help make the dressing, but I've never cooked in my life, so I've been more of a nuisance than a help. Sky is doing the baking because she makes the best cookies in the world, according to Holder.

When I drop the second egg in two minutes, Six finally regrets her choice. "Just go hang out with Holder and Breckin in the living room," she says. "I feel like it'll be easier without you in the kitchen."

I don't take any offense because it's the truth.

I go to the living room and sit next to Breckin. He's playing a video game with Holder. "You winning, Powder Puff?"

He lazily turns his head and looks at me, annoyed. "We went an entire week without you calling me that. I thought you actually learned something in college."

"What could I learn that would make me stop calling you Powder Puff?"

"Oh, I don't know. Decency?"

Holder laughs from the recliner he's sprawled out in. I glare in his direction. "What are you laughing at, Pimple Dick?"

"Breckin's right," Holder says. "Sometimes I think maybe you're maturing, but then you go and say something ignorant again to set me straight. Still the same ol' Daniel."

I shake my head. "I thought that was why you like me, because I don't change. I'm myself all the time."

"I think that's the problem," Breckin says. "You don't evolve. But you're getting better. I haven't heard you use the *R* word in a derogatory way since you've been home."

"What's the *R* word?" I ask. I have no idea what he's talking about.

He begins to spell it out for me. "R-E-T-A-R—"

I cut Breckin off. "Oh. That," I say. "Yeah, I learned not to say that when a chick in my economics class smacked me in the back of the head with her notebook."

"Maybe there's hope for you yet," Breckin says. "Come to think of it, I did seem to hate you a lot more in high school. But I wouldn't hate you at all if you'd stop calling me Powder Puff."

"Aren't you on Twitter?" Holder asks. "Don't you see what happens to people like you?"

"People like me?"

"Yeah. Guys who say insensitive shit because they think it makes them look cool and careless."

"I don't think I'm cool and careless. I just had no idea Powder Puff was insensitive."

"Bullshit," Holder says with a fake cough.

"Okay, so maybe I knew it was insensitive," I admit, looking back at Breckin. "But it's a joke."

"Well," Breckin says, "as someone who identifies as a gay male, I feel it's my duty to teach you how to be more sensitive. Powder Puff is insulting. So is the *R* word. And *most* of the nicknames you give to people."

"Yeah," Holder says. "Stop calling my girlfriend Cheese Tits."

"But . . . it's a joke. I don't even know what Cheese Tits or Powder Puff mean."

Holder turns his head and looks at me. "I know you don't. Neither do I. But Breckin is right. You're an asshole sometimes, and you should stop being an asshole sometimes."

Shit. I seem to be learning a lot of what people think about me over Thanksgiving break, whether I want to or not. So far, I've learned I'm insensitive. I'm an asshole. I'm annoying. I'm a guy. *What else is wrong with me?*

"That means I have to come up with a new nickname for you," I say to Breckin.

"You could just call me Breckin."

I nod. "I will. For now."

That seems to satisfy him. I lean back, just as my phone rings. I fish it out of my pocket and look at the incoming call. It's an unknown number.

I stand up, but it feels like my heart is still on the couch.

Adrenaline rushes through me as I swipe to answer the phone. It might be a telemarketer, but it might not be, so I rush across the living room and go outside to take the call in private.

"Hello?" No one says anything, so I repeat myself. "Hello? It's Daniel. Hello?"

If it is a telemarketer, they've probably never heard a guy sound so desperate to talk to one of them before.

A man clears his throat, and then says, "Hi. Daniel Wesley?"

I'm pacing the front yard, gripping the back of my neck. "Yes. Who is this?"

"I'm . . . well, I'm your child's father."

I stop pacing. In fact, I bend over at the waist when I hear those words. I feel like my stomach just fell onto the ground. I feel like *I'm* about to fall to the ground.

Holy. Fucking. Shit. Don't say anything stupid, Daniel. Don't screw this up.

"Do you have a second to chat?" the guy asks.

I nod frantically. "Yes. Yes, of course." I walk to the front patio and take a seat. I can barely feel my legs. "Thank you for calling, sir. Thank you so much. Can I just ask how he's doing? Is he good? Healthy? Is he happy?"

I should probably get Six for this conversation. I feel awful being feet away from her and she has no idea that I'm on the phone with a man who knows where our son is. But I'm worried there's a chance he's not calling with good news, so I stay seated until I can find out more information.

"He's . . ." The man is hesitant. He pauses for a moment. "Listen, Daniel. I don't know you. And I don't know my son's biological mother. But I know my wife, and she has been through hell. The last thing I want to do is bring stress or pain back into her life, because she's in such a good place right now. I need to know what your intentions are before I tell her you've reached out. Before I decide to share anything with you. I hope you understand that."

"She doesn't know you're talking to me right now?"

"No. She doesn't. And I haven't decided if I'm even going to tell her about this conversation yet."

Yet.

I cling to that word. That word means this phone call is the one deciding factor in whether or not Six and I will know what happened to our child.

Yeah, no pressure or anything. *Christ.*

I think about what Hannah said. *Be persistent.*

"Okay. Well. My name is Daniel. I'm nineteen. My girlfriend, Six . . . she's the biological mother. And . . ." I stand up again, feeling the pressure of this entire conversation and just how much is riding on my shoulders right now. "Sorry. I just need a minute."

The man says, "It's okay. Take all the time you need."

I blow out a calming breath. I look at the house and into the window of the kitchen. Six is in there, oblivious to what's going on out here. Oblivious to the fact that I'm speaking to a man who knows where her child is.

Our child.

But honestly . . . her child. The baby she grew and carried for nine months. The burden she still carries.

I know he's my son, but I'd be lying to myself if I said I was talking to this man and feeling this nervous because of how I feel about a child I've never met. I'm not doing this for him. I'm confident Six made the right choice.

Everything I'm doing, I'm doing for Six. And I don't want to let her down. She needs this more than anyone has ever needed anything. And sadly, the future of her happiness is in my hands. My tiny, tiny hands.

I blow out a calming breath, hoping I can be as candid as I need to be with this guy.

"Can I ask you a question?" I ask him.

"Go ahead."

"Why did you adopt him? Can you and your wife not have children?"

The man is silent for a moment. "No. We can't. We tried for several years, and then my wife had a hysterectomy."

I can hear in his voice how hard it was just for him to say that, much less live through it. It makes me think his wife has been through the same kind of pain Six has been through. "Would you have stayed married to her no matter what? If you adopted a baby or not?"

"Of course," the man says. "She's the love of my life. But this child means the world to us, so if you're thinking about trying to—"

"Just hear me out," I say. "Six is the love of *my* life. I

know I'm only nineteen, but she's the best thing that's ever happened to me. And seeing her sad is just . . . it's unbearable, man. It's fucking unbearable. She just needs to know he's okay. She needs to know she made the right decision. And I'd be lying to you if I said I need this, too, because I don't. Not as much as she does. I just want her to be whole again. This broke her. And until she knows her little boy is happy and healthy I don't know that she'll ever heal. So yeah, I guess that's all I'm asking for. I want to see her happy, and right now, you and your wife are literally the only people in the world who can give her that."

I press my hand to my forehead. I shouldn't have cussed. I said *fucking* and that probably annoyed him. I feel every bit of the immature teenager that I still am while talking to this man.

There's a long silence, but I know he's still on the phone because I hear him sigh heavily. Then he says, "I'll talk to my wife. I'm going to let this be her decision and I'm going to support whatever that decision is. I have your contact information. If you don't hear from us, I need to ask you to let this go. As much as I wish I could help you, I can't promise anything."

I pump my fist in the air. I try not to sound too excited when I say, "Okay. Thank you. That's all I was hoping for. Thank you."

"Daniel?" he says.

"Yes, sir?"

"However this turns out . . . *thank you.*"

He hasn't said a single word about our son, but I hear it all in that *thank you*. It has to mean our little boy is doing well and making them happy.

He hangs up after saying that.

And then I'm left with this emptiness. My God, it's so heavy.

Being so close but still so fucking far away.

I take a seat on the patio chair again. Part of me wants to run inside and swing Six around and tell her everything that just happened. Every word of that conversation. But the realistic side of me knows that the conversation I just had might mean absolutely nothing. I may never hear from him again. And if I don't, that means no matter how much I reach out to whoever I can reach out to, this couple's decision is final. And we're legally bound to accept that.

All our hope has been placed on this one conversation. This one woman.

We're in the middle of the biggest trial of our lives and we have a jury of one deciding our future.

"Hey."

I wipe my eyes and look away from the front door Six just walked out of. I stand up, with my back to her. I shove my phone into my pocket.

"Daniel? Are you crying?"

I run my hands under my eyes again. "No. Allergies." I turn and face her, plastering on the fakest smile I've ever given anyone.

"You don't have allergies."

"I don't?"

"No." She steps closer to me and puts her hands on my chest. Her eyes are filled with concern. "What's wrong? Why are you crying? You never cry."

I take her face in my hands and press my forehead to hers. I feel her arms snake around my waist. "Six, I tell you everything," I whisper. "But I don't want to talk about this. Not yet. Just give me time to process it, okay?"

"You're scaring me."

"I'm fine. Perfectly fine. I just had a moment and I need you to trust me." I wrap my arms around her and hug her tight. "I'm hungry. I just want to eat all the food and hang out with you and my friends and not think about anything else today. I'm fine. I promise."

She nods against my shoulder. "Okay. But I ruined the dressing, so pizza is on the way."

I laugh. "I figured as much."

Chapter Five

It's been eight hours since the man called. I've checked my phone every five minutes for an email or a missed call or a text.

Nothing.

He didn't say when he was going to talk to his wife. He might be waiting for the perfect moment. That could be weeks or months. Or maybe he already talked to her and she decided she didn't want communication.

Maybe I'm going to spend the rest of my life looking down at my phone, waiting for them to contact me. I should have told him to at least tell me if they chose not to communicate with us. At least then I would have a definitive answer.

"Your turn, Daniel," Jack says to me.

I rest my phone back on the table and roll the dice. I suggested we all play Monopoly when Jack and Karen got home earlier. I needed my mind to be on something else, but this game is so damn slow. Holder demands to be the banker because he doesn't trust me, and he counts everyone's money three times.

I move my thimble and land on Park Place. "I'll buy it," I say.

"That'll be three hundred and fifty dollars," Holder says.

I pay him in fives because, for some reason, it's all I have. I watch him count it. Then he counts it again. He starts to put it in the tray, but then he picks up the wad of fives and starts to count for a *third* time.

"*Christ*. Hurry the hell up," I groan.

"Language," Jack says.

"Sorry," I mutter.

Holder stops counting the money. He's just staring at me from across the table.

"You okay?" Six asks, concerned.

"I'm fine," I reassure her. "This game is just taking forever because Holder counts money like a blind mole."

"Bite me," Holder says as he resumes counting my money for the *third* time.

"Moles are actually blind, so saying *blind mole* is redundant," Breckin says.

I turn my head and glare at him. "Shut up, Powder Puff."

"Okay," Holder snaps, grabbing the Park Place card back from me. "You're done. Go home."

I snatch the card back from him. "No, we aren't finished. We're finishing this damn game."

"You're making this not fun," Sky says.

"Seriously," Six says. She squeezes my leg under the table, a little forcefully. "Let's take a break. We can go to my house and make out. That might make you feel better."

That actually sounds way better and a lot more distracting than this stupid game. I toss my Park Place card on the center of the Monopoly board. "Good idea."

"Good riddance," Holder mutters.

I ignore them and walk toward the front door. Six apologizes on my behalf and that makes me feel like shit, but I don't stop her. I'll apologize to everyone tomorrow.

I've just never felt this pent-up before. That phone call left me wondering if this is how Six has felt this whole time. Maybe she's felt this way since the day she put him up for adoption, and if so, I'm a complete asshole for never recognizing it or trying to do something about it before this week.

We've walked around to the side of her house because she still uses her bedroom window whenever she returns home from Sky's. Right before she pushes it open, I pull her to me by her waist.

"I'm sorry. I love you."

"I love you, too," she says.

"I'm sorry I'm in a bad mood."

"It's okay. You were definitely a dick in there just now, but I know you. You'll make it right."

"I will."

"I know," she says.

"I love you. No matter what."

"I know." She pushes open the window and says, "Come on, I'll let you touch my boobs. Maybe that'll get your mind off things."

"Both of them?"

"Sure." She climbs through the window and I follow her, wondering how I ended up with the only girl in the world who gets me.

And, despite knowing exactly who I am, she somehow still loves me.

When we're standing next to her bed, I kiss her and it's a good kiss. A distracting kiss. Right when I'm about to lower her to her bed, my phone vibrates in my pocket.

My adrenaline begins pumping even harder. I immediately pull away from her and look at the incoming text. I practically deflate when I see it's just a text from Holder.

You okay, man? Need to talk?

"It's just Holder," I say, as if Six was even wondering who texted me. I slide my phone back into my pocket.

Six sits on the bed and pulls me on top of her, and even though I've been a complete asshole tonight, she lets me make out with her for fifteen minutes straight. She even lets me take off her bra. We haven't had sex since the day in the maintenance closet, and that's been a long damn time.

But I like that we still have that to look forward to, and even though I can't wait for it to happen, tonight is not the night I want it to happen. I've been a brat tonight. She deserves to have sex with me when I'm not acting like a brat.

My phone vibrates again, but I ignore it this time. Holder can wait.

"I think you got another text," Six whispers.

"I know. It can wait."

Six pushes against my chest. "I have to pee, anyway."

I roll onto my back and watch her walk into the bathroom. I pull my phone out of my pocket and see a notification from my Gmail.

My heart twists into a knot and I hit the notification so hard I'm surprised I don't drop my phone.

It's an email from someone named Quinn Wells.

I don't know that name.

I don't know that name and that's good. This could be good. I'm standing now. Pacing. The toilet is flushing. I read the subject line.

Hi.

That's it. It just says *Hi.* I don't even know how to interpret that, so I keep reading.

Dear Six and Daniel,

 Graham told me about your conversation. It's odd, because I've written countless letters to the

biological mother of my child before, letters I knew I
would never send, but now that I know you'll actually
read this, I don't even know how to start.

"Oh my God, holy shit, fuck, fuck, *fuck yes!*" I cover my
mouth with my hand and stop reading because this isn't
something I should be reading alone. Six needs to read this,
too. She walks out of the bathroom and sees me standing by
her bed. I motion for her to hurry up and sit down.

"What?"

"Sit. Sit." I pat the bed and sit next to her and she's so
confused, but I can't find my words right now to explain
what's happening, so I just start rambling and hope she can
decipher it all. "So, I made some phone calls the other day.
And then this guy called me today and I didn't know if we
would hear anything back, so I didn't say anything to you,
but . . ."

I shove my phone into her hands. "Look. Look at this. I
haven't read it yet, but . . ."

Six grabs my phone, eyeing me with warranted concern.
She breaks our stare and looks at the phone screen. "Dear
Six and Daniel," she says aloud. "Graham told me about
your conversation. It's odd, because I've written countless
letters to the biological mother of my child before, letters I
knew . . ."

Six stops reading and looks up at me. I can see in her
eyes she has no idea what this is, and that she's hoping it's
what she thinks it is, but she's too scared to think that.

"It's them," I say, pointing down at my phone. "Quinn Wells. That's her name. And her husband's name must be Graham. Quinn and Graham. They have our baby."

Six drops the phone and covers her mouth. I've never seen eyes fill with tears as fast as hers just did. "Daniel?" she whispers. Her voice is cautious. She's scared to believe this.

I pick up the phone. "It's them," I say again.

"How?" She's shaking her head in complete disbelief. "I don't understand. You talked to her husband? But . . . *how*?"

She's too scared to read the email. I probably should have explained it all earlier so this moment wouldn't be so chaotic, but I didn't know he'd talk to her today and that she'd actually reach out, and *holy shit, I can't believe this is happening.*

"I called that teacher you mentioned. Ava. Hannah said I was annoying and that I needed to be persistent, and so I was and I literally begged her, Six. I didn't know if it would work, but then he called today and said he was going to leave the decision up to his wife. I'm sorry I didn't tell you, but I didn't want to get your hopes up because I wasn't sure if she would ever reach out. But she did."

Six's whole body is shaking from the sobs. She's crying so hard now. Way too hard to read an email. I pull her to me. "It's okay, babe. It's okay. This is good."

"How do you know?" she says through her tears. "What if she's emailing to tell us to leave them alone?"

She's terrified, but she doesn't need to be. I don't know how I know, because I haven't read the email yet, but something about her reaching out tells me it's good. Quinn's husband seemed to really hear me out today, and I just don't believe they would email us if it wasn't good.

"You want me to read it out loud?"

Six nods, tucking herself against me. I wrap my arm around her as she presses her face against my chest like she doesn't want to see the email. I pick up my phone and begin to read the letter out loud. I start from the very beginning again.

> **Dear Six and Daniel,**
>
> Graham told me about your conversation. It's odd, because I've written countless letters to the biological mother of my child before, letters I knew I would never send, but now that I know you'll actually read this, I don't even know how to start.
>
> First, I want to take this opportunity to introduce myself. My name is Quinn Wells and my husband's name is Graham. We were both born and raised in Connecticut. Circumstances led us to Italy for a time, however, where we were fortunate enough to be given the gift of adopting your beautiful baby boy.

I have to put my phone down and take a breath. Six lifts her face from my chest and looks up at me, alarmed by my pause. I smile at her and wipe a tear away. "She said he's beautiful."

Six smiles.

"I don't think I can read this out loud," I say. "Let's read it together."

Both of us are complete wrecks now, so I reach over and grab some tissues from her bedside table and hand some to her. She sits up straighter and I hold up the phone. We lean our heads together and continue reading the email.

Our struggle with infertility has been a long one. It was very difficult for us to conceive, and when we finally did, it resulted in an unviable pregnancy and a hysterectomy. I don't want to inundate you with all the painful details, but please know that because of the struggles Graham and I have been through, our marriage has turned out stronger and full of more love than I could ever imagine.

And now, thanks to you, it is nothing short of perfect.

Being the young expectant mother you were, Six, I can't possibly imagine how difficult it must have been for you to make the decision to put your child up for adoption. Because I am unable to comprehend the pain you must have faced, I sometimes wonder if you are unable to comprehend our absolute elation and gratefulness to you.

My sister was the one who told us about you. You know her. Ava. She grew to love and respect you not only as one of her favorite students, but as a person.

Forgive me if I have any of the details wrong, as not a lot of information was disclosed about your situation. We were told that you were an American student in Italy on a foreign exchange. Ava informed us that you were looking for a family to adopt your child. We didn't want to get our hopes up because Graham and I have been let down many times in the past, but we wanted this more than anything.

The night Ava came to discuss the opportunity with us, I immediately told her to stop speaking. I didn't want to hear it. I was scared to death that it would be a situation that might not work out in the end. The thought of it not working out after getting my hopes up was more terrifying to me than never entertaining the idea of it.

After Ava left that night, Graham spoke to me about my fears. I will never forget the words he said that made me change my mind and open up my heart to the possibility. He said, "If you weren't completely terrified right now, I would be convinced that we aren't the right parents for this child, because becoming a parent should be the most terrifying thing to ever happen to a person."

As soon as he said that I knew he was absolutely right. Becoming a mother isn't about securing your own happiness. It's about taking the chance of being terrified and even devastated for the sake of a child.

That also applies to you, Six, as his biological

mother. I know it was a hard decision for you. But for whatever reason, you accepted a future of unknown fear in return for your child's happiness and security. I will never be able to thank you enough for that.

I'm still not sure why you chose us. Maybe it's because Ava was able to vouch for us or maybe it's because they told you our story. Or maybe it was chance. Whatever your reasons, I can assure you there are no two people in this world who could love your little boy more than Graham and I do.

We were advised by the lawyer to make it a closed adoption for various reasons. The main one being that it was supposed to give us peace of mind knowing that if you changed your mind and wanted to locate your child in the future, we would be protected.

However, the fact that you were unable to reach out to us because of the closed nature of the adoption has brought me very little peace of mind. I have been full of fear. Not an irrational fear of losing our son to you, but a substantial fear that you might go a lifetime not knowing this beautiful human you brought into the world.

Even though he's not quite a year old yet, he is the most incredible child. Sometimes, when I hold him, I wonder so many things. I wonder where he got the adorable heart shape of his mouth. I wonder if the head full of brown hair came from his mother or his father. I wonder if his playful personality is a reflection of the people who created him. There are so many wonderful things about him, and we want nothing more than to share those wonderful things with the people who blessed us with him.

We decided to name him Matteo Aaron Wells. We chose the name Aaron because it means "miraculous," and we chose Matteo because it's an Italian name meaning "gift." And that is exactly what Matteo is to us. A miraculous gift.

Graham and I made the decision to at least entertain the idea of reaching out to you a few weeks ago. We contacted our lawyer and requested your information, but I hadn't reached out yet because I was hesitant. Even this morning, after Graham told me about the phone call, I was still hesitant.

But then something happened about an hour ago. Matteo was in his high chair and Graham was feeding him mashed potatoes, and as soon as Matteo saw me when I walked into the room, he lifted his hands and said, "Mama."

It wasn't his first word, and it wasn't even the first time he said Mama, but it was the first time he applied the term specifically to me. I didn't know how hard it would hit me. How much it would mean to me. I immediately picked him up and pulled him to my chest and cried. Then Graham pulled me to his chest, and we stood there and cried together for several minutes. It was a ridiculous moment and maybe we were both way too excited about it, but it wasn't until this moment that it felt so real and permanent.

We're a family.

He's our son and we're his parents and none of this would have been possible without you.

As soon as Graham released me, I told him I needed to write this email. I want Matteo to know that not only does he have a mother and father in me and Graham, but he has an extra mother and father who care for him as deeply as we do. A biological mother who cares enough for him that she sacrificed her own happiness to see him have a life that she, for whatever reasons, felt she was unable to give him at the time of his birth.

We would love for you to meet him someday. Feel free to call us at the number below, or email us if you'd prefer. We would be honored to finally have the opportunity to thank you in person.

I've attached some photos of him. He's the happiest little boy I know, and I can't wait for him to become a significant part of both of your lives.

Thank you for our miraculous gift.

Sincerely,

Quinn, Graham, and Matteo Wells

We hug.
We hug and we cry. So hard.

Chapter Six

I don't even know how to describe this moment Six and I are sharing. It's the best thing that's ever happened to me. I don't know that I've ever cried tears of happiness. I don't know that I've ever seen Six cry so hard while laughing. We're just a big, stupid mess and it feels really, really phenomenal.

Every time I start to speak, we cry. Every time she starts to speak, we cry. We can't even talk and it's been five minutes since we finished the email.

We keep waiting for the attachments to load on my phone, but they're taking forever, so Six grabs her laptop. I log in to my email and hit download.

When the first picture loads, there isn't even enough air in the room to fill our collective gasps.

He looks just like me.

But he also looks just like her.

It's so weird and amazing, seeing this life we created, and it somehow makes me feel even closer to her.

"Oh my God," she whispers. "He's perfect."

"Scroll down," I say, too impatient to wait for more of him now that we got this small glimpse of him. We linger over each picture. We zoom in on his features. He has Six's mouth and my eyes and a headful of brown hair.

We even zoom in on his surroundings. It looks like he has a big backyard. A whole playset he's still too little to use. There are five pictures total, and after we look at them each twenty times, I say, "We should call them."

Six nods. "Yes." She clenches her stomach. "I'm so nervous."

"Me too. Me too, babe."

She sits on the edge of her bed and I stand and pace while I dial the number Quinn listed in the email. I put it on speaker, and when it starts ringing I sit down next to Six.

"This is Graham."

"Hi. Hey, it's me. Daniel. We just got your email." I feel like I should say more. Like *thank you* or *we love you* or *can we come meet him tonight?*

"Great," Graham says. "Let me grab Quinn."

The line goes quiet and Six and I look at each other nervously. Then a woman says, "Hi. This is Quinn. Is this Six and Daniel?"

"Yes," we both say at once.

"Thank you," Six blurts out. She's crying, but also smiling bigger than I've ever seen her smile. "Thank you so much. He's so perfect. We're so happy to see him so happy. Thank you." She covers her own mouth so she'll stop talking.

Quinn laughs. "Thank *you*," she says softly. "I meant every word."

"Where do you guys live?" I ask. "Are you still in Italy?"

"Oh. No, I forgot to mention that in the email. We moved back to Connecticut a few months ago. We wanted to be closer to Graham's parents."

"So, Matteo is here? In the same country?" I ask.

"Yep."

Six wipes at her eyes. "And you really don't mind if we meet him?"

"We would love that. But we know very little about either of you. Could you tell us a little about yourselves first? Where do you live?"

"We both go to college in Dallas," I say. "Six wants to be a psychologist."

"Psychiatrist," Six corrects him between tears.

"Something that ends in *ist*," I say. "I don't know what I want to be yet. We're both freshmen, so we're figuring things out as we go."

"And you're a couple? Still?"

"Yes. Well, we weren't technically a couple until after the baby was adopted. But we are now."

"I love that," Quinn says.

"Daniel is the best," Six says. "You'll love him." She looks at me and smiles. I squeeze her hand.

"You'll love Six more."

"I already love you both because of what you've given us," Quinn says. "Well, we know you guys are dying to meet him, but we don't want you to miss too much college. We would say come next weekend, but we'd like you to be able to stay more than just a day or two. How does Christmas break sound? It's just a few weeks away."

That sounds like a lifetime.

I can see Six feels the same way because she deflates a little. But then she says, "That's perfect. We'll be there."

"Yes. We'll be there," I confirm.

Quinn says, "Do you need help with the cost of flights?"

"No, you guys have done enough," Six says. "Truly."

There's a pause, and then Graham takes over the phone. "We have each other's numbers now. We'll text you our address. Just let us know what days you want to come and we'll work our schedules around it. We're looking forward to it."

"Thank you," Six says again.

"Yes. Thank you," I add.

Six is squeezing my hand so hard, it kind of hurts. Graham and Quinn both say goodbye. When I hang up the phone, we sit in silence for a moment, letting it all sink in.

"Shit," I mutter.

"What?"

I look at Six. "This means we have to tell our parents that they're grandparents."

Six looks worried, but only for a second. Then she grins. "My brothers are going to hate you."

I would expect that to alarm me, but it doesn't. "I don't care. Nothing can bring me down from this high."

Six laughs and then stands up, pulling my hands. "We have to go tell Sky and Holder!" Six crawls out her window and then through Sky's bedroom window. I'm right on her heels.

When we burst into the living room from the hallway, everyone looks up at us. They're still playing Monopoly.

"We found him!" Six says.

I'm sure they can all tell we've been crying, which would explain why they seem so alarmed by the sight of us.

"Found who?" Karen asks.

Sky immediately knows what we're talking about and why we look so disheveled and elated. She stands up slowly and covers her mouth. Then she says, "No."

Six nods. "Yes. We just got off the phone with them. We get to meet him next month."

"Meet who?" Breckin says.

"The baby?" Holder says.

I nod. "Yes. His name is Matteo. And he's adorable. He looks just like us."

"Who is Matteo?" Karen asks.

"What is everyone talking about?" Jack asks.

Holder and Sky are rushing across the room. Holder must not even care that I lost my cool with him earlier because he pulls me in for a hug. Six and Sky are hugging and squealing. Then all four of us are hugging. *God, I've done a lot of hugging this week.*

When we all let go, Jack and Karen and Breckin are still staring at us. More than annoyed. "What's going on?" Karen asks Sky.

Sky answers for us. "Daniel got Six pregnant and she had the baby in Italy and put it up for adoption and they found him!"

"I didn't know I got her pregnant," I say. I don't know why I say that.

"I didn't know it was Daniel who got me pregnant," Six says.

"It's complicated," Holder adds.

Karen's eyes are wide. She's staring at Six. "You . . . you had a *baby*?"

Six nods. "Yeah, and no offense, but we don't have time to explain right now. We've got to go tell our parents that they're grandparents now."

"Your parents don't know?" Jack says. For some reason, he looks at Holder and glares at him. "Anything you and Sky want to share with us now that this is all out in the open?"

Holder shakes his head. "No. No, sir. No babies here. Not yet. I mean, not for a long time. Years."

As much as I like seeing Holder nervous, Six and I have stuff to do. People to inform. Parents to piss off. I grab her hand and lead her to the front door. "Sorry I was a dick earlier!" I yell back to everyone. Then I look at Breckin. "I'll never call you Powder Puff again. I'm a dad now, I have to set a good example."

Breckin nods. "Thanks. I think."

Six pushes me out the door. "Let's tell your parents first," she says. "We'll tell mine in the morning. They're already in bed."

Chapter Seven

Six and I are seated on the love seat together. She's clutching my hand. Hannah and Chunk are on the couch. My parents are too worried to sit down, so they're pacing the living room.

"You're scaring us, Daniel," my mother says.

"What is this about?" my father asks me. "You never call Wesley family meetings." He looks at Six. "Oh my God. Are you pregnant? Did Daniel get you pregnant?"

We glance at each other and then Six says, "No. Well . . . not . . . technically."

"You want to *get* pregnant?" he asks, still throwing out guesses.

"No," Six says.

"You're engaged?" my mother asks me.

"No," I say.

"Sick?" she asks.

I wish they'd just shut up and let me form my thoughts. This is a tough thing to blurt out.

"You're breaking up?" my father asks.

"You dropped out of college?" my mother asks.

"For Pete's sake, they had a baby!" Chunk yells, annoyed. Then she immediately slaps her hand over her mouth and looks at me with eyes as wide as saucers. "Sorry, Daniel. I was getting really irritated with all the guessing."

"It's fine," I assure her.

My parents look at me in dumbfounded silence. And confusion. "You . . . *what?*"

"Six and I . . . we um . . ." I struggle to find my words.

"We had sex in a dark closet about a year before we formally met," Six says. "I got pregnant. Found out on a foreign exchange in Italy. I didn't know who I had sex with, which meant I didn't know who the father was, so I gave the baby up for adoption. But when I moved back and started dating Daniel, we figured it out. And now we know where our baby is and we're going to meet him over Christmas break."

That wasn't as delicate as I was hoping it would be, but it's out there now.

And my parents are still silent.

"Sorry," I mutter. "We used a condom."

I expect them to be angry or sad, but instead, my father begins to laugh.

So does my mother.

"Good one," my father says. "But we aren't falling for it."

"It's not a prank," I say.

I look to Hannah and Chunk for backup, but their jaws are practically dragging the floor. "Wait," Hannah says. "You found him? You actually *found* him?"

Oh yeah. I forgot Hannah and Chunk didn't know that part.

Six nods and pulls out her phone to show Hannah. "They emailed us tonight."

Hannah grabs the phone from Six.

My mother looks at Chunk like she's the only one who will be honest with her. "It's true," Chunk says. "Daniel told us a couple days ago. It really happened."

"We have pictures," I say, pulling out my phone.

My mother shakes her head and starts pacing again. "Daniel, if this is a joke, I will never forgive you."

"It isn't a joke, Mrs. Wesley," Six says. "I would never joke about something like this."

"Look, I know it's a shock."

My father holds his hand up to shut me up. "You had a baby and put him up for adoption and didn't tell us?"

"He didn't know until after it happened," Six says in my defense. "I didn't know who the father was."

My father is standing next to my mother, still glaring down at me. "How could you not—"

My mother puts a hand on my father's shoulder so he won't finish that sentence. "We need a minute," my mother says to us.

Six and I look at each other. We've been so excited I

don't think we really thought about how this would go down with our parents. We go to my bedroom, but we wait with the door slightly open so we can listen to what they have to say. But nothing is said. Just sighs. Lots of sighs.

My father is the first to speak. "Do we ground him?" he asks my mother.

"He's nineteen."

Another pause. Then, "We're *grand*parents?" my mother says.

"We aren't old enough to be grandparents."

"Obviously, we are. And they said it was a boy?" she asks.

"Yeah. A boy. Our boy had a boy. Our son has a son. *My* son has his own son. I have a grandson."

"So do I," my mother mutters disbelievingly.

Six and I just wait patiently and listen as they work it out.

"I'm not ready to be a grandmother," my mother says.

"Well, you are."

"I wonder what his name is?" she asks my father.

I take it upon myself to answer this one. "Matteo!" I yell down the hallway as I poke my head out of the bedroom.

My father peeks down the hallway from the living room. When I see him, I open my door all the way. We stare at each other for a moment. He looks disappointed. I'd almost rather him look angry. "Well," he says, motioning for us to come back to the living room, "let's see the pictures."

We take a seat at our dining room table and my parents

and my sisters pass my phone around, taking turns looking at the pictures. It takes a good ten minutes to sink in before my mother starts crying. "He's so beautiful," she says.

Six is squeezing my hand again. Then she starts to cry, because when Six sees anyone else cry, it makes *her* cry. "I'm sorry I let someone adopt him," she says to my parents. "I didn't know what else to do."

My mother's eyes swing to Six and she's immediately out of her chair. She takes Six's hands and locks eyes with her. "You have nothing to apologize for. Nothing at all. We love you so much, Six."

They hug, and dammit if it doesn't make *me* tear up. As much as they embarrass me, I really did get lucky when it comes to parents.

Hell. I might have even gotten lucky when it comes to sisters, too.

"I want to meet him," Chunk says. "When can we meet him?"

"Hopefully you all will. But we think it should just be the two of us this first trip."

Everyone seems to be in agreement with that.

"Oh, and one more thing," I add, turning to my parents. "Could you buy us plane tickets to Connecticut?"

Chapter Eight

Three weeks later

We agreed to take an Uber to their house from the airport. Meeting our child for the first time in an airport seemed too stale.

We don't speak much on the way there. It's been the longest three weeks of both of our lives, and as much as we wanted to call them every day, we held off. We didn't want to scare them away.

"Neighborhood seems nice," I say as we grow closer. All the houses are decorated for Christmas. I look over at Six and she looks so nervous. Her skin is pale.

When we pull up to the address, we stare out the window for a moment. It's a nice house. Bigger than anything Six and I would be raising him in. Not that the size of the house matters, but I can't help but want the very best for him.

"You ready?" I ask Six.

She shakes her head. Her eyes are red, and I can tell she's trying not to cry.

This is a huge moment for us. It's terrifying. But our Uber driver doesn't get that because he says, "Hey, I don't get paid for you guys to sit in my back seat and cry."

That irritates the hell out of me. I bump the back of his headrest. "She's about to meet her child for the first time, Dick Prick! Give us a minute! Also, it smells like tacos in here. Get an air freshener."

The Uber driver meets my glare in the rearview mirror and then mutters, "Sorry. Take your time. Didn't know this was a big moment."

"Well, it is," I mutter.

Six rolls her eyes at me. "It's fine," she says, sniffling. "I'm ready. Let's do this."

We get out of the car and I go around to the trunk to grab our suitcases. One of them is filled with a week's worth of our clothes. The other one is filled with toys and clothes from everyone: Sky and Holder, Karen and Jack, Breckin, both sets of our parents. Even Six's brothers, who really did give me a hard time after they found out, pitched in a few presents before we left.

The Uber driver actually makes himself useful and helps me with one of the suitcases. When he shuts the trunk, he looks at me. "Does it really smell like tacos in my car?"

I shrug. "Yeah. But the good kind."

"I had tacos for lunch. You have a good nose."

I kind of feel bad for snapping at the guy now, but he shouldn't rush his passengers like that. "I wasn't trying to insult you. I love tacos."

The driver shrugs it off. "It's cool. And hey, I'm also an Uber Eats driver. I can actually go get you tacos if you want some. There's this really great taco stand over on Jackson Street."

I *am* hungry. "How good? I'm from Texas and we have really good tacos in Texas."

"Dude, they're the best tacos you'll ever—"

"Daniel?" Six interrupts our conversation. She lifts a hand and waves it at the house behind her. "We're about to meet our son in a matter of seconds and you're seriously going to sit here and make me wait while you have a full-on conversation about *tacos*?"

"I . . . Sorry. I just love tacos."

"Tacos are great," the driver mutters. "Good luck with your kid and stuff." He gets back in the car and cranks it. We look up at the house just as the front door opens. A man walks out. I guess this is Graham.

"Shit," I whisper. "He's good-looking. I don't know why that makes me even more nervous."

"His socks don't match," Six says as we make our way up the driveway. "I like him already."

We meet Graham at the front door. He shakes my hand and introduces himself. "You must be Daniel," he says. He looks at Six and hugs her. "And Six." He pulls back and opens the front door. "How was your flight?"

We follow him inside and I set the two suitcases by their front door. "It was good," I say, looking around. This is so weird. Being here. I feel like I'm about to puke. I can't imagine how Six feels right now.

There are pictures lining the hallway that leads to the living room. Six and I walk slowly and look at them. Most we've seen, but some we haven't.

Quinn appears around the corner and she's exactly how I assumed she would be. Welcoming and happy and full of just as many emotions as Six. She introduces herself and then we're all just kind of awkwardly standing around.

"Are you ready to meet Matteo?" Quinn asks.

Six blows out a breath, shaking out her hands. "I don't want to scare him. I have to collect myself."

"Don't worry about that," Graham says. "We've spent the first year of his life emotional wrecks. Sometimes we just burst into tears while we're holding him because we're so damn lucky." Graham and Quinn smile at each other.

Graham motions for us to follow them into the living room, where we finally see our son. He's lying on the floor, surrounded by toys.

Seeing him in pictures was one thing but seeing him in person is an entirely different experience. Six squeezes my hand and we both gasp. I suddenly don't feel good enough to be here. Worthy enough.

And now all I can picture is Wayne and Garth, bowing down and chanting, *"We're not worthy. We're not worthy."* I kind of want to drop to my knees in front of this beautiful little boy and do the same thing.

Quinn picks up Matteo and walks him over to us.

We both start to cry. Six touches his arm with her fingers and then his hair. Then she pulls her hand back and covers her mouth.

"You want to hold him?" Quinn asks.

Six nods, so Quinn hands Matteo over to her. Six pulls him against her chest and presses her cheek against his head. She closes her eyes and just stands there, breathing him in.

It's fucking beautiful.

I want to take pictures, but that would be weird. I just never want to forget this. This whole damn moment. Seeing Six with our baby. Our happy and healthy and perfect baby. Seeing Six smiling. Seeing that piece of her that's been missing for so long finally reconnect all the broken parts of her.

We sit down on the couch with Matteo and take turns holding him.

"What's he like?" I ask. "Is he shy? Outgoing? Does he cry a lot? My mom said I was a crier."

"He's really friendly," Graham says. "Like he's never met a stranger."

Six laughs. "He gets that from Daniel."

Graham and Quinn are seated on the sofa opposite us. They don't look nervous at all about us being here. Quinn is snuggled against Graham, her hand on his chest. They're both smiling. It's almost as if a part of them was needing this, too.

"He's not a crier," Quinn says. "But he has a good set of lungs on him. Likes to hear himself jabber."

"He also gets that from me," I say.

We chat for a while, both of us continuing to take turns with Matteo. After we've been there for about an hour, Quinn is showing Six an album full of baby pictures.

Graham stands up and stretches out his arms, then drops his hands to his hips. He nudges his head toward the kitchen.

"Wanna help me with dinner, Daniel?"

I stand up, but I feel like I should warn him. "I can try, but I tend to only make the cooking experience worse."

Graham laughs, but heads into the kitchen anyway, expecting me to follow him. He takes vegetables out of the refrigerator and sets them on the counter. He slides a knife toward me and then rolls a tomato across the island. "Think you can cut a tomato?"

"First time for everything," I say. I start to cut the tomato while Graham assembles the rest of the salad. I feel like I should thank him, but I'm so awkward when it comes to having sincere conversations. I clear my throat. When he looks at me, I keep my eyes on the tomato I'm butchering. "I can't thank you enough for doing this for Six."

Graham says nothing. When I glance up at him, he's staring at me. He smiles a little and then says, "I didn't do it for Six. I did it for you."

That makes me pause.

"When I called you that day on the phone, I was honestly prepared to tell you to take a hike."

I release the knife and the tomato and then press my palms into the counter. "Really?"

Graham nods as he meticulously chops up an onion. "I had no interest in bringing potential stress into Quinn's life. I didn't think it would be good in any capacity to have Matteo's biological parents in the picture. I've seen the stories on the news, in the papers. The devastating custody battles. I didn't want to open that door. But when I called you . . . I don't know. I could hear the desperation in your voice. I could relate to the fact that all you wanted in that moment was to see the woman you loved happy." He makes eye contact with me across the island. "You reminded me of myself, and what that felt like. The agony that comes along with not being able to take the pain away from the person you love more than yourself."

Dammit. Maybe it's the onions. I don't know. I have to look away from him because I feel my eyes dampen. I grab my shirtsleeve and dab at them. "Those are some strong onions, man," I mutter.

Graham laughs. "Yeah. I guess so."

When I've composed myself, I go back to helping Graham with the salad. Quinn walks into the kitchen and looks at the tomato on my cutting board. She laughs.

"What have you done to that poor tomato?"

"I tried to warn Graham that I'm bad luck in a kitchen."

Quinn motions for the knife. "I'll take over. Go hang out in the living room with your family."

I smile at her and let her take over. But when I leave the kitchen, I have to pause to collect myself in the hallway.

She just called us a family.

"Fucking onions," I mutter to myself.

I walk back into the living room and sit down on the couch next to my girlfriend and our little boy. I spend the whole time watching them together as I try not to cry. But damn, my emotions are being tested more today than any other time in my life.

Today has honestly been filled with the best moments I've ever spent with Six. Better than the maintenance closet, better than our first date, better than all the days we've ever spent together combined. The last three agonizing weeks of waiting to be sitting here with our son have been torture.

But this?

This is perfection.

A damn Christmas miracle.

Chapter Nine

We'll be staying in their guest room for the week. At first, we were hesitant about it because we didn't want to impose. But they insisted, and we're two broke kids in college, so free sounded better than any other option. Apparently, Quinn's sister, Ava, spoke so highly of Six they felt like they knew her before they even invited us to meet Matteo. I'm sure it was hard for them, trusting us enough to not only bring us into their lives, but to also welcome us into their home.

I'm glad we chose to stay with the Wellses because we really like them. Graham seems like a stand-up guy. He laughs at my jokes. That's important to me. And Quinn and Six hit it off immediately.

After they put Matteo to sleep, we stayed up for two hours, the four of us, just talking and sharing our stories. They've been through a lot, but knowing the outcome and how happy they seem makes me think that Six and I can keep what we have forever. True love exists and the people in this house are proof of that.

"Matteo seems so happy," Six says, falling onto the bed.

"So do they," I say. "Did you see the way Graham looks at Quinn? Eleven years of marriage and he still looks at her like I look at you."

Six rolls onto her side and smiles at me. She rests a gentle hand on my cheek and brushes her thumb over my lips. "Thank you," she whispers. "You have no idea how much you've changed my life."

"Yeah?"

She nods. "Yeah. I know he's okay now. That's all I've ever wanted. And he's going to know us. We'll see him as often as we can. And I love them so much. *So* much. I was worried that meeting Matteo and the people who adopted him might make it worse. But when I see him with them, it's like he's theirs and I'm okay with that. He is theirs. He's ours *and* theirs." She leans forward. "I love you, Daniel Wesley," she whispers, her mouth brushing mine. "I finally feel connected again."

Six and I have kissed a lot since we've been together, but it's never felt quite like this. Now it's peaceful and good. Like we're both in the best place either of us has ever been.

I love her so much. Sometimes I love her so much it makes me feel like I might puke. Like there's so much love, it fills me up until I'm nauseated. In a good way. If nausea can ever be good.

Six rolls on top of me, and I don't know what's about to happen or how far this kiss will go. Maybe really far. Like all the way. Or maybe not far at all.

It doesn't even matter because today is perfect. Today is the best day of my life and it'll always be the best day of my life. No matter what.

Six pulls the covers over our heads. "I'm really proud of you," she says. "You went the whole night without cussing. And you didn't even give Matteo a nickname. I was sure you were going to slip up and call him Salty Balls or something."

That makes me laugh. "We'll be here for a week. There's plenty of time for me to slip up."

Six kisses my chin. Then my mouth. Then she kisses my . . .

Well. What happens next is no one's business but ours.

Don't miss the highly anticipated sequel to the
"riveting" (*Kirkus Reviews*, starred review)
#1 *New York Times* bestselling novel

IT ENDS WITH US

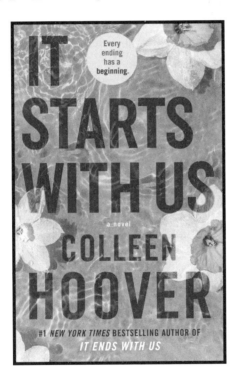

All Your
Perfects

All Your
Perfects

A Novel

Colleen Hoover

ATRIA PAPERBACK

New York   London   Toronto   Sydney   New Delhi

ATRIA
PAPERBACK

An Imprint of Simon & Schuster, Inc.
1230 Avenue of the Americas
New York, NY 10020

First Atria Paperback edition July 2018

ATRIA PAPERBACK and colophon are trademarks of Simon & Schuster, Inc.

For information about special discounts for bulk purchases, please contact Simon & Schuster Special Sales at 1-866-506-1949 or business@simonandschuster.com.

The Simon & Schuster Speakers Bureau can bring authors to your live event. For more information, or to book an event, contact the Simon & Schuster Speakers Bureau at 1-866-248-3049 or visit our website at www.simonspeakers.com.

Interior design by Alexis Minieri

Manufactured in China

40   39   38   37   36   35   34

Library of Congress Cataloging-in-Publication Data

Names: Hoover, Colleen, author.
Title: All your perfects : a novel / Colleen Hoover.
Description: First Atria Books hardcover edition. | New York : Atria Books, 2018.
Identifiers: LCCN 2017053852 (print) | LCCN 2017055146 (ebook) | ISBN 9781501171604 (eBook) | ISBN 9781501171598 (hardcover)
Classification: LCC PS3608.O623 (ebook) | LCC PS3608.O623 A45 2018 (print) | DDC 813/.6—dc23
LC record available at https://lccn.loc.gov/2017053852

ISBN 978-1-5011-9332-3
ISBN 978-1-5011-7160-4 (ebook)

To Heath.
I love you more today than any day that has come before it.
Thank you for being legit.

All Your
Perfects

Chapter One

Then

The doorman didn't smile at me.

That thought plagues me during the entire ride up the elevator to Ethan's floor. Vincent has been my favorite doorman since Ethan moved into this apartment building. He always smiles and chats with me. But today, he simply held the door open with a stoic expression. Not even a, *"Hello, Quinn. How was your trip?"*

We all have bad days, I guess.

I look down at my phone and see that it's already after seven. Ethan should be home at eight, so I'll have plenty of time to surprise him with dinner. *And myself.* I came back a day early but decided not to tell him. We've been doing so much planning for our wedding; it's been weeks since we had an actual home-cooked meal together. Or even sex.

When I reach Ethan's floor, I pause as soon as I step out

of the elevator. There's a guy pacing the hallway directly in front of Ethan's apartment. He takes three steps, then pauses and looks at the door. He takes another three steps in the other direction and pauses again. I watch him, hoping he'll leave, but he never does. He just keeps pacing back and forth, looking at Ethan's door. I don't think he's a friend of Ethan's. I would recognize him if he were.

I walk toward Ethan's apartment and clear my throat. The guy faces me and I motion toward Ethan's door to let him know I need to get past him. The guy steps aside and makes room for me but I'm careful not to make further eye contact with him. I fish around in my purse for the key. When I find it, he moves beside me, pressing a hand against the door. "Are you about to go in there?"

I glance up at him and then back at Ethan's door. *Why is he asking me that?* My heart begins to race at the thought of being alone in a hallway with a strange guy who's wondering if I'm about to open a door to an empty apartment. *Does he know Ethan isn't home? Does he know I'm alone?*

I clear my throat and try to hide my fear, even though the guy looks harmless. But I guess evil doesn't have a telling exterior, so it's hard to judge. "My fiancé lives here. He's inside," I lie.

The guy nods vigorously. "Yeah. He's inside all right." He clenches his fist and taps the wall next to the door. "Inside my fucking girlfriend."

I took a self-defense class once. The instructor taught us to slide a key between our fingers, poking outward, so if you're attacked you can stab the attacker in the eye. I do this, prepared for the psycho in front of me to lunge any second now.

He blows out a breath and I can't help but notice the air between us fills with the smell of cinnamon. What a strange thought to have in the moment before I'm attacked. What an odd lineup that would be at the police station. *"Oh, I can't really tell you what my attacker was wearing, but his breath smelled good. Like Big Red."*

"You have the wrong apartment," I tell him, hoping he'll walk away without an argument.

He shakes his head. Tiny little fast shakes that indicate I couldn't be more wrong and he couldn't be more right. "I have the right apartment. I'm positive. Does your fiancé drive a blue Volvo?"

Okay, so he's stalking Ethan? My mouth is dry. Water would be nice.

"Is he about six foot tall? Black hair, wears a North Face jacket that's too big for him?"

I press a hand against my stomach. *Vodka would be nice.*

"Does your fiancé work for Dr. Van Kemp?"

Now *I'm* the one shaking my head. Not only does Ethan work for Dr. Van Kemp . . . his father *is* Dr. Van Kemp. *How does this guy know so much about Ethan?*

"My girlfriend works with him," he says, glancing at the apartment door with disgust. "*More* than works with him, apparently."

"Ethan wouldn't . . ."

I'm interrupted by it. *The fucking.*

I hear Ethan's name being called out in a faint voice. At least it's faint from this side of the door. Ethan's bedroom is against the far side of his apartment, which indicates that whoever she is, she isn't being quiet about it. She's screaming his name.

While he fucks her.

I immediately back away from the door. The reality of what is happening inside Ethan's apartment makes me dizzy. It makes my whole world unstable. My past, my present, my future—all of it is spinning out of control. The guy grips my arm and stabilizes me. "You okay?" He steadies me against the wall. "I'm sorry. I shouldn't have blurted it out like that."

I open my mouth, but uncertainty is all that comes out. "Are you . . . are you sure? Maybe those sounds aren't coming from Ethan's apartment. Maybe it's the couple in the apartment next door."

"That's convenient. Ethan's neighbor is named Ethan, too?"

It's a sarcastic question, but I immediately see the regret in his eyes after he says it. That's nice of him—finding it in himself to feel compassion for me when he's obviously experiencing the same thing. "I followed them," he says. "They're in there together. My girlfriend and your . . . boyfriend."

"Fiancé," I correct.

I walk across the hallway and lean against the wall, then eventually slide down to the floor. I probably shouldn't plop myself on the floor because I'm wearing a skirt. Ethan likes skirts, so I thought I'd be nice and wear one for him, but now I want to take my skirt off and tie it around his neck and choke him with it. I stare at my shoes for so long, I don't even notice that the guy is sitting on the floor next to me until he says, "Is he expecting you?"

I shake my head. "I was here to surprise him. I've been out of town with my sister."

Another muffled scream makes its way through the door. The guy next to me cringes and covers his ears. I cover mine, too. We sit like this for a while. Both of us refusing to allow the noises to penetrate our ears until it's over. It won't last long. Ethan can't last more than a few minutes.

Two minutes later I say, "I think they're finished." The guy pulls his hands from his ears and rests his arms on his knees. I wrap my arms around mine, resting my chin on top of them. "Should we use my key to open the door? Confront them?"

"I can't," he says. "I need to calm down first."

He seems pretty calm. Most men I know would be breaking down the door right now.

I'm not even sure I want to confront Ethan. Part of me wants to walk away and pretend the last few minutes didn't happen. I could text him and tell him I came home early and he could tell me he's working late and I could remain blissfully ignorant.

Or I could just go home, burn all his things, sell my wedding dress, and block his number.

No, my mother would never allow that.

Oh, God. My mother.

I groan and the guy immediately sits up straight. "Are you about to be sick?"

I shake my head. "No. I don't know." I pull my head from my arms and lean back against the wall. "It just hit me how pissed my mother is going to be."

He relaxes when he sees I'm not groaning from physical illness, but rather from the dread of my mother's reaction when she finds out the wedding is off. Because it's definitely off. I lost count of how many times she's mentioned how much the deposit was in order to get on the waiting list at the venue. "Do you realize how many people wish they could get married at Douglas Whimberly Plaza? Evelyn Bradbury was married there, Quinn. *Evelyn Bradbury!*"

My mother loves to compare me to Evelyn Bradbury. Her family is one of the few in Greenwich who is more prominent than my stepfather's. So of course my mother uses Evelyn Bradbury as an example of high-class perfection at every opportunity. I don't care about Evelyn Bradbury. I have half a mind to text my mother right now and simply say, The wedding is off and I don't give a fuck about Evelyn Bradbury.

"What's your name?" the guy asks.

I look at him and realize it's the first time I've really taken him in. This might be one of the worst moments of his life, but even taking that into consideration, he's extremely handsome. Expressive dark brown eyes that match his unruly hair. A strong jaw that's been constantly twitching with silent rage since I walked out of the elevator. Two full lips that keep being pressed together and thinned out every time he glances at the door. It makes me wonder if his features would appear softer if his girlfriend weren't in there with Ethan right now.

There's a sadness about him. Not one related to our current situation. Something deeper . . . like it's embedded in him. I've met people who smile with their eyes, but he frowns with his.

"You're better looking than Ethan." My comment takes him off guard. His expression is swallowed up in confusion because he thinks I'm hitting on him. That's the last thing I'm doing right now. "That wasn't a compliment. It was just a realization."

He shrugs like he wouldn't care either way.

"It's just that if you're better looking than Ethan, that

makes me think your girlfriend is better looking than me. Not that I care. Maybe I do care. I *shouldn't* care, but I can't help but wonder if Ethan is more attracted to her than he is to me. I wonder if that's why he's cheating. Probably. I'm sorry. I'm usually not this self-deprecating but I'm so angry and for some reason I just can't stop talking."

He stares at me a moment, contemplating my odd train of thought. "Sasha is ugly. You have nothing to worry about."

"Sasha?" I say her name incredulously, then I repeat her name, putting emphasis on the *sha*. "Sa*sha*. That explains a lot."

He laughs and then *I* laugh and it's the strangest thing. Laughing when I should be crying. Why am I not crying?

"I'm Graham," he says, reaching out his hand.

"Quinn."

Even his smile is sad. It makes me wonder if his smile would be different under different circumstances.

"I would say it's good to meet you, Quinn, but this is the worst moment of my life."

That is a very miserable truth. "Same," I say, disappointed. "Although, I'm relieved I'm meeting you now rather than next month, after the wedding. At least I won't be wasting marriage vows on him now."

"You're supposed to get married next month?" Graham looks away. "What an asshole," he says quietly.

"He really is." I've known this about Ethan all along. He's an asshole. Pretentious. But he's good to me. *Or so I thought.* I lean forward again and run my hands through my hair. "God, this sucks."

As always, my mother has perfect timing with her incoming text. I retrieve my phone and look down at it.

Your cake tasting has been moved to two o'clock on Saturday. Don't eat lunch beforehand. Will Ethan be joining us?

I sigh with my whole body. I've been looking forward to the cake tasting more than any other part of the wedding planning. I wonder if I can avoid telling anyone the wedding is off until Sunday.

The elevator dings and my attention is swept away from my phone and to the doors. When they open, I feel a knot form in my throat. My hand clenches in a fist around my phone when I see the containers of food. The delivery guy begins to walk toward us and my heart takes a beating with every step. *Way to pour salt on my wounds, Ethan.*

"Chinese food? Are you kidding me?" I stand up and look down at Graham who is still on the floor, looking up at me. I wave my hand toward the Chinese food. "That's *my* thing! Not his! *I'm* the one who likes Chinese food after sex!" I turn back toward the delivery guy and he's frozen, staring at me, wondering if he should proceed to the door or not. "Give me that!" I take the bags from him. He doesn't even question me. I plop back down on the floor with the two bags of Chinese food and I rifle through them. I'm pissed to see that Ethan simply duplicated what I always order. "He even ordered the same thing! He's feeding Sasha my Chinese food!"

Graham jumps up and pulls his wallet out of his pocket. He pays for the food and the poor delivery guy pushes open the door to the stairwell just to get out of the hallway faster than if he were to walk back to the elevator.

"Smells good," Graham says. He sits back down and grabs the container of chicken and broccoli. I hand him a fork and let him eat it, even though the chicken is my favorite. This isn't a time to be selfish, though. I open the Mongolian beef and start eating, even though I'm not hungry. But I'll be damned if Sasha or Ethan will eat any of this. "Whores," I mutter.

"Whores with no food," Graham says. "Maybe they'll both starve to death."

I smile.

Then I eat and wonder how long I'm going to sit out here in the hallway with this guy. I don't want to be here when the door opens because I don't want to see what Sasha looks like. But I also don't want to miss the moment when she opens the door and finds Graham sitting out here, eating her Chinese food.

So I wait. And eat. With Graham.

After several minutes, he sets down his container and reaches into the takeout bag, pulling out two fortune cookies. He hands one to me and proceeds to open his. He breaks open the cookie and unfolds the strip of paper, then reads his fortune out loud. "You will succeed in a great business endeavor today." He folds the fortune in half after reading it. "Figures. I took off work today."

"Stupid fortune," I mutter.

Graham wads his fortune into a tiny ball and flicks it at Ethan's door. I crack open my cookie and slip the fortune out of it. "If you only shine light on your flaws, all your perfects will dim."

"I like it," he says.

I wad up the fortune and flick it at the door like he did. "I'm a grammar snob. It should be your *perfections*."

"That's what makes me like it. The one word they misuse is *perfects*. Kind of ironic." He crawls forward and grabs the fortune, then scoots back against the wall. He hands it to me. "I think you should keep it."

I immediately brush his hand and the fortune away. "I don't want a reminder of this moment."

He stares at me in thought. "Yeah. Me neither."

I think we're both growing more nervous at the prospect of the door opening any minute, so we just listen for their voices and don't speak. Graham pulls at the threads of his blue jeans over his right knee until there's a small pile of threads on the floor and barely anything covering his knee. I pick up one of the threads and twist it between my fingers.

"We used to play this word game on our laptops at night," he says. "I was really good at it. I'm the one who introduced Sasha to the game, but she would always beat my score. Every damn night." He stretches his legs out. They're a lot longer than mine. "It used to impress me until I saw an eight-hundred-dollar charge for the game on her bank statement. She was buying extra letters at five dollars a pop just so she could beat me."

I try to picture this guy playing games on his laptop at night, but it's hard. He looks like the kind of guy who reads novels and cleans his apartment twice a day and folds his socks and then tops off all that perfection with a morning run.

"Ethan doesn't know how to change a tire. We've had two flats since we've been together and he had to call a tow truck both times."

Graham shakes his head a little and says, "I'm not looking for reasons to excuse the bastard, but that's not so bad. A lot of guys don't know how to change a tire."

"I know. That's not the bad part. The bad part is that I *do* know how to change a tire. He just refused to let me because it would have embarrassed him to have to stand aside while a girl changed his tire."

There's something more in Graham's expression. Something I haven't noticed before. Concern, maybe? He pegs me with a serious stare. "Do *not* forgive him for this, Quinn."

His words make my chest tighten. "I won't," I say with complete confidence. "I don't want him back after this. I keep wondering why I'm not crying. Maybe that's a sign."

He has a knowing look in his eye, but then the lines around his eyes fall a little. "You'll cry tonight. In bed. That's when it'll hurt the most. When you're alone."

Everything suddenly feels heavier with that comment. I don't want to cry but I know this is all going to hit me any minute now. I met Ethan right after I started college and we've been together four years now. That's a lot to lose in one moment. And even though I know it's over, I don't want to confront him. I just want to walk away and be done with him. I don't want to need closure or even an explanation, but I'm scared I'll need both of those things when I'm alone tonight.

"We should probably get tested."

Graham's words and the fear that consumes me after he says them are cut off by the sound of Ethan's muffled voice.

He's walking toward the door. I turn to look at his apartment door but Graham touches my face and pulls my attention back to him.

"The worst thing we could do right now is show emotion, Quinn. Don't get angry. Don't cry."

I bite my lip and nod, trying to hold back all the things I know I'm about to need to scream. "Okay," I whisper, right as Ethan's apartment door begins to open.

I try to hold my resolve like Graham is doing, but Ethan's

looming presence makes me nauseous. Neither of us looks at the door. Graham's stare is hard and he's breathing steadily as he keeps his gaze locked on mine. I can't even imagine what Ethan will think in two seconds when he opens the door fully. He won't recognize me at first. He'll think we're two random people sitting on the hallway floor of his apartment building.

"Quinn?"

I close my eyes when I hear Ethan say my name. I don't turn toward his voice. I hear Ethan take a step out of his apartment. I can feel my heart in so many places right now, but mostly I feel it in Graham's hands on my cheeks. Ethan says my name again, but it's more of a command to look at him. I open my eyes, but I keep them focused on Graham.

Ethan's door opens even wider and a girl gasps in shock. *Sasha.* Graham blinks, holding his eyes closed for a second longer as he inhales a calming breath. When he opens them, Sasha speaks.

"Graham?"

"Shit," Ethan mutters.

Graham doesn't look at them. He continues to face me. As if both of our lives aren't falling apart around us, Graham calmly says to me, "Would you like me to walk with you downstairs?"

I nod.

"Graham!" Sasha says his name like she has a right to be angry at him for being here.

Graham and I both stand up. Neither of us look toward Ethan's apartment. Graham has a tight grip on my hand as he leads me to the elevator.

She's right behind us, then next to us as we wait for the

elevator. She's on the other side of Graham, pulling on his shirtsleeve. He squeezes my hand a little harder, so I squeeze his back, letting him know we can do this without a scene. Just walk onto the elevator and leave.

When the doors open, Graham ushers me on first and then he steps on. He doesn't leave room for Sasha to step on with us. He blocks the doorway and we're forced to face the direction of the doors. The direction of Sasha. He hits the button for the lobby and when the doors begin to close, I finally look up.

I notice two things.

1) Ethan is no longer in the hallway and his apartment door is closed.
2) Sasha is so much prettier than me. Even when she's crying.

The doors close and it's a long, quiet ride to the bottom. Graham doesn't let go of my hand and we don't speak, but we also don't cry. We walk quietly out of the elevator and across the lobby. When we reach the door, Vincent holds it open for us, looking at us both with apology in his eyes. Graham pulls out his wallet and gives Vincent a handful of bills. "Thanks for the apartment number," Graham says.

Vincent nods and takes the cash. When his eyes meet mine, they're swimming in apology. I give Vincent a hug since I'll likely never see him again.

Once Graham and I are outside, we just stand on the sidewalk, dumbfounded. I wonder if the world looks different to him now because it certainly looks different to me. The sky, the trees, the people who pass us on the sidewalk. Everything seems slightly more disappointing than it did before I walked into Ethan's building.

"You want me to hail you a cab?" he finally says.

"I drove. That's my car," I say, pointing across the street.

He glances back up at the apartment building. "I want to get out of here before she makes it down." He looks genuinely worried, like he can't face her at all right now.

At least Sasha is trying. She followed Graham all the way to the elevator while Ethan just walked back inside his apartment and closed his door.

Graham looks back at me, his hands shoved in his jacket pockets. I wrap my coat tightly around myself. There's not much left to say other than goodbye.

"Goodbye, Graham."

His stare is flat, like he's not even in this moment. He backs up a step. Two steps. Then he spins and starts walking in the other direction.

I look back at the apartment building, just as Sasha bursts through the doors. Vincent is behind her, staring at me. He waves at me, so I lift a hand and wave back to him. We both know it's a goodbye wave, because I'm never stepping foot inside Ethan's apartment building again. Not even for whatever stuff of mine litters his apartment. I'd rather him just throw it all away than face him again.

Sasha looks left and then right, hoping to find Graham. She doesn't. She just finds me and it makes me wonder if she even knows who I am. Did Ethan tell her he's supposed to get married next month? Did he tell her we just spoke on the phone this morning and he told me he's counting down the seconds until he gets to call me his wife? Does she know when I sleep over at Ethan's apartment that he refuses to shower without me? Did he tell her the sheets he just fucked her on were an engagement gift from my sister?

Does she know when Ethan proposed to me, he cried when I said yes?

She must not realize this or she wouldn't have thrown away her relationship with a guy who impressed me more in one hour than Ethan did in four years.

Chapter Two

Now

Our marriage didn't collapse. It didn't suddenly fall apart.

It's been a much slower process.

It's been *dwindling*, if you will.

I'm not even sure who is most at fault. We started out strong. Stronger than most; I'm convinced of that. But over the course of the last several years, we've weakened. The most disturbing thing about it is how skilled we are at pretending nothing has changed. We don't talk about it. We're alike in a lot of ways, one of them being our ability to avoid the things that need the most attention.

In our defense, it's hard to admit that a marriage might be over when the love is still there. People are led to believe that a marriage ends only when the love has been lost. When anger replaces happiness. When contempt replaces bliss. But

Graham and I aren't angry at each other. We're just not the same people we used to be.

Sometimes when people change, it's not always noticeable in a marriage, because the couple changes together, in the same direction. But sometimes people change in opposite directions.

I've been facing the opposite direction from Graham for so long, I can't even remember what his eyes look like when he's inside me. But I'm sure he has every strand of hair on the back of my head memorized from all the times I roll away from him at night.

People can't always control who their circumstances turn them into.

I look down at my wedding ring and roll it with my thumb, spinning it in a continuous circle around my finger. When Graham bought it, he said the jeweler told him the wedding ring is a symbol for eternal love. An endless loop. The beginning becomes the middle and there's never supposed to be an end.

But nowhere in that jeweler's explanation did he say the ring symbolizes eternal *happiness*. Just eternal love. The problem is, love and happiness are not concordant. One can exist without the other.

I'm staring at my ring, my hand, the wooden box I'm holding, when out of nowhere, Graham says, "What are you doing?"

I lift my head slowly, completely opposite of the surprise I'm feeling at his sudden appearance in the doorway. He's already taken off his tie and the top three buttons of his shirt are undone. He's leaning against the doorway, his curiosity pulling his eyebrows together as he stares at me. He fills the room with his presence.

I only fill it with my absence.

After knowing him for as long as I have, there's still a mysteriousness that surrounds him. It peeks out of his dark eyes and weighs down all the thoughts he never speaks. The quietness is what drew me to him the first day I met him. It made me feel at peace.

Funny how that same quietness makes me uneasy now.

I don't even try to hide the wooden box. It's too late; he's staring straight at it. I look away from him, down at the box in my hands. It's been in the attic, untouched, rarely even thought of. I found it today while I was looking for my wedding dress. I just wanted to see if the dress still fit. It did, but I looked different in it than I did seven years ago.

I looked lonelier.

Graham walks a few steps into the bedroom. I can see the stifled fear in his expression as he looks from the wooden box to me, waiting for me to give him an answer as to why I'm holding it. Why it's in the bedroom. Why I thought to even pull it out of the attic.

I don't know why. But holding this box is certainly a conscious decision, so I can't respond with something innocent like "I don't know."

He steps closer and the crisp smell of beer drifts from him. He's never been much of a drinker, unless it's Thursday, when he goes to dinner with his coworkers. I actually like the smell of him on Thursday nights. I'm sure if he drank every day I'd grow to despise the smell, especially if he couldn't control the drinking. It would become a point of contention between us. But Graham is always in control. He has a routine and he sticks to it. I find this aspect of his personality to be one of his sexiest traits. I used to look forward to his return on Thursday nights. Sometimes I would dress up for him and wait for him right here on the bed, anticipating the sweet flavor of his mouth.

It says something that I forgot to look forward to it tonight.

"Quinn?"

I can hear all his fears, silently smashed between each letter of my name. He walks toward me and I focus on his eyes the whole time. They're uncertain and concerned and it makes me wonder when he started looking at me this way. He used to look at me with amusement and awe. Now his eyes just flood me with pity.

I'm sick of being looked at this way, of not knowing how to answer his questions. I'm no longer on the same wavelength as my husband. I don't know how to communicate with him anymore. Sometimes when I open my mouth, it feels like the wind blows all my words straight back down my throat.

I miss the days when I needed to tell him everything or I would burst. And I miss the days when he would feel like time cheated us during the hours we had to sleep. Some mornings I would wake up and catch him staring at me. He would smile and whisper, *What did I miss while you were sleeping?* I would roll onto my side and tell him all about my dreams and sometimes he would laugh so hard, he would have tears in his eyes. He would analyze the good ones and downplay the bad ones. He always had a way of making me feel like my dreams were better than anyone else's.

He no longer asks what he misses while I sleep. I don't know if it's because he no longer wonders or if it's because I no longer dream anything worth sharing.

I don't realize I'm still spinning my wedding ring until

Graham reaches down and stills it with his finger. He gently threads our fingers together and carefully pulls my hand away from the wooden box. I wonder if his intention is to react like I'm holding an explosive or if that's truly how he feels right now.

He tilts my face upward and he bends forward, pressing a kiss to my forehead.

I close my eyes and subtly pull away, making it appear as though he caught me while I was already mid-movement. His lips brush across my forehead as I push off the bed, forcing him to release me as I watch him take a humbling step back.

I call it the divorce dance. Partner one goes in for the kiss, partner two isn't receptive, partner one pretends he didn't notice. We've been dancing this same dance for a while now.

I clear my throat, my hands gripping the box as I walk it to the bookshelf. "I found it in the attic," I say. I bend down and slide the box between two books on the bottom shelf.

Graham built me this bookshelf as a gift for our first wedding anniversary. I was so impressed that he built it from scratch with his bare hands. I remember he got a splinter in the palm of his hand while moving it into the bedroom for me. I sucked it out of his palm as a thank-you. Then I pushed him against the bookshelf, knelt down in front of him, and thanked him some more.

That was back when touching each other still held hope. Now his touch is just another reminder of all the things I'll never be for him. I hear him walking across the room toward me so I stand up and grip the bookshelf.

"Why did you bring it down from the attic?" he asks.

I don't face him, because I don't know how to answer him.

He's so close to me now; his breath slides through my hair and brushes the back of my neck when he sighs. His hand tops mine and he grips the bookshelf with me, squeezing. He brings his lips down against my shoulder in a quiet kiss.

I'm bothered by the intensity of my desire for him. I want to turn and fill his mouth with my tongue. I miss the taste of him, the smell of him, the sound of him. I miss when he would be on top of me, so consumed by me that it felt like he might tear through my chest just so he could be face-to-face with my heart while we made love. It's strange how I can miss a person who is still here. It's strange that I can miss making love to a person I still have sex with.

No matter how much I mourn the marriage we used to have, I am partly—if not wholly—responsible for the marriage it's turned into. I close my eyes, disappointed in myself. I've perfected the art of avoidance. I'm so graceful in my evasion of him; sometimes I'm not sure if he even notices. I pretend to fall asleep before he even makes it to bed at night. I pretend I don't hear him when my name drips from his lips in the dark. I pretend to be busy when he walks toward me, I pretend to be sick when I feel fine, I pretend to accidentally lock the door when I'm in the shower.

I pretend to be happy when I'm breathing.

It's becoming more difficult to pretend I enjoy his touch. I don't enjoy it—I only *need* it. There's a difference. It makes me wonder if he pretends just as much as I do. Does he want me as much as he professes to? Does he wish I wouldn't pull away? Is he thankful I do?

He wraps an arm around me and his fingers splay out against my stomach. A stomach that still easily fits into my wedding dress. A stomach unmarred by pregnancy.

I have that, at least. A stomach most mothers would envy.

"Do you ever . . ." His voice is low and sweet and completely terrified to ask me whatever he's about to ask me. "Do you ever think about opening it?"

Graham never asks questions he doesn't need answers to. I've always liked that about him. He doesn't fill voids with unnecessary talk. He either has something to say or he doesn't. He either wants to know the answer to something or he doesn't. He would never ask me if I ever think about opening the box if he didn't need to know the answer.

Right now, this is my least favorite thing about him. I don't want this question because I don't know how to give him his answer.

Instead of risking the wind blowing my words back down my throat, I simply shrug. After years of being experts of avoidance, he finally stops the divorce dance long enough to ask a serious question. The one question I've been waiting for him to ask me for a while now. And what do I do?

I shrug.

The moments that follow my shrug are probably why it's taken him so long to ask the question in the first place. It's the moment I feel his heart come to a halt, the moment he presses his lips into my hair and sighs a breath he'll never get back, the moment he realizes he has both arms wrapped around me but he still isn't holding me. He hasn't been able to hold me for a while now. It's hard to hold on to someone who has long since slipped away.

I don't reciprocate. He releases me. I exhale. He leaves the bedroom.

We resume the dance.

Chapter Three

Then

The sky turned upside down.

Just like my life.

An hour ago, I was engaged to the man I've been in love with for four years. Now I'm not. I turn the windshield wipers on and watch out the window as people run for cover. Some of them run inside Ethan's apartment building, including Sasha.

The rain came out of nowhere. No sprinkles to indicate what was coming. The sky just tipped over like a bucket of water and huge drops are falling hard against my window.

I wonder if Graham lives close by or if he's still walking. I flip on my blinker and pull out of my usual parking spot at Ethan's for the very last time. I head in the direction Graham began walking a few minutes ago. As soon as I turn left, I see him duck into a restaurant to take cover from the storm.

Conquistadors. It's a Mexican restaurant. One I'm not too fond of. But it's close to Ethan's apartment and he likes it, so we eat here at least once a month.

A car is pulling out of a space in front of the restaurant, so I patiently wait for them to leave and then I ease my car into their spot. I get out of the car without knowing what I'll say to Graham once I walk inside.

"Need a ride home?"

"Need company?"

"Up for a night of revenge sex?"

Who am I kidding? The last thing I want tonight is revenge sex. That's not why I'm following him, so I hope he doesn't assume that's the case once he sees me. I still don't know why I'm following him. Maybe it's because I don't want to be alone. Because like he said, the tears will come later, in the silence.

When the door closes behind me and my eyes adjust to the dim lighting in the restaurant, I spot Graham standing at the bar. He's removing his wet coat and laying it over the back of the chair when he sees me. He doesn't appear at all shocked to see me. He pulls out the chair next to him with the confident expectation that I'll walk over to him and take it.

I do. I sit right next to him and neither of us says a word. We just commiserate in our silent misery.

"Can I get you two any drinks?" a bartender asks.

"Two shots of whatever will help us forget the last hour of our lives," Graham says.

The bartender laughs, but neither of us laughs with him. He sees how serious Graham is being, so he holds up a finger. "I have just the thing." He walks to the other end of the bar.

I can feel Graham watching me, but I don't look at him.

I don't really want to see how sad his eyes are right now. I almost feel worse for him than I do for myself.

I pull a bowl of pretzels in front of me. They're a mixture of shapes, so I begin to pull out all the sticks and I lay them on the bar in the shape of a grid. Then I pull out all the O-shaped pretzels and scoot the bowl of the traditionally shaped pretzel knots toward Graham.

I lay my pretzel in the center of the grid. I look at Graham and wait quietly. He looks at the pretzels I've strategically placed on the bar and then he looks back at me. A very slow and guarded smile makes its appearance. Then he reaches into the bowl, pulls out a pretzel knot and places it in the square above mine.

I pick the spot to the left of the center square, placing my pretzel carefully in my square.

The bartender lays two shots down in front of us. We pick them up at the same time and swing our chairs so that we're facing each other.

We sit in silence for a good ten seconds, waiting for the other to make the toast. Graham finally says, "I have absolutely nothing to toast to. Fuck today."

"Fuck today," I say in complete agreement. We clink our shot glasses together and tilt our heads back. Graham's goes down a lot smoother than mine. He slams his glass on the counter and then picks up another pretzel. He makes the next move.

I'm picking up the next pretzel when my phone starts buzzing in my jacket pocket. I pull it out. Ethan's name is flashing across the screen.

Graham then pulls his phone out and sets it on the bar. Sasha's name is flashing across his screen. It's comical, really.

What must the two of them think, walking out and seeing both of us sitting on the floor together, eating their Chinese food.

Graham places his phone on the bar, faceup. He puts his finger on his phone, but instead of answering it, he gives his phone a shove. I watch as it slides across the bar and disappears over the edge. I hear his phone crash against the floor on the other side of the bar, but Graham acts as if he isn't at all fazed with the idea of having a broken phone.

"You just broke your phone."

He pops a pretzel into his mouth. "It's full of nothing but pictures and texts from Sasha. I'll get a new one tomorrow."

I lay my phone on the bar and I stare at it. It's silent for a moment, but Ethan calls for a second time. As soon as his name flashes across the screen, I have the urge to do exactly what Graham just did. I'm due for a new phone, anyway.

When the ringing stops and a text from Ethan comes through, I give my phone a shove. We watch as my phone slips over the other side of the bar.

We go back to playing tic-tac-toe. I win the first game. Graham wins the second. Third is a draw.

Graham picks up another one of the pretzels and eats it. I don't know if it was the shot I took or if I'm just confused by the turmoil of today, but every time Graham looks at me, I can feel the look trickle down my skin. And my chest. Everywhere, actually. I can't tell if he makes me nervous or if I just have a buzz. Either way, this feeling is better than the devastation I would be feeling right now if I were at home alone.

I replace the piece of pretzel grid that Graham just ate. "I have a confession," I say.

"Nothing you say can beat the past couple of hours of my life. Confess away."

I lean my elbow against the bar and prop my head on my hand. I give him a sidelong glance. "Sasha came outside. After you walked away."

Graham can see the shame in my expression. His eyebrows raise in curiosity. "What did you do, Quinn?"

"She asked which way you went. I refused to tell her." I sit up straight and swing the chair so that I'm facing him. "But before I got in my car, I turned around and said, 'Eight hundred dollars on a *word* game? *Really*, Sasha?'"

Graham stares at me. Hard. It makes me wonder if I crossed a line. I probably shouldn't have said that to her, but I was bitter. I don't regret it.

"What'd she say?"

I shake my head. "Nothing. Her mouth kind of fell open in shock, but then it started raining and she ran back inside Ethan's apartment building."

Graham is staring at me with so much intensity. I hate it. I wish he'd laugh or get angry that I interfered. *Something*.

He says nothing.

Eventually, his eyes lower until he's staring down between us. We're facing each other, but our legs aren't touching. Graham's hand that's resting on his knee moves forward a little until his fingers graze my knee, just below the hem of my skirt.

It's both subtle and obvious. My entire body tenses at the contact. Not because I don't like it, but because I can't remember the last time Ethan's touch sent this much heat through me.

Graham traces a circle over the top of my knee with his

finger. When he looks up at me again, I'm not confused by the look in his eyes. It's very clear what he's thinking now.

"You want to get out of here?" His voice is both a whisper and a plea.

I nod.

Graham stands and pulls his wallet out of his pocket. He lays some cash on the bar and then slips into his jacket. He reaches down and threads his fingers through mine, leading me through the restaurant, out the door and hopefully toward something that makes this day worth waking up for.

Chapter Four

Now

Graham once asked me why I take such long showers. I don't remember what my excuse was. I'm sure I said they were relaxing, or that the hot water was good for my skin. But I take such long showers because it's the only time I allow myself to grieve.

I feel weak for needing to grieve since no one has died. It doesn't make sense that I grieve so much for those who never even existed.

I've been in the shower for half an hour now. When I woke up this morning, I incorrectly assumed it would be a quick, painless shower day. But that changed when I saw the blood. I shouldn't be shocked. It happens every month. It's happened every month since I was twelve.

I'm standing flat against the shower wall, allowing the spray of the shower to fall over my face. The stream of water dilutes my tears and it makes me feel less pathetic. It's easier to convince myself I'm not crying *that* hard when most of what's falling down my cheeks is water.

I'm doing my makeup now.

Sometimes this happens. One second I'm in the shower, the next second I'm not. I lose myself in the grief. I get so lost that by the time I climb my way out of the dark, I'm in a new place. This new place is me, naked, in front of the bathroom mirror.

I slide the lipstick over my bottom lip and then my top. I set it down and stare at my reflection. My eyes are red from the grief but my makeup is in place, my hair has been pulled back, my clothes are folded neatly on the counter. I look at my body in the mirror, covering both breasts with my hands. From the outside, I look healthy. My hips are wide, my stomach is flat, my breasts are average and perky. When men look at me, sometimes their eyes linger.

But inside, I am not at all attractive. I am not internally appealing by Mother Nature's standards, because I do not have a working reproductive system. Reproduction is why we exist, after all. Reproduction is required to complete the circle of life. We are born, we reproduce, we raise our offspring, we die, our offspring reproduce, they raise *their* offspring, *they* die. Generation after generation of birth, life, and death. A beautiful circle not meant to be broken.

Yet . . . I am the break.

I was born. That's all I'm able to do until I die. I'm standing on the outside of the circle of life, watching the world spin while I am at a standstill.

And because he is married to me . . . Graham is at a standstill.

I pull on my clothes, covering up the body that has repeatedly failed us.

I walk into our kitchen and find Graham standing in front of the coffeepot. He looks up at me and I don't want him to know about the blood or the grief in the shower so I make the mistake of smiling at him. I quickly wipe the smile away but it's too late. He thinks it's a good day. My smiles give him hope. He walks up to me because, like an idiot, I'm not holding any of my usual weapons. I normally make sure I have both hands full with either a purse, a drink, an umbrella, a jacket. Sometimes all those things at once. Today I have nothing to shield myself from his love, so he hugs me good morning. I'm forced to hug him back.

My face fits perfectly between his neck and shoulder. His arms fit perfectly around my waist. I want to press my mouth against his skin and feel the chills that break out against my tongue. But if I do that I know what would follow.

His fingers would be skimming my waist.

His mouth, hot and wet, would find mine.

His hands would be freeing me from my clothes.

He would be inside me.

He would make love to me.

And when he stopped, I would be filled with hope.

And then all that hope would eventually escape with the blood.

I would be left devastated in the shower.

And then Graham would say to me, "Why do you take such long showers?"

And I would respond, "Because they're relaxing. The hot water is good for my skin."

I close my eyes and press my hands against his chest, easing myself away from him. I push away from him so often now, I sometimes wonder if my palms have imprinted against his chest.

"What time is dinner at your sister's house?" My questions ease the rejection. If I push away as I'm asking a question, the distraction makes it seem less personal.

Graham moves back to the coffeemaker and picks up his cup. He blows on it as he shrugs. "She gets off work at five. So probably seven."

I grab my weapons. My purse, a drink, my jacket. "'K. See you then. Love you." I kiss his cheek with my weapons safely separating us.

"I love you, too."

He says the words to the back of my head. I rarely give him the opportunity to say them to my face anymore.

When I get to my car, I send a text to Ava, my sister.

Not this month.

She's the only one I discuss it with anymore. I stopped talking to Graham about my cycle last year. Every month since we started trying for a baby years ago, Graham would console me when I'd find out I wasn't pregnant. I appreciated it in the beginning. Longed for it, even. But month after month, I grew to dread having to tell him how broken I was. And I knew if I was growing to dread him having to console me, that he was more than likely already tired of the disappointing routine. I decided early last year to only bring it up if the outcome were ever different.

So far, the outcome is always the same.

Sorry Babe,

my sister texts back.

You busy? I have news.

I back out of my driveway and set my phone to Bluetooth right before I call her. She answers in the middle of the first ring. Instead of hello, she says, "I know you don't want to talk about it, so let's talk about me."

I love that she gets me. "What's new with you?"

"He got the job."

I grip the steering wheel and force my voice to sound excited. "Did he? Ava, that's great!"

She sighs, and I can tell she's forcing herself to sound sad. "We move in two weeks."

I feel the tears threaten my eyes, but I've cried enough for one day. I really am happy for her. But she's my only sibling and now she's moving halfway across the world. Her husband, Reid, is from a huge family in France, and before they even got married, Ava said they would eventually move to Europe. The thought of it has always excited her so I know she's holding back her giddiness out of respect for my sadness over the distance this will put between us. I knew Reid applied for a few jobs last month, but a small part of me was selfishly hoping he wouldn't receive an offer.

"Will you guys be moving to Monaco?"

"No, Reid's job will be in Imperia. Different country, but it's only an hour drive to Monaco. Europe is so tiny, it's weird. You drive an hour here and you end up in New York. You drive an hour in Europe and you end up in a country that speaks a whole different language."

I don't even know where Imperia is but it already sounds like a better fit for her than Connecticut. "Have you told Mom yet?"

"No," she says. "I know how dramatic she's going to be,

so I figured I'd tell her in person. I'm on my way to her house right now."

"Good luck with that."

"Thanks," she says. "I'll call you and let you know how thick she lays on the guilt. See you at lunch tomorrow?"

"I'll be there. And it'll give her a whole day to calm down."

When we end the call, I find myself stuck at a red light on an empty street.

Literally *and* figuratively.

————

My father died when I was only fourteen. My mother remarried not long after that. It didn't surprise me. It didn't even upset me. My mother and father never had a relationship worth envying. I'm sure it was good in the beginning, but by the time I was old enough to know what love was, I knew they didn't have it.

I'm not sure my mother ever married for love, anyway. Money is her priority when it comes to seeking out a soul mate. My stepfather didn't win her over with his personality. He won her over with his beach house in Cape Cod.

Contrary to her wardrobe and attitude, my mother isn't rich. She grew up in a meager life in Vermont, the second of seven children. She married my father when he was moderately wealthy, and as soon as they had my sister and me, she demanded he buy her a home in Old Greenwich, Connecticut. It didn't matter that he had to work twice as hard to afford her lavish spending. I think he liked being at work more than he liked being home.

When my father passed away, there were assets, but not

enough to afford my mother the same lifestyle she was used to. It didn't take her long to rectify it, though. She married my stepfather in a private ceremony within a year of burying my father. She barely had to go eight months on a budget.

Even though my sister and I grew up in a wealthy lifestyle, we were not, and *are* not wealthy. Our mother has long spent anything my father left all those years ago. And my stepfather has biological children of his own who will receive his wealth when he dies. Because of all these factors, Ava and I have never considered ourselves wealthy, despite growing up and being raised by people who were.

It's why, as soon as we both graduated college, we immediately started working and paying our own bills. I never ask my mother for money. One, because I think it's inappropriate for a grown, married woman to have to ask her parents for help. And two, because she doesn't give freely. Everything comes with stipulations when it's given by my mother.

She will occasionally do things for Ava and me that we're both very grateful for. She paid off our vehicles for Christmas last year. And when I graduated college before meeting Graham, she helped me find an apartment and paid the first month's rent. But mostly, she spends her money on us in ways that benefit her. She'll buy us clothes she thinks we should wear because she doesn't like the ones we buy ourselves. She'll buy us spa days for our birthday and force us to spend it with her. She'll visit our homes and complain about our furniture and two days after she leaves, a delivery person will show up with all new furniture she picked out herself.

Graham absolutely hates it when she does this. He says a gift is a nice gesture, but an entire couch is an insult.

I'm not ungrateful for the things she does for me. I just know that I have to make my own way in life because even though money surrounds me, it doesn't line my pockets.

One of the things I've always been grateful for is our weekly lunches. Without fail, Ava and I join her for lunch at the country club near her house. I absolutely hate the place, but I enjoy time with Ava and we tolerate our mother enough to be able to look forward to our weekly lunches.

However, I have a feeling all that is going to change now that Ava is moving to Europe. She'll be preparing to move for the next week, which makes this our last lunch. The fullness that was just added to her life has made mine feel even emptier.

"Can't you fly home for lunch every week?" I ask Ava. "How am I supposed to entertain your mother all by myself?" We always refer to our mom as *your* mother when we're discussing her. It started as a joke in high school, but now we say it so often, we have to watch ourselves in front of her so that we don't slip up.

"Bring an iPad and Skype me in," she says.

I laugh. "Don't tempt me."

Ava picks up her phone and perks up when she reads a message. "I have an interview!"

"That was fast. What's the job?"

"It's for an English tutor at a local high school there. Doesn't pay shit but if I get the job, I'll learn how to cuss in French and Italian a lot faster."

Reid makes enough money that Ava doesn't have to work, but she's always had a job. She says the housewife role isn't a fit for her and I think that's what drew Reid to her. Neither of them want kids and Ava has always liked staying busy, so it works for them.

There are moments I envy her lack of desire for children. So many issues in my life and marriage would be nonexistent if I didn't feel so incomplete without a child.

"It's going to feel so weird without you, Ava," my mother says, claiming her seat at the table. I ordered her usual, a martini with extra olives. She sets her purse down in the chair next to her and pulls an olive from the toothpick. "I didn't think your move would bother me this much," my mother continues. "When are you coming home to visit?"

"I haven't even left yet," Ava says.

My mother sighs and picks up her menu. "I can't believe you're leaving us. At least you don't have kids. I can't imagine how I'd feel if you whisked grandchildren away from me."

I laugh under my breath. My mother is the most dramatic person I know. She hardly wanted to be a mother when Ava and I were little and I know for a fact she's in no hurry to be a grandmother. That's one aspect of her personality I'm able to find relief in. She doesn't nag me about having a baby. She only prays I never adopt.

Ava brought up adoption at one of our lunches with my mother two years ago. My mother actually scoffed at the idea. *"Quinn, please tell me you aren't pondering the idea of raising someone else's child,"* she said. *"It could have . . . issues."*

Ava just looked at me and rolled her eyes, then texted me under the table. *Yes, because biological children never have issues. Your mother needs to take a look in the mirror.*

I'm going to miss her so much.

I already miss you so much, I text her.

Still here.

"Honestly, girls, do neither of you know table etiquette by now?"

I look up and my mother is glaring at our phones. I lock mine and shove it in my purse.

"How is Graham?" my mother asks. She only asks out of courtesy. Even though Graham and I have been married for over seven years, she still wishes he were anyone else. He's never been good enough for me in her eyes, but not because she wants the best for me. If it were up to my mother, Graham would be Ethan and I'd be living in a house as big as hers and she'd be able to brag to all her friends about how much richer her daughter is than Evelyn Bradbury.

"He's great," I say, without elaborating. Because honestly, I'm only assuming Graham is great. I can't tell anymore what he's feeling or thinking or if he's great or good or miserable. "Really great."

"Are you feeling okay?"

"I feel fine. Why?"

"I don't know," she says, giving me the once-over. "You just look . . . tired. Are you getting enough sleep?"

"Wow," Ava mutters.

I roll my eyes and pick up my menu. My mother has always had a knack for direct insults. It never bothers me much because she jabs both Ava and me an even amount. Probably because we look so much alike. Ava is only two years older than me. We both have the same straight brown hair that reaches just past our shoulders. We have the same eyes that are identical in color to our hair. And according to our mother, we both look tired a lot.

We order our food and make small talk until it arrives.

Lunch is almost in the bag when someone approaches our table. "Avril?"

Ava and I both look up as Eleanor Watts adjusts her baby blue Hermès bag from one shoulder to the other. She tries to make it appear subtle, but she might as well hit us over the head with it while screaming, "Look at me! I can afford a fifteen-thousand-dollar purse!"

"Eleanor!" my mother exclaims. She stands and they air kiss and I force a smile when Eleanor looks at us.

"Quinn and Ava! Ladies, you are as beautiful as ever!" I have half a mind to ask her if I look tired. She takes an empty seat and cradles her arms around her bag. "How are you, Avril? I haven't seen you since . . ." She pauses.

"Quinn's engagement party to Ethan Van Kemp," my mother finishes.

Eleanor shakes her head. "I can't believe it's been that long. Look at us, we're grandparents now! How did that even happen?"

My mother picks up her martini glass and sips from it. "I'm not a grandmother yet," she says, almost as if she's bragging about it. "Ava is moving to Europe with her husband. Children interfere with their wanderlust," she says, waving her hand flippantly toward Ava.

Eleanor turns to me, her eyes scanning my wedding ring before they move back to my face. "And what about you, Quinn? You've been married a while now." She says this with ignorant laughter.

My cheeks burn, even though I should be used to this conversation by now. I know people don't mean to be insensitive but the intention doesn't make the comments hurt any less.

"When are you and Graham going to have a baby?"

"Do you not want children?"

"Keep trying, it'll happen!"

I clear my throat and pick up my glass of water. "We're working on it," I say, right before taking a sip. I want that to be the end of it, but my mother ensures it isn't. She leans in toward Eleanor like I'm not even here.

"Quinn is struggling with infertility," my mother says, as if it's anyone's business other than mine and Graham's.

Eleanor tilts her head and looks at me with pity. "Oh, honey," she says, placing her hand over mine. "I'm so sorry to hear that. Have the two of you considered IVF? My niece and her husband couldn't conceive naturally, but they're expecting twins any day now."

Have we considered IVF? *Is she serious right now?* I should probably just smile and tell her that's a great idea, but I'm suddenly aware that I have a limit and it was just reached. "Yes, Eleanor," I say, pulling my hand from hers. "We've been through three unsuccessful rounds, actually. It drained our savings account and we had to take out a second mortgage on our home."

Eleanor's face reddens and I'm immediately embarrassed by my reply, which means my mother is probably mortified. I don't look at her to validate my assumption, though. I can see Ava taking a swig of her water, trying to hide her laughter.

"Oh," Eleanor says. "That's . . . I'm sorry."

"Don't be," my mother interjects. "There's a reason for everything we go through, right? Even the struggles."

Eleanor nods. "Oh, I believe that wholeheartedly," she says. "God works in mysterious ways."

I laugh quietly. Her comment is reminiscent of the many

comments my mother has said to me in the past. I know she doesn't mean to be, but Avril Donnelly is the most insensitive of anyone.

Graham and I decided to start trying for a baby after only one year into our marriage. I was so naïve, thinking it would happen right away. After the first few unsuccessful months, I started to worry. I brought it up to Ava . . . and my *mother*, of all people. I told them my concerns before I even brought them up to Graham. My mother actually had the nerve to say that maybe God didn't think I was ready for a child yet.

If God doesn't give babies to people who aren't ready for them, He's got a lot of explaining to do. Because some of the mothers He chose to be fertile are very questionable. My own mother being one of them.

Graham has been supportive throughout the entire ordeal, but sometimes I wonder if he gets as frustrated as I do with all the questions. They get harder to answer over and over. Sometimes when we're together and people ask why we haven't had children yet, Graham blames it on himself. "I'm sterile," he'll say.

He's far from sterile, though. He had his sperm count tested in the beginning and it was fine. Actually, it was *more* than fine. The doctor used the word *lavish*. "You have a lavish amount of sperm, Mr. Wells."

Graham and I joked about that forever. But even though we tried to turn it into a joke, it meant the issue was all me. No matter how *lavish* his sperm count was, they weren't any good to my uterus. We had sex on a strict ovulation schedule. I took my temperature regularly. I ate and drank all the right foods. Still nothing. We pinched every penny we had and tried IUI and then IVF and were met with unsuccessful results.

We've discussed surrogacy, but it's just as expensive as IVF, and according to our doctor, due to the endometriosis I was diagnosed with at twenty-five, my eggs just aren't very reliable.

Nothing has been successful and we can't afford to keep repeating things we've already attempted, or even trying new techniques. I'm starting to realizc it might never happen.

This past year has been the absolute hardest of all the years. I'm losing faith. Losing interest. Losing hope.

Losing, losing, losing.

"Are you interested in adoption?" Eleanor asks.

My eyes swing to hers and I do my best to hide my exasperation. I open my mouth to answer her, but my mother leans in. "Her husband isn't interested in adoption," she says.

"*Mother*," Ava hisses.

She dismisses Ava with a flip of her hand. "It's not like I'm telling the whole world. Eleanor and I are practically best friends."

"You haven't seen each other in almost a decade," I say.

My mother squeezes Eleanor's hand. "Well, it certainly doesn't feel like that long. How is Peter?"

Eleanor laughs, welcoming the change of subject as much as I do. She starts telling my mother about his new car and his midlife crisis, which technically can't be a midlife crisis because he's well into his sixties, but I don't correct them. I excuse myself and head to the restroom in an attempt to run away from the constant reminder of my infertility.

I should have corrected her when my mother said Graham isn't interested in adoption. It's not that he's not interested, we just haven't had any luck in getting approved with an agency due to Graham's past. I don't understand how an adoption agency won't take into consideration that outside of that devastating conviction when he was a teenager, he's never so much as had a parking ticket. But, when you're only one of thousands of couples applying to adopt, even one strike against you can rule you out.

My mother is wrong. Neither of us is opposed to the idea, but we just can't get approved and we can no longer afford to keep trying. The treatments drained our bank account and now that we have a second mortgage on our home, we wouldn't even know how to afford the process if we *were* approved.

There are so many factors, and even though people think we haven't considered all of our options, we've considered them many times.

Hell, Ava even bought us a fertility doll when she went to Mexico three years ago. But nothing—not even superstition—has worked in our favor. Graham and I decided early last year to leave it up to chance, hoping it will happen naturally. It hasn't. And to be honest, I'm tired of swimming upstream.

The only thing holding me back from giving up completely is Graham. I know deep down if I let go of the dream of children, I will be letting go of Graham. I don't want to take the possibility of becoming a father away from him.

I'm the infertile one. Not Graham. Should he be punished by my infertility, too? He says kids don't matter to him as much as I matter to him, but I know he says that because he doesn't want to hurt me. And because he still has hope. But ten or twenty years from now, he'll resent me. He's human.

I feel selfish when I have these thoughts. I feel selfish

every time Graham and I have sex because I know I'm clinging to a hope that isn't there, dragging him along in a marriage that will eventually become too dull for either of us.
Which is why I spend hours every day online, searching for
something that might give me an answer. Anything. I'm in
support groups, I read all the message boards, the stories of
"miracle conceptions," the private adoption groups. I'm even
in several parenting groups just in case I do eventually have
a child. I'll be well prepared.

The one thing I don't participate in online is social media. I deleted all my accounts last year. I just couldn't take the
insensitive people on my timeline. April Fools' Day was the
worst. I lost track of how many of my friends think it's funny
to announce a fake pregnancy.

They have absolutely no compassion for people in my
situation. If they knew how many women have spent years
dreaming of a positive result, they'd never even think to
make light of it.

And don't get me started on the number of my friends
who complain about their children on their timeline. *"Evie
was up all night crying! Ugh! When will she sleep through the freaking night?"* or *"I can't wait for school to start back! These boys are
driving me insane!"*

If those mothers only knew.

If I were a mother, I wouldn't take a single moment of
my child's life for granted. I'd be grateful for every second
they whined or cried or got sick or talked back to me. I'd
cherish every second they were home during the summer
and I'd miss them every second they were away at school.

That's why I deleted social media. Because with every
status I saw, I became more and more bitter. I know those

mothers love their children. I know they don't take them for granted. But they don't understand what it's like not to be able to experience the things that bring them stress. And rather than despise every person I'm friends with online, I decided to delete my accounts in hopes it would bring me a small semblance of peace. But it hasn't.

Even without social media, not a single day goes by without being reminded that I might never be a mother. Every time I see a child. Every time I see a pregnant woman. Every time I run into people like Eleanor. Almost every movie I watch, every book I read, every song I hear.

And lately . . . every time my husband touches me.

Chapter Five

Then

I've never brought a guy to my apartment who wasn't Ethan. In fact, Ethan rarely came here, either. His apartment is nicer and much larger, so we always stayed there. But here I am, about to have rebound sex with a complete stranger just hours after I caught my fiancé having an affair.

If Ethan is capable of an affair, I am certainly capable of revenge sex with an extremely attractive guy. This entire day has been one bizarre event after another. _What's one more?_

I open the door and make a quick scan of the apartment in case there's anything I need to hide. In doing so, I realize I'd have to hide _everything_ and that's not possible with Graham one step behind me. I step aside and allow him to enter my apartment.

"Come in," I say.

Graham walks in after me, taking in my apartment with

his sad eyes. It's a small one-bedroom, but all the pictures of Ethan and me make it feel even smaller. Suffocating.

Leftover wedding invitations are still spread out over the dining room table.

The wedding dress I bought two weeks ago hangs from the entryway closet door. Seeing it makes me angry. I pull it down, fold the wedding bag over, and shove it in the closet. I don't even bother to hang it. I *hope* it gets wrinkled.

Graham walks over to my bar and picks up a photo of Ethan and me. In the picture, Ethan had just proposed and I said yes. I was flashing my ring at the camera. I stand next to Graham and look at the photo with him. His thumb brushes over the glass. "You look really happy here."

I don't respond, because he's right. I look happy in that photo because I *was* happy. Extremely happy. And oblivious. How many times had Ethan cheated on me? Did it happen before he even proposed to me? I have so many questions but I don't think I want the answers enough to eventually subject myself to an interrogation of Ethan.

Graham sets the photo down on the bar, facedown. And just like we did with our phones, he presses his finger against it and gives it a shove across the bar. It flies over the edge and shatters when it hits my kitchen floor.

Such a careless, rude thing to do in someone else's apartment. But I like that he did it.

There are two more pictures on the bar. I take the other one of Ethan and me and place it facedown. I push it across the bar and when that one shatters, I smile. So does Graham.

We both stare at the last photo. Ethan isn't in this one. It's a picture of me and my father, taken just two weeks before he died. Graham picks it up and brings it in closer for inspection. "Your dad?"

"Yeah."

He sets the photo back on the counter. "This one can stay."

Graham makes his way to the table where the leftover wedding invitations are laid out. I didn't choose the invitations. My mother and Ethan's mother did. They even mailed them out for us. My mother dropped these off two weeks ago and told me to look on Pinterest for crafts to make out of leftover invitations, but I had no desire to do anything with the invitations.

I'll definitely be throwing them away now. I don't want a single keepsake from this disaster of a relationship.

I follow Graham to the table and I take a seat on it, pulling my legs up. I sit cross-legged as Graham picks up one of the invitations and begins reading it aloud.

"The honor of your presence is requested at the nuptials of Quinn Dianne Whitley, daughter of Avril Donnelly and the late Kevin Whitley of Old Greenwich, Connecticut, to Ethan Samson Van Kemp, son of Dr. and Mrs. Samson Van Kemp, also of Old Greenwich. The event will take place at the prestigious Douglas Whimberly Plaza on the evening of . . ."

Graham pauses reading and looks at me. He points at the wedding invitation. "Your wedding invitation has the word *prestigious* in it."

I can feel the embarrassment in my cheeks.

I hate those invitations. When I saw them for the first time, I threw a fit at the pretentiousness of the entire thing, but my mother and pretentious go hand in hand. "My mother's doing. Sometimes it's easier to just let her get her way than put up a fight."

Graham raises an eyebrow and then tosses the invitation back onto the pile. "So, you're from Greenwich, huh?"

I can hear the judgment in his voice, but I don't blame him. Old Greenwich was recently rated one of the wealthiest cities in America. If you're a part of that wealth, it's commonplace to assume you're better than those who aren't. If you *aren't* part of that wealth, you judge those who are. It's a trend I refuse to be a part of.

"You don't come across as a girl who hails from Old Greenwich," he adds.

My mother would find that insulting, but his comment makes me smile. I take it as the compliment he meant it to be. And he's right . . . my microscopic apartment and the furnishings herein in no way resemble the home I grew up in.

"Thank you. I try very hard to separate myself from the dredges of high society."

"You'd have to try even harder if you wanted to convince people you're a *part* of high society. And I mean that in a good way."

Another comment my mother would be insulted by. I'm starting to like this guy more and more.

"Are you hungry?" I glance into the kitchen, wondering if I even have food to offer him. Luckily, he shakes his head.

"Nah. I'm still kind of full from all the Chinese food and infidelity."

I laugh quietly. "Yeah. Me too."

Graham scans my apartment once more, from my kitchen, to the living room, to the hallway that leads to the bedroom. Then his eyes land on me so hard I suck in a breath. He stares at me, then at my legs. I watch him as his eyes take in every part of me. It feels different, being looked at this way by someone who isn't Ethan. I'm surprised I like it.

I wonder what Graham thinks when he looks at me. Is he just as shocked as me that he ended up here, in my apartment, staring at me, rather than in his own apartment, standing by his own table, staring at Sasha?

Graham slips a hand inside his jacket pocket and pulls out a small box. He opens it and hands it to me. There's a ring inside of it. An obvious engagement ring, but it's significantly smaller than the one Ethan bought for me. I actually like this one better than mine. I wanted something a little subtler, but Ethan went with the most expensive one his father could afford.

"I've been carrying it around for two weeks," Graham says. He leans against the table next to me and stares down at the ring in my hand. "I haven't had the chance to propose because she kept blowing me off. I've been suspicious for a while now. She's such a good liar."

He says the last part of that sentence like he's impressed.

"I like it." I take the ring out of the box and slide it onto my right hand.

"You can keep it. I don't need it anymore."

"You should return it. It was probably expensive."

"I got it off eBay. It's nonrefundable."

I hold both hands out in front of me and compare the two rings. I look at my engagement ring and wonder why I never thought to tell Ethan beforehand that I didn't need something ostentatious. It's like I was so desperate to marry him, I lost my voice. My opinions. *Me.*

I slide my engagement ring off my left hand and put it in

the box, replacing the one that Graham bought Sasha. I hand the box to Graham, but he won't take it.

"Take it," I say, shoving it at him in an attempt to trade rings.

He leans back on his hands so that I can't offer it to him. "That ring could buy you a new car, Quinn."

"My car is paid for."

"Then give the ring back to Ethan. He can give it to Sasha. She'd probably like it better than the one I bought for her."

He won't take the ring, so I place it on the table. I'll mail it to Ethan's mother. She can decide what to do with it.

Graham stands up and shoves his hands in his jacket pockets. He really is better looking than Ethan. I wasn't saying that to flatter him earlier. Ethan's good looks derive mostly from confidence and money. He's always been well groomed, well dressed and a little bit cocky. If a person believes they're good-looking enough, the rest of the world eventually believes it, too.

But Graham's attractiveness is more sincere. He doesn't have any spectacular features that stand out individually. His hair isn't a unique shade of brown. His eyes are dark, but they don't verge on black or unusual. If anything, the flat chestnut makes his eyes look even more sad than they would if his eyes were blue or green. His lips are smooth and full, but not in a way that would make me think about their distinctiveness if they weren't right in front of me. He's not extremely tall to where his height would be something one would point out. He's probably right at six feet tall.

His attractiveness comes from the combination of all the many pieces of him. His unspectacular features somehow come together to create this pull in my chest. I love the way he looks at the world through a pair of calm eyes when his life is in complete turmoil. I'm completely drawn in by the way he smiles with only half of his mouth. When he speaks sometimes, he pauses and runs a thumb over his bottom lip. It's unintentionally sexy. I'm not sure I've ever been so physically attracted to someone I know so little.

Graham looks at the front door and I wonder if he changed his mind. Did I do something to turn him off? Is he still thinking about Sasha? He looks like he's about to call it a night. He pushes off the table and I remain seated, waiting on him to give me all the reasons why this isn't a good idea. He moves his body so that he's standing directly in front of me. It's like he doesn't know what to do with his hands before he tells me goodbye, so he just shoves them in the pockets of his jeans. His gaze falls to my neck before traveling back up to my face. It's the first time his eyes have looked more intense than anything else. "Where's your bedroom?"

I'm shocked by his forwardness.

I try to hide my internal conflict because I would love more than anything to get back at Ethan by fucking his lover's hot boyfriend. But knowing that's also why Graham is here makes me wonder if I want to be someone else's revenge sex.

It beats being alone right now.

I slide off the table and stand up. Graham doesn't step back, so our bodies touch briefly before I move past him. I feel it everywhere, but mostly in my lungs. "Follow me."

I'm still nervous, but not nearly as nervous as when I was putting the key into the front door. Graham's voice calms me. His entire presence calms me. It's hard to be intimidated by someone so sad.

"I never make my bed," I admit as I open the door to my

messy bedroom. I turn on a lamp and Graham's frame fills the doorway.

"Why not?" He takes a couple steps into my bedroom and it's the strangest sight. This guy I don't know at all, standing in my bedroom. The same bedroom where I should be wallowing on my bed in brokenhearted anguish right now.

And what about Graham? Does this feel just as strange to him? I know he's had doubts about Sasha or he wouldn't have been following her to Ethan's apartment building with an engagement ring burning a hole in his pocket.

Has Graham been looking for an out? Have I? Am I just now realizing it? Because right now, I'm nervous and anxious and everything I shouldn't be just hours after my life took a turn for the worse.

I'm staring wordlessly at Graham when I realize I haven't answered his question about why I don't make my bed. I clear my throat. "It takes approximately two minutes to properly make a bed. That means the average person wastes an entire thirty-eight days of their life making a bed they're just going to mess up."

Graham looks amused. He gives me one of his half smiles and then glances at my bed. Watching him take in my bed makes me feel unprepared for this. I was prepared for a reunion with Ethan tonight. Not for sex with a stranger. I don't know that I want the lights on. I don't even know that I want to be wearing what I'm wearing. I don't want Graham to have to take clothes off my body that were intended for another man. I need a moment to collect myself. I haven't had a moment yet and I think I need one.

"I need to . . ." I point toward the bathroom door. "I need a minute."

Graham's lips curl up into a slightly bigger smile and I realize in this moment that those incredible lips are about to be touching mine and I suddenly don't feel worthy. It's a weird feeling because I am a confident woman. But Graham sets a standard for confidence that I'm not used to. His confidence makes mine feel like uncertainty.

I shut myself in the bathroom and stare at the closed door. For a moment, I forget what I'm even doing in here, but then I remember I'm about to have sex with a guy who isn't Ethan for the first time in four years. I kick it into high gear. I open my closet door and sift through it to find the most unassuming thing I can find. It's a blush-colored nightgown with spaghetti straps. It isn't see-through, but he'll be able to tell I'm not wearing the bra I'm currently ripping off. I pull the gown on and walk over to the bathroom sink. I pull my hair up into a loose bun to get it out of my face and then I brush my teeth and my tongue until I'm convinced my mouth won't remind him of the Chinese food we stole earlier.

I check myself in the mirror and stare for a little too long. I just can't seem to wrap my mind around the fact that today is ending this way. Me . . . anticipating sex with a man who isn't my fiancé.

I blow out a calming breath and then open my bathroom door.

I'm not sure what I expected, but Graham looks the same. He's still standing in front of the bathroom door, still wearing his jeans and his T-shirt. And his jacket. *And* his shoes. I'm looking at his shoes when he whispers, "Wow."

I look back up at him. He's closer. His face is so close to mine and I really want to reach up and touch his jaw. I don't usually pay attention to a person's jaw, but his is strong and covered in stubble, leading all the way up to his mouth that looks as sad as his eyes.

I think he notices our proximity because he immediately takes a step back and waves his hand toward my bed.

My pillows are all lined up and my duvet is tucked under the mattress and completely wrinkle-free. The corner of it is neatly folded over, revealing the sheet beneath it.

"You made my bed?" I walk toward the bed and take a seat on it. This isn't how I envisioned this starting, but it's only because I've been stuck in an Ethan routine for the last four years.

Graham lifts my duvet and I pull my legs up and climb into my bed. I scoot over far enough for him to join me, but he doesn't. He just pulls the covers over me and sits down on the bed, facing me. "It's nice, huh?"

I adjust my pillow and roll over onto my side. He tucked the end of my blanket beneath the mattress, so it doesn't give way. It feels snug and tight around my feet and legs. I actually kind of like it. And somehow even the top of the blanket seems to be snuggling me.

"I'm impressed."

He reaches a hand to a loose strand of hair and tucks it behind my ear. The gesture is sweet. I don't know Graham very well at all, but I can tell he's good. I could tell he was good the second Ethan opened the door and Graham didn't physically attack him. It takes someone with a healthy amount of confidence and self-control to walk away quietly from a situation like that.

Graham's hand comes to rest on my shoulder. I'm not sure what changed in him since we walked out of the bar, or even since walking into my bedroom. But I can tell his thoughts are no longer where they were earlier. He slides his hand down the blanket, coming to rest on my hip. His entire expression seems rife with indecision. I try to ease the conflict a little.

"It's okay," I whisper. "You can go."

He sighs heavily with relief. "I thought I could do this. Me and you. Tonight."

"I thought I could, too, but . . . it's way too soon for a rebound."

I can feel the heat of his hand through the duvet. He moves it up a little and grips my waist as he leans forward. He kisses me softly on the cheek. I close my eyes and swallow hard, feeling his lips move to my ear. "Even if it wasn't too soon, I still wouldn't want to be your rebound." I feel him pull away. "Goodnight, Quinn."

I keep my eyes closed as he lifts off the bed. I don't open them until he turns off my lamp and closes my bedroom door.

He wouldn't want to be my rebound?

Was that a compliment? Or was that him saying he's not interested?

I mull over his parting words for a moment, but I soon shove them to the back of my mind. I'll think about Graham's words tomorrow. All I feel like thinking about in this moment is everything I've lost in the past few hours.

My entire life changed today. Ethan was supposed to be my other half for the rest of my life. Everything I thought I knew about my future has been derailed. Everything I thought I knew about Ethan has been a lie.

I hate him. I hate him because no matter what happens from this point forward, I will never be able to trust someone like I trusted him.

I roll onto my back and stare up at my ceiling. "Fuck you, Ethan Van Kemp."

What kind of last name is that, anyway? I say my name out loud and add his last name to it. "Quinn Dianne Van Kemp."

It's never sounded as stupid as it sounds right now. I'm relieved it will never be my name.

I'm relieved I caught him cheating.

I'm relieved I had Graham to walk me through it.

I'm relieved Graham decided to leave just now.

In that heated moment with Graham in the restaurant, I felt revengeful. I felt like sleeping with him would somehow ease the pain Ethan caused me today. But now that Graham has left, I realize nothing will cushion this feeling. It's just one huge, inconvenient, painful wound. I want to lock my front door and never leave my apartment. Except for ice cream. Tomorrow I'll leave for ice cream but after that, I'm never leaving my apartment again.

Until I run out of ice cream.

I toss the covers away and walk to the living room to lock the front door. When I reach up to the chain lock, I notice a yellow Post-it stuck to the wall next to the door. There's a phone number on it. Beneath the phone number is a short message.

Call me someday. After *your rebound guy.*

Graham

I have a mixed reaction to his note. Graham seems nice and I've already established my attraction to him, but at this point, I'm not sure I can stomach the thought of dating again.

It's only been a couple of hours since my last relationship. And even if I got to a point where I felt like dating again, the last person I would want to date would be the ex-boyfriend of the girl who had a hand in ruining everything good in my life.

I want as far from Ethan and Sasha as I can get. And sadly, Graham would only remind me of them.

Even still, his note makes me smile. But only for a second.

I go back to my room and crawl under my covers. I pull them over my head, and the tears begin to fall. Graham was right when he said, *"You'll cry tonight. In bed. That's when it'll hurt the most. When you're alone."*

Chapter Six

Now

The day Ava left for Europe, she left me a gift. It was a bag of exotic tea that's supposed to help with infertility. The problem was, it tasted like I had ripped open a bag of tea and poured it straight on my tongue, then washed it down with coffee beans.

So . . . the miracle fertility tea is out of the question. I'm leaving it up to chance again. I've decided I'll try for one more month. Maybe two, before I tell Graham I'm finished trying.

Two more months before I tell him I really am ready to open that wooden box on my bookshelf.

I'm sitting on our kitchen counter in one of Graham's T-shirts when he walks through the door. My bare legs are dangling, feet pointing toward the floor. He doesn't immediately notice me, but once he does, I become his entire focus. I grip the counter between my legs, opening them just enough to let him in on my plans for the night. His eyes are locked on my hands as he pulls at his tie, sliding it from his collar, dropping it to the floor.

That's one of my favorite things about him working later than me. I get to watch him take his tie off every day.

"Special occasion?" He grins as he takes me in with one fell swoop. He's walking toward me and I give him my best seductive smile. The one that says I want to put all the pretending behind us for the night. Pretending we're okay, pretending we're happy, pretending this is exactly the life we'd choose if the choice were ours.

By the time he reaches me, his jacket is off and the first few buttons of his shirt are undone. He slips off his shoes at the same time his hands slide up my thighs. I wrap my arms around his neck and he presses against me, ready and eager. His lips meet my neck and then my jaw and then he presses them gently against my mouth. "Where would you like me to take you?" He picks me up and secures me against him as I lock my legs around his waist.

I whisper in his ear. "Our bedroom sounds nice."

Even though I've all but given up on the chances of becoming pregnant, I'm obviously still clinging to that small sliver of hope on at least a monthly basis. I don't know if that makes me strong or pathetic. Sometimes I feel I'm both.

Graham drops me on the bed, our clothes covering the distance from the kitchen to our room like scattered breadcrumbs. He settles himself between my legs and then pushes inside me with a groan. I take him in with silence.

Graham is consistent in every possible way outside of the bedroom. But inside the bedroom, I never know what I'm going to get. Sometimes he makes love to me with patience and selflessness, but sometimes he's needy and quick and selfish. Sometimes he's talkative while he's inside me, whispering words that make me fall even more in love with him. But sometimes he's angry and loud and says things that make me blush.

I never know what I'm going to get with him. That used to excite me.

But now I tend to want only one of the many sides of him in the bedroom. The needy, quick, and selfish side of him. I feel less guilt when I get this side of him because lately, the only thing I really want out of sex is the end result.

Sadly, tonight is not the selfish version of Graham in the bedroom. Tonight he's the exact opposite of what I need from him right now. He's savoring every second of it. Pushing into me with controlled thrusts while he tastes all the parts of my neck and upper body. I try to be as involved as he is, occasionally pressing my lips to his shoulders or pulling at his hair. But it's hard to pretend I don't want him to get it over with. I turn my head to the side so he can leave his mark on my neck while I wait.

He eventually begins to pick up the pace and I tense a little, anticipating the end, but he pulls out of me unexpectedly. He's lowering himself down my body, drawing my left nipple into his mouth when I recognize this pattern. He's going to make his way down, slowly tasting every part of me until he eventually slides his tongue between my legs, where he'll waste a precious ten minutes and I'll have to think too much about what day it is, what time it is, what fourteen days from now will be, what I would do or say if the test is finally positive, how long I'll cry in the shower if it's negative again.

I don't want to think tonight. I just want him to hurry.

I pull his shoulders until his mouth is back near mine and I whisper in his ear, "It's okay. You can finish." I try to guide him back inside of me but he pulls back. I make eye contact with him for the first time since we were in the kitchen.

He brushes my hair back gently. "Are you not in the mood anymore?"

I don't know how to tell him I was never in the mood to begin with without hurting his feelings. "It's fine. I'm ovulating."

I try to kiss him, but before my lips meet his, he rolls off me.

I stare at the ceiling, wondering how he can possibly be upset with me for that comment. We've been trying to get pregnant for so long now. This routine is nothing new.

I feel him leave the bed. When I look at him, his back is to me and he's pulling on his pants.

"Are you seriously mad because I'm not in the mood?" I ask, sitting up. "If you don't recall, we were just having sex less than a minute ago, regardless of my mood."

He spins around and faces me, taking a pause to gather his thoughts. He pulls a frustrated hand through his hair and then steps closer to the bed. The clench of his jaw reveals his irritation, but his voice is quiet and calm when he speaks. "I'm tired of fucking for the sake of science, Quinn. It would be nice if just one time I could be inside you because you *want* me there. Not because it's a requirement to getting pregnant."

His words sting. Part of me wants to lash out and say something hurtful in return, but most of me knows he's only saying it because it's true. Sometimes I miss the spontaneous lovemaking, too. But it got to a point where all our failed attempts at getting pregnant began to hurt too much. So much that I realized the less sex we had, the less disappointment I would feel. If we only had sex during the days I was ovulating, I would be disappointed a fewer number of times.

I wish he could understand that. I wish he knew that sometimes the trying is harder for me than the failing. I try to empathize with his feelings, but it's hard because I don't know that he truly empathizes with mine. How could he? He's not the one failing every time.

I can be disappointed in myself later. Right now, I just need him back on this bed. Back inside me. Because he's right. Sex with my husband is definitely a requirement to getting pregnant. And today is our best chance this month.

I kick the covers off me so that I'm sprawled out on the bed. I press one of my hands against my stomach and pull his attention there. "I'm sorry," I whisper, trailing my fingers upward. "Come back to bed, Graham."

His jaw is still clenched, but his eyes are following my hand. I watch his struggle as part of him wants to storm out of the room and part of him wants to storm me. I don't like that he's not convinced I want him yet, so I roll over onto my stomach. If there's one thing about me physically that Graham loves the most, it's the view of me from behind. "I want you inside me, Graham. That's all I want. I promise." *I lie.*

I'm relieved when he groans.

"Dammit, Quinn." And then he's on the bed again, his hands on my thighs, his lips against my ass. He slips one hand beneath me and presses it flat against my stomach, lifting me enough so that he can easily slide into me from behind. I moan and grasp the sheets convincingly.

Graham grips my hips and lifts himself up onto his knees, pulling me back until he's all the way inside me.

I no longer have the patient Graham. He's a mixture of emotions right now, thrusting into me with impatience and anger. He's focused on finishing and not at all focused on me and that's exactly how I want it.

I moan and meet his thrusts, hoping he doesn't recognize that the rest of me is disconnected to this moment. After a while, we somehow move from both being on our knees, to me being pressed stomach first into the mattress as all his weight bears down on me. He grips my hands that are gripping the sheets and I relax as he releases a groan. I wait for him to fill me with hope.

But he doesn't.

Instead, he pulls out of me, pressing himself against the small of my back. Then he groans one final time against my neck. I feel it meet my skin, warm and wet as it slides down my hip and seeps into the mattress.

Did he just . . .

He did.

Tears sting at my eyes when I realize he didn't finish inside me. I want to climb out from under him, but he's too heavy and he's still tense and I can't move.

As soon as I feel him begin to relax, I attempt to lift up. He rolls over onto his back. I roll away from him, using the sheet beneath me to wipe myself clean. Tears are streaming down my cheeks and I swipe at them angrily. I am so angry I can't even speak. Graham just watches me as I try to conceal the anger I'm feeling. And the embarrassment.

Graham is my husband, but tonight he was a means to an end. And even though I tried to convince him otherwise, he just proved that to himself by not giving me the only thing I wanted from him tonight.

I can't stop the tears from falling, but I try anyway. I pull the blanket up to my eyes and Graham rolls off the bed and grabs his pants. My quiet tears begin to turn to sobs and my shoulders begin to shake. It's not like me to do this in front of him. I usually save this for my long showers.

As Graham grabs his pillow off the bed, part of him looks like he wants to console me while the other part looks like he wants to scream at me. The angry part wins out and he begins to walk toward the door.

"Graham," I whisper.

My voice stops him in his tracks and he turns around and faces me. He seems so heartbroken, I don't even know what to say. I wish I could say I'm sorry for wanting a baby more than I want him. But that wouldn't help, because it would be a lie. I'm not sorry. I'm bitter that he doesn't understand what sex has become to me over the last few years. He wants me to continue to want him, but I can't when sex and making love have always given me hope that it might be that one in a million chance I'll get pregnant. And all the sex and love-making that leads to the hope then leads to the moment all that hope is overcome by devastation.

Over the years, the entire routine and the emotions it brings started running together. I couldn't separate the sex from the hope and I couldn't separate the hope from the devastation. Sex became hope became devastation.

SexHopeDevastation. Devastation. Devastation.

Now it *all* feels devastating to me.

He'll never understand that. He'll never understand that it isn't *him* I don't want. It's the devastation.

Graham watches me, waiting for me to follow his name up with something else. But I don't. I can't.

He nods a little, turning away from me. I watch the muscles in his back tense. I watch his fist clench and unclench. I can see him release a heavy sigh even though I can't hear it. And then he opens the bedroom door with ease before slamming it shut with all his strength.

A loud thud hits the door from the other side. I squeeze my eyes shut and my whole body tenses as it happens again. And then again.

I listen as he punches the door five times from the other side. I listen as he releases his hurt and rejection against the wood because he knows there's nowhere else it can go. When everything is silent again . . . I shatter.

Chapter Seven

Then

It's been difficult getting over Ethan. Well, not *Ethan* per se. Losing the relationship was harder than losing Ethan. When you associate yourself with another person for so long, it's difficult becoming your own person again. It took a few months before I finally deleted him from my apartment completely. I got rid of the wedding dress, the pictures, the gifts he'd given me over the years, clothes that reminded me of him. I even got a new bed, but that probably had more to do with just wanting a new bed than being reminded of Ethan.

It's been six months now and the only reason I'm on my second date with this Jason guy is because the first one wasn't a complete disaster. And Ava talked me into it.

As much as my mother loved Ethan and still wishes I'd forgive him, I think she would like Jason even more. That should probably be a positive but it isn't. My mother and I have very different tastes. I'm waiting for Jason to say or do something that my mother would hate so that I can be drawn to him a little more than I am.

He's already repeated several questions he asked me last Friday. He asked how old I was. I told him I was twenty-five, the same age I was last Friday. He asked me when my birthday was and I told him it was still July 26.

I'm trying not to be a bitch, but he makes it difficult when it's clear he didn't pay attention to a single thing I said last week.

"So you're a Leo?" he asks.

I nod.

"I'm a Scorpio."

I have no idea what that says about him. Astrology has never been my thing. Besides, it's hard to pay attention to Jason because there's something much more interesting behind him. Two tables away, smirking in my direction, is Graham. As soon as I recognize him, I immediately look down at my plate.

Jason says something about the compatibility of Scorpios and Leos and I look him in the eyes, hoping he can't see the chaos I'm feeling right now. But my resolve is broken because Graham is standing now. I can't help but look over Jason's shoulder and watch as Graham excuses himself from his table. He locks eyes with me again and begins to head in our direction.

I'm squeezing the napkin in my lap, wondering why I'm suddenly more nervous at the sight of Graham than I've ever been around Jason. I make eye contact with Graham right before he approaches the table. But as soon as I look at him, he looks away. He nods his head once, in the direction he's walking. He passes our table, his hand just barely touching my elbow. A one second graze of his finger across my skin. I suck in air.

"How many siblings do you have?"

I lay my napkin on the table. "Still just the one." I push my chair back. "I'll be right back. I need to use the restroom."

Jason scoots back, half standing as I push my chair in. I smile at him and turn toward the restrooms. Toward Graham.

Why am I so nervous?

The bathrooms are at the rear of the restaurant. You have to make a turn behind a partition to find the hallway. Graham has already disappeared around the corner, so I pause before I make the turn. I put my hand on my chest, hoping it will somehow calm what's happening inside of it. And then I blow out a quick breath and walk into the hallway.

Graham is leaning casually against a wall, his hand in the pocket of his suit. The sight of him both excites me and comforts me, but I'm also nervous because I feel bad for never calling him.

Graham smiles his lazy half smile at me. "Hello, Quinn." His eyes still frown a little with his smile and I'm happy to see that. I don't know why. I like that he always looks to be battling some inner perpetual turmoil.

"Hey." I stand awkwardly a few feet away from him.

"Graham," he says, touching his chest. "In case you forgot."

I shake my head. "I didn't. It's kind of hard to forget every detail of the worst day of your life."

My comment makes him smile. He pushes off the wall and takes a step closer to me. "You never called."

I shrug like I haven't given his phone number much

thought. But in reality, I look at it every day. It's still stuck to the wall where he left it. "You said to call you after my rebound guy. I'm just now getting around to the rebound guy."

"Is that who you're with tonight?"

I nod. He takes a step closer, leaving only two feet between us. But it feels like he's suffocating me.

"What about you?" I ask. "Are you with your rebound girl?"

"My rebound was two girls ago."

I hate that answer. I hate it enough to be done with this conversation. "Well . . . congratulations. She's pretty."

Graham narrows his eyes as if he's trying to read all the things I'm not saying. I take a step toward the women's restroom and put my hand on the door. "It was good to see you, Graham."

His eyes are still narrowed and he tilts his head a little. I'm not sure what else to say. I walk into the women's restroom and allow the door to swing shut behind me. I let out a huge sigh. That was intense.

Why was that so intense?

I walk over to the sink and turn on the water. My hands are shaking, so I wash them in warm water, hoping the lavender soap helps calm my nerves. I dry them and then look at them in the mirror, trying to convince myself I wasn't that affected by Graham. But I was. They're still shaking.

For six months I've wanted to call him, but for six months I've talked myself out of it. And now, knowing he's moved on and he's with someone else, I might have blown my chance. Not that I wanted one. I still hold fast to the belief that he would remind me too much of what happened. If I do decide to start something up with someone, I'd want it to be someone brand-new. Someone completely unrelated to the worst days of my life.

Someone like Jason, maybe?

"Jason," I whisper. *I should get back to my date.*

When I open the door, Graham is still in the same spot. Still looking at me with his head tilted. I stop short and the door hits me in the back when it swings shut, pushing me forward a step.

I glance toward the end of the hallway and then look back at Graham. "Were we not finished?"

He inhales a slow breath as he takes a step toward me. He stops only a foot from me this time, sliding both hands back into his pockets. "How are you?" His voice is quiet, like it's hard for him to get it out. The way his eyes are searching mine makes it obvious he's referring to everything I've been through with the breakup. Calling off the wedding.

I like the sincerity in his question. I'm feeling all the same comfort his presence brought me that night six months ago. "Good," I say, nodding a little. "A few residual trust issues, but other than that I can't complain."

He looks relieved. "Good."

"What about you?"

He stares at me a moment, but I don't see what I'm hoping to see in his eyes. Instead, I see regret. Sadness. Like maybe he still hasn't recovered from losing Sasha. He shrugs, but doesn't answer with words.

I try not to let my pity show, but I think it does. "Maybe this new girl will be better than Sasha. And you'll finally be able to get over her."

Graham laughs a little. "I'm over Sasha," he says with conviction. "Pretty sure I was over Sasha the moment I met you."

He gives me absolutely zero time to absorb his words before he throws more of them at me. "We better get back to our dates, Quinn." He turns and walks out of the hallway.

I stand still, dumbfounded by his words. *"Pretty sure I was over Sasha the moment I met you."*

I can't believe he just said that to me. He can't say something like that and then just walk away! I stalk after him, but he's already halfway to his table. I catch Jason's eye and he smiles when he sees me, standing up. I try to compose myself, but it's hard as I watch Graham lean down and give his date a quick kiss on the side of her head before he takes his seat across from her again.

Is he trying to make me jealous? If he is, it's not working. I don't have time for frustrating men. I barely have time for boring men like Jason.

Jason has walked around the table to pull out my chair for me. Before I take my seat, Graham makes eye contact with me again. I swear I can see him smirk a little. I don't know why I stoop to his level, but I lean over and give Jason a quick kiss on the mouth.

Then I sit.

I have a clear shot of Graham as Jason walks back around to his side of the table. Graham is no longer smirking.

But I am.

"I'm ready to get out of here," I say.

Chapter Eight

Now

Ava and I talked on the phone almost every day when she lived in Connecticut, but now that she's halfway across the world, we seem to talk even more. Sometimes twice a day, even with the time difference.

"I have to tell you something."

There's a trepidation in her voice. I close my front door and walk my things to the kitchen counter. "Are you okay?" I set down my purse, pull the phone from between my shoulder and ear, and grip the phone in my hand.

"Yes," she says. "I'm fine. It's nothing like that."

"Well, what is it? You're scaring me, so it's obviously bad news."

"It's not. It's . . . good news actually."

I sink to the living room sofa. If it's good news, why does she sound so unhappy?

And then it clicks. She doesn't even have to say it. "You're pregnant?" There's a pause. It's so quiet on her end of the phone, I look down at mine to make sure we're still connected. "Ava?"

"I'm pregnant," she confirms.

Now *I'm* the quiet one. I put my hand against my chest, feeling the remnant pounding of my heart. For a moment, I feared the worst. But now that I know she's not dying, I can't help but wonder why she doesn't sound happy. "Are you okay?"

"Yeah," she says. "It's unexpected of course. Especially finding out so soon after moving here. But we've had a couple of days to let it sink in now. We're actually excited."

My eyes well up with tears but I'm not sure why I feel like crying. This is good. She's excited. "Ava," I whisper. "That's . . . wow."

"I know. You're going to be an aunt. I mean, I know you already are because of Graham's sister's children, but I just never thought you'd be an aunt because of me."

I force a smile but realize it isn't enough, so I force a laugh. "Your mother is going to be a grandma."

"That's the craziest part," she says. "She didn't know how to take the news. She's either drowning in martinis today or out shopping for baby clothes."

I swallow down the immediate envy, knowing my mother knew before I did. "You . . . you told her already?"

Ava releases a sigh full of regret. "Yesterday. I would have told you first but . . . I wanted Mom's advice. On how to tell you."

I lean my head back against the couch. She was scared to tell me? Does she think I'm that unstable? "Did you think I'd be jealous of you?"

"No," she says immediately. "I don't know, Quinn. Upset, maybe? Disappointed?"

Another tear falls, but this time it isn't a tear of joy. I quickly wipe it away. "You know me better than that." I stand up in an attempt to compose myself, even though she can't see me. "I have to go. Congratulations."

"Quinn."

I end the call and stare down at my phone. How could my own sister think I wouldn't be happy for her? She's my best friend. I'm happy for her and Reid. I'd never resent her for being able to have children. The only thing I resent is that she conceived so easily by *accident*.

Oh, God. I'm a terrible person.

No matter how much I'm trying to deny it, I do feel resentment. *And* I hung up on her. This should be one of the best moments of her life, but she loves me too much to be fully excited about it. And I'm being too selfish to allow that.

I immediately call her back.

"I'm sorry," I blurt out as soon as she answers.

"It's okay."

"No, it's not. You're right. I'm grateful that you were trying to be sensitive to what Graham and I are going through, but really, Ava. I am so happy for you and Reid. And I'm excited to be an aunt again."

I can hear the relief in her voice when she says, "Thank you, Quinn."

"There is one thing, though."

"What?"

"You told your *mother* first? I will never forgive you for that."

Ava laughs. "I regretted it as soon as I told her. She

actually said, '*But will you raise it in Europe? It'll have an accent!*'"

"Oh, God help us."

We both laugh.

"I have to name a *human,* Quinn. I hope you help me because Reid and I are never going to agree on a name."

We chat a little longer. I ask her the typical questions. How she found out. *Routine doctor's visit.* When she's due. *April.* When they'll find out what they're having. *They want it to be a surprise.*

When the conversation comes to an end, Ava says, "Before you hang up . . ." She pauses. "Have you heard back from the last adoption agency you applied to?"

I stand up to walk toward the kitchen. I'm suddenly thirsty. "I have," I tell her. I grab a water out of the refrigerator, take the cap off, and bring it to my mouth.

"That doesn't sound good."

"It is what it is," I say. "I can't change Graham's past and he can't change my present. No point in dwelling on it."

It's quiet on Ava's end of the line for a moment. "But what if you can find a baby through private adoption?"

"With what money?"

"Ask your mother for the money."

"This isn't a purse, Ava. I'm not letting your mother buy me a human. I'd be indebted to her for eternity." I look at the door just as Graham walks into the living room. "I have to go. I love you. Congratulations."

"Thank you," she says. "Love you, too."

I end the call just as Graham's lips meet my cheek. "Ava?" He reaches for my water and takes a drink.

I nod. "Yep. She's pregnant."

He nearly chokes on the water. He wipes his mouth and laughs a little. "Seriously? I thought they didn't want kids."

I shrug. "Turns out they were wrong."

Graham smiles and I love seeing that he's genuinely happy for them. What I hate, though, is that his smile fades and concern fills his eyes. He doesn't say it, but he doesn't have to. I see the worry. I don't want him to ask me how I feel about it, so I smile even wider and try to convince him I'm perfectly fine.

Because I am. Or I will be. Once it all sinks in.

————

Graham made spaghetti carbonara. He insisted on cooking tonight. I usually like when he cooks, but I have a feeling he only insisted tonight because he's afraid I might be having a negative reaction to the fact that my sister can get pregnant by accident and I can't even get pregnant after six years of trying on purpose.

"Have you heard back from the adoption agency yet?"

I look up from my plate of food and stare at Graham's mouth. The mouth that just produced that question. I grip my fork and look back down at my plate.

We've gone a month without discussing our infertility issues. Or the fact that neither of us has initiated sex since the night he slept in the guest room. I was hoping we could go *another* month.

I nod. "Yeah. They called last week."

I see the roll of his throat as he breaks eye contact with me and scoots his fork aimlessly around his plate. "Why didn't you tell me?"

"I'm telling you now."

"Only because I asked."

I don't respond to him again. He's right. I should have told him when I got the call last week, but it hurts. I don't like talking about things that hurt. And lately everything hurts. Which is why I barely talk anymore.

But I also didn't tell him because I know how much guilt he still holds over that incident. The incident that has been responsible for our third rejection from an adoption agency.

"I'm sorry," he says.

His apology creates an ache in my chest because I know he isn't apologizing for our snippy exchange. He's apologizing because he knows we were turned down because of his past conviction.

It happened when he was only nineteen. He doesn't talk about it a lot. Hardly ever. The wreck wasn't his fault, but because of the alcohol in his system, it didn't matter. The charge still lingers on his record and will forever put us out of the running when couples *without* criminal charges are approved in place of us.

But that was years ago. It's not something he can change and he's been punished enough for what happened when he was just a teenager. The last thing he needs is for his own wife to blame him, too.

"Don't apologize, Graham. If you apologize for not being approved for adoption then I'll have to apologize for not being able to conceive. It is what it is."

His eyes momentarily meet mine and I see a flash of appreciativeness in him.

He runs his finger around the rim of his glass. "The adoption issue we're having is a direct result of a poor decision

I made. You can't control the fact that you can't conceive. There's a difference."

Graham and I aren't a perfect example of a marriage, but we are a perfect example of knowing when and where the blame should be placed. He never makes me feel guilty for not being able to conceive and I've never wanted him to feel guilty for a choice he already holds way too much guilt for.

"There may be a difference, but it isn't much of one. Let's just drop it." I'm tired of this conversation. We've had it so many times and it changes nothing. I take another bite, thinking of a way we can change the subject, but he just continues.

"What if . . ." He leans forward now, pushing his plate toward the center of the table. "What if you applied for adoption on your own? Left me out of the equation?"

I stare at him, thinking of all that question entails. "I can't. We're legally married." He doesn't react. Which means he knew exactly what he was suggesting. I lean back in my chair and eye him cautiously. "You want us to get a divorce so I can apply on my own?"

Graham reaches across the table and covers my hand with his. "It wouldn't mean anything, Quinn. We would still be together. But it might make our chances better if we just . . . you know . . . pretended I wasn't in the picture. Then my past conviction couldn't affect our chances."

I contemplate his idea for a moment, but it's just as preposterous as the fact that we keep trying to conceive. Who would approve a divorced, single woman to adopt a child over a stable, married couple with more income and more opportunity? Becoming approved by an agency isn't an easy process, so actually being selected and the birth mother going through with the adoption are even harder. Not to mention the fees. Graham brings in twice as much money as me and we still might not be able to afford it, even if I were somehow approved for the process.

"We don't have the money." I expect that to be the end of it, but I can tell by his expression that he has another suggestion. I can also tell by the way he's not readily suggesting whatever it is he's thinking that it must include my mother. I immediately shake my head and grab my plate. I stand up. "We aren't asking her. The last time I spoke to her about adoption, she told me God would give me a child when I was ready. And like I told Ava earlier, the last thing we need is for her to feel like she owns a piece of our family." I walk the plate to the sink. Graham scoots back in his chair and stands.

"It was just an idea," he says, following me into the kitchen. "You know, there's a guy at my work who said his sister tried for seven years to get pregnant. She found out three months ago that she's having a baby. Due in January."

Yes, Graham. That's called a miracle. And it's called a miracle because the chances of it happening are slim to none.

I turn on the water and wash my plate. "You talk about it to people at work?"

Graham is next to me now, lowering his plate into the sink. "Sometimes," he says quietly. "People ask why we haven't had kids."

I can feel the pressure building in my chest. I need to be done with the conversation. I want Graham to be done, too, but he leans against the counter and dips his head. "Hey."

I give him a sidelong glance to let him know I'm listening, but then I move my attention back to the dishes.

"We barely talk about it anymore, Quinn. I don't know if that's good or bad."

"It's neither. I'm just tired of talking about it. It's all our marriage has become."

"Does that mean you're accepting it?"

"Accepting what?" I still don't look at him.

"That we'll never be parents."

The plate in my hand slips out of my grasp. It lands against the bottom of the sink with a loud clutter.

But it doesn't break like I do.

I don't even know why it happens. I'm gripping the sink now and my head is hanging between my shoulders and tears just start falling from my eyes. *Fuck.* I really can't stand myself sometimes.

Graham waits several seconds before he moves to console me. He doesn't put his arms around me, though. I think he can tell I don't want to be crying right now and hugging me is something he's learned doesn't help in these situations. I don't cry in front of him near as much as I cry alone, but I've done it enough for him to know that I'd rather do it alone. He runs his hand over my hair and kisses the back of my head. Then he just touches my arm and moves me out of the way of the sink. He picks up the plate and finishes washing the dishes. I do what I do best. I walk away until I'm strong enough to pretend the conversation never happened. And he does what he does best. He leaves me alone in my grief because I've made it so hard for him to console me.

We're getting really good at playing our parts.

Chapter Nine

Then

I'm on my bed. I'm making out with Jason.

I blame Graham for this.

I would have never invited Jason back to my apartment had I not seen Graham. But for some reason, seeing him there filled me with . . . *feelings*. And then watching him kiss his date on the side of her head filled me with jealousy. And then watching him grab her hand across the table as we walked past them filled me with regret.

Why did I never call him?

I should have called him.

"Quinn," Jason says. He's been kissing my neck, but now he's not. He's looking down at me, his expression full of so many things I don't want to be there right now. "Do you have a condom?"

I lie and tell him no. "I'm sorry. I wasn't expecting to bring you back here tonight."

"It's fine," he says, lowering his mouth to my neck again. "I'll come prepared next time."

I feel bad. I'm almost positive I'll never have sex with Jason. I am positive he won't be coming back to my apartment after tonight. I'm even *more* positive I'm about to ask him to leave. I wasn't this positive before dinner. But after running into Graham, I realize how it should feel to be with another person. And the way I feel around Jason pales in comparison to how I feel when I'm around Graham.

Jason whispers something inaudible against my neck. His fingers have made their way up my shirt and over my bra.

Thank God the doorbell rings.

I slide off the bed in a hurry. "It's probably my mother," I say to him, straightening out my clothes. "Wait here. I'll be right back."

Jason rolls onto his back and watches me leave the room. I rush to the door, knowing exactly who I hope it is before I even open it. But even still, I gasp when I look through the peephole.

Graham is standing at my door, looking down at his feet.

I press my forehead to my door and close my eyes.

What is he doing here?

I attempt to straighten out my shirt and my hair before opening the door. When I'm finally face-to-face with him, I grow irritated at the way I feel in his presence. Graham doesn't even touch me and I feel it everywhere. Jason touches me everywhere and I feel it nowhere.

"What . . ." The word that just left my mouth is somehow full of more breath than voice. I clear my throat and try again. "What are you doing here?"

Graham smiles a little, lifting a hand to the doorframe. The smirk on his face and the fact that he's chewing gum are two of the sexiest things I've ever seen at one time. "I thought this was the plan."

I am so confused. "The plan?"

He laughs halfheartedly. But then he tilts his head. He points behind me, into my apartment. "I thought . . ." He points behind him, over his shoulder. "At the restaurant. There was this look . . . right before you left. I thought you were asking me to come over."

His voice is louder than I need it to be right now. I check over my shoulder to make sure Jason hasn't come out of the bedroom. Then I try to shield Graham from my apartment a little better by slipping more on the other side of the door. "What *look*?"

Graham's eyes narrow a bit. "You didn't give me a look?"

I shake my head. "I did not give you a look. I wouldn't even know what look to give you that would say, '*Hey, ditch your date and come over to my place tonight.*'"

Graham's lips form a tight line and he looks down at the floor with a hint of embarrassment. He raises his eyes, but his head is still dipped when he says, "Is he here? Your date?"

Now *I'm* the one who's embarrassed. I nod. Graham releases a sigh as he leans against the doorjamb. "Wow. I read that one wrong."

When he looks at me again, I notice the left side of his face is red. I step closer to him and reach up to his cheek. "What happened?"

He grins and pulls my hand from his cheek. He doesn't let go of it. I don't want him to.

"I got slapped. It's fine. I deserved it."

That's when I see it. The outline of a handprint. "Your date?"

He lifts a shoulder. "After what happened with Sasha, I vowed to be completely honest in every aspect of my relationships from then on. Jess . . . my date tonight . . . didn't see that as a good quality."

"What did you say to her?"

"I broke it off with her. I told her I was into another girl. And that I was going to her apartment to see her."

"Because this other girl supposedly gave you a look?"

He smiles. "I *thought* she did, anyway." He brushes his thumb across the top of my hand and then he releases it. "Well, Quinn. Maybe another time."

Graham takes a step back and it feels like he pulls all my emotions with him as he turns to walk away.

"Graham," I say, stepping out into the hallway. He turns around, and I don't know if I'm going to regret what I'm about to say, but I'll regret it even more if I don't. "Come back in fifteen minutes. I'll get rid of him."

Graham shoots me the perfect thank-you smile, but before he walks away, his eyes move past me. To someone behind me. I turn around and see Jason standing in the doorway. He looks pissed. Rightfully so.

He swings open the door and walks out into the hallway. He walks past Graham, shoving him with his shoulder. Graham just stands silent, staring at the floor.

I feel terrible. But if it hadn't happened this way, I would have shot him down on his way out of my apartment later. Rejection sucks, no matter how it's presented.

The door to the stairwell slams shut and neither of us speak as we listen to Jason's footsteps fade down the stairs.

When all is quiet, Graham finally lifts his head and makes eye contact with me. "You still need that fifteen minutes?"

I shake my head. "Nope."

Graham walks toward me as I step back into my apartment. I hold the door open for him, certain that he won't be leaving here as quickly as he did last time. Once he's inside, I close the door and then turn around. Graham is smiling, looking at the wall beside my head. I follow his line of sight to the Post-it he left six months ago.

"It's still here."

I smile sheepishly. "I would have called you eventually. Maybe."

Graham pulls down the sticky note and folds it in half, sliding it into his pocket. "You won't be needing it after tonight. I'll make sure you have my number memorized before I leave here tomorrow."

"That confident you're staying over?"

Graham takes an assured step closer. He places a hand against the door beside my head, forcing my back against the door. It isn't until he does this that I realize why I find him so attractive.

It's because he makes *me* feel attractive. The way he looks at me. The way he talks to me. I'm not sure anyone has ever made me feel as beautiful as he makes me feel when he looks at me. Like it's taking everything in him to keep his mouth away from mine. His eyes fall to my lips. He leans in so close, I can smell the flavor of gum he's chewing. *Spearmint.*

I want him to kiss me. I want him to kiss me even more than I wanted Jason to *stop* kissing me. And that was a lot. But I feel like whatever is about to start with me and Graham, it needs to start with complete transparency. "I kissed Jason. Earlier. Before you got here."

My comment doesn't seem to dismay him. "I figured as much."

I put my hands on his chest. "I just . . . I want to kiss you, too. But it's weird because I just kissed someone else. I'd like to brush my teeth first."

Graham laughs. *I love his laugh*. He leans in and presses his forehead to the side of my head, causing my knees to lock. His lips are right over my ear when he whispers. "Hurry. Please."

I slip around him and rush to my bathroom. I pull open the drawer and grab my toothbrush and toothpaste like I'm racing against time. My hands are shaking as I squeeze the toothpaste onto my toothbrush. I turn on the water and start brushing my teeth furiously. I'm brushing my tongue when I look in the mirror and see Graham walk into the bathroom behind me. I laugh at how ridiculous this is.

I haven't kissed a guy in six months. Now I'm brushing away the germs of one guy while the next one waits in line.

Graham seems to be enjoying the ridiculousness of this moment just as much as I am. He's now leaning against the sink next to me, watching as I spit toothpaste into the sink. I rinse my toothbrush and then toss it aside, grabbing an empty glass. I fill it with water and take a sip, swishing the water around in my mouth until I'm certain my mouth is as clean as it's going to get. I spit the water out and take another sip. This time I just swallow the water, though, because Graham takes the cup from me and sets it near the sink. He pulls the piece of gum out of his mouth, tossing it in the trash can, then he slides his other hand around my head and doesn't even ask if I'm ready yet. He brings his mouth to mine, assured and eager, like the last sixty seconds of preparation have been pure torture. The moment our lips touch, it's as if an ember that's been slow-burning for six long months finally bursts into flames.

He doesn't even bother with an introductory, slow kiss. His tongue is in my mouth like he's been there many times before and knows exactly what to do. He turns me until my back is against the sink and then he lifts me, setting me down on my bathroom counter. He settles himself between my legs, grabbing my ass with both hands, pulling me against him. I wrap my arms around him, lock my legs around him. I try to convince myself I did not go my whole life never realizing this kind of kiss existed.

The way his lips move against mine makes me question the skills of every guy that came before him.

He starts to ease the pressure and I catch myself pulling him against me, not wanting him to stop. But he does. Slowly. He gives me a small peck on the corner of my mouth before pulling back.

"Wow," I whisper. I open my eyes and he's staring at me. But he's not looking at me in awe like I'm looking at him. There's a very noticeable dejected look on his face.

He shakes his head slowly, his eyes narrowing. "I can't believe you never called me. We could have been kissing like this for months."

His comment throws me off. So much so, I stumble over my words when I attempt a response. "I just . . . I guess I thought being around you would remind me of Ethan too much. Of everything that happened that night."

He nods like he understands. "How many times have you thought of Ethan since seeing me at the restaurant tonight?"

"Once," I say. "Just now."

"Good. Because I'm not Ethan." He lifts me, carrying me to the bed. He lays me down and then he backs away, pulling off his shirt. I'm not sure I've ever touched skin that smooth and tight and beautiful and tanned. Graham without a shirt is near perfection.

"I like your . . ." I point at his chest and make a circular motion with my finger. "Your body. It's very nice."

He laughs, pressing a knee into the mattress. He lies down next to me. "Thank you," he says. "But you can't have this body right now." He adjusts the pillow beneath his head, getting comfortable. I lift up onto my elbow and scowl at him.

"Why not?"

"What's the rush? I'll be here all night."

Surely he's kidding. Especially after that kiss. "Well, what are we supposed to do while we wait? *Talk?*"

He laughs. "You sound like conversation with me is the worst idea in the world."

"If we talk too much before we have sex, I might find out things I don't like about you. Then the sex won't be as fun."

He reaches up and tucks my hair behind my ear with a grin. "Or . . . you might find out we're soul mates and the sex will be mind-blowing."

He has a point.

I fold my arms over my pillow and lay my head on them as I roll onto my stomach. "We better get to talking, then. You go first."

Graham runs his hand over my arm. He traces the scar on my elbow. "Where'd you get this scar?"

"My older sister and I were racing through the house when I was fourteen. I didn't know the sliding glass door was shut and I ran through it. Shattered the glass and cut myself in like ten different places. That's the only scar, though."

"Damn."

"You have any scars?"

Graham lifts up a little and points to a spot on his collarbone. There's about a four-inch scar that looks like it must have been pretty bad at the time of the injury. "Car wreck." He scoots closer to me and wraps his leg over both of mine. "What's your favorite movie?"

"Anything by the Coen brothers. My favorite is *Oh Brother, Where Art Thou?*"

He looks at me like maybe he has no clue what movie I'm talking about. But then he says, "We thought . . . you was . . . a toad."

I laugh. "Damn! We're in a tight spot!"

"Jesus Saves, George Nelson withdraws!" We're both laughing now. My laughter ends with a sigh, and then Graham smiles at me appreciatively. "See? We like the same movie. Our sex is going to be amazing."

I grin. "Next question."

"Name something you hate."

"Infidelity and most vegetables."

Graham laughs. "Do you live off chicken nuggets and French fries?"

"I love fruit. And tomatoes. But I'm not really a fan of anything green. I've tried to love vegetables but I finally decided last year to accept that I hate them and force nutrition into my diet in other ways."

"Do you like to work out?"

"Only in emergencies," I admit. "I like doing stuff outdoors, but not if it's routine exercise."

"I like to run," he says. "It clears my head. And I love every single vegetable *except* tomatoes."

"Uh-oh. Not looking good, Graham."

"No, it's perfect. You'll eat my tomatoes, I'll eat every other vegetable on your plate. Nothing goes to waste. It's a perfect match."

I like his way of looking at it. "What else? Movies and food only scratch the surface."

"We could talk politics and religion but we should probably save those two for after we're in love."

He says that so confidently, but also like he's kidding. Either way, I agree we should avoid politics and religion. Those lead to arguments even when people agree. "Definitely cool with not touching those two."

Graham grabs my wrist and slides it out from under my head. He threads his fingers through mine and rests our hands between us. I try not to focus too much on how sweet I think it is. "What's your favorite holiday?" he asks.

"All of them. But I'm partial to Halloween."

"Not what I expected you to say. Do you like it for the costumes or the candy?"

"Both, but mostly the costumes. I love dressing up."

"What's the best costume you ever wore?"

I think about it for a moment. "Probably when my friends and I went as Milli Vanilli. Two of us talked the whole night while the other two stood in front of us and mouthed everything we said."

Graham rolls onto his back and laughs. "That's pretty spectacular," he says, staring up at the ceiling.

"Do you dress up for Halloween?"

"I'm not opposed to it but I never dressed up with Sasha

because she always went as something typical and slutty. A slutty cheerleader. A slutty nurse. A slutty prude." He pauses for a second. "Don't get me wrong, I love a slutty costume. Nothing wrong with a woman showing off her assets if that's what she wants to do. It's just that Sasha never really asked me to dress up. I think she wanted all the attention and didn't really want to do the couples costume thing."

"That sucks. So much missed opportunity."

"Right? I could have dressed up as her slutty quarterback."

"Well, if we're still talking when Halloween rolls around, we can wear matching slutty costumes."

"*Still* talking? Quinn, Halloween is over two months away. We'll practically be living together by then."

I roll my eyes. "You're way too confident."

"You could call it that."

"Most men push for sex right away. But you turn me down one night and show up six months later just to turn me down again and force me into conversation. I can't tell if I should be worried."

Graham raises an eyebrow. "Don't mistake me for something I'm not. I'm normally all for the sex up front, but you and I have an eternity to get to it."

I can tell he's kidding by the straight face he tries to keep. I lift up on my pillow and raise my brow. "Sex I'm okay with. Eternal commitment is pushing it."

Graham slides an arm beneath me and pulls me against him so that my head is now resting on his chest. "Whatever you say, Quinn. If you want us to pretend for a few more months that we aren't soul mates, that's fine with me. I'm a great actor."

I laugh at his sarcasm. "Soul mates don't exist."

"I know," he says. "We aren't soul mates. Soul mates are dumb."

"I'm serious."

"Me too. Completely serious."

"You're an idiot."

He presses his lips into my hair, kissing me on top of the head. "What is today's date?"

He is so random. I lift my head and look at him. "The eighth of August. Why?"

"Just want to make sure you never forget the date the universe brought us back together."

I lay my head against him again. "You're coming on way too strong. It's probably going to scare me away."

His chest moves with his quiet laughter. "No, it won't. You'll see. Ten years from now on August eighth, I'm going to roll over in our bed at midnight and whisper, *'I told you so'* in your ear."

"Are you that petty?"

"The pettiest."

I laugh. I laugh a lot while we talk. I don't know how long we lay in the same position talking, but I still have a million questions left when I start yawning. I fight it because talking to him is somehow even more relaxing than sleep and I want to ask him questions all night.

Graham eventually goes to the kitchen to get a glass of water. When he comes back to the bedroom, he turns off the lamp and climbs in bed behind me, spooning me. It's honestly not what I expected tonight. Especially with the way he approached me at the restaurant and then showed up at my apartment. I thought he had one thing on his mind.

I couldn't have been more wrong.

I wrap my arms over his and close my eyes. "I thought you were kidding about the no sex," I whisper.

I feel him laugh a little. "Keeping my pants on is not as easy as I'm making it look." He pushes against my ass to let me know how serious he is. I can feel him straining against his jeans.

"That must be painful," I tease. "You sure you don't want to change your mind?"

He squeezes me tighter, pressing a kiss close to my ear. "I've never been more comfortable."

His words make me blush in the dark, but I don't respond to him. I don't have a reply good enough. I'm quiet for several minutes as I listen to his breathing slow into a peaceful pattern. Right before I fall asleep, Graham whispers against my ear. "I thought you were the one that got away."

I smile. "I still could be."

"Don't be."

I try to say, *"I won't be,"* but he puts his hand between my cheek and the pillow and tilts my head until his mouth reaches mine. We kiss just enough. Not too short, but not too long that it leads to something else. It's the perfect kiss for the perfect moment.

Chapter Ten

Now

"Two more lipsticks," Gwenn says. She slides the bright red tube of lipstick over my top lip but goes so far outside of the edges, I feel it touch my nose.

"You're really good at this," I say with a laugh.

We're at Graham's parents' house, having dinner with his family. Graham is on the floor playing with his sister Caroline's five-year-old daughter, Adeline. The three-year-old, Gwenn, is on the couch next to me, putting makeup on me. Graham's parents are in the kitchen, cooking.

This is how most of our Sundays are spent. I've always enjoyed Sundays here, but lately they've become my favorite days of the month. I don't know why things are easier here, surrounded by Graham's family, but they are. It's easier for me to laugh. It's easier for me to look happy. It's even easier for me to let Graham love me.

I've noticed there's a difference with how I am toward Graham in public compared to when we're at home. At home, when it's just the two of us, I'm more withdrawn. I avoid his touch and his kiss because in the past, those things have always led to sex. And now that I dread sex so much, I dread the stuff that leads up to it, too.

But when we're in a setting like this, when his affection leads to nothing, I crave it. I like it when he puts his hands on me. When he kisses me. I love snuggling up to him on the couch. I don't know if he notices the difference in me between our house and other places. If he does, he's never let on.

"I finish," Gwenn says. She struggles putting the cap back on the lipstick she just applied to my mouth. I take it from her and help her close it.

Graham looks up at me from the floor. "Hot damn, Quinn. That is . . . yeah."

I smile at Gwenn. "Did you make me pretty?"

She starts giggling.

I make my way to the bathroom and laugh when I look in the mirror. I'm convinced they only make blue eye shadow for this exact purpose. So three-year-olds can put it on adults.

I'm washing my face when Graham walks into the bathroom. He looks at me in the mirror and makes a face.

"What? You don't like it?"

He kisses my shoulder. "You look beautiful, Quinn. Always."

I finish washing the makeup from my face, but Graham's lips don't leave my shoulder. He traces a soft trail of kisses up my neck. Knowing that this kiss won't lead to *sexhopedevastation* makes me enjoy it more than if this were happening in our own bathroom at our own house.

It sounds so fucked up. I don't understand how his actions can elicit different responses from me depending on the setting. But right now, I'm not going to question it, because he doesn't seem to be questioning it. He seems to be enjoying it.

He remains behind me, pressing me against the sink as his hand runs over my hip and slides around to the front of my thigh. I grip the sink and watch him in the mirror. He lifts his eyes and stares at my reflection as he begins to bunch up the front of my dress with his fingers, crawling it up the front of my thighs.

It's been over a month and a half now since he's initiated sex. The longest we've ever gone. I know, based on how things ended the last time we had sex, he's waiting for me to initiate it. But I haven't.

It's been so long since he's touched me, my reaction seems to be intensified.

I close my eyes when his hand slips inside my panties. I'm covered in chills from head to toe, and knowing this can't go too far makes me want him and his mouth and his hands all over me.

The door is open and someone could walk down the hall at any moment, but that only serves as further affirmation that this make-out session will stop any second now. Which is why my mind is allowing me to enjoy it as much as I am.

He slips a finger inside of me and runs his thumb down the center of me and it's the most I've felt from his touch in over a year. My head falls back against his shoulder and he tilts my mouth toward his. I moan, just as his lips cover mine. He kisses me with hunger and impatience, like he's desperate to get all he can out of this moment before I push him away.

Graham kisses me with urgency the whole time he touches me. He kisses me until I come, and even as I whimper and tremble in his arms, he doesn't stop kissing and touching me until the moment passes completely.

He slowly pulls his hand out of my panties, diving his tongue into my mouth one last time before pulling back. I grip the sink in front of me, breathing heavily. He kisses me on the shoulder, grinning as he walks out of the bathroom, smiling like he just conquered the world.

I take several minutes to collect myself. I make sure my face is no longer flushed before I walk back to the living room. Graham is lying on the couch, watching television. He makes room for me on the couch, pulling me against him. Every now and then, he'll kiss me or I'll kiss him and it feels just like it used to. And I pretend that everything is okay. I pretend every other day of the week is just like Sundays at Graham's parents' house. It's like everything else falls away when we're here, and it's just me and Graham without a single trace of failure.

After dinner, Graham and I offer to do the dishes. He turns on the radio and we stand at the sink together. I wash and he rinses. He talks about work and I listen. When an Ed Sheeran song starts to play, my hands are covered in soapy suds, but Graham pulls me to him anyway and starts dancing with me. We cling to each other and barely move while we dance—his arms around my waist and mine around his neck. His forehead is pressed to mine and even though I know he's watching me, I keep my eyes closed and pretend we're perfect. We dance alone until the song almost comes to an end, but Caroline walks into the kitchen and catches us.

She's due with her third child in a few weeks. She's holding a paper plate with one hand and holding her lower back with the other. She rolls her eyes at the sight of us. "I can't imagine what it must be like when you're in private if you two are this handsy in public." She throws the plate in the trash can and heads back toward the living room. "You're probably that annoyingly perfect couple who has sex twice a day."

When the door to the kitchen closes, we're alone and the song is over and Graham is just staring at me. I know his sister's comment has made him think about my affection. I can tell he wants to ask me why I love his touch so much in public, but recoil from it in private.

He doesn't say anything about it, though. He hands me a towel to dry my hands. "You ready to go home?"

I nod, but I also feel it start to happen. The nerves building in my stomach. The worry that being so affectionate with him at his mother's will make him think I want his affection at the house.

It makes me feel like the worst wife in the world. I don't do this because I don't love him. But maybe if I could somehow love him better, I wouldn't do this.

Even knowing how unfair I am to him doesn't stop me from lying to him on our way home. "I feel like I'm getting a migraine," I say, pressing my forehead to the passenger window of our car.

When we make it home, Graham tells me to go to bed and get some rest. Five minutes later, he brings me a glass of water and some aspirin. He turns out my lamp and leaves the room and I cry because I hate what I've turned this marriage into.

My husband's heart is my saving grace, but his physical touch has become my enemy.

Chapter Eleven

Then

I can feel the heat of his body next to me. I like that the sun is up and he's still here.

I feel Graham move before I open my eyes. His hand finds mine beneath my pillow and he threads our fingers together. "Good morning."

When I open my eyes, I'm smiling. He lifts his other arm and brushes his thumb across my cheek. "What'd I miss while you were asleep? Did you dream?"

I think that might be the sweetest thing anyone has ever said to me. I don't know if that's good or bad. "I had kind of a strange dream. You were in it."

He perks up, releasing my hand and lifting onto his elbow. "Oh yeah? Tell me about it."

"I had a dream that you showed up here in head-to-toe scuba gear. And you told me to put my scuba gear on because we were going to swim with sharks. I told you I was scared of sharks and you said, *'But Quinn. These sharks are actually cats!'* And then I said, *'But I'm scared of the ocean.'* And you said, *'But Quinn. This ocean is actually a park.'*"

Graham laughs. "What happened next?"

"I put on my scuba gear, of course. But you didn't take me to an ocean or a park. You took me to meet your mother. And I was so embarrassed and so mad at you because I was wearing a scuba-diving suit at her dinner table."

Graham falls onto his back with laughter. "Quinn, that is the best dream in the history of dreams."

His reaction makes me want to tell him every dream I ever have for the rest of my life.

I like that he rolls toward me and looks at me like there's nowhere else he'd rather be. He leans forward and presses his mouth to mine. I want to stay in bed with him all day, but he pulls away and says, "I'm hungry. You got anything to eat?"

I nod, but before he can climb out of bed, I pull him back and press my lips against his cheek. "I like you, Graham." I roll off him and head to my bathroom.

He calls out after me. "Of course you like me, Quinn! I'm your soul mate!"

I laugh as I close the door to the bathroom. And then I want to scream when I look in the mirror. Holy shit. I have mascara smeared everywhere. A pimple that appeared on my forehead overnight. My hair is a mess, but not in that sexy, come-hither way. It's just a mess. Like a rat slept in it all night.

I groan and then yell, "I'm taking a shower!"

Graham yells back from the kitchen. "I'm looking for food!"

I doubt he finds much. I don't keep a lot of groceries at my house because I rarely cook since I live alone.

I step into the shower. I have no idea if he's staying after breakfast, but while I shower, I make sure to pay special attention to certain areas just in case.

I've been in the shower all of three minutes when I hear the bathroom door open.

"You don't have anything to eat."

The sound of his voice in my bathroom surprises me so much, I almost slip and fall. I grip the shower bar and steady myself, but immediately let go of the bar and cover my breasts when I see the shower curtain move.

Graham peeks his head inside the shower. He looks straight at my face and nowhere else, but I'm still doing everything I can to shield myself.

"You have absolutely no food. Crackers and a stale box of cereal." He says this like it's not at all unusual that he's looking at me naked. "Want me to go grab breakfast?"

"Um . . . okay." I'm wide-eyed, still shocked from his confident intrusion.

Graham grins, pulling his bottom lip in with his teeth. His eyes begin to slowly trail down my body. "My God, Quinn," he whispers. He closes the shower curtain and says, "I'll be back in a little while." Right before he walks out of my bathroom I hear him whisper, "Fuck."

I can't help but smile. I love how that just made me feel.

I turn back around and face the shower spray as I close my eyes and let the warm water beat down on my face. I can't figure Graham out. He's just the right amount of confident and cocky. But he balances that out with his reverent side. He's funny and smart and he comes on way too strong, but it all feels genuine.

Genuine.

If I had to describe him in one word, that would be it.

It surprises me because I never thought of Ethan as genuine. There was always a part of me that felt his seeming perfection was part of an act. Like he had been taught how to say all the right things but it wasn't inherent with him. It was as if he studied how to be the version of himself he presented to everyone.

But with Graham, I have a feeling he's been who he is all his life.

I wonder if I'll learn to trust him. After what I went through with Ethan, I've felt like that would never happen.

When I'm finished in the shower, I dry off and pull on a T-shirt and a pair of yoga pants. I have no idea if Graham has intentions of hanging out today, but until I find that out, I'll be dressing for comfort.

When I walk back into the bedroom, I grab my phone off the nightstand and notice several missed texts.

I saved my contact in your phone. This is Graham. Your soul mate.

What do you want for breakfast?

McDonald's? Starbucks? Donuts?

Are you still in the shower?

Do you like coffee?

I can't stop thinking about you in the shower.

Okay, then. I'll get bagels.

I'm in my bedroom hanging up laundry when I hear Graham walk through the front door. I walk to the living room and he's at the table, laying out breakfast. *A lot* of breakfast.

"You didn't specify what you wanted, so I got everything."

My eyes scan the box of donuts, the McDonald's, the Chick-fil-A. He even got bagels. And Starbucks. "Are you trying to replicate the breakfast scene from *Pretty Woman* when Richard Gere orders everything off the menu?" I smile and take a seat at the table.

He frowns. "You mean this has been done before?"

I take a bite of a glazed donut. "Yep. You're gonna have to be more original if you want to impress me."

He sits down across from me and pulls the lid off a Starbucks cup. He licks the whipped cream. "I guess I'll have to cancel the white limo that's supposed to pull up to your fire escape this afternoon."

I laugh. "Thank you for breakfast."

He leans back in his seat, placing the lid back on his coffee. "What are your plans today?"

I shrug. "It's Saturday. I'm off work."

"I don't even know what you do for a living."

"I write for an advertising firm downtown. Nothing impressive."

"Nothing about you is unimpressive, Quinn."

I ignore his compliment. "What about you?"

"Nothing impressive. I'm an accountant for a company downtown."

"A math guy, huh?"

"My first choice was an astronaut, but the idea of leaving the earth's atmosphere is kind of terrifying. Numbers don't really pose a threat to my life, so I went with that." He opens one of the bags and pulls out a biscuit. "I think we should have sex tonight." He takes a bite of the biscuit. "All night," he says with a mouthful.

I almost choke on the bite I just swallowed. I pull the extra coffee toward me and take a sip. "You do, huh? What's so different about tonight than last night?"

He tears off a piece of the biscuit and pops it into his mouth. "I was being polite last night."

"So your politeness is just a façade?"

"No, I really am a decent guy. But I'm also extremely attracted to you and want to see you naked again." He smiles at me. It's a shy smile and it's so cute, it makes *me* smile.

"Some men get cheated on and they become revengeful. You get cheated on and become brutally honest."

He laughs, but he doesn't bring up the potential sex again. We both eat in silence for a minute and then he says, "What'd you do with your engagement ring?"

"I mailed it to Ethan's mother."

"What'd you do with the one I left here?"

A reserved smile creeps across my lips. "I kept it. Sometimes I wear it. It's pretty."

He watches me for a moment and then he says, "You want to know what I kept?"

I nod.

"Our fortunes."

It takes me a moment before I realize what he's talking about. "From the Chinese food and infidelity?"

"Yep."

"You kept those?"

"Sure did."

"Why?"

"Because." He looks down at his coffee and moves the cup in small circles. "If you saw what was on the back of them, you wouldn't be questioning it."

I lean back in my seat and eye him suspiciously. Ethan and I got those fortune cookies all the time. I know exactly what's on the back of them because I always thought it was odd. Most fortunes have a set of numbers, but this place only puts a single number on the fortunes. "The backs of those fortune cookies just have a number on them."

"Yep." He has a mischievous gleam in his eyes.

I tilt my head. "What? Did they have the same number or something?"

He looks at me seriously. "The number eight."

I hold his stare and think about that for a few seconds. Last night he asked me the date. August 8.

8/8.

The day we reconnected.

"Are you serious?"

Graham holds his resolve for a moment, but then he relaxes and lets out a laugh. "I'm kidding. Yours had a seven on the back of it and mine had like a five or something." He stands up and takes his trash to the kitchen. "I kept them because I'm a neat freak and I didn't like littering on the floor of the hallway. I forgot they were in my pocket until I got home that night."

I wonder how much of that is true. "Do you really still have them, though?"

He steps on the trash can lever and the lid pops open. "Of course." He walks back to the table and pulls me out of my chair. He slides his arms around my waist and kisses me. It's a sweet kiss and he tastes like caramel and sugar. He moves his mouth to my cheek and kisses it, then pulls me against his chest. "You know I'm only teasing you, right? I don't actually believe we'll spend the rest of our lives together. *Yet.*"

I kind of like his teasing. A lot. I open my mouth to respond to him, but his phone rings. He holds up a finger and pulls it out of his pocket, then immediately answers it. "Hey, beautiful," he says. He covers his phone and whispers, "It's my mother. Don't freak out."

I laugh and leave him to his phone call while I walk to the table to gather all the breakfast he brought. I don't think it'll all fit in the fridge.

"Not much," Graham says. "Is Dad golfing today?" I watch him chat with his mother. He does it with such ease. When I chat with my mother, I'm tense and on edge and rolling my eyes through most of the conversation. "Yeah, dinner sounds good. Can I bring a date?" He covers his phone and looks at me. "Get your scuba gear ready, Quinn."

I don't know whether to laugh at his joke or start freaking out. I don't even know the guy's last name yet. I don't want to meet his parents. I just mouth, "No" very firmly.

He winks at me. "Her name is Quinn," he says, answering his mother's question. He's watching me while he continues the conversation. "Yeah, it's pretty serious. Been seeing her for a while now."

I roll my eyes at his lies. He's unrelenting.

"Hold on, I'll ask her." He doesn't cover his phone this time. Actually, he yells louder than he needs to because we're just a few feet apart. "Babe! Do you want pie or cobbler for dessert?"

I step closer to him so he can hear the seriousness in my voice. "We haven't even been on a *date* yet," I whisper. "I don't want to meet your mother, Graham."

He covers his phone this time and motions at the table. "We just had like five dates," he whispers. "Chick-fil-A, Mc-Donald's, donuts, Starbucks . . ." He pulls his phone back to his ear. "She prefers pie. We'll see you around six?" There's a pause. "Okay. Love you, too."

He ends the call and slides the phone into his pocket. I'm glaring at him, but it doesn't last long because he walks up to me and tickles me until I laugh. Then he pulls me against him. "Don't worry, Quinn. Once you taste her cooking, you won't ever want to leave."

I sigh heavily. "You are nothing like I expected."

He presses a kiss to the top of my head. "Is that good or bad?"

"I honestly have no idea."

Chapter Twelve

Now

When I pull onto Caroline's street, I see Graham's car parked in her driveway. But it looks like other than his sister and her husband, we're the only ones here. I'm relieved by that.

Caroline had her baby boy yesterday morning. A home birth. It's the first boy born in Graham's family since him, actually.

Caroline is the only sister of Graham's who lives in Connecticut. Tabitha lives in Chicago with her wife. Ainsley is a lawyer and lives all over. She travels almost as much as Ava and Reid do. Sometimes I'm a little envious of their carefree lifestyles, but I've always had other priorities.

Graham and I are very involved in the lives of Caroline's two daughters. Outside of the time we spend with them on Sundays, we also occasionally take them for outings or to the movies to give Caroline and her husband time alone. I suspect with the birth of their son, we'll be spending even more time with the girls.

I love watching Graham with them. He's playful and loves to make them laugh. But he's also very invested in their mental health and well-being. He answers every "but why" question with patience and honesty. And even though they're only three and five, he treats them as equals. Caroline jokes that when they return home after spending time at our house, they start every sentence with, "But Uncle Graham said . . ."

I love the relationship he has with his nieces so much, seeing him with his baby nephew makes me even more excited to see him as an uncle. I do occasionally let the thoughts get to me in moments like this about what a great father he would make, but I refuse to let our depressing situation dampen Graham's experience with his family. So, I plaster on my happy face and make sure to never allow the sadness to show.

I practice smiling in my rearview mirror. Smiling used to come naturally to me, but almost every smile that appears on my face nowadays is a façade.

When I reach the front door, I don't know whether to ring the bell or just walk in. If the baby or Caroline are sleeping, I'd feel terrible for waking them up. I push open the door and the front of the house is quiet. No one is seated in the living room, although there are unwrapped gifts lining the sofa. I walk to the living room and place Graham's and my gift on the coffee table next to the couch.

I make my way through a quiet kitchen and toward the den where Caroline and her family spend most of their time. It was an add-on they completed right after Gwenn was born.

Half of the room serves as a living room and the other half serves as a playroom for the girls.

I'm almost to the den, but I pause just outside the door when I see Graham. His back is to me and he's standing near the couch, holding his new nephew. He's swaying from side to side with the newborn cocooned in a blanket in his arms. I suppose if our situation were different, this would be a moment where I would have nothing but pure adoration for my husband—watching him hold his newborn nephew. Instead, I ache inside. It makes me question the thoughts that might be going through his head right now. Does a small part of him resent that I haven't been able to create a moment like this for him?

No one can see me from where I'm standing since Graham has his back to me and I'm out of the line of sight of his sister, who is probably seated on the sofa. I hear her voice when she says, "You're such a natural."

I watch Graham's reaction to her words, but he has none. He just continues staring down at his nephew.

And then Caroline says something that makes me grip the wall behind me. "You would make such a good father, Graham." Her words fly through the air and reach me all the way in the next room.

I'm convinced she wouldn't have said what she said if she knew I could hear her. I wait for Graham's response, curious if he'll even have one.

He does.

"I know," he says quietly, looking over at Caroline. "It devastates me that it still hasn't happened yet."

I slip my hand over my mouth because I'm scared of what might happen if I don't. I might gasp, or cry, or vomit.

I'm in my car now.

Driving.

I couldn't face him after that. Those few sentences confirmed all of my fears. Why would Caroline bring it up? Why would he respond to her with such bluntness, but never tell *me* the truth about how he feels?

This is the first moment I've felt like I'm disappointing his family. What do his sisters say to him? What does his mother say? Do they wish he could have children more than they wish he would stay married to me?

I've never thought about this from their perspective. I don't like how these thoughts are making me feel. Ashamed. Like maybe I'm not only preventing Graham from ever having a child, but I'm preventing his family from being able to love a child that Graham would be perfectly capable of creating if not for me.

I pull into a parking lot to gather myself. I wipe my tears and tell myself to forget I ever heard that. I pull my phone out of my purse to text Graham.

Traffic is terrible. Tell Caroline I won't be able to stop by until tomorrow.

I hit send and lean back in my seat, trying so hard to get their conversation out of my head, but it plays over and over again.

"You would make such a good father, Graham."

"I know. It devastates me that it still hasn't happened yet."

———

I'm standing at the refrigerator two hours later when Graham finally returns home from Caroline's. I know I'm stressed when I clean out the refrigerator and that's exactly what I've spent the last half hour doing. He lays his things on the kitchen counter. His keys, his briefcase, a bottle of water. He walks over to me and leans in, kissing me on the cheek. I force a smile and when I do, I notice this is the hardest I've ever had to force a smile.

"How was the visit?" I ask him.

He reaches around me into the refrigerator. "Good." He grabs a soda. "The baby is cute."

He's acting so casual about it all, like he didn't admit out loud today that he's devastated he isn't a father.

"Did you get to hold him?"

"No," Graham says. "He was sleeping the whole time I was there."

I snap my eyes back to his. *Why did he just lie to me?*

It feels like the inside walls of my chest are being torched as I try to keep my emotions from surfacing but I can't let go of his admission that he's devastated he hasn't become a father yet. *Why does he stay?*

I close the refrigerator door even though I haven't cleaned out the side drawers. I need to get out of this room. I feel too much guilt when I look at him. "I'll be up late tonight. I have a lot of work to catch up on in my office. Dinner's in the microwave if you're hungry." I walk toward my office. Before I close the door all the way, I glance back into the kitchen.

Graham's hands are pressed against the counter and his head is hanging between his shoulders. He stays like this for almost an entire minute, but then he pushes off the bar with force, as if he's angry at something. Or someone.

Before I can close the door to my office, he looks in my

direction. Our eyes meet. We stare at each other for a few seconds and it's the first time I've ever felt like he was a complete stranger. I have absolutely no clue what he's thinking right now.

This is the moment when I know I should ask him what he's thinking. This is the moment when I should tell him what I'm thinking. This is the moment I should be honest with him and admit that maybe we should open that box.

But instead of being brave and finally speaking truth, I choke on my inner coward. I look away from him and close the door.

We resume the dance.

Chapter Thirteen

Then

Every minute I've spent with him today surprises me more than the last.

Every time he opens his mouth or smiles or touches me, all I can think is, "What would possess Sasha to cheat on this man with *Ethan*?"

Her trash, my treasure.

His childhood home is everything I imagined it would be. Full of laughter and stories and parents who look at him like he was sent straight from heaven. He's the youngest of four kids and the only boy. I didn't get to meet any of his sisters today because two of them live out of state and one of them had to cancel dinner.

Graham gets his looks from his father. His father is a solid man with sad eyes and a happy soul. His mother is petite.

Shorter than me, but carries herself with a confidence even bigger than Graham's.

She's cautious of me. I can tell she wants to like me, but I can also tell she doesn't want to see her son get his heart broken again. She must have liked Sasha at one point. She tries to pry about our "relationship" but Graham feeds her nothing but fiction.

"How long have you two been seeing each other?"

He puts his arm around my shoulders and says, "A while."

A day.

"Has Graham met your parents yet, Quinn?"

Graham says, "A few times. They're great."

Never. And they're terrible.

His mother smiles. "That's nice. Where did you meet?"

"In my office building," he says.

I don't even know where he works.

Graham is having fun with this. Every time he makes up a story about us, I squeeze his leg or nudge him as I try to stifle my laughter. At one point, he tells his mother we met at a vending machine. He says, "Her Twizzlers were stuck in the machine, so I put a dollar in and bought Twizzlers so that hers would get unstuck. But you wouldn't believe what happened." He looks at me and urges me to finish the lie. "Tell them what happened next, Quinn."

I squeeze his leg so hard he winces. "His Twizzlers got stuck in the machine, too."

Graham laughs. "Can you believe it? Neither one of us got Twizzlers. So I took her to lunch in the food court and the rest is history."

I have to bite my cheek to keep from laughing. Luckily, he was right about his mother's food, so I spend most of the meal with my mouth full. His mother is an amazing cook.

When she goes to the kitchen to finish the pie, Graham says, "You want a tour of the house?"

I grab his hand as he leads me out of the dining room. As soon as we're in private, I shove him in the chest. "You lied to your parents like twenty times in under an hour!"

He grabs my hands, pulling me to him. "But it was fun, wasn't it?"

I can't deny the smile that's breaking through. "Yeah. It really was."

Graham lowers his mouth to mine and kisses me. "You want a typical tour of a typical house or do you want to go to the basement and see my childhood bedroom?"

"That's not even a question."

He leads me to the basement and flips on the light. There's a faded poster of the table of elements hanging on the wall of the stairwell. He flips on another light when we reach the bottom of the stairs, revealing a teenage boy's bedroom that looks like it hasn't been touched since he moved out. It's like a secret portal straight into the mind of Graham Wells. *I finally learned his last name over dinner.*

"She refuses to redecorate it," he says, walking backward into the room. "I still have to sleep in here when I visit." He kicks at a basketball lying on the floor. It's flat, so it barely rolls away from him. "I hate it. It reminds me of high school."

"You didn't like high school?"

He makes a quick gesture around the room. "I liked science and math more than I liked girls. Imagine what high school was like for me."

His dresser is covered in science trophies and picture

frames. Not a single sports award in sight. I pick up one of his family photos and bring it in closer for inspection. It's a picture of Graham and his three older sisters. They all favor their mother heavily. And then there's the lanky preteen with braces in the middle. "Wow."

He's standing right behind me now, looking over my shoulder. "I was the poster child for awkward phases."

I place the picture back on the dresser. "You'd never know it now."

Graham walks to his bed and takes a seat on the Star Wars comforter. He leans back on his hands and admires me as I continue to look around the room. "Did I already tell you how much I like that dress?"

I look down at my dress. I wasn't prepared to meet the parents of a man I'm not even dating, so I didn't have a whole lot of clean laundry. I chose a simple navy blue cotton dress and paired it with a white sweater. When I walked out of my bedroom before we left my apartment, Graham saluted me like I was in the navy. I immediately turned around to go change, but he grabbed me and told me I looked really beautiful.

"You did tell me that," I say, leaning back on my heels.

His eyes drag up my legs, slowly. "I'm not gonna lie, though. I really wish you would have worn your scuba gear."

"I'm never telling you my dreams again."

Graham laughs and says, "You have to. Every day for as long as I know you."

I smile and then spin around to read some of the awards on his wall. There are so many awards. "Are you smart?" I glance over at him. "Like *really* smart?"

He shrugs. "Just a little above average. A by-product of

being a nerd. I had absolutely no game with the girls so I spent most of my time in here studying."

I can't tell if he's kidding because if I had to guess what he was like in high school based off what I know about him now, I'd say he was the high school quarterback who dated the head cheerleader.

"Were you still a virgin when you graduated high school?"

He crinkles up his nose. "Sophomore in college. I was nineteen. Hell, I was eighteen before I even kissed a girl." He leans forward, clasping his hands between his knees. "In fact, you're the first girl I've ever brought down here."

"No way. What about Sasha?"

"She came to dinner a few times, but I never showed her my old bedroom. I don't know why."

"Whatever. You probably tell that to all the girls you bring down here. Then you seduce them on your Star Wars comforter."

"Open that top drawer," he says. "I guarantee you there's a condom in there that's been there since I was sixteen."

I pull open the drawer and push things out of the way. It looks like a junk drawer. Old receipts, file folders, loose change. *A condom in the back.* I laugh and pull it out, flipping it over in my fingers. "It expired three years ago." I look at Graham and he's staring at the condom in my hand like he's wondering how accurate expiration dates are. I slip the condom into my bra. "I'm keeping it."

Graham smiles appreciatively at me. I like the way he looks at me. I've felt cute before. Beautiful, even. But I'm not sure I've ever known what sexy felt like until him.

Graham leans forward again, scooting to the edge of his bed. He crooks his finger, wanting me to come closer. He has that look in his eyes again. The look he had that night in the restaurant when he touched my knee. That look sends the same heat through me now, just like it did then.

I take a few steps, but stop a couple of feet from him. He sits up straight. "Come closer, Quinn." The desire in his voice whirls through my chest and stomach.

I take another step. He slides his hand around the back of my knee and pulls me the last step toward him. Chills break out on my legs and arms from his touch.

He's looking up at me and I'm looking down at him. His bed sits low to the floor, so his mouth is dangerously close to my panty line. I swallow when the hand he has wrapped around my leg begins to slide slowly up the back of my thigh.

I'm not prepared for the sensation his touch sends through me. I close my eyes and sway a little, steadying myself with two firm hands on his shoulders. I look down at him again, just as he presses his lips against the dress covering my stomach.

He holds eye contact with me as he slides his other hand to the back of my other thigh. I'm completely engulfed by my own heartbeat. I feel it everywhere, all at once.

Graham begins to bunch my dress up in his hands, little by little, crawling it up my thighs. He slides his hands and the dress up to my waist, then presses his mouth to the top of my thigh. I move my hands to his hair, gasping quietly as his lips move over my panties.

Holy shit.

I can feel the intense heat from his mouth as he kisses me there. It's a soft kiss, right against the front of my panties, but it doesn't matter how soft it is. I feel it all the way to my core and it makes me shudder.

I clench my fingers in his hair, pressing myself closer to his mouth. His hands are on my ass now, pulling me toward him. The soft kisses begin to turn into firm kisses and before he even has the chance to pull down my panties, a tremor starts to rush through me, unexpected, sudden, explosive.

I pull away from him with a whimper, but he pulls me back to his mouth, kissing me there harder until I'm gripping his shoulders, needing his strength to continue standing. My whole body begins to shudder and I struggle to remain quiet and remain upright as the whole bedroom spins around me.

My arms are shaking and my legs are weak as his kisses come to a stop. He slides his mouth against my thigh and looks up at me. It takes everything in me to hold eye contact with him as he pushes my dress up a little more and presses a kiss against the bare skin of my stomach.

Graham grips me at the waist. I'm completely out of breath and a little in shock at what just happened. And how fast it happened. And the fact that I want more of him. I want to lower myself on top of him and put this condom to use.

As if he can read my mind, Graham says, "How accurate do you think that expiration date is?"

I lower myself onto his lap and straddle him, feeling just how serious his question was. I brush my lips across his. "I'm sure the expiration date is just a precaution."

Graham grabs the back of my head and dips his tongue inside my mouth, kissing me with a groan. He slips his fingers in my bra and pulls out the condom, then stops kissing me long enough to tear it open with his teeth. He turns me, pushing me onto his Star Wars comforter. I hook my thumbs inside my panties and slide them off as he unzips his jeans.

I'm lying back on the bed as he kneels onto the mattress and puts the condom on. I don't even get a good look at him before he lowers himself on top of me.

He kisses me as he begins to slowly push himself into me. My whole body tenses and I moan. Maybe a little too loudly, because he laughs against my mouth. "Shh," he says against my lips with a smile. "We're supposed to be touring the house right now. Not each other."

I laugh, but as soon as he begins to push into me again, I hold my breath.

"Jesus, Quinn." He breathes against my neck and then thrusts against me. We're both a little too loud now. He holds still once he's inside me, both of us doing our best to stay as quiet as we can. He begins to move, causing me to gasp, but he covers my mouth with his, kissing me deeply.

He alternates between kissing me and watching me, doing both things with an intensity I'm not sure I've ever experienced. He pauses his lips so that they hover just above mine, occasionally brushing them as we fight to remain silent. He keeps his eyes focused on mine while he moves inside of me.

He's kissing me again when he starts to come.

His tongue is deep inside my mouth and the only reason I know he's about to finish is because he holds his breath and stops moving for a few seconds. It's so subtle as he fights to remain as quiet as possible. The muscles in his back clench beneath my palms and he never once breaks eye contact when he finally does pull away from my lips.

I wait for him to collapse on top of me, out of breath, but he doesn't. He somehow holds himself up after it's over, watching me like he's scared he might miss something. He dips his head and kisses me again. And even when he pulls out of me, he still doesn't collapse on top of me. He puts all his weight on his side as he eases down beside me without breaking the kiss.

I slide my hand through his hair and hold him against my mouth. We kiss for so long, I almost forget where I am.

When he breaks for air, he watches me silently for a moment, his hand still on my cheek, and then he dips his head and kisses me again like he doesn't know how to stop. I don't think I know how to stop this, either. I wish more than anything we were somewhere else. My place . . . his place . . . anywhere other than a place where we have to stop and go back upstairs eventually.

I am not inexperienced when it comes to sex. But I think I am inexperienced when it comes to this. The feeling of not wanting it to be over long after it's over. The feeling of wishing I could bury myself inside his chest so I could be closer to him. Maybe this isn't new for him, but based on the way he's looking at me between all the kissing, I would say there's more confusion in his expression than familiarity.

Several seconds pass as we stare at each other. Neither of us speaks. Maybe he doesn't have anything to say, but I can't speak because of the severe intensity building inside my chest. The sex was great. Quick, but incredible.

But this thing that's happening right now . . . the not being able to let go . . . the not wanting to stop kissing . . . the not being able to look away . . . I can't tell if this is just a side to sex I've never experienced or if this goes deeper than that. Like maybe sex isn't as deep as it gets. Maybe there's a whole level of connection I didn't know could exist.

Graham closes his eyes for a few seconds, then presses

his forehead against mine. After releasing a quick sigh, he pushes himself off me, almost as if he had to force his eyes shut in order to separate us. He helps me up and I look for my panties while he disposes of the condom and zips up his jeans.

It's quiet while I dress. We don't look at each other. He picks up the empty condom wrapper from the floor and tosses it into the trash can beside his bed.

Now we're facing each other. My arms are crossed over my chest and he's looking at me like he isn't sure if the last fifteen minutes actually happened. I'm looking at him like I wish it could happen again.

He opens his mouth like he's about to say something, but then he just gives his head a quick shake and steps forward, grabs my face and kisses me again. It's a rough kiss, like he isn't finished with me. I kiss him back with just as much intensity. After a minute of the kiss, he starts to walk me backward toward the stairs. We break for air and he just laughs, pressing his lips into my hair.

We make it up two steps before I realize I haven't looked in a mirror. I just had sex with this man and I'm about to have to go smile at his parents. I frantically comb my fingers through my hair and straighten out my dress. "How do I look?"

Graham smiles. "Like you just had sex."

I try to shove him in the chest, but he's faster than me. He grabs my hands and turns us until my back is against the wall of the stairwell. He straightens out a few strands of hair and then wipes his thumbs under my eyes. "There," he says. "You look beautiful. And innocent, like you just took a typical tour of the house." He kisses me again and I know he probably means for it to be short and sweet, but I grab his head and pull him closer. I can't get enough of the taste of him. I just want to be back at my apartment, in my bed with him, kissing him. I don't want to have to go upstairs and pretend I want pie when all I want is Graham.

"Quinn," he whispers, grabbing my wrists and pushing them against the wall. "How fast do you think you can eat a slice of pie?"

It's good to know our priorities are aligned. "Pretty damn fast."

Chapter Fourteen

Now

Despite all the Thursday nights that Graham has returned home smelling like beer, I've never actually seen him drunk. I think he chooses not to drink more than one or two beers at a time because he's still so full of guilt over losing his best friend, Tanner, all those years ago. The feeling of being drunk probably reminds him of his devastation. Much like how sex reminds me of *my* devastation.

I wonder what he's devastated about tonight?

This is the first time he's ever had to be escorted home by a coworker on a Thursday night. I watch from the window as Graham stumbles toward the front door, one arm thrown haphazardly around a guy who is struggling to get him to the house.

I move to the front door and unlock it. As soon as I open it, Graham looks up and smiles widely at me. "Quinn!"

He waves toward me; turning his head to the guy he's with. "Quinn, this is my good friend Morris. He's my good friend."

Morris nods apologetically.

"Thanks for getting him home," I say. I reach out and pull Graham from him, wrapping his arm around my shoulders. "Where is his car?"

Morris throws a thumb over his shoulder, just as Graham's car pulls into the driveway. Another of Graham's co-workers steps out of the car. I recognize him from Graham's office. I think his name is Bradley.

Bradley walks toward the front door while Graham puts both arms around me, placing even more of his weight on me. Bradley hands me the keys and laughs.

"First time we could get him to drink more than two," he says, nudging his head toward Graham. "He's good at a lot of things, but the man can't hold his alcohol."

Morris laughs. "Lightweight." They both wave goodbye and walk toward Morris's car. I step into the house with Graham and close the front door.

"I was gonna take a cab," Graham mutters. He releases me and walks toward the living room, falling onto the sofa. I would laugh and find this humorous if I weren't so worried that the reason he decided to drink too much tonight might have something to do with how upset he was after holding his new nephew. Or maybe it's his feelings about our marriage as a whole that he wanted to numb for a while.

I walk to the kitchen to get him a glass of water. When I take it back to him in the living room, he's sitting up on the couch. I hand him the water, noticing how different his eyes look. He's smiling at me as he takes a sip. He hasn't looked this happy or content in a very long time. Seeing him drunk makes me realize just how sad he looks now when he's sober. I didn't notice his sadness consumed him even more than it used to. I probably didn't notice because sadness is like a spiderweb. You don't see it until you're caught up in it, and then you have to claw at yourself to try to break free.

I wonder how long Graham has been trying to break free. I stopped trying years ago. I just let the web consume me.

"Quinn," Graham says, letting his head fall back against the couch. "You are so fucking beautiful." His eyes scroll down my body and then stop at my hand. He wraps his fingers around my wrist and pulls me to him. I'm stiff. I don't give in to the pull. I wish he were drunk enough that he would pass out on the couch. Instead, he's just drunk enough to forget he hasn't initiated sex since that night he slept in the guest room. He's just drunk enough to pretend we haven't been struggling as much as we have.

Graham leans forward and grabs me by my waist, pulling me down onto the couch next to him. His kiss is inebriated and fluid as he pushes me onto my back. My arms are above my head and his tongue is in my mouth and he tastes so good that I forget to be turned off by him for a moment. That moment turns into two and soon he has my T-shirt pushed up around my waist and his pants undone. Every time I open my eyes and look at him, he's looking back at me with eyes so different from my own. So far from the despondence I've permanently acquired.

The lack of sadness in him is intriguing enough for me to let him have me, but not intriguing enough for me to respond to him with as much need as he's taking me.

In the beginning of our marriage, we used to have sex

almost daily, but Thursdays were the day I looked forward to the most. It was one of my favorite nights of the week. I'd put on lingerie and wait for him in the bedroom. Sometimes I would throw on one of his T-shirts and wait for him in the kitchen. It really didn't matter what I was wearing. He'd walk in the door and I'd suddenly not be wearing it anymore.

We've had so much sex in our marriage, I know every inch of his body. I know every sound he makes and what those sounds mean. I know that he likes to be on top the most, but he's never minded when I wanted to take over. I know he likes to keep his eyes open. I know that he loves to kiss during sex. I know that he likes it in the mornings but prefers it late at night. I know everything there is to know about him sexually.

Yet in the last two months . . . we haven't had sex at all. The closest we've come until now is when he made out with me in the bathroom at his parents' house.

He hasn't initiated it since then and neither have I. And we haven't talked about the last time we had sex since it happened. I haven't had to keep up with my ovulation cycle since then and honestly it's been a big relief. After finally going a couple of months without tracking my cycle, I realize how much I would prefer never having sex again. That way, every month when my period comes, it would be completely expected and not at all devastating.

I try to reconcile my need to avoid sex with my need for Graham. Just because I don't desire sex doesn't mean I don't desire him. I've just forced it to be a different kind of desire now. An emotional one. It's my physical desires that never end well. I desire his touch, but if I allow it, it leads to sex. I desire his kiss, but if I kiss him too much, it leads to sex. I desire his flirtatious side, but if I enjoy it too much, it leads to sex.

I want so much to enjoy my husband without the one thing I know he needs the most and the one thing I want the least. But he makes so many sacrifices for me; I know I should sometimes do the same for him. I just wish sex wasn't a sacrifice for me.

But it is. And it's one I decide to make for him tonight. It's been too long, and he's been way too patient.

I lift one leg over the back of the couch and lower one to the floor, just as he pushes into me. His warm breath rolls down my throat as he thrusts into me repeatedly.

Today is the thirteenth.

What is fourteen days from today?

"Quinn," he whispers, his lips barely touching mine. I keep my eyes closed and my body limp, allowing him to use me to fuck the drunkenness out of himself. "Kiss me, Quinn."

I open my mouth but keep my eyes closed. My arms are resting loosely above my head and I'm counting on my fingers how many days it's been since I last had a period. Am I even ovulating? I'm almost finished counting when Graham grabs my right hand and wraps it around his neck. He buries his face into my hair while gripping one of my legs, wrapping it around his waist.

I'm not.

I'm five days past ovulation.

I sigh heavily; disappointed that there won't even be a chance this leads to anything. It's difficult enough bringing myself to make love at all anymore, so the fact that this time doesn't even count fills me with regret. Why couldn't this have happened last week, instead?

Graham pauses above me. I wait for his release, but nothing about him tenses. He just pulls his face away from my hair and looks down at me. His eyebrows are drawn together and he shakes his head, but then drops his face to my neck again, thrusting against me. "Can't you at least pretend you still want me? Sometimes I feel like I'm making love to a corpse."

His own words make him pause.

Tears are falling down my cheeks when he pulls out of me with regret.

His breath is hot against my neck, but this time I hate the way it feels. The way it smells just like the beer that gave him the uninhibited nerve to say those words to me. "Get off me."

"I'm sorry. I'm sorry."

I press my hands against his chest, ignoring the immediate and intense regret in his voice. "Get the fuck off me."

He rolls onto his side, grabbing my shoulder, attempting to roll me toward him. "Quinn, I didn't mean it. I'm drunk, I'm sorry . . ."

I push off the couch and practically run out of the living room without entertaining his apologies. I go straight to the shower and wash him out of me while I let the water wash away my tears.

"Can't you at least pretend you still want me?"

I squeeze my eyes shut as the mortification rolls through me.

"Sometimes I feel like I'm making love to a corpse."

I swipe angrily at my tears. Of course he feels like he's making love to a corpse. It's because he *is*. I haven't felt alive inside in years. I've slowly been rotting away, and that rot is now eating at my marriage to the point that I can no longer hide it.

And Graham can no longer stand it.

When I finish in the shower, I expect to find him in our bed, but he isn't there. He's probably so drunk; he just passed out on the sofa. As angry as I am at him for saying what he said, I also feel enough compassion to check on him and make sure he's okay.

When I walk through the dark kitchen toward the living room, I don't even see him standing at the counter until I pass him and he grabs my arm. I gasp from the unexpectedness of it.

I look up at him, ready to yell at him, but I can't. It's hard to yell at someone for speaking their truth. The moon is casting just enough light into the windows and I can see the sadness has returned to his eyes. He doesn't say anything. He just pulls me to him and holds me.

No . . . he *clings* to me.

The back of my T-shirt is clenched into two solid fists as he tightens his grip around me. I can feel his regret for allowing those words to slip from his mouth, but he doesn't tell me he's sorry again. He just holds me in silence because he knows at this point, an apology is futile. Apologies are good for admitting regret, but they do very little in removing the truth from the actions that caused the regret.

I allow him to hold me until my hurt feelings put a wedge between us. I pull away and look down at my feet for a moment, wondering if I want to say anything to him. Wondering if he's going to say anything to me. When the room remains silent, I turn and walk to our bedroom. He follows me, but all we do is crawl into bed, turn our backs toward each other and avoid the inevitable.

Chapter Fifteen

Then

I ate the slice of pie in five bites.

Graham's parents seemed a little confused by our hasty exit. He told his mother we had tickets to a fireworks show and we needed to go before we missed the grand finale. I was relieved she didn't catch the metaphorical part of his lie.

We do very little speaking on the way home. Graham says he likes to drive with the windows down at night. He turns the music up and grabs my hand, holding it all the way back to my place.

When we reach my apartment, I open the door and make it halfway across the living room before I realize he hasn't followed me inside. I turn around and he's leaning against the frame of the door like he has no intention of coming in.

There's a look of concern in his eye, so I walk back to the door. "Are you okay?"

He nods, but his nod is unconvincing. His eyes flitter around the room and then lock on mine with way too much seriousness. I was getting used to the playful, sarcastic side of Graham. Now the intense, serious side has reappeared.

Graham pushes off the door and runs a hand through his hair. "Maybe this is . . . too much. Too fast."

Heat immediately rises to my cheeks, but not the good kind of heat. It's the kind when you get so angry, your chest burns. "Are you kidding me? You're the one who forced me to meet your parents before I even knew your last name." I press a hand to my forehead, completely blown away that he decides to back down now. *After* he fucks me. I laugh incredulously at my own stupidity. "This is unreal."

I step back to close the door, but he steps forward and pushes it open, pulling me to him by my waist. "No," he says, shaking his head adamantly. "No." He kisses me, but pulls back before I would even have the chance to deny him. "It's just . . . *God,* I feel like I can't even find words right now." His head falls back like he can't figure out how to process his confusion. He releases me and steps out into the hallway. He starts pacing back and forth while he gathers his thoughts. He looks just as torn as he did the first time I saw him. He was pacing then, too, outside of Ethan's door.

Graham takes a step toward me, gripping the doorframe. "We've spent one day together, Quinn. *One.* It's been perfect and fun and you are so beautiful. I want to pick you up and carry you to your bed and stay inside you all night and tomorrow and the next day and it's . . ." He runs a hand through his unruly hair and then grips the back of his neck. "It's making my head swim and I feel like if I don't back off now, I'm gonna be real disappointed when I find out you don't feel the same way."

I take at least ten seconds to catch up to everything he just said. My mouth opens and before I can tell him he's right, that it's too soon and too fast, I say, "I know what you mean. It's terrifying."

He steps closer. "It is."

"Have you ever felt like this before? This fast?"

"Never. Not even close."

"Me neither."

He slips his hand against my neck and slides his fingers through my hair. His other hand presses against my lower back as he pulls me to him. He asks the question in a whisper against my lips. "Do you want me to leave?"

I answer him with a kiss.

Everything that happens next isn't questioned by either of us. There's no second-guessing as he kicks my door shut. No worrying if this is too fast when we tear away each other's clothes. Neither of us hesitates on the way to my bedroom.

And for the next hour, the only question he asks me is, "Do you want to be on top now?"

He only needs my answer once, but I say yes at least five times before we're finished.

Now he's lying on his back and I'm wrapped around him like there's not two feet of mattress on either side of us. My legs are intertwined with his and my hand is tracing circles over his chest. We've been mostly quiet since we finished, but not because we don't have anything to say. I think we're just reflecting on what life was like two days ago compared to what it's like now.

It's a lot to take in.

Graham trails his fingers up and down my arm. His lips meet the top of my head in a quick kiss. "Did Ethan ever try to get you back?"

"Yeah, he tried for a few weeks." I think it goes without saying that he wasn't successful. "What about Sasha?"

"Yep," he says. "She was relentless. She called me three times a day for a month. My voice mail stayed full."

"You should have changed your number."

"I couldn't. It's the only form of contact you had for me."

His admission makes me smile. "I probably never would have called you," I admit. "I kept your number on my wall because I liked how it made me feel. But I didn't think it was a good idea, given how we met."

"Do you still feel that way?"

I slide on top of him and his concerned expression is won over by a smile. "At this point I don't really care how we met. I only care that we met."

Graham kisses the corner of my mouth, threading our hands together. "I actually thought you took Ethan back and that's why you never called me."

"There's no way I would have taken him back. Especially after he tried to blame the whole affair on Sasha. He painted her out to be some kind of temptress who seduced him. He actually called her a whore once. That was the last time I spoke to him."

Graham shakes his head. "Sasha isn't a whore. She's a relatively good person who sometimes makes terrible and selfish decisions." He rolls me onto my back and begins to run a lazy finger over my stomach in circles. "I'm sure they did it because they thought they wouldn't get caught."

I have no idea how he talks so calmly about it. I was so

angry in the weeks following Ethan's affair. I took it personally, like they had the affair just to spite us. Graham looks at the affair like they did it *despite* us.

"Do you still talk to her?"

"Hell, no," he says with a laugh. "Just because I don't think she's a malicious person doesn't mean I want anything to do with her."

I smile at that truth.

Graham kisses the tip of my nose and then pulls back. "Are you relieved it happened? Or do you miss him?"

His questions don't seem to come from a place of jealousy at all. Graham just seems curious about the things that have happened in my life. Which is why I answer him with complete transparency. "I missed him for a while, but now that I've had a chance to reflect, we really had nothing in common." I roll onto my side and prop my head up on my hand. "On paper we had a lot in common. But in here," I touch my chest. "It didn't make sense. I loved him, but I don't think it was the kind of love that could withstand a marriage."

Graham laughs. "You say that like marriage is a Category 5 hurricane."

"Not all the time. But I definitely think there are Category 5 *moments* in every marriage. I don't think Ethan and I could have survived those moments."

Graham stares up at the ceiling in thought. "I know what you mean. I would have disappointed Sasha as a husband."

"Why in the world do you think that?"

"It's more a reflection of her than myself." Graham reaches up to my cheek and wipes something away.

"Then that would make her a disappointing wife. It wouldn't make you a disappointing husband."

Graham smiles at me appreciatively. "Do you remember what your fortune cookie said?"

I shrug. "It's been a while. Something about flaws, accompanied by a grammatical error."

Graham laughs. "It said, *If you only shine light on your flaws, all your perfects will dim.*"

I love that he kept my fortune. I love it even more that he has it memorized.

"We're all full of flaws. Hundreds of them. They're like tiny holes all over our skin. And like your fortune said, sometimes we shine too much light on our own flaws. But there are some people who try to ignore their own flaws by shining light on other people's to the point that the other person's flaws become their only focus. They pick at them, little by little, until they rip wide open and that's all we become to them. One giant, gaping flaw." Graham makes eye contact with me, and even though what he's saying is kind of depressing, he doesn't seem disappointed. "Sasha is that type of person. If I had married her, no matter how much I would have tried to prevent it, she would eventually be disappointed in me. She was incapable of focusing on the positive in other people."

I'm relieved for Graham. The thought of him being in an unhappy marriage makes me sad for him. And the thought of potentially being in an unhappy marriage hits a little too close to home. I frown, knowing I almost went through with that same type of marriage. I stare down at my hand, unconsciously rubbing my naked ring finger. "Ethan used to do that. But I didn't notice until after we broke up. I realized I felt better about myself without him than I did with him." I look back up at Graham. "For so long, I thought he was good for me. I feel so naive. I no longer trust my own judgment."

"Don't be so hard on yourself," he says. "Now you know exactly what to look for. When you meet someone who is good for you, they won't fill you with insecurities by focusing on your flaws. They'll fill you with inspiration, because they'll focus on all the best parts of you."

I pray he can't feel the intense pounding of my heart right now. I swallow hard and then choke out a pathetic sentence. "That's . . . really beautiful."

His pointed stare doesn't waver until he closes his eyes and presses his mouth to mine. We kiss for a quiet moment, but it's so intense, I feel like I can't breathe when we separate. I look down and suck in a quiet breath before looking him in the eye again. I force a grin in an attempt to ease the intensity in my chest. "I can't believe you kept that fortune."

"I can't believe you kept my number on your wall for six months."

"Touché."

Graham reaches to my face and runs his thumb over my lips. "What do you think is one of your biggest flaws?"

I kiss the tip of his thumb. "Does family count as a flaw?"

"Nope."

I think on it a moment longer. "I have a lot. But I think the one I would like to change if I could is my inability to read people. It's hard for me to look at someone and know exactly what they're thinking."

"I don't think many people can read people. They just think they can."

"Maybe."

Graham readjusts himself, wrapping my leg over him

while his eyes fill with playfulness. He leans forward and brushes his lips across mine, teasing me with a swipe of his tongue. "Try to read me right now," he whispers. "What am I thinking?" He pulls back and looks down at my mouth.

"You're thinking you want to move to Idaho and buy a potato farm."

He laughs. "That is *exactly* what I was thinking, Quinn." He rolls onto his back, pulling me on top of him. I push against his chest and sit up, straddling him.

"What about you? What's your biggest flaw?"

The smile disappears from Graham's face and his eyes are suddenly sad again. The variance in his expressions is so extreme. When he's sad, he looks sadder than anyone I've ever known. But when he's happy, he looks happier than anyone I've ever known.

Graham threads his fingers through mine and squeezes them. "I made a really stupid choice once that had some devastating consequences." His voice is quieter and I can tell he doesn't want to talk about it. But I love that he does anyway. "I was nineteen. I was with my best friend, Tanner. His sixteen-year-old brother, Alec, was with us. We had been at a party and I was the least drunk of the three of us, so I drove us the two miles home."

Graham squeezes my hands and inhales a breath. He's not looking me in the eye, so I know his story doesn't end well and I hate it for him. It makes me wonder if this is the flaw that makes him look as sad as he does sometimes.

"We had a wreck half a mile from my house. Tanner died. Alec was thrown from the vehicle and broke several bones. The wreck wasn't our fault. A truck ran a stop sign, but it didn't matter because I wasn't sober. They charged me with a DUI and I spent a night in jail. But since I didn't have a record, I was only charged with injury to a child and put on a year of probation for what happened to Alec." Graham releases a heavy sigh. "Isn't that fucked up? I got charged for the injuries Alec received in the wreck, but wasn't charged in the death of my best friend."

I can feel the weight of his sadness in my chest as I stare at him. There's so much of it. "You say that like you feel guilty you weren't charged for his death."

Graham's eyes finally meet mine. "I feel guilty every day that I'm alive and Tanner isn't."

I hate that he felt he had to tell me this. It's obviously hard to talk about, but I appreciate that he did. I bring one of his hands up to my mouth and I kiss it.

"It does get better with time," Graham says. "When I tell myself it could have just as easily been me in that passenger seat and Tanner behind the wheel. We both made stupid decisions that night. We were both at fault. But no matter what consequences I suffer as a result, I'm alive and he isn't. And I can't help but wonder if my reactions could have been faster had I not been drinking. What if I hadn't decided I was sober enough to drive? What if I'd been able to swerve and miss that truck? I think that's what feeds most of my guilt."

I don't even try to offer him reassuring words. Sometimes situations don't have a positive side. They just have a whole lot of sad sides. I reach down and touch his cheek. Then I touch the corners of his sad eyes. My fingers move to the scar on his collarbone that he showed me last night. "Is that where you got this scar?"

He nods.

I lower myself on top of him and press my lips to his scar. I kiss it from one end to the other and then lift up and look Graham in the eye. "I'm sorry that happened."

He forces a smile, but it fades as fast as it appeared. "Thank you."

I move my lips to his cheek and kiss him there, softly. "I'm sorry you lost your best friend."

I can feel Graham release a rush of air as his arms wrap around me. "Thank you."

I drag my lips from his cheek to his mouth and I kiss him gently. Then I pull back and look at him again. "I'm sorry," I whisper.

Graham watches me in silence for a few brief seconds, then he rolls me over so that he's on top of me. He presses his hand against my throat, gripping my jaw with gentle fingers. He watches my face as he pushes inside me, his mouth waiting in eagerness for my gasp. As soon as my lips part, his tongue dives between them and he kisses me the same way he fucks me. Unhurried. Rhythmic. Determined.

Chapter Sixteen

Now

The first time I dreamt Graham was cheating on me, I woke up in the middle of the night drenched in sweat. I was gasping for air because in my dream, I was crying so hard I couldn't breathe. Graham woke up and immediately put his arms around me. He asked me what was wrong and I was so mad at him. I remember pushing him away because the anger from my dream was still there, as if he'd actually cheated on me. When I told him what happened, he laughed and just held me and kissed me until I was no longer angry. Then he made love to me.

The next day he sent me flowers. The card said, *"I'm sorry for what I did to you in your nightmare. Please forgive me tonight when you dream."*

I still have the card. I smile every time I think about it. Some men can't even apologize for the mistakes they make in reality. But my husband apologizes for the mistakes he makes in my dreams.

I wonder if he'll apologize tonight.

I wonder if he actually has anything to apologize for.

I don't know why I'm suspicious. It started the night he came home too drunk to remember it the next morning and the suspicion continued to last Thursday, when he came home and didn't smell like beer at all. I've never been suspicious of him before this month, even after the trust issues Ethan left me with. But something didn't feel right this past Thursday. He came straight home and changed clothes without kissing me. And it hasn't felt right since that night.

The fear hit me hard today, right in the chest. So hard, I gasped and covered my mouth.

It's as if I could feel his guilt from wherever he was in that second. I know that's impossible—for two people to be so connected that they can feel each other even when they aren't in each other's presence. I think it was more of my denial inching its way forward until it was finally front and center in my conscience.

Things are at their worst between us. We hardly communicate. We aren't affectionate. Yet still, we walk around every other room in our house and pretend we're still husband and wife. But since that drunken night, it seems like Graham stopped sacrificing. The goodbye kisses started becoming more infrequent. The hello kisses have stopped completely. He's finally stooped to my level in this marriage.

He either has something to feel guilty for or he's finally done fighting for the survival of this marriage.

Isn't that what I wanted, though? For him to stop fighting so hard for something that will only bring him more misery?

I don't drink very often but I keep wine on hand for emergencies. This certainly feels like an emergency. I drink the first glass in the kitchen while I watch the clock.

I drink the second glass on the couch while I watch the driveway.

I need the wine to still the doubts I'm having. My fingers are trembling as I stare down at the wine. My stomach feels full of worry, like I'm inside one of my nightmares.

I'm sitting on the far-right side of the couch with my feet curled beneath me. The TV isn't on. The house is dark. I'm still watching the driveway when his car finally pulls in at half past seven. I have a clear view of him as he turns off the car and the headlights fade to black. I can see him, but he can't see me.

Both of his hands are gripping the steering wheel. He's just sitting in the car like the last place he wants to be is inside this house with me. I take another sip of wine and watch as he rests his forehead against his steering wheel.

One, two, three, four, five . . .

Fifteen seconds he sits like this. Fifteen seconds of dread. Or regret. I don't know what he's feeling.

He releases the steering wheel and sits up straight. He looks in his rearview mirror and wipes his mouth. Adjusts his tie. Wipes his neck. *Breaks my heart.* Sighs heavily and then finally exits his car.

When he walks through the front door, he doesn't notice me right away. He crosses the living room, heading for the kitchen, which leads to our bedroom. He's almost to the kitchen when he finally sees me.

My wineglass is tilted to my lips. I hold his stare as I take another sip. He just watches me in silence. He's probably wondering what I'm doing sitting in the dark. Alone. Drinking wine. His eyes follow the path from me to the living room window. He sees how visible his car is from my position. How visible his actions must have been to me as he was sitting in his car. He's wondering if I saw him wipe the remnants of her off his mouth. Off his neck. He's wondering if I saw him adjust his tie. He's wondering if I saw him press his head to the steering wheel in dread. Or regret. He doesn't bring his eyes back to mine. Instead, he looks down.

"What's her name?" I somehow ask the question without it sounding spiteful. I ask it with the same tone I often use to ask him about his day.

How was your day, dear?

What's your mistress's name, dear?

Despite my pleasant tone, Graham doesn't answer me. He lifts his eyes until they meet mine, but he's quiet in his denial.

I feel my stomach turn like I might physically be sick. I'm shocked at how much his silence angers me. I'm shocked at how much more this hurts in reality than in my nightmares. I didn't think it could get worse than the nightmares.

I somehow stand up, still clenching my glass. I want to throw it. Not at him. I just need to throw it at *something*. I hate him with every part of my soul right now, but I don't blame him enough to throw the glass at him. If I could throw it at myself, I would. But I can't, so I throw it toward our wedding photo that hangs on the wall across the room.

I repeat the words as my wineglass hits the picture, shattering, bleeding down the wall and all over the floor. "What's her *fucking* name, Graham?!"

My voice is no longer pleasant.

Graham doesn't even flinch. He doesn't look at the wedding photo, he doesn't look at the bleeding floor beneath it, he doesn't look at the front door, he doesn't look at his feet. He looks me right in the eye and he says, "Andrea."

As soon as her name has fallen from his lips completely, he looks away. He doesn't want to witness what his brutal honesty does to me.

I think back to the moment I was about to have to face Ethan after finding out he cheated on me. That moment when Graham held my face in his hands and said, *"The worst thing we could do right now is show emotion, Quinn. Don't get angry. Don't cry."*

It was easier then. When Graham was on *my* side. It's not so easy being over here alone.

My knees meet the floor, but Graham isn't here to catch me. As soon as he said her name, he left the room.

I do all the things Graham told me not to do the last time this happened to me. I show emotion. I get angry. I cry.

I crawl over to the mess I made on the floor. I pick up the smaller glass shards and I place them into a pile. I'm crying too hard to see them all. I can barely see through my tears as I grab a roll of napkins to soak up the wine from the wood floor.

I hear the shower running. He's probably washing off remnants of Andrea while I wash away remnants of red wine.

The tears are nothing new, but they're different this time. I'm not crying over something that never came to be. I'm crying for something that's coming to an end.

I pick up a shard of the glass and scoot to the wall, leaning against it. I stretch my legs out in front of me and I stare down at the piece of glass. I flip my hand over and press the glass against my palm. It pierces my skin, but I continue to press harder. I watch as it goes deeper and deeper into my palm. I watch as blood bubbles up around the glass.

My chest still somehow hurts worse than my hand. *So much worse.*

I drop the shard of glass and wipe the blood away with a napkin. Then I pull my legs up and hug my knees, burying my face in them. I'm still sobbing when Graham walks back into the room. I hug myself tighter when he kneels next to me. I feel his hand in my hair, his lips in my hair. His arms around me. He pulls me against him and sits against the wall.

I want to scream at him, punch him, run from him. But all I can do is curl up into myself even tighter as I cry.

"Quinn." His arms are clasped firmly around me and his face is in my hair. My name is full of agony when it falls from his lips. I've never hated it so much. I cover my ears because I don't want to hear his voice right now. But he doesn't say another word. Not even when I pull away from him, walk to our bedroom, and lock the door.

Chapter Seventeen

Then

Inseparable.

That's what we are.

It's been two and a half months since I supposedly gave him a "look" that night at the restaurant.

Even after spending every waking moment together outside of our respective jobs, I still miss him. I have never been this wrapped up in someone in my life. I never thought it was possible. It's not an unhealthy obsession, because he gives me my space if I want it. I just don't want the space. He's not possessive or overprotective. I'm not jealous or needy. It's just that the time we spend together feels like this euphoric escape and I want as much of it as I can get.

We've only slept apart once in the ten weeks we've been seeing each other. Ava and Reid got into a fight, so I let her stay with me and we talked shit about guys and ate junk food all night. It was depressingly fun, but five minutes after she walked out the door I was calling Graham. Twenty minutes after she left, he was knocking on my door. Twenty-one minutes after she left, we were making love.

That's basically what it's been. Ten weeks of nothing but sex, laughter, sex, food, sex, laughter, and more sex.

Graham jokes that we have to plateau at some point. But that point is not today.

"Jesus, Quinn." He groans against my neck as he collapses on top of me. He's out of breath and I'm no help because I can't catch mine, either.

This wasn't supposed to happen. It's Halloween and we're supposed to be at a party at Ava and Reid's house, but as soon as I pulled on my slutty T-shirt dress, Graham couldn't keep his hands off me. We almost had sex in the hallway, near the elevator, but he carried me back inside to save our dignity.

He held me to the Halloween costumes I suggested back in August. We decided to go as ourselves, only sluttier. We couldn't really figure out what a slutty slut costume of ourselves should look like, so we decided to just barely wear clothes. I have a ton of makeup on. Graham says his job is to just feel me up all night and make sure we have plenty of public displays of affection.

Our clothes are on the floor now, though, with the addition of a new rip in my shirt. The wait for that damn elevator gets us every time.

Graham leans in to me and buries his head against my neck again, kissing me until I break out in chills. "When am I going to meet your mother?"

That one question rips a hole in the moment and I feel all my joy seep out. "Never, if I can pull it off."

Graham pulls away from my neck and looks down at me. "She can't be that bad."

I release a halfhearted laugh. "Graham, she's the one who put the word *prestigious* in my wedding invitations."

"Did you judge me based on my parents?"

I loved his parents. "No, but I met them the first day we were together. I didn't even know you enough to judge you."

"You knew me, Quinn. You didn't know anything about me, but you knew *me*."

"You sound so sure of yourself."

He laughs. "I am. We figured each other out the night we met in that hallway. Sometimes people meet and none of the surface-level stuff matters because they see past all that." Graham lowers his mouth to my chest and places a kiss over my heart. "I knew everything I needed to know the first night I met you. Nothing external could ever influence my opinion of you. Even my judgment of the woman who raised you."

I want to kiss him. Or marry him. Or *fuck* him.

I settle on a kiss, but I keep it fairly quick because I'm scared if I don't pull away from him I might tell him I'm in love with him. It's right there on the tip of my tongue and it's harder keeping it in than letting it out. But I don't want to be the first one to say it. Not yet, anyway.

I quickly roll off the bed and pick up our costumes. "Fine. You can meet my mother next week." I toss him his clothes. "But tonight you're meeting Ava. Get dressed, we're late."

When I get my costume situated, Graham is still sitting on the bed, staring at me.

"What about your panties?" he asks.

My skirt is really short, and any other night I wouldn't be caught dead in it. I look down at my panties on the floor and

COLLEEN HOOVER

think about how crazy it would drive him if he knew I wasn't wearing anything under this already-too-short skirt all night. I leave them on the floor and grin at him. "They don't really go with my costume."

Graham shakes his head. "You're killing me, Quinn." He stands up and gets dressed while I touch up my makeup.

We make it out the door.

We make it down the hallway.

But once again, we get distracted while we wait for the elevator.

———

"You're late." It's the only thing Ava says when she opens the door and sees me standing there with Graham. She's dressed in a two-piece pantsuit and her hair is styled like she's straight out of *Stepford Wives*. She waits until we're inside her house and then she slams the door shut. "Reid!" She yells his name and turns to look for him, but he's standing right next to her. "Oh." She tosses a hand toward Graham. "He's here."

Reid reaches out and shakes Graham's hand. "Nice to meet you."

Ava gives Graham the once-over. Then me. "Your costumes are so undignified." She walks away without looking back.

"What the hell?" I say, looking at Reid. "Why is she being so rude?"

Reid laughs. "I tried to tell her it wasn't an obvious costume."

"What is she supposed to be? A bitch?"

Reid's face reddens. He leans in to Graham and me. "She's dressed up as your mother."

Graham immediately starts to laugh. "So she's not normally that . . . unpleasant?"

I roll my eyes and grab his hand. "Come on, I need to reintroduce you to my sister."

Ava is actually nice to Graham the second time she meets him. But then she goes into character the rest of the night and pretends to be our mother. The funniest part is that no one at the party has any idea who she's supposed to be. That's just a secret among the four of us, which makes it even better every time I hear her tell someone how tired they look or how much she hates children.

At one point, she walked up to Graham and said, "How much money do you make?"

Then Ava said, "Make sure you sign a prenup before you marry my daughter."

She's so good at being our mother, I'm relieved the party is winding down because I don't think I could take another second of it.

I'm in the kitchen with her now, helping her wash dishes. "I thought you and Reid used to have a dishwasher. Have I lost my mind?" Ava lifts her foot and points toward the mini-fridge with the glass door a few feet away. "Is that a wine refrigerator? Where your dishwasher used to be?"

"Yep," she says.

"But . . . *why?*"

"Downside of marrying a French guy. He thinks an ample supply of chilled wine is more important than a dishwasher."

"That's terrible, Ava."

She shrugs. "I agreed to it because he promised he'd do most of the dishes."

"Then why are we doing the dishes?"

COLLEEN HOOVER

Ava rolls her eyes. "Because your boyfriend is a shiny new toy and my husband is enamored."

It's true. Graham and Reid have spent most of the night chatting. I hand Ava the last plate. "Reid pulled me aside earlier and told me he already likes Graham more than he ever liked Ethan."

"That makes two of us," Ava says.

"*Three* of us."

When we finish with the dishes, I peek into the living room and Graham is saying something to Reid that's requiring a lot of arm movement. I don't think I've ever seen him so animated. Reid is doubled over with laughter. Graham catches my eye and the smile that appears on his face during our quick glance sends a warmth through me. He holds my stare for a couple of seconds and then focuses his attention back on Reid. When I turn around, Ava is standing in the doorway, watching as I try to wipe the smile off my face.

"He's in love with you."

"Shh." I walk back into the kitchen and she follows me.

"That *look*," she says. She picks up a paper plate and fans herself. "That man is in love with you and he wants to marry you and he wants you to have all his babies."

I can't help but smile. "God, I hope so."

Ava stands up straight and straightens out her pantsuit. "Well, Quinn. He is very decent-looking, but as your mother, I must admit that I think you can do much richer. Now where is my martini?"

I roll my eyes. "Please stop."

Chapter Eighteen

Now

I don't know if Graham slept in the guest room or on the couch last night, but wherever he slept, I doubt he actually got any sleep. I tried to imagine what he looked like with his sad eyes and his hands in his hair. Every now and then I'd feel sorry for him, but then I'd try to imagine what Andrea looks like. What she looked like through my husband's sad eyes while he kissed her.

I wonder if Andrea knows that Graham is married. I wonder if she knows he has a wife at home who hasn't been able to get pregnant. A wife who has spent the entire night and the entire day locked inside her bedroom. A wife who finally pulled herself out of bed long enough to pack a suitcase. A wife who is . . . _done_.

I want to be gone before Graham returns home.

I haven't called my mother to tell her I'm coming to stay

with her yet. I probably won't call her. I'll just show up. I dread the conversation with her enough to put as much time between now and having to speak with her about it.

"I warned you," she'll say.

"You should have married Ethan," she'll say. *"They all eventually cheat, Quinn. At least Ethan would have been a* rich *cheater."*

I unlock my bedroom door and walk to the living room. Graham's car isn't in the driveway. I walk around the house to see if there's anything I want to take with me. It feels reminiscent of when I was cleaning Ethan out of my apartment. I wanted nothing to do with him. Not even the things that reminded me of him.

I scour my home as my eyes fall over the years of stuff Graham and I have accumulated. I wouldn't even know where to start if I wanted to take anything. So I start nowhere. I just need clothes.

When I make it back to the bedroom, I close my suitcase and zip it up. As I'm pulling it off the bed, my eyes lock on the wooden box on the bottom shelf of my bookcase. I immediately walk to the bookcase and grab the box, then take it back to the bed. I jiggle the lock, but it doesn't budge. I remember Graham taping the key to it so we'd never lose it. I flip the box over and dig my nail beneath the piece of tape. I guess I'll finally get to see what's inside of it after all.

"Quinn."

I jump when I hear his voice. But I don't look at him. I cannot look at him right now. I keep my eyes downcast and finish pulling at the tape until I can pry the key loose.

"Quinn." Graham's voice is full of panic. I freeze, waiting for him to say whatever it is he needs to say. He walks into the room and sits down on the bed next to me. His hand clasps

my hand that's gripping the key. "I did the absolute worst thing I could possibly do to you. But please give me a chance to make things right before you open this."

I can feel the key in the palm of my hand.

He can keep it.

I grab his hand and flip it over. I place the key in his palm and then close his fist. I look him in the eye. "I won't open the box. But only because I don't give a *fuck* what's inside of it anymore."

I don't even remember the grief between leaving my house and driving over here, but I'm now parked in my mother's driveway.

I stare up at it. At the huge Victorian-style home that means more to my mother than anything outside of it. Including me.

She'd never admit to that, though. It would look bad, admitting out loud that she never really wanted to be a mother. Sometimes I resent her for that. She was able to get pregnant—by accident—and carry a child to term. Twice. And neither of those times was exciting for her. She talked for years about the stretch marks my sister and I left on her. She hated the baby weight she never lost. On the days we were really stressing her out, she'd call the nanny she had on speed dial and she'd say, *"Honestly, Roberta. I can't take this another minute. Please come as soon as you can, I need a spa day."*

I sit back in my seat and stare up at the bedroom that used to be mine. Long before she turned it into a spare closet for her empty shoeboxes. I remember standing at my window once, staring out over our front yard. Graham was with me. It was the first time I'd ever taken him home to meet her.

I'll never forget what he said that day. It was the most

honest and beautiful thing he's ever said to me. And it was that moment—standing with him at my bedroom window—that I fell in love with him.

That's the best memory I have inside my mother's house and it isn't even a memory I share with her. It's a memory I share with Graham. The husband who just cheated on me.

I feel like being inside my mother's house would be worse than being inside my own. I can't face her right now. I need to figure out my shit before I allow her to stick her nose in it.

I begin to back out of the driveway, but it's too late. The front door opens and I see her step outside, squinting to see who is in her driveway.

I lean my head back against the seat. So much for escaping.

"Quinn?" she calls out.

I get out of the car and walk toward her. She holds the front door open, but if I go inside, I'll feel trapped. I take a seat on the top step and look out over the front yard.

"You don't want to go inside?"

I shake my head and then fold my arms over my knees and I just start crying. She eventually takes a seat next to me. "What's the matter?"

It's times like these when I wish I had a mother who actually cared when I was crying. She just goes through the motions, patting a stiff hand against my back.

I don't even tell her about Graham. I don't say anything because I'm crying too hard to speak at first. When I finally do calm down enough to catch my breath, all I can ask her is something that comes out way worse than I mean for it to.

"Why would God give someone like you children but not me?" My mother stiffens when I say that. I immediately lift up and look at her. "I'm sorry. I didn't mean for that to sound so heartless."

She doesn't look all that offended. She just shrugs. "Maybe it isn't God's fault," she says. "Maybe reproductive systems just work or they don't." That would make more sense. "How did you know I never wanted kids?"

I laugh halfheartedly. "You said it. Many times."

She actually looks guilty. She glances away from me and stares out over the front yard. "I wanted to travel," she says. "When your father and I got married, we had plans to move to a different country every year for five years before buying a house. Just so we could experience other cultures before we died. But one crazy night, we weren't careful and it turned into your sister, Ava." She looks at me and says, "I never wanted to be a mother, Quinn. But I've done my best. I truly have. And I'm grateful for you and Ava. Even if it's hard for me to show it." She grabs my hand and squeezes it. "I didn't get my first choice at the perfect life, but I sure as hell did the best I could with my second choice."

I nod, wiping a tear away. I can't believe she's admitting all of this to me. And I can't believe I can sit here and be okay with her telling me my sister and I weren't what she wanted in life. But the fact that she's being honest and even said she's grateful is more than I ever imagined I'd get from her. I put my arms around her.

"Thank you."

She hugs me back, albeit stiffly and not like I would hug my own children if I had any. But she's here and she's hugging me and that should count for something.

"Are you sure you don't want to come inside? I could put on some hot tea."

I shake my head. "It's late. I should probably get back home."

She nods, although I can tell she's hesitant to leave me out here alone. She just doesn't know what to do or say beyond what she's already said without it becoming too awkward. She eventually goes inside, but I don't leave right away. I sit on her porch for a while because I don't want to go back home yet.

I also don't want to be here.

I kind of wish I didn't have to be anywhere at all.

Chapter Nineteen

Then

"I miss you." I try not to pout, but it's a phone conversation and he can't see me, so I push my lip out.

"I'll see you tomorrow," he says. "Promise. I just worry I'm smothering you but you're too nice to tell me."

"I'm not. I'm mean and blunt and I would tell you to leave if I wanted you to leave." It's true. I would tell him if I wanted space. And he would give it to me without question.

"I'll come over as soon as I get off work tomorrow and pick you up. Then I meet your mother."

I sigh. "Okay. But let's have sex before we go to her house because I'm already stressed."

Graham laughs and I can tell by his laugh he's thinking dirty thoughts because of my sentence. He has different laughs for different reactions and it's been one of my favorite things, differentiating them all. My favorite laugh is in the morning when I tell him about what I dreamt the night before. He always thinks my dreams are funny and there's a dry throatiness to his morning laugh because he's not fully awake yet.

"See you tomorrow." He says it quietly, like he already misses me.

"Goodnight." I hang up in a hurry. I don't like talking to him on the phone because he still hasn't told me he loves me yet. I haven't told him, either. So when we're saying goodbye to each other, I'm always scared that's when he'll choose to say it. I don't want him to say it for the first time during a phone conversation. I want him to say it when he's looking at me.

I spend the next two hours trying to remember what my life was like before Graham. I take a shower alone, watch TV alone, play on my phone alone. I thought maybe it would be nice, but I'm mostly just bored with it.

It's odd. I was with Ethan for four years and probably spent one or two nights a week with him. I loved my alone time when Ethan and I were dating. Even in the beginning. Being with him was nice, but being alone was just as nice.

It's not like that with Graham. After two hours, I'm bored out of my mind. I finally turn off the television, turn off my phone, turn off the lamp. When all is dark, I try to clear my thoughts so I'll fall asleep and be able to dream about him.

———

My alarm starts to buzz, but it's too bright, so I grab a pillow and throw it over my face. Graham is normally here and he always cuts off the alarm for me and gives me a couple of minutes to wake up. Which means my alarm will go off forever if I don't adult.

I move the pillow and just as I'm about to reach for the alarm, it cuts off. I open my eyes and Graham is rolling back over to face me. He's not wearing a shirt and it looks like he just woke up.

He smiles and pecks me on the lips. "I couldn't sleep," he says. "Finally gave up and came over here after midnight."

I smile, even though it's way too early for me to feel like smiling. "You missed me."

Graham pulls me against him. "It's weird," he says. "I used to be fine when I was alone. But now that I have you, I'm *lonely* when I'm alone."

Sometimes he says the sweetest things. Words I want to write down and keep forever so that I'll never forget them. But I never write them down because every time he says something sweet, I take off his clothes and need him inside me more than I need to write down his words.

That's exactly what happens. We make love and I forget to write down his words. We've been trying to catch our breath for the last minute when he turns to me and says, "What did I miss while you were sleeping?"

I shake my head. "It's too weird."

He lifts up onto his elbow and looks at me like I'm not getting out of this. I sigh and roll onto my back. "Okay, fine. We were at your apartment in the dream. Only your apartment was a really tiny shit-hole in Manhattan. I woke up before you because I wanted to do something nice and make you breakfast. But I didn't know how to cook and all you had were boxes of cereal, so I decided to make you a bowl of Lucky Charms. But every time I would pour the cereal into the bowl, the only thing that would come out of the box were tiny little comedians with microphones."

"Wait," Graham says, interrupting me. "Did you say *comedians*? Like as in people who tell jokes?"

"I told you it was weird. And yes. They were telling knock-knock jokes and yo-momma jokes. I was getting so angry because all I wanted to do was make you a bowl of Lucky Charms, but there were hundreds of tiny, annoying comedians climbing all over your kitchen, telling lame jokes. When you woke up and walked into the kitchen, you found me crying. I was a sobbing mess, running around your kitchen, trying to squash all the little comedians with a mason jar. But instead of being freaked out, you just walked up behind me and wrapped your arms around me. You said, 'Quinn, it's okay. We can have toast for breakfast.'"

Graham immediately drops his face into the pillow, stifling his laughter. I shove him in the arm. "Try and decipher that one, smartass."

Graham sighs and pulls me to him. "It means that I should probably cook breakfast from now on."

I like that plan.

"What do you want? French toast? Pancakes?"

I lift up and kiss him. "Just you."

"Again?"

I nod. "I want seconds."

I get exactly what I want for breakfast. Then we shower together, drink coffee together, and leave for work.

We couldn't even spend an entire night apart, but I don't think this means we live together. That's a huge step neither of us are willing to admit we took. I think if anything, this just means we no longer live alone. If there's a difference.

His mother probably thinks we already live together since she thinks we've been dating a lot longer than we have. I've been to Graham's parents' house at least once a week since the first night he took me there. Luckily, he stopped with the fictional stories. I was worried I wouldn't be able to keep up with everything he told her the first night.

His mother absolutely loves me now and his father already refers to me as his daughter-in-law. I don't mind it. I know we've only been together three months, but Graham will be my husband one day. It's not even a question. It's what happens when you meet your future husband. You eventually marry him.

And eventually . . . you introduce him to your mother.

Which is what is happening tonight. Not because I want him to meet her, but because it's only fair since I've met his. *I show you mine, you show me yours.*

————

"Why are you so nervous?" Graham reaches across the seat and puts pressure on my knee. The knee I've been bouncing up and down since we got in the car. "I'm the one meeting your mother. I should be the nervous one."

I squeeze his hand. "You'll understand after you meet her."

Graham laughs and brings my hand to his mouth, kissing it. "Do you think she'll hate me?"

We're on my mother's street now. So close. "You aren't Ethan. She already hates you."

"Then why are you nervous? If she already hates me, I can't disappoint her."

"I don't care if she hates you. I'm scared you'll hate *her*."

Graham shakes his head like I'm being ridiculous. "I could never hate the person who gave you life."

He says that now . . .

I watch Graham's expression as he pulls into the driveway. His eyes take in the massive home I grew up in. I can feel his thoughts from where I'm sitting. I can also hear them because he speaks them out loud.

"Holy shit. You grew up here?"

"Stop judging me."

Graham puts the car in park. "It's just a home, Quinn. It doesn't define you." He turns in his seat to face me, placing his hand on the seat rest behind my head as he leans in closer. "You know what else doesn't define you? Your mother." He leans forward and kisses me, then reaches around me and pushes open my door. "Let's get this over with."

No one greets us at the door, but once we're inside, we find my mother in the kitchen. When she hears us, she turns around and assesses Graham from head to toe. It's awkward because Graham goes in for a hug at the same time she goes in for a handshake. He falters a little, but that's the only time he falters. He spends the entire dinner as the adorably charming person he is.

The whole time, I watch him, completely impressed. He's done everything right. He greeted my mother as if he were actually excited to meet her. He's answered all her questions politely. He's talked just enough about his own family while making it seem he was more interested in ours. He complimented her décor, he laughed at her lame jokes, he ignored her underhanded insults. But even as I watch him excel, I've seen nothing but judgment in her eyes. I don't even have to hear what she's thinking because she's always worn her thoughts in her expressions. Even through years of Botox.

She hates that he drove up in his Honda Accord and not something flashier.

She hates that he dared to show up for his first introduction in a T-shirt and a pair of jeans.

She hates that he's an accountant, rather than the millionaires he does the accounting *for*.

She hates that he isn't Ethan.

"Quinn," she says as she stands. "Why don't you give your friend a tour of the house."

My friend.

She won't even dignify us with a label.

I'm relieved to have an excuse to leave the sitting room, even if it's just for a few minutes. I grab Graham's hand and pull him out of the sitting room as my mother returns the tea tray to the kitchen.

We start in the great room, which is just a fancier name for a living room no one is allowed to sit in. I point to the wall of books and whisper, "I've never even seen her read a book. She just pretends to be worldly."

Graham smiles and pretends to care while we walk slowly through the great room. He pauses in front of a wall of photos. Most of them are of my mother and us girls. Once our father died and she remarried, she put away most of the photos of him. But she's always kept one. It's a picture of our father with Ava on one knee and me on the other. As if Graham knows the exact photo I'm studying, he pulls it off the wall.

"You and Ava look more alike now than you did here."

I nod. "Yeah, we get asked if we're twins every time we're together. We don't really see it, though."

"How old were you when your father died?"

"Fourteen."

"That's so young," he says. "Were you very close?"

I shrug. "We weren't *not* close. But he worked a lot. We only saw him a couple of times a week growing up, but he made the most of the times we did see him." I force a smile. "I like to imagine that we'd be a lot closer now if he were alive. He was an older father, so I think it was just hard for him to connect with little girls, you know? But I think we would have connected as adults."

Graham places the picture back on the wall. He pauses at every single picture and touches my photo, as if he can learn more about me through the pictures. When we finally make it through the sitting room, I lead him toward the back door to show him the greenhouse. But before we pass the stairs, he rests his hand against the small of my back and whispers against my ear. "I want to see your old bedroom first."

His seductive voice makes his intentions clear. I get excited at the thought of recreating what happened in his childhood bedroom. I grab his hand and rush him up the stairs. It's probably been a year or more since I actually came up to my old bedroom. I'm excited for him to see it because after being in his, I feel like I learned a lot more about him as a person.

When we reach my bedroom, I push open the door and let him walk in first. As soon as I flip on the light, I'm filled with disappointment. This experience won't be the same as the one we had in Graham's old bedroom.

My mother has boxed up everything. There are empty designer shoe boxes stacked up against two of the walls, floor to ceiling. Empty designer purse boxes cover a third wall. All of my things that once covered the walls of my bedroom are now boxed up in old moving boxes with my name sprawled across them. I walk over to the bed and run my hands over one of the boxes.

"I guess she needed the spare bedroom," I say quietly.

Graham stands next to me and rubs a reassuring hand against my back. "It's a tiny house," he says. "I can see why she'd need the extra room."

I laugh at his sarcasm. He pulls me in for a hug and I close my eyes as I curl into his chest. I hate that I was so excited for him to see my old bedroom. I hate that it makes me this sad to know my mother will never love me like Graham's mother loves him. There are two guest bedrooms in this house, yet my mother chooses to use my old bedroom as the storage room. It embarrasses me that he's witnessing this.

I pull back and suck up my emotions. I shrug, hoping he can't tell how much it bothers me. But he can. He brushes my hair back and says, "You okay?"

"Yeah. I just . . . I don't know. Meeting your family was an unexpected quality about you. I was kind of hoping you could have the same experience." I laugh a little, embarrassed I even said that. "Wishful thinking."

I walk over to my bedroom window and stare outside. I don't want him to see the disappointment on my face. Graham walks up behind me and slips his arms around my waist.

"Most people are products of their environment, Quinn. I come from a good home. I grew up with two great, stable parents. It's expected that I would grow up and be relatively normal." He spins me around and puts his hands on my shoulders. He dips his head and looks at me with so much sincerity in his eyes. "Being here . . . meeting your mother and seeing where you came from and who you somehow turned out to be . . . it's *inspiring*, Quinn. I don't know how you did it, you selfless, amazing, incredible woman."

A lot of people can't pinpoint the exact moment they fall in love with another person.

I can.

It just happened.

And maybe it's coincidence or maybe it's something more, but Graham chooses this exact moment to press his forehead to mine and say, "I love you, Quinn."

I wrap my arms around him, grateful for every single part of him. "I love you, too."

Chapter Twenty

Now

I turn off my car and scoot my seat back, propping my leg against the steering wheel. The only light on inside the house is the kitchen light. It's almost midnight. Graham is probably sleeping because he has to work tomorrow.

This morning when I woke up, I expected Graham to still be outside our bedroom door, knocking, begging for forgiveness. It made me angry that he left for work. Our marriage is crumbling, he admitted to seeing another woman, I holed myself up in our bedroom all night . . . but he woke up, got dressed, and traipsed off to work.

He must work with Andrea. He probably wanted to warn her that I knew in case I flew off the handle and showed up at his office to kick her ass.

I wouldn't do that. I'm not mad at Andrea. She's not the one who made a commitment to me. She has no loyalty to me or I to her. I'm only mad at one person in this scenario and that is my husband.

The living room curtain moves. I debate ducking, but I know from experience what a clear view it is from the living room to our driveway. Graham sees me, so there's no point in hiding. The front door opens and Graham steps outside. He begins to head toward my car.

He's wearing the pajama pants I bought him for Christmas last year. His feet are covered in two mismatched socks. One black, one white. I always thought that was a conflicting personality trait of his. He's very organized and predictable in a lot of ways, but for some reason, he never cares if his socks match. To Graham, socks are a practical necessity, not a fashion statement.

I stare out my window as he opens the passenger door and takes a seat inside the car. When he closes the door, it feels as though he cuts off my air supply. My chest is tight and my lungs feel like someone took a knife and ripped a hole in them. I roll down my window so I can breathe.

He smells good. I hate that no matter how much he hurt my heart, the rest of me never got the memo that it's supposed to be repulsed by him. If a scientist could figure out how to align the heart with the brain, there would be very little agony left in the world.

I wait for his apologies to start. The excuses. Possibly even the blame. He inhales a breath and says, "Why did we never get a dog?"

He's sitting in the passenger seat, his body half facing me as his head rests against the headrest. He's staring at me very seriously despite the unbelievable question that just fell from his lips. His hair is damp, like he just got out of the shower.

His eyes are bloodshot. I don't know if it's from lack of sleep or if he's been crying, but all he wants to know is why we never got a *dog*?

"Are you kidding me, Graham?"

"I'm sorry," he says, shaking his head. "It was just a thought I had. I didn't know if there was a reason."

His first *I'm sorry* since he admitted to having an affair and it's an apology unrelated to his infidelity. It's so unlike him. Having an *affair* is so unlike him. It's like I don't even know this man sitting next to me. "Who *are* you right now? What did you do with my husband?"

He faces forward and leans back against his seat, covering his eyes with his arm. "He's probably somewhere with my wife. It's been a while since I've seen her."

So this is how it's going to be? I thought he'd come out here and make this entire ordeal a little easier to bear, but instead, he's giving me every reason in the world to justify my rage. I look away from him and focus my attention out my window. "I hate you right now. So much." A tear slides down my cheek.

"You don't hate me," he says quietly. "In order to hate me you'd have to love me. But you've been indifferent toward me for a long time now."

I wipe away a tear. "Whatever helps you excuse the fact that you slept with another woman, Graham. I'd hate for you to feel guilty."

"I never slept with her, Quinn. We just . . . it never got that far. I swear."

I pause with his confession.

He didn't sleep with her? Does that make a difference?

Does it hurt less? No. Does it make me less angry at him?

No. Not even a little bit. The fact is, Graham was intimate with another woman. It wouldn't matter if that consisted of a conversation, a kiss, or a three-day fuck-a-thon. Betrayal hurts the same on any level when it's your husband doing the betraying.

"I never slept with her," he repeats quietly. "But that shouldn't make you feel any better. I thought about it."

I clasp my hand over my mouth and try to stifle a sob. It doesn't work because everything he's saying, everything he's doing . . . it's not what I expected from him. I needed comfort and reassurance and he's giving me nothing but the opposite. "Get out of my car." I unlock the doors, even though they're already unlocked. I want him far away from me. I grip the steering wheel and pull my seat up straighter, waiting for him to just go. I start the engine. He doesn't move. I look at him again. "Get out, Graham. *Please*. Get out of my car." I press my forehead to the steering wheel. "I can't even look at you right now." I squeeze my eyes shut and wait for the door to open, but instead, the engine cuts off. I hear him pull my keys out of the ignition.

"I'm not going anywhere until you know every detail," he says.

I shake my head, swiping at more tears. I reach for my door but he grabs my hand. "Look at me." He pulls me toward him, refusing to let me out of the car. "Quinn, *look* at me!"

It's the first time he's ever yelled at me.

It's actually the first time I've ever heard him *yell*.

Graham has always been a silent fighter. The strength of his voice and the way it reverberates inside the car makes me freeze. "I need to tell you why I did what I did. When I'm finished, you can decide what to do, but *please*, Quinn. Let me speak first."

I close my door and lean back in my seat. I squeeze my eyes shut and the tears continue to fall. I don't want to listen to him. But part of me needs to know every detail because if I don't get the facts, I'm scared my imagination will make it even worse. "Hurry," I whisper. I don't know how long I can sit here without completely losing it.

He inhales a calming breath. It takes him a moment to figure out where to start. Or how to start. "She was hired on by our firm a few months ago."

I can hear the tears in his voice. He tries to keep it steady, but the regret is there. It's the only thing that helps ease the pain—knowing he's suffering, too.

"We interacted a few times, but I never looked at her as anything more than a coworker. I've never looked at any woman how I look at you, Quinn. I don't want you to think that's how it started."

I can feel him looking at me, but I keep my eyes shut. My pulse is pounding so hard, I feel like the only thing that could make it stop is getting out of this claustrophobic car. But I know he won't let me until I hear him out, so I focus on breathing steadily while he speaks.

"There were things she would do sometimes that would catch my attention. Not because I found her intriguing or attractive, but because . . . her mannerisms reminded me of you."

I shake my head and open my mouth to speak. He can tell I'm about to interrupt, so he whispers, "Just let me finish."

I close my mouth and lean forward, crossing my arms over the steering wheel. I press my forehead against my arms and pray he gets this over with.

"Nothing happened between us until last week. We were assigned to work on a job together Wednesday, so we spent a lot of the day together. I noticed as the hours passed that I was . . . drawn to her. Attracted to her. But not because she had something you didn't. I was drawn to her because of how much she reminded me of you."

I have so much I want to scream at him right now, but I hold back.

"Being around her all day Wednesday made me miss you. So I left work early, thinking maybe if I just took you out for a nice dinner or did something to make you happy, you would smile at me like you used to. Or you'd be interested in my day. Or *me*. But when I got home and walked through the front door, I saw you walking out of the living room. I know you heard me opening the door. But for some reason, instead of being excited to see me come home an hour early, you went to your office so you could avoid me."

I'm not only full of anger now. I'm also full of shame. I didn't think he noticed all the times I try to avoid him.

"You spoke one word to me Wednesday night. *One*. Do you remember what it was?"

I nod, but I keep my head buried against my arms. "Goodnight."

I can hear the tears in his voice when he says, "I was so angry at you. Figuring you out is like a fucking riddle sometimes, Quinn. I was tired of trying to figure out how to be around you the right way. I was so mad at you, I didn't even kiss you goodbye when I left for work Thursday."

I noticed.

"When we finished up the project on Thursday, I should have come home. I should have left, but instead . . . I stayed.

186

And we talked. And . . . I kissed her." Graham runs his hands down his face. "I shouldn't have done it. And even after it started, I should have stopped it. But I couldn't. Because the whole time I had my eyes closed, I pretended it was you."

I lift my head off my arms and look at him. "So it's *my* fault? Is that what you're saying?" I turn my whole body toward him in my seat. "You don't get the attention you want from me, so you find someone who reminds you of me? I guess as long as you pretend it's your wife, it shouldn't count." I roll my eyes and fall back against my seat. "Graham Wells, first man in the world to find an ethical way around an affair."

"Quinn."

I don't let him speak. "You obviously didn't feel very guilty if you had the entire fucking weekend to think about it, but then went back to work and did it all over again."

"It was twice. Last Thursday and last night. That's it. I swear."

"What if I wouldn't have caught on? Would you have even stopped it?"

Graham runs his hand over his mouth, squeezing his jaw. His head shakes a little and I'm hoping it's not an answer to my question. I'm hoping he's just shaking it in regret.

"I don't know how to answer that," he says, looking out his window. "Nobody deserves this. Especially you. Before I left tonight, I swore to myself that it would never happen again. But I also never believed I would be capable of something like this to begin with."

I look up at the roof of the car and press my palm to my chest, blowing out a quick breath. "Then why did you do it?" My question comes out in a sob.

Graham turns to me as soon as I start crying. He leans

across the seat and grips my face, silently pleading for me to look at him. When I finally do meet his desperate stare, it makes me cry even harder. "We walk around inside that house like everything is okay, but it's *not*, Quinn. We've been broken for years and I have no idea how to fix us. I find solutions. It's what I do. It's what I'm good at. But I have no idea how to solve me and you. Every day I come home, hoping things will be better. But you can't even stand to be in the same room with me. You hate it when I touch you. You hate it when I talk to you. I pretend not to notice the things you don't want me to notice because I don't want you to hurt more than you already do." He releases a rush of air. "I am not blaming you for what I did. It's my fault. It's *my* fault. *I* did that. *I* fucked up. But I didn't fuck up because I was attracted to *her*. I fucked up because I miss *you*. Every day, I miss you. When I'm at work, I miss you. When I'm home, I miss you. When you're next to me in bed, I miss you. When I'm *inside* you, I miss you."

Graham presses his mouth to mine. I can taste his tears. Or maybe they're my tears. He pulls back and presses his forehead to mine. "I miss you, Quinn. So much. You're right here, but you aren't. I don't know where you went or when you left, but I have no idea how to bring you back. I am so alone. We live together. We eat together. We sleep together. But I have never felt more alone in my entire life."

Graham releases me and falls back against his seat. He rests his elbow against the window, covering his face as he tries to compose himself. He's more broken than I've ever seen him in all the years I've known him.

And I'm the one slowly tearing him down. I'm making him unrecognizable. I've strung him along by allowing him to believe there's hope that I'll eventually change. That I'll miraculously turn back into the woman he fell in love with.

But I can't change. We are who our circumstances turn us into.

"Graham." I wipe at my face with my shirt. He's quiet, but he eventually looks at me with his sad, heartbroken eyes. "I haven't gone anywhere. I've been here this whole time. But you can't see me because you're still searching for someone I used to be. I'm sorry I'm no longer who I was back then. Maybe I'll get better. Maybe I won't. But a good husband loves his wife through the good *and* the bad times. A good husband stands at his wife's side through sickness *and* health, Graham. A good husband—a husband who *truly* loves his wife—wouldn't cheat on her and then blame his infidelity on the fact that he's *lonely*."

Graham's expression doesn't change. He's as still as a statue. The only thing that moves is his jaw as he works it back and forth. And then his eyes narrow and he tilts his head. "You don't think I love you, Quinn?"

"I know you used to. But I don't think you love the person I've become."

Graham sits up straight. He leans forward, looking me hard in the eye. His words are clipped as he speaks. "I have loved you every single second of every day since the moment I laid eyes on you. I love you more now than I did the day I married you. I love you, Quinn. I fucking *love* you!"

He opens his car door, gets out and then slams it shut with all his strength. The whole car shakes. He walks toward the house, but before he makes it to the front door, he spins around and points at me angrily. "I *love* you, Quinn!"

He's shouting the words. He's angry. *So* angry.

He walks toward his car and kicks at the front bumper with his bare foot. He kicks and he kicks and he kicks and then pauses to scream it at me again. "I *love* you!"

He slams his fist against the top of his car, over and over, until he finally collapses against the hood, his head buried in his arms. He remains in this position for an entire minute, the only thing moving is the subtle shaking of his shoulders. I don't move. I don't even think I breathe.

Graham finally pushes off the hood and uses his shirt to wipe at his eyes. He looks at me, completely defeated. "I love you," he says quietly, shaking his head. "I always have. No matter how much you wish I didn't."

Chapter Twenty-one

Then

I never ask my mother for favors for obvious reasons. Which is precisely why I called my stepfather to ask permission to use his beach house in Cape Cod. He only uses it as a rental property now and it stays booked up in the summers. But it's February and the house has been sitting empty for most of the winter. It took a lot to swallow my pride and ask him, but it was a lot easier than if I'd asked her. She has stated numerous times since she met Graham that she thinks I could do better. In her eyes, better means meeting someone with his own beach house so that I'll never have to ask to borrow theirs for the weekend.

Graham walked around for an hour after we got here, pointing things out with the excitement of a kid on Christmas morning.

Quinn, come look at this view!

Quinn, come look at this bathtub!
Quinn, did you see the fire pit?
Quinn, they have kayaks!

His excitement has waned a little since we got here earlier today. We just ate dinner and I took a shower while Graham built a fire in the fire pit. It's an unusually warm day for a February in Massachusetts, but even on a warmer winter day, it barely tops out in the fifties during the day and the thirties at night. I bring a blanket to the fire pit with me and curl up next to Graham on the patio sofa.

He pulls me even closer, wrapping an arm around me while I rest my head on his shoulder. He tucks the blanket around both of us. It's cold, but the warmth from both him and the fire make it bearable. Comfortable, even.

I've never seen Graham more at peace than when he's out here, listening to the sounds of the ocean. I love how he looks out over the water as if it holds all the answers to every question in the world. He looks at the ocean with the respect it deserves.

"What a perfect day," he says quietly.

I smile. I like that a perfect day to him includes me. It's been six months since we started dating. Sometimes I look at him and feel such an overwhelming appreciation for him, I almost want to write thank-you notes to our exes. It's the best thing that's ever happened to me.

It's funny how you can be so happy with someone and love them so much, it creates an underlying sense of fear in you that you never knew before them. The fear of losing them. The fear of them getting hurt. I imagine that's what it's like when you have children. It's probably the most incredible kind of love you'll ever know, but it's also the most terrifying.

"Do you want kids?" I practically blurt the question out. It was so quiet between us and then I sliced through that quiet with a question whose answer could determine our future. I don't know how to do anything with subtlety.

"Of course. Do you?"

"Yeah. I want a lot of kids."

Graham laughs. "How many is a lot?"

"I don't know. More than one. Less than five." I lift my head off his shoulder and look at him. "I think I would make a great mom. I don't brag on myself, but if I had kids, I'm pretty sure they would be the best kids ever."

"I have no doubt."

I lay my head back on his shoulder. He covers my hand that's pressed against his chest. "Have you always wanted to be a mom?"

"Yes. It's kind of embarrassing how excited I am to be a mother. Most girls grow up dreaming of a successful career. I was always too embarrassed to admit that I wanted to work from home and have a bunch of babies."

"That's not embarrassing."

"Yes it is. Women nowadays are supposed to want to amount to more than just being a mother. Feminism and all that."

Graham scoots me off his chest to tend to the fire. He grabs two small logs and walks them over to the fire pit, then reclaims his seat next to me. "Be whatever you want to be. Be a soldier if you want. Or a lawyer. Or a CEO. Or a housewife. The only thing you shouldn't be is embarrassed."

I love him. I love him so much.

"A mom isn't the only thing I want to be. I want to write a book someday."

"Well you certainly have the imagination for it based on all the crazy dreams you have."

"I should probably write them down," I laugh.

Graham is smiling at me with an unfamiliar look on his face. I'm about to ask him what he's thinking, but he speaks first.

"Ask me again if I want kids," he says.

"Why? Are you changing your answer?"

"I am. Ask me again."

"Do you want kids?"

He smiles at me. "I only want kids if I can have them with you. I want to have lots of kids with you. I want to watch your belly grow and I want to watch you hold our baby for the first time and I want to watch you cry because you're so deliriously happy. And at night I want to stand outside the nursery and watch you rock our babies to sleep while you sing to them. I can't think of anything I want more than to make you a mother."

I kiss his shoulder. "You always say the sweetest things. I wish I knew how to express myself like you do."

"You're a writer. You're the one who's good with words."

"I'm not arguing about my writing skills. I could probably write down what I feel for you, but I could never put it into words verbally like you do."

"Then do that," he says. "Write me a love letter. No one's ever written me a love letter before."

"I don't believe that."

"I'm serious. I've always wanted one."

I laugh. "I'll write you a love letter, you sappy man."

"It better be more than a page long. And I want you to tell me everything. What you thought of me the first time you saw me. What you felt when we were falling in love. And I want you to spray your perfume on it like the girls in high school do."

"Any other requests?"

"I wouldn't be opposed to you slipping a nude pic in the envelope."

I can probably make that happen.

Graham tugs me onto his lap so that I'm straddling him. He pulls the blanket over us, cocooning us inside of it. He's wearing a pair of cotton pajama pants, so I get a clear sense of what he's thinking right now. "Have you ever made love outdoors in thirty-degree weather before?"

I grin against his mouth. "Nope. But funny enough, that's precisely why I'm not wearing any underwear right now."

Graham's hands fall to my ass and he groans as he lifts my nightgown. I rise a little so that he can free himself, and then I lower myself on top of him, taking him in. We make love, cocooned under a blanket with the sound of the ocean as our background song. It's the perfect moment in a perfect place with the perfect person. And I know without a doubt that I'll be writing about this moment when I write my love letter to him.

Chapter Twenty-two

Now

He kissed another woman.

I stare at the text I'm about to send Ava, but then I remember she's several hours ahead where she lives. I would feel bad, knowing this is the text she'll wake up to. I delete it.

It's been half an hour since Graham gave up and went back inside, but I'm still sitting in my car. I think I'm too wounded to move. I have no idea if any of this is my fault or if it's his fault or if it's no one's fault. The only thing I know is that he hurt me. And he hurt me because I've been hurting him. It doesn't make what he did right in any sense, but a person can understand a behavior without excusing it.

Now we're both full of so much pain, I don't even know where to go from here. No matter how much you love someone—the capacity of that love is meaningless if it outweighs your capacity to forgive.

Part of me wonders if we'd even be having any of these problems if we would have been able to have a baby. I'm not sure that our marriage would have taken the turn it did because I would have never been as devastated as I've been the last few years. And Graham wouldn't have had to walk on eggshells around me.

But then part of me wonders if this was inevitable. Maybe a child wouldn't have changed our marriage and instead of just being an unhappy couple, we would have been an unhappy family. And then what would that make us? Just another married couple staying together for the sake of the children.

I wonder how many marriages would have survived if it weren't for the children they created together. How many couples would have continued to live together happily without the children being the glue that holds their family together?

Maybe we should get a dog. See if that fixes us.

Maybe that's exactly what Graham was thinking when he sat in my car earlier and said, *"Why did we never get a dog?"*

Of course, that's what he was thinking. He's just as aware of our problems as I am. It only makes sense our minds would head in the same direction.

When it grows too cold in the car, I walk back into our house and sit on the edge of the sofa. I don't want to go to my bedroom where Graham is sleeping. A while ago he was screaming that he loves me at the top of his lungs. He was so loud, I'm sure all the neighbors woke up to the sound of him yelling and the pounding of his fist against metal.

But right now, our house is silent. And that silence between us is so loud; I don't think I'll ever be able to fall asleep.

We've tried therapy in the past, hoping it would help with the infertility issues we struggled with. I got bored with it. *He* got bored with it. And then we bonded over how boring therapy was. Therapists do nothing but try to make you recognize the wrongs within yourself. That's not Graham's issue and it's not my issue. We know our faults. We recognize them. My fault is that I can't have a baby and it makes me sad. Graham's fault is that he can't fix me and it makes *him* sad. There's no magical cure that therapy will bring us. No matter how much we spend on trying to fix our issue, no therapist in the world can get me pregnant. Therefore, therapy is just a drain on a bank account that has already had one too many leaks.

Maybe the only cure for us is divorce. It's weird, having thoughts of divorcing someone I'm in love with. But I think about it a lot. I think about how much time Graham is wasting by being with me. He would be sad if I left him, but he'd meet someone new. He's too good not to. He'd fall in love and he could make a baby and he'd be able to rejoin that circle of life that I ripped him out of. When I think about Graham being a father someday, it always makes me smile . . . even if the thought of him being a father doesn't include me being a mother.

I think the only reason I never completely let him go is because of the miracles. I read the articles and the books and the blog posts from the mothers who tried to conceive for years and then just as they were about to give up, *voilà! Pregnant!*

The miracles gave me hope. Enough hope to hang on to Graham just enough in case we ever got a miracle of our own. Maybe that miracle would have fixed us. Put a Band-Aid on our broken marriage.

I want to hate him for kissing someone else. But I can't, because part of me doesn't blame him. I've been giving him every excuse in the world to walk out on me. We haven't had sex in a while, but I know that's not why he strayed outside of our marriage. Graham would go a lifetime without sex if I needed him to.

The reason he allowed himself to fuck up is because he gave up on us.

Back when I was in college, I was assigned to do an article on a couple who had been married for sixty years. They were both in their eighties. When I showed up to the interview, I was shocked at how in tune they were with each other. I assumed, after living with someone for sixty years, you'd be sick of them. But they looked at each other like they still somehow respected and admired each other, even after all they'd been through.

I asked them a number of questions during the interview, but the question I ended the interview with left such an impact on me. I asked, "What's the secret to such a perfect marriage?"

The old man leaned forward and looked at me very seriously. "Our marriage hasn't been perfect. *No* marriage is perfect. There were times when she gave up on us. There were even more times when *I* gave up on us. The secret to our longevity is that we never gave up at the same time."

I'll never forget the honesty in that man's answer.

And now I truly feel like I'm living that. I believe that's why Graham did what he did. Because he finally gave up on us. He's not a superhero. He's human. There isn't a person in this world who could put up with being shut out for as long as Graham has put up with it. He has been our strength in the past and I've continually been our weakest link. But now the tables have turned and Graham was momentarily our weakest link.

The problem is—I feel like I've given up, too. I feel like we've both given up at the same time and there may be no turning back from that. I know I could fix it by forgiving him and telling him I'll try harder, but part of me wonders if that's the right choice.

Why fight for something that will likely never get better? How long can a couple cling to a past they both prefer in order to justify a present where neither of them is happy?

There is no doubt in my mind that Graham and I used to be perfect for each other. But just because we used to be perfect for each other doesn't mean we're perfect together now. We're far from it.

I look at the clock, wishing it would magically fast forward through tomorrow. I have a feeling tomorrow is going to be so much worse than today was. Because tomorrow I feel like we'll be forced to make a decision.

We'll have to decide if it's finally time to open that wooden box.

The thought of it makes my stomach turn. A pain rips through me and I clench at my shirt as I lean forward. I am so heartbroken; I can actually physically feel it. But I don't cry, because in this situation, my tears cause me even more pain.

I walk to our bedroom with dry eyes. It's the longest stretch of time I've gone in the last twenty-four hours without crying. I push open our bedroom door, expecting Graham to be asleep. Instead, he's sitting up against the headboard. His reading glasses are at the tip of his nose and he's holding a book in his lap. His bedside lamp is on and we make eye contact for a brief second.

I crawl in bed beside him, my back turned to him. I think we're both too broken tonight to even continue the argument. He continues reading his book and I do my best to try to fall asleep. My mind runs, though. Several minutes pass and just knowing he's right next to me prevents me from relaxing. He must realize I'm still awake because I hear him as he closes his book and places it on the nightstand. "I quit my job today."

I don't say anything in response to his confession. I just stare at the wall.

"I know you think I left for work this morning and that I just left you here, locked up in this bedroom."

He's right. That's exactly what I thought.

"But I only left the house because I needed to quit my job. I can't work in the place where I made the worst mistake of my life. I'll start looking for a new job next week."

I squeeze my eyes shut and pull the covers up to my chin. He turns out the lamp, indicating he doesn't need a response from me. After he rolls over, I let out a quiet sigh, knowing he won't be working around Andrea anymore. He stopped giving up. He's trying again. He still believes there's a possibility that our marriage will go back to how it used to be.

I feel sorry for him. What if he's wrong?

These thoughts plague me for the next hour. Graham somehow falls asleep—or I think he's asleep. He's playing the part well.

But I can't sleep. The tears keep threatening to fall and the pain in my stomach gets worse and worse. I get up and take some aspirin, but when I'm back in the bed I start to question whether emotional turmoil can actually manifest as physical pain.

Something isn't right.

It shouldn't hurt this much.

I feel a sharp pain. A deep pain. A pain strong enough to force me onto my side. I clench my fists around my blanket and curl my legs up to my stomach. When I do this, I feel it. Slippery and wet, all over the sheets.

"Graham." I try to reach for him, but he's rolling over to turn on the light. Another pain, so profound it makes me gasp for breath.

"Quinn?"

His hand is on my shoulder. He pulls the covers away. Whatever he sees sends him flying off the bed, the lights are on, he's picking me up, telling me it'll be okay, he's carrying me, we're in the car, he's speeding, I'm sweating, I look down, I'm covered in blood. "Graham."

I'm terrified and he takes my hand and he squeezes it and he says, "It's okay, Quinn. We're almost there. We're almost there."

Everything after that runs together.

There are glimpses of things that stick out to me. The fluorescent light over my head. Graham's hand around mine. Words I don't want to hear, like, *miscarriage* and *hemorrhaging* and *surgery*.

Words Graham is saying into the phone, probably to his mother, while he holds my hand. He whispers them because he thinks I might be asleep. Part of me is, most of me isn't. I know these aren't things he's saying *might* happen. They've *already* happened. I'm not going into surgery. I've just come out of it.

Graham ends the call. His lips are against my forehead and he whispers my name. "Quinn?" I open my eyes to meet his. His eyes are red and there's a deep wrinkle between his brows that I've never noticed before. It's new, probably brought on by what's currently happening. I wonder if I'll think of this moment every time I look at that wrinkle.

"What happened?"

The crease between his eyes deepens. He brushes his hand over my hair and carefully releases his words. "You had a miscarriage last night," he confirms. His eyes search mine, preparing for whatever reaction I might have.

It's weird that my body doesn't feel it. I know I'm probably heavily medicated, but it seems like I would know that there was a life growing inside of me that is no longer there. I put a hand on my stomach, wondering how I missed it. How long had I been pregnant? How long has it been since we last had sex? Over two months. Closer to three.

"Graham," I whisper. He takes my hand and squeezes it. I know I should be full of so much devastation right now that not even a sliver of happiness or relief could find its way into my soul. But somehow, I don't feel the devastation that should accompany this moment. I feel hope. "I was pregnant? We finally got pregnant?"

I don't know how I'm focusing on the only positive thing about this entire situation, but after years of constant failure, I can't help but take this as a sign. *I got pregnant. We had a partial miracle.*

A tear slips out of Graham's eye and lands on my arm. I look down at the tear and watch it slide over my skin. My eyes flick back up to Graham's and not a single part of him is able to see the positive in this situation.

"Quinn . . ."

Another tear falls from his eye. In all the years I've known him, I've never seen him look this sad. I shake my head, because whatever has him this terrified to speak is not something I want to hear.

Graham squeezes my hand again and looks at me with so much devastation in his eyes, I have to turn away from him when he speaks. "When we got here last night . . ."

I try to stop listening, but my ears refuse to fail me.

"You were hemorrhaging."

The word *no* is repeating and I have no idea if it's coming from my mouth or if it's inside my head.

"You had to have a . . ."

I curl up and hug my knees, squeezing my eyes shut. As soon as I hear the word *hysterectomy* I start crying. *Sobbing.*

Graham crawls into the hospital bed and wraps himself around me, holding me as we let go of every single ounce of hope that was left between us.

Chapter Twenty-three

Then

It's our last night at the beach house. We leave in the morning to head back to Connecticut. Graham has a meeting he has to be back for tomorrow afternoon. I have laundry to do before I go back to work on Tuesday. Neither of us is ready to leave yet. It's been peaceful and perfect and I'm already looking forward to coming back here with him. I don't even care if I have to kiss my mother's ass for the next month in order to plan our next getaway. It's a price I'll gladly pay for another weekend of perfection.

It's a little bit colder tonight than the last two nights we've been here, but I kind of like it. I have the heater turned up high in the house. We freeze our asses off for hours near the fire pit and then cuddle up in bed to thaw out. It's a routine I would never get bored of.

I just finished making us both cups of hot chocolate. I

take them outside and hand Graham his, then sit down next to him.

"Okay," he says. "Next question."

Graham found out this morning that, even though I love looking at it, I've never actually stepped foot in the ocean. He spent the majority of the day trying to figure out other things about me that he didn't know. It's become a game to us now and we're alternating questions so we can find out everything there is to know about each other.

He mentioned the first night we were together that he doesn't talk about religion or politics. But it's been six months now and I'm curious to know his opinions. "We've still never discussed religion," I say. "Or politics. Are those still topics that are off the table?"

Graham edges the cup with his lips and sucks a marshmallow into his mouth. "What do you want to know?"

"Are you a Republican or a Democrat?"

He doesn't even hesitate. "Neither. I can't stand the extremists on either side, so I sort of hover in the middle."

"So you're one of *those* people."

He tilts his head. "What people?"

"The kind who pretend to agree with every opinion just to keep the peace."

Graham arches an eyebrow. "Oh, I have opinions, Quinn. Strong ones."

I pull my legs up and tuck them under me, facing him. "I want to hear them."

"What do you want to know?"

"Everything," I challenge. "Your stance on gun control. Immigration. Abortion. *All* of it."

I love the look of excitement on his face, as if he's preparing for a presentation. It's adorable that a presentation would even excite him.

He sets his mug of hot chocolate on the table beside him. "Okay . . . let's see. I don't think we should take away a citizen's right to own a gun. But I do think it should be one hell of a difficult process to get your hands on one. I think women should decide what to do with their own bodies, as long as it's within the first trimester or it's a medical emergency. I think government programs are absolutely necessary but I also think a more systematic process needs to be put in place that would encourage people to get off of welfare, rather than to stay on it. I think we should open up our borders to immigrants, as long as they register and pay taxes. I'm certain that life-saving medical care should be a basic human right, not a luxury only the wealthy can afford. I think college tuition should automatically be deferred and then repaid over a twenty-year period on a sliding scale. I think athletes are paid way too much, teachers are paid way too little, NASA is underfunded, weed should be legal, people should love who they want to love, and Wi-Fi should be universally accessible and free." When he's finished, he calmly reaches for his mug of hot chocolate and brings it back to his mouth. "Do you still love me?"

"More than I did two minutes ago." I press a kiss to his shoulder and he wraps his arm around me, tucking me against him.

"Well, that went better than I thought it would."

"Don't get too comfortable," I warn. "We still haven't discussed religion. Do you believe in God?"

Graham breaks eye contact and looks out at the ocean. He caresses my shoulder and thinks about my question for a moment. "I didn't used to."

"But you do now?"

"Yeah. I do now."

"What changed your mind?"

"A few things," he says. He nudges his head toward the ocean. "*That* being one of them. How can something exist that is that magnificent and powerful without something even more magnificent and powerful creating it?"

I stare out at the water with him when he asks me what I believe. I shrug. "Religion isn't one of my mother's strong suits, but I've always believed there was something out there greater than us. I just don't know exactly what it is. I don't think anyone knows for sure."

"That's why they call it faith," he says.

"So how does a man of math and science reconcile his knowledge with his faith?"

Graham smiles when I ask him that question, like he's been dying to discuss it. I love that about him. He has this adorable inner nerd that appears sometimes and it makes him even more attractive.

"Do you know how old the earth is, Quinn?"

"No, but I bet I'm about to find out."

"Four and a half *billion* years old," he says. His voice is full of wonder, like this is his absolute favorite thing to talk about. "Do you know how long ago our specific species appeared?"

"No idea."

"Only two hundred thousand years ago," he says. "Only two hundred thousand years out of four and a half *billion* years. It's unbelievable." He grabs my hand and lays it palm down on his thigh. He begins tracing over the back of my hand with a lazy finger. "If the back of your hand represented the age of this earth and every species that has ever lived, the entire human race wouldn't even be visible to the naked eye. We are that insignificant." He drags his fingers to the center of the back of my hand and points to a small freckle. "From the beginning of time until now, we could combine every single human that has ever walked this earth, and all their problems and concerns as a whole wouldn't even amount to the size of this freckle right here." He taps my hand. "Every single one of your life experiences could fit right here in this tiny freckle. So would mine. So would Beyoncé's."

I laugh.

"When you look at the earth's existence as a whole, we're nothing. We haven't even been here long enough to earn bragging rights. Yet humans believe we're the center of the universe. We focus on the stupidest, most mundane issues. We stress about things that mean absolutely nothing to the universe, when we should be nothing but grateful that evolution even gave our species a chance to *have* problems. Because one of these days . . . humans won't exist. History will repeat itself and earth will move on to a different species altogether. Me and you . . . we're just two people out of an entire race that, in retrospect, is still way less impressive at sustainability than a dinosaur. We just haven't reached our expiration date yet." He slides his fingers through mine and squeezes my hand.

"Based on all the scientific evidence that proves how insignificant we are, it was always hard for me to believe in God. The more appropriate question would have been, '*Could a God believe in me?*' Because a lot has happened on this earth in four and a half billion years to think that a God would give a shit about me or my problems. But, I recently concluded that there's no other explanation for how you and I could end up on the same planet, in the same species, in the same century, in the same country, in the same state, in the same town, in the same hallway, in front of the same door for the same reason at the exact same time. If God didn't believe in me, then I'd have to believe you were just a coincidence. And you being a coincidence in my life is a lot harder for me to fathom than the mere existence of a higher power."

Oh.

Wow. I'm breathless.

Graham has said so many sweet things to me, but this wasn't sweet. This was pure poetry. This was beyond an expression of his intelligence, because I know he's incredibly smart. This was sacrificial. He gave me purpose. He made me incredibly relevant—crucial—to him, when I've never felt relevant, vital, or crucial to anyone else before. "I love you so much, Graham Wells." It's all I can say because I can't compete with what he just said. I don't even try.

"Do you love me enough to marry me?"

I lift off his arm and sit up straight, still facing him.

Did he seriously just ask me that?

It was so spontaneous. He probably hasn't even thought it through. He's still smiling but in a few seconds I think he's probably going to laugh because he accidentally blurted it out without even thinking. He doesn't even have a ring, which proves it was an accident.

"Graham . . ."

He slips his hand under the blanket. When he pulls his hand back out, he's holding a ring. No box, no gift wrap, no pretenses. It's just a ring. A ring he's been carrying in his pocket for a moment he obviously *did* think through.

I bring my hands up to my mouth. They're shaking because I wasn't expecting this and I'm speechless and I'm scared I won't be able to answer him out loud because everything is caught in my throat but I somehow still whisper the words, "Oh my God."

Graham pulls my left hand from my mouth and he holds the ring near my ring finger, but he doesn't attempt to slip it on. Instead, he dips his head to bring my focus back to him. When our eyes meet, he's looking at me with all the clarity and hope in the world. "Be my wife, Quinn. Weather the Category 5 moments with me."

I'm nodding before he's even finished speaking. I'm nodding, because if I try to say *yes*, I'll start crying. I can't even believe he somehow made this perfect weekend even better.

As soon as I start nodding, he laughs with a heavy sigh of relief. And when he slips the ring on my finger, he bites his lip because he doesn't want me to see that he's getting choked up, too. "I didn't know what ring to get you," he says, looking back up at me. "But when the jeweler told me that the wedding ring symbolizes an endless loop without a beginning, middle, or end, I didn't want to break up that endless loop with diamonds. I hope you like it."

The ring is a delicate, thin gold band with no stones. It's not a reflection of how much money Graham has or doesn't have. It's a reflection of how long he believes our love will last. An eternity.

"It's perfect, Graham."

Chapter Twenty-four

Now

". . . cervical ectopic pregnancy," she says. "Very rare. In fact, the chances of a woman experiencing this type of ectopic pregnancy are less than one percent."

Graham squeezes my hand. I lay back in the hospital bed, wanting nothing more than for the doctor to leave the room so I can go back to sleep. The medicine has me so drowsy, it's hard to pay attention to everything she's saying. I know I don't have to though, because Graham is focused on every word that comes out of her mouth. "Bed rest for two weeks," is the last thing I hear her say before I close my eyes. I know Graham is the one who loves math, but I feel like I'm going to be obsessing over that less than one percent. The chances of me getting pregnant after so many years of trying were greater than the chances of a pregnancy resulting in a cervical ectopic abruption.

"What was the cause?" Graham asks.

"More than likely the endometriosis," she replies. She goes into a little more detail, but I tune her out. I tilt my head toward Graham and open my eyes. He's staring at the doctor, listening to her response. But I can see the worry in him. His right hand is covering his mouth, his left hand still has a grip on mine.

"Could . . ." He glances down at me and there is so much worry in his eyes. "Could stress have caused the miscarriage?"

"Miscarriage was inevitable with this type of pregnancy," she says. "Nothing could have been done to prolong it. It ruptured because ectopic pregnancies aren't viable."

My miscarriage happened nineteen hours ago. It isn't until this moment that I realize Graham has spent the last nineteen hours thinking he was somehow responsible. He's been afraid that the stress from our fight led to this.

After the doctor leaves the room, I brush my thumb across his hand. It's a small gesture, and one that is very hard to make due to the amount of anger I still hold, but one he notices immediately. "You have a lot to feel guilty for, but my miscarriage is not one of them."

Graham stares at me a moment with vacant eyes and a broken soul. Then he releases my hand and walks out of the room. He doesn't come back for half an hour, but it looks like he's been crying.

He's cried a few times during our marriage. I've never actually seen him cry until yesterday, but I've seen him in the aftermath.

Graham spends the next few hours making sure I'm comfortable. My mother comes to visit, but I pretend to be asleep. Ava calls, but I tell Graham to tell her I'm asleep. I spend most of the day and night trying not to think about everything that's happening, but every time I close my eyes I find myself wishing I would have just known. Even if the pregnancy would have ended the same way, I'm angry with myself for not paying more attention to my body so I could have enjoyed it while it lasted. If I had paid more attention, I would have suspected I was pregnant. I would have taken a test. It would have been positive. And then, just once, Graham and I would have known what it felt like to be parents. Even if it would have been a fleeting feeling.

It's a little morbid that I would go through this entire thing again if I could have just known I was pregnant for one single day. After so many years of trying, it seems cruel that our payoff was a miscarriage followed by a hysterectomy without the cushion of feeling like parents, if even for a moment.

The entire ordeal has been unfair and painful. More so than my recovery will be. Because of the rupture and the hemorrhaging, the doctors had to perform an emergency abdominal hysterectomy, rather than a vaginal one. Which means a longer recovery time. I'll likely be in the hospital another day or two before I'll be discharged. Then I'll be confined to our bed for two weeks.

Everything feels so unfinished between us. We hadn't resolved anything before the miscarriage and now it just feels like the decision we were about to make has been put on hold. Because I'm in no place to discuss the future of our marriage right now. It'll probably be weeks before things are back to normal.

As normal as things can get without a uterus.

"You can't sleep?" Graham asks. He hasn't left the hospital all day. He only left the room earlier for half an hour, but then he returned and has been alternating between the couch and the chair next to my bed. Right now he's in the chair, seated on the edge of it, waiting for me to speak. He looks exhausted, but I know Graham and he isn't going anywhere until I do. "Do you want something to drink?"

I shake my head. "I'm not thirsty." The only light on in the room is the one behind my bed and it makes it look like Graham is in a spotlight on a lonely stage.

His need to console me is warring with his awareness of the tension that's been between us for so long. But he fights the tension and reaches for the rail. "Do you mind if I lay with you?" He already has the rail down and is crawling into the bed with me when I shake my head. He's careful to turn me so that my IV doesn't pull. He fits himself into less than half the bed next to me and slips a hand under my head, sacrificing his comfort for mine. He kisses me on the back of my head. Part of me wasn't sure I wanted him in the bed with me, but I soon realize that falling asleep in our shared sadness is somehow more comforting than falling asleep alone.

———

"I'm flying home," Ava blurts out, before I even have the chance to say hello.

"No you aren't. I'm fine."

"Quinn, I'm your sister. I want to come stay with you."

"No," I repeat. "I'll be fine. You're pregnant. The last thing you need is to spend all day on an airplane."

She sighs heavily.

"Besides," I add. "I'm thinking about coming to visit you,

instead." It's a lie. I haven't thought about it until this very moment. But my impending two weeks on bed rest makes me realize how much I'll need to put space between our house and myself when I'm finally recovered.

"Really? Can you? When do you think you'll be released to fly?"

"I'll ask the doctor when she discharges me."

"Please don't say that if you aren't serious."

"I am serious. I think it'll do me some good."

"What about Graham? Won't he be using all his vacation time during your recovery?"

I don't talk about my marriage troubles to anyone. Not even Ava. "I want to come alone," I say. I don't elaborate. I haven't told her Graham quit his job and I didn't tell her about him kissing another woman. But by the pause Ava gives me, I can tell she knows something is up. I'll wait to tell her about everything until I actually see her in person.

"Okay," she says. "Talk to your doctor and let me know a date."

"Okay. Love you."

"Love you, too."

After I end the call, I look up from the hospital bed to see Graham standing in the doorway. I wait for him to tell me it's not a good idea to plan travel after just having surgery. Instead, he just looks down at the coffee cup in his hand. "You're going to visit Ava?"

He doesn't say *we*. Part of me feels guilty. But surely he understands that I need space.

"Not until I get cleared to fly. But yeah. I need to see her."

He doesn't look up from his cup. He just nods a little and says, "Are you coming back?"

"Of course."

Of course.

I don't say it with a lot of conviction, but there's enough in my voice to assure him that this isn't a separation. It's just a break.

He swallows heavily. "How long will you be gone?"

"I don't know. Maybe a couple of weeks."

Graham nods and then takes a sip from his cup while kicking off the door. "We have some airline miles on our card. Let me know when you want to leave and I'll book your flight."

Chapter Twenty-five

Then

I don't remember Ethan's and my wedding plans being this stressful.

That might have been because I let my mother take the reins back then and had very little to do with the planning. But this is different. I want Graham and I to decide on what flavor of cake we want. I want Graham and I to decide who to invite and where it should be and what time of day we want to commit to each other for the rest of our lives. But my mother won't stop making decisions that I don't want her to make, no matter how many times I ask her to stop.

"I just want your day to be perfect, Quinn," she says.

"Graham can't afford these things, so I'm only trying to help out," she says.

"Don't forget to have him sign a prenup," she says.

COLLEEN HOOVER

"You never know if your stepfather will leave you an inheritance," she says. *"You need to protect your assets."*

She says things that make me feel like marriage is nothing more than a loan to her, rather than a commitment of love. She's brought up the idea of a prenuptial agreement so many times, she forgets that as it stands, I have no assets to protect. Besides, I know Graham isn't marrying me for the money or property my stepfather may or may not leave me one day. Graham would marry me even if I were up to my eyeballs in debt.

I feel myself starting to resent the whole idea of a lavish wedding. I would vent my frustration to Graham, but if I did that, I'd have to tell him why my mother is frustrating me. The last thing I want to do is share with Graham all the underhanded things my mother says about him.

I look down at my phone as another text comes through from my mother.

You should rethink the buffet, Quinn. Evelyn Bradbury hired a private chef for her wedding and it was so much classier.

I roll my eyes and flip my phone over so I won't be subjected to more of her texts.

I hear the front door to my apartment close, so I grab my brush. I pretend I'm just brushing my hair rather than moping in the bathroom when Graham walks in. The sight of him alone instantly calms me. My frustration is now long gone and replaced with a smile. Graham wraps his arms around me from behind and kisses me on the neck. "Hey, beautiful." He smiles at me in the mirror.

"Hey, handsome."

He spins me around and gives me an even better kiss. "How was your day?"

"Fine. How was yours?"

"Fine."

I push against his chest because he's staring at me too hard and I might accidentally let my true emotions out and then he'll ask me what's wrong and I'll have to tell him how much this wedding is stressing me out.

I turn around and face the mirror, hoping he'll go to the living room or the kitchen or anywhere that isn't somewhere he can stare at me like he's staring at me right now.

"What's bothering you?"

Sometimes I hate how well he knows me.

Except during sex. It comes in handy during sex.

"Why can't you be oblivious to a woman's emotional state like most men?"

He smiles and pulls me to him. "If I was oblivious to your emotional state, I would merely be a man in love with you. But I'm more than that. I'm your soul mate and I can feel everything you're feeling." He presses his lips to my forehead. "Why are you sad, Quinn?"

I sigh, exasperated. "My *mother*." He releases me and I walk to the bedroom and sit on my bed. I fall backward and stare up at the ceiling. "She's trying to turn our wedding into the wedding she had planned for me and Ethan. She's not even asking me what we want, Graham. She's just making decisions and telling me after the fact."

Graham crawls onto the bed and lays beside me, propping his head up on his hand. He rests his other hand on my stomach.

"Yesterday she told me she put down a deposit at the Douglas Whimberly Plaza for the date of our wedding. She's not even asking what we want, but because she's paying for everything, she thinks it earns her the right to make all the decisions. Today she texted and said she ordered the invitations."

Graham makes a face. "You think that means our wedding invitations will have the word *prestigious* in them?"

I laugh. "I'd be more shocked if they didn't." My head flops to the side and I give him the most pathetic look, short of pouting. "I don't want a huge wedding in a fancy plaza with all my mother's friends there."

"What *do* you want?"

"At this point I don't even know that I *want* a wedding." Graham tilts his head, a little concerned by my comment. I quickly rectify it. "I don't mean I don't want to marry you. I just don't want to marry you in my mother's dream wedding."

Graham gives me a reassuring smile. "We've only been engaged for three months. We still have five months before the wedding date. There's plenty of time to put your foot down and make sure you get what you want. If it'll make things easier for you, just blame everything on me. Tell her I said no and she can hate me for ruining her dream wedding while keeping the peace between the two of you."

Why is he so perfect? "You really don't care if I blame you?"

He laughs. "Quinn, your mother already hates me. This will give her a little more justification for her hatred and then everyone wins." He stands up and slips off his shoes. "We going out tonight?"

"Whatever you want to do. Ava and Reid are ordering some kind of fight on Pay-Per-View and invited us over."

Graham undoes his tie. "That sounds fun. I have some emails I need to send but I can be ready in an hour."

I watch as he leaves the room. I fall back onto the bed and

smile because it feels like he just might have come up with a solution to some of my issues in less than two minutes. But even though the solution sounds like a good one—*just blame Graham for everything*—my mother will never go for it. She'll just point out that Graham isn't paying for the wedding, so Graham doesn't get a say.

But still. He *tried* to solve my issues. That's what counts, right? He's willing to take the blame for something just to keep the peace between my mother and me.

I can't believe I get to marry that man in five months. I can't believe I get to spend the rest of my life with him. Even if that life together will start in the Douglas Whimberly Plaza, surrounded by people I barely know and food that's so expensive, it guarantees ample trays full of raw meat and ceviche that no one actually likes to eat, but pretends to because it's fancy.

Oh, well. The wedding may not be ideal, but it will only be a few painful hours, followed by a lifetime of perfection.

I drag myself off the bed, committed to somehow remaining sane for the next five months. I spend the next half hour getting ready for our night out. Graham and I have a handful of friends we sometimes spend time with on the weekends, but we mostly spend our time with Ava and Reid. They got married just before I met Graham. Ava was smart. She married Reid on a whim in Vegas. My mother wasn't able to order her invitations or book her venue or even choose which cake tasted best to her. I was the only one who knew they were jetting off to Vegas to get married and I've secretly been envious of their decision.

I'm buttoning my jeans when Graham walks into the bathroom. "Are you ready?"

"Almost. Let me grab some shoes." I walk to my closet and Graham follows me in there. He leans against the doorway and watches me while I look for a pair of shoes. I have to dress up for work every day, so a lazy night at Ava and Reid's is a nice respite from the heels and business attire I wear daily. I'm looking through all the shoes on my shelf, trying to find my favorite comfy pair. Graham is watching me the whole time. I glance at him a couple of times and I can't help but think he's up to something. There's a smirk on his face. It's barely there, but it's there.

"What is it?"

He unfolds his arms and slides his hands into the pockets of his jeans. "What if I told you I just spent the last half hour reworking the plans for our wedding?"

I stand up straight. He definitely has all my attention now. "What do you mean?"

He inhales a breath, like he's trying to calm his nerves. Knowing he's nervous about whatever he's about to say makes *me* nervous for what he's about to say.

"I don't care about the details of our wedding, Quinn. We can have whatever kind of wedding you want as long as the final result is that you'll be my wife. But . . ." He walks into my closet and pauses a foot away from me. "If the only thing you want from this wedding is me, then why are we waiting? Let's just go ahead and get married. This weekend." Before I can speak, he grabs my hands and squeezes them. "I just booked the beach house through next Monday. I spoke to a minister who is willing to come marry us there. He'll even bring a witness so we don't have to tell anyone. It'll just be you and me. We'll get married by the ocean tomorrow afternoon and then tomorrow night we can sit by the fire where I proposed to you. We'll spend the whole night eating s'mores and asking each other questions, and then we'll make love and fall asleep and wake up married on Sunday."

I'm almost as speechless as I was the moment he proposed to me. And just like three months ago when I was too excited and shocked to say *yes*, I nod. Profusely. And I laugh and I hug him and I kiss him.

"It's perfect, it's perfect, I love you, it's *perfect*."

We grab a suitcase out of my closet and start packing. We decide we aren't telling anyone. Not even his mother.

"We can call them tomorrow, after we're married," Graham says.

I can't stop smiling, even though I know my mother is going to completely lose it when I call her tomorrow night and tell her we're already married. "My mother is going to kill us."

"Yes, she probably will. But it's a lot easier to ask for forgiveness than permission."

Chapter Twenty-six

Now

Tomorrow will mark three weeks since I've been at Ava's and I haven't heard Graham's voice since the day he dropped me off at the airport.

He called me once last week but I didn't answer my phone. I texted him and told him I needed time to think. He responded and said *Call me when you're ready.* He hasn't texted me since then and I'm still not ready to call him.

As miserable as I feel inside, I really do like it here at Ava's. I can't determine if I like it because it's new and different or if I like it because I feel further away from all of my problems. I haven't done a lot of sightseeing because of the recovery. My body is still sore and weaker than what I'm used to. But Ava and Reid's home is beautiful and relaxing, so I don't mind spending most of my time here. It's been so long since Ava and I had quality time together, I've actually been enjoying myself despite the circumstances of my marriage.

I do miss Graham, though. But I miss the Graham that was married to the happier version of myself. We fit together better in the beginning than we do now. I know that's because my piece of the puzzle has changed shape more than his. But even though I feel more at fault over the downfall of our relationship, it still does nothing to change the trajectory.

This trip has been exactly what my soul was craving—a much-needed change of pace. I spoke openly to Ava about everything going on with Graham for the first time. The thing I love most about Ava is that she listens more than she gives advice. I don't really want advice. Advice won't change how I feel. Advice won't change the fact that I can't get pregnant. Advice won't change the fact that Graham said he was devastated he hasn't become a father yet. The only thing advice is good for is to pad the esteem of the person giving it. So instead of advice, she's just given me distraction. Not only from Graham, but from our mother. From work. From infertility. Connecticut. *My whole life*.

"What about this color?" Ava holds up a swatch of yellow paint.

"Too . . . canary," I say.

She looks down at the swatch and laughs. "That's actually what it's called. Canary."

Reid walks to the stove and lifts a lid from a pot, taking a whiff of the sauce he's been cooking. I'm sitting on the bar with Ava, looking through possible wall colors for their nursery. "If we'd just find out what we're having, it would make this process a lot easier," Reid says, putting the lid back on the pot. He turns off the burner.

"Nope," Ava says, sliding off the bar. "We decided we aren't finding out. We only have ten weeks left. Be patient." She gathers three plates from the cabinet and walks them to the table. I take silverware and napkins to the table while Reid brings the pasta.

Neither of them have made me feel as if I'm overstaying my welcome, but I'm starting to worry that I might be. Three weeks is a long time to host someone. "I'll probably fly home this week," I say as I spoon pasta onto my plate.

"Don't leave on our account," Reid says. "I like having you here. Brings me a little peace of mind while I'm traveling."

Reid spends two or three nights a week away from home and with Ava being pregnant, he worries about leaving her alone more than she wants him to. "I don't know why my presence brings you peace of mind. Ava is braver than I am."

"It's true," she says. "One time we went to a haunted house and Freddy Krueger jumped out at us. Quinn pushed me toward him and ran back to the entrance."

"Did not," I say. "I pushed you toward Jason Voorhees."

"Either way, I almost died," Ava says.

"Do you think you'll fly back in two months when Ava has the baby?"

"Of course I will."

"Bring Graham this time," Reid says. "I miss the guy."

Graham and Reid have always gotten along well. But I can tell by the look Ava gives me that she hasn't told Reid about Graham's and my issues. I appreciate that.

I twist my fork in the pasta, reflecting on how lonely I've felt since Ava and Reid moved away from Connecticut, but this is the first time I've realized how much their move probably affected Graham, too. He lost a friend in Reid with

231

their move. Probably his closest friend since Tanner. But he's never once talked about it because my sadness fills our house from wall to wall, leaving no room for his sadness.

For the rest of dinner, all I can think about are all the things Graham probably doesn't tell me because he doesn't want to put his sadness onto me. When we're finished eating, I offer to do the dishes. Reid and Ava are sitting at the table, poring over more color options for the nursery when their doorbell rings.

"That's weird," Ava says.

"Really weird," Reid agrees.

"Do you two never have visitors?"

Reid scoots back from the table. "Never. We don't really know anyone here well enough yet for them to come to our house." He walks to the door and Ava and I are both watching him when he opens it.

The last person I expect to see standing in that doorway is Graham.

My hands are submersed in suds and I remain frozen as Reid and Graham hug hello. Reid helps him with his suitcase and as soon as he walks through the door, Graham's eyes go in search of mine.

When he finally sees me, it's as if his whole body relaxes. Reid is smiling, looking back and forth between us expectantly, waiting on the surprised reunion. But I don't run to Graham and he doesn't run to me. We just stare at each other in silence for a beat. The beat is a little too long. Long enough for Reid to sense the tension in this reunion.

He clears his throat and takes Graham's suitcase. "I'll um . . . put this in the guest room for you."

"I'll help you," Ava says, quickly standing. When they've

both disappeared down the hallway, I finally break out of my shocked trance long enough to pull my hands out of the water and dry them on a dish towel. Graham slowly makes his way into the kitchen, eyeing me carefully the whole time.

My heart is pounding at the sight of him. I didn't realize how much I missed him, but I don't think that's why my heart is pounding. My pulse is out of control because his presence means confrontation. And confrontation means a decision. I'm not sure I was ready for that yet. It's the only reason I've still been hiding out at my sister's house halfway across the world from him.

"Hey," he says. It's such a simple word, but it feels more serious than anything he's ever said to me. I guess that's what almost three weeks of not speaking to your husband feels like.

"Hi." My reply comes out cautious. But not as cautious as the hug I eventually give him. It's quick and meaningless and I want a redo as soon as I pull away from him, but instead I reach toward the sink and remove the drain. "This is a surprise."

Graham shrugs, leaning against the counter next to me. He gives the kitchen and living room a quick once-over before bringing his eyes back to mine. "How are you feeling?"

I nod. "Good. I'm still a little sore, but I've been getting plenty of rest." Surprisingly, I do feel good. "I thought I might be sadder than I am, but I've realized I had already come to terms with the fact that my uterus was useless, so what does it matter that it's no longer in my body?"

Graham stares at me in silence, not really knowing how to respond to that. I don't expect him to, but his silence makes me want to scream. I don't know what he's doing here. I don't know what I'm supposed to say. I'm angry that he showed up without warning and angry that I'm happy to see him.

I wipe my hand across my forehead and press my back into the counter next to him.

"What are you doing here, Graham?"

He leans in to me, looking at me sincerely. "I can't take this another day, Quinn." His voice is low and pleading. "I need you to make a choice. Either leave me for good or come home with me." He reaches for me, pulling me to his chest. "Come home with me," he repeats in a whisper.

I close my eyes and inhale the scent of him. I want so bad to tell him I forgive him. That I don't even blame him for what he did.

Yes, Graham kissing someone who wasn't me is the single worst thing he's done during our relationship. But I'm not completely innocent in this situation.

Forgiving him isn't even what I've been worried about.

I'm worried about what happens *after* I forgive him. We had issues before he kissed another woman. We'll still have those same issues if I forgive him. That night in the car, before the miscarriage, Graham and I fought about the affair. But as soon as we open this floodgate tonight . . . that's when the real fight will happen. That's when we'll talk about the issues that caused all the other issues that lead to our current issues. This is the talk I've been trying to avoid for a couple of years now.

The talk that's about to happen because he just flew halfway around the world to confront me.

I pull away from Graham, but before I can speak, Reid and Ava interrupt us, but only momentarily. "We're going out for dessert," Ava says, pulling on her jacket.

Reid opens the front door. "See you two in an hour."

He closes the door and Graham and I are suddenly alone in their house, half a world away from our home. Half a world away from the comfort of our avoidance.

"You must be exhausted," I say. "Do you want to sleep first? Or eat?"

"I'm fine," he says quickly.

I nod, realizing just how imminent this conversation is. He doesn't even want food or water before we do this. And I can do nothing but stand here like I'm trying to decide if I want to talk it out or run from him so we can continue to avoid it. There's never been so much tension between us as we contemplate our next moves.

He eventually walks to the table. I follow him, taking a seat across from him. He folds his arms over the table and looks at me.

He's so handsome. As many times as I've turned away from him in the past, it's not because I'm not attracted to him. That's never been the issue. Even now after a full day of travel, he looks better than he did the day I met him. It always works that way with men, doesn't it? They somehow look manlier into their thirties and forties than they did in the pinnacle of their youth.

Graham has always taken good care of himself. Still, like clockwork, he wakes up every day and goes for a run. I love that he stays in shape, but not because of the physical attributes it's given him. My favorite part of him is that he never talks about it. Graham isn't the type to prove anything to anyone or turn his fitness routine into a pissing match with his friends. He runs for himself and no one else and I love that about him.

He reminds me a lot in this moment of how he looked the

morning after we got married. *Tired.* Neither of us got much sleep the night of our wedding and by morning, he looked like he'd aged five years overnight. His hair was in disarray; his eyes were slightly swollen from lack of sleep. But at least that morning he looked *happy* and tired.

Right now, he's nothing but sad and tired.

He presses his palms and fingertips together and brings his hands against his mouth. He looks nervous, but also ready to get this over with. "What are you thinking?"

I hate the feeling I'm experiencing right now. It's like all my worries and fears have been bound together in a tight ball and that ball is bouncing around inside of me, pounding against my heart, my lungs, my gut, my throat. It's making my hands shake, so I clasp them together on the table in front of me and try to still them.

"I'm thinking about everything," I say. "About where you went wrong. Where *I* went wrong." I release a quick rush of air. "I'm thinking about how right it used to feel and how I wish it was still like that."

"We can get back to that, Quinn. I know we can."

He's so hopeful when he says it. And naïve. "How?"

He doesn't have an answer for that question. Maybe that's because he doesn't feel broken. Everything broken in our marriage stems from me, and he can't fix me. I'm sure if he could somehow fix our sex life, that would be enough to appease him for a few more years.

"Do you think we should have sex more often?" *Graham almost looks offended by my question.* "That would make you happier, right?"

He traces an invisible line on the table, looking down at it until he begins to speak. "I won't lie and say I'm happy with our sex life. But I'm also not going to pretend that's the only thing I wish were different. What I want more than anything is for you to want to be my wife."

"No, what you want is for me to be the wife I used to be. I don't think you want me as I am now."

Graham stares at me a moment. "Maybe you're right. Is it so bad that I missed it when I was convinced that you were in love with me? When you would get excited to see me? When you wanted to make love to me because you wanted to and not because you just wanted to get pregnant?" He leans forward, pegging me with his stare. "We can't have kids, Quinn. And you know what? I'm okay with that. I didn't marry you for the potential kids we might have had together one day. I fell in love with you and I committed to you because I wanted to spend the rest of my life with you. That's all I cared about when I said my vows. But I'm starting to realize that maybe you didn't marry me for the same reasons."

"That's not fair," I say quietly. He can't insinuate that I wouldn't have married him if I'd known he couldn't have kids. And he can't say he still would have married me if he'd had that knowledge prior to our marriage. A person can't confidently proclaim what they would have done or how they would have felt in a situation they've never been in.

Graham stands up and walks to the kitchen. He grabs a bottle of water out of the fridge and I sit silently as he drinks it. I wait for him to come back to the table to continue the conversation, because I'm not ready to speak again. I need to know everything he's feeling before I decide what to say. What to do. When he takes his seat again, he reaches across the table and puts his hand over mine. He looks at me sincerely.

"I will never put a single ounce of blame on you for what

I did. I kissed someone who wasn't you and that was my fault. But that's only one issue out of a dozen issues we have in this marriage and they are *not* all my fault. I can't help you when I don't know what's going on in your head." He pulls my hand closer and cradles it between both of his. "I know that I have put you through hell these past few weeks. And I am so, so sorry for that. More than you know. But if you can forgive me for putting you through the worst thing imaginable, then I know we can get through the rest of it. I *know* we can."

He's looking at me with so much hope in his expression. I guess that's easy to do when he honestly believes him kissing someone else is the worst thing that's ever happened to me.

If I weren't so outraged, I would laugh. I pull my hand away from him.

I stand up.

I try to suck in a breath, but I had no idea anger settled in the lungs.

When I'm finally able to respond to him, I do it slowly and quietly because if there's anything I need for Graham to understand, it's everything I'm about to say. I lean forward and press my palms against the table, staring directly at him.

"The fact that you think what you did with that woman was the worst thing that could possibly happen to me proves that you have *no* idea what I've been through. You have no idea what it's like to experience infertility. Because *you* aren't experiencing infertility, Graham. *I* am. Don't get that confused. You can fuck another woman and make a baby. *I* can't fuck another man and make a baby." I push off the table and spin around. I planned to take a moment and gather my thoughts, but apparently, I don't need a moment, because I immediately turn and face him again. "And I *loved* making love to you,

Graham. It's not you I didn't want. It was the agony that came afterward. Your infidelity is a walk in the park compared to what I experienced month after month every time we had sex and it lead to nothing but an orgasm. An *orgasm*! Big *fucking* deal! How was I supposed to admit that to you? There was no way I could admit that I grew to despise every hug and every kiss and every touch because all of it would lead to the worst day of my life every twenty-eight fucking days!" I push past the chair and walk away from the table. "Fuck you and your affair. I don't give a *fuck* about your affair, Graham."

I walk into the kitchen as soon as I'm finished. I don't even want to look at him right now. It's the most honest I've ever been and I'm scared of what it did to him. I'm also scared that I don't care what it did to him.

I don't even know why I'm arguing issues that are irrelevant. I can't get pregnant now no matter how much we fight about the past.

I pour myself a glass of water and sip from it while I calm down.

A few silent moments go by before Graham moves from the table. He walks into the kitchen and leans against the counter in front of me, crossing his feet at the ankles. When I work up the courage to look at his eyes, I'm surprised to see a calmness in them. Even after the harsh words that just left my mouth, he somehow still looks at me like he doesn't absolutely hate me.

We stare at each other, both of us dry-eyed and full of years' worth of things we should never have kept bottled up. Despite his calmness and his lack of animosity, he looks deflated by everything I just yelled at him—like my words were safety pins, poking holes in him, letting all the air out.

I can tell by the exhaustion in his expression that he's given up again. I don't blame him. Why keep fighting for someone who is no longer fighting for *you*?

Graham closes his eyes and grips the bridge of his nose with two fingers. He cycles through a calming breath before folding both arms over his chest. He shakes his head, like he's finally come to a realization that he never wanted to come to. "No matter how hard I try . . . no matter how much I love you . . . I can't be the one thing you've always wanted me to be, Quinn. I will never be a father."

A tear immediately falls from my eye. And then another. But I remain stoic as he steps toward me.

"If this is what our marriage is . . . if this is all it will ever be . . . just me and you . . . will that be enough? Am I enough for you, Quinn?"

I'm confounded. Speechless.

I stare at him in utter disbelief, unable to answer him. Not because I can't. I know the answer to his question. I've *always* known the answer. But I stay silent because I'm not sure I *should* answer him.

The silence that lingers between his question and my answer creates the biggest misunderstanding our marriage has ever seen. Graham's jaw hardens. His eyes harden. Everything—even his heart—hardens. He looks away from me because my silence means something different to him than what it means to me.

He walks out of the kitchen, toward the guest room. Probably to get his suitcase and leave again. It takes everything in me not to run after him and beg him to stay. I want to fall to my knees and tell him that if on our wedding day, someone had forced me to choose between the possibility of having children or spending a life with Graham, I would have chosen life with him. Without a doubt, I would have chosen him.

I can't believe our marriage has come to this point. The point where my behavior has convinced Graham that he's not enough for me. He *is* enough for me.

The problem is . . . he could be so much more *without* me.

I blow out a shaky breath and turn around, pressing my palms into the counter. The agony of knowing what I'm doing to him makes my entire body tremble.

When he emerges from the hallway, he's not holding his suitcase. He's holding something else.

The box.

He brought our box with him?

He walks into the kitchen and sets it beside me on the counter. "If you don't tell me to stop, we're opening it."

I lean forward and press my arms into the counter, my face against my arms. I don't tell him to stop, though. All I can do is cry. It's the kind of cry I've experienced in my dreams. The cries that hurt so much, you can't even make a sound.

"Quinn," he pleads with a shaky voice. I squeeze my eyes shut even harder. "*Quinn*." He whispers my name like it's his final plea. When I still refuse to ask him to stop, I hear him move the box closer to me. I hear him insert the key into the lock. I hear him pull the lock off, but instead of it clinking against the counter, it crashes against the kitchen wall.

He is so angry right now.

"Look at me."

I shake my head. I don't want to look at him. I don't want to remember what it felt like when we closed that box together all those years ago.

He slides his hand through my hair and leans down, bringing his lips to my ear. "This box won't open itself, and I sure as hell am not going to be the one to do it."

His hand leaves my hair and his lips leave my ear. He slides the box over until it's touching my arm.

There have only been a handful of times I've cried this hard in my life. Three of those times were when the IVF rounds didn't take. One of those times was the night I found out Graham kissed another woman. One of those times was when I found out I had a hysterectomy. Out of all the times I've cried this hard, Graham has held me every single time. Even when the tears were because of him.

This time feels so much harder. I don't know if I'm strong enough to face this kind of devastation on my own.

As if he knows this, I feel his arms slide around me. His loving, caring, selfless arms pull me to him, and even though we're on opposite sides of this war, he refuses to pick up his weapons. My face is now pressed against his chest and I am so broken.

So broken.

I try to still the war inside me, but all I hear are the same sentences that have been repeating over and over in my head since the moment I first heard them.

"You would make such a great father, Graham."

"I know. It devastates me that it still hasn't happened yet."

I press a kiss to Graham's chest and whisper a silent promise against his heart. *Someday it'll happen for you, Graham. Someday you'll understand.*

I pull away from his chest.

I open the box.

We finally end the dance.

Chapter Twenty-seven

Then

It's been five hours since we said I do on a secluded beach in the presence of two strangers we met just minutes before our vows. And I don't have a single regret.

Not one.

I don't regret agreeing to spend the weekend with Graham at the beach house. I don't regret getting married five months before we planned to. I don't regret texting my mother when it was over, thanking her for her help, but letting her know it's no longer needed because we're already married. And I don't regret that instead of a fancy dinner at the Douglas Whimberly Plaza, Graham and I grilled hot dogs over the fire pit and ate cookies for dessert.

I don't think I'll ever regret any of this. Something so perfect could never become a regret.

Graham opens the sliding glass door and walks onto the balcony. It was too cold to sit up here when we were here three months ago, but it's perfect tonight. A cool breeze is coming off the water, blowing my hair just enough to keep it out of my face. Graham takes a seat next to me, tugging me toward him. I snuggle against him.

Graham leans forward slightly and places his phone next to mine on the railing in front of us. He's been inside breaking the news to his mother that there won't be a wedding.

"Is your mother upset?" I ask.

"She's pretending to be happy for us but I can tell she would have liked to have been there."

"Do you feel guilty?"

He laughs. "Not at all. She's been through two weddings with two of my sisters and she's in the middle of planning the last one's wedding. I'm sure a huge part of her is relieved. It's my sisters I'm worried about."

I didn't even think about them. I texted Ava on the way here yesterday, but I think she's the only one who knew. Ava and all three of Graham's sisters were going to be bridesmaids in the wedding. We had just told them last week. "What did they say?"

"I haven't told them yet," he says. "I'm sure I won't have to because ten bucks says my mother is on the phone with all three of them right now."

"I'm sure they'll be happy for you. Besides, they met my mother on Easter Sunday. They'll understand why we ended up doing it this way."

My phone pings. Graham reaches forward and grabs it for me. He naturally glances at it as he's handing it to me. When I see the text is from my mom, I try to pull the phone from him, but it's too late. He pulls it back to him and finishes reading the text.

"What is she talking about?"

I read the text and feel panic wash over me. "It's nothing." *Please just let it go, Graham.*

I can tell he isn't, because he urges me to sit up and look at him. "Why did she text you that?"

I look down at my phone again. At her terrible text.

You think he jumped the gun because he was excited to marry you? Wake up, Quinn. It was the perfect way for him to avoid signing.

"Sign what?" Graham asks.

I press my hand against his heart and try to find the words, but they're somehow even harder to find tonight than they have been the last three months I've avoided talking about it.

"She's talking about a prenuptial agreement."

"For what?" Graham says. I can already hear the offense in his voice.

"She's concerned my stepfather has changed the will to add me to it. Or maybe he already has, I don't know. It would make more sense, since she's been wanting me to talk to you about it so bad."

"Why haven't you?"

"I was going to. It's just . . . I don't feel like I need to, Graham. I know that's not why you're marrying me. And even if my mother's husband does leave me money in the future, I don't care that it would go to both of us."

Graham hooks his thumb under my chin. "First, you're right. I don't give a damn about your bank account. Second, your mother is mean to you and it makes me angry. But . . .

as mean as she speaks to you sometimes, she's right. You shouldn't have married me without a prenup. I don't know why you never talked to me about it. I would have signed one without question. I'm an accountant, Quinn. It's the smart thing to do when assets are involved."

I don't know what I was expecting, but I wasn't expecting him to agree with her. "Oh. Well . . . I should have brought it up to you, then. I didn't think the conversation would be this easy."

"I'm your husband. My goal is to make things easier on you, not more difficult." He kisses me, but the kiss is interrupted by my phone going off.

It's another text from my mother. Before I can finish reading it, Graham takes the phone from me. He types out a text to her.

Graham agreed to sign a postnup. Have your lawyer draft
it up. Problem solved.

He sets the phone on the railing and, similar to the first night we met, he pushes the phone over the edge of the balcony. Before my phone lands in the bushes below, Graham's phone receives an incoming text. And then another. And another.

"Your sisters."

Graham leans forward and gives his phone a shove, too. When we hear it land in the bushes below, we both laugh.

"Much better," he says. He stands up and reaches for my hand. "Come on. I have a present for you."

I grab his hand and jump up with excitement. "Really? A wedding present?"

He pulls me behind him, walking me into the bedroom. "Have a seat," he says, motioning to the bed. "I'll be right back."

246

I hop onto the center of the bed and wait giddily for him to get back with the gift. It's the first gift I've ever received from my husband, so I'm making a way bigger deal out of it than it probably needs to be. I don't know when he would have had time to buy me something. We didn't know we were getting married until half an hour before we came here.

Graham walks back into the room holding a wooden box. I don't know if the box is my present or if there's something inside of it, but the box itself is so beautiful, I wouldn't mind if the actual box was my present. It's a dark mahogany wood and it looks hand-carved, with intricate detailing on the top of the lid.

"Did you make this?"

"A few years ago," he says. "I used to build stuff in my father's garage. I like working with wood."

"I didn't know that about you."

Graham smiles at me. "Side effect of marrying someone you've known less than a year." He takes a seat across from me on the bed. He won't stop smiling, which excites me even more. He doesn't hand me the present, though. He opens the lid and pulls something out of the box. It's familiar. An envelope with his name on it.

"You know what this is?"

I take the envelope from him. The last time we were at this beach house, Graham asked me to write him a love letter. As soon as we got home, I spent an entire evening writing him this letter. I even sprayed it with my perfume and slipped a nude pic in the envelope before I sealed it.

After I gave it to him, I wondered why he never mentioned it again. But I got so caught up in the wedding, I forgot about it. I flip over the envelope and see that it's never even been opened. "Why haven't you opened it?"

He pulls another envelope out of the box, but he doesn't answer me. This one is a larger envelope with my name on it.

I grab it from him, more excited for a love letter than I've ever been in my life. "You wrote me one, too?"

"First love letter I've ever written," he says. "I think it's a decent first attempt."

I grin and use my finger to start to tear open the flap, but Graham snatches it out of my hands before I can get it open.

"You can't read it yet." He holds the letter against his chest like I might fight him for it.

"Why not?"

"Because," he says, putting both envelopes back in the box. "It's not time."

"You wrote me a letter I'm not allowed to read?"

Graham appears to be enjoying this. "You have to wait. We're locking this box and we're saving it to open on our twenty-fifth wedding anniversary." He grabs a lock that goes to the box and he slides it through the attached loop.

"Graham!" I say, laughing. "This is like the worst gift ever! You gave me twenty-five years of torment!"

He laughs.

As frustrating as the gift is, it's also one of the sweetest things he's ever done. I lift up onto my knees and lean forward, wrapping my arms around his neck. "I'm kind of mad I don't get to read your letter yet," I whisper. "But it's a really beautiful gift. You really are the sweetest man I know, Mr. Wells."

He kisses the tip of my nose. "I'm glad you like it, Mrs. Wells."

I kiss him and then sit back down on the bed. I run my

hand over the top of the box. "I'm sad you won't see my picture for another twenty-five years. It required a lot of flexibility."

Graham arches an eyebrow. "Flexibility, huh?"

I grin. I look down at the box, wondering what his letter to me says. I can't believe I have to wait twenty-five years. "There's no way around the wait?"

"The only time we're allowed to open this box before our twenty-fifth anniversary is if it's an emergency."

"What kind of emergency? Like . . . death?"

He shakes his head. "No. A relationship emergency. Like . . . divorce."

"Divorce?" I hate that word. "Seriously?"

"I don't see us needing to open this box for any other reason than to celebrate our longevity, Quinn. But, if one of us ever decides we want a divorce—if we've reached the point where we think that's the only answer—we have to promise not to go through with it until we open this box and read these letters. Maybe reminding each other of how we felt when we closed the box will help change our minds if we ever need to open it early."

"So this box isn't just a keepsake. It's also a marriage survival kit?"

Graham shrugs. "You could say that. But we have nothing to worry about. I'm confident we won't need to open this box for another twenty-five years."

"I'm *more* than confident," I say. "I would bet on it, but if I lose and we get divorced, I won't have enough money to pay out on our bet because you never signed a prenup."

Graham winks at me. "You shouldn't have married a gold digger."

"Do I still have time to change my mind?"

Graham clicks the lock shut. "Too late. I already locked it." He picks up the key to the lock and walks the box to the dresser. "I'll tape the key to the bottom of it tomorrow so we'll never lose it," he says.

He walks around the bed to get closer to me. He grabs me by the waist and lifts me off the bed, throwing me over his shoulder. He carries me over the patio threshold and back outside to the balcony where he slides me down his body as he sits on the swing.

I'm straddling his lap now, holding his face in my hands. "That was a really sweet gift," I whisper. "Thank you."

"You're welcome."

"I didn't get you a gift. I didn't know I was getting married today so I didn't have time to shop."

Graham slides my hair over my shoulder and presses his lips against the skin of my neck. "I can't think of a single gift in the world I would push you off my lap for."

"What if I bought you a huge flat screen TV? I bet you'd push me off your lap for a flat screen."

He laughs against my neck. "Nope." His hand slides up my stomach until he's cupping my breast.

"What about a new car?"

He slowly drags his lips up my throat. When his mouth reaches mine, he whispers *hell no* against my lips. He tries to kiss me, but I pull back just enough.

"What if I bought you one of those fancy calculators that cost like two grand? I bet you'd push me off your lap for math."

Graham slides his hands down my back. "Not even for math." His tongue pushes between my lips and he kisses me with such assurance, my head starts to spin. And for the next half hour, that's all we do. We make out like teenagers on the outdoor balcony.

Graham eventually stands up, holding me against him without breaking our kiss. He carries me inside and lays me down on the bed. He turns out the light and pushes the sliding glass door all the way open so we can hear the waves as they crash against the shore.

When he returns to the bed, he pulls off my clothes, one piece at a time, ripping my shirt in the process. He kisses his way down my neck and down my throat, all the way to my thighs, giving attention to every single part of me.

When he finally makes it back to my mouth, he tastes like me.

I roll him onto his back and return the favor until I taste like him.

When he spreads my legs and connects us, it feels different and new, because it's the first time we've made love as husband and wife.

He's still inside me when the first ray of sun begins to peek out from the ocean.

Chapter Twenty-eight

Now

Graham does nothing after I open the box. He just stands next to me in silence as I grab the envelope with his name on it. I slide it to him and look back down in the box.

I lift the envelope with my name on it, assuming it would be the only thing left inside the box since all we put in it before closing it were these two letters. But beneath our two letters, there are a few more letters, all addressed to me with dates on them. *He's been adding letters.* I look up at him, silently questioning him.

"There were things I needed to say that you never really wanted to hear." He grabs his envelope and walks out the back door, onto Ava and Reid's back porch. I take the box to the guest bedroom and close the door.

I sit alone on the bed, holding the only envelope from him that I expected to find in the box. The one from our wedding night. He wrote the date in the top right corner of the envelope. I open the other envelopes and I pile the pages on top of each other in the order they were written. I'm too scared to read any of it. Too scared not to.

When we locked this box all those years ago, there wasn't a doubt in my mind that we wouldn't need to open it before our twenty-fifth wedding anniversary. But that was back before reality set in. Back before we knew that our dream of having kids would never come true. Back before we knew that the more time that passed and the more devastating moments I experienced and the more Graham made love to me, that it would *all* start to hurt.

My hands are shaking as I press the pages to the blanket, smoothing them out. I lift the first page and begin to read it.

I don't think I'm prepared for this. I don't think anyone who gets married for the right reasons ever expects this moment to come. I stiffen like I'm bracing myself for impact as I begin to read.

Dear Quinn,

I thought I would have more time to prepare this letter. We aren't supposed to get married yet, so this gift is all very last minute. I'm not even that great of a writer, so I'm not sure I'm even going to be able to convey what I need to say to you in words. I'm better with numbers, but I don't want to bore you with a bunch of math equations, like Me plus you equals infinity.

If you think that's cheesy, you're lucky you met me later in life, rather than when I was in junior high. When I was in the seventh grade, I concocted a love

*poem that I was going to write down and give to my
first girlfriend. Thank God it was years later before
I actually got my first girlfriend. By then, I realized
what a bad idea it was to rhyme a love poem with the
Periodic Table of Elements.*

*However, I'm so comfortable in my masculinity
around you, I think this is the perfect time to finally
put that Periodic Table of Elements love poem to use.
Because yes, I still remember it. Some of it.*

> *Hey, girl, you're looking mighty fine*
> *Feels like I'm breathing Iodine*
>
> *Your smile gets all up in my head*
> *Feel so heavy, like I'm dragging Lead*
>
> *Your skin is smooth, it looks so sleek*
> *It's like someone dipped you in Zinc*
>
> *Kissing you would never get old*
> *Marry me girl, I'll flank you in Gold*

*That's right. You're the lucky girl who gets to marry
the author of that poem today.*

*Good thing it'll be twenty-five years before you read
it, because as soon as we're married this afternoon, I'm
never letting you out of this marriage. I'm like Hotel
California. You can love Graham any time you like,
but you can never leave.*

*The minister will be here in two hours. You're
upstairs getting ready for our wedding as I write this*

letter. On our way here yesterday, we stopped at a bridal store and you made me wait in the car while you ran inside to pick out a wedding dress. When you got back to the car with the dress hidden inside of a garment bag, you couldn't stop laughing. You said the ladies who were helping you thought you were insane, buying a dress just a day before your wedding. You said they gasped when you told them you're a procrastinator and that you still haven't picked out a groom.

I can't wait to see what you look like walking down that aisle of sand. It'll just be you in your dress on a beach with no decorations, no guests, no fanfare. And the entire ocean will be our backdrop. But let's just pray none of your dream from last night comes true.

This morning when you woke up, I asked what I had missed while you were sleeping. You told me you had a dream that we were getting married on the beach, but right before we said I do, a tsunami came and washed us away. But we didn't die. We both turned into aquatic killers. You were a shark and I was a whale, and we were still in love, even though you were a fish and I was a mammal. You said the rest of your dream was just us trying to love one another in an ocean full of creatures who didn't approve of our interspecies relationship.

That's probably my favorite dream of yours to date.

I'm sitting out here on the patio, writing the love letter I thought I had five more months to write. Part of me is a little nervous because, like I said, I've never been much of a writer. My imagination isn't as wild as yours, as evidenced by the things you dream about.

*But writing a letter to you about how much I love you
should come pretty easily, so hopefully this letter and
this gift to you will serve its purpose.*

*Honestly, Quinn, I don't even know where to start.
I guess the beginning is the most obvious choice, right?*

*I could begin by talking about the day we met in
the hallway. The day I realized that maybe my life was
thrown off course because fate had something even
better in store for me.*

*But instead, I'm going to talk about the day we
didn't meet. This will probably come as a surprise to you
because you don't remember it. Or maybe you do have a
memory of it but you just didn't realize it was me.*

*It was a few months before we met in the hallway.
Ethan's father held a Christmas party for their
employees and I was Sasha's date. You were Ethan's
date. And while I will admit I was still wrapped up in
all things Sasha at the time, something about you was
engraved in my memory after that night.*

*We hadn't been formally introduced, but you were
just a few feet away and I knew who you were because
Sasha had pointed you and Ethan out a few minutes
before. She said Ethan was in line to be her next boss
and you were in line to be his wife.*

*You were wearing a black dress with black heels.
Your hair was up in a tight bun and I overheard you
joking with someone about how you looked just like
the caterers. They all wore black and the girls had
their hair styled the same way as yours. I don't know
if the catering team was shorthanded that night, but I
remember seeing someone walk up to you and ask for a*

*refill on his champagne. Rather than correct him, you
just walked behind the bar and refilled his champagne.
You then took the bottle and started refilling other
people's glasses. When you finally made it over to me
and Sasha, Ethan walked up and asked what you were
doing. You told him you were refilling drinks like it
was no big deal, but he didn't like it. I could tell by the
look on his face that it embarrassed him. He told you
to put down the champagne bottle because there was
someone he wanted you to meet. He walked off and I'll
never forget what you did next.*

*You turned to me and you rolled your eyes with a
laugh, then held up the champagne bottle and offered
me a refill.*

*I smiled at you and held out my glass. You refilled
Sasha's glass and proceeded to offer refills to other
guests until the bottle was finally empty.*

*I don't remember much else about that night. It was
a mundane party and Sasha was in a bad mood most
of the time so we left early. And to be honest, I didn't
think about you much after that.*

*Not until the day I saw you again in the hallway.
When you stepped off the elevator and walked
toward Ethan's door, I should have been filled with
nothing but absolute dread and disgust over what was
happening inside Ethan's apartment. But for a brief
moment, I felt myself wanting to smile when I laid
eyes on you. Seeing you reminded me of the party and
how easy-going you were. I liked how you didn't care if
people thought you were a caterer or the girlfriend of
the Ethan Van Kemp. And it wasn't until the moment*

258

*you joined me in the hallway—when your presence
somehow brought me to the brink of smiling during
the worst moment of my life—that I knew everything
would be fine. I knew that my inevitable breakup with
Sasha wasn't going to break* me.

*I don't know why I never told you that. Maybe
because I liked the idea of us meeting in a hallway
under the same circumstances. Or maybe because I
was worried you wouldn't remember that night at the
party or refilling my glass of champagne. Because why
would you? That moment held no significance.*

Until it did.

*I would write more about our meeting in the
hallway, but you know all about it. Or maybe I could
write more about the first night we made love, or
the fact that once we finally reconnected, we never
wanted to spend a single second apart. Or I could
write about the day I proposed to you and you so
stupidly agreed to spend the rest of your life with
a man who couldn't possibly give you all that you
deserve in this world.*

*But I don't really want to talk about any of that.
Because you were there for all of it. Besides, I'm almost
positive your love letter to me details every minute
of us falling in love, so I'd hate to waste my letter on
repeating something you more than likely put into
words more eloquently than I ever could.*

*I guess that means I'm left with talking about the
future.*

*If all goes as planned, you'll be reading this letter
on our twenty-fifth wedding anniversary. You might*

cry a few tears and smear the ink a little. Then you'll lean over and kiss me and we'll make love.

But . . . if for some reason, you're opening this box because our marriage didn't work out how we thought it would, let me first tell you how sorry I am. Because I know we wouldn't read these letters early unless we did absolutely everything we could to prevent it.

I don't know if you'll remember this, but we had a conversation once. I think it was only the second night we spent together. You mentioned how all marriages have Category 5 moments, and how you didn't think your previous relationship would have made it through those moments.

I think about that sometimes. About what could make one couple survive a Category 5 moment, but a different couple might not. I've thought about it enough to come up with a possible reason.

Hurricanes aren't a constant threat to coastal towns. There are more days with great weather and perfect beach days than there are hurricanes.

Marriages are similar, in that there are a lot of great days with no arguments, when both people are filled with so much love for each other.

But then you have the threatening-weather days. There might only be a few a year, but they can do enough damage that it takes years to repair. Some of the coastal towns will be prepared for the bad-weather days. They'll save their best resources and most of their energy so that they'll be stocked up and prepared for the aftermath.

But some towns won't be as prepared. They'll put

all their resources into the good weather days in hopes that the severe weather will never come. It's the lazier choice and the choice with greater consequences.

I think that's the difference in the marriages that survive and the marriages that don't. Some people think the focus in a marriage should be put on all the perfect days. They love as much and as hard as they can when everything is going right. But if a person gives all of themselves in the good times, hoping the bad times never come, there may not be enough resources or energy left to withstand those Category 5 moments.

I know without a doubt that we're going to have so many good moments. No matter what life throws at us, we're going to make great memories together, Quinn. That's a given. But we're also going to have bad days and sad days and days that test our resolve.

Those are the days I want you to feel the absolute weight of my love for you.

I promise that I will love you more during the storms than I will love you during the perfect days.

I promise to love you more when you're hurting than when you're happy.

I promise to love you more when we're poor than when we're swimming in riches.

I promise to love you more when you're crying than when you're laughing.

I promise to love you more when you're sick than when you're healthy.

I promise to love you more when you hate me than when you love me.

And I promise . . . I swear . . . that I love you more as you read this letter than I did when I wrote it.

I can't wait to spend the rest of my life with you. I can't wait to shine light on all your perfects.

I love you.

So much.

Graham

———

Dear Quinn,

I'm going to start this letter off with a little apology. I'm sorry I opened the box again. I'm sorry I needed to write another letter. But I feel like you'll appreciate it more than you'll be upset about it.

Okay, now for math. I know you hate math, but I love it and I need to math for you. It's been exactly one year to the day since we decided to start a family. Which means there have been approximately 365 days between that day and this one.

Of those 365 days, we have had sex an average of about 200 days. Roughly four nights a week. Of those 200 days, you were ovulating only 25% of the time. About fifty days. But the chances of a woman getting pregnant while they ovulate is only twenty percent. That's ten days out of fifty. Therefore, by my calculations, out of the total 365 days that have passed between the day we first started trying and today, only ten of those days counted. Ten is nothing.

It's almost like we just started trying.

I'm only writing this down because I can tell you're starting to get worried. And I know by the time you read this letter on our 25th anniversary, we'll probably be just a few years away from being grandparents and none of this math will even be relevant. But just as I want you to remember the perfect days, I feel like I should probably talk a little about our not so perfect days, too.

You're asleep on the couch right now. Your feet are in my lap and every now and then, your whole body jerks, like you're jumping in your dream. I keep trying to write you this letter, but your feet keep knocking my arm, making the pen slide off the page. If my handwriting is shit, it's your fault.

You never fall asleep on the couch, but it's been a long night. Your mother had another one of her fancy charity events. This one was actually kind of fun. It was casino themed and they had all kinds of tables set up where you could gamble. Of course, it was for charity, so you can't really win, but it was better than a lot of the stuffier events where we have to sit at tables with people we don't like, and listen to speeches from people who do nothing but brag on themselves.

The night was fine, but I noticed pretty early on that you were getting drained from the questions. It's just harmless, casual conversation, but sometimes that casual conversation can be really tiresome. Hurtful, even. I listened, over and over, as people would ask you when we were going to have a baby. Sometimes people just naturally assume pregnancy follows a marriage. But people don't think about the questions they ask others and they don't realize how many times someone has already been forced to answer their question.

The first few times you were asked, you just smiled and said we just started trying.

But by the fifth or sixth time, your smile was becoming more forced. I started answering for you, but even then, I could see in your eyes that the questions were painful. I just wanted to get you out of there.

Tonight was the first time I could see your sadness. You're always so hopeful and positive about it, even when you're worried. But tonight you seemed like you were over it. Like maybe tonight is going to be the last event we'll ever attend until we actually do have a baby in our arms.

But I get it. I'm tired of the questions, too. It's breaking me seeing you so sad. I feel so . . . ineffectual. I hate it. I hate not being in control of this. I hate not being able to fix this for you.

But even though we've been trying for over a year, I have hope. It'll happen someday. It'll just have to happen a different way than we thought it would.

Hell, I don't even know why I'm writing about this, because you'll be a mother when you read this letter. Five times over, maybe.

I guess I'm just processing all of it. And we have so much to be grateful for. You love your job. I tolerate mine. After work we get to spend our evenings together. We make love all the time and we laugh a lot. Life is perfect, really. Of course there's the one element of *you getting pregnant that we hope makes life even better, but that will come with time. And honestly, the longer it takes, we might even appreciate it a little more. Gratitude is born in the struggle. And we have definitely struggled.*

Our niece Adeline is beautiful and happy and she likes you way more than she likes me. Caroline agreed to let her sleep over last year and it hasn't stopped. And you look so forward to when we get to keep her. I think it has made me fall a little more in love with you. I know how much it hurts that we haven't had a baby of our own yet, but seeing how genuinely happy you are for my sister and her family reaffirms just how selfless you are. You don't equate our struggles with their success and it makes me love that strength about you.

You're still asleep on the couch, but you're snoring now and I need to stop writing this letter so I can go find my phone and record it. You argue with me and tell me you don't snore, so I'm about to get the proof.

I love you, Quinn. And even though the tone of this letter was kind of depressing, the strength of my love for you is at its greatest. This isn't a Category 5 moment. Maybe more of a Category 2. But I promise you I am loving you harder this year than any year that came before it.

I love you.
So much.

Graham

Dear Quinn,

I would apologize for opening the box yet again, but I have a feeling it's going to happen again. Sometimes you don't want to talk about the things that make you sad, but I feel like someday you'll want to know my thoughts. Especially this year. It's been our toughest yet.

We've been married for more than five years now. I don't want to dwell on it too much because I feel like it's all our life has become, but in the last few years, nothing has been successful as far as our fertility issues are concerned. We went through three rounds of IVF before calling it quits. We would have gone a fourth round, despite the doctor advising against it, but we just couldn't afford it.

There are a lot of things I want to document during this marriage, Quinn, but the devastation following each of those failed attempts is not one of them. I'm sure you remember how hard it was for both of us, so there's no point in detailing it.

You know how I always ask you about your dreams? I think I'm going to stop doing that for a while.

Last Sunday when you woke up, I asked you what I missed while you were sleeping. You stared at me with this blank look in your eyes. You were silent for a little while and I thought you were trying to figure out how to relay your dream, but then your chin started to quiver. When you couldn't stop it, you pressed your face into your pillow and you started to cry.

God, Quinn. I felt so guilty. I just put my arm around you and held you until you stopped crying.

I didn't push you to talk about what your dream was because I didn't want you to have to think about it again. I don't know if you dreamt that you were pregnant or that we had a baby but whatever it was, it was something that devastated you when you woke up and realized it was merely a dream.

It's been six days since that happened, and I haven't asked you about your dreams since that morning. I just don't want to put you through that again. Hopefully one day we'll get back to that, but I promise I won't ask you again until you finally are a mother.

It's tough. I know when we got married we didn't expect to face these kinds of hurdles together. And honestly, Quinn, I try to carry you over them but you're so damn independent. You try not to cry in front of me. You force your smiles and your laughter and you pretend to still be hopeful, but it's changing you. It's making you sad and filling you with guilt.

I know you sometimes feel bad because you think you're taking away my opportunity to be a father. But I don't care about that. If you tell me today that you want to stop trying for a baby, I'll be relieved, because that would mean you might stop being sad. I'm only going through this fertility process with you because I know you want to be a mother more than anything. I would walk through fire to see you happy. I'd give up everything I have to see a genuine smile on your face. If we had to forego sex forever, I would. Hell, I'd even give up cheese to see you finally get your dream of becoming a mother. And you know how much I love cheese.

I would never tell you this because I know part

of you would take it the wrong way, but I think my favorite moments in the past year are all the moments when we aren't home. When we go out with our friends or visit our parents. I've noticed when we're home, you've become a little more withdrawn when I touch you or kiss you. It used to be that we couldn't keep our hands off each other, but something changed earlier this year. And I know it's only because sex has become so clinical between us, that it's starting to feel routine to you. Maybe even a little painful, because it never leads to what you hope it leads to. Sometimes when we're alone and I kiss you, you don't kiss me back like you used to. You don't turn away, but you barely reciprocate.

You tend to enjoy me more when you know a kiss has to stop at a kiss. In public, you reciprocate and you lean on me and I know it's a subtle difference, but there's a difference. I think our friends think we're the most affectionate couple they know because we always have our hands all over each other. They probably imagine our private life is even more affectionate.

But it's actually our private life that has stalled. And I am not complaining, Quinn. I didn't marry you just for the good years. I didn't marry you just for the amazing chemistry we have. And I'd be foolish to think our marriage could last an eternity without a few tough moments. So, while this year has been our toughest yet, I know one thing with complete certainty. I love you more this year than any year that came before it.

I know I sometimes get frustrated. Sometimes I miss when we made love on a whim, rather than on a schedule. But I ask that even in the times I get

*frustrated, please remember that I'm only human.
And as much as I promise to be your pillar of strength
for as long as you need one, I'm sure I will sometimes
fail you. My whole purpose in life is to make you
happy, and sometimes I feel like I'm unable to do that
anymore. Sometimes I give up on myself.*

But I just pray that you don't give up on me, too.

*I love you, Quinn. I hope this is the last depressing
letter I ever write to you. My hope is that next year, my
letter will be full of good news.*

*Until then, I will continue to love you more and
more with every struggle we face than I loved you
when all was perfect.*

Graham

*P.S. I don't know why I only vent about the stressful
stuff. So much good has happened in the last couple of years.
We bought a house with a big backyard and we spent the first
two days christening every room. You got a promotion a few
months ago. Now you only have to go into the office one or
two days a week. You do most of the writing for the advertising firm from home, which you love. And we've talked about
the possibility of me opening my own accounting firm. I'm
working on a business plan for that. And Caroline gave us
another niece.*

All good things, Quinn.

So many good things.

———

Dear Quinn,

    We've been trying.
      Trying to have a baby. Trying to adopt a baby. Trying to pretend we're okay. Trying to hide from each other when we cry.
      It's all our marriage has become. A whole lot of trying and not much succeeding.
      I truly believed we could make it through all the Category 5s we faced, but I think this year has been a Category 6. As much as I hope I'm wrong and as much as I don't want to admit it, I have a feeling we'll be opening this box soon. Which is why I'm on a flight to your sister's house right now as I write this letter. I'm still fighting for something I don't even know that you still want me to fight for.
      I know I failed you, Quinn. Maybe it was self-sabotage or maybe I'm not the man I thought I could be for you. Either way, I am so disappointed in myself. I love you so much more than my actions have shown and I could spend this whole letter telling you how sorry I am. I could write an entire novel that's nothing more than an apology and it still wouldn't detail my regret.
      I don't know why I did what I did. I can't even explain it, even when I tried to tell you about it that night in the car. It's hard to put into words because I'm still trying to process it. I didn't do it because of some intense attraction I couldn't fight. I didn't do it because

I missed having sex with you. And even though I tried to convince myself that I was doing it because she reminded me of you, I know how stupid that sounds. I never should have said that to you. You're right, in a way it sounded like I was blaming you, and that was never my intention. You had nothing to do with what I did.

 I don't want to talk about it, but I need to. You can skip this part of the letter if you don't want to read it, but I need to work through it and for some reason, writing about things in these letters always seems to help sort through my thoughts. I know I should be better at communicating them, but I know you don't always want to hear them.

 I think the way I've been feeling started during a moment I had at my sister's house. I guess you could say it was an epiphany, but that sounds like such a positive word for what I was feeling. It was the day we were supposed to meet our new nephew, but you said you got stuck in traffic.

 I know that was a lie, Quinn.

 I know, because when I was leaving Caroline's house, I saw the gift we bought her in the living room. Which means you had been there at some point during my visit, but for whatever reason, you didn't want me to know.

 I thought about it during my whole drive home after leaving her house. And the only thing I can think of that would make you not want to admit you were there is if you saw me standing in Caroline's living room, holding Caleb. And if you saw that, you might have heard what Caroline said to me, and what I said to her in return. About how I was devastated I still hadn't become a father yet. As much as I wish I could take that away, I can't. But I do need you to know why I said it.

I couldn't stop staring at him as I held him because he kind of looks like me. I had never held the girls when they were that young, so Caleb was the tiniest human I had ever held. And it made me wonder, had you been there, what would that have made you feel? Would you have been proud, seeing me with my nephew? Or would you have been disappointed that you would never see me holding a newborn of our own like that?

I think Caroline saw the look on my face while I was holding him and thought I was looking at him with such intensity because I wanted one of my own. But I was actually looking at him and wondering if you would continue to love me if I never became the one thing you wished I could be.

I know Caroline was merely complimenting me when she said I'd make a good father. But the reason I said I was devastated it still hadn't happened yet is because I was devastated for you. For our future. Because it wasn't until that moment that I realized I might never be enough for you.

Not long after that, I was walking out of my sister's house and saw the gift and knew you had been there. I didn't want to go home. I didn't want to confront you because I was afraid you might confirm my fears, so I drove around aimlessly. Later that night when I got home, you asked if I got to hold Caleb. I lied to you because I wanted to see your reaction to my lie. I was hoping maybe I was wrong and you weren't actually at my sister's house. Maybe the gift was from someone else and it was just similar to the one we had bought. But as soon as I saw your reaction, I knew you had been there.

And because you were hiding it, I knew you must have overheard our conversation. Which meant you also saw me holding Caleb. I was worried that the image of me holding a newborn like I was a father would be stuck in your head and it would make you sad every time you looked at me and I wasn't *a father. You would realize that the only way to get those images out of your head is if I were out of your life for good.*

I've worried about a lot of things since we got married, but I don't think I've ever worried about us *until after that moment. I've been fighting for so long to be the strength you need, but that was the first time it occurred to me that I may not be what brings you strength anymore. What if I'm part of what brings you pain?*

I wanted you to call me out for lying to you. I wanted you to scream at me for telling Caroline I was devastated I wasn't a father yet. I wanted something *from you, Quinn. Anything. But you keep all your thoughts and feelings bottled up so tight; it's becoming impossible to read you anymore.*

But you aren't the only one who is impossible to read anymore. I should have been honest with you about it that night. The moment I knew you had been to Caroline's, I should have said so. But somewhere between our wedding day and today, I lost my courage. I became too scared to hear what you truly feel inside that head

273

and heart of yours, so I've done my share of keeping it just below the surface. If I didn't press you to talk about it, I would never have to confront the possibility that our marriage was in trouble. Confrontation leads to action. Avoidance leads to inaction.

I have been an inactive husband for the past few years and I am so sorry for that.

The night I lied to you about holding Caleb, I remember you walking to your office. It was the first moment I ever had the thought that we might need a divorce.

I didn't have that thought because I wasn't happy with you. I had that thought because I felt I was no longer making you happy. I felt like my presence was bringing you down, causing you to sink further and further into yourself.

I walked to the living room and sat down on the couch, wondering if new possibilities would open up for you if I left you. Maybe if you weren't tied to me, somewhere down the line you could meet a man who already had children. You could fall in love with him and be a stepmother to his children and have some semblance of happiness brought back into your life.

I broke down, Quinn. Right there in our living room. It's the moment I realized that I was no longer bringing you happiness. I had become one of the many things adding to your pain.

I think that's been the case for a while now, but for some reason, I wasn't able to recognize it until recently. And even then, it took me a while before I finally allowed myself to believe it.

I felt like I had failed you. But even knowing that, I never would have made the decision to leave you. I knew that about myself. Even if I believed that you might be happier after I left, I was too selfish to give that to you. I knew what it would do to me if I left you and that terrified me. My fear of not having you in my life sometimes overpowered my desire to see you happy.

I think that's why I did what I did. Because I knew I would never be selfless enough to leave you. I allowed myself to do something completely out of character for me because if I felt I was no longer worthy of you, it would be easier to convince myself that you deserved better.

It's so fucked up.

I don't even know how it got to this point. I can't look back on our marriage and pinpoint the day that my love for you became something you resented and not something you cherished.

I used to believe if you loved someone enough, that love could withstand anything. As long as two people remained in love, then nothing could tear them apart. Not even tragedy.

But now I realize that tragedy can tear down even the strongest of things.

You could have one of the greatest singing voices of all time, but one injury to the throat could end your entire career. You could be the fastest runner in the world, but one back injury could change all of that. You could be the most intelligent professor at Harvard, but one stroke could send you into early retirement.

You could love your wife more than any man

has ever loved a wife, but one harrowing battle with infertility could turn a couple's love into resentment.

But even after years of tragedy wearing us down, I refuse to give in just yet. I don't know if flying to Europe with the box we closed on our wedding night will make it better or worse. I don't know that a grandiose gesture will convince you of how incomplete my life is without you. But I can't go another day without trying to prove to you how inconsequential children are when it comes to the fate of my future with you. I don't need children, Quinn. I only need you. I don't know how I can stress that enough.

But even still, no matter how content I am with this life, it doesn't mean you are content with yours.

When I get to Europe, a final decision will be made and I have a feeling I'm not going to want to agree to that decision. If I could avoid the conversation with you forever just to keep you from deciding to open the box, I would. But that's where we went wrong. We stopped talking about all the things that should never have been silenced.

I have no idea what's best for us anymore. I want to be with you, but I don't want to be with you when my presence causes you so much pain. So much has changed between us in the time since we closed the box on our wedding night to now. Our circumstances changed. Our dreams changed. Our expectations changed. But the most important thing between us never changed. We lost a lot of ourselves in this marriage, but we have never stopped loving each other. It's the one thing that stood strong against those Category 5 moments. I realize now that sometimes two people can lose their hope or their desire or their happiness, but losing all those things doesn't mean you've lost.

We haven't lost yet, Quinn.

And no matter what has happened since we closed this box or what will happen after we open it, I promise to love you through it all.

I promise to love you more when you're hurting than when you're happy.

I promise to love you more when we're poor than when we're swimming in riches.

I promise to love you more when you're crying than when you're laughing.

I promise to love you more when you're sick than when you're healthy.

I promise to love you more when you hate me than when you love me.

I promise to love you more as a childless woman than I would love you as a mother.

And I promise . . . I swear . . . that if you choose to end things between us, I will love you more as you're walking out the door than on the day you walked down the aisle.

I hope you choose the road that will make you the happiest. Even if it's not a choice I'll love, I will still always love you. Whether I'm a part of your life or not. You deserve happiness more than anyone I know.

I love you. Forever.

Graham

I don't know how long I cry after reading the final letter. Long enough that my head hurts and my stomach aches and I've gone through half a box of Kleenex. I cry for so long, I get lost in the grief.

Graham is holding me.

I don't know when he walked into the room, or when he knelt on the bed, or when he pulled me to his chest.

He has no idea what I've even decided. He has no idea if the words about to come out of my mouth are going to be nice ones or hateful ones. Yet here he is, holding me as I cry, simply because it hurts him to see me cry.

I press a kiss to his chest, right over his heart. And I don't know if it takes five minutes or half an hour, but when I finally stop crying long enough to speak, I lift my head from his chest and look at him.

"Graham," I whisper. "I love you more in this moment than any moment that has come before it."

As soon as the words are out of my mouth, the tears begin to fall from his eyes. "Quinn," he says, holding my face. "*Quinn* . . ."

It's all he can say. He's crying too hard to say anything else. He kisses me and I kiss him back with everything in me in an attempt to make up for all the kisses I denied him.

I close my eyes, repeating the words from his letter that reached me the deepest.

We haven't lost yet, Quinn.

He's right. We might have finally given up at the same time, but that doesn't mean we can't get back that hope. I want to fight for him. I want to fight for him as hard as he's been fighting for me.

"I'm so sorry, Quinn," he whispers against my cheek. "For everything."

I shake my head, not even wanting an apology. But I know he needs my forgiveness, so I give it to him. "I forgive you. With everything I am, Graham. I forgive you and I don't blame you and I am so sorry, too."

Graham wraps his arms around me and holds me. We remain in the same position for so long, my tears have dried, but I'm still clinging to him with everything in me. And I'll do everything I can to make sure I never let go of him again.

Chapter Twenty-nine

Then

I couldn't imagine a better way to end our first anniversary—wrapped up in a blanket outside, listening to the waves crash against the shore. It's the perfect moment for the perfect gift.

"I have something for you," I say to Graham.

He's the one who usually surprises me with gifts, so the fact that I have one for him grabs his attention. He looks at me with anticipation and pulls the blanket away from me, pushing me out of the chair. I run inside and then return with his package. It's wrapped in Christmas paper, even though it's not even close to Christmas.

"It's all I could find," I say. "I didn't have time to wrap it before I left, so I had to wrap it with what was in the closet here."

He begins to open it, but before he even has the wrapping paper off, I blurt out, "It's a blanket. I made it."

He laughs. "You are so terrible at surprises." He pulls away the tissue paper and reveals the blanket I made out of ripped pieces of our clothing. "Are these . . ." He lifts up one of his ripped work shirts and laughs.

We sometimes have issues with keeping our clothing intact when we're pulling them off each other. I think I've ripped a half dozen of Graham's shirts, at least. Graham has ripped several of mine. Sometimes I do it because I love the dramatics of the buttons popping off. I don't remember when it started, but it's become a game to us. A pricey game. Which is why I decided to put some of the discarded clothing to good use.

"This is the best gift anyone has ever given me." He throws the blanket over his shoulder and then picks me up. He carries me inside and lays me on the bed. He rips my nightgown off of me and then he rips his own shirt for show. The whole scene has me laughing until he climbs on top of me and smothers my laugh with his tongue.

Graham lifts my knee and starts to push himself inside me, but I press against his chest. "We need a condom," I whisper breathlessly.

I was on antibiotics last week for a cold I was trying to get over so I haven't been taking my pill. We've had to use condoms all week as a preventative measure.

Graham rolls off me and walks to his duffel bag. He grabs a condom, but he doesn't immediately come back to the bed. He just stares at it. Then he tosses it back onto the bag.

"What are you doing?"

With a heavy amount of assuredness, he says, "I don't want to use one tonight."

I don't respond. He doesn't want to use a condom? Am I reading his intent wrong?

Graham walks back to the bed and lowers himself on top of me again. He kisses me, then pulls back. "I think about it sometimes. About you getting pregnant."

"You do?" I was not expecting that. I hesitate a moment before saying, "Just because you think about it doesn't mean you're ready for it."

"But I am. When I think about it, I get excited." He rolls onto his side and puts his hand on my stomach. "I don't think you should get back on the pill."

I grip the top of his hand, shocked at how much I want to kiss him and laugh and take him inside me. But as sure as I am about having children, I don't want to make that choice unless he's just as certain as I am. "Are you positive?"

The thought of us becoming parents fills me with an overwhelming amount of love for him. So much, I feel a tear fall down my cheek.

Graham sees the tear and he smiles as he brushes it away with his thumb. "I love that you love me so much, it sometimes makes you cry. And I love that the idea of us having a baby makes you cry. I love how full of love you are, Quinn."

He kisses me. I don't think I tell him enough what a great kisser he is. He's the best I've ever had. I don't know what makes his kisses different from the men I've kissed in the past, but it's so much better. Sometimes I'm scared he'll get tired of kissing me someday because of how much I kiss him. I just can't be near him without tasting him. "You're a really good kisser," I whisper.

Graham laughs. "Only because it's you I'm kissing."

We kiss even more than we usually do when we make

love. And I know we've made love a hundred times before tonight. Maybe even a thousand times. But this time feels different. It's the first time we don't have some kind of barrier preventing us from creating a new life together. It's like we're making love with a purpose.

Graham finishes inside of me and it's the most incredible feeling, knowing that our love for each other might be creating something even bigger than our love for each other. I don't know how that can even be possible. How can I possibly love anyone as much or even *more* than I love Graham?

It's been such a perfect day.

I've experienced a lot of perfect moments, but entire perfect days are hard to come by. You need the perfect weather, the perfect company, the perfect food, the perfect itinerary, the perfect mood.

I wonder if things will always be this perfect. Now that we've decided to start a family, part of me wonders if there's a level of perfection that we haven't even reached yet. What will things be like next year when we're possibly parents? Or five years from now? Ten? Sometimes I wish I had a crystal ball that could actually see into the future. I'd want to know everything.

I'm tracing my fingers in an invisible pattern over his chest when I look up at him. "Where do you think we'll be ten years from now?"

Graham smiles. He loves talking about the future. "Hopefully we'll have our own house in ten years," he says. "Not too big, not too small. But the yard will be huge and we'll play outside with the kids all the time. We'll have two—a boy and a girl. And you'll be pregnant with the third."

I smile at that thought. He reacts to the smile on my face and he continues to talk.

"You'll still write, but you'll work from home and you'll only work when you feel like it. I'll own my own accounting firm. You'll drive a minivan because we're totally gonna be those parents who take the kids to soccer games and gymnastics." Graham grins at me. "And we'll make love all the time. Probably not as often as we do now, but more than all of our friends."

I press my hand over his heart. "That sounds like the perfect life, Graham."

Because it does. But *any* life with Graham sounds perfect.

"Or . . ." he adds. "Maybe nothing will change. Maybe we'll still live in an apartment. Maybe we'll be struggling financially because we keep moving from job to job. We might not even be able to have kids, so we won't have a big yard or even a minivan. We'll be driving our same, shitty cars ten years from now. Maybe absolutely nothing will change and ten years from now, our lives will be the same as they are now. And all we'll have is each other."

Just like after he described the first scenario, a serene smile spreads across my face. "That sounds like the perfect life, too." And it does. As long as I have Graham, I don't know that this life could be anything less than what it is now. And right now, it's wonderful.

I relax against his chest and fall asleep with the most peaceful feeling in my heart.

Chapter Thirty

Now

"Quinn."

His voice is raspy against my ear. It's the first morning in a long time that I've been able to wake up with a smile on my face. I open my eyes and Graham looks like a completely different person than the broken man who walked through Ava and Reid's front door last night. He presses his lips to my cheek and then pulls back, pushing my hair off my face. "What did I miss while you were sleeping?"

I've missed those words so much. It's one of the things I've missed the most about us. It means even more to me now, knowing he only stopped asking me because he didn't want me to hurt. I reach my hand out to his face and brush my thumb across his mouth. "I dreamt about us."

He kisses the pad of my thumb. "Was it a good dream or a bad dream?"

COLLEEN HOOVER

"It was good," I say. "It wasn't a typical weird dream, though. It was more of a memory."

Graham slips a hand between his head and the pillow. "I want to know every detail."

I mirror his position, smiling when I begin telling him about the dream. "It was our first anniversary. The night we decided to start a family. I asked you where you thought we'd be ten years from now. Do you remember?"

Graham shakes his head. "Vaguely. Where did I think we'd be?"

"You said we'd have kids and I'd drive a minivan and we'd live in a house with a big yard where we played with our children." Graham's smile falters. I brush his frown away with my thumb, wanting his smile back. "It's strange, because I forgot all about that conversation until I dreamt about it last night. But it didn't make me sad, Graham. Because then you said we might not have any of that. You said there was a chance that we'd be moving from job to job and that we wouldn't be able to have kids. And that maybe nothing between us would change after ten years, and all we'd have was each other."

"I remember that," he whispers.

"Do you remember what I said to you?"

He shakes his head.

"I said, 'That sounds like the perfect life, too.'"

Graham blows out a breath, like he's been waiting a lifetime for the words I'm giving him.

"I'm sorry I lost sight of that," I whisper. "Of us. You've always been enough for me. Always."

He looks at me like he's missed my dreams as much as he's missed me. "I love you, Quinn."

"I love you, too."

He presses his lips to my forehead, then my nose. I kiss him on the chin and we lie snuggled together.

At least until the moment is ruined by the growl from my stomach.

"Does your sister have anything to eat around here?" Graham pulls me out of the bed and we quietly make our way to the kitchen. It's not even eight in the morning yet and Ava and Reid are still asleep. Graham and I scour the kitchen for all the food we need to make pancakes and eggs. He turns on the stove and I'm mixing the batter when I notice the wooden box he made me still sitting at the end of the counter.

I put down the mixer and walk over to the box. I run my hand over it, wondering if things would be different today had he not made this gift for us to close on our wedding night. I still remember writing him the love letter. I also remember slipping the nude pic inside the envelope. I wonder how different I look now than when I snapped that picture.

I open the box to pull out his letter, but when I pick it up, I notice a few scraps of paper at the bottom of the box. One of them is the yellow Post-it note I left stuck to my wall for six months. The other two are our fortunes.

I pick them up and read them. "I can't believe you kept these all this time. It's so cute."

Graham walks over to me. "Cute?" He pulls one of the fortunes out of my hands. "This isn't cute. It's proof that fate exists."

I shake my head and point to his fortune. "Your fortune says you would succeed in a business endeavor that day, but you didn't even go to work. How is that proof that we're soul mates?"

His lips curl up into a grin. "If I had been at work I never would have met you, Quinn. I'd say that's the biggest work-related success I've ever had."

I tilt my head, wondering why I never thought of his fortune from that point-of-view.

"Also . . . there's this." Graham flips his fortune over and holds it up, pointing at the number eight on the back.

I look down and also read the number on the back of mine. An eight.

Two number eights. *The date we reconnected all those years ago.*

"You lied to me," I say, looking back up at him. "You said you were kidding about these having eights on the back."

Graham takes the fortune out of my hand and carefully places both of them back in the box. "I didn't want you to fall in love with me because of fate," he says, closing the box. "I wanted you to fall in love with me simply because you couldn't help yourself."

I smile as I stare up at him with appreciation. I love that he's sentimental. I love that he believes in fate more than he believes in coincidences. I love that he believes *I'm* his fate.

I stand on the tips of my toes and kiss him. He grabs the back of my head with both hands and returns my kiss with just as much appreciation.

After several moments of kissing and a couple of failed efforts at stopping, he mutters something about the pancakes burning and forces himself away from me as he steps to the stove. I bring my fingers to my lips and smile when I realize he just kissed me and I had absolutely no desire to pull away from him. In fact, I wanted the kiss to last even longer than it did. It's a feeling I wasn't sure I would be capable of again.

I debate pulling him back to me because I really want to kiss him again. But I also really want pancakes, so I let him resume cooking. I turn toward the wooden box and reach for the letter I wrote to him. Now that I feel like we're on a path to recovery, it makes me want to read the words I wrote to him when we were first starting this journey together. I flip over the envelope to pull out the letter, but the envelope is still sealed. "Graham?" I turn back around. "You didn't read yours?"

Graham glances over his shoulder and smiles at me. "I didn't need to, Quinn. I'll read it on our twenty-fifth anniversary." He faces the stove and resumes cooking like he didn't just say something that feels more healing than anything he's ever said or done.

I look back down at the letter with a smile on my face. Even with the temptation of nude pictures, he was secure enough in his love for me that he didn't need any reassurance from reading this letter.

I suddenly want to write him another letter to go along with this one. In fact, I might even start doing what he's been doing all these years and add more letters to the box. I want to write him so many letters that when we finally reopen this box for the right reasons, he'll have enough letters to read for a week.

"Where do you think we'll be on our twenty-fifth anniversary?" I ask.

"Together," he says, matter-of-fact.

"Do you think we'll ever leave Connecticut?"

He faces me. "Do you want to?"

I shrug. "Maybe."

"I think about it sometimes," he admits. "I've already got

a few personal clients lined up. If I secured a few more, it would allow for that, but it probably wouldn't pay as much. But we could travel for a year or two. Maybe longer if we enjoy it enough."

This conversation reminds me of the night I spoke to my mother on the steps outside of her home. I don't think I give her enough credit, but she's right. I can spend my time focusing on the perfect version of the life I'll never have or I can spend my time enjoying the life I *do* have. And the life I have would provide me with so much opportunity if I would get out of my own head long enough to chase those opportunities.

"I used to want to be so many things before I became obsessed with the idea of being a mother."

Graham smiles sweetly at me. "I remember. You wanted to write a book."

It's been so long since I've talked about it, I'm surprised he remembers. "I did. I still do."

He's smiling at me when he turns to flip the rest of the pancakes. "What else do you want to do besides write a book?"

I move to stand next to him near the stove. He wraps one arm around me while he cooks with his other hand. I rest my head against his shoulder. "I want to see the world," I say quietly. "And I would really like to learn a new language."

"Maybe we should move here to Italy and piggyback off Ava's language tutor."

I laugh at his comment, but Graham sets down the spatula and faces me with an excited gleam in his eyes. He leans against the counter. "Let's do it. Let's move here. We have nothing tying us down."

I tilt my head and eye him. "Are you serious?"

"It would be fun to try something new. And it doesn't even have to be Italy. We can move anywhere you want."

My heart begins to beat faster with the anticipation of doing something that insane and spontaneous.

"I do really like it here," I say. "A lot. And I miss Ava."

Graham nods. "Yeah, I kind of miss Reid. But don't repeat that."

I push myself up onto the counter next to the stove. "Last week I went for a walk and saw a cottage a few streets over for rent. We could try it out temporarily."

Graham looks at me like he's in love with the idea. Or maybe he's looking at me like he's in love with *me*. "Let's go look at it today."

"Okay," I say, full of giddiness. I catch myself biting my cheek in an attempt to hide my smile, but I immediately stop trying to hide it. If there's one thing Graham deserves, it's for my happiness to be transparent. And this moment is the first moment in a long time I've felt this much happiness. I want him to feel it, too.

It's like this is the first time I've truly felt like I might be okay. That *we'll* be okay. It's the first time I don't look at him and feel guilty for everything I can't give him because I know how grateful he is for everything I *can* give him. "Thank you," I whisper. "For everything you said in your letters."

He stands between my legs, placing his hands on my hips. I wrap my arms around his neck, and for the first time in a long time, I kiss my husband and feel full of gratitude. I know my life as a whole hasn't been perfect, but I'm finally starting to appreciate all the perfect things within it. There are so many of them. My flexible job, my husband, my in-laws, my sister, my nieces, my nephew.

That thought makes me pause. I pull back and look up at Graham. "What did my fortune say? Do you have it memorized?"

"If you only shine light on your flaws, all your perfects will dim."

I think about it for a moment. About how fitting that fortune is for my life. I've spent way too much time putting all of my focus on my infertility. So much so, my husband and all the other things that are perfect in my life were being forced to take a backseat.

Since the moment we cracked open those fortune cookies, I've never really taken them seriously. But maybe Graham is right. Maybe those fortunes are more than a coincidence. And maybe Graham was right about the existence of fate.

If so, I think my fate is standing right in front of me.

Graham touches my mouth with the tips of his fingers and slowly traces the smile on my lips. "You have no idea what this smile means to me, Quinn. I've missed it so much."

Epilogue

"Wait, look at this one!" I pull on Graham's hand, making him stop in his tracks on the sidewalk again. But I can't help it. Almost every store on this street has the cutest children's clothes I've ever seen and Max would be adorable in the outfit displayed in the window.

Graham tries to keep moving forward, but I pull on his hand until he relents and follows me into the store. "We were almost to the car," he says. "So close."

I shove the bags of kids clothes I've already bought into Graham's hands and then find the rack with the toddler sizes. "Should I get the green pants or the yellow ones?"

I hold them up to Graham and he says, "Definitely yellow."

The green pants are cuter, but I go with Graham's choice simply because he volunteered an answer. He hates shopping for clothes, and this is only the ninth store I've forced him to follow me into. "I swear this is the last one. Then we can go home." I give Graham a quick peck on the lips before walking to the register.

Graham follows me and pulls his wallet out of his pocket. "You know I don't care, Quinn. Shop all day if you want. He only turns two once."

I hand the clothes to the cashier. In a thick Italian accent, she says, "This outfit is my absolute favorite." She looks up at us and says, "How old is your little boy?"

"He's our nephew. Tomorrow is his second birthday."

"Ah, perfect," she says. "Would you like this in a gift box?"

"No, a bag is fine."

She tells Graham the total, and as he's paying, the cashier looks at me again. "What about the two of you? Any children of your own?"

I smile at her and open my mouth, but Graham beats me to the punch. "We have six children," he lies. "But they're all grown now and out of the house."

I try not to laugh, but once we decided to start lying to strangers about our infertility, it's become a competition with who can be the most ridiculous. Graham usually wins. Last week he told a lady we had quadruplets. Now he's trying to convince someone that a couple our age could have six children already grown and out of our home.

"All girls," I add. "We kept trying for a boy, but it just wasn't in the cards."

The cashier's mouth falls open. "You have *six* daughters?"

Graham takes the bag and the receipt from her. "Yes. And two granddaughters."

He always takes it a little too far. I grab Graham's hand

and mutter a thank-you to the cashier, pulling him outside as fast as I pulled him inside. When we're on the sidewalk again, I slap him on the arm. "You are so ridiculous," I say, laughing.

He threads our fingers together as we begin to walk. "We should make up names for our imaginary daughters," he says. "In case someone probes for details."

We're passing a kitchen store when he says this, and my eyes automatically fall on a spice rack in the window. "Coriander," I tell him. "She's the oldest."

Graham pauses and looks at the spice rack with me. "Parsley is the youngest. And Paprika and Cinnamon are the oldest set of twins."

I laugh. "We have two sets of twins?"

"Juniper and Saffron."

As we're walking toward our car, I say, "Okay, let me make sure I have this right. In order of birth: Coriander, Paprika, Cinnamon, Juniper, Saffron and Parsley."

Graham smiles. "Almost. Saffron was born two minutes before Juniper."

I roll my eyes, and he squeezes my hand as we cross the street together.

It still amazes me how much has changed since we opened the box two years ago. We came so close to losing everything we had built together because of something that was out of our control. Something that should have brought us closer together but instead pulled us further apart.

Avoidance sounds like such a harmless word, but that one word can cause some severe damage to a relationship. We avoided so much in our marriage, simply out of fear. We avoided communicating. We avoided talking about the challenges we faced. We avoided all the things that made us the saddest. And after time, I began to avoid the other half of my life altogether. I avoided him physically, which led to emotional avoidance, which led to a lot of feelings that were left unsaid.

Opening that box made me realize that our marriage wasn't in need of a minor repair. It needed to be rebuilt from the ground up, with an entirely different foundation. I started out our life together with certain expectations, and when those expectations weren't met, I had no idea how to move forward.

But Graham has been the constant fighting force behind my healing. I finally stopped being as sad about our fate. I stopped focusing on what we would never have together and started focusing on all the things we did have and could have. It didn't eliminate my pain altogether, but I'm happier than I've been in a very long time.

Of course opening the box didn't miraculously solve everything. It didn't immediately take away my desire for children, although it did increase my lust for a life outside of being a mother. It didn't completely dissolve my aversion to sex, although it did open the door to slowly learning how to separate the sex from the hope from the devastation. And I occasionally still cry in the shower, but I never cry alone. I cry while Graham holds me, because he made me promise I would stop trying to hide the brunt of my heartache.

I no longer hide it. I embrace it. I'm learning how to wear my struggle as a badge and not be ashamed of it. I'm learning to not be so personally offended by other people's ignorance in relation to infertility. And part of what I've learned is that I have to have a sense of humor about it all. I never thought I would be at a point where we could turn all the painful questions into a game. Now when we're out in public, I actually look forward to when someone asks if we have kids. Because I know Graham is going to say something that will make me laugh.

I've also learned that it's okay to have a little hope.

For so long, I was so worn down and emotionally exhausted that I thought if I figured out a way to lose all hope, I would also lose all expectation and all disappointment. But it didn't work that way. The hope has been the only positive thing about being infertile.

I will never lose hope that we might actually have a child of our own. I still apply to adoption agencies and talk to lawyers. I don't know that we'll ever stop trying to make it happen. But I've learned that even though I'm still hoping to become a mother, it doesn't mean I can't live a fulfilling life while I continue to try.

For once, I'm happy. And I know that I'll be happy twenty years from now, even if it's still just me and Graham.

"Shit," Graham mutters as we reach our car. He points at the tire. "We have a flat."

I glance at the car, and the tire is definitely flat. So flat, no amount of air could salvage it. "Do we have a spare?"

We're in Graham's car, so he opens the trunk and lifts the floor portion, revealing a spare and a jack. "Thank God," he says.

I put our bags in the backseat of the car and watch as he pulls out the tire and the jack. Luckily the flat is on the passenger side, which is flush with the sidewalk rather than the road. Graham rolls the tire near the flat one and then moves the jack. He looks up at me with an embarrassed look on his

face. "Quinn . . ." He kicks at a pebble on the sidewalk, breaking eye contact with me.

I laugh, because I can tell by his embarrassment that he
has no idea what to do next. "Graham Wells, have you never
changed a flat tire?"

He shrugs. "I'm sure I could google it. But you mentioned to me once that Ethan never let you change a flat." He
motions toward the tire. "I'm giving you first dibs."

I grin. I'm loving this way too much. "Put the parking
brake on."

Graham sets the parking brake while I position the jack
under the car and begin to raise it.

"This is kind of hot," Graham says, leaning against a light
pole as he watches me. I grab the wrench and begin removing the lug nuts from the tires.

We're on a busy sidewalk, so two people stop to ask if they
can help, because they don't realize Graham is with me. Both
times, Graham says, "Thank you, but my wife has got this."

I laugh when I realize what he's doing. The entire time
I'm changing the tire, Graham brags about it to everyone
who walks by. "Look! My wife knows how to change a tire."

When I finally finish, he puts the jack and the flat tire
back in the trunk. My hands are covered in grease.

"I'm going to run inside this store and wash my hands."

Graham nods and opens the driver's side door while I
rush into the nearest store. When I walk inside, I'm taken off
guard as I look around. I was expecting this to be another
clothing store, but it isn't. There are pet crates displayed in
the window and a bird—a parakeet—perched on top of a
cage near the front door.

"Ciao!" the bird says loudly.

300

I raise an eyebrow. "Hello."

"Ciao!" it screeches again. "Ciao! Ciao!"

"That's the only word he knows," a lady says as she approaches me. "You here to adopt or are you here for supplies?"

I hold up my greasy hands. "Neither. I'm hoping you have a sink."

The woman points me in the direction of the restroom. I make my way through the store, pausing to look at all the various animals in their cages. There are rabbits and turtles and kittens and guinea pigs. But when I make it to the back of the store, near the restroom, I pause in my tracks and suck in a breath.

I stare at him for a moment because he's staring right back at me. Two big brown eyes, looking at me like I'm the fiftieth person to walk past him today. But he still somehow has hope in those eyes—like maybe I'll be the first one to actually consider adopting him. I step closer to his cage, which is flanked by several empty cages. He's the only dog in the whole store.

"Hey, buddy," I whisper. I read the note at the bottom left corner of his cage. Beneath the Italian description is a description written in English.

German Shepherd
Male
Seven weeks old
Available for adoption

I stare at the note for a moment and then force myself to walk to the bathroom. I scrub my hands as fast as I can, because I can't stand for that puppy to think I'm just another one of the dozens of people who walked past him today and didn't want to take him home.

I've never been much of a dog person, because I've never had a dog before. I honestly thought I'd never own a dog, but I have a feeling I'm not walking out of this store without this puppy. Before I leave the bathroom, I pull my phone from my pocket and shoot Graham a text.

Come inside to the back of the store. Hurry.

I walk out of the bathroom, and when the puppy sees me again, his ears perk up. He lifts a paw and presses it against the cage as I come closer. He's sitting on his hind legs, but I can see his tail twitching, like he wants my attention but he's scared it'll just be fleeting and he'll be spending another night in this cage.

I slip my fingers between the bars of his cage, and he sniffs them, then licks me. I feel a tightening in my chest every time we make eye contact, because seeing him so full of hope but so scared of disappointment makes me sad. This puppy reminds me of me. Of how I used to feel.

I hear someone walking up behind me, so I spin around to see Graham staring at the puppy. He walks up to the cage and tilts his head. The puppy looks from me to Graham and then finally stands up, unable to stop his tail from wagging.

I don't even have to say anything. Graham just nods his head and says, "Hey, little guy. You want to come home with us?"

———

"It's been three days," Ava says. "That poor puppy needs a name."

She's clearing off the table, preparing to go home. Reid left with Max about an hour ago to put him to bed. We all try to eat dinner together a few times a week, but we usually go to their house, since Max goes to bed early. But now we're the ones with a new baby, and even though that new baby is a puppy, he naps and pees and poops as much as a human newborn.

"It's so hard coming up with a good name, though," I groan. "I want to give him a name that'll mean something, but we've tossed out every idea we've had."

"You're being too picky."

"It took you eight months to choose a name for your child. Three days isn't that long for a dog."

Ava shrugs. "Good point." She wipes down the table as I cover the leftover food and put it in the fridge.

"I thought about giving him a math-related name, since Graham loves math so much. Like maybe naming him after a number."

Ava laughs. "It's so weird that you say that. I just got my files at work today for the high school foreign exchange students I'll be tutoring when they arrive in a couple of weeks. One of them is a girl from Texas. Her birth name is Seven Marie Jacobs, but she goes by Six. I thought of Graham when I saw that."

"Why does she go by Six if her birth name is Seven?"

Ava shakes her head. "I don't know, but it's quirky. I haven't even met her yet but I already like the girl." Ava pauses and looks up at me. "What about naming it after one of the characters in your book?"

I shake my head. "Already thought of that, but those characters feel like actual people now that the book is finished. I know it's weird, but I want the dog to have his own name. I'd feel like he was being forced to share."

"Makes sense," Ava says, resting her hands on her hips. "Any news from your agent?"

"She hasn't submitted to publishers yet. It's being reviewed by an in-house editor and then they're going to try and sell it."

Ava smiles. "I hope it happens, Quinn. I'm going to freak the fuck out if I walk into a bookstore and see your book on the shelf."

"You and me both."

Graham walks inside with the puppy and Ava meets him at the door. "It's late, I gotta go," she says, talking to the puppy while scratching him on his head. "I hope when I see you tomorrow you have a name."

Graham and I tell her goodbye and he locks the door behind her. He cradles the puppy in his arms and walks over to me. "Guess who used the bathroom twice so his mommy and daddy can get a few hours of sleep?"

I pull the puppy out of Graham's arms and squeeze him. He licks my cheek and then rests his head in the crease of my elbow. "He's tired."

"I'm tired, too," Graham says, yawning.

I put the puppy into his crate and cover it with a blanket. Neither of us knows anything about dogs, so we've been reading as much as we possibly can about how to crate-train them, what they eat, how they should be disciplined, how much they should sleep.

Sleep has definitely been the most difficult thing to tackle so far. Being the owner of a new puppy comes with new hurdles, but the biggest of those hurdles is exhaustion. I wouldn't trade it for anything, though. Every time that little puppy looks at me, I melt.

Graham and I make our way to the bedroom. We leave our door open so we can hear the puppy if he starts to cry. When we crawl into bed, I roll toward Graham and rest my head on his chest.

"I can't imagine what having a newborn must be like if a puppy is this tiring," I say.

"You're forgetting about all our sleepless nights with Coriander, Paprika, Cinnamon, Saffron, Juniper, and Parsley."

I laugh. "I love you."

"I love you, too."

I curl even more into Graham, and he tightens his hold around me. I do my best to fall asleep, but my mind keeps running through potential puppy names until I'm positive I've exhausted every name in existence.

"Quinn." Graham's voice is against my ear, warm and quiet. "Quinn, wake up." I open my eyes and pull away from his chest. He points behind me and says, "Look."

I half-turn and glance over at the alarm clock, right as it changes to midnight. Graham leans in to my ear and whispers, "It's the eighth of August. Ten years later and we're happily married. *I told you so.*"

I sigh. "Why am I not surprised that you remembered that?"

I don't know how I didn't expect this moment. The number eight holds so much meaning to us that the date should have been obvious to me, but I've been so preoccupied with the puppy the last few days, I didn't even realize today was the eighth of August.

"August," I whisper. "That's what we'll name the puppy."

Acknowledgments

With every book I write, there are people in the beginning who get the scraps I end up throwing away. I ruin plot twists for them. I change story lines. I make reading my words a little bit of a confusing chore. Especially with the many versions of *All Your Perfects*. A huge thank-you to Kay Miles, Vilma Gonzalez, Marion Archer, Karen Lawson, Lauren Levine, Vannoy Fite, Kim Jones, Jo Popper, Brooke Howard, and Joy Nichols for always being honest. And there.

To Tarryn Fisher. I love you and your whole stupid family.

Thank you to my agent, Jane Dystel, and her amazing team!

Thank you to the amazing Atria Books team. To my publisher, Judith Curr, for the past five years of support. To Ariele Stewart, my NPTBF. We can probably drop the first letter of our acronym now. To Melanie Iglesias Pérez, thank you for all you do! Which is a ton! And to my editor, Johanna Castillo. When I try to write how much I appreciate you, words seem dumb. I love you.

Thank you to CoHorts. A group of book-loving people who boost my ego and remind me daily of who I want to be.

Thank you to FP. The original 21. I credit all the good in this career to that first year. The love, support, and excitement we all held for one another is a thing of beauty. I will never forget it. I will always appreciate each one of you.

To my boys. My beautiful, wonderful men. Thanks to your father, my life would still be complete if I never had any of you. But I will never take for granted that I do have you. You bring joy to my life every single day. I hope you never stop asking me to tuck you in at night. You make me so proud.

And to my husband, Heath Hoover. The only times I've ever seen you come close to crying are when you're proud of your family. Nothing makes me love and appreciate you more. Almost everything good in my life is because of you.

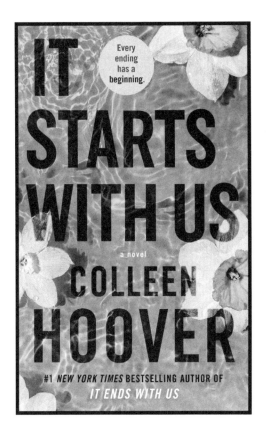

Finding
Cinderella

Also by Colleen Hoover

Slammed
Point of Retreat
Hopeless
This Girl
Losing Hope

Finding Cinderella

A Novella

Colleen Hoover

ATRIA PAPERBACK

NEW YORK LONDON TORONTO SYDNEY NEW DELHI

ATRIA PAPERBACK

Atria Paperback
A Division of Simon & Schuster, Inc.
1230 Avenue of the Americas
New York, NY 10020

First Atria Paperback edition March 2014

ATRIA Paperback and colophon are trademarks of Simon & Schuster, Inc.

The Simon & Schuster Speakers Bureau can bring authors to your live event. For more information or to book an event, contact the Simon & Schuster Speakers Bureau at 1-866-248-3049 or visit our website at www.simonspeakers.com.

Cover design by Sarah Hansen
Cover photograph © Image Source/Getty Images

Manufactured in China

20   19   18   17   16

ISBN 978-1-4767-8328-4
ISBN 978-1-4767-7143-4

For Stephanie and Craig.
Fist bump.

A Note to My CoHorts

So many amazing things have happened over the past two years, and it's all thanks to each and every one of my readers. I originally released *Finding Cinderella* online for free as a thank-you to everyone who has made my life what it is today.

Never did I expect the reaction *Finding Cinderella* received. The feedback was one thing, but the fact that you all rallied together and begged for it in print was something I never expected. Here you all were with a free ebook in your hands. You had already read it, yet you still wanted it in paperback to grace your shelves. That is the highest compliment an author can receive, knowing her words mean that much to her readers.

After months of pleas, I have never been more excited for the release of a book than I am for this one. Because this one isn't on shelves because of me. It's on shelves because of *you*.

I dedicate this book to all of the awesomely insane CoHorts for their endless, unmatched support. I love you all!

My Cinderella Story

Two years ago I was living in a mobile home with my husband and three sons, and working at a job that paid $9 per hour. I was happy with what I had been given, but it was not exactly the life I had envisioned for my family or myself.

Since childhood, I dreamed of being a writer, but for thirty-one years I made excuse after excuse as to why I couldn't be one:

> *"I have no spare time."*
> *"My writing isn't good enough."*
> *"I'll never get published."*
> *"I'm too busy writing excuses to write a novel."*

In reality, the only reason I was not pursuing my dream was because I thought dreams were just that . . . *dreams*. Intangible. Unrealistic. Childish.

I've always been a realist, never looking at the glass half empty *or* half full. I'm the type of person who is just thankful to have a glass at *all*. That was exactly how I viewed my life two years ago. I never allowed myself to be ungrateful or wish for more.

My husband and I both come from low-income families, and we did our best to make ends meet and put ourselves through college. I took out student loans and we both worked full-time, trading days off so we didn't have to pay for child care. I received a Bachelor of Social Work from Texas A&M University–Commerce in December 2005, two months before giving birth to our third child.

After a few years of our moving around from rent-house to rent-house and my working as a social worker, my parents helped us buy a three-bedroom, two-bath singlewide mobile home that was barely more than one thousand square feet. I felt blessed to have three healthy children, a wonderful, supportive husband, and a roof over our heads.

As happy as I was, I felt like something was missing. That childhood dream of writing a book kept resurfacing and I kept pushing it back down with more excuses.

Then in October 2011, after watching one of my own children follow one of his dreams, I began to entertain the thought that maybe dreams *are* tangible.

My middle child, who was eight years old at the time, wanted to audition for the local community theater. I was thrilled at his bravery, but when he actually got the part, I was forced to face reality. There was no way I could work eleven-hour days and take him to rehearsals five evenings a week. My husband was working as a long-haul truck driver at the time and was home only a few days each month, so I was essentially a single mother. However, my children's happiness has always been my priority, and I was not about to let my son down. I received help from a friend who dropped him off at my work after school so we could make it to his rehearsals, while my mother watched my other two children.

For the next two months, I sat in the audience for three hours each evening watching rehearsals. I watched my son on stage and was filled with pride at seeing him pursue his passion at such a young age. Those moments prompted me to think about my own childhood passions and how much I dreamed of becoming a writer. When I was younger, I wrote during every free moment and on any surface I could find. My mother would enthusiastically read my "Mystery Bob" stories that I penned from crayon on scraps of paper stapled together. I continued to write for fun throughout high school and even pursued journalism my first year in college. However, after I married my high school sweetheart and had our first son by the age of twenty, my childhood dream began to fade as the responsibilities of real life set in. As much as I wanted to be a writer, it seemed impossible. Instead, I held on to my self-doubt and insecurities for ten years, allowing responsibility after responsibility to become my crutch.

As I sat in the audience of my son's rehearsals, I saw something in him that had long been dormant in myself—*creative passion*.

While it was a remarkable moment to see my son pursuing his dream, it was also a rude awakening. I was doing my children a disservice by setting the example that it's okay to put yourself last . . . to put your own desires on the back burner while you take care of everyone else. I made a promise to myself that night that I would start writing again, even if it was only for my own enjoyment. After coming to this realization, I began to find inspiration and motivation from other areas.

One of my biggest motivators came from an Avett Brothers concert I attended with my sister. It was one of the best experiences of my life, not because we were in the front row, but because of a few powerful seconds during their song "Head Full of Doubt, Road Full of Promise." I had heard these lyrics sung many times before, yet the meaning had never resonated with me until that very moment.

"Decide what to be, and go be it."

The sentence was simple and straightforward; yet it left a profound impression on me. For days, the words continued to repeat in my head until they finally sunk in: if I wanted to be a writer, there was no reason I couldn't *"go be it."* I pulled out my laptop at one of the play rehearsals, and I wrote the very first line to *Slammed*:

"Kel and I load the last two boxes into the U-Haul."

It was the first sentence to the book that would change my life.

At the time, I was writing the book only for myself, but my mother was a huge supporter of my writing. After all, she still had the riveting "Mystery Bob" stories I'd written in crayon. Even though I knew her opinion would be biased, I let her read what I had completed. She loved it, as any good mother would, and began pestering me for the next chapters.

I also allowed my boss and both of my sisters to read the first several chapters and they, too, asked for more. The fact that they wanted more of the story gave me the inspiration to continue. I enjoyed it so much that I wrote at every opportunity. I would put my children to bed at night, write until well after midnight and then have to be at work at seven o'clock the next morning. By the end of December, I had traded so much sleep in favor of writing that I had a complete manuscript. I also had three children who were now very adept at working a microwave.

When I reached those two final words, *The End*, I felt like I had just achieved my childhood dream, despite not having a real book, a publisher, or even an audience.

After word spread that I had written a book, friends and family began requesting to read it. I couldn't afford to have paperbacks printed, so I researched and found Amazon's Kindle Direct Publishing program. After days of more research and attempting to learn everything I could about self-publishing, I uploaded my book to Amazon.

I had no expectations. I never even tried to get the book traditionally published, because in my mind I had already achieved my dream of writing the book. I didn't think there was a chance that people who didn't know me would ever read it.

The opposite happened. Hundreds of people, complete strangers, started to order my book. I began receiving requests for a sequel from those readers and, since I enjoyed writing the first book so much, I was more than thrilled to deliver a sequel. I released *Point of Retreat* in February 2012. Soon after, I began receiving royalty payments. Everything was happening so fast, I held on to every moment, afraid it would all end overnight. Since the sales weren't guaranteed, I refused to accept the possibility that things could improve from there. I was waiting for the excitement, positive reviews, and requests for more books to come to an end, because it was all too good to be true.

But it didn't end. Every day brought new readers until the books eventually hit the *New York Times* Best Sellers List. Publishers took notice of the rapid success of both books and, after signing up with a literary agent, I accepted a publishing offer from Atria Books.

My life became so busy that I had to quit my job in order to focus on writing full-time. I was worried there wouldn't be enough money in it to support my family, but with the release of my third book, *Hopeless*, in December 2012, I was finally convinced that this was now my career. *Hopeless* went on to hit #1 on the *New York Times* Best Sellers List and was Amazon's best selling self-published e-book of 2013, and their sixteenth bestselling e-book overall of 2013.

We moved out of our mobile home less than ten months ago and now live in a lake house that we never thought could be ours. Each morning I wake up and I'm consumed with disbelief that this is now our life. We've been able to pay off all our debt and create college funds for our boys. We've also donated to several charities as a way to give back for all the incredible things that have happened to us.

In the past two years, I have gone from a mother who refused to believe that a childhood fantasy could become a reality, to a writer with five books that have all become *New York Times* Best Sellers, a free novella, and two more novels to be published this year.

Each of those books is tangible proof that if you have the courage to make them happen, dreams are very real and attainable. All you have to do is find what inspires you, which can be something as simple as a song lyric or a child's smile on stage. Then you have to make the long, brave effort, which can be as daunting as sitting down at a computer, facing a blank page, and not giving up until you reach the finish line.

Despite all the great experiences and accomplishments that have come after it, I still consider my proudest moment to be the first time I typed the words *The End.*

For that was my beginning.

Colleen Hoover

Finding
Cinderella

Prologue

"You got a tattoo?"

It's the third time I've asked Holder the same question, but I just don't believe it. It's out of character for him. Especially since I'm not the one who encouraged it.

"Jesus, Daniel," he groans on the other end of the line. "Stop. And stop asking me why."

"It's just a weird thing to tattoo on yourself. *Hopeless.* It's a very depressing term. But still, I'm impressed."

"I gotta go. I'll call you later this week."

I sigh into the phone. "God, this sucks, man. The only good thing about this entire school since you moved is fifth period."

"What's fifth period?" Holder asks.

"Nothing. They forgot to assign me a class, so I hide out in this maintenance closet every day for an hour."

Holder laughs. I realize as I'm listening to it that it's the first time I've heard him laugh since Les died two months ago. Maybe moving to Austin will actually be good for him.

The bell rings and I hold the phone with my shoulder and fold up my jacket, then drop it to the floor of the maintenance closet. I flip off the light. "I'll talk to you later. Nap time."

"Later," Holder says.

I end the call and set my alarm for fifty minutes later, then place my phone on the counter. I lower myself to the floor and lie down. I close my eyes and think about how much this year sucks. I hate that

Holder is going through what he's having to go through and there isn't a damn thing I can do about it. No one that close to me has ever died, much less someone as close as one of my sisters. A *twin* sister to be exact.

I don't even try to offer him advice, but I think he likes that. I think he needs me to just continue being myself, because God knows everyone else in this whole damn school has no clue how to act around him. If they weren't all such stupid assholes he'd probably still be here and school wouldn't suck half as bad as it does.

But it does suck. Everyone in this place sucks and I hate them all. I hate everybody but Holder and they're the reason he isn't here anymore.

I stretch my legs out in front of me and cross my ankles, then fold my arm over my eyes. At least I have fifth period.

Fifth period is nice.

•   •   •

My eyes flick open and I groan when something lands on me. I hear the sound of the door slam shut.

What the hell?

I place my hands on whatever just fell on me and begin to roll it off me when my hands graze a head full of soft hair.

It's a human?

A girl?

A chick just fell on me. In the maintenance closet. And she's crying.

"Who the hell are you?" I ask cautiously. Whoever she is, she tries to push off me but we both seem to be taking turns moving in the same direction. I lift up and try to roll her to my side but our heads crash together.

"Shit," she says.

I fall back onto my makeshift pillow and grab my forehead. "Sorry," I mumble.

Neither one of us moves this time. I can hear her sniffling, trying not to cry. I can't see two inches in front of me because the light is still out but I suddenly don't mind that she's still on top of me because she smells incredible.

"I think I'm lost," she says. "I thought I was walking into the bathroom."

I shake my head, even though I know she can't see it. "Not a bathroom," I say. "But why are you crying? Did you hurt yourself when you fell?"

I feel her whole body sigh on top of me. Even though I have no idea who she is or what she looks like, I can feel the sadness in her and it makes me a little sad in return. I'm not sure how it happens, but my arms go around her and her cheek falls against my chest. In the course of five seconds we go from extremely awkward to kind of comfortable, like we do this all the time.

It's weird and normal and hot and sad and strange and I don't really want to let go. It feels kind of euphoric, like we're in some sort of fairytale. Like she's Tinkerbell and I'm Peter Pan.

No, wait. I don't want to be Peter Pan.

Maybe she can be like Cinderella and I'll be her Prince Charming.

Yeah, I like that fantasy better. Cinderella's hot when she's all poor and sweaty and slaving over the stove. She also looks good in her ball gown. It also doesn't hurt that we're meeting in a broom closet. Very fitting.

I feel her pull a hand up to her face, more than likely wiping away a tear. "I hate them," she says softly.

"Who?"

"Everybody," she says. "I hate everybody."

I close my eyes and lift my hand, then run it down her hair, doing my best to comfort her. *Finally, someone who actually gets it.* I'm not sure why she hates everybody but I have a feeling she's got a pretty valid reason.

"I hate everybody too, Cinderella."

She laughs softly, probably confused as to why I just referred to her as Cinderella, but at least it's not more tears. Her laugh is intoxicating and I try to think of how I can get her to do it again. I'm trying to think of something funny to say when she lifts her face off my chest and I feel her scoot forward. Before I know it, I feel lips on mine and I'm not sure if I should shove her away or roll on top of her. I begin to lift my hands to her face, but she pulls back just as quick as she kissed me.

"Sorry," she says. "I should go." She places her palms beside me on the floor and starts to lift up, but I grab her face and pull her back down on top of me.

"No," I say. I bring her mouth back to mine and I kiss her. I keep our lips pressed firmly together as I lower her to my side. I pull her against me so that her head is resting on my jacket. Her breath tastes like Starburst and it makes me want to keep kissing her until I can identify every single flavor.

Her hand touches my arm and she gives it a tight squeeze just as my tongue slips inside her mouth. That would be strawberry on the tip of her tongue.

She keeps her hand on my arm, periodically moving it to the back of my head, then returning it to my arm. I keep my hand on her waist, never once moving it to touch any other part of her. The only thing we explore is each other's mouths. We kiss without making another sound. We kiss until the alarm sounds on my phone. Despite the noise, neither of us stops kissing. We don't even hesitate. We kiss for another solid minute until the bell rings in the hallway outside and suddenly lockers are slamming shut and people are talking and everything about our moment is stolen from us by all the inconvenient external factors of school.

I still my lips against hers, then slowly pull back.

"I have to get to class," she whispers.

I nod, even though she can't see me. "Me, too," I reply.

She begins to scoot out from beneath me. When I roll onto my back, I feel her move closer to me. Her mouth briefly meets mine one more time, then she pulls away and stands up. The second she opens the door, the light from the hallway pours in and I squeeze my eyes shut, throwing my arm over my face.

I hear the door shut behind her and by the time I adjust to the brightness, the light is gone again.

I sigh heavily. I also remain on the floor until my physical reaction to her subsides. I don't know who the hell she was or why the hell she ended up here, but I hope to God she comes back. I need a whole hell of a lot more of that.

• • •

She didn't come back the next day. Or the day after that. In fact, today marks exactly a week since she literally fell into my arms, and I've convinced myself that maybe that whole day was a dream. I did stay up most of the night before watching zombie movies with Chunk, but even though I was going on two hours of sleep, I don't know that I would have been able to imagine that. My fantasies aren't that fun.

Whether she comes back or not, I still don't have a fifth period and until someone calls me out on it, I'll keep hiding out in here. I actually slept way too much last night, so I'm not tired. I pull my phone out to text Holder when the door to the closet begins to open.

"Are you in here, kid?" I hear her whisper.

My heart immediately picks up pace and I can't tell if it's that she came back or if it's because the light is on and I'm not really sure I want to see what she looks like when she opens this door.

"I'm here," I say.

The door is still barely cracked. She slips a hand inside and slides it around the wall until she finds the light, then she flicks it off. The door opens and she slips into the room, then quickly shuts it behind her.

"Can I hide with you?" she asks. Her voice sounds a little different than last time. It sounds happier.

"You're not crying today," I say.

I feel her make her way over to me. She grazes my leg and can feel that I'm seated on a countertop, so she feels around me until she finds a clear spot. She pushes herself up beside me and takes a seat next to me.

"I'm not sad today," she says, her voice much closer this time.

"Good." It's quiet for several seconds, but it's nice. I'm not sure why she came back or why it took her a week, but I'm glad she's here.

"Why were you in here last week?" she asks. "And why are you in here now?"

"Schedule mishap. I was never assigned a fifth period, so I hide out and hope administration doesn't notice."

She laughs. "Smart."

"Yep."

It's quiet again for a minute or so. Our hands are gripping the edge of the counter and every time she swings her legs, her fingers barely touch mine. I eventually just move my hand on top of hers and pull it onto my lap. It seems odd to just grab her hand like this, but we pretty much made out for fifteen minutes straight last week so holding hands is actually reversing a base.

She slides her fingers between mine and our palms meet, then

I fold my fingers over hers. "This is nice," she says. "I've never held anyone's hand before."

I freeze.

How the hell old is she?

"You're not in junior high, are you?"

"*God* no. I've just never held anyone's hand before. The guys I've been with seem to forget this part. But it's nice. I like it."

"Yeah," I agree. "It is nice."

"Wait," she says. "*You* aren't in junior high, are you?"

"No. Not yet," I say.

She swings her leg out to the side and kicks me, then we both laugh.

"This is kind of weird, isn't it?" she asks.

"Elaborate. Lots of things could be considered weird, so I'm not sure what you're referring to."

I feel her shoulders shrug. "I don't know. This. Us. Kissing and talking and holding hands and we don't even know what the other looks like."

"I'm really good looking," I say.

She laughs.

"I'm serious. If you could see me right now, you'd be on your knees begging me to be your boyfriend so you could flaunt me around the school."

"Highly unlikely," she says. "I don't do boyfriends. Overrated."

"If you don't hold hands and you don't do boyfriends, then what *do* you do?"

She sighs. "Pretty much everything else. I've got quite a reputation, you know. In fact, it's possible the two of us may have had sex before and we don't even realize it."

"Not possible. You'd remember me."

She laughs again and as much as I'm having fun talking to her, that laugh makes me want to drag her to the floor with me and do nothing but kiss her again.

"Are you actually good looking?" she asks skeptically.

"Terribly good looking," I reply.

"Let me guess. Dark hair, brown eyes, great abs, white teeth, Abercrombie & Fitch."

"Close," I say. "*Light* brown hair, correct on the eyes, abs, and teeth, but American Eagle Outfitters all the way."

"Impressive," she says.

"My turn," I say. "Thick blonde hair, big blue eyes, an adorable little white dress with a matching hat, royal blue skin, and you're about two feet tall."

She laughs loudly. "You have a thing for Smurfette?"

"A guy can dream."

The sound of her laughter actually makes my heart hurt. It hurts because I really want to know who this chick is but I know once I find out, I more than likely won't want her like I want her right now.

She inhales a breath and then the room becomes quiet. So quiet, it's almost uncomfortable.

"I'm not coming back in here after today," she says softly.

I squeeze her hand, surprised by the sadness I feel at that confession.

"I'm moving. Not right away, but soon. This summer. I just think it'd be silly if I came back here, because eventually we'll have to turn on the light or we'll slip up and say our names and I just don't think I want to know who you are."

I graze my thumb over her hand. "Why'd you come back today, then?"

She exhales a delicate breath. "I wanted to thank you."

"For what? Kissing you? That's all I did."

"Yeah," she says, matter-of-fact. "Exactly. For kissing me. For *just* kissing me. Do you know how long it's been since a guy has actually *just* kissed me? After I left last week I tried to remember, but I couldn't. Every time a guy has ever kissed me, he's always been in such a hurry to move on to what comes after the kisses that I don't think anyone has ever taken the time to give me an honest to God, genuine kiss before."

I shake my head. "That's really depressing," I say. "But don't give me too much credit. I've been known to want to rush past that part in the past. I just didn't really care to rush past it last week because you're a pretty phenomenal kisser."

"Yeah," she says confidently. "I know. Imagine what making love to me could feel like."

I swallow the sudden lump in my throat. "Believe me, I have. For about seven days straight now."

Her legs stop swinging next to me. I don't know if I just made her uncomfortable with that comment.

"You know what else is sad?" she asks. "No one's ever made love to me before."

This conversation is headed in a weird direction. I can already tell.

"You're young. Plenty of time for that. Virginity is actually a turn-on, so you have nothing to worry about."

She laughs, but it's a sad laugh this time.

Weird how I can already differentiate her laughs.

"I am *so* not a virgin," she says. "That's why it's sad. I'm pretty skilled in the sex department, but looking back . . . I've never loved any of them. None of them have ever loved me, either. Sometimes I wonder if sex with someone who actually loves you is different. Better."

I think about her question and realize that I don't have an answer. I've never loved anyone, either. "Good question," I say. "It's kind of sad that we've both had sex, multiple times it sounds like, but neither of us has ever loved anyone we've done it with. Says a lot about our characters, don't you think?"

"Yeah," she says quietly. "Sure does. A lot of sad truth."

It's quiet for a while and I still have hold of her hand. I can't stop thinking about the fact that no one's ever held her hand before. It makes me wonder if I've ever held the hands of any of the girls I've had sex with. Not that there have been a ton, but enough that I should be able to recall holding one of their hands.

"I might be one of those guys," I ashamedly admit. "I don't know if I've ever held a girl's hand before."

"You're holding mine," she says.

I nod slowly. "So I am."

A few more beats of silence pass before she speaks again.

"What if I leave here in forty-five minutes and never hold another guy's hand again? What if I go through life like I am right now? What if guys continue to take me for granted and I do nothing to change it and I'll have lots of sex, but never know what it's like to make love?"

"So don't do that. Find you a good guy and tie him down and make love to him every night."

She groans. "That terrifies me. As curious as I am about the difference between making love and having sex, my stance on relationships makes it impossible to find out."

I think about her comment for a while. It's weird, because she sounds a little like the female version of me. I'm not sure I'm as opposed to relationships as she is, but I've definitely never told a girl I loved her and I really hope that doesn't happen for a hell of a long time.

"You're really never coming back?" I ask.

"I'm really not coming back," she says.

I let go of her hand and press my palms onto the cabinet, then jump down. I move and stand in front of her, then place my hands on either side of her. "Let's solve our dilemma right now."

She leans back. "Which dilemma?"

I move my hands and place them on her hips, then pull her to me. "We have a good forty-five minutes to work with. I'm pretty sure I could make love to you in forty-five minutes. We can see what it's like and if it's even worth going through relationships in the future. That way when you leave here, you won't worry about never knowing what it's like."

She laughs nervously, then leans toward me again. "How do you make love to someone you aren't in love with?"

I lean forward until my mouth is next to her ear. "We pretend."

I can hear the breath catch in her lungs. She turns her face slightly toward mine and I feel her lips graze my cheek. "What if we're bad actors?" she whispers.

I close my eyes, because the possibility that I might actually be making love to this chick in a matter of minutes is almost too much to take in.

"You should audition for me," she says. "If you're convincing then I just might agree to this absurd idea of yours."

"Deal," I say.

I take a step back and remove my shirt, then lay it on the floor. I grab my jacket off the counter and unfold it, then lay it on the floor as well. I turn back to the counter, then scoop her up. She locks herself around me, burying her head in my neck.

"Where's your shirt?" she asks, running her hands across my shoulder. I lower her to the floor, onto her back. I ease myself to her side and pull her against me.

"You're lying on it," I respond.

"Oh," she says. "That was considerate of you."

I bring my hand up to her cheek. "That's what people do when they're this in love."

I feel her smile. "How in love are we?"

"All the way," I say.

"Why? What is it about me you love so much?"

"Your laugh," I say immediately, not sure how much of that is actually made up. "I love your humor. I also love the way you tuck your hair behind your ears when you're reading. And I love how you hate to talk on the phone almost as much as I do. I really love that you leave me those little notes all the time in your adorable handwriting. And I love that you love my dog so much, because he really likes you. I also love taking showers with you. Those are always fun."

I slide my hand from her cheek to the nape of her neck. I ease my mouth forward and rest my lips against hers.

"Wow," she says against my mouth. "You're really convincing."

I smile and pull away. "Stop breaking character," I tease. "Now it's your turn. What do you love about me?"

"I do love your dog," she says. "He's a great dog. I also love how you open doors for me even though I'm supposed to want to open doors for myself. I love that you don't try to pretend you like old black and white movies like everyone else does, because they bore the hell out of me. I also love it when I'm at your house and every time your parents turn the other way, you steal little kisses from me. My favorite part about you though is when I catch you staring at me. I love that you don't look away and you stare unapologetically, like you aren't ashamed that you can't stop watching me. It's all you want to do because you think I'm the most amazing thing you've ever laid eyes on. I love how much you love me."

"You're absolutely right," I whisper. "I love staring at you."

I kiss her mouth, then trail kisses across her cheek and up her jawline. I press my lips against her ear and even though I know we're pretending, my mouth runs dry at the thought of the words about to pass my lips. I hesitate, almost deciding against it. But an even bigger part of me wants to say it. A huge part of me wishes I could mean it and a small part of me thinks I probably could.

I run my hands up and through her hair. "I love you," I whisper.

The next breath she draws in is a deep one. My heart is hammering against my chest and I'm quiet, waiting on her next move. I have no idea what comes next. Then again, neither does she.

Her hands move from my shoulders and slowly make their way up to my neck. She tilts her head until her mouth is flush against my ear. "I love you more," she whispers. I can feel the smile on her lips and I wonder if it matches the smile on my face. I don't know why I'm suddenly enjoying this so much, but I am.

"You're so beautiful," I whisper, moving my lips closer to her mouth. "So damn beautiful. And every single one of those guys who somehow passed this up is a complete fool."

She closes the gap between our lips and I kiss her, but this time the kiss seems so much more intimate. For a brief moment, I actually feel like I really do love all those things about her and she really does love all those things about me. We're kissing and touching and pulling the rest of our clothes off in such a hurry, it feels as if we're on a timer.

I guess we technically are.

I pull my wallet out of the pocket of my jeans and grab a condom, then ease myself back against her.

"You can change your mind," I whisper, hoping to hell she doesn't.

"So can you," she says.

I laugh.

She laughs.

Then we both shut the hell up and spend the rest of the hour proving exactly how much we love each other.

•   •   •

I'm on my knees now, quietly gathering our clothes. After I slip my shirt over my head, I pull her up and help her with her own shirt. I stand up and pull on my jeans, then help her to her feet. I rest my chin on top of her head and pull her against me, recognizing the perfect fit.

"I could turn on the light before you leave," I say. "Aren't you a little curious to see the face of the guy you're madly in love with?"

She shakes her head against my chest with her laugh. "It'll ruin everything," she says. Her words are muffled by my shirt, so she lifts her head away from my chest and tilts her face up to mine. "Let's not ruin it. Once we find out who the other is, we'll find something we don't like. Maybe *lots* of things we don't like. Right now it's perfect. We can always have this perfect memory of that one time we loved somebody."

I kiss her again, but it doesn't last long because the bell rings. She doesn't release her hold from around my waist. She just presses her head against my chest again and squeezes me tighter. "I need to go," she says.

I close my eyes and nod. "I know."

I'm surprised by just how much I don't want her to go, knowing I'll never see her again. I almost beg her to stay, but I also know she's right. It only feels perfect because we're *pretending* it's perfect.

She begins to pull away from me, so I lift my hands to her cheeks one last time. "I love you, babe. Wait for me after school, okay? In our usual spot."

"You know I'll be there," she says. "And I love you, too." She stands on her tiptoes and presses her lips to mine—hard and desperate and sad. She pulls away and makes her way to the door. As soon as she begins to open it, I walk swiftly to her and push the door shut with my hand. I press my chest against her back and I lower my mouth to her ear.

"I wish it could be real," I whisper. I put my hand on the doorknob and open it, then turn my head when she slips out the door.

I sigh and run my hands through my hair. I think I need a few minutes before I can leave this room. I'm not sure I want to forget the way she smells just yet. In fact, I stand here in the dark and try my hardest to commit every single thing about her to my memory, since that's the only place I'll ever see her again.

Chapter One

"Oh, my *God*!" I say, frustrated. "Lighten up." I crank the car just as Val climbs inside and slams her door in a huff, then pushes herself back against the seat.

As soon as she's inside the car, the overwhelming amount of perfume she has on begins to suffocate me. I crack the window, but just enough so that she won't think I'm insulting her. She knows how much perfume bothers me, especially when chicks smell like they bathe in it, but she never seems to care what I think, because she continues to douse it on by the gallon.

"You're so immature, Daniel," she mutters. She flips the visor down and pulls her lipstick from her purse, then begins to reapply it. "I'm beginning to wonder if you'll *ever* change."

Change?

What the hell is *that* supposed to mean?

"Why would I change?" I ask, cocking my head out of curiosity.

She sighs and drops her lipstick back into her purse, smacks her lips together, then turns toward me. "So you're telling me you're happy with the way you act?"

What?

With the way *I* act? Is she really commenting on the way *I* act? The same girl I've seen curse at waitresses for something as simple as too much ice in her glass is seriously commenting on the way *I* act?

I've been seeing her off and on for months now and I haven't had a single clue that she was hoping I would eventually change. Hoping I'd become someone I'm not.

Come to think of it, I keep getting back together with her, thinking *she'll* be the one to change. To be *nice* for once. In reality, people are who they are and they'll never really change. So why the hell are Val and I even wasting our time on this exhausting relationship if we don't even really like who the other is?

"I didn't think so," she says smugly, incorrectly assuming my silence was admission that I'm not happy with how I act. In actuality, my silence was the moment of clarity I've needed since the day I met her.

I remain silent until we pull into her driveway. I leave the car running, indicating that I have no plans on going inside with her tonight.

"You're leaving?" she asks.

I nod and stare out the driver's side window. I don't want to look at her, because I'm a guy and she's hot and I know if I look at her, then my moment of clarity regarding our relationship will become foggy and I'll end up inside her house, making up with her on her bed like I always do.

"You aren't the one who gets to be mad, Daniel. You acted ridiculous tonight. And in front of my parents, no less! How do you expect them to ever approve of you if you act the way you do?"

I have to exhale a slow, calming breath so that I don't raise my voice like she's doing right now. "How do I act, Val? Because I was myself at dinner tonight, just like I'm myself every other minute of the day."

"Exactly!" she says. "There's a time and a place for your stupid nicknames and immature antics and dinner with my parents isn't the time *or* the place!"

I rub my hands over my face out of frustration, then I turn and look at her. "This is me," I say, gesturing toward myself. "If you don't like all of me, then we've got serious issues, Val. I'm not changing and honestly, it wouldn't be fair of me to ask you to change, either. I would never ask you to pretend to be something you're not, which is exactly what you're asking of me right now. I'm *not* changing, I'll *never* change and I would really like it if you would get the hell out of my car right now because your perfume is making me fucking nauseous."

Her eyes narrow and she grabs her purse off the console and pulls it toward her. "Oh, that's nice, Daniel. Insult my perfume to get back at me. See what I mean? You're the epitome of immature." She opens the car door and unbuckles her seatbelt.

"Well at least I'm not asking you to *change* your perfume," I say mockingly.

She shakes her head. "I can't do this anymore," she says, getting out of the car. "We're done, Daniel. For good this time."

"Thank *God*," I say loud enough for her to hear me. She slams her door and marches toward her house. I roll down her window to air out the perfume and I back out of the driveway.

Where the hell is Holder? If I don't get to complain to someone about her, I'll fucking scream.

•   •   •

I climb into Sky's window and she's sitting on the floor, rummaging through pictures. She looks up and smiles as I make my way into her room. "Hey, Daniel," she says.

"Hey, Cheese Tits," I say as I drop down onto her bed. "Where's your hopeless boyfriend?"

She nudges her head toward her bedroom door. "They're in the kitchen making ice cream. You want some?"

"Nah," I say. "I'm too heartbroken to eat anything right now."

"Val having a bad day?"

"Val's having a bad *life*," I say. "And after tonight I've finally realized I don't want to be a part of it."

She raises her eyebrows. "Oh, yeah? Sounds serious this time."

I shrug. "We broke up an hour ago. And who's *they*?"

She shoots me a confused look, so I clarify my question. "You said *they* were in the kitchen making ice cream. Who's *they*?"

Sky opens her mouth to answer me when her bedroom door swings open and Holder walks in with two bowls of ice cream in his hands. A girl is following behind him with her own bowl of ice cream and a spoon hanging out of her mouth. She pulls the spoon from her lips and kicks the bedroom door shut with her foot, then turns toward the bed and stops when she sees me.

She looks vaguely familiar, but I can't place her. Which is odd because she's cute as hell and I feel like I should probably know her name or remember where I've seen her, but I don't.

She walks to the bed and sits down on the opposite end of it, eyeing me the whole time. She dips her spoon into her ice cream, then puts the spoon back in her mouth.

I can't stop staring at that spoon. I think I love that spoon.

"What are you doing here?" Holder asks. I regretfully take my eyes off the Ice Cream Girl and watch as he takes a seat on the floor next to Sky and picks up a few of the pictures.

"I'm done with her, Holder," I say, stretching my legs out in front of me on the bed. "For good. She's fucking crazy."

"But I thought that's why you loved her," he says mockingly.

I roll my eyes. "Thanks for the insight, Dr. Shitmitten."

Sky takes one of the pictures out of Holder's hands. "I think he's actually serious this time," she says to him. "No more Val." Sky tries to look sad for my sake, but I know she's relieved. Val never really fit in with the two of them. Now that I think about it, she never really fit in with me, either.

Holder looks up at me curiously. "Done for good? Really?" He sounds oddly impressed.

"Yeah, *really*, really."

"Who's Val?" Ice Cream Girl asks. "Or better yet, who are *you*?"

"Oh, my bad," Sky interrupts. She points back and forth between Ice Cream Girl and me. "Six, this is Dean's best friend, Daniel. Daniel, this is my best friend, Six."

I'll never get used to hearing Sky call him Dean, but her introduction gives me an excuse to look over at that spoon again. Six pulls it out of her mouth and points it at me. "Nice to meet you, Daniel," she says.

How in the hell can I steal that spoon before she leaves?

"Why does your name sound familiar?" I ask her.

She shrugs. "I dunno. Maybe because six is a fairly common number? Either that or you've heard of what a raging whore I am."

I laugh. I don't know why, though, because her comment really wasn't funny. It was actually a little disturbing. "No, that's not it," I say, still confused as to why her name sounds so familiar. I don't think Sky has ever mentioned her in front of me before.

"The party last year," Holder says, forcing me to look at him again. I'm pretty sure I roll my eyes when I have to look away from her, but I don't mean to. I'd just much rather stare at her than at Holder. "Remember?" he says. "It was the week I got back from Austin and a few days before I met Sky. The night Grayson pummeled you on the floor for saying you took Sky's virginity?"

"Oh, you mean the night you pulled me off of him before I even got the chance to kick his ass?" It still irritates me just thinking about it. I could have had him if Holder hadn't stepped in.

"Yeah," Holder confirms. "Jaxon mentioned something that night about Sky and Six, but I didn't know who they were at the time. I think that's where you heard her name."

"Wait, wait, wait," Sky says, waving her hands in the air and looking at me like I'm crazy. "What do you mean Grayson pummeled you because you said you took my *virginity*? What the *hell*, Daniel?"

Holder puts a reassuring hand on Sky's lower back. "It's cool, babe. He just said it to piss Grayson off because I was about to kick the idiot's ass for the way he was talking about you."

Sky is shaking her head, still confused. "But you didn't even know me. You just said it was a few days before you met me, so why would you be pissed that Grayson was talking shit about me?"

I stare at Holder, too, waiting for his answer. I never thought about it then, but that is odd that he was pissed over Grayson's comments when he didn't even know Sky at the time.

"I didn't like how he was talking about you," he says, leaning in to kiss Sky on the side of the head. "It made me think he probably talked about Les the same way and it pissed me off."

Shit. Of course he would think that. Now I *really* wish he had let me kick Grayson's ass that night.

"That's sweet, Holder," Six says. "You were protecting her before you even knew her."

Holder laughs. "Oh, you don't know the half of it, Six."

Sky looks up at him and they smile at each other, almost like they have some sort of secret, then they both turn their attention back to the pictures on the floor in front of them.

"What are those?" I ask, inquiring about the pictures they're looking through.

"For the yearbook," Six says, answering me. She sets the bowl of ice cream on the bed beside her, then pulls her feet up and sits cross-legged. "Apparently we're supposed to submit pictures of ourselves as kids for the senior page, so Sky is going through the pics Karen gave her."

"You go to the same school as us?" I ask, referring to the fact that she included herself in the explanation of the assignment. I know we go to a huge school, but I have a feeling I would remember her, especially if she's Sky's best friend.

"I haven't been to that school since junior year," she says. "But I'll be there once Monday rolls around." She says it like she's not at all looking forward to it.

I can't help but smile at her reply, though. I wouldn't mind having to see this girl on a recurring basis. "So does that mean you'll be joining our lunchroom alliance?" I lean forward and grab the bowl of ice cream she didn't finish. I pull it to me and take a bite.

She watches me as I close my lips around the spoon and pull it out of my mouth. She scrunches up her nose, staring at the spoon. "I could have herpes, you know," she says.

I grin at her and wink. "You somehow just made herpes sound appealing."

She laughs, but her bowl is suddenly ripped from my hands by Holder and he's pulling me off the bed. My feet hit the floor and he shoves me toward the window. "Go home, Daniel," he says, releasing his grip on my shirt as he lowers himself back to the floor next to Sky.

"What the *hell*, man?" I yell.

Seriously, though. *What the hell?*

"She's Sky's best friend," he says, waving a hand in Six's direction. "You're not allowed to flirt with her. If the two of you mess around it'll just cause tension and make things weird and I don't want that. Now leave and don't come back until you can be around her without having the perverted thoughts I know are going through your head right now."

For the first time in my life, I think I'm actually speechless. Perhaps I should nod and agree with him, but the idiot just made the biggest mistake he could possibly make.

"Shit, Holder," I groan, running my palms down my face. "Why the hell did you have to go and *do* that? You just made her off-limits, man." I begin to make my way back out the window. Once I'm outside, I stick my head back through and look at him. "You should have told me I should date her, then I more than likely wouldn't have been interested. But you had to go and make her forbidden, didn't you?"

"Gee, Daniel," Six says, unenthusiastically. "Glad to know you think of me as a human being and not a challenge." She looks at Holder as she stands up from the bed. "And I didn't realize I had a fifth overprotective brother," she says, making her way toward the window. "I'll see you guys later. I probably need to go rummage through my own pictures before Monday, anyway."

Holder glances back at me as I step aside and allow Six to climb out the window. He doesn't say anything, but the look he gives me is a silent warning that Six is completely off-limits to me. I raise my hands in defense, then pull the window shut after Six is outside. She walks a few feet to the house next door and begins to climb through that window.

"Do you take shortcuts through windows all the time, or do you happen to live in that house?" I ask, walking toward her. Once she's inside, she spins around and leans her head out. "This would be *my* window," she says. "And don't even think about following me inside. This window has been out of commission for almost a year and I have no plans to reopen for business."

She tucks her shoulder-length blonde hair behind her ears and I take a step back, hoping a little distance will allow my heart to stop attacking the walls of my chest. But now all I want to do is figure out a way to recommission her window.

"You really have four older brothers?"

She nods. I hate the fact that she has four older brothers, but only because it presents four more reasons why I shouldn't date her. Add that to Holder making her off-limits and I know she's the only thing I'll be able to think about now.

Thanks, Holder. Thanks a lot.

She rests her chin in her hands and stares at me. It's dark outside, but the moon overhead is casting a light right on her face and she looks like a fucking angel. I don't even know if people should use the words *fucking* and *angel* in the same thought structure, but *shit*. She really looks like a fucking angel with her blonde hair and big eyes. I'm not even sure what color her eyes are because it's dark and I didn't really pay attention when we were in Sky's bedroom, but whatever color they are, it's my new favorite color.

"You're very charismatic," she says.

Jesus. Her voice completely slays me. "Thanks. You're pretty cute yourself."

"I didn't say you were cute, Daniel. I said you were charismatic. There's a difference."

"Not much of one," I say. "You like Italian?"

She frowns and pulls back a few inches like I just insulted her. "Why would you ask me that?"

Her reaction confuses me. I have no idea how that comment could have offended her. "Uh, have you never been asked out on a date before?"

The scowl disappears from her face and she leans forward again. "Oh. You mean food. I'm sort of tired of Italian food, actually. Just got back from a seven-month exchange there. If you're asking me out on a date, I'd rather have sushi."

"I've never had sushi," I admit, trying to process the fact that I'm pretty sure she just agreed to go out on a date with me.

"When?"

This was way too easy. I figured she'd put up a fight and make me beg a little like Val always does. I love that she isn't playing games. She's straightforward and I like that about her already.

"I can't take you tonight," I say. "I had my heart completely broken about an hour ago by a psychotic bitch and I need a little more time to recover from that relationship. How about tomorrow night?"

"Tomorrow is Sunday," she says.

"Do you have an issue with Sundays?"

"Not really, I guess. It just seems odd to go on a first date on a Sunday night. Meet me here at seven o'clock, then."

"I'll meet you at your front door," I say. "And you might not want to tell Sky where you're going unless you want to see me get my ass kicked."

"What's to tell?" she says sarcastically. "It's not like we're going on a random Sunday night date or anything."

I smile and back away, slowly heading backward to my car. "It was nice to meet you, Six."

She places her hand on her window to pull it down. "Likewise. I think."

I laugh, then turn to head toward my car. I'm almost to the door when she calls my name. I spin back around and she's leaning out her window.

"I'm sorry about your broken heart," she whispers loudly. She ducks back into her bedroom and the window closes.

What broken heart? I'm pretty sure this is the first time my heart has actually felt any form of relief since the moment I started dating Val.

Chapter Two

"Does this look okay?" I ask Chunk when I make it into the kitchen. She turns and looks me up and down, then shrugs.

"I guess. Where ya going?"

I step in front of one of the mirrors lining the hallway and check my hair again. "A date."

She groans, then turns back around to the table in front of her. "You've never cared before what you look like. You better not be proposing to her. I'll divorce this family before I allow you to make her my sister."

My mother walks past me and pats me on the shoulder. "You look great, honey. I wouldn't wear those shoes, though."

I look down at my shoes. "Why? What's wrong with my shoes?"

She opens a cabinet, takes out a pan, then turns to face me. Her eyes fall to my shoes again. "They're too bright." She turns and walks to the stove. "Shoes should never be neon."

"They're yellow. Not neon."

"*Neon* yellow," Chunk says.

"Not saying I think they're ugly," my mother says. "I just know Val, and Val is more than likely going to hate your shoes."

I walk to the kitchen counter and grab my keys, then put my cell phone in my pocket. "I don't give a shit what Val thinks."

My mother turns and looks at me curiously. "Well you're asking your thirteen-year-old sister if you look good enough for your date, so I think you kind of *do* care what Val thinks."

"I'm not going out with Val. I broke up with Val. I have a new date tonight."

Chunk's arms go up in the air and she looks up to the ceiling. "Thank the *Lord!*" she proclaims loudly.

My mother laughs and nods. "Yes. Thank the Lord," she says, relieved. She turns back toward the stove and I can't stop looking back and forth between the both of them.

"What? Neither of you like Val?" I know Val is a bitch, but my family seemed to like her. Especially my mom. I honestly thought she'd be upset we broke up.

"I hate Val," Chunk says.

"God, me, too," my mother groans.

"Me three," my father says, walking past me.

None of them are looking at me, but they're all responding like this has been a previously discussed topic.

"You mean all of you hated Val?"

My father turns to face me. "Your mother and I are masters at reverse psychology, Danny-boy. Don't act so surprised."

Chunk raises her hand in the air toward my father. "Me, too, Dad. I reverse psychologized him, too."

My dad reaches over and high-fives Chunk's hand. "Well played, Chunk."

I lean against the frame of the door and stare at them. "You guys were just pretending to like Val? What the hell for?"

My dad sits at the table and picks up a newspaper. "Children are naturally inclined to make choices that will displease their parents. If we had told you how we really felt about Val, you probably would have ended up marrying her just to spite us. Which is why we pretended to love her."

Assholes. All three of them. "You're never meeting another one of my girlfriends again."

My father chuckles, but doesn't seem at all disappointed.

"Who is she?" Chunk asks. "The girl you're actually making an effort for."

"None of your damn business," I reply. "Now that I know how this family works, I'm never bringing her around any of you."

I turn to head out the door and my mother calls after me. "Well if it helps, we already love her, Daniel! She's a sweetheart!"

"And beautiful," my dad says. "She's a keeper!"

I shake my head. "Y'all suck."

• • •

"You're late," Six says when she appears at her front door. She walks out of her house with her back to me, inserting her key in the lock.

"You don't want me to meet your parents?" I ask, wondering why she's locking her door this early in the evening. She turns around and faces me.

"They're old. They ate dinner like ten hours ago and went to bed at seven."

Blue. Her eyes are blue.

Holy shit, she's cute. Her hair is lighter than I thought it was last night in Sky's room. Her skin is flawless. It's like she's the same girl from last night, only now she's in HD. And I was right. She really does look like a fucking angel.

She steps out of the way and I shut the screen door, still unable to take my eyes off her. "I actually got here early," I say, finally replying to her first comment. "Holder was dropping Sky off at her house and I swear it took them half an hour to say their good-byes. I had to wait until the coast was clear."

She slides her house key into her back pocket and nods. "Ready?"

I eye her up and down. "Did you forget your purse?"

She shakes her head. "Nope. I hate purses." She pats her back pocket. "All I need is my house key. I didn't bother bringing money since this date was your idea. You're paying, right?"

Whoa.

Back up.

Let's assess the last thirty seconds, shall we?

She hates purses. That means she didn't bring makeup. Which means she won't constantly be reapplying that shit like Val does. It also means she's not hiding a gallon of perfume anywhere on her person. And it also means she had no plans at all to offer to pay for her half of dinner, which seems a little old-fashioned, but for some reason I like it.

"I love that you don't carry a purse," I say.

"I love that you don't carry one, either," she says with a laugh.

"I do. It's in my car," I say, nudging my head toward my car.

She laughs again and begins walking toward the porch steps. I do the same until I see Sky standing just inside her room with her window wide open. I immediately grab Six by her shoulders and pull her until both of our backs are flat against the front door. "You can see Sky's window from the front yard. She'll see us."

Six glances up at me. "You're really taking this *off-limits* order seriously," she says in a hushed voice.

"I *have* to," I whisper. "Holder doesn't kid around when he forbids me to date people."

She arches a curious eyebrow. "Does Holder usually dictate who you can and can't date?"

"No. You're actually the first."

"Then how do you know he'll actually get mad over it?"

I shrug. "I don't, really. But the thought of hiding it from him just seems sort of fun. Is it not a little bit exciting for you, hiding this date from Sky?"

"Yeah," she says with a shrug. "I guess it is."

Our backs are still pressed against the door and for some reason, we're still whispering. It's not like Sky could hear us from here, but again, the whispering makes it more fun. And I really like the sound of Six's voice when she whispers.

"How do you propose we get out of this situation, Six?"

"Well," she says, pondering my question for a moment. "Normally when I'm attempting a risky, clandestine, secret date and I need to escape my house undetected, I ask myself, 'What would MacGyver do?'"

Oh, my god, this chick just mentioned MacGyver?

Hell.

Yes.

I break my eyes away from hers long enough to hide the fact that I think I just fell for her and also to assess our escape route. I glance at the swing on the porch, then look back at Six when I'm sure the cheesy grin is gone from my face.

"I think MacGyver would take your porch swing and build an invisible force field out of grass and matches. Then he would attach a jet engine to it and fly it out of here undetected. Unfortunately I'm all out of matches."

"Hmmm," she says, squinting her eyes like she's coming up with some brilliant plan. "That's an unfortunate inconvenience." She glances toward my car parked in her driveway, then back up to me. "We could just crawl to your car so she doesn't see us."

And a brilliant plan it would be if it didn't involve a girl getting dirty. I've learned in my six months of on-again off-again with Val that girls like to stay clean.

"You'll get dirt on your hands," I warn her. "I don't think you can walk into a fancy sushi restaurant with dirty hands and jeans."

She looks down at her jeans, then back up to me. "I know this great Bar-B-Q restaurant we could go to, instead. The floor is covered in discarded peanut shells. One time I saw this really fat guy eating at a booth and he wasn't even wearing a shirt."

I smile at the same time I fall a little harder for her. "Sounds perfect."

We both drop to our hands and knees and crawl our way off her porch. She's giggling, and the sound of it makes me laugh. "Shh," I whisper when we reach the bottom of the steps. We crawl across the yard in a hurry, both of us glancing toward Sky's house every few feet. Once we reach the car, I reach up to my door handle. "Crawl through the driver's side," I say to her. "She'll be less likely to see you."

I open the door for her and she crawls into the front seat. Once she's inside the car, I climb in after her and slide into my seat. We're both crouched down, which is pointless if you think about it. If Sky were to look out her bedroom window, she'd see my car parked in Six's driveway. It wouldn't matter if she saw our heads or not.

Six wipes the dirt from her hands onto the legs of her jeans and it completely turns me on. She turns her head to face me and I'm still staring at the dirt smeared across the thighs of her jeans. I somehow tear my gaze away and look her in the eyes.

"You'll have to disguise your car next time you come over," she says. "This is way too risky."

I like her comment a little too much.

"Confident there'll be a next time already?" I ask, smirking at her. "The date just started."

"Good point," she says with a shrug. "I might hate you by the end of the date."

"Or I might hate *you*," I say.

"Impossible." She props her foot up on the dash. "I'm unhateable."

"Unhateable isn't even a real word."

She peers over her shoulder into the backseat, then faces forward again with a scowl. "Why does it smell like you had a harem of whores in here?" She pulls her shirt up over her nose to cover up the smell.

"Does it still smell like perfume?" I don't even smell it anymore. It's probably seeped into my pores and I'm now immune to it.

She nods. "It's awful," she says, her voice muffled by her shirt. "Roll down a window." She makes a fake spitting sound like she's trying to get the taste of it out of her mouth and it makes me laugh.

I crank the car, then put it in reverse and begin to back out.

"The wind will mess up your hair if I roll down the windows. You didn't bring a purse, which means you didn't bring a brush, which means you won't be able to fix your hair when we get to the restaurant."

She reaches to her door and presses the button to roll down her window. "I'm already dirty and I'd rather have messy hair than smell like a harem," she says. She rolls the window down completely, then motions for me to roll mine down as well, so I do.

I put the car in drive and press on the gas. The car immediately fills with wind and fresh air and her hair begins flying around in all directions, but she just relaxes into the seat.

"Much better," she says, grinning at me. She closes her eyes while inhaling a deep breath of the fresh air.

I try to pay attention to the road, but she makes it pretty damn hard.

•   •   •

"What are your brothers' names?" I ask her. "Are they numbers, too?"

"Zachary, Michael, Aaron, and Evan. I'm ten years younger than the youngest."

"Were you an accident?"

She nods. "The best kind. My mother was forty-two when she had me, but they were excited when I came out a girl."

"I'm glad you came out a girl."

She laughs. "Me, too."

"Why'd they name you Six if you were actually the fifth child?"

"Six isn't my name," she says. "Full name is Seven Marie Jacobs, but I got mad at them for moving me to Texas when I was fourteen so I started calling myself Six to piss them off. They didn't really care, but I was stubborn and refused to give up. Now everyone calls me Six but them."

I love that she gave herself a nickname. My kind of girl.

"Question still applies," I say. "Why did they name you *Seven* if you were actually the fifth child?"

"No reason, really. My dad just liked the number."

I nod, then take a bite of food, eyeing her carefully. I'm waiting for that moment. The one that always comes with girls, where the pedestal you place them on in the beginning gets kicked out from under them. It's usually the moment they start talking about ex-boyfriends or mention how many kids they want or they do something really annoying, like apply lipstick in the middle of dinner.

I've been waiting patiently for Six's flaws to stand out, but so far I can't find any. Granted, we've only interacted with each other for a collective three or four hours now, so hers may just be buried deeper than other people's.

"So you're a middle child?" she asks. "Do you suffer from middle-child syndrome?"

I shake my head. "Probably about as much as you suffer from fifth-child syndrome. Besides, Hannah is four years older than me and Chunk is five years younger, so we have a nice spread."

She chokes on her drink with her laugh. "Chunk? You call your little sister Chunk?"

"We all call her Chunk. She was a fat baby."

"You have nicknames for everyone," she says. "You call Sky

Cheese Tits. You call Holder *Hopeless.* What do you call me when I'm not around?"

"If I give people nicknames, I do it to their faces," I point out. "And I haven't figured yours out yet." I lean back in my seat and wonder myself why I haven't given her one yet. The nicknames I give people are usually pretty instant.

"Is it a bad thing you haven't nicknamed me yet?"

I shrug. "Not really. I'm just still trying to figure you out is all. You're kind of contradictory."

She arches an eyebrow. "I'm contradictory? In what ways?"

"All of them. You're cute as hell, but you don't give a shit what you look like. You look sweet, but I have a feeling you're just the right mix of good and evil. You seem really easygoing, like you aren't the type to play games with guys, but you're kind of a flirt. And I'm not judging at all by this next observation, but I'm aware of your reputation, yet you don't seem like the type who needs a guy's attention to stroke your self-esteem."

Her expression is tight as she takes in everything I've just said. She reaches to her glass and takes a sip without breaking her stare. She finishes her drink, but holds the glass against her lips while she thinks. She eventually lowers it back to the table and looks down at her plate, picking up her fork.

"I'm not like that anymore," she says softly, avoiding my gaze.

"Like what?" I hate the sadness in her voice now. Why do I always say stupid shit?

"I'm not how I used to be."

Way to go, Daniel. Dumbass.

"Well, I didn't know you back then, so all I can do is judge the girl sitting in front of me right now. And so far, she's been a pretty damn cool date."

The smile spreads back to her lips. "That's good," she says, looking back up at me. "I wasn't sure what type of date I'd be, considering this is the first one I've ever been on."

"No need to stroke my ego," I say. "I can handle the fact that I'm not the first guy to ever express an interest in you."

"I'm serious," she says. "I've never been on a real date before. Guys tend to skip this whole part with me so they can just get to what they really want me for."

My smile disappears. I can tell by the look on her face she's being completely serious. I lean forward and look her hard in the eyes. "Those guys were all fucktards."

She laughs, but I don't.

"I'm serious, Six. Those guys all need a good kick to the clit, because dinner talk is by far the best part of you."

When the sentence leaves my mouth, the smile leaves her face. She looks at me like no one's ever given her a genuine compliment before. It pisses me off.

"How do you know this is the best part of me?" she asks, somehow finding that teasing, flirtatious tone in her voice again. "You haven't had the pleasure of kissing me yet. I'm pretty sure that's the best part of me, because I'm a phenomenal kisser."

Jesus Christ. I don't know if that was an invitation, but I want to send her my RSVP right this second. "I have no doubt being kissed by you would be fantastic, but if I had to choose, I'd take dinner talk over a kiss any day."

She narrows her eyes. "I call bullshit," she says with a challenging glare. "There's no way any guy would pick dinner talk over a good make-out session."

I attempt to return her challenging look, but she makes a good point.

"Okay," I admit. "Maybe you're right. But if I had my way, I'd pick kissing you *during* dinner talk. Get the best of both worlds."

She nods her head, impressed. "You're good," she says, leaning back in her seat. She folds her arms over her chest. "Where'd you learn those smooth moves?"

I wipe my mouth with my napkin, then set it on top of my plate. I lift my elbows until they're resting on the back of the booth and I smile at her. "I don't have smooth moves. I'm just charismatic, remember?"

Her mouth curls up into a grin and she shakes her head like she knows she's in trouble. Her eyes are smiling at me and I realize I've never felt like this before with any other girl. Not that I have it in my head that we're about to fall in love or we're soulmates or some shit like that. I've just never been around a girl where being myself was actually a good thing. With Val, I was always trying my hardest not to piss her off. With past girlfriends, I always found myself holding back from all the shit I really wanted to say. I've always felt like being myself with a girl wasn't necessarily a positive, because I'll be the first to admit, I can be a little over the top.

It's different with Six, though. Not only does she get my sense of humor and my personality, but I feel like she encourages it. I feel like the real me is what she likes the most and every time she laughs or smiles at the perfect moment, I want to fist bump her.

"You're staring at me," she says, breaking me out of my thoughts.

"So I am," I say, not bothering to look away.

She stares right back at me, but her demeanor and expression grow competitive as she narrows her eyes and leans forward. She's silently challenging me to a staring contest.

"No blinking," she says, confirming my thoughts.

"Or laughing," I say.

And it's on. We silently stare at each other for so long, my eyes begin to water and my grip tightens on the table. I try my hardest to keep my eyes locked on hers but they want to stare at every inch of her. I want to stare at her mouth and those full, pink lips and that soft, silky blonde hair. Not to mention her smile. I could stare at her smile all day.

In fact, I'm staring at it right now so I'm pretty sure that means I just lost the staring contest.

"I win," she says, right before she takes another drink of her water.

"I want to kiss you," I say bluntly. I'm a little shocked I said it, but not really. I'm pretty impatient and I really want to kiss her and I usually say whatever I'm thinking, so . . .

"Right now?" she asks, looking at me like I'm insane. She sets her glass back down on the table.

I nod. "Yep. Right now. I want to kiss you over dinner talk so I can have the best of both worlds."

"But I just ate onions," she says.

"So did I."

She's working her jaw back and forth, actually contemplating an answer. "Okay," she says with a shrug. "Why not?"

As soon as she gives me permission, I glance down at the table between us, wondering what the best way to do this would be. I could go sit with her on her side of the booth, but that might be invading her personal space too much. I reach in front of me and push my glass out of the way, then scoot hers to the left.

"Come here," I say, placing my hands on top of the table as I lean toward her. She must have thought I was kidding by the way her eyes dart nervously around us, taking in the fact that we're about to experience our first kiss in public.

"Daniel, this is awkward," she says. "Do you really want our first kiss to be in the middle of a restaurant?"

I nod. "So what if it's awkward? We'll have a do-over later. People put way too much stock in first kisses, anyway."

She tentatively places her palms facedown on the table, then pushes herself up and slowly leans in toward me. "Okay, then," she says, following her words up with a sigh. "But it would be so much better if you waited until the end of our date when you walk me to my front door and it'll be dark and we could be really nervous and you could accidentally touch my boob. That's how first kisses are supposed to be."

I laugh at her comment. We still aren't close enough for me to kiss her yet, but we're getting there. I lean forward a little more, but her eyes leave mine and focus on the table behind me.

"Daniel, there's a woman in the booth behind you changing her baby's diaper on the table. You're about to kiss me and the last thing I'll see before your lips touch mine is a woman wiping her infant's ass."

"Six. Look at me." She brings her eyes back to mine and we're finally close enough that I could reach her mouth. "Ignore the diaper," I command. "And ignore the two men in the booth to our left who are swigging their beer and watching us like I'm about to bend you over this table."

Her eyes dart to the left, so I catch her chin in my hand and force her attention back to me. "Ignore it all. I want to kiss you and I want you to want me to kiss you and I don't really feel like waiting until I walk you to your porch tonight because I've never really wanted to kiss someone this much before."

Her eyes drop to my mouth and I watch as everything around us disappears from her field of vision. Her tongue slips out of her mouth and glides nervously across her lips before it disappears again. I slide my hand from her chin to the nape of her neck and I pull her forward until our lips meet.

And holy shit, do they meet. Our mouths meld together like they used to be in love and they're just now seeing each other for the first time in years. My stomach feels like it's in the middle of a damn rave and my brain is trying to remember how to do this. It's like I suddenly forgot how to kiss, even though it's only been a day since I broke up with Val. I'm pretty sure I kissed Val yesterday, but for some reason my brain is acting like this is all new and it's telling me I should be parting my lips or teasing her tongue, but the signals just aren't making it to my mouth yet. Or my mouth is just ignoring me because it's been paralyzed by the soft warmth pressed against it.

I don't know what it is, but I've never held a girl's lips between mine for this long without breathing or moving or taking the kiss as far as I can possibly take it.

I inhale, even though I haven't taken a breath in almost a minute. I loosen my grip on the back of Six's head and begin to slowly pull my lips from hers. I open my eyes and hers are still closed. Her lips haven't moved and she's taking in shallow, quiet breaths as I remain poised close to her face, watching her.

I don't know if she expected more of a kiss. I don't know if she's ever had a peck last more than a minute before. I don't know what she's thinking, but I love the look on her face.

"Don't open your eyes," I whisper, still staring at her. "Give me ten more seconds to stare, because you look absolutely beautiful right now."

She tucks her bottom lip in with her teeth to hide her smile, but she doesn't move. My hand is still on the back of her head and I'm silently counting down from ten when I hear the waitress pause at our table.

"Y'all ready for your ticket?"

I hold up a finger, asking the waitress to give me a second. Well, five seconds to be exact. Six never moves a muscle, even after hearing the waitress speak. I count down silently until my ten seconds are up, then Six slowly opens her eyes and looks up at me.

I back away from her, putting several inches of space between us. I keep my eyes locked with hers. "Yes, please," I say, giving the waitress her answer. I hear her tear off the ticket and slap it down on the table. Six smiles, then begins laughing. She backs away from me and falls back down in her booth.

I breathe and it feels like the air is all brand new.

I slowly take my seat in the booth again, watching her laugh. She scoots the ticket toward me. "Your treat," she says.

I reach into my pocket and pull out my wallet, then lay cash down on top of the ticket. I stand up and reach out for Six's hand. She looks at it and smiles, then takes it. When she stands, I wrap my arm around her shoulder and pull her against me.

"Are you going to tell me how awesome that kiss was or are you going to ignore it?"

She shakes her head and laughs at me. "That wasn't even a real kiss," she says. "You didn't even try to put your tongue in my mouth."

I push open the doors to walk outside, but step aside and let her out first.

"I didn't have to put my tongue in your mouth," I say. "My kisses are that intense. I don't even really have to do anything. The only reason I pulled back was that I was sure we were about to experience a classic 'When Harry met Sally' moment."

She laughs again.

God, I love that she thinks I'm funny.

I open the passenger door for her and she pauses before climbing inside. She looks up at me. "You realize that classic scene is Sally proving a point about how easy it is for women to fake orgasms, right?"

God, I love that I think she's funny.

"Do I have to take you home yet?" I ask.

"Depends on what you have in mind next."

"Nothing really," I admit. "I just don't want to take you home yet. We could go to the park next to my house. They have a jungle gym."

She grins. "Let's do it," she says, holding up a tight fist in front of her.

I naturally bring my fist up and bump hers. She hops into the car and I shut her door, dumbfounded over the fact that she just fist bumped me.

The girl just fist bumped me and it was probably the hottest thing I've ever seen.

I walk to my side of the car and open the door, then take a seat. Before I crank the car I turn to look at her. "Are you really a guy?"

She raises an eyebrow, then pulls the collar of her shirt out and takes a quick glance down at her chest. "Nope. Pretty damn girl," she says.

"Are you dating someone?"

She shakes her head.

"Are you leaving the country tomorrow?"

"Nope," she says, her face obviously confused by my line of questions.

"What's your deal, then?"

"What do you mean?"

"Everyone has something and I can't figure yours out. You know, that one thing about themselves that's eventually a deal-breaker." I crank the car and begin to back out. "I want to know what yours is right now. My heart can't take another second of these tiny little things you do that drive me completely insane."

Her smile changes. It grows from a genuine smile to a guarded one. "We all have deal breakers, Daniel. Some of us just hope we can keep them hidden forever."

She rolls down her window again and the noise makes it impossible to continue the conversation. I'm almost positive the overwhelming scent of perfume is gone, so I'm curious if her need for the noise is why she rolled down the window this time.

•   •   •

"Do you bring all your dates here?" she asks.

I think about her question for a minute before answering. "Pretty much," I finally say after silently tallying the ends of all my dates. "I did take this chick out once in eleventh grade, but I took her home during the middle of the date because she got a stomach virus. I think she's the only one I never brought here."

She digs her heels into the dirt and comes to a stop in the swing. I'm standing behind her, so she turns around and looks up at me. "Seriously? You've brought all but one girl here?"

I shrug. Then nod. "Yeah. But none of them has ever wanted to literally *play* before. We usually just make out."

We've been here half an hour and already she's made me watch her on the monkey bars, push her on the merry-go-round and now I've been pushing her while she's been swinging for the last ten minutes. I'm not complaining, though. It's nice. Really nice.

"Have you ever had sex out here?" she asks.

I'm not sure how to take her bluntness. I've never really met anyone who asks the same straightforward questions I would, so I'm beginning to feel a little sympathetic to the people I put on the spot like this. I glance around the park until I see the makeshift wooden castle. I point to it. "You see the castle?"

She turns her head to look at the castle. "You had sex in there?"

I drop my arm and slide both my hands into the back pockets of my jeans. "Yep."

She stands and begins to walk in that direction.

"What are you doing?" I ask her. I'm not sure why she's heading toward the castle, but I'm almost positive it's not because she's weird and wants to have sex in the same spot I had sex with Val two weeks ago.

Does she?

God I hope not.

"I want to see where you had sex," she says, matter-of-fact. "Come show me."

This girl confuses the hell out of me. What's strange is how much I freaking love it. I begin jogging until I catch up with her. We walk until we reach the castle. She looks at me expectantly, so I point to the doorway. "Right in there," I say.

She walks to the doorway and peeks inside. She looks around for a minute, then pulls back out. "Looks really uncomfortable," she says.

"It was."

She smiles. "If I tell you something will you promise not to judge me?"

I roll my eyes. "It's human nature to judge."

She inhales a breath, then releases it. "I've had sex with six different people."

"At once?" I say.

She shoves my arm. "Stop. I'm trying to be honest with you here. I'm only eighteen and I lost my virginity when I was sixteen. Plus, I haven't had sex in about a year, so if you add it up, that's six people in just a little over fifteen months. That's like a whole new person every two and a half months. Only sluts do that."

"Why have you not had sex in over a year?"

She rolls her eyes and begins to walk past me. I follow her. When she reaches the swings, she takes her seat again. I sit in the swing beside her and twist my body until I'm facing her, but she faces forward.

"Why have you not had sex in over a year?" I say again. "You didn't like any of the boys you met in Italy?"

I can't see her face, but her body language reveals that this could be that *one thing*. The thing that changes it all for me.

"There was this one boy in Italy," she says softly. "But I don't want to talk about him. And yes, he's why I haven't had sex in over a year." She looks back at me. "Look, I know my reputation precedes me and I don't know if that's why you brought me here or what you expect to happen at the end of this date, but I'm not that girl anymore."

I lift my legs until my swing spins forward again. "The only thing I was hoping for at the end of this date was a kiss on your front porch," I say. "And maybe an accidental boob grab."

She doesn't laugh. I suddenly hate that I brought her here.

"Six, I didn't bring you here expecting anything. Yes, I've brought girls here in the past but that's only because I live across the street and I come here a lot. And yes, maybe I brought all those other girls here to have a little privacy while we made out, but that's only because I more than likely just wanted them to shut up and kiss me because they were getting on my everlasting nerves. But I only brought you here because I wasn't ready to take you home yet. I don't even really want to make out with you because I like talking to you too much."

I close my eyes, wishing I hadn't just said all that. I know girls like guys who play the uninterested asshole part. I'm usually pretty good at playing that part, but not with Six. Maybe because I usually am an uninterested asshole, but with her I'm as interested and curious and hopeful as I can possibly be.

"Which house is yours?" she asks.

I point across the street. "That one," I say, pointing to the one with the living room light on.

"Really?" she asks, sounding genuinely interested. "Is your family home?"

I nod. "Yeah, but you aren't meeting them. They're evil liars and I already told them I was never bringing you home to meet them."

I can feel her turn and look at me. "You told them you were never bringing me to meet them? So you already mentioned me?"

I meet her gaze. "Yes. I might have mentioned you."

She smiles. "Which one is your bedroom?"

"First window on the left side of the house. Chunk's bedroom is the window on the right. The one with the light on."

She stands up again. "Is your window unlocked? I want to see what your bedroom looks like."

Jesus, she's nosey.

"I don't want you to see my bedroom. I'm unprepared. It's messy."

She begins walking toward the street. "I'm going anyway."

I lean my head back and groan, then stand up and follow her toward the house.

"You're a piece of work," I say as we reach my window. She presses her palms against the glass and pushes up. The window doesn't budge, so I push her aside and open it for her. "I've never snuck into my own bedroom before," I admit. "I've snuck *out* before, but never in."

She begins to lift herself up over the ledge, so I grab her by the waist and assist her. She throws her leg over the edge of it and slips inside. I climb in behind her, then walk to the dresser and turn on my lamp. I make a scan of the room to ensure there isn't anything I don't want her to see. I kick a pair of underwear under the bed.

"I saw those," she whispers. She walks to my bed and presses her palms into the mattress, then straightens back up. She scans the room slowly, taking in everything about me. It feels weird, like I'm being exposed.

"I like your room," she says.

"It's a room."

She disagrees with a shake of her head. "No, it's more than that. This is where you live. This is where you sleep. This is where you feel the most privacy in your whole entire life. This is more than just a room."

"It doesn't feel very private right now," I say, watching as she skims her hand across every surface of my room. She turns and looks at me, then faces me full-on.

"What's the one thing in this room that tells the biggest secret about you?"

"I'm not telling you that."

She tilts her head. "So I'm right. You have secrets."

"I never said I didn't."

"Give me one," she asks. "Just one."

I'll give them all to her if she keeps looking at me like this. She's so damn adorable. I walk slowly toward her and she swallows a gulp of air. I stop when I'm several inches from her, then I nod my head down toward my mattress. "I've never kissed a girl on this bed," I whisper.

She looks down at my mattress, then back up to me. "I hope you really don't expect me to believe you've never made out with a girl in your room before."

"I didn't say that. I stated I had never kissed a girl on this particular bed. I was being honest, because it's a brand-new mattress. I just got it last week."

I can see the change in her eyes. The heavy rise and fall of her chest. She likes that I'm so close to her and she likes that I'm insinuating I want to kiss her on my bed.

Her eyes fall to the bed. "Are you saying you want to kiss me on your bed?"

I lean in closer until my lips are right next to her ear. "Are you saying you would let me?"

She sucks in a soft rush of air and I love that we're both feeling this. I want to kiss her on my bed so damn bad. I want it more than I even wanted the damn bed. Hell, I don't even care if it's on the bed. I just want to kiss her. I don't care where it is. I'll kiss her anywhere she'll allow me to kiss her.

I close the small gap between our bodies by resting my hands on her hips and pulling her to me. Her hands fly up to my forearms and she gasps. I dig my fingers into her hips and rest my cheek against hers. My mouth is still grazing her ear as I close my eyes, enjoying the feel of this.

I love the way she smells. I love the way she feels. And even though I haven't really given her an honest to God kiss yet, I already love the way she kisses.

"Daniel," she whispers. My name crashes against my shoulder when it rushes out of her mouth. "Will you take me home now?"

I wince at her words, immediately wondering what I just did wrong. I remain still for several long seconds, waiting until the feel of her against me no longer has me completely paralyzed.

"You didn't do anything wrong," she says, immediately easing the doubt building inside me. "I just think I should go home."

Her voice is soft and sweet and I suddenly hate every single guy in her past who has ever failed to get to know this side of her.

I don't release her immediately. I turn my head slightly until my forehead is touching the side of her head. "Did you love him?" I ask, allowing my brilliant brain to completely ruin this moment between us.

"Who?"

"The guy in Italy," I clarify. "The one who hurt you. Did you love him?"

Her forehead meets my shoulder and the way she fails to respond to that question reveals her answer, but it also fills me with so many more questions. I want to ask her if she still loves him. If she's still with him. If they still talk.

I don't say anything, though, because I have a feeling she wouldn't be here with me right now if any of that were the case. I bring my hand up to the back of her head and I press my lips into her hair. "Let's get you home," I whisper.

•   •   •

"Thanks for buying me dinner," she says when we reach her front door.

"You didn't really give me a choice. You left your house without a penny and then you shoved the bill in my face."

She laughs as she unlocks her front door, but doesn't open it yet. She turns back around and lifts her eyes, looking at me through lashes so long and thick, I have to refrain from reaching out and touching them.

Kissing her at dinner was definitely spontaneous, but I was sure it would make this moment a breeze.

It isn't.

If anything, I feel even more pressure to kiss her because it's already happened once tonight. And the fact that it's already happened and I know how damn good it feels makes me want it even more, but now I'm scared I've built it up too much.

I begin to lean in toward her when her lips part.

"Are you gonna use tongue this time?" she whispers.

I squeeze my eyes shut and take a step back, completely thrown off by her comment. I rub my palms down my face and groan.

"Dammit, Six. I was already feeling inadequate. Now you've just put expectations on it."

She's smiling when I look at her again. "Oh, there are definitely expectations," she says teasingly. "I expect this to be the most mind-blowing thing I've ever experienced, so you better deliver."

I sigh, wondering if the moment can possibly be recovered. I doubt it. "I'm not kissing you now."

She nods her head. "Yes you are."

I fold my arms over my chest. "No. I'm not. You just gave me performance anxiety."

She takes a step toward me and slides her hands between my folded arms, pushing against them until they unlock. "Daniel Wesley, you owe me a do-over since you made me kiss you in a crowded restaurant next to a dirty diaper."

"It wasn't crowded," I interject.

She glares at me. "Put your hands on my face and push me against this wall and slip me some tongue! Now!"

Before she can laugh at herself, my hands are casing her face and her back is pressed against the wall of her house and my lips are on hers. It happens so fast, it catches her off guard and she gasps, which causes her lips to part farther than she probably meant for them to. As soon as I caress the tip of her tongue with mine, she's clenching my shirt in two tight fists, pulling me closer. I tilt my head and take the kiss deeper, wanting to give her all the feels she can possibly get from a kiss and I want her to have them all at once.

My mouth isn't having a problem remembering what to do this time. What it's having a problem with is remembering how to slow down. Her hands are now in my hair and if she moans into my damn mouth one more time I'm afraid I might carry her to the backseat of my car and try to cheapen this date.

I can't do that. I can't, I can't, I can't. I like this girl too much already and I'll be damned if this isn't our first date and she already has me thinking about the next one. I brace my hands on the wall behind her head and I force myself to push off of her.

We're both panting. Gasping for breath. I'm breathing heavier than any kiss has ever made me breathe before. Her eyes are closed and I absolutely love how she doesn't immediately open them when I'm finished kissing her. I like that she seems to want to savor the way I make her feel, just like I want to savor her.

"Daniel," she whispers.

I groan and drop my forehead to hers, touching her cheek with my hand. "You make me love my name so damn much."

She opens her eyes and I pull back, looking down on her, still stroking her cheek. She's looking at me the same way I'm looking at her. Like we can't believe our luck.

"You better not turn out to be an asshole," she says quietly.

"And you better be done with that guy in Italy," I reply.

She nods. "I am," she says, although her eyes seem to tell a different story. I try not to read into it because whatever it is, it doesn't matter now. She's here with me. And she's happy about that. I can tell.

"You better not take back the girl who broke your heart last night," she adds.

I shake my head. "Never. Not after this. Not after you."

She seems relieved by my answer.

"This is scary," she whispers. "I've never had a boyfriend before. I don't know how this works. Do people become exclusive this fast? Are we supposed to pretend we're not that interested for a few more dates?"

Oh, dear God.

I've never been turned on by a girl laying claim to me before. I usually run in the other direction. She's obliterating every single thing I thought I knew about myself with every new sentence that passes those lips.

"I have no interest in faking disinterest," I say. "If you want to call yourself my girlfriend half as much as I wish you would, then it would save me a whole lot of begging. Because I was literally about to drop to my knees and beg you."

She squints her eyes playfully. "No begging. It screams desperation."

"You make me desperate," I say, pressing my lips to hers again. I choose to keep this kiss simple, even though I want to grab her face again and hold her against the wall. I pull away from her and we stare at each other. We stare at each other for so long I begin to worry that she's put some kind of spell on me, because I've never wanted to just stare at a girl like I want to stare at her. Just looking at her causes my heart to burn and my chest to constrict and I'm sort of freaking out that I barely know her at all and we've just made ourselves exclusive.

"Are you a witch?" I ask.

Her laugh returns and I suddenly don't care if she's a witch. If this is some kind of spell she's put on me, I hope it never breaks.

"I have no idea who you even are and now you're my damn girlfriend. What the hell have you done to me?"

She holds her palms up defensively. "Hey, don't blame me. I've gone eighteen years swearing off boyfriends and then you show up out of the blue with your vulgar mouth and terribly awkward first kisses and now look at me. I'm a hypocrite."

"I don't even know your phone number," I say.

"I don't even know your birthday," she says.

"You're the worst girlfriend I've ever had."

She laughs and I kiss her again. I notice I have to kiss her every time she laughs and she laughs a lot. Which means I have to kiss her a lot. God, I hope she doesn't laugh in front of Sky or Holder, because it's going to be so damn hard not to kiss her.

"You better not tell Sky about us," I say. "I don't want Holder to know yet."

"What about school? I enroll tomorrow. You don't think it'll be obvious when we interact?"

"We'll pretend we hate each other. It could be fun."

She tilts her face up and finds my mouth again, giving me a light peck. "But how do you plan on keeping your hands off me?"

I slide my other hand to her waist. "I won't keep my hands off you. I'll just touch you when they aren't looking."

"This is gonna be so much fun," she whispers.

I smile and pull her against me again. "Damn right it is." I dip my head and kiss her one last time. I release her, then reach behind her and turn the doorknob, pushing open her front door. "See you tomorrow."

She backs up two steps until she's in her doorway. "See you tomorrow."

She begins to turn and head into her house, but I grab her wrist and pull her back out. I wrap an arm around her lower back and lean in until my lips touch hers. "I forgot to accidentally touch your boob."

I catch her laugh with my mouth and graze her breast with the palm of my hand, then I immediately pull away from her. "Oops. Sorry."

She's covering her laugh with her hand as she backs into her house. She closes the door and I immediately fall to my knees, then onto my back. I stare straight up at the roof of her porch, wondering what in the hell just happened to my heart.

The door slowly reopens and she looks down at me, sprawled across her front porch like an idiot.

"I just needed a minute to recover," I say, smiling up at her. I'm not even excusing the fact that I'm shamelessly affected by her. She winks, then begins to close the door.

"Six, wait," I say, pushing myself up. She opens the door again and I reach up and grab the doorframe, then lean in toward her. "I know I just broke up with someone last night, but I need you to know you aren't a rebound. You know that, right?"

She nods. "I know," she says confidently. "Neither are you."

With that, she steps back into her house and closes her door.

Christ.

Motherfucking angel.

Chapter Three

"Let's go!" I tell Chunk for the fifth time.

She grabs her backpack and groans, then stands up and pushes her chair in. "What's your freakin' deal, Daniel? You're never in a hurry to get to school." She downs the rest of her orange juice. I'm standing at the door where I've been standing for five minutes, ready to leave. I hold open the front door and follow her outside.

Once we're in the car I don't even wait for her to shut her door before I'm putting it in reverse.

"Seriously, why are you in such a hurry?" she asks.

"I'm not in a hurry," I say defensively. "You were just being really slow."

The last thing she needs to know is how utterly pathetic I am. So pathetic I've been awake for two hours now, waiting until we could leave. I probably won't even see Six until lunch if we don't have classes together, so I really don't know why I'm in a hurry.

I didn't think about that. I hope we *do* have classes together.

"How was your date last night?" Chunk asks as she puts on her seatbelt.

"Good," I say.

"Did you kiss her?"

"Yep."

"Do you like her?"

"Yep."

"What's her name?"

"Six."

"No, really. What's her name?"

"*Six.*"

"No, not whatever nickname you gave her. What does everyone else call her?"

I roll my head and look at her. "Six. They call her Six."

Chunk scrunches up her nose. "Weird."

"It fits her."

"Do you love her?"

"Nope."

"Do you want to?"

"Ye—"

Whoa.

Hold up.

Do I want to?

I don't know. Maybe. Yes? Shit. I don't know. How screwed up is it that I broke up with a girl two days ago and I'm already contemplating the possibility of loving someone else?

Well, technically, I don't think I really loved Val. I sort of thought I did on occasion, but I think if a person is really, truly in love then it has to be unconditional. How I felt about Val was definitely not unconditional. I had conditions for every single feeling I had about her. Hell, the only reason I ever asked her out in the first place is that for about fifteen seconds, I thought she was Cinderella.

After that experience in the closet last year, that mystery girl was all I could think about. I looked for her everywhere, even though I had no idea what she looked like. I was pretty sure she had blonde hair, but it was dark, so I could have been wrong. I listened to every single girl's voice I walked past to see if they sounded like her. The problem was, they *all* sounded like her. It's hard to memorize a voice when you don't have a face to back it up with, so I would always find small things that reminded me of her in every girl I spoke to.

With Val, I actually convinced myself she was Cinderella. I was walking past her in the hallway one afternoon on my way to history class. I'd seen her in the past but never paid much attention because she seemed a little high-maintenance for me. I accidentally bumped her shoulder when I passed her because my head was turned and I was talking to someone else. She called out after me, "Watch it, kid."

I froze in my tracks. I was too scared to turn around because hearing her use the term "kid" had me convinced I was about to come face to face with the girl from the closet. When I finally gained the courage to turn around, I was floored by how hot she was. I always hoped if I ever found out who Cinderella was that I'd be attracted to her. But Val was way hotter than how I'd been fantasizing.

I walked back up to her and made her repeat what she said. She looked shocked, but she repeated it anyway. When the words fell from her mouth again, I immediately leaned forward and kissed her. As soon as I kissed her I knew she wasn't Cinderella. Her mouth was different. Not *bad* different, just different. When I pulled back after realizing it wasn't her, I was a little annoyed with myself for not just letting it go. I was never going to find out who the girl was, so there was no point in dwelling on it. Plus, Val really was hot. I forced myself to ask her out that day and thus began "the relationship."

"You just passed my school," Chunk says.

I slam on the brakes when I realize she's right. I kick the car into reverse and back up, then pull over to let her out. She looks out the passenger window and sighs.

"Daniel, we're so early there isn't even anyone else here yet."

I lean forward and look out her window, scanning the school. "Not true," I say, pointing to someone pulling into a parking spot. "There's someone."

She shakes her head. "That's the maintenance guy. I beat the freaking maintenance guy to school." She opens her door and steps out, then turns and leans into the car before shutting her door. "Do I need to plan for you to be here to pick me up an hour early, too? Is your brain stuck in eastern time today?"

I ignore her comment and she shuts the door, then I hit the gas and drive toward my school.

•   •   •

I don't know what kind of car she drives, so I pull into my usual spot and wait. There are a few other cars here, including Sky and Holder's, but I know they're at the track running like they do every morning.

I can't believe I don't know what kind of car she drives. I also still don't know her phone number. Or her birthday. Or her favorite color or what she wants to be when she's older or why the hell she chose Italy for her foreign exchange or what her parents' names are or what kind of food she eats.

My palms begin to sweat, so I wipe them on my jeans, then grip my steering wheel. What if she's really annoying around other people? What if she's a junkie? What if . . .

"Hey."

Her voice breaks me out of my near–panic attack. It also calms me the hell down because as soon as I see her sliding into the front seat of my car, my unjustified fears are replaced by pure relief.

"Hey."

She shuts her door and pulls her leg up, turning to face me in the car. She smells so good. She doesn't smell like perfume at all. She just smells good. Kind of fruity.

"Have you had your panic attack yet?" she asks.

Confusion clouds my face. I don't have time to answer her before she begins talking again.

"I had one this morning," she says, looking at everything else around us, unable to make eye contact with me. "I just keep thinking we're idiots. Like maybe this connection we think we have is all in our heads and we didn't really have as much fun as we thought we did last night. I don't even know you, Daniel. I don't know your birthday, your middle name, Chunk's real name, if you have any pets, what your major will be in college. I know it's not like we made this huge commitment or got married or had sex, but you have to understand that I have never thought the idea of having a boyfriend was even remotely appealing and maybe I still don't think it's all that appealing, but . . ."

She finally looks at me and makes eye contact. "But you're so funny and this entire past year has been the worst year of my life and for some reason when I'm with you it feels good. Even though I hardly know you, the parts of you I do know I really, really like." She leans her head into the headrest and sighs. "And you're cute. Really cute. I like staring at you."

I turn in my seat and mirror her position by resting my head against my own headrest. "Are you finished?"

She nods.

"I had my panic attack right before you got in the car just now. But when you opened your door and I heard your voice, it went away. I think I'm good now."

She smiles. "That's good."

I smile back at her and we both just stare at each other for several seconds. I want to kiss her, but I also kind of like just staring at her. I would hold her hand, but she's running her fingers up and down the seam of the passenger seat and I like watching her do that.

"I should go inside and register for classes now," she says.

"Make sure you get second lunch."

She nods. "I can't wait to pretend I hate you today."

"I can't wait to pretend I hate you more."

I can tell she's about to turn, so I lean forward and slip my hand behind her neck, then pull her to me. I kiss her good morning, hello and good-bye all at once. When I pull back, I glance over her shoulder and see Sky and Holder making their way off the track and toward the parking lot.

"Shit!" I push her head down between us. "They're coming this way."

"Crap," she whispers.

She begins humming the theme to *Mission Impossible* and I start laughing. I start to crouch down with her, but if they reach my car they'll see us whether our heads are down or not.

"I'll get out of the car so they don't come over here."

"Good idea," she says, her voice muffled by her arms. "I think you just gave me whiplash."

I lean over and kiss the back of her head. "Sorry. I'll see you later. Lock my doors when you get out."

I open the car door just as Holder begins to head in my direction. I start walking their way to intercept them. "Good run?" I ask when I reach them.

They both nod, out of breath. "I need my change of clothes," Sky says to Holder, pointing to her car. "Want me to grab yours?" Holder nods and she heads in that direction. Holder's eyes move from hers over to mine.

"Why are you here so early?" he asks. He doesn't ask it like he's accusing me of anything. He's probably just making small talk, but I already feel defensive.

"Chunk had to be at school early," I say.

He nods and grabs the hem of his shirt, then wipes sweat off his forehead. "You still coming tonight?"

I think about his question. I think really hard, but I'm drawing a blank about what could be going on tonight that I would need to go to.

"Daniel, do you even know what the hell I'm talking about?"

I shake my head. "No idea," I admit.

"Dinner at Sky's house. Karen invited you and Val? They're having a big welcome-back thing for Sky's best friend."

That gets my attention. "Yeah, of course I'll be there. Not bringing Val, though. We broke up, remember?"

"Yeah, but dinner is still ten hours away. You might love her again by then."

Sky walks up and hands Holder his bag. "Daniel, have you seen Six?"

"No," I immediately blurt out.

Sky glances toward the school, not having noticed the defensiveness in my immediate response. "She must be registering for classes inside." She turns to Holder. "I'm gonna go find her." She reaches up and kisses him on the cheek, but Holder's eyes remain on mine.

They're narrowed.

This isn't good.

Sky walks away and I begin to walk right behind her, toward the school. Holder's hand lands on my shoulder when I pass him, so I pause. I turn around, but it takes me a few seconds to look him in the eyes. When I do, he doesn't look happy.

"Daniel?"

I raise an eyebrow to match his expression. "Holder?"

"What are you up to?"

"I do not know what you are talking about," I reply innocently.

"You do know what I am talking about because when you are lying, you do not use contractions when you speak."

I ponder his observation for a few seconds. *Is that true?*

Shit. It's true.

I breathe out a heavy breath and do my best to look like I'm giving him a confession. "Fine," I say, kicking at the dirt beneath my feet. "I had sex with Val just now. In my car. I didn't want you to know because you and Sky seemed excited that we broke up."

Tension releases from Holder's shoulders and he shakes his head. "Dude, I could care less who you date. You know that." He begins walking toward the school, so I follow suit. "Unless it's Six," he adds. "You aren't allowed to date Six."

I keep walking forward, even though that comment makes me want to freeze. "I have no desire to date Six," I say. "She's not really that cute, anyway."

He stops in his tracks and spins around to face me. He holds up a finger like he's about to lecture me. "You're not allowed to talk shit about her, either."

Christ. Hiding our relationship from him may be more exhausting than it is fun. "No loving her, no hating her, no screwing her, no dating her. Got it. Anything else you want to add?"

He thinks for a second, then lowers his arm. "Nope. That covers it. See you at lunch." He turns and walks inside. I glance back to the parking lot in time to see Six sneaking out of my car. She gives me a quick wave. I wave back, then turn and head inside.

•   •   •

I walk my tray toward the table and internally rejoice when I see the only available spot is right next to Six. She glances at me as I walk up and her eyes smile, but only briefly. I set my tray down across from Holder and find my way into the current conversation. Everyone is discussing the dinner at Sky's house tonight, but I've had dinner there before. Karen doesn't know what real food is. She's vegan, so I normally turn down meals at their house. Not tonight, though.

"Will there be meat?" I ask.

Sky nods. "Yeah. Jack's actually cooking, so the food should be good. I also baked a chocolate cake."

I reach across the table for the salt, even though I don't need it. It gives me an excuse to lean in ridiculously close to Six.

"So, Six. How do you like your classes?" I ask casually.

She shrugs. "They're okay."

"Let me see your schedule."

She narrows her eyes like I'm doing something wrong. I give her a look to let her know she has nothing to worry about. Even if I wasn't into her, I'm not an asshole. I'd still be making conversation with her.

"It sucks we don't have any classes together," Sky says. "Who do you have for history?"

Six pulls her schedule out of her pocket and hands it to me. I open it and make a quick scan of the classes, but none are the same as mine. "Carson for history," I say, replying to Sky's question. I hand Six back her schedule and give her a look to let her know we don't have any classes together. She looks bummed, but says nothing.

"Can you speak Italian very well?" Breckin asks Six.

"Not well at all. I speak better Spanish than I do Italian. I chose Italy because I had enough funding and I'd rather have spent half a year there than in Mexico."

"Good choice," Breckin says. "The men are hotter in Italy."

Six nods. "Yes they are," she says appreciatively.

I immediately lose my appetite and drop my fork onto my plate. It makes a loud clanking noise, so naturally everyone turns to look at me. It's quiet and awkward and everyone is still staring, so I say the first thing on my mind. "Italian men are too hairy."

Sky and Breckin laugh, but Six purses her lips together and looks back down at her plate.

God, I suck at this.

Luckily, Val walks up and takes everyone's attention off me.

Wait. Did I just say luckily? Because Val walking up is *not* a good thing.

"Can I talk to you?" she says, glaring down at me.

"Do I have a choice?"

"Hallway," she says, spinning on her heels. She heads toward the exit to the cafeteria.

"Do us all a favor and go see what Val wants," Sky says. "If you don't meet her out there she'll come back to the table."

"*Please*," Breckin mutters.

I'm watching all their reactions and I don't know if they've always reacted this way when it comes to Val or if I'm only recognizing it for the first time because I finally have clarity.

"Why is everyone referring to Tessa Maynard as *Val?*" Six asks, confused.

Breckin points over his shoulder in the direction Val walked off in. "Tessa is Val. Val is Tessa. Daniel can't seem to call anyone by their actual name, if you haven't noticed."

I watch as Six inhales a slow breath, then looks directly at me. She looks really disgusted. "Your girlfriend is Tessa Maynard? You have sex with Tessa Maynard?"

"*Ex*-girlfriend and *had* sex," I clarify. "And yes. Probably coincided with the same time you were falling in love with a hairy Italian."

Six's eyes narrow, then she quickly looks away. I instantly feel bad for what I said, but I was only kidding. Sort of. We're *supposed* to be mean to each other. I can't tell if I really hurt her feelings or if she's just a really good actress.

I sigh, then stand up and head toward the cafeteria doors in a hurry so I can get back to the table and somehow make sure Six really isn't pissed at me.

I make it out to the hallway and Val is standing right outside the cafeteria doors. "I'll take you back under one condition," she says.

I'm curious what the condition is, but it doesn't really matter at this point.

"Not interested."

Her mouth literally drops open. It's not even that cute a mouth now that I'm looking at it. I don't know how I fell for it all those other times.

"I'm serious, Daniel," she says firmly. "If you screw up one more time, I'm done."

I let my head fall backward until I'm looking up at the ceiling. "Jesus, Tessa," I say. She's not really worthy of my nicknames anymore. I look her in the eyes again. "I don't want you to take me back. I don't want to date you. I don't even want to make out with you. You're mean."

She scoffs, but stands frozen. "Are you serious?" she says, dumbfounded.

"Serious. Positive. Convinced. Enlightened. Take your pick."

She throws her hands up in the air and spins around, then walks back into the cafeteria. I walk to the doors and open them. Six is staring at me from our table, so I make a quick glance around at the rest of the group. No one is paying attention, so I motion for her to come out into the hallway. She takes a quick drink of her water, then stands, making up an excuse to the rest of the table. I step out of view while she makes her way to the exit. When the doors open I immediately grab her by the wrist and pull her until we reach the lockers. I push her against them and crash my mouth to hers. Her hands immediately fly up to my hair and we rush our kisses like we might get caught.

And we really might.

After a good solid minute, she pushes lightly against my chest, so I pull away from her.

"Are you mad?" I ask her, almost blurting out the question between heavy breaths.

"No," she says, shaking her head. "Why would I be mad?"

"Because Val is Tessa and you obviously don't like Tessa very much and because I had a jealous moment and called Italian men hairy."

She laughs. "We're acting, Daniel. I was actually a little impressed. And kind of turned on when you got jealous. But highly *un*impressed with the fact that Val is Tessa. I can't believe you had sex with Tessa Maynard."

"I can't believe you had sex with pretty much everyone else," I reply teasingly.

She grins. "You're a jerk."

"You're a slut."

"Will you be at my dinner tonight?" she asks.

"That's a really dumb question."

A smile spreads slowly across her face and it's so damn sexy I have to kiss her again.

"I should get back," she whispers when I pull away.

"Yes, you should. So should I."

"You first. I'm supposed to be in the administration office clearing up an issue with my schedule."

"Okay," I say. "I'll go first, but I'll miss you until you get back to the table."

"Don't make me puke," she says.

"I bet you're adorable when you puke. I bet your actual puke is even adorable. It's probably bubble-gum pink."

"You're seriously disgusting." She laughs and reaches up to kiss me again. She pushes against my chest, then slips out from between me and the locker. She puts both of her hands on my back and pushes me toward the cafeteria doors. "Act natural."

I turn and wink at her, then walk back through the doors. I casually make my way back to the table and take a seat.

"Where's Six?" Breckin asks.

I shrug. "How should I know? I was busy making out with Val in the hallway."

Sky shakes her head and lays her fork down. "I just lost my appetite, Daniel. Thanks."

"You'll have your appetite back by dinner tonight," I say.

Sky shakes her head. "Not with you and Val there. You'll probably be sucking face next to my food. If you drool on my chocolate cake you aren't getting any."

"Sorry, Cheese Tits," I say. "But Val won't be at your dinner tonight. I'll be there, though."

"I bet you will," Breckin says under his breath.

I glance over at him and he looks at me challengingly.

"What'd you just mumble, Powder Puff?" He absolutely hates it when I call him Powder Puff, but he should know I only give nicknames to the people I like. I think he does know that, though, because he doesn't really give me too much shit about it.

"I said I bet you will," he repeats louder this time. He turns to Sky, who is seated right next to him. "Six, right?"

Sky nods. "Six or six-thirty."

"I'll be there at six," Breckin says. He looks back at me and smirks. "I bet you'll be there at six, too, right, Daniel? You like six? Is six good for you?"

He's on to us. Fucker.

"Six is perfect," I say, holding his stare. "My absolute favorite time of day."

He smiles knowingly, but I'm not worried. I have a feeling he's going to have just as much fun with this as I am.

"All cleared up?" Sky asks Six when she returns to the table. Six nods and takes her seat. Her hand brushes across my outer thigh when she adjusts herself. I press my knee against hers and we both pick our forks up at the same time and take a bite of food.

Having her here just inches from me and not being allowed to touch her is complete torture. I'm beginning to think I'd rather just lean over and kiss her and take Holder's ass beating than have to pretend I don't want her.

Since the moment she disappeared into her house last night I've felt more restless than I've ever felt before. I've been fidgeting all day. I can't stop tapping my fingers and shaking my leg. It feels like I want to scratch at my skin when she's not around, like I'm coming down from a high.

That's exactly what this feels like. Like she's a drug I've become immediately addicted to, but I have none in supply. The only thing that satiates the craving is her laugh. Or her smile or her kiss or the feel of her pressed against me.

God, it's so hard not to touch her. So hard.

She begins laughing loudly at something Sky said and the craving becomes almost intolerable because of the intense need I have to catch that sound with my mouth.

I drop my fork onto my plate and lower my head into my hands and groan. "Stop laughing," I say quietly.

She's obviously laughing too loud to hear me, so I turn toward her and say it again. "Six. Stop laughing. Please."

Her jaw clamps shut and she turns to look at me. "Excuse me?"

About that same time, Holder kicks the shit out of my knee. I scoot back and immediately pull my leg up and rub the spot he kicked. "What the hell, man?"

Holder looks at me like I'm clueless. "What the hell is wrong with you? I told you not to be mean to her."

Ha. He thinks I'm being mean? If he only knew how nice I want to be to her right now.

"You don't like my laugh?" Six says. I can tell in her voice she knows how much I like her laugh, but she's enjoying the fact that Holder is clueless to what her laugh does to me.

"No," I grumble, scooting back toward the table.

She laughs again and the sound of it causes me to wince.

"Are you always this grumpy?" she asks. "Do you want me to go get your girlfriend and bring her back to the table so she can put you in a better mood?"

"No!" Sky and Breckin yell in unison.

I look at Six. "You think my girlfriend could put me in a better mood?"

She grins. "I think your *girlfriend* is a pathetic idiot for agreeing to date you."

I shake my head. "My girlfriend makes incredibly wise decisions. I can't wait until tonight when I get to show her just how smart she was when she decided to lay claim to me."

"I thought you said she wasn't coming to dinner," Sky says, disappointed.

Six's hand slips under the table and she begins to gently rub at the spot on my knee that Holder just finished kicking.

"Jesus Christ," I mutter, leaning forward. I put my elbows on the table and run my hands up and down my face, attempting to appear unaffected by the fact that it feels like Six just crawled her way inside my chest and is wrapping herself around my heart.

"Is lunch over yet?" I say to no one in particular. "I need to get out of here."

Holder looks at his phone. "Five more minutes." He looks back up at me. "Are you sick, Daniel? You're not being yourself today. It's starting to freak me out a little bit."

Six's hand is still on my knee. I casually lower my hand and slide it under the table, then place it over hers. She flips her hand over and I lace our fingers together and squeeze her hand.

"I know," I say to Holder. "I'm just having a weird day. Girlfriends. They have that effect on you."

He's still looking at me suspiciously. "You seriously need to make up your mind when it comes to her. It's past the point that any of us feel sorry for you, because now it's just irritating."

"Doesn't help that she used to be a slut," Six says.

"Six!" Sky says with a laugh. "That was so mean."

Six shrugs. "It's true. Daniel's girlfriend used to be a big, fat slut. I heard she had sex with six different guys in just over a year."

"Don't talk about my girlfriend that way," I say. "Who gives a shit what she did in the past? I sure as hell don't."

Six squeezes my hand, then pulls hers away and brings her hand back up to the table. "Sorry," she says. "That wasn't nice. If it helps, I heard she's a good kisser."

I grin. "*Phenomenal* kisser."

The bell rings and everyone picks up their trays. I notice Six isn't in any hurry, so I take my time as well. Sky kisses Holder on the cheek, then walks off with Breckin toward the exit. Holder picks up both their trays and lifts his eyes to mine. "I'll see you tonight," he says. "And I hope to hell the real Daniel shows up, because you aren't making a whole lot of sense today."

"I know," I say, pointing briefly at my head. "She's got me all screwed up in here, man. All screwed up. I'm losing my mind."

Holder shakes his head. "That right there is exactly what I'm talking about. You seem more affected by Val today than you ever have. It's just weird." He walks off, still looking confused. I feel sort of bad for lying to him, but it's his own fault. He shouldn't try to tell me who I can date, then I wouldn't have to hide it from him.

"That was fun," Six says quietly. She begins to pick up her tray, but I intercept it. I take a step toward her and look her hard in the eyes.

"Don't you ever insult my girlfriend again. You hear me?"

She tightens her lips to hide her smile. "Noted."

"I want to walk you to your locker. Wait for me."

Her smile becomes harder for her to hide as she nods her head. I take both of our trays and place them on the tray pile, then walk back to the table. I glance around us and don't really see anyone paying attention, so I quickly lean in and kiss her briefly on the lips, then pull away.

"Daniel Wesley, you're gonna get caught," she says with a grin. She turns and begins walking toward the exit, so I discreetly place a hand on her lower back and walk next to her.

"God, I hope so," I say. "If I have to sit through another lunch like that, I'll lose my shit and you'll end up on your back on top of the table."

She laughs. "What a way with words you have."

We exit the cafeteria and I walk her to her locker. It's on the opposite hall from mine, which couldn't be more inconvenient. We don't have a single class together and I won't even see her in the hallway while we're at school. I know I haven't even been dating her for an entire day, but I already miss her.

"Can I come over before dinner?" I ask her.

She shakes her head. "No, I'll be helping Karen and Sky prep. I'm going over there right after school."

"What about after dinner?"

She shakes her head again while she switches her books. "Sky crawls through my window every night. You can't be in my room."

"I thought your window was out of commission."

"Only to people with penises."

I laugh. "What if I told you I didn't have a penis?"

She glances at me. "I would probably rejoice. My experiences with people who have penises never end well."

I shake my head. "That's not something my penis wants to hear you say. He has a very sensitive ego."

She smiles and shuts her locker, then leans against it. "Well, maybe you should go home after school and stroke his ego a little bit until he feels better."

I cock an eyebrow. "You just made a masturbation joke."

She nods. "So I did."

"I have the coolest girlfriend in the world."

She nods again. "So you do."

"I'll see you at dinner."

"So you will," she says.

"Can we sneak off and make out while everyone's eating?"

She squints her eyes as if she's actually contemplating it. "Don't know. We'll play it by ear."

I nod and lean my shoulder against the locker next to hers. We're just a few inches apart and we're staring at each other again. I love how she looks at me like she actually enjoys staring at me.

"Give me your phone number," I say.

"As long as you aren't planning to text me pics of your ego stroking after school."

I clutch at my heart. "Dammit, Six. I love every single word that comes out of your mouth."

"Cock," she says dryly.

She's evil.

"Except that word," I say. "I don't love cock."

She laughs and opens her locker again. She takes out a pen, then turns and grabs my hand. She writes her phone number down, then puts the pen back in her locker. "I'll see you tonight, Daniel." She begins backing away. All I can do is nod, because I'm pretty sure her voice just hardcore made out with my ears. She turns and disappears down the hallway just as something appears in my line of sight.

I look to the eyes that are now glaring at me.

"What do you want, Powder Puff?" I ask him, pushing off the locker.

"You like her?"

"Who?" I ask, playing dumb. I don't know why I'm trying to play dumb. We both know who he's referring to.

"I think it's adorable," he says. "She likes you, too. I can tell."

"Really?"

"You're too easy. And yes, I don't know how, but I can tell she likes you. Y'all are cute. Why are you hiding it? Or better yet, who are you hiding it from?"

"Holder. He says I can't date her." I begin walking toward class and Breckin falls into step with me.

"Why not? Because you're an asshole?"

I stop and look at him. "I'm an asshole?"

Breckin nods. "Yeah. I thought you knew that."

I laugh, then start walking again. "He thinks it'll screw everything up since we're all best friends."

"He's right. It will."

I stop walking again. "Who's to say things won't work out with me and Six?"

"Didn't you just meet her? Like two days ago?"

"Doesn't matter," I say defensively. "She's different. I have a good feeling about her."

Breckin studies me for a moment, then he smiles. "This should be fun. I'll see you tonight." He turns and walks in the opposite direction, but he stops and faces me again. "Call me Powder Puff again and your secret is out."

"Okay, Powder Puff."

He laughs and points at me. "See? Such an *ass*hole."

He spins and heads toward his class. I pull my phone out of my pocket and open up Val's contact information. I hit delete, then add Six's number into my phone. I'll wait until I make it to my classroom before I text her.

Don't want to seem desperate.

Chapter Four

Me: Pretend you're going to the bathroom or something.

I place my phone back down on the table and begin eating again. I've been here almost an hour and Six and I have barely had a chance to talk. I don't know if I'll even need Breckin to out us, because I'm about to lose my patience and do it myself.

I know everyone's curious about her trip to Italy, but she seems uncomfortable talking about it. Her answers are short and clipped and I hate that I'm the only one who seems to notice how much she doesn't want to bring up Italy. I also like that I'm the only one who notices, because it proves that whatever connection I feel with her is more than likely genuine. I feel like I know her better than anyone else here. Maybe even better than Sky knows her.

Although it's absurd to feel that way, since I still don't even know her birthday.

Six: There's only one bathroom in the hallway. Even if I were to go there it would be obvious if you got up and followed me.

I read her text and groan out loud.

"Everything okay?" Jack asks. He's seated next to me at the table, which is fine any other time but I really wanted Six to be in his chair. I nod, then put my phone facedown on the table.

"Irritating girlfriend drama," I say.

He nods and turns back to Holder, continuing with their conversation. Six is involved in a discussion with Sky and Karen. Breckin ended up not being able to come, which was probably a good thing. Not sure I could have handled the fact that he knows.

Right now it's just me and my impatience having a silent war at the dinner table.

"That reminds me," Six says loudly. "I bought you all presents. I forgot." She scoots back from the table. "They're at my house. I'll be right back." She stands and takes two steps before turning back toward us. "Daniel? They're kind of heavy. Mind giving me a hand?"

Don't act too excited, Daniel.

I sigh heavily. "I guess," I say as I scoot back from the table. I look at Holder and roll my eyes, then follow Six outside. Neither of us says a word while we make our way to the side of the house. She reaches her window, then turns around.

"I lied," she says. Her eyes are worried, which causes me to worry. "About what?"

She shakes her head. "I didn't buy anyone presents. I just can't take another second of all the questions, and then seeing you across the table and knowing how much I just wish it could be the two of us is making this whole dinner really irritating. But now I don't have presents. How do I go back in there without presents?"

I try not to laugh, but I love that she's been just as irritated as I've been. I was starting to worry I might have a few issues.

"We could just stay out here and never go back inside."

"We could," she says in agreement. "But they'd eventually come look for us. Not to mention it would be rude, since Jack and Karen went through all this trouble to cook for me and oh, my God, what if it's true, Daniel?"

I don't know if it's me or if she's just really difficult to keep up with, but I have no idea what she's talking about. "What if what's true?"

She exhales a quick breath. "What if our feelings are just reverse psychology? What if Holder had told you to date me Saturday night? You might not have been interested in me after that. What if the only reason we like each other so much is that it's forbidden? What if the second they all find out the truth, we can't stand each other?"

I hate that the worry in her voice sounds genuine, because that means she actually believes the shit she's saying right now.

"You think there's a chance I only like you because I'm not supposed to like you?"

She nods.

I grab her hand and yank her back toward the front of the house.

"Daniel, I don't have presents!"

I ignore her and walk her up the front steps, open the door, and march her straight into the kitchen.

"Hey!" I yell. Everyone turns around and looks at us. I glance at Six and her eyes are wide. I inhale a deep breath, then turn back to the table. Specifically to Holder.

"She fist bumped me," I say, pointing at Six. "It's not my fault. She hates purses and she fist bumped me, then she made me push her on the damn merry-go-round. After that, she demanded to see where I had sex in the park, then she forced me to sneak into my own bedroom. She's weird and half the time I can't keep up with her, but she thinks I'm funny as hell. And Chunk asked me this morning if I wanted to love her someday, and I realized I've never hoped I could love someone more than I want to love her. So every single one of you who has an issue with us dating is going to have to get over it because . . ." I pause and turn toward Six. "Because you fist bumped me and I could care less who knows we're together. I'm not going anywhere and I don't want to go anywhere so stop thinking I'm into you because I'm not supposed to be into you." I lift my hands and tilt her face toward mine. "I'm into you because you're awesome. And because you let me accidentally touch your boob."

She's smiling wider than I've ever seen her smile. "Daniel Wesley, where'd you learn those smooth moves?"

"Not moves, Six. Charisma."

She throws her arms around my neck and kisses me. I wait for the moment Holder yanks me away from her, but that moment doesn't come. We kiss for a solid thirty seconds before people begin clearing their throats. When Six pulls away from me, she's still smiling.

"Does it feel different now that they know?" I ask her. "Because it actually feels better to me."

She shoves my chest. "Stop! Stop saying things that make me grin like an idiot. My face has been hurting since the second I met you."

I pull her to me and hug her, then suddenly become aware that we're still standing in Sky's kitchen and everyone is still staring at us. I hesitantly turn and look at Holder to gauge his level of anger. He's never actually hit me before, but I've seen what he can do and I sure as hell don't want to experience it.

When my eyes meet his, he's . . . smiling. He's actually smiling.

Sky has a napkin to her eyes and she's wiping tears away.

Karen and Jack are both smiling.

It's weird.

Too weird.

"Do you guys talk to my parents?" I ask cautiously. "Did they teach you their dirty reverse psychology tricks?"

Karen is the first to speak. "Sit down, you two. Your food is getting cold."

I kiss Six on the forehead, then take my seat back at the table. I keep glancing at Holder, but he doesn't look upset at all. He actually looks a little impressed.

"Where the hell is my present?" Jack asks Six.

She clears her throat. "I decided to wait until Christmas." She picks up her glass and brings it to her lips, then glances at me. I smile at her.

Everyone else resumes whatever conversations were going on before my interruption. It's like no one is even that shocked. They act like it's completely normal. Like it's a natural thing . . . me and Six.

And I totally get it, because it is. Whatever we have is good, and even though I still don't know her birthday, I know this is right. And based on the look on her face right now, so does she.

•　　•　　•

"I really like this one," I say, looking at the picture in my hands. I'm leaning against the wall, sitting on the floor in Sky's bedroom. Six is passing around pictures she took in Italy to Sky, Holder, and me.

"Which pic are you looking at?" she says. She's lying next to me on the floor. I look down at her and flip the photo over so she can see it. She shakes her head with a quick roll of her eyes. "You only like that one because my cleavage looks great."

I immediately turn the photo back around. She's right. It does look great. But that's not at all why I liked it at first. She looks happy in this one. Peaceful.

"I took that picture the day I got to Italy," she says. "You can keep it."

"Thank you. I wasn't planning on giving it back to you, anyway."

"Consider it an anniversary present," she says.

I immediately look down at the time on my phone. "Oh. Wow. It really is our anniversary." I readjust myself until I'm leaning over her. "I almost forgot. I'm the worst boyfriend ever. I can't believe you haven't dumped me yet."

She grins. "That's okay. You can remember the next one." She slips her hand to the back of my neck and pulls me forward until our lips meet.

"*Anniversary?*" Sky says, confused. "Exactly how long have the two of you been dating?"

I pull away from Six and sit back up against the wall. "Precisely twenty-four hours."

An awkward silence follows, then of course Holder fills it. "Am I the only one who has a bad feeling about this?"

"I think it's great," Sky says. "I've never seen Six so . . . nice? Happy? Spoken for? It's a good look for her."

Six sits up and wraps her arms around my neck, then pulls me to the floor with her. "That's because I've never met anyone as vulgar and inappropriate and horrible at first kisses as Daniel." She pulls my mouth to hers and kisses me while she laughs at herself.

This is a first. A kiss and a laugh at the same time? I think I might be in heaven.

"Six has a bedroom, too, you know," Holder says.

Six stops laughing. *And* she stops kissing me.

Holder is about to be put on my shit list.

"Six doesn't allow penises in her bedroom," I reply to him while still staring down at her.

Six moves her mouth to my ear. "As long as you don't expect me to stroke his ego tonight, I kind of want to kiss you on my bed."

I didn't know people could move as fast as I'm moving right now. This has to be some sort of record, because my hands are under her back and knees and I'm scooping her up in my arms before her sentence even completely registers. She throws her arms around my neck and squeals as I head straight for Sky's window. I put her down gently, but then practically shove her outside. I begin to follow right behind her without even telling Sky or Holder good-bye.

"They are so strange together," I hear Sky say right before I'm out the window.

"Yeah," Holder says in agreement. "But also oddly . . . *right*."

I pause.

Did Holder just compliment my relationship with Six? I don't know why I always want his approval so much, but hearing him say that fills me with this weird sense of pride. I turn around and take a step back to the window and lean inside. "I heard that."

He looks at the window and sees me leaning inside, so he rolls his eyes. "Go away," he says with a laugh.

"No. We're having a moment."

He cocks an eyebrow, but doesn't respond.

"You're my best friend, Holder."

Sky shakes her head and laughs, but Holder is still looking at me like I've lost my mind.

"For real," I say. "You're my best friend and I love you. I'm not ashamed to admit that I love a guy. I love you, Holder. Daniel Wesley loves Dean Holder. Always and forever."

"Daniel, go make out with your girlfriend," he says, waving me off.

I shake my head. "Not until you tell me you love me, too."

His head falls back against Sky's headboard. "I fucking love you, now GO AWAY!"

I grin. "I love you more."

He picks up a pillow and tosses it at the window. "Get the hell out of here, dipshit. "

I smile and back away from the window.

"You two are so strange together," Sky says to him.

I pull the window shut, then turn around to find Six. She's already in her bedroom, leaning out her window with her chin in her hands. She's grinning.

"Daniel and Holder, sittin' in a tree," she says in a singsong voice.

I walk toward her and improvise the next line of the song. "But then Daniel climbs down," I finish the rest of the sentence in a hurry, "and goes to Six's window and climbs inside her bedroom and throws her on the bed and kisses her until he can't take any more and has to go home and stroke his ego."

She's laughing and backing into her bedroom to make room for me to climb inside.

Once I'm inside, I look around and observe her room. I finally understand what she meant when she said my bedroom was more than just a room. This is like a secret glimpse into who Six really is. I feel like I could study this room and everything in it and find out everything I ever need to know about her.

Unfortunately, she's standing at the foot of her bed and she looks a little bit nervous and way more beautiful than I deserve, and I can't take my eyes off of her long enough to even study her bedroom.

I can't help but smile at her. I can already tell this is about to be the best anniversary I've ever had. The lights are off, so the mood is already perfect for making out. It's quiet, though. So quiet I can hear her breaths increase with each deliberately slow step I take toward her.

Shit. Maybe those are *my* breaths. I can't tell, because every inch closer I get requires an extra intake of air.

When I reach her, she's looking up at me with an odd mixture of peaceful anticipation. I want to push her onto the bed right now and climb on top of her and kiss the hell out of her.

I could do that, but why do the one thing she's expecting me to do?

I lean in slowly. Very slowly . . . until my mouth is so close to her neck she more than likely can't even tell if I'm touching her skin or not. "I have three questions I need to ask you before we do this," I say quietly, but very seriously. I pull back just far enough to see her gulp softly.

"Before we do what?" she asks hesitantly.

I lift a hand to the back of her head, then pull back from her neck and position my lips close to hers. "Before we do what we both want to do. Before I lean in one more inch. And before you part your lips for me just enough for me to steal a taste. Before I put my hands on your hips and back you up until you have nowhere to go but onto your bed."

I can feel her breath teasing my lips and it's so tempting I have to force myself to lean in to her ear again so I'm not so close to her mouth. "Before I slowly lower myself on top of you and our hands become curious and brave. Before my fingers slip under the hem of your shirt. Before my hand begins to explore its way up your stomach, and I discover I've never touched skin as soft as yours."

She gasps, then exhales a shaky breath and it's almost as sexy as the fist bump.

It may even be sexier.

"Before I finally get to touch your boob on *purpose*."

She laughs at that one, but her laugh is cut short when I press my thumb to the center of her lips.

"Before your breaths pick up pace and our bodies are aching because everything we're feeling is just making us want more and more and more of each other. Until I'm afraid I'll beg you not to ask me to slow down. So instead, I regrettably tear my mouth from yours and force myself away from your bed and you lift up unto your elbows and look at me, disappointed, because you kind of wished I would have kept going, but at the same time you're relieved I didn't, because you know you would have given in. So instead of giving in, we just stare. We watch each other silently as my heart rate begins to slow down and your breaths are easier to catch and the insatiable need is still there, but our minds are clearer now that I'm not pressed against you anymore. I turn around and walk to your window and leave without even saying good-bye, because we both know if either of us speaks . . . it'll be the collective demise of our willpower and we'll cave. We'll cave so hard."

I move my hand to her cheek. She whimpers and looks like she's about to collapse onto the bed, so I wrap my other arm around her lower back and pull her against me.

"So yeah . . . three questions first."

I let go of her and immediately turn around two seconds before I hear her fall onto her bed. I walk straight to the desk chair and take a seat, for two reasons. One, I want her to think I mean business and that everything I just said to her didn't affect me like it did her. And two, because I want her more than I've ever wanted anything and my knees were about to give out on me if I didn't sit down.

"Question number one," I say, watching her from across her room. She's lying on her back with her eyes closed and I hate that I'm not watching her up close right now. "When's your birthday?"

"October . . ." She clears her throat, obviously still recovering. "Thirty-first. Halloween."

How could the date of a birthday make me fall even harder for her? I have no idea, but it somehow does.

"Question number two. What's your favorite food?"

"Homemade mashed potatoes."

Never would have guessed that one. Glad I asked.

"Question number three," I say. "It's a big one. Are you ready?"

She nods, but keeps her eyes closed.

"What's the one thing in this room that tells the biggest secret about you?"

As soon as the question leaves my mouth, she's completely still. Her exaggerated breaths come to a halt. She remains motionless for almost a whole minute before she slowly pushes herself up until she's seated on the edge of the bed, facing me. "It has to be something inside this room?"

I nod slowly.

She lifts her hand and touches a finger to her heart, pointing at it. "This," she whispers. "My biggest secret is right in here."

Her eyes are moist and sad and somehow with that answer, the air instantly changes between us. In a dangerous way. A terrifying way. Because it feels like her air just became *my* air and I suddenly want to take in fewer breaths in order to ensure she never runs out.

I stand up and walk to the bed. Her eyes follow me closely until I'm directly in front of her. "Stand up."

She stands slowly.

I weave both hands through the locks of her hair until I'm holding the back of her head. I stare at her until my heart can't take anymore, then I press my lips to hers. I've lost count of how many times I've kissed her over the past day. Every time I kiss her, the feeling I get is like nothing I've ever experienced. The closest I've ever come to feeling this way is the day I was pretending to be in love with the girl in the closet. But even that day, the day I thought would surpass every day after it, doesn't come close to this.

Her mouth is warm and inviting and everything it always is when I kiss her, but it's also so much more. The fact that I have this reaction to her after one day scares the living shit out of me.

One day.

I've been doing this with her for one day and I have no idea what's happening. I don't know if it's a full moon or if I have a tumor wrapped around my heart or if she really is a witch. Whatever it is still doesn't explain how this kind of thing can exist between two people this ridiculously fast . . . and actually last.

I feel like deep down my heart knows she's too good to be true. My mind and my whole body know she's too good to be true, so I kiss her harder, hoping to convince myself that this is real. It's not some fairy tale. It's not an hour of make-believe.

This is reality, but even in our imperfect reality, people don't fall for each other like this. They don't develop feelings like this for someone they barely know.

The only thing my entire thought process is proving to me right now is how much I need to grab her tight and hang on, because wherever she goes, I want to go, too. And right now, she's going backward, down onto the bed. I'm easing myself on top of her in the same way I just told her this would happen. And we're kissing, just like I said we would, only this time it may just be a little more frantic and needy and holy *shit*.

Her skin.

It really is the softest skin I've ever touched.

I move my hand from her waist and inch my fingers underneath the hem of her shirt, then slowly begin to work my way to her stomach.

She pushes my hand away.

"Daniel."

She immediately lifts up and I immediately lift off her. She's breathing so heavily I catch myself holding my own breath, scared I'm hogging too much of her air.

She looks both regretful and embarrassed that she suddenly asked me to stop. I lift my hand and stroke her cheek reassuringly.

My eyes scroll over her features, taking in her nervous demeanor. She's afraid of what might happen between us. I can see on her face and in the way she's looking at me that she's just as scared as I am. Whatever this is between us, neither one of us was searching for it. Neither one of us knew it even existed. Neither one of us is even remotely prepared for it, but I know we both want it. She wants this to work with me as much as I want it to work with her and seeing the look in her eyes right now makes me believe that it will. I've never believed in anything like I believe in the possibility of the two of us.

I can tell by the way she's looking at me that if I tried to kiss her again, she'd let me. It's almost as if she's torn between the girl she used to be and the girl she is now and she's afraid if I try to kiss her again, she'll cave.

And I'm afraid if I don't get up and walk away, I'll let her.

We don't even have to speak. She doesn't even have to ask me to leave, because I know that's what I need to do. I nod, silently answering the question I don't want her to have to ask. I begin to ease off her bed and a silent *thank you* flashes in her eyes. I stand up, back away from her and climb out her window without a word. I walk a few feet until I reach the edge of her house, then I lean against it and slide down to the ground.

I lean my head back and close my eyes, attempting to figure out where I went right in my life to deserve her.

"What the hell are you doing?" Holder asks. I look up and he's halfway out Sky's window. Once he makes it all the way out, he turns and pulls her window shut.

"Recovering," I say. "I just needed a minute."

He walks toward me and takes a seat on the ground across from me, then leans against Sky's house. He pulls his legs up and rests his elbows on his knees.

"You're already leaving?" I ask him. "It's not even nine o'clock yet."

He reaches down to the ground and rips up a few blades of grass, then spins them between his fingers. "Got kicked out for the night. Karen walked in and my hand was up Sky's shirt. She didn't like that too much."

I laugh.

"So," he says, glancing back up at me. "You and Six, huh?"

Despite my effort not to smile, I do it anyway. I smile pathetically and nod. "I don't know what it is about her, Holder. I . . . she just . . . yeah."

"I know what you mean," he says quietly, looking back down at the grass between his fingers.

Neither one of us says anything else for several moments until he drops the blades of grass and wipes his hands on his jeans, preparing to stand up. "Well . . . I'm glad we had this talk, Daniel, but the fact that we already professed our mutual love for each other tonight is leaving me a little overwhelmed. I'll see you tomorrow." He stands up and begins walking toward his car.

"I love you, Holder!" I yell after him. "Best friends forever!"

He keeps walking forward, but lifts his hand in the air and flips me off.

It's almost as cool as a fist bump.

Chapter Five

"You're wrong," she says.

We're standing in my kitchen. Her back is pressed against the counter and I'm standing in front of her with my arms on either side of her. I catch her lips with mine and shut her up. It doesn't last long because she pushes my face away.

"I'm serious," she whispers. "I don't think they like me."

I bring a hand up and wrap it around the nape of her neck and look her directly in the eyes. "They like you. I promise."

"No we don't," my dad says as he makes his way into the kitchen. "We can't stand her. In fact, we hope you never bring her back." He refills his cup with ice, then walks back to the living room.

Six's eyes follow him as he exits the room, then she looks back up at me, wide-eyed.

"See?" I say with a smile. "They love you."

She points toward the living room. "But he just . . ."

My father's voice cuts her off when he walks back into the kitchen. "Kidding, Six," he says, laughing. "Inside joke. We actually like you a lot. I tried to give Danny-boy Grandma Wesley's ring earlier, but he says it's still too soon to make you a Wesley."

Six laughs at the same time she breathes a sigh of relief. "Yeah, maybe so. It's only been a month. I think we should wait at least two more weeks before we talk proposals."

My dad walks farther into the kitchen and leans against the counter across from us. I feel a little awkward standing so close to Six now, so I move next to her and lean against the bar.

"Did you come back in here so you could think of things to say that would embarrass me?" I ask. I know that's why he's standing here. I can see the glimmer in his eyes.

He takes a drink of his tea. He scrunches his nose up. "Nah," he says. "I would never do that, Danny-boy. I'm not the type of dad who would tell his son's girlfriend how he talks about her incessantly. I would also never tell my son's girlfriend that I'm proud of her for not having sex with him yet."

Holy shit. I groan and slap myself in the forehead. I should have known better than to bring her here.

"You talk to him about the fact that we haven't had sex?" Six says, completely embarrassed.

My father shakes his head. "No, he doesn't have to. I know because every night he comes home he goes straight to his bedroom and takes a thirty-minute shower. I was eighteen once."

Six covers her face with her hands. "Oh, my God." She peeks through her hands at my dad. "I guess I know who Daniel gets his personality from."

My father nods. "Tell me about it. His mother is terribly inappropriate."

Right on cue, my mother and Chunk walk through the front door with dinner. I glare at my father, then walk toward my mother and grab the pizza boxes out of her hands. She sets her purse down, walks over to Six, and gives her a quick hug.

"I'm sorry I didn't cook for you. Busy day today," she says.

"It's fine," Six replies. "Nothing like inappropriate conversation over pizza."

I watch as my mother spins around and eyes my father. "Dennis? What have you been up to?"

He shrugs. "Just telling Danny-boy how I would never embarrass him in front of Six."

My mother laughs. "Well, as long as you aren't embarrassing him, then. I'd hate for Six to find out about his lengthy showers every night."

I slap the table. "Mom! Jesus Christ!"

My dad winks at her. "Already covered that one."

Six walks to the table, shaking her head. "Your parents actually make you seem like a gentleman." She takes a seat at the table and I sit in the chair next to her.

"I'm so sorry," I whisper to her. She looks at me and smiles.

"Are you kidding me? I *love* this."

"Why would long showers embarrass you?" Chunk says to me, taking a seat across from Six. "I would think wanting to be clean is a good thing." She picks up a slice of pizza and begins to take a bite, but then her eyes squeeze shut and she drops the pizza onto her plate. By the look on her face, the meaning behind the long showers has just hit her. "Oh, gross. *Gross!*" she says, shaking her head.

Six begins to laugh and I rest my forehead against my hand, convinced this is more than likely the most uncomfortable, embarrassing five minutes of my life. "I hate all of you. Every last one of you." I quickly look at Six. "Except you, babe. I don't hate you."

She smiles and wipes her mouth with a napkin. "I know exactly what you mean. I hate everybody, too."

As soon as the words fall from her mouth, she looks away like she didn't just punch me in the gut, rip out my intestines, and stomp them into the ground.

I hate everybody too, Cinderella.

The words I said that day in the closet are screaming loudly inside my head.

There's no way.

There's no way I wouldn't have noticed she was Cinderella.

I bring my hands to my face and close my eyes, trying hard to remember something about that day. Her voice, her kiss, her smell. The way we seemed to connect almost instantly.

Her *laugh*.

"Are you okay?" Six asks quietly. No one else can tell something major is going on with me right now, but she notices. She notices because we're in sync. She notices because we have this unspoken connection. We've had it since the second I laid eyes on her in Sky's bedroom.

We've had it since the second she fell on top of me in the maintenance closet.

"No," I say, bringing my hands down. "I'm not okay." I grip the edge of the table, then slowly turn to face her.

Soft hair.

Amazing mouth.

Phenomenal kisser.

My mouth is dry, so I reach to my cup and down a huge gulp of water. I slam my cup back down on the table, then turn and face her. I'm trying not to smile, but this whole thing is slightly overwhelming. Realizing that the girl from my past that I wished I could know is the same girl from my present that I'm thankful to have is practically one of the best moments of my life. I want to tell Six, I want to tell Chunk, I want to tell my parents. I want to scream it from the rooftops and print it in all the papers.

Cinderella is Six! Six is Cinderella!

"Daniel. You're scaring me," she says, watching as my face grows paler and my heart pounds faster.

I look at her. *Really* look at her this time.

"You want to know why I haven't given you a nickname yet?"

She looks confused that this is what I decide to say in the middle of my silent freak-out. She nods cautiously. I place one hand on the back of her chair and one hand on the table in front of her, then lean in toward her.

"Because I already gave you one, Cinderella."

I pull back slightly and watch her face closely, waiting on the realization she's about to have. The flashback. The clarity. She's about to wonder how the hell she failed to realize it, too.

Her eyes slowly move up my face until they meet mine. "No," she says, shaking her head.

I nod slowly. "Yes."

She's still shaking her head. "No," she says again with more certainty. "Daniel there's no way it could . . ."

I don't let her finish. I grab her face and kiss her harder than I've ever kissed her. I don't give a shit that we're seated at a dinner table. I don't care that Chunk is groaning. I don't care that my mom is clearing her throat. I keep kissing her until she begins to back away from me.

She's pushing on my chest, so I pull away from her just in time to see the regret wash over her entire face. I focus on her eyes long enough to see them squeeze shut as she stands to leave the kitchen. I watch her rush away long enough to see her stifle a sob by slapping her hand over her mouth. I remain in my seat until the front door slams shut and I realize she's gone.

I'm immediately out of my seat. I rush out the front door and run straight to her car, which is now backing out of my driveway. I slam my fist against her hood as I rush to catch up to her window. She's not looking at me. She's wiping tears away, trying her hardest not to look out the window I'm banging on.

"Six!" I yell, repeatedly banging on her window with my fist. I see her hand reach down to put the car in drive. I don't even think. I sprint to the front of the car and slap my hands down on the hood, standing directly in front of it so she can't take off. I'm watching her do everything she can to avoid looking at me.

"Roll down your window," I yell.

She doesn't move. She continues to cry as she focuses on everything other than what's right in front of her.

Me.

I slap the hood of the car again until she finally brings her eyes up to meet mine. Seeing her heartache confuses the hell out of me. I couldn't have been happier finding out she was Cinderella, yet she seems embarrassed as hell that I realized it.

"Please," I say, wincing from the ache that just reached my chest. I hate seeing her upset and I really hate that this is why she's upset.

She puts the car in park, then reaches a hand to her door and lowers the driver's side window. I'm not so sure she still won't drive away if I move out from in front of her car. I carefully and very slowly begin to make my way toward her window, the whole time keeping an eye on her hand to ensure she doesn't put the car back into drive.

When I reach her window, I bend my knees and lower myself until I'm face to face with her. "Do I even need to ask?"

She looks up at the roof and leans her head against the headrest. "Daniel," she whispers through her tears. "You wouldn't understand."

She's right.

She's absolutely right.

"Are you embarrassed?" I ask her. "Because we had sex?"

She squeezes her eyes shut, giving away the fact that she thinks I'm judging her. I immediately reach a hand through her window and pull her gaze back to mine. "Don't you dare be embarrassed by that. Ever. Do you know how much that meant to me? Do you know how many times I've thought about you? I was there. I made that choice right along with you, so please don't think for a second that I would ever judge you for what happened between us."

She begins to cry even harder. I want her to get out of the car. I need to hold her because I can't see her this upset and not do whatever I can to take it away.

"Daniel, I'm sorry," she says through her sobs. "This was a mistake. This was a huge mistake." Her hand reaches down to the gearshift and I'm already reaching into the car, trying to stop her.

"No. No, Six," I plead. She puts the car in drive and reaches to the door, then places her finger on the window button.

I make one last attempt to lean in and kiss her before the window begins to rise on me. "Six, *please*," I say, shocked at the sadness and desperation in my own voice. She continues to raise the window until I'm completely out of it and it's all the way up. I press my palms to her window and slap the glass, but she drives away.

There's nothing left for me to do but watch the back of the car as it disappears down the street.

What the hell was that?

I pull my hands through my hair and look up at the sky, confused as to what just happened.

That wasn't her.

I hate that she had the complete opposite reaction from me when she found out who I was.

I hate that she's embarrassed about that day, like she just wants to forget it. Like she wants to forget *me*.

I hate it because I've done everything I possibly can to commit that day to my memory, like no one or nothing else I've ever experienced.

She can't do this. She can't just push me away like this without an explanation.

Chapter Six

I couldn't give my parents an explanation when I went back inside to grab my keys. They were apologetic, thinking they did something wrong. They felt bad about their jokes, but I didn't even have it in me to reassure them that they weren't the problem. I couldn't reassure them, because I don't even know what the problem is.

I'll be damned if I don't find out tonight, though. Right now.

I put my car in park and turn off the engine, relieved to see her car parked in her driveway. I get out of my car and shut my door, then head to her front door. Before I make it to her front porch, I detour to the side of the house. I know with the shape she left my house in a few minutes ago, there's no way she would have walked through her front door. She would have taken the window.

I reach her bedroom and the window is shut, as well as the curtains. The room is dark, but I know she's inside. Knocking won't do me any good, so I don't even bother. I push the window up, then slide the curtains to the side.

"Six," I say firmly. "I'm respecting your window rule, but it's really hard right now. We need to talk."

Nothing. She says nothing. I know she's in her room, though. I can hear her crying, but barely.

"I'm going to the park. I want you to meet me there, okay?"

Several silent moments pass before she responds.

"Daniel, go home. Please." Her voice is soft and weak, but the message behind that sad, angelic voice is like a stab to my heart. I back away from the window, then kick the side of the house out of frustration. Or anger. Or sadness or . . . *shit*. All of it.

I lean back into her window and grip the frame. "Meet me at the goddamned park, Six!" I say loudly. My voice is angry. *I'm* angry. She's pissing me the hell off. "We don't do this kind of thing. You don't play these games. You owe me a fucking explanation."

I push away from her window and turn to walk back to my car. I make it five feet before my palms are running down my face and I'm wishing I could punch the actual air in front of me. I stop walking and pause for several moments while I search for patience. It's in here somewhere.

I walk back to her window and hate that she's crying much louder now, even though she's trying to stifle the sounds with her pillow.

"Listen, babe," I say quietly. "I'm sorry I said goddamned. And fucking. I shouldn't cuss when I'm upset, but . . ." I inhale a deep breath. "But *dammit*, Six. *Please. Please* just meet me at the park. If you aren't there in half an hour, I'm done. I had enough of this bullshit with Val and I'm not putting myself through it again."

I turn to leave and make it all the way to my car this time before pausing and kicking at the ground. I walk back to her window again. "I didn't mean it just now when I said I'd be done if you didn't show up. If you don't show up to the park, I'll still want to be with you. I'll just be sad that you didn't show up. Because we show up, Six. It's what we do. It's me and you, babe."

I wait for a reply for a lot longer than I even need to. She never responds, so I go back to my car and climb inside, then head to the park and hope she shows up.

•   •   •

Twenty-seven minutes pass before her car finally pulls into a parking spot.

I'm not surprised she showed up. I knew she would. Her reaction was uncharacteristic of her and I know she just needed time to let everything soak in.

I watch her as she slowly makes her way toward me, never once looking up at me. She keeps her eyes trained to the ground the whole time until she passes me. She sinks into the swing next to me and grabs the chains, then leans her head against her arm. I wait for her to speak first, knowing she more than likely won't.

She doesn't.

I run my hands up the chain rope until they're even with my head, then I lean into my arm and mirror her position. We're both staring quietly into the dark night in front of us.

"After you left that day," I say. "I wasn't sure of what you wanted me to do. I wondered if you thought about me, too, and if you had changed your mind. If maybe you wanted me to try and find you."

I tilt my head and look at her. Her blonde hair is tucked behind her ears and her eyes are closed. Even with her eyes closed I can see the pain in her features.

"For days I wondered if that's what you wanted me to do. I waited and waited for you to come back, but you never did. I know we both said we would be better off not knowing who the other was, but honestly, you were all I could think about. I wanted you to come back so fucking bad that I spent every single fifth period in that damn closet for the rest of the semester. The last day of school was the absolute worst. When the bell rang and I had to walk out of that closet for the last time, it absolutely sucked. So much. I felt like an idiot for being so consumed by the thought of you. When I met Val, I forced myself to go forward with her because it helped to not think about that damn closet so much."

I twist the swing until I'm facing her. "I like you, Six. A lot. And I know this sounds all kinds of jacked up and crazy, but pretending to make love to you that day was the closest I've ever been to actually loving someone until now."

I turn my swing to face forward again, then I stand up. I walk to her and kneel down on both knees in front of her, then wrap my arms around her waist. I look up at her and see the pain flash across her face when I touch her. "Six. Don't let what happened between us become a negative thing. *Please*. Because that day was one of the best days of my life. Actually, it was *the* best day of my life."

She lifts her head away from her arm and opens her eyes, then looks directly at me. Tears are streaming down her face. It breaks my damn heart.

"Daniel," she whispers through her tears. She squeezes her eyes shut and turns her head like she can't even look at me. "I got pregnant."

Chapter Seven

Sometimes when I'm almost asleep, I'll hear something that pulls me right back into a state of high alert. I'll listen closely, wondering if I actually heard a sound or if it's just my imagination playing tricks on me. I'll hold my breath and be really still, and I'll just listen quietly.

I'm quiet.

I'm still.

I'm holding my breath.

I'm listening.

I'm concentrating really hard while my head rests on her thighs. I don't know when I lowered it here, but my hands are still gripping her waist. I'm trying to figure out if those words are going to hit me and completely knock my heart around like a punching bag all over again, or if it was just my imagination.

God, I hope it was my imagination.

A tear hits my cheek that just fell straight from her eyes.

"I didn't find out until I was already in Italy," she says, her voice coated and laced with sorrow and shame. "I'm so sorry."

In my head, I'm counting backward. Counting the days and the weeks and the months and trying to make sense of what she's saying, because she's obviously not pregnant now. My mind is still churning, crunching numbers, erasing errors, crunching more numbers.

She was in Italy for almost seven months.

Seven months there, three months before she left and one month since she returned.

That's almost a year.

My mind hurts. Everything hurts.

"I didn't know what to do," she says. "I couldn't raise him by myself. I was already eighteen when I found out, so . . ."

I immediately lift up and look at her face. "*Him?*" I ask, shaking my head. "How do you know . . ." I close my eyes and blow out a steady breath, then release my grip on her waist. I stand up and turn around, then pace back and forth, absorbing everything that's happening.

"Six," I say, shaking my head. "I don't . . . are you saying . . ." I pause, then turn and face her. "Are you telling me you had a fucking *baby*? That *we* had a baby?"

She's crying again. Sobbing, even. Hell, I don't know if she ever even stopped. She nods like it's painful to do.

"I didn't know what to do, Daniel. I was so scared."

She stands up and walks toward me, then places her hands delicately on my cheeks. "I didn't know who you were, so I didn't know how to tell you. If I knew your name or what you looked like I never would have made that decision without you."

I bring my hands up to hers, and I pull them away from my face. "Don't," I say as I feel the resentment building within me. I'm trying so hard to hold it back. To understand. To let it all soak in.

I just can't.

"How could you not tell me? It's not like you found a puppy, Six. This is . . ." I shake my head, still not getting it. "You had a *baby*. And you didn't even bother telling me!"

She grasps my shirt in her fists, shaking her head, wanting me to see her side of things. "Daniel, that's what I'm trying to tell you! What was I supposed to do? Did you expect me to plaster flyers all over the school asking for information on who knocked me up in the maintenance closet?"

I look her directly in the eyes. "Yes," I say in a low voice.

She takes a step back, so I take a step forward. "*Yes*, Six! That's *exactly* what I would have expected you to do. You should have plastered it all over the hallways, aired it on the radio, taken an ad out in the motherfucking newspaper! You get pregnant with my kid and you worry about your *reputation*? Are you *kidding* me?"

My hand covers my cheek a second after she slaps me.

The pain in her eyes can't even come close to matching the pain in my heart, so I don't feel bad for saying what I said. Even when she begins to cry harder than I knew people were capable of crying.

She rushes back to her car.

I let her go.

I walk back to the swing and I sit.

Fucking life.

Motherfucking life.

Daniel: Where are you?

Holder: Just left Sky's house. Almost home. What's up?

Daniel: I'll be there in five.

Holder: Everything okay?

Daniel: Nope.

Five minutes later Holder is standing on his curb waiting for me. I pull onto the side of the street and he opens the passenger door, then climbs inside. I put my car in park and prop my foot on the dash, then look out my window.

I'm surprised at how pissed I am. I'm even surprised at how sad I am. I don't know how to separate everything I'm feeling in order to get a grip on the core of what's upsetting me the most. Right now I can't tell if it's the fact that I didn't have a say in whatever decision she made or if it's because she was even put into that situation to have to make that kind of decision to begin with.

I'm pissed I wasn't there to help her. I'm pissed I was careless enough to make a girl go through something like that.

I'm sad because . . . *hell*. I'm sad that I'm so mad at her. I'm sad I have to know something this overwhelming and there isn't a damn thing I can do about it now, even if I wanted to. I'm sad because I'm sitting here in a parked car and I'm about to have a breakdown in front of my best friend and I really don't want to do that but it's too late.

I punch the steering wheel the second I begin to cry. I punch it several times, over and over, until the car begins to close in on me and I need to get the hell out of it. I open the door and climb out, then turn around and kick my tire. I kick it over and over until my foot starts to go numb, then I collapse against the hood onto my elbows. I press my forehead against the cold metal of the car and focus on burying this anger.

It's not her fault.

It's not her fault.

It's not her fault.

When I'm finally calm enough to return to the car, Holder is sitting quietly in the passenger seat, watching me closely.

"You want to talk about it?" he asks.

I shake my head. "Nope."

He nods. He's probably relieved I don't want to talk about it.

"What do you want to do?" he asks.

I wrap my fingers around the steering wheel, then crank the car. "I don't care what we do."

"Me neither."

I put the car in drive.

"We could go to Breckin's house and let you get your aggression out on a video game," he suggests.

I nod, then begin to drive toward Breckin's house. "You better not fucking tell him I cried."

Chapter Eight

"You look like hell," Holder says, leaning against the locker next to mine. "Did you even sleep last night?"

I shake my head. Of course I didn't. How the hell could I have slept? I knew she wasn't sleeping, so there's no way in hell I could have.

"You gonna tell me what happened?" he asks. I shut my locker, but keep my hand on it as I look down at the floor and slowly inhale.

"No. I know I usually tell you everything, but not this, Holder."

He taps the locker next to him a couple of times with his fist, then he pushes off of it. "Six isn't telling Sky anything, either. Not sure what happened, but . . ." He looks at me until I make eye contact with him. "I like you with her. Get it worked out, Daniel."

He walks away and I close my locker. I wait next to it for a few minutes more than necessary because my next class is down the hallway where Six's locker is. I haven't seen her since she left the park last night and I'm not sure I really want to see her. I'm not sure about anything. I have so many questions, but just thinking about having to ask her any of them makes my chest hurt so bad I can't fucking breathe.

After the final bell rings, I decide to walk to my next class. I debated staying home from school altogether, but I figured it would be worse just sitting in my room thinking about it all day. I'd rather be preoccupied for as long as I can today because I know as soon as school is out I need to confront her.

Or maybe I'm supposed to confront her right now, because as soon as I round the corner, my eyes land on her.

I come to a quiet stop and watch her. She's the only one in the hallway. She's standing still, facing her locker. I want to walk away before she sees me, but I can't stop watching her. Her whole demeanor is heartbroken and I want so bad to rush over to her and wrap my arms around her but . . . I can't. I want to scream at her and hug her and kiss her and blame her for every single jumbled-up emotion I've spent the last day trying to process.

I sigh heavily and she turns to look at me. I'm far enough away that I can't hear her crying, but close enough I can see the tears. Neither one of us moves. We just stare. Several moments pass and I can see she's hoping I say something to her.

I clear my throat and begin walking toward her. The closer I get, the louder her soft cry becomes. I get about five feet away, then I pause. The closer I get to her, the harder it is to breathe.

"Is he . . ." I close my eyes and pass a calming breath, then open them again and try my hardest to finish my sentence with dry eyes. "When you talked about the boy who broke your heart in Italy . . . you were referring to him, weren't you? The baby?"

I can barely see the nod of her head when she confirms my thoughts. I squeeze my eyes shut and tilt my head back.

I didn't know hearts could literally ache like this. It hurts so much I want to reach inside and rip it out of my chest so I'll never feel this again.

I can't do this. Not right here. We can't stand in the hallway of a high school and have this discussion.

I turn around before I open my eyes so I don't have to see the look on her face again. I walk straight to my classroom and open the door, then walk inside without looking back at her.

Chapter Nine

I don't know why I'm still here. I don't want to be here and I'm pretty sure I'll leave in half an hour. I just can't leave before then because I'm scared of what she might think if I don't show up to lunch. I could text her and tell her I'll talk to her later, but I'm not even sure I feel like sending her a text yet. There's still so much I have to process, I'd rather just ignore it all until I find the strength to sort through everything.

I walk through the cafeteria doors and head straight to our table. There's no way I can eat lunch so I don't even bother getting food. Breckin is sitting in my usual spot next to Six, but that's probably a good thing. Not so sure I could sit by her right now, anyway.

Her eyes are focused on the textbook in front of her. She's not crying anymore. I take a seat across from her and I know she knows I just sat down, but her eyes never move. Sky and Holder are deep in conversation with Breckin, so I watch them, trying to find a spot to jump in.

I can't though, because I'm completely unable to pay attention. I keep stealing glances at her to make sure she isn't crying or to see if she's looking at me. She never does either of those things.

"You're not eating?" Breckin says, catching my attention.

I shake my head. "Not hungry."

"You need to eat something," Holder says. "And a nap might do you some good, too. Maybe you should go home."

I nod, but don't say anything.

"If you do go home, you should take Six with you," Sky says. "You both look like you could use a nap."

I don't even respond to that with a nod. My eyes fall back to Six just in time to see a tear land on a page in front of her. She quickly swipes it away with her hand and flips the page over.

Fuck if that just didn't make me feel like complete shit.

I continue to watch her and tears continue to fall onto the pages, one by one. Her hand is always quick to wipe them away before anyone notices and she always flips to a new page before she can even possibly have read the last one.

"Get up, Breckin," I say. He looks at me blankly, but doesn't make an effort to move. "I want your seat. Get up."

He finally realizes what I'm saying, so he quickly stands up. I stand and walk around the table. I sit down beside her and when I do, she brings her arms onto the table. She folds them and buries her head into the crease in her elbow. I watch as her shoulders begin to shake and dammit if I can allow her to keep feeling this way. I wrap an arm around her and lower my forehead to the side of her head and I close my eyes. I don't say anything. I don't do anything. I just hold her while she cries into her arms.

"Daniel," I hear her say through her muffled tears. She lifts her head and looks up at me. "Daniel, I'm so sorry. I'm so, so sorry." Her tears become sobs and her sobs become too much. It's too fucking much.

I pull her to my chest. "Shh," I say into her hair. "Don't. Don't apologize."

Her body becomes limp against mine and everyone in the cafeteria is beginning to stare at us. I want to hold her and tell her how sorry I am for allowing her to walk away last night, but she needs privacy. I wrap my arm tighter around her, then scoop her legs up into my other arm. I pull her against me, then stand up and carry her out into the hallway. I keep walking until I round the corner and find our room. She's still crying against my chest, wrapped tightly around me. I open the door to the maintenance closet, then I close it behind us. I back up to the door and slide down until I meet the floor, still holding her in my arms.

"Six," I say, lowering my mouth to her ear. "I want you to try to stop crying, because I have so much I want to say to you."

I feel her nod against my chest and I remain quiet, waiting on her to calm down. Several minutes pass before she's finally quiet enough for me to continue.

"First of all, I am so sorry for letting you walk away last night, but I don't want you to think for one second it was because I was judging your choices. Okay? I'm not about to put myself in your shoes and tell you that you made a bad choice, because I wasn't there and I have no clue how hard that must have been for you."

I adjust her and straighten out my legs so she's forced to sit up and look at me. I pull one of her legs to the other side of me until she's facing me. "I'm just sad, okay? That's all this is. I'm allowed to be sad about this and I need you to let me be sad because this is a whole hell of a lot to process in a day."

She pulls her lips into a thin line and she nods while I wipe away her tears with both my thumbs. "I have so many questions, Six. And I know you'll answer them when you're ready, but I can wait. If you need me to give you time I can."

She shakes her head. "Daniel. He's your son. I'll answer any question you ask me. I just don't know if you want to hear the answers because . . ." She squeezes her eyes shut to hold back more tears. "Because I think I made the wrong choice and it's too late. It's too late to go back now."

She's crying hard again, so I wrap my arms around her and hug her.

"If I knew he was yours or that I would eventually find you I would have never done it, Daniel. I would have never given him up.

But I did and now you're here and it's too late because I don't know where he is and I'm sorry. God, I'm so sorry."

I shake my head, wishing she would stop. It's hurting me more to see her upset with herself than anything else about this whole situation.

"Listen to me, Six." I pull back and look her in the eyes, holding her face firmly between my hands. "You made a choice for *him*. Not for yourself. Not for me. You did what was best for him and I will never be able to thank you enough for that. And please don't think this changes how I feel about you. If anything, it just lets me know that I'm not crazy. For the past month I've been thinking my feelings for you couldn't be real because there are so many of them and they're so much. *Too* much sometimes. I constantly have to bite my tongue when I'm around you because all I've been wanting to do lately is tell you how much I love you. But it's only been a month since we met and the only other time I've said those words out loud to a girl was over a year ago. Right here on this floor. And you wouldn't believe how real I wanted that moment to be for us, Six. I know I didn't know you but my *God*, I wished I did. And now that I do know you . . . *really* know you . . . I know it's real. I love you. And knowing what we shared last year and now knowing what you had to go through and how it's made you exactly who you are right now . . . it just blows my mind. It blows my mind that I get to love you."

I feel her hands wiping tears from my cheeks when I lean in to kiss her. I pull her against me and she pulls me against her and I have no plans to ever let her go. I kiss her until her hands move up to my face and she pulls her lips from mine. Our foreheads meet and she's still crying, but her tears are different now. I feel like they're tears of relief rather than tears of worry.

"I'm so happy it's you," she says, keeping her hands locked on my face. "I'm so happy it was you."

I pull her against me and hold her. I hold her for so long that the bell rings and the hallway fills and empties and another bell rings and we're still sitting here together, holding on to each other when the silence in the hallway returns. I'm periodically pressing kisses into her hair, stroking her back, kissing her forehead.

"He looked like you," she says quietly. Her hand is lightly trailing up and down my arm and her cheek is pressed against my chest. "He had your brown eyes and he was kind of bald, but I could tell he was going to have brown hair. And he had your mouth. You have a great mouth."

I rub my hand up her back and kiss the top of her head. "He's got it made," I say. "Looks just like his daddy, hopefully acts like his mommy, and he'll have a nice Italian accent. Kid won't have any problems in life."

She laughs and hearing that sound immediately brings tears to my eyes again. I squeeze her tight against me, rest my cheek against the top of her head, and sigh.

"It's probably for the best that it all happened like it did," I say. "If we had decided to keep him I would have ruined him with some stupid nickname. I probably would have called him Salty Balls or some shit like that. I'm not cut out to be a dad yet, obviously."

She shakes her head. "You'd be a great dad. And one of these days, Salty Balls will be the perfect nickname for one of our kids. Just not yet."

Now I'm the one laughing. "What if we have all girls?"

She shrugs. "Even better."

I smile and keep her held close against me. After last night and being apart from her, knowing how much she was hurting, I know I'll never want to feel that way again. I never want *her* to feel that way again.

"You know what I just realized?" she says. "We've already had sex. I've been kind of bummed because if I had sex with you, it would have made you the seventh person I've ever had sex with and that's a lot. But you'll still be the sixth, because I was already counting you and I didn't even know it."

"I like six," I say. "That's a good number to be. It's actually my favorite number."

"Don't get too excited now that you know we've already had sex," she says. "I'm still making you wait."

"I'll wear you down soon enough," I tease.

I bring one of my hands up to her head and I hold it while I lean forward and kiss her softly on the lips. I stay close to her mouth and make a confession. "I haven't brought this up because we haven't been together that long and I didn't want to scare you off. But now that I know we have a kid together, it makes it less embarrassing."

"Oh, no. What is it?" she asks nervously.

"We graduate in less than a month. I know you and Sky and Holder were planning on going to the same college in Dallas after the summer. I had already applied to a college in Austin, but after I met you I might have applied to Dallas, too. You know . . . in case things worked out with us. I didn't like the thought of being five hours apart."

She tilts her head and looks up at me. "When did you apply?"

I shrug like it's not a big deal. "The night Sky had that dinner for you."

She sits up and looks at me. "That was twenty-four hours after we went out for the first time. You applied to my college after knowing me for one day?"

I nod. "Yeah, but technically I knew you for a whole year. If you look at it that way, it's way less creepy."

She smiles at my logic. "Well? Did you get accepted?"

I nod. "I might have already made living arrangements with Holder, too."

She grins and it's probably the most I've ever loved a smile. "Daniel? This is serious. This thing with us. It's pretty intense, huh?"

I nod. "Yeah. I think we might really be in love this time. No more pretending."

She nods. "Things are so serious now, I think it's time I introduced you to all my brothers."

I stop nodding and start shaking my head back and forth. "I may be exaggerating. I don't love you *that* much."

She laughs. "No, you love me. You love me so much, Daniel. You've loved me since the second I let you accidentally touch my boob."

"No, I think I've loved you since you forced me to stick my tongue in your mouth."

She shakes her head. "No, you've loved me since I let you kiss me in a crowded restaurant next to a dirty diaper."

"Nope. I've loved you since you walked through Sky's bedroom door with that spoon in your mouth."

"Actually, you've loved me since the first time you told me you loved me a year ago. Right here in this room."

I shake my head. "I've loved you since the moment you fell on top of me and said you hated everybody."

She stops smiling. "I've loved you since the moment you said you hated everybody, too."

"I used to hate everybody," I say. "Until I met you."

"I told you I was unhateable." She grins.

"And I told you unhateable isn't even a real word."

Her eyes focus on mine and she takes both my hands, then laces her fingers through them. We stare at each other like we've done so many times before, but this time I feel it in every single part of me. I feel *her* in every part of me and the feeling is new and heavy and intense. I realize in this moment that we just became so much more together than we could ever possibly be alone.

"I love you, Daniel Wesley," she whispers.

"I love you Seven Marie Six Cinderella Jacobs."

She laughs. "Thank you for not turning out to be an asshole."

"Thank you for never asking me to change." I lean forward and kiss the smile that just spread across her lips as I silently thank the universe for sending her back to me.

My fucking angel.

Epilogue

"What in the world is wrong with you, Daniel?" Chunk says, slapping her pen down on the table.

I pause the drumming of my fingers against the wooden tabletop. "Nothing." I didn't realize my nervousness was so obvious. Especially to a thirteen-year-old.

"Something's wrong with you," she says. She pushes her homework aside and folds her arms across the table, leaning forward. "Did you break up with Six?"

I shake my head. "No."

"She break up with you?"

"*Hell* no," I say defensively.

"Get in trouble at school?"

I shake my head and look down at the time on my phone. Ten more minutes and I'll leave. I just need ten more minutes.

"You get her pregnant?" Chunk asks.

My eyes dart up to hers and my pulse increases. I technically can't answer that with a no, because . . . well.

"Oh, my god," Chunk says. "You got her pregnant? Daniel! Mom and Dad are gonna *kill* you!"

She pushes away from the table just as my mother walks into the kitchen. Chunk's hands go up to her mouth in disbelief and she's shaking her head, still staring at me. She doesn't know my mother is behind her now. "Daniel, are you stupid? I'm only thirteen, but even *I* know what safe sex is. Christ, I can't believe you got her *pregnant*!"

I'm shaking my head, too flustered to tell her Six isn't pregnant.

My mother is frozen, staring at me with wide eyes. She covers her mouth with her hand at the same moment my father walks into the kitchen. Chunk hears him and spins around.

"What's wrong?" my father asks. "You all look like you've seen a ghost."

Before I have the chance to defend myself or dismiss the words that just came out of Chunk's mouth, my mother turns to face my father. She points at me.

"He got her pregnant," she whispers disbelievingly. "Your son got his girlfriend pregnant."

My father stares silently at my mother. I know I should be standing up right now—denying everything before they all get too worked up, but everything they're saying is technically true.

I *did* get Six pregnant.

However, that was over a year ago and none of them know about that, nor do they *need* to know about it. But Six sure as hell isn't pregnant right now. I know that for a fact. We've been dating for over three months, and I'm sure it'll be at least three more months before she allows me to break that bread.

I don't like that analogy. Doesn't even make sense.

Jump that fence?

Nah, that's not sexy enough.

Cross that finish line?

Nope. It'll be more like a starting *line.*

Tap that ass?

Meh. Too tacky.

Poke that potato?

"Daniel?" my father asks, pulling my gaze to his. He doesn't look happy, but he also doesn't look angry. Which is weird, since he's just been told he'll likely be a grandfather, and he's only forty-five. He's looking at me like he's confused. "How can Six be pregnant?" he asks, shaking his head. "Every time you're with her you still come home and take those embarrassingly long showers."

I swear to God. Why do these people continue to bring that up?

I look over at Chunk and shake my head. "Six isn't pregnant," I tell all of them. "Chunk just has an overactive imagination."

A collective sigh comes from the three of them. My mother slaps her hand to her heart and releases a quick "Oh dear good lord, Jesus Christ, holy shit, thank *god!*" She blows out a calming breath after her slew of blasphemy.

Chunk rolls her eyes when she realizes I'm telling the truth. She takes her seat across from me and pulls her homework back in front of her. "Well, if she's not pregnant then what in the heck are you so nervous about?"

Oh yeah. This little distraction almost helped me forget everything that's about to happen. As soon as the night's plans invade my mind again, I have to inhale slowly through my nose to remind my lungs they need air.

"What is it, Danny boy?" my father asks. "She break up with you?"

I drop my head into my hands, frustrated at how damn nosey they all are.

"No," I groan. "She didn't break up with me. I also didn't break up with her. She's not pregnant, we aren't having sex, and I didn't get in trouble at school!" I'm standing now, pacing back and forth. The three of them are watching me practically have a meltdown. I finally turn and face them with my hands planted firmly on my hips. "I'm just freaking out a little bit, okay? I'm supposed to be at her house right now, because she wants me to meet her brothers. *All* of them. Like *right now.*"

My father looks amused, and it kind of pisses me off.

"How many brothers does she have?" my mother asks. Her voice is soothing, like she's about to give me the pep talk I'm desperately in need of.

"Four. And they're all older than she is."

My mother's mouth presses into a thin line as she gently nods her head. "Oh, boy," she says in a whisper. "You're screwed, Daniel." She turns around and walks into the kitchen. I'm stuck in the same position, wondering where her words of advice went.

My father is nodding his head, still with that annoying smile plastered on his face. "I really don't like Six," he says. "I'm starting to hate her, actually. Three months now, and she's *still* holding firm to that trophy?"

"Stop, Dad," I say immediately. "You are *not* allowed to talk about my sex life. And you're especially not allowed to use shitty analogies to reference the fact that Six is making me wait."

He holds his palms up defensively. "Sorry." He laughs. "Besides, I forget that your sister isn't an adult sometimes." He pats Chunk on her shoulder. "Sorry, Chunk. I'll never mention in front of you again how your brother's girlfriend won't allow him to kill that mocking-bird." He pulls out a chair and sits at the table. Chunk and I groan at the same time.

"Dad," she says. "You just ruined my favorite book with that comparison. Thanks a lot."

He winks at her before turning to face me again. "You'll be fine, Danny boy. Just don't be yourself at all, and they'll have no choice but to love you."

I grab my jacket off the back of the chair and pull it on as I exit the kitchen. "You all still suck," I mumble as I walk out the front door.

• • •

I don't remember walking into her house. I don't remember anything I said as I was being introduced to any of them. I don't even remember how I made it to my seat, but here I am—being stared down across the kitchen table by four of the most intimidating men I've ever met. I was hoping we were going to make it through the meal with everyone stuffing his face and no one addressing me directly.

That didn't even last a whole bite.

One of them just asked what my plans are after graduation, but I'm not sure which one he is. He's the one who looks the most like Six because he's the only blond, but he's also the largest of the four. His hands make his fork look like a toothpick.

I look down at my hands and frown, because they make my fork look like a spatula. I set my fork down on the table before they notice how tiny they all make my hands look.

Six taps my leg under the table, reminding me to speak. I gently clear my throat. "I'm not sure."

My voice sounds like a damn child's, compared to the four of their voices. I've never even thought about my voice or how it might sound to an outsider until this moment. I've never really thought about how my hands might make a fork look until now, either. I've also never really thought about breaking up with Six before, but . . . *nah*. I don't care how scary they are or how much they hate me. There's no way in hell I'm breaking up with Six.

"Well, are you at least going to college?" Evan asks.

I know Evan's name. He's the one closest in age to Six. He's also the only one who smiled at me when he introduced himself, so I made sure to remember him. That way, if the other three decide to jump me, I can scream Evan's name for help, since he'd be the only one likely to defend me.

"I am going to college," I say with a nod. *Finally. A question I can answer.* "I'm attending the same one Six will be at."

Evan nods his head slowly, digesting that response with a bite of food.

"What if the two of you aren't dating after graduation?" the big one says.

"Aaron, shut up," Six says with a roll of her eyes. She squeezes my leg under the table. "Stop antagonizing him."

Aaron's eyes are still locked with mine. "Do you think I'm antagonizing you?" he asks coolly. "I just thought we were having polite conversation."

I swallow the lump in my throat and shake my head. "You're fine," I say. "I get it. I have two sisters. Granted, one of them is older than me but I still give the douchebags she brings home a hard time. And don't even get me started on Chunk. The first guy she brings home doesn't stand a chance. I already hate him, and the kid probably doesn't even know she exists yet."

The brother directly across from me smiles a little bit. It might be my imagination, but I know for a fact he's not frowning anymore.

"Chunk?" Aaron asks. "Six said you give nicknames to people. That's what you call your little sister?"

I nod.

"What do you call Six?" the brother across from me says. I'm pretty sure his name is Michael. I have a fifty-fifty chance of being right, considering the brother on the end could also be named Michael. It's either that or Zachary.

Six bumps my leg again, and I realize I haven't answered him. "Cinderella," I blurt out.

They're all staring at me now, waiting for an explanation for that one. I don't think I want to give them one. How do you tell four brothers that you call their little sister Cinderella because you had random hot sex with her in the maintenance closet of a school?

"Why do you call her that?" Aaron asks. He turns toward the brother at the end. "Zach, didn't you used to have a turtle named Cinderella?"

Zach. Zach is the quietest one.

He shakes his head. "Ariel," he says, correcting Aaron. "I had a thing for the little mermaid."

The one I can now assume is Michael, based on the process of elimination, says, "You didn't answer the question. Why do you call her Cinderella?"

Six laughs under her breath, and I know she finds this extremely amusing, even though I sort of wish I would choke to death on a turkey bone so I could be put out of my misery.

"I call her Cinderella because the first time I laid eyes on her, I thought she was so beautiful she couldn't be real. Girls like her were reserved for fairy tales and fantasies."

I'm proud of my own answer. Didn't know I could bullshit under pressure like this.

The quiet one straightens up in his seat. *Zach.* "So you're saying you fantasize about our little sister?"

What the . . .

"Jesus, Zach!" Six yells. "Stop it! All four of you, stop it! You're just interrogating him to amuse yourselves."

All four of them begin to laugh. Evan winks at me, and they all begin eating again.

I'm still not brave enough to pick up my fork in front of them.

"We're just messing with you," Zach says with a laugh. "We never get to do this, because you're the first guy Six has ever let us meet."

I turn and look at Six. I didn't know this little fact, and I think I kind of love it. "Am I, really?" I ask her. "You've never introduced anyone to your brothers before?"

Six smiles and gives her head a small shake. "Why would I?" she says. "No other guy has ever deserved to meet them."

I immediately pull her to me, and I give her a loud smack on the lips. "Dammit, I love you, girl," I say, finding the confidence to finally pick up my fork again. It looks like a fork now rather than a spatula.

I dig in to the food and take a huge bite.

All four of her brothers are quietly staring back at me.

All four are smiling.

•   •   •

I fall onto Sky's bed with a huge sigh, landing on my back next to Holder, who is propped up against the headboard.

"I see you survived the meeting of the brothers," he says, looking down at me.

"Barely," I say. "But I think I won them over in the end."

"How'd you manage that?" Sky asks. She's sitting on the other side of Holder, messing with her phone.

"I gave them all nicknames. They found me highly amusing."

Holder laughs. "Only you, Daniel."

"Where's Six?" Sky asks me.

"She didn't feel like coming over." I pull myself up to a standing position. "I just wanted to let Holder know I'm still alive. I'm gonna head back over there."

Before I walk back to her bedroom window, I see a frown form on Sky's face. I don't like it, because she never frowns. She's one of the happiest people I've ever met.

Come to think of it, I also didn't like the fact that Six didn't want to come over here tonight. It was weird, because she didn't feel like it last night, either.

It hits me that something is up between the two of them.

"What's wrong, Cheese Tits?"

Her eyes shoot up to mine and she forces a smile. "Nothing."

I take a step back toward the bed. "I call bullshit," I say. "When's the last time you spoke to my girl?"

She glances down at her phone again and shrugs. Holder sees what I've noticed, and he puts an arm around her.

"Hey," he says reassuringly. "What's wrong, babe?" He pulls her in close to him and kisses her on the side of the head, just as a tear falls from her eyes. She quickly pulls her hand up to wipe it away, but Holder notices. He sits up straighter and turns to face her at the same time I take a seat back down on the bed.

"Sky, what's wrong?" he says, urging her to look up at him.

She shrugs it off, shaking her head. "It's probably nothing," she says. "I'm sure she's just tired or something."

"Who's tired?" I ask her. "Six?"

She nods.

Her assumption confuses me, because Six isn't tired. She seemed fine tonight.

"It's just that she hasn't been over here in the three days we've been out for Christmas break," Sky says. "She also hasn't texted or called me back. I think she's mad at me, but I have no idea what I did."

I immediately stand up. "Well, we have to fix this," I say, somewhat panicked. "She can't be mad at you. Y'all aren't allowed to fight." I begin pacing the room. Holder is watching me with those narrowed, intimidating eyes of his.

"Daniel, calm down. They're girls. Girls argue sometimes."

I shake my head, refusing to accept it. I'm pacing again. "Not Sky and Six. They aren't like all the other girls, Holder. You know that. They don't fight. They *can't* fight. We're supposed to go to college together. They're supposed to be roommates." I turn and face him, coming to a pause. "We're a team, man. Me and Six and you and Sky. Me and you. Six and Sky. They can't break up. I won't let it happen." I'm already heading to the window. Sky is pleading with me not to make a big deal out of it, but it's too late for that. I'm climbing in Six's bedroom window and my heart is racing, and there's no way I can let them keep this up for another day.

Six is lying on her bed, staring up at the ceiling. She doesn't turn to look at me when I enter her room. "What's the matter?" I ask her.

"Nothing," she says immediately.

Bullshit.

I kneel down on the bed and move toward her until I'm on top of her, looking down at her face. "Bullshit."

She turns away from me, so I grab her chin and make her look at me again. "Why are you mad at Sky?"

She shakes her head, and I can see in her eyes that she isn't mad at Sky. "I'm not mad at her," she says, sounding offended. I want to feel relieved, but something is still bothering her.

She looks worried. Scared, even. I feel like an asshole for not recognizing it earlier, but she *was* more quiet than usual during dinner.

And last night. She was really quiet last night.

Shit. Maybe she's mad at *me.*

"I'm sorry," I tell her. She looks up at me, confused.

"For what?"

I shrug. "I don't know. For whatever I did. Sometimes I do or say really stupid shit, and I don't even realize I'm doing it until I hurt someone's feelings. So if that's what's wrong, I'm sorry." I lower my head and kiss her. "I'm really, really sorry."

She pushes against my chest, and I sit back on my knees. She pulls herself to a seated position in front of me. "You didn't do anything wrong, Daniel. You're perfect."

I love that answer, but hate that I still don't know what's upsetting her.

"It's just that . . ." Her voice grows quiet, and she looks down at her lap. "If I tell you something . . . you swear you'll never ever tell Holder?"

I immediately nod my head. As much as I'll always be there for Holder, there's no way in hell I'd ever break Six's trust. "I swear."

Her eyes meet mine, and she's silently telling me I better be serious, because whatever she's about to tell me is a big deal.

I don't like this look in her eyes. Luckily, she scoots off the bed and walks to her desk. She picks up her laptop and brings it back to the bed with her. "I want to show you something." She opens the laptop and pulls up a minimized screen before turning it to face me. "And please never bring this up again, Daniel."

I pull the laptop in front of me and begin reading.

Words like *missing child* and *reward* and dates and statements and pictures are all flooding my eyes. I'm shaking my head, because the words on the screen don't make any sense when they're referring to the picture of the little girl who looks just like Sky.

"What is this, Six?" I ask.

She pulls the laptop back out of my hands. "I'm not sure," she says. "I left my computer here while I was in Italy. I just noticed a few days ago that this was in my search history from several months ago. I don't know what to do, Daniel," she says, looking down at the screen. "It's her. This is Sky. I would ask her about it, but I think if she knew about it, she would have said something to me."

I'm still trying to process what I just saw on the computer and all the words coming out of Six's mouth.

"What if it was Karen who used my computer? Or Holder? Or someone else entirely? I don't know for sure that Sky was the one looking this up, and I'm scared if I say anything to her, I'll be bringing up something she doesn't even want to know."

I don't even hesitate. I grab the laptop and stand up. "Six? This isn't something you keep to yourself. If you don't tell her now, nothing will ever be the same between the two of you, because you'll feel too guilty to talk to her." I grab her hand. "Come on. Let's just rip off the Band-Aid."

Her eyes are wide and scared, but I don't care. She can't keep something like this bottled up. And if this little girl really is Sky, she has every right to know.

We stand up but before we head to the window, I pull Six in for a tight hug. I kiss her on top of the head and tell her it'll be fine. "It might not even have anything to do with her," I say. "It could just be a coincidence."

•　　•　　•

We're standing at the foot of Sky's bed, watching her. Holder has the laptop and Sky's hand is covering her mouth. They're both staring wide-eyed at the screen.

They're both quiet.

"I'm sorry," Six says. "I don't know what it is or who was looking it up . . . but I didn't know how to tell you. I also didn't know how *not* to tell you."

Sky finally pulls her eyes away from the computer, but they don't fall on Six. They slide up to Holder's face. He looks at her calmly and expels a deep breath, then gently closes the laptop.

Their reactions are way too weird. I expected a little crying. A little bit of yelling, maybe. Perhaps a few flying objects I'd have to duck from.

Holder pushes the laptop back toward Six. "We don't need to see it," he says. "She already knows."

Six gasps, and I grab her hand. Sky stands up at the same time Holder does. She walks toward us and places her hands on Six's shoulders, looking at her calmly. "I would have told you, Six," she says. "But if this ever gets out . . . it's not me that would be affected. It's Karen. That's the only reason I haven't told you."

Six's eyes are wide and hurt, but I can tell she's also trying to be understanding. "So it was Karen?" Six whispers, backing away from Sky.

Sky nods her head. "Everything you read about my childhood was true," she says. She looks at Holder for permission to continue. He nods, but looks at me and shoots me that look. The look that tells me that whatever I'm about to hear will never leave this room.

"Karen did what she had to do because my father was a monster," Sky says. Tears fill her eyes and Holder steps up behind her and places his hands on her shoulders. He kisses the top of her head, pulling her back against his chest. "I found out everything after Holder told me. While you were in Italy."

I look over at Holder. "How did *you* know?"

He regards me silently for a few seconds. He looks as if he regrets not telling me, but I don't blame him. It's not my business. "I recognized her. Me and Les . . . we used to live next door to them before we moved here. We were all friends. I was there when it happened."

Six and I both begin to pace the room. It's too much to take in. I'm not sure I even want to know something like this about them. That's a lot of pressure . . . having this kind of knowledge in my head. I don't like that they know I know this now. I liked how things were yesterday. I liked how easy it was, before all this new information was planted in my head. Now I have to bury it and pretend it's not there, but it's so huge. It's too much for Sky and Holder to have to trust us with this kind of thing.

"I got Six pregnant!" I blurt out, feeling somewhat relieved that I'm giving them a secret, too. "Last year. She was the girl in the closet," I say to Holder. I told him about her once before, so I know he'll know what I'm referring to. "We had sex without even knowing what the other looked like. She got pregnant and found out when she was in Italy. She didn't know who I was and she was scared, so she gave our son up for adoption and . . . *yeah*," I say, pausing to face all of them. I drop my hands to my hips and take a calming breath. "We had a baby."

They're all facing me now. Six is looking at me like I'm suddenly not perfect anymore. "Daniel?" she whispers. "What the hell?"

She's mad at me. She's hurt that I would just blurt out the biggest secret she's ever had in her entire life.

I walk to her and place my hands on her shoulders. "I had to make the score even. We had to tell them. We know this really huge thing about them and unless they know *our* really huge thing, it wouldn't be even between us. Things would be weird."

I don't know if I'm making any sense to her.

"Six?" Sky whispers. "Is that true?"

Six pulls away from me and looks down. She nods, ashamed.

"Why didn't you tell me?"

Six looks back up at Sky. "Why didn't you tell me your name isn't even *Sky*?" Six says in defense.

Sky nods her head slowly, understanding that she can't really blame Six and Six can't really blame her. We're all even now. We stand quietly, each of us absorbing everything that's been revealed.

"Let's spit on it," I say. I hold my palm up and spit into my hand. "None of this will ever leave the room." I hold my hand out between the four of them and urge them to do the same.

"I'm not swapping spit with you," Sky says with a disgusted look on her face.

Six lifts her eyes to meet mine. "Me, neither," she says, crinkling up her nose.

I shake my head in confusion. "It's *spit*," I say. "You don't have a problem sticking your tongue in my mouth, but you won't touch a little spit with your hand?"

She winces. "That's different."

Holder steps forward and holds up his pinky. I laugh at him. "Really, Holder? You want us to *pinky* swear?"

He glares at me. "I'd like you to know there is nothing wrong with holding pinkies," he says defensively. "Now wipe the spit off your hand like a man and hold my damn pinky."

I can't believe I'm about to pinky swear. What are we, five?

I do what he asks and wipe my hand on my jeans, then we all step toward him. We wrap our pinkies together, and we all look each other in the eyes. No one says a word, because we don't have to. We all know that no matter what happens, everything we've learned about each other tonight will never leave this room.

Once we all release our pinkies, we step back and observe the moment silently. After several minutes of awkwardness, I turn to Six.

"Want to go make out at the park?"

She nods and expels a breath of relief. "Yep."

Thank God.

I turn to Holder and Sky. "We all still on for dinner at my house tomorrow night?"

Holder nods. "Sure. As long as you tell your dad he's not allowed to bring up anything embarrassing."

Has Holder not learned anything from watching me?

"He's my dad, Holder. If I tell him that, he'd take it as a dare."

Holder laughs. I step forward and pull him and Sky both in for a hug. I reach my arm behind me and grab Six, pulling her in with us. "Best friends forever," I tell them. "I love y'all so damn much."

They all groan and pull away from me. "Go make out with your girlfriend, Daniel," Holder says.

I wink at Six and push her toward the window.

I know it won't be tonight, but I'm still curious how long it'll be before she finally lets me pop her cork.

Nope. Still not sexy enough.

Smash her burger?

Oh God, no.

Plant my flower in her garden?

What the hell, Daniel?

Make love to her?

Yeah. That's it. That's the one.

•   •   •

The end.

Sneak Peek

Enjoy an excerpt from Colleen Hoover's new novel *Maybe Someday*, available now!

prologue

Sydney

I just punched a girl in the face. Not just *any* girl. My best friend. My roommate.

Well, as of five minutes ago, I guess I should call her my *ex*-roommate.

Her nose began bleeding almost immediately, and for a second, I felt bad for hitting her. But then I remembered what a lying, betraying whore she is, and it made me want to punch her again. I would have if Hunter hadn't prevented it by stepping between us.

So instead, I punched *him*. I didn't do any damage to him, unfortunately. Not like the damage I'd done to my hand.

Punching someone hurts a lot worse than I imagined it would. Not that I spend an excessive amount of time imagining how it would feel to punch people. Although I am having that urge again as I stare down at my phone at the incoming text from Ridge. He's another one I'd like to get even with. I know he technically has nothing to do with my current predicament, but he could have given me a heads-up a little sooner. Therefore, I'd like to punch him, too.

Ridge: Are you OK? Do u want to come up until the rain stops?

Of course I don't want to come up. My fist hurts enough as it is, and if I went up to Ridge's apartment, it would hurt a whole lot worse after I finished with him.

I turn around and look up at his balcony. He's leaning against his sliding-glass door; phone in hand, watching me. It's almost dark, but the lights from the courtyard illuminate his face. His dark eyes lock with mine and the way his mouth curls up into a soft, regretful smile makes it hard to remember why I'm even upset with him in the first place. He runs a free hand through the hair hanging loosely over his forehead, revealing even more of the worry in his expression. Or maybe that's a look of regret. As it should be.

I decide not to reply and flip him off instead. He shakes his head and shrugs his shoulders, as if to say, *I tried*, and then he goes back inside his apartment and slides his door shut.

I put the phone back in my pocket before it gets wet, and I look around at the courtyard of the apartment complex where I've lived for two whole months. When we first moved in, the hot Texas summer was swallowing up the last traces of spring, but this courtyard seemed to somehow still cling to life. Vibrant blue and purple hydrangeas lined the walkways leading up to the staircases and the fountain affixed in the center of the courtyard.

Now that summer has reached its most unattractive peak, the water in the fountain has long since evaporated. The hydrangeas are a sad, wilted reminder of the excitement I felt when Tori and I first moved in here. Looking at the courtyard now, defeated by the season, is an eerie parallel to how I feel at the moment. Defeated and sad.

I'm sitting on the edge of the now empty cement fountain, my elbows propped up on the two suitcases that contain most of my belongings, waiting for a cab to pick me up. I have no idea where it's going to take me, but I know I'd rather be anywhere except where I am right now. Which is, well, homeless.

I could call my parents, but that would give them ammunition to start firing all the *We told you so*'s at me.

We told you not to move so far away, Sydney.

We told you not to get serious with that guy.

We told you if you had chosen prelaw over music, we would have paid for it.

We told you to punch with your thumb on the outside *of your fist.*

Okay, maybe they never taught me the proper punching techniques, but if they're so right all the damn time, they *should* have.

I clench my fist, then spread out my fingers, then clench it again. My hand is surprisingly sore, and I'm pretty sure I should put ice on it. I feel sorry for guys. Punching sucks.

Know what else sucks? Rain. It always finds the most inappropriate time to fall, like right now, while I'm homeless.

The cab finally pulls up, and I stand and grab my suitcases. I roll them behind me as the cab driver gets out and pops open the trunk. Before I even hand him the first suitcase, my heart sinks as I suddenly realize that I don't even have my purse on me.

Shit.

I look around, back to where I was sitting on the suitcases, then feel around my body as if my purse will magically appear across my shoulder. But I know exactly where my purse is. I pulled it off my shoulder and dropped it to the floor right before I punched Tori in her overpriced Cameron Diaz nose.

I sigh. And I laugh. Of course I left my purse. My first day of being homeless would have been way too easy if I'd had a purse with me.

"I'm sorry," I say to the cab driver, who is now loading my second piece of luggage. "I changed my mind. I don't need a cab right now."

I know there's a hotel about a half-mile from here. If I can just work up the courage to go back inside and get my purse, I'll walk there and get a room until I figure out what to do. It's not as if I can get any wetter.

The driver takes the suitcases back out of the cab, sets them on the curb in front of me, and walks back to the driver's side without ever making eye contact. He just gets into his car and drives away, as if my canceling is a relief.

Do I look that pathetic?

I take my suitcases and walk back to where I was seated before I realized I was purseless. I glance up to my apartment and wonder what would happen if I went back there to get my wallet. I sort of left things in a mess when I walked out the door. I guess I'd rather be homeless in the rain than go back up there.

I take a seat on my luggage again and contemplate my situation. I could pay someone to go upstairs for me. But who? No one's outside, and who's to say Hunter or Tori would even give the person my purse?

This really sucks. I know I'm going to have to end up calling one of my friends, but right now, I'm too embarrassed to tell anyone how clueless I've been for the last two years. I've been completely blindsided.

I already hate being twenty-two, and I still have 364 more days to go.

It sucks so bad that I'm . . . *crying*?

Great. I'm crying now. I'm a purseless, crying, violent, homeless girl. And as much as I don't want to admit it, I think I might also be heartbroken.

Yep. Sobbing now. Pretty sure this must be what it feels like to have your heart broken.

"It's raining. Hurry up."

I glance up to see a girl hovering over me. She's holding an umbrella over her head and looking down at me with agitation while she hops from one foot to the other, waiting for me to do something. "I'm getting soaked. *Hurry.*"

Her voice is a little demanding, as if she's doing me some sort of favor and I'm being ungrateful. I arch an eyebrow as I look up at her, shielding the rain from my eyes with my hand. I don't know why she's complaining about getting wet, when there isn't much clothing to *get* wet. She's wearing next to nothing. I glance at her shirt, which is missing its entire bottom half, and realize she's in a Hooters outfit.

Could this day get any weirder? I'm sitting on almost everything I own in a torrential downpour, being bossed around by a bitchy Hooters waitress.

I'm still staring at her shirt when she grabs my hand and pulls me up in a huff. "Ridge said you would do this. I've got to get to work. Follow me, and I'll show you where the apartment is." She grabs one of my suitcases, pops the handle out, and shoves it at me. She takes the other and walks swiftly out of the courtyard. I follow her, for no other reason than the fact that she's taken one of my suitcases with her and I want it back.

She yells over her shoulder as she begins to ascend the stairwell. "I don't know how long you plan on staying, but I've only got one rule. Stay the hell out of my room."

She reaches an apartment and opens the door, never even looking back to see if I'm following her. Once I reach the top of the stairs, I pause outside the apartment and look down at the fern sitting unaffected by the heat in a planter outside the door. Its leaves are lush and green as if they're giving summer the middle finger with their refusal to succumb to the heat. I smile at the plant, somewhat proud of it. Then I frown with the realization that I'm envious of the resilience of a plant.

I shake my head, look away, then take a hesitant step inside the unfamiliar apartment. The layout is similar to my own apartment, only this one is a double split bedroom with four total bedrooms. My and Tori's apartment only had two bedrooms, but the living rooms are the same size.

The only other noticeable difference is that I don't see any lying, backstabbing, bloody-nosed whores standing in this one. Nor do I see any of Tori's dirty dishes or laundry lying around.

The girl sets my suitcase down beside the door, then steps aside and waits for me to . . . well, I don't know what she's waiting for me to do.

She rolls her eyes and grabs my arm, pulling me out of the door-way and further into the apartment. "What the hell is wrong with you? Do you even speak?" She begins to close the door behind her but pauses and turns around, wide-eyed. She holds her finger up in the air. "Wait," she says. "You're not . . ." She rolls her eyes and smacks herself in the forehead. "Oh, my God, you're deaf."

Huh? What the hell is wrong with this girl? I shake my head and start to answer her, but she interrupts me.

"God, Bridgette," she mumbles to herself. She rubs her hands down her face and groans, completely ignoring the fact that I'm shaking my head. "You're such an insensitive bitch sometimes."

Wow. This girl has some serious issues in the people-skills de-partment. She's sort of a bitch, even though she's making an effort not to be one. Now that she thinks I'm deaf. I don't even know how to respond. She shakes her head as if she's disappointed in herself, then looks straight at me.

"I . . . HAVE . . . TO . . . GO . . . TO . . . WORK . . . NOW!" she yells very loudly and painfully slowly. I grimace and step back, which should be a huge clue that I can hear her practically yelling, but she doesn't notice. She points to a door at the end of the hallway. "RIDGE . . . IS . . . IN . . . HIS . . . ROOM!"

Before I have a chance to tell her she can stop yelling, she leaves the apartment and closes the door behind her.

I have no idea what to think. Or what to do now. I'm standing, soaking wet, in the middle of an unfamiliar apartment, and the only person besides Hunter and Tori whom I feel like punching is now just a few feet away in another room. And speaking of Ridge, why the hell did he send his psycho Hooters girlfriend to get me? I take out my phone and have begun to text him when his bedroom door opens.

He walks out into the hallway with an armful of blankets and a pillow. As soon as he makes eye contact with me, I gasp. I hope it's not a noticeable gasp. It's just that I've never actually seen him up close before, and he's even better looking from just a few feet away than he is from across an apartment courtyard.

I don't think I've ever seen eyes that can actually speak. I'm not sure what I mean by that. It just seems as if he could shoot me the tiniest glance with those dark eyes of his, and I'd know exactly what they needed me to do. They're piercing and intense and—oh, my God, I'm staring.

The corner of his mouth tilts up in a knowing smile as he passes me and heads straight for the couch.

Despite his appealing and slightly innocent-looking face, I want to yell at him for being so deceitful. He shouldn't have waited more than two weeks to tell me. I would have had a chance to plan all this out a little better. I don't understand how we could have had two weeks' worth of conversations without his feeling the need to tell me that my boyfriend and my best friend were screwing.

Ridge throws the blankets and the pillow onto the couch.

"I'm not staying here, Ridge," I say, attempting to stop him from wasting time with his hospitality. I know he feels bad for me, but I hardly know him, and I'd feel a lot more comfortable in a hotel room than sleeping on a strange couch.

Then again, hotel rooms require money.

Something I don't have on me at the moment.

Something that's inside my purse, across the courtyard, in an apartment with the only two people in the world I don't want to see right now.

Maybe a couch isn't such a bad idea after all.

He gets the couch made up and turns around, dropping his eyes to my soaking-wet clothes. I look down at the puddle of water I'm creating in the middle of his floor.

"Oh, sorry," I mutter. My hair is matted to my face; my shirt is now a see-through pathetic excuse for a barrier between the outside world and my very pink, very noticeable bra. "Where's your bathroom?"

He nods his head toward the bathroom door.

I turn around, unzip a suitcase, and begin to rummage through it while Ridge walks back into his bedroom. I'm glad he doesn't ask me questions about what happened after our conversation earlier. I'm not in the mood to talk about it.

I select a pair of yoga pants and a tank top, then grab my bag of toiletries and head to the bathroom. It disturbs me that everything about this apartment reminds me of my own, with just a few subtle differences. This is the same bathroom with the Jack-and-Jill doors on the left and right, leading to the two bedrooms that adjoin it. One is Ridge's, obviously. I'm curious about who the other bedroom belongs to but not curious enough to open it. The Hooters girl's one rule was to stay the hell out of her room, and she doesn't seem like the type to kid around.

I shut the door that leads to the living room and lock it, then check the locks on both doors to the bedrooms to make sure no one can walk in. I have no idea if anyone lives in this apartment other than Ridge and the Hooters girl, but I don't want to chance it.

I pull off my sopping clothes and throw them into the sink to avoid soaking the floor. I turn on the shower and wait until the water gets warm, then step in. I stand under the stream of water and close my eyes, thankful that I'm not still sitting outside in the rain. At the same time, I'm not really happy to be where I am, either.

I never expected my twenty-second birthday to end with me showering in a strange apartment and sleeping on a couch that belongs to a guy I've barely known for two weeks, all at the hands of the two people I cared about and trusted the most.

1.

Sydney

I slide open my balcony door and step outside, thankful that the sun has already dipped behind the building next door, cooling the air to what could pass as a perfect fall temperature. Almost on cue, the sound of his guitar floats across the courtyard as I take a seat and lean back into the patio lounger. I tell Tori I come out here to get homework done, because I don't want to admit that the guitar is the only reason I'm outside every night at eight, like clockwork.

For weeks now, the guy in the apartment across the courtyard has sat on his balcony and played for at least an hour. Every night, I sit outside and listen.

I've noticed a few other neighbors come out to their balconies when he's playing, but no one is as loyal as I am. I don't understand how someone could hear these songs and not crave them day after day. Then again, music has always been a passion of mine, so maybe I'm just a little more infatuated with his sound than other people are. I've played the piano for as long as I can remember, and although I've never shared it with anyone, I love writing music. I even switched my major to music education two years ago. My plan is to be an elementary music teacher, although if my father had his way, I'd still be prelaw.

"A life of mediocrity is a waste of a life," he said when I informed him that I was changing my major.

A life of mediocrity. I find that more amusing than insulting, since he seems to be the most dissatisfied person I've ever known. And he's a lawyer. Go figure.

One of the familiar songs ends and the guy with the guitar begins to play something he's never played before. I've grown accustomed to his unofficial playlist since he seems to practice the same songs in the same order night after night. However, I've never heard him play this particular song before. The way he's repeating the same chords makes me think he's creating the song right here on the spot. I like that I'm witnessing this, especially since after only a few chords, it's already my new favorite. All his songs sound like originals. I wonder if he performs them locally or if he just writes them for fun.

I lean forward in the chair, rest my arms on the edge of the balcony, and watch him. His balcony is directly across the courtyard, far enough away that I don't feel weird when I watch him but close enough that I make sure I'm never watching him when Hunter's around. I don't think Hunter would like the fact that I've developed a tiny crush on this guy's talent.

I can't deny it, though. Anyone who watches how passionately this guy plays would crush on his talent. The way he keeps his eyes closed the entire time, focusing intently on every stroke against every guitar string. I like it best when he sits cross-legged with the guitar upright between his legs. He pulls it against his chest and plays it like a stand-up bass, keeping his eyes closed the whole time. It's so mesmerizing to watch him that sometimes I catch myself holding my breath, and I don't even realize I'm doing it until I'm gasping for air.

It also doesn't help that he's cute. At least, he seems cute from here. His light brown hair is unruly and moves with him, falling across his forehead every time he looks down at his guitar. He's too far away to distinguish eye color or distinct features, but the details don't matter when coupled with the passion he has for his music. There's a confidence to him that I find compelling. I've always admired musicians who are able to tune out everyone and everything around them and pour all of their focus into their music. To be able to shut the world off and allow yourself to be completely swept away is something I've always wanted the confidence to do, but I just don't have it.

This guy has it. He's confident and talented. I've always been a sucker for musicians, but more in a fantasy way. They're a different breed. A breed that rarely makes for good boyfriends.

He glances at me as if he can hear my thoughts, and then a slow grin appears across his face. He never once pauses the song while he continues to watch me. The eye contact makes me blush, so I drop my arms and pull my notebook back onto my lap and look down at it. I hate that he just caught me staring so hard. Not that I was doing anything wrong; it just feels odd for him to know I was watching him. I glance up again, and he's still watching me, but he's not smiling anymore. The way he's staring causes my heart to speed up, so I look away and focus on my notebook.

Way to be a creeper, Sydney.

"There's my girl," a comforting voice says from behind me. I lean my head back and tilt my eyes upward to watch Hunter as he makes his way onto the balcony. I try to hide the fact that I'm shocked to see him, because I'm pretty sure I was supposed to remember he was coming.

On the off chance that Guitar Boy is still watching, I make it a point to seem really into Hunter's hello kiss so that maybe I'll seem less like a creepy stalker and more like someone just casually relaxing on her balcony. I run my hand up Hunter's neck as he leans over the back of my chair and kisses me upside down.

"Scoot up," Hunter says, pushing on my shoulders. I do what he asks and slide forward in the seat as he lifts his leg over the chair and slips in behind me. He pulls my back against his chest and wraps his arms around me.

My eyes betray me when the sound of the guitar stops abruptly, and I glance across the courtyard once more. Guitar Boy is eyeing us hard as he stands, then goes back inside his apartment. His expression is odd. Almost angry.

"How was school?" Hunter asks.

"Too boring to talk about. What about you? How was work?"

"Interesting," he says, brushing my hair away from my neck with his hand. He presses his lips to my neck and kisses his way down my collarbone.

"What was so interesting?"

He tightens his hold on me, then rests his chin on my shoulder and pulls me back in the chair with him. "The oddest thing happened at lunch," he says. "I was with one of the guys at this Italian restaurant. We were eating out on the patio, and I had just asked the waiter what he recommended for dessert, when a police car rounded the corner. They stopped right in front of the restaurant, and two officers jumped out with their guns drawn. They began barking orders toward us when our waiter mumbled, 'Shit.' He slowly raised his hands, and the police jumped the barrier to the patio, rushed toward him, threw him to the ground, and cuffed him right at our feet. After they read him his rights, they pulled him to his feet and escorted him toward the cop car. The waiter glanced back at me and yelled, 'The tiramisu is really good!' Then they put him in the car and drove away."

I tilt my head back and look up at him. "Seriously? That really happened?"

He nods, laughing. "I swear, Syd. It was crazy."

"Well? Did you try the tiramisu?"

"Hell, yeah, we did. It was the best tiramisu I've ever had." He kisses me on the cheek and pushes me forward. "Speaking of food, I'm starving." He stands up and holds out his hand to me. "Did you cook tonight?"

I take his hand and let him pull me up. "We just had salad, but I can make you one."

Once we're inside, Hunter takes a seat on the couch next to Tori. She's got a textbook spread open across her lap as she halfheartedly focuses on both homework and TV at the same time. I take out the containers from the fridge and make his salad. I feel a little guilty that I forgot tonight was one of the nights he said he was coming. I usually have something cooked when I know he'll be here.

We've been dating for almost two years now. I met him during my sophomore year in college, when he was a senior. He and Tori had been friends for years. After she moved into my dorm and we became friends, she insisted I meet him. She said we'd hit it off, and she was right. We made it official after only two dates, and things have been wonderful since.

Of course, we have our ups and downs, especially since he moved more than an hour away. When he landed the job in the accounting firm last semester, he suggested I move with him. I told him no, that I really wanted to finish my undergrad before taking such a huge step. In all honesty, I'm just scared.

The thought of moving in with him seems so final, as if I would be sealing my fate. I know that once we take that step, the next step is marriage, and then I'd be looking at never having the chance to live alone. I've always had a roommate, and until I can afford my own place, I'll be sharing an apartment with Tori. I haven't told Hunter yet, but I really want to live alone for a year. It's something I promised myself I would do before I got married. I don't even turn twenty-two for a couple of weeks, so it's not as if I'm in any hurry.

I take Hunter's food to him in the living room.

"Why do you watch this?" he says to Tori. "All these women do is talk shit about each other and flip tables."

"That's exactly why I watch it," Tori says, without taking her eyes off the TV.

Hunter winks at me and takes his food, then props his feet up on the coffee table. "Thanks, babe." He turns toward the TV and begins eating. "Can you grab me a beer?"

I nod and walk back into the kitchen. I open the refrigerator door and look on the shelf where he always keeps his extra beer. I realize as I'm staring at "his" shelf that this is probably how it begins. First, he has a shelf in the refrigerator. Then he'll have a toothbrush in the bathroom, a drawer in my dresser, and eventually, his stuff will infiltrate mine in so many ways it'll be impossible for me ever to be on my own.

I run my hands up my arms, rubbing away the sudden onset of discomfort washing over me. I feel as if I'm watching my future play out in front of me. I'm not so sure I like what I'm imagining.

Am I ready for this?

Am I ready for this guy to be the guy I bring dinner to every night when he gets home from work?

Am I ready to fall into this comfortable life with him? One where I teach all day and he does people's taxes, and then we come home and I cook dinner and I "grab him beers" while he props his feet up and calls me *babe*, and then we go to our bed and make love at approximately nine P.M. so we won't be tired the next day, in order to wake up and get dressed and go to work and do it all over again?

"Earth to Sydney," Hunter says. I hear him snap his fingers twice. "Beer? Please, babe?"

I quickly grab his beer, give it to him, then head straight to my bathroom. I turn the water on in the shower, but I don't get in. Instead, I lock the door and sink to the floor.

We have a good relationship. He's good to me, and I know he loves me. I just don't understand why every time I think about a future with him, it's not an exciting thought.

Ridge

Maggie leans forward and kisses my forehead. "I need to go."

I'm on my back with my head and shoulders partially propped against my headboard. She's straddling my lap and looking down at me regretfully. I hate that we live so far apart now, but it makes the time we do spend together a lot more meaningful. I take her hands so she'll shut up, and I pull her to me, hoping to persuade her not to leave just yet.

She laughs and shakes her head. She kisses me, but only briefly, and then she pulls away again. She slides off my lap, but I don't let her make it very far before I lunge forward and pin her to the mattress. I point to her chest.

"You"—I lean in and kiss the tip of her nose—"need to stay one more night."

"I can't. I have class."

I grab her wrists and pin her arms above her head, then press my lips to hers. I know she won't stay another night. She's never missed a day of class in her life, unless she was too sick to move. I sort of wish she was feeling a little sick right now, so I could make her stay in bed with me.

I slide my hands from her wrists, delicately up her arms until I'm cupping her face. Then I give her one final kiss before I reluctantly pull away from her. "Go. And be careful. Let me know when you make it home."

She nods and pushes herself off the bed. She reaches across me and grabs her shirt, then pulls it on over her head. I watch her as she walks around the room and gathers the clothes I pulled off her in a hurry.

After five years of dating, most couples would have moved in together by now. However, most peoples' other halves aren't Maggie. She's so fiercely independent it's almost intimidating. But it's understandable, considering how her life has gone. She's been caring for her grandfather since I met her. Before that, she spent the majority of her teenage years helping him care for her grandmother, who died when Maggie was sixteen. Now that her grandfather is in a nursing home, she finally has a chance to live alone while finishing school, and as much as I want her here with me, I also know how important this internship is for her. So for the next year, I'll suck it up while she's in San Antonio and I'm here in Austin. I'll be damned if I ever move out of Austin, especially for San Antonio.

Unless she asked, of course.

"Tell your brother I said good luck." She's standing in my bedroom doorway, poised to leave. "And you need to quit beating yourself up, Ridge. Musicians have blocks, just like writers do. You'll find your muse again. I love you."

"I love you, too."

She smiles and backs out of my bedroom. I groan, knowing she's trying to be positive with the whole writer's block thing, but I can't stop stressing about it. I don't know if it's because Brennan has so much riding on these songs now or if it's because I'm completely tapped out, but the words just aren't coming. Without lyrics I'm confident in, it's hard to feel good about the actual musical aspect of writing.

My phone vibrates. It's a text from Brennan, which only makes me feel worse about the fact that I'm stuck.

Brennan: It's been weeks. Please tell me you have something.

Me: Working on it. How's the tour?

Brennan: Good, but remind me not to allow Warren to schedule this many gigs on the next leg.

Me: Gigs are what gets your name out there.

Brennan: OUR name. I'm not telling you again to stop acting like you aren't half of this.

Me: I won't be half if I can't work through this damn block.

Brennan: Maybe you should get out more. Cause some unnecessary drama in your life. Break up with Maggie for the sake of art. She'll understand. Heartache helps with lyrical inspiration. Don't you ever listen to country?

Me: Good idea. I'll tell Maggie you suggested that.

Brennan: Nothing I say or do could ever make Maggie hate me. Give her a kiss for me, and get to writing. Our careers are resting squarely on your shoulders.

Me: Asshole.

Brennan: Ah! Is that anger I detect in your text? Use it. Go write an angry song about how much you hate your little brother, then send it to me. ;)

Me: Yeah. I'll give it to you after you finally get your shit out of your old bedroom. Bridgette's sister might move in next month.

Brennan: Have you ever met Brandi?

Me: No. Do I want to?

Brennan: Only if you want to live with two Bridgettes.

Me: Oh, shit.

Brennan: Exactly. TTYL.

I close out the text to Brennan and open up a text to Warren.

Me: We're good to go on the roommate search. Brennan says hell no to Brandi. I'll let you break the news to Bridgette, since you two get along so well.

Warren: Well, motherfucker.

I laugh and hop off the bed, then head to the patio with my guitar. It's almost eight, and I know she'll be on her balcony. I don't know how weird my actions are about to seem to her, but all I can do is try. I've got nothing to lose.

About the Author

Colleen Hoover is the #1 *New York Times* bestselling author of *Slammed*, *Point of Retreat*, *Hopeless*, *This Girl*, and *Losing Hope*. Colleen lives in Texas with her husband and their three boys. Please visit her Facebook page at www.facebook.com/authorcolleenhoover and her website at ColleenHoover.com.

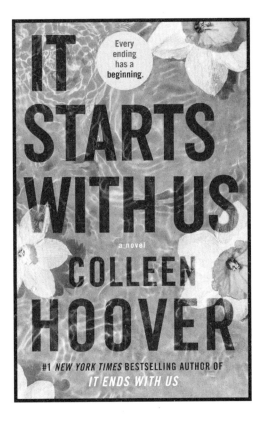

Losing
Hope

Also by Colleen Hoover

Slammed
Point of Retreat
Hopeless
This Girl

Losing Hope

A Novel

Colleen Hoover

ATRIA PAPERBACK

NEW YORK   LONDON   TORONTO   SYDNEY   NEW DELHI

ATRIA PAPERBACK

A Division of Simon & Schuster, Inc.

1230 Avenue of the Americas

New York, NY 10020

First Atria Paperback edition October 2013

ATRIA PAPERBACK and colophon are trademarks of Simon & Schuster, Inc.

For information about special discounts for bulk purchases, please contact Simon & Schuster Special Sales at 1-866-506-1949 or business@simonandschuster.com.

The Simon & Schuster Speakers Bureau can bring authors to your live event. For more information or to book an event, contact the Simon & Schuster Speakers Bureau at 1-866-248-3049 or visit our website at www.simonspeakers.com.

Manufactured in China

10   9   8   7   6   5   4   3   2   1

Library of Congress Cataloging-in-Publication Data is available.

ISBN 978-1-4767-4655-5
ISBN 978-1-4767-4656-2 (ebook)

This book is dedicated to my husband and sons,
for their endless, selfless support.

Chapter One

My heart rate is signaling for me to just walk away. Les has reminded me more than once that it's not my business. She's never been a brother before, though. She has no idea how hard it is to sit back and *not* let it be my business. That's why, right now, this son-of-a-bitch is my number-one priority.

I slide my hands into the back pockets of my jeans and hope to hell I can keep them there. I'm standing behind the couch, looking down at him. I don't know how long it'll take him to notice I'm here. Considering the grip he has on the chick straddling his lap, I doubt he'll notice for a while. I remain behind them for several minutes while the party continues around us, everyone completely unaware that I'm a fraction away from losing my mind. I would take out my phone so that I'd have evidence, but I couldn't do that to Les. She doesn't need a visual.

"Hey," I finally say, unable to contain my silence a second longer. If I have to watch him palm this chick's breast one more time without a single ounce of respect for his relationship with Les, I'll rip his fucking hand off.

Grayson tears his mouth away from hers and tilts his head back, looking up at me with glossed-over eyes. I can see the fear settle in when it clicks—when he finally realizes that the last person he thought would be here tonight actually showed up.

"Holder," he says, pushing the girl off his lap. He struggles to his feet but can hardly stand up straight. He looks at me pleadingly, pointing at the girl, who's now adjusting her barely-there skirt. "This isn't . . . it's not what it looks like."

I slide my hands out of my back pockets and fold my arms across my chest. My fist is closer to him now and I have to clench it, knowing how good it would feel to punch his face in.

I look down to the floor and inhale a breath. Then another. And one more just for show, since I'm really enjoying watching him squirm. I shake my head and raise my eyes back to his. "Give me your phone."

The confusion on his face would be comical if I weren't so pissed. He laughs and attempts to back up a step, but bumps into the coffee table. He catches himself by pressing his hand onto the glass and straightens back up. "Get your own fucking phone," he mumbles. He doesn't look back at me as he maneuvers his way around the coffee table. I calmly walk around the couch and intercept him, holding out my hand.

"Give me your phone, Grayson. *Now.*"

I'm not really at an advantage sizewise, since we're about the same build. However, I'm definitely at an advantage if you take my anger into consideration, and Grayson can clearly see that. He takes a step back, which probably isn't a very smart move considering he's backing himself straight into the corner of the living room. He fumbles with his pocket and finally pulls out his phone.

"What the hell do you want my phone for?" he says. I grab it out of his hands and dial Les's number without hitting send. I hand it back to him.

"Call her. Tell her what a bastard you are and end it."

Grayson looks down at his phone, then back up at me. "Go fuck yourself," he spits.

I inhale a calming breath, then roll my neck and pop my jaw. When that doesn't help ease my urge to make him bleed, I reach forward, grab the collar of his shirt and shove him hard against the wall, pinning his neck with my forearm. I remind myself that if I kick his ass before he makes the call, my remaining calm for the past ten minutes will have been pointless.

My teeth are clenched, my jaw is tight, and my pulse is pounding in my head. I've never hated anyone more than in this moment. The intensity of what I wish I could do to him right now is even scaring *me*.

I look him hard in the eyes and let him know how the next few minutes are about to play out. "Grayson," I say through clenched teeth. "Unless you want me to do what I really want to do to you right now, you will put the phone to your ear, you will call my sister, and you will end it. Then you're going to hang up the phone and never speak to her again." I press my arm harder against his neck, taking note of the fact that his face is now redder than his shirt, due to lack of oxygen.

"Fine," he grumbles, attempting to free himself from the hold I have on him. I wait until he looks down at the phone and hits send before I release my arm and let go of his shirt. He puts the phone to his ear and never stops looking at me as we both stand still and wait for Les to answer.

I know what this will do to her, but she has no idea what he does behind her back. No matter how many times she hears it from other people, he's somehow able to weasel his way back into her life every time.

Not this time. Not if I have any control over it. I won't sit back and let him do this to my sister anymore.

"Hey," he says into the phone. He tries to turn away from me to speak to her, but I shove his shoulder back against the wall. He winces.

"No, babe," he says nervously. "I'm at Jaxon's house." There's a long pause while he listens to her speak. "I know that's what I said, but I lied. That's why I'm calling. Les, I . . . I think we need some space."

I shake my head, letting him know that he needs to make it an absolute break-up. I'm not looking for him to give her space. I'm looking for him to give my sister permanent freedom.

He rolls his eyes and flips me off with his free hand. "I'm breaking up with you," he says flatly. He allows her to talk while he remains silent. The fact that he's showing no remorse whatsoever proves what a heartless dick he is. My hands are shaking and my chest tightens, knowing exactly what this is doing to Les right now. I hate myself for forcing this to happen, but Les deserves better, even if she doesn't think she does.

"I'm hanging up now," he says into the phone.

I shove his head back against the wall and force him to look at me. "Apologize to her," I say quietly, not wanting her to hear me in the background. He closes his eyes and sighs, then ducks his head.

"I'm sorry, Lesslie. I didn't want to do this." He pulls the phone from his ear and abruptly ends the call. He stares at the screen for several seconds. "I hope you're happy," he says, looking back up at me. "Because you just broke your sister's heart."

That's the last thing Grayson says to me. My fist meets his jaw twice before he hits the floor. I shake out my hand, back away from him, and make my way to the exit. Before I even reach my car, my phone is buzzing in my back pocket. I pull it out and don't even look at the screen before answering it.

"Hey," I say, attempting to control the trembling anger in my voice when I hear her crying on the other end. "I'm on my way, Les. It'll be okay, I'm on my way."

It's been an entire day since Grayson made the call, but I still feel guilty, so I tack on an extra two miles to my evening run for self-inflicted punishment. Seeing Les torn up like she was last night wasn't something I had expected. I realize now that having him call her like I did probably wasn't the best way of handling things, but there's no way I could just sit back and allow him to dick around on her like he was.

The most unexpected thing about Les's reaction was that her anger wasn't solely placed on Grayson. It was as if she was pissed at the entire male population. She kept referring to men as "sick bastards," pacing her bedroom floor back and forth, while I just sat there and watched her vent. She finally broke down, crawled into bed, and cried herself to sleep. I lay awake, knowing I had a hand in her heartache. I stayed in her room the whole night, partly to make sure she was okay, but mostly because I didn't want her picking up the phone and calling Grayson in a moment of desperation.

She's stronger than I give her credit for, though. She didn't attempt to call him last night and she's made no attempt to call him today. She didn't get much sleep last night, so she went to her room before lunch to nap. However, I've been pausing outside her bedroom door throughout the day just to make sure I couldn't hear her on the phone, so I know she hasn't made any attempts to call him. At least while I've been home. In fact, I'm pretty sure the heartless phone call from him last night was exactly what she needed to finally see him for who he really is.

I kick my shoes off at the door and walk to the kitchen to refill my water. It's Saturday night and I would normally be heading out with Daniel, but I already texted him to let him know I was staying in tonight. Les made me promise I would stay in with her because she didn't want to go out and chance running into Grayson yet. She's lucky she's cool, because I don't know many seventeen-year-old guys who would give up a Saturday night to watch chick flicks with his heartbroken sister. But then again, most siblings don't have what Les and I have. I don't know if our close relationship has anything to do with the fact that we're twins. She's my only sibling, so I don't have anything to compare us to. She might argue that I'm too protective of her, and there may be some truth to that argument, but I don't plan on changing anytime soon. Or ever.

I run up the stairs, pull my shirt off, and push open the bathroom door. I turn the water on, then walk across the hall and knock on her bedroom door. "I'm taking a quick shower, will you order the pizza?"

I brace my hand against her door and reach down to pull my socks off. I turn around and toss them into the bathroom, then beat on her door again. "Les!"

When she doesn't respond, I sigh and look up at the ceiling. If she's on the phone with him, I'll be pissed. But if she's on the phone with him, it probably means he's telling her the break-up was all my fault and *she'll* be the one who's pissed. I wipe my palms on my shorts and open the door to her bedroom, preparing for another heated lecture on how I need to mind my own business.

I see Les on her bed after I walk into her room, and I'm immediately taken back to when I was a little boy. Back to the moment that changed me. Everything about me. Everything about the world *around* me. My whole world turned from a place full of vibrant colors to a dull, lifeless gray. The sky, the grass, the trees . . . all the things that were once beautiful were stripped of their magnificence the moment I realized I was responsible for our best friend Hope's disappearance.

I never looked at people the same way. I never looked at nature the same way. I never looked at my future the same way. Everything went from having a meaning, a purpose, and a reason, to simply being a second-rate version of what life was *supposed* to be like. My once effervescent world was suddenly a blurred, gray, colorless photocopy.

Just like Les's eyes.

They aren't hers. They're open. They're looking right at me from her position on the bed.

But they aren't hers.

The color in her eyes is gone. This girl is a gray, colorless photocopy of my sister.

My Les.

I can't move. I wait for her to blink, to laugh, to revel in the twisted aftermath of the sick, fucking joke she's playing right now. I wait for my heart to start beating again, for my lungs to start working again. I wait for control of my body to return to me because I don't know who has control of it right now. *I* sure as hell don't. I wait and I wait and I wonder how long she can keep this up. How long can people keep their eyes open like that? How long can people not breathe before their body jerks for that desperately needed gasp of air?

How fucking long before I do something to *help* her?

My hands are touching her face, grabbing her arm, shaking her whole body until she's in my arms and I'm pulling her onto my lap. The empty pill bottle falls out of her hand and lands on the floor but I refuse to look at it. Her eyes are still lifeless and she's no longer looking at me as the head between my hands falls backward every time I try to lift it up.

She doesn't flinch when I scream her name, and she doesn't wince when I slap her, and she doesn't react when I start to cry.

She doesn't do a goddamned thing.

She doesn't even tell me it'll be okay when every single ounce of whatever was left inside my chest is propelled out of me the moment I realize that the very best part of me is dead.

Chapter Two

"Will you look for her pink top and the black pleated pants?" my mother asks. She keeps her eyes trained on the paperwork laid out in front of her. The man from the funeral home reaches across the table and points to a spot on the form.

"Just a few more pages, Beth," he says. My mother mechanically signs the forms without question. She's trying to keep it together until they leave, but I know as soon as they walk out the front door she'll break down again. It's only been forty-eight hours, but I can tell just by looking at her that she's about to experience it all over again.

You would think a person could only die once. You would think you would only find your sister's lifeless body once. You would think you would only have to watch your mother's reaction once after finding out her only daughter is dead.

Once is so far from accurate.

It happens repeatedly.

Every single time I close my eyes I see Les's eyes. Every time my mother looks at me, she's watching me tell her that her daughter is dead for the second time. For the third time. For the thousandth time. Every time I take a breath or blink or speak, I experience her death all over again. I don't sit here and wonder if the fact that she's dead will ever sink in. I sit here and wonder when I'll stop having to watch her die.

"Holder, they need an outfit for her," my mother repeats again after noticing I haven't moved. "Go to her room and get the pink shirt with the long sleeves. It's her favorite one, she'd want to wear it."

She knows I don't want to go into Les's bedroom any more than she does. I push my chair away from the table and head upstairs. "Les is dead," I mutter to myself. "She doesn't give a shit what she's wearing."

I pause outside her door, knowing I'll have to watch her die all over again the moment I open it. I haven't been in here since I found her and I really had no intention of *ever* coming back in here.

I walk inside and shut the door behind me, then make my way to her closet. I do my best not to think about it.

Pink shirt.

Don't think about her.

Long sleeves.

Don't think about how you would do anything to go back to Saturday night.

Pleated black pants.

Don't think about how much you fucking hate yourself right now for letting her down.

But I do. I think about it and I become hurt and angry all over again. I grab a fistful of shirts hanging in the closet and rip them as hard as I can off their hangers until they fall to the closet floor. I grip the frame on top of the door and squeeze my eyes shut, listening to the sound of the now empty hangers swinging back and forth. I try to focus on the fact that I'm in here to grab two things and leave, but I can't move. I can't stop replaying the moment that I walked into this bedroom and found her.

I fall to my knees on the floor, look over at her bed, and watch her die one more time.

I sit back against the closet door and close my eyes, remaining in this position for however long it takes me to realize that I don't want to be in here. I turn around and rummage through the shirts that are now on the closet floor until I find the long-sleeved pink one. I look up at the pants hanging from their hangers and I grab a pair of black pleated ones. I toss them to the side and begin to push up from the floor, but immediately sit back down when I see a thick, leather-bound notebook on the bottom shelf of her closet.

I grab it and pull it onto my lap, then lean back against the wall and stare at the cover. I've seen this notebook before. It was a gift to her from Dad about three years ago, but Les told me she'd never use it because she knew the notebook was just a request made by her therapist. Les hated therapy, and I was never sure why Mom encouraged her to go. We both went for a while after Mom and Dad split up, but I stopped attending the sessions once they started interfering with junior high football practice. Mom didn't seem to mind that I didn't go, but Les continued with the weekly sessions up until two days ago . . . when her actions made it clear the therapy wasn't exactly helping.

I flip the notebook open to the first page and it doesn't surprise me that it's blank. I wonder, if she had used the notebook like the therapist suggested, would it have made a difference?

I doubt it. I don't know what could have saved Les from herself. Certainly not a pen and paper.

I pull the pen out of the spiral binding, then press the tip of the pen to the paper and begin to write her a letter. I don't even know why I'm writing her. I don't know if she's in a place where she can see me right now, or if she's even in a place at *all*, but in case she can see this . . . I want her to know how her selfish decision affected me. How hopeless she left me. *Literally* hopeless. And completely alone. And so, so incredibly sorry.

Chapter Two-and-a-half

Les,

You left your jeans in the middle of your bedroom floor. It looks like you just stepped out of them. It's weird. Why would you leave your jeans on the floor if you knew what you were about to do? Wouldn't you at least throw them in the hamper? Did you not think about what would happen after I found you and how someone would eventually have to pick your jeans up and do something with them? Well, I'm not picking them up. And I'm not hanging all your shirts back up, either.

Anyway. I'm in your closet. On the floor. I just don't really know what I want to say to you right now, or what I want to ask you. Of course the only question on everyone else's mind right now is "Why did she do it?" But I'm not going to ask you why you did it for two reasons.

1) You can't answer me. You're dead.
2) I don't know if I really care why you did it. There isn't anything about your life that would give you a good enough reason to do what you did. And you probably already know that if you can see Mom right now. She's completely devastated.

You know, I never really knew what it meant to actually be devastated. I thought we were devastated after we lost Hope. What happened to her was definitely tragic for us, but the way we felt was nothing compared to how you've made Mom feel. She's so incredibly devastated; she gives the word a whole new meaning. I wish the use of the word could be restricted to situations like this. It's absurd that people are allowed to use it to describe anything other than how a mother feels when she loses her child. Because that's the only situation in this entire world worthy of the term.

Dammit, I miss you so much. I'm so sorry I let you down. I'm sorry I wasn't able to see what was really going on behind your eyes every time you told me you were fine.

So, yeah. Why, Les? Why did you do it?

H

Chapter Two-and-three-quarters

Les,

Well, congratulations. You're pretty popular. Not only did you fill the parking lot of the funeral home with cars, but you also filled the lot next door and both churches down the street. That's a lot of cars.

I held it together, though; mostly for Mom's sake. Dad looked almost as bad as Mom. The whole funeral was really weird. It made me wonder, had you died in a car wreck or from something more mainstream, would people's reactions have been different? If you hadn't purposely overdosed (that's the term Mom prefers), then I think people might have been a little less weird. It was like they were scared of us, or maybe they thought purposely overdosing was contagious. They discussed it like we weren't even in the same room. So many stares and whispers and pitiful smiles. I just wanted to grab Mom and pull her out of there and protect her from the fact that I knew she was reliving your death with every hug and every tear and every smile.

Of course I couldn't help but think everyone was acting like they were because they blamed us in a way. I could tell what they were thinking.

How could a family not know this would happen?

How could they not see the signs?

What kind of mother is she?

What kind of brother doesn't notice how depressed his own twin sister is?

Luckily, once your funeral began, everyone's focus was momentarily taken off us and placed on the slideshow. There were a lot of pictures of you and me. You were happy in all of them. There were a lot of pictures of you and your friends, and you were happy in all of those, too. Pictures of you with Mom and Dad before the divorce; pictures of you with Mom and Brian after she remarried; pictures of you with Dad and Pamela after he remarried.

But it wasn't until the very last picture came up on the screen that it hit me. It was the picture of you and me in front of our old house. The one that was taken about six months after Hope went missing? You still had the bracelet on that matched the one you gave her the day she was taken. I noticed you stopped wearing it a couple of years ago, but I've never asked about it. I know you don't really like to talk about her.

Anyway, back to the picture. I had my arm around your neck and we were both laughing and smiling at the camera. It's the same smile you flashed in all the other pictures. It got me to thinking about how every picture I've ever seen of you; you have that same exact, identical smile. There isn't a single picture of you with a frown on your face. Or a scowl. Or a blank expression. It's like you spent your whole life trying to keep up this false appearance. For whom, I don't know. Maybe you were scared that a camera would permanently capture an honest feeling of yours.

Because let's face it, you weren't happy all the time. All those nights you cried yourself to sleep? All those nights you needed me to hold you while you cried, but you refused to tell me what was wrong? No one with a genuine smile would cry to themselves like that. And I realize you had issues, Les. I knew our life and the things that happened to us affected you differently than they did me. But how was I supposed to know that they were as serious as they were if you never let it show? If you never told me?

Maybe... and I hate to think this. But maybe I didn't know you. I thought I did, but I didn't. I don't think I knew you at all. I knew the girl who cried at night. I knew the girl who smiled in the pictures. But I didn't know the girl that linked that smile with those tears. I have no idea why you flashed fake smiles, but cried real tears. When a guy loves a girl, especially his sister, he's supposed to know what makes her smile and what makes her cry.

But I didn't. And I don't. So I'm sorry, Les. I'm so sorry I let you go on pretending that you were okay when obviously you were so far from it.

H

Chapter Three

"Beth, why don't you go to bed?" Brian says to my mother. "You're exhausted. Go get some sleep."

My mother shakes her head and continues stirring, despite the pleas from my stepdad for her to take a break. We've got enough food in the refrigerator to feed an army, yet she insists on cooking for everyone just so we don't have to eat the *sympathy food*, as she refers to it. I'm so sick of fried chicken. It seems to be the go-to meal for anyone dropping food off at the house. I've had fried chicken for every meal since the morning after Les died, and that was four days ago.

I walk to the stove and take the spoon out of her hands, then rub her shoulder with my free hand while I stir. She leans against me and sighs. It's not a good sigh, either. It's a sigh that all but says, "I'm done."

"Please, go sit on the couch. I can finish this," I say to her. She nods and walks aimlessly into the living room. I watch from the kitchen as she takes a seat and leans her head back into the couch, looking up to the ceiling. Brian takes a seat next to her and pulls her to him. I don't even have to hear her to know she's crying again. I can see it in the way she slumps against him and grabs hold of his shirt.

I look away.

"Maybe you should come stay with us, Dean," my father says, leaning against the counter. "Just for a little while. It might do you some good to get away."

He's the only one who still calls me Dean. I've been going by Holder since I was eight, but the fact that I was named after him may be why he never took to calling me anything other than Dean. I only see him a couple of times a year, so it doesn't bother me too much that he still calls me Dean. I still hate the name, though.

I look at him, then back to my mother still holding on to Brian in the living room. "I can't, Dad. I'm not leaving her. Especially now."

He's been trying to get me to move to Austin with him since they divorced. The truth is, I like it here. I haven't liked visiting my old hometown since I moved away. Too many things remind me of Hope when I'm there.

But I guess too many things are going to start reminding me of Les, here.

"Well, my offer doesn't expire," he says. "You know that."

I nod and switch off the burner. "It's ready," I say.

Brian comes back to the kitchen with Pam and we all take seats at the table, but my mother remains in the living room, softly crying into the couch throughout dinner.

I'm waving good-bye to my father and Pam when Amy pulls up in front of our house. She waits for my father's car to clear, then she pulls into our driveway. I walk to the driver's side door and open it for her.

She smiles half-heartedly and flips the visor down, wiping the mascara from underneath the frame of her sunglasses. It's been dark for over an hour now, yet she's still wearing sunglasses. That can only mean she's been crying.

I haven't really talked to her much in the past four days, but I don't have to ask her how she's holding up. She and Les have been best friends for seven years. If there's anyone that feels like I do right now, it's her. And I'm not even sure if *I'm* holding up all that well.

"Where's Thomas?" I ask when she steps out of the car.

She pushes her blonde hair away from her face with her sunglasses, adjusting them on top of her head. "He's at his house. He had to go help his dad with some yard stuff after school."

I don't know how long the two of them have been dating, but they were together before Les and I even moved here. And we moved here in the fourth grade, so it's been a while.

"How's your mom?" she asks. As soon as she says it, she shakes her head apologetically. "I'm sorry, Holder. That was a really stupid question. I promised myself I wouldn't be one of those people."

"Believe me, you're not," I assure her. I motion behind me. "You coming inside?"

She nods and glances at the house, then to me. "Do you mind if I go up to her room? It's fine if you don't want me up there yet. It's just that she had a few pictures I'd really like to have."

"No, it's fine." Based on the relationship she had with Les, Amy has just as much right to be in Les's bedroom as I do. I know Les would want Amy to take whatever it is she wants.

She follows me into the house and up the stairs. I notice my mother isn't on the couch anymore. Brian must have finally coaxed her into going to bed. I walk to the top of the stairs with Amy, but have no desire to go into Les's room with her. I nudge my head toward my bedroom. "I'll be in my room if you need me."

She inhales a deep, nervous breath and nods while releasing it. "Thanks," she says, eyeing Les's door warily. She takes a reluctant step toward the bedroom, so I turn away and head to my room. I shut the door behind me and take a seat on the bed, picking up Les's notebook while I lean back against my headboard. I've already written her today, but I grab a pen because I've got nothing better to do than write to her again. Or at least there's nothing else I *want* to do because it all leads back to thoughts of her anyway.

Chapter Three-and-a-half

Les,

Amy's here. She's in your room, going through your shit.
   I wonder if she had any clue as to what you were
about to do? I know sometimes girls share stuff with
their girlfriends that they wouldn't share with anyone
else—even twin brothers. Did you ever tell her how you
really felt? Did you give her any hints at all? I'm
really hoping you didn't, because that would mean she
probably feels pretty damn guilty right about now. She
doesn't deserve to feel guilty over what you did, Les.
She's been your best friend for seven years now, so
I hope to hell you thought about that before you made
such a selfish decision.
   I feel guilty for what you did, but I deserve to feel
guilty. There's a responsibility that comes along with
being a brother that doesn't necessarily come along with
being a best friend. It was my job to protect you, not
Amy's. So she doesn't deserve to feel guilty.
   Maybe that was my problem. Maybe I spent so much
time trying to protect you from Grayson that I never
thought who I really needed to be protecting you from
was yourself.

   H

*   *   *

There's a light tap on my bedroom door, so I close the notebook and set it on the nightstand. Amy pushes open the door and I sit up on the bed. I motion for her to come in so she eases through the door and shuts it behind her. She walks over to my dresser and sets the pictures she collected down, running her finger over the top one. Tears are silently streaming down her cheeks.

"Come here," I say, holding a hand out to her. She walks closer to me and takes my hand, then completely breaks down the second she makes eye contact with me. I continue to pull her forward until she's on the bed and I wrap my arms around her. She curls up against my chest, sobbing uncontrollably. She's shaking so hard and it's almost a devastated cry, but like I said before, *devastated* should be reserved for mothers.

I close my eyes tightly and try not to let it all hit me like it's hitting Amy right now, but it's hard. I can hold it in for my mother because she needs me to be strong for her. Amy doesn't, though. If Amy feels anything like I do, then she just needs to know there's someone else out there just as blindsided and heartbroken as she is.

"Shh," I say, stroking her hair. I know she doesn't want me to console her with empty, overused words. She just needs someone to understand how she feels and I may be the only one she knows who truly does. I don't tell her to try to stop crying, because I know it's impossible. I press my cheek against her head, hating the fact that I'm now crying, too. I've done a pretty damn good job of keeping it in, but I can't anymore. I continue to hold her and she continues to hold on to me because it's nice to be able to find solace in such an ugly, lonely situation.

Listening to Amy cry reminds me of all the nights I used to be in this same position with Les. She wouldn't want me to talk to her or help her stop crying. Les just needed me to hold her and let her cry, even if I had no idea why she needed it. Just being able to be here for Amy in this same small way gives me that familiar sense of being needed like I used to feel with Les. I haven't felt needed since Les decided she didn't need *anyone*.

"I'm so sorry," Amy says, her voice muffled by my shirt.

"For what?"

She catches her breath and attempts to stop crying, but her effort is wasted with the new tears that follow. "I should have known, Holder. I had no idea. I was her best friend and I feel like everyone blames me and . . . I don't know. Maybe they should. I don't know. Maybe I've been so wrapped up in my relationship with Thomas that I missed something she was trying to tell me."

I continue stroking her hair, empathizing with every word coming out of her mouth. "You and me both," I sigh. I wipe the moisture away from my eyes with the back of my hand. "You know, I keep trying to pinpoint moments that might have changed the outcome. Things I might have said to her or things she might have said to me. But even if I was able to go back and change something about the past, I'm not sure that it would have changed the outcome. You don't know that, either. Les is the only one who knows for sure why she went through with it and unfortunately she's the only one not here to enlighten us."

Amy lets out a small laugh, although I'm not sure why. She pulls back slightly and looks at me with a solemn expression. "She better be glad she's not here, because I'm so mad at her, Holder." Her somberness gives way to another sob and she brings a hand to her eyes. "I'm so, so mad at her for not confiding in me and I feel like I can't say that to anyone but you," she whispers.

I move her hand away from her face and look her in the eyes because I don't want her to feel like I'm judging her for that comment. "Don't feel guilty, Amy. Okay?"

She nods and smiles a sympathetic smile, then looks down at our hands resting on the pillow between us. I lay my hand on top of hers and smooth reassuring strokes across the top of it with my fingers. I know how she feels and she knows how I feel and it's good to have that, even if only for a moment.

I want to tell her thank you for being there for Les all these years, but it seems so inappropriate to thank her for being there when she's feeling the exact opposite right now. Instead, I remain quiet and bring my hand up to her face. I don't know if it's the magnitude of the moment or the fact that she made me feel somewhat needed again or if it's simply because my head and my heart have been numb for so many days. Whatever it is, it's here and I don't want it to go away yet. I just let it completely take over while I slowly lean forward and press my mouth to hers.

I didn't intend to kiss her. In fact, I expect myself to pull away any second, but I don't. I expect her to push me away, but she doesn't. The moment my mouth meets hers, she parts her lips and sighs as if this is exactly what she needs from me. Oddly enough, that makes me want to kiss her even more. I kiss her, knowing she's my sister's best friend. I kiss her, knowing she has a boyfriend. I kiss her, knowing this isn't something I would do with her under any circumstance other than in this moment.

She slides her hand up my arm and slips her fingers inside the sleeve of my shirt, lightly tracing the contours of the muscles in my arm. I pull her closer to the middle of the bed with me and deepen our kiss. The more we kiss, the more we both recognize the fact that desire and need might just be the only thing that can minimize grief. We simultaneously grow more impatient, doing whatever we can to rid ourselves of the grief completely. Every stroke of her hand against my skin pulls me farther out of my own mind and more into the moment with her, so I kiss her more desperately, needing her to take my mind *completely* away from my life right now. My hand makes its way up her shirt and the second I cup her breast, she moans and digs her nails into my forearm, arching her back.

That's a nonverbal cue for *yes* if I've ever seen one.

I've only got two things remaining on my mind as she begins to pull off my shirt and my hands are eagerly fumbling with the zipper on her jeans.

1. *I need to get these clothes off her.*
2. *Thomas.*

I normally don't make a habit of thinking about other guys while I'm making out with girls, but I normally don't make a habit of making out with other guys' *girls*. Amy isn't mine to kiss, but here I am doing it anyway. Her clothes aren't mine to be helping her out of, but here I am doing it anyway. Her panties aren't something I should be slipping my hand inside of, but here I am doing it anyway.

I pull away from her mouth when I touch her and watch as she moans and presses her head back against my pillow. I keep doing what I'm doing to her with one hand while I lean across the bed and pull a condom out of the drawer with my other hand. I tear it open with my teeth, watching her intently the whole time. I know that neither of us is in the right frame of mind right now or this wouldn't be happening. Regardless if we're in the right frame of mind or not, at least we're in the *same* frame of mind. I'm hoping we are, anyway.

I know how incredibly and completely wrong it is to ask a girl about her boyfriend when she's thirty seconds away from completely forgetting all about him, but I have to. I don't want her regretting this any more than she already will. Than we *both* will.

"Amy?" I whisper. "What about Thomas?"

She whimpers slightly and keeps her eyes closed, bringing her palms up to my chest. "He's at his house," she mutters, giving no hint that the mention of his name is making her want to stop what we're doing. "He had to go help his dad with some yard stuff after school."

Her exact repetition of the answer she gave me when I asked about him in the driveway makes me laugh. She opens her eyes and looks up at me, probably confused about why I would laugh at a time like this. She just smiles, though. I'm thankful she smiled, because I'm really sick of everyone's tears. I'm so damn sick of all the tears.

And *shit*. If she doesn't feel guilty right this second, then I'm *sure* as hell not about to feel guilty. We can regret this all we need to later.

I lower my mouth to hers at the exact moment she gasps, then moans loudly—completely and wholeheartedly forgetting all about her boyfriend. Every last bit of her attention is one hundred percent focused on the movement of my hand, and every last bit of my attention is one hundred percent focused on getting this condom on before she starts thinking about her boyfriend again.

I ease myself on top of her, ease my mouth back to hers, ease myself inside her, and completely take advantage of the situation, knowing how much I'll regret it later. Knowing how much I *already* regret it.

But here I am, doing it anyway.

She's dressed and sitting on the edge of my bed, putting on her shoes. I've already got my jeans on and I'm walking to the bedroom door, not sure what to say. I have no idea how or why any of that just happened, and based on the look on her face, neither does she. She stands up and walks toward the door, picking up the pictures she grabbed from Les's room as she passes by my dresser. I hold the door open, unsure if I should follow her out or kiss her good-bye or tell her I'll call her.

What the hell did I just do?

She walks into the hallway and pauses, then turns around to face me. She doesn't make eye contact, though. She just stares at the pictures in her hands. "I just came for pictures, right?" she asks cautiously. A worried frown consumes her face and I realize she's afraid I might think what just happened between us was more than it actually was.

I want to reassure her that I'm not going to say anything. I lift her chin so that she's looking me in the eyes and I smile at her. "You came for pictures. That's it, Amy. And Thomas is at home, helping his dad with the yard work."

She laughs, if you can even call it that, then she looks at me appreciatively. There's an awkward silence for a moment before she finally laughs again. "What the hell *was* that, anyway?" she says, waving her hand in the direction of my bedroom. "That's not us, Holder. We're not that type of people."

We're *not* that type of people. I agree with that. I lean my head against the doorframe and already feel the regret seeping in. I don't know what came over me or why the fact that she's not remotely mine for the taking didn't stop me in my tracks. The only excuse I can come up with is that whatever happened between us just now is a direct product of our grief. And our grief is a direct product of Les's selfish decision.

"Let's blame it on Les," I say, only half-teasing. "It wouldn't have happened if she had been here."

Amy smiles. "Yeah," she says, squinting playfully. "What a bitch, making us do something despicable like that. How dare she."

I laugh. "Right?"

She holds up the pictures in her hand. "Thanks for . . ." she looks at the pictures and pauses for a moment, then brings her eyes back to mine. "Just . . . thank you, Holder. For listening."

I acknowledge her thanks with a single nod and watch as she turns to head down the stairs. I close the door and walk back to my bed, picking up the notebook on the way over. I open it up to the letter where I left off before Amy walked into my room an hour earlier.

Chapter Three-and-three-quarters

Les,

What happened with Amy just now was all your fault.
Just so we're clear.

   H

Chapter Four

Les,

Happy two-week deathiversary. Harsh? Maybe so, but I'm not apologizing. I have to go back to school Monday and I'm not looking forward to it at all. Daniel has been keeping me up to date on all the rumors, despite the fact that I keep telling him I don't give a shit. Of course everyone thinks you killed yourself because of Grayson, but I know that isn't true. You were pretending to be alive long before you ever met Grayson.

And then there's the whole incident that I still haven't told you about. The one that involved me forcing Grayson to break up with you? It's a complicated story, but because of that night, everyone is now saying that I was indirectly responsible for your suicide. Daniel says people are even sympathizing with Grayson and the asshole is eating it up.

The best part about this particular rumor is that apparently my immense guilt over the hand I played in your suicide is causing me to be suicidal. And if that's what the masses are saying, then it must be true, right?

To be honest, I'm way too scared to kill myself. Don't tell anyone that. (Not that you could now, even if you *wanted to.) But it's true. I'm a pussy when it comes to the fact that I have no idea what to expect after this life. What if the afterlife is worse than the life you're running from? Willingly taking a dive headfirst into the unknown takes some serious courage. I have to hand it to you Les, you're way braver than I am.*

Okay, I'm signing off. I'm not used to writing so much. Texting would be way more convenient, but you like to do everything the hard way, don't you?

If I see Grayson at school on Monday, I'll rip his balls off and mail them to you. What's your new address?

H

* * *

Daniel is waiting for me by his car when I pull into the parking lot.

"What's the game plan?" he says as soon as I open my door.

I'm racking my brain for anything I might have missed. I don't remember anything significant about today that would require a game plan.

"Game plan for what?" I ask.

"The game plan for today, dipshit." He points his clicker toward his car and locks his doors, then begins walking toward the school with me. "I know how much you didn't want to come back, so maybe we need a game plan to counteract all the attention. Do you want me to be all sad and mopey with you so people won't want to confront us? I doubt it," he answers himself. "That might encourage people to approach you with words of encouragement that resemble condolences and I know you're sick of that shit. If you want, I can be super excitable and take all the attention off you. As much as you don't want to admit it, you're all everyone's been talking about for two weeks. I'm so fucking sick of it," he says.

I hate that people don't have anything better to talk about, but I like that it bothers Daniel as much as it bothers me.

"Or we could just be normal and hope people have better things to talk about than what happened with Les. Ooh! Ooh!" he says giddily, turning to face me while he walks backward. "I could act all pissed off and walk in front of you like a bodyguard, even though you're bigger than me. And if anyone tries to approach you I'll punch them in the face. Please? Will you play the part of pissed-off, grieving brother? For me? Please?"

I laugh. "I think we'll be just fine without a game plan."

He frowns at my unwillingness to participate. "You underestimate the enjoyment other people gain from gossip and speculation. Just stay quiet and if anything needs to be said today, I'll be the one to say it. I've been dying to yell at these people for two weeks now."

I appreciate his concern, but I really anticipate today being just like any other day. If anything, I think it would be too awkward for people to mention it when I'm actually in their presence. They'll be too uncomfortable to say anything to me at all, which is exactly how I prefer it.

The bell for first period hasn't rung yet, so everyone's still standing outside. It's the first time I'm walking into the school without Les by my side. Just the thought of her takes me right back to that moment when I walked into her bedroom and found her. I don't want to relive that moment again. Not right now. I pull my phone out of my pocket and pretend to be interested in it for the sake of just taking my mind off the fact that Daniel could be right. Everyone around us is way too quiet and I hope to hell it's back to normal soon.

Daniel and I don't have class together until third period so when we make it inside the building he waves me off and heads in the opposite direction. I open the door to my homeroom and almost immediately, a sudden hush falls over the classroom. Every single pair of eyes is staring back at me, quietly watching me walk to my desk.

I keep my phone out and continue to pretend I'm engaged in it, but I'm acutely aware of everyone around me. It keeps me from having to make eye contact with anyone, though. If I don't make eye contact, they'll be less likely to approach me. I wonder if I'm just imagining a difference in the way people are acting today as opposed to before Les killed herself. Maybe it's just me. I don't want to think it's just me, though. If that's the case, then how long does this last? How long will I have to go through every second of the day thinking about her death and how it affects every aspect of my life?

I compare losing Les to losing Hope all those years ago. It seemed back then that everything that happened for months after Hope was taken somehow led to thoughts of her. I would wake up in the morning and wonder where *she* was waking up. I would brush my teeth and wonder if whoever took her thought to buy her a new toothbrush, since she didn't get to take anything with her. I would eat breakfast and wonder if whoever took her knew that Hope didn't like orange juice and whether or not they were letting her have white milk, because that was her favorite. I would go to bed at night and look out my bedroom window that used to face hers, and I would wonder if she even had a bedroom window where she was.

I try to think of when the thoughts finally stopped, but I'm not so sure they have. I still think about her more than I should. It's been years now, but every time I look up at the sky I think about her. Every time someone calls me Dean instead of Holder, I think about her and how I used to laugh at the way she said my name when we were kids. Every time I see a bracelet on a girl I think about the bracelet Les gave her just minutes before she was taken from us.

So many things remind me of her and I hate knowing that it's just going to be worse now that Les is gone, too. Every single thing I think or see or do or say reminds me of Les. Then every single time I'm reminded of Les, it leads to thoughts of Hope. Then every single time I think about Hope, I'm reminded of how I let them down. I failed them both. It's as if the day I gave them their nickname, I was somehow nicknaming myself the same. Because I sure as hell feel pretty fucking hopeless right now.

I've somehow made it through two classes without a single person speaking to me. Not that they aren't discussing it, though. It's like they think I'm not even here, the way they whisper and stare and speculate about what's going on in my head.

I take a seat next to Daniel once I arrive in Mr. Mulligan's classroom. Daniel silently asks how I'm doing with just a look. Over the past few years we seem to have formed some sort of nonverbal communication between us. I shrug, letting him know that it's going. Of course it sucks and I'd rather not be here at all right now, but what can I do? Suck it up. That's what.

"I heard Holder's not speaking to anyone," the girl in front of me whispers to the girl seated in front of her. "Like, *at all*. Not since he found her."

It's obvious by the volume at which she's speaking that she has no idea I'm sitting right behind her. Daniel lifts his head to look at them and I can see the disgust on his face, knowing I can hear their conversation.

"Maybe he's taking a vow of silence," the other girl speculates.

"Yeah, maybe. It wouldn't have hurt Lesslie to take a vow of silence every now and then. Her laugh was so freaking annoying."

I instantly see red. I clench my fists and find myself wishing for the first time in my life that it wasn't wrong for a guy to hit a girl. I'm not angry that they're talking about her behind her back, I expected as much. I'm not even angry that they're talking about her beyond the grave. I'm angry because the *one thing* I loved the most about Les was her laugh. If they're going to say anything about her, they better not mention her fucking laugh again.

Daniel grips the edges of his desk and lifts his leg, then kicks the girl's desk as hard as he can, scooting her a good twelve inches across the floor. She squeals and immediately turns in her seat to face him.

"What the hell is wrong with you, Daniel?"

"What's *wrong* with me?" he asks, raising his voice. He leans forward in his chair and glares at her. "I'll tell you what's wrong with me. I'm pissed that you're a girl because if you had a dick, I'd be punching you in your disrespectful, fat mouth right now."

Her mouth drops open and it's obvious she's confused why he's targeted her. Her confusion is instantly cleared up the second she notices that I'm right behind her, though. Her eyes grow wide and I smile at her, lifting my hand in a half-hearted wave.

I don't say anything, though. I don't really feel the need to add to anything Daniel just said and apparently I'm taking a vow of silence, so I just keep my mouth shut. Besides, Daniel said he's been dying to yell at these people for two weeks now. Today might be his only chance, so I just let him do his thing. The girl immediately turns and faces the front without even offering up the slightest hint of an apology.

The classroom door opens and Mr. Mulligan enters, breaking up the tension and naturally replacing it with his own. Les and I did everything we could to avoid having him at all this year, but we weren't very lucky. Well, *I'm* not, anyway. Les doesn't have to worry about sitting through his tedious, hour-long lectures anymore.

"Dean Holder," he says as soon as he reaches his desk. "I'm still waiting for your research paper that was due last week. I hope you have it with you, because we're presenting today."

Shit. I haven't even thought about what I might have had due over the past two weeks.

"No, I don't have it with me."

He looks up from whatever it is he's looking at on his desk and eyes me. "See me after class, then."

I nod and maybe even roll my eyes a little. Eye rolling is inevitable in his class. He's a douchebag who gets off on the control he thinks he has over a classroom. It's obvious he was bullied as a kid and anyone not wearing a pocket-protector is the recipient of his misguided revenge.

I ignore the presentations during the rest of the period and try to make a list of what assignments I might have due. Les was the organized one of the two of us. She always let me know what was due and when it was due and which class it was due in.

After what seems like hours, the bell finally rings. I remain seated until the class clears out so that Mr. Mulligan can practice his retaliation on me. Once the classroom is occupied by just the two of us, he walks to the front of his desk and leans against it, folding his arms over his chest.

"I know your family has been through quite the ordeal and I'm sorry for your loss." *Here we go.* "I just hope you understand that unfortunate things like this are going to happen throughout your life, but that doesn't give you the excuse to not live up to what's expected of you."

Jesus Christ. It's a fucking *research* paper. It's not like I'm rewriting the Constitution. I know I should just nod and agree with him, but he picked the wrong day to play preacher.

"Mr. Mulligan, Les was the only sibling I had, so I actually *don't* foresee this happening again. As much as it seems like it happens repeatedly, she can only kill herself once."

The way his eyebrows crease together and his lips tighten into a firm line make it apparent that he doesn't find me amusing at all. Which is good, because I wasn't trying to be amusing.

"Some situations should remain off-limits to your sarcasm," he says flatly. "I would hope you would have a little more respect for your sister than that."

As much as I hate that I can't hit girls today, I hate the fact that I can't punch teachers even more. I immediately stand up and walk swiftly to where he's standing, stopping just inches from him, my fists down at my sides. My proximity causes his body to go rigid and I can't help but feel a sense of satisfaction knowing I've scared him. I look him directly in the eyes, clench my teeth, and lower my voice.

"I don't give a shit if you're a teacher, a student, or a goddamned priest. Don't you ever mention my sister again." I stare at him for several more seconds, seething, waiting on his reaction. When he fails to say anything, I turn around and grab my backpack. "You'll get your report tomorrow," I say, exiting the classroom.

I've been convinced I was minutes away from being expelled. However, Mr. Mulligan apparently chose not to report our little interaction, because nothing has been said or done and it's now lunch break.

Moving along.

"Holder," someone says from behind me in the hallway. I turn around to find Amy catching up to me.

"Hey, Amy." I wish her presence gave me even the slightest hint of comfort, but it doesn't. Seeing her standing here just reminds me of two weeks ago, then that reminds me of the pictures she was at my house for, then that reminds me of Les, then that reminds me of Hope. Then of course I'm consumed with guilt again.

"How are you?" she asks hesitantly. "I haven't heard from you since . . ." Her voice trails off, so I answer her quickly, not wanting her to feel she has to go into more detail.

"I'm okay," I reply, feeling guilty that she seems disappointed I didn't call her. I thought she was pretty clear with what happened between us. I hope she is, anyway. "Did you um . . ." I look down at my feet and sigh, unsure how to bring it up without sounding like a complete asshole. I shift my weight from one foot to the other and look back up at her. "Did you *want* me to call you? Because I thought what happened . . ."

"No," she says quickly. "No. You thought right. I just . . . I don't know." She shrugs and looks as though she already regrets this conversation. "Holder, I just wanted to make sure you were okay. I've been hearing rumors and I'd be lying if I didn't say they have me worried. I felt like I made that day at your house all about me, and I never even thought to ask you how you were holding up at all."

She looks guilty for even bringing up the rumors, but she shouldn't feel that way. She's the only person all day to actually make an active effort to ensure the rumors aren't true. "I'm okay," I assure her. "Rumors are rumors, Amy."

She smiles, but doesn't seem to believe the words coming out of my mouth. The last thing I want her to do is worry about me. I wrap my arms around her and whisper in her ear. "I promise, Amy. You don't need to worry about me, okay?"

She nods, then pulls away from me, looking nervously down the hall to her left, then to her right. "Thomas," she whispers, excusing the fact that she pulled away from me. I smile at her reassuringly.

"Thomas," I say, nodding. "Not at home helping his dad with yard stuff, I guess?"

She purses her lips together and shakes her head. "Take care, Holder," she says, turning to walk away.

I put my things in my locker, then head to the cafeteria. I walk in several minutes after the cafeteria has filled up with people, and at first it's like any other day at lunch. But once people begin to spot me as I make my way to the table where Daniel is seated, the voices drop entire octaves and eyes can't seem to mind their own business.

The amount of drama I've witnessed today is comical, really. Everyone I pass, even people I've been friends with for years, all seem to think if they don't quietly watch my every move, they might miss the moment that I completely break down and lose it. I hate to disappoint them, but I've got a pretty good handle on things today. Nobody's going to be losing it, so they might as well go back to their regular routine.

By the time I actually reach the table, the entire sound of the lunchroom has dropped to a dull murmur. All eyes are on me and I seriously wish I could tell everyone to go fuck themselves. But that would be giving them exactly the meltdown they want, so instead I keep my mouth shut.

The one thing I don't do, though, is tell Daniel *he* can't say what I'm wishing I could say. I look him straight in the eyes as I approach the table and we have one of our quick, nonverbal conversations. A nonverbal conversation in which I give him the go-ahead to release any pent-up frustration he might still be harboring.

He grins mischievously and loudly slaps his palms down on the table. "Holy motherfucking shit!" he yells, climbing up onto his chair. He gestures wildly toward me. "Look, everybody! It's Dean Holder!" He proceeds to climb on top of the lunchroom table, pulling all the attention away from me and placing it on himself.

"Why is everyone staring at *me*?" he yells, motioning with huge, exaggerated gestures toward me. "We have *the* Dean Holder here! The one and only!" When only a few people look away from him toward me, he throws his hands up in the air like he's disappointed in them. "Come on, guys! We've been anticipating this moment for two *weeks* now! Now that he's finally here, you all decide to shut the hell up? What's up with that?" He looks down at me and frowns, slumping his shoulders in defeat. "I'm sorry, Holder. I thought today would be a little more interesting for you. I was hoping for a Q&A session to kind of clear the air, but I didn't realize every single person in this school is a spineless dipshit." He begins to climb down from the table but then shoots his arm up into the air and holds up a finger. "Wait!" he says, spinning to face the entire crowd. "That's actually a very good idea!"

I look around and expect one of the cafeteria monitors to be making their way over to him to put a stop to his spectacle, but the only monitor in the cafeteria right now is just watching him like everyone else, waiting to see what he's up to.

Daniel jumps from our table to the table next to us, stepping on a few trays in the process. He spills chocolate milk all over the table and almost slips, but presses his hand onto the top of a guy's head and straightens himself back up. The entire spectacle is pretty damn entertaining, so I take a seat at our table and watch him like I'm not even the reason behind his whole outburst.

He looks down at a girl seated at the table beneath his feet and he extends his arm, pointing his finger down at her. "What about you, Natalie? Now that we have Dean Holder here and live in person, would you like to ask him if your theory about why Les killed herself is correct?"

Natalie's face reddens and she stands up. "You're an asshole, Daniel!" She grabs her tray and walks away from the table. Daniel remains standing on top of the table, but his extended index finger follows her across the cafeteria.

"Wait, Natalie! What if Lesslie *did* kill herself because Grayson dumped her the same week he took her virginity? Don't you want to know if you're right? Don't you want to know what you've won?"

Natalie exits the cafeteria, so he immediately turns his attention to Thomas, who is seated next to Amy a few tables down. She's got her hand over her mouth and she's looking at Daniel in shock like the rest of the cafeteria. He points to Thomas, then hops across three cafeteria tables to get to him. "Thomas!" Daniel yells excitably. "What about you? Would you like to participate in the Q&A? I heard your theory this morning during first period and it was a doozy."

Thomas stands up and grabs his tray just like Natalie did. "Daniel, you're being a jerk." He nods toward me. "He doesn't need this right now."

I don't say anything, but I actually hope Thomas gets away unscathed. I don't know what rumor he started, but even so. I'm pretty sure what I did with Amy was retaliation enough, even though he'll likely never know about it.

"Oh?" Daniel says, pulling his hand up to his mouth in false shock. He looks over at me. "Holder? Do you not need this right now? Are you like, in *mourning* or something? Should we be respecting that?"

I try not to smile, but Daniel's doing a damn good job of turning this shitty day upside down. He steps from one table to the next, moving back toward our table.

"Do you not want to participate in the Q&A, Holder? I thought maybe you would want to set the record straight." He spins around and addresses the entire cafeteria again without waiting on an answer from me. Several students begin picking their trays up and exiting the cafeteria in fear that they'll be pointed out next. "Where's everyone going? None of you seem to mind discussing it any other time. Why not right now when we can actually get some honest answers? Maybe Holder could tell us all why Les really did it. Or better yet, *how* she did it. Maybe we could even find out the truth behind the speculation that he's suicidal, too!" Daniel looks at me again and props his hands on his hips. "Holder? Are the rumors true? Do you actually have the date set for when you plan to kill yourself?"

Now all eyes are definitely on me. Before I can answer, and not that I was going to, Daniel holds up his arms and faces his palms out toward me. "Wait! Don't answer that, Holder." He spins around to address the quickly dwindling crowd again. "I think we should open it up for bets! Somebody find me a pen and paper! I've got dibs on next Thursday," he says, pulling his wallet out of his pocket.

Apparently the cafeteria monitor draws the line at illegal betting, because she's now walking determinedly toward Daniel. He notices the monitor stalking toward him, so he shoves his wallet back into his pocket. "We'll take bets after school, then," he says quickly, jumping off the table.

I turn and head toward the doors to the cafeteria and he follows behind me. As soon as the doors swing shut behind us, the murmur of the cafeteria returns, but much louder this time. Once we're both back in the hallway near our lockers, I turn to face him.

I can't decide whether I want to punch him for what he just did or bow down to him. "You're messed up, man." I laugh.

He runs his palms down his face and falls against the lockers with a big sigh. "Yeah. I didn't really mean for it to go on like that. I just couldn't take another second of this shit. I don't know how you're doing it."

"Me either," I say. I open my locker and grab my car keys. "I think I'm just gonna call it a day. I really don't want to stick around right now."

Daniel opens his mouth to respond, but he's interrupted by someone clearing his throat behind me. I turn around to find Principal Joiner eyeing Daniel angrily. I turn back to Daniel and he lifts his shoulders innocently. "I guess I'll see you tomorrow then. Looks like me and Principal Joiner have a lunch date."

"More like a detention date," Principal Joiner says firmly from behind me. Daniel rolls his eyes and follows the principal toward the office.

I grab the book I need to finish Mr. Mulligan's research paper and shut my locker, then walk down the hall toward the exit. Before I round the hallway, I hear someone say Les's name and it causes me to stop in my tracks. I peer around the corner and there is a small group of four people leaning up against their lockers. One of the guys is holding a cell phone and they're all leaning over him, watching the video he's playing. Daniel's voice is coming from the speaker. Apparently someone recorded his display during lunch just now and it's already circulating. *Great.* Even more fuel for the gossip.

"I don't understand why Daniel made such a big deal out of it," the guy holding the phone says. "Does he really expect us *not* to talk about it? If someone is pathetic enough to kill themselves, we're obviously going to talk about it. If you ask me, Les should have tried to stick it out rather than take the easy—"

I don't wait for him to finish his sentence. His phone shatters when I throw it against the locker, but the sound doesn't even come close to the sound my fist makes when it meets his jaw for the first time. I don't know if the punches get louder after that, though, because everything around me is instantly tuned out. He's on his back on the floor of the hallway now and I'm on top of him, hitting him hard enough that I hope he's never able to open his fucking mouth again. People are pulling on my shoulders and my shirt and my arms, but I continue hitting him. I put my rage on repeat and watch as my fist grows redder and redder from the blood that smears my hand every time I swing at him.

I guess they're getting their wish after all. I'm breaking down.

I'm losing it.

And I don't really give a fuck.

Chapter Five

Les,

Happy five-week deathiversary.

Sorry I haven't kept you up to speed lately, but a lot has happened. You're going to love this. I, Dean Holder, got arrested.

I got into a fight at school defending your honor two weeks ago. Well, I guess I can't really call it a fight, per se. I think two people have to be involved to constitute a fight and this incident was definitely one-sided.

Anyway, I was taken into custody. I was barely there for three hours before Mom bailed me out, though, so it sounds more badass than it actually was. I will admit, it was the first time I've ever been thankful she's a lawyer.

I'm a little more than upset right now and I don't really know what to do about it. Mom has been struggling a lot lately and my little incident at school really didn't help matters. She thinks she failed us. You killing yourself left her completely doubting her abilities as a mother, which is really hard for me to watch. Now that I went and fucked up, too, she's doubting herself even more. So much so that she's forcing me to go stay with Dad for a while.

I think it's all too much for her. After I beat that asshole up at school, she admitted to me that she thinks I need more help than she's able to give me right now. I did everything I could to change her mind, but after my court hearing this morning, it seems the judge agrees with her. Dad is on his way here right now to pick me up. Five more hours and I'll be heading back to our hometown.

Back to where the downhill slope began.

Do you remember how things used to be when we were kids? Before I let Hope climb into that car?

Things were good. Really good. Mom and Dad were happy. We were happy. We loved our neighborhood, our house, our cat that kept jumping in that damn well in the backyard. I don't even remember that cat's name, but I remember him being the stupidest damn cat I've ever encountered.

It wasn't until the day I walked away from Hope, leaving her crying in the front yard, that our lives began going downhill. After that day everything changed. The reporters showed up, the stress intensified, and our innocent trust in other people completely disappeared.

Mom wanted to move out of town and Dad didn't want to leave his job. She didn't like the fact that we still lived next door to where it happened. Remember how she wouldn't let us go outside alone for years after Hope was kidnapped? She was so scared the same thing would happen to us.

They tried to not let the stress affect their marriage, but it eventually ended up being too much. I remember the day they told us they were divorcing and selling the house, and that Mom was moving us here to be closer to her family. I'll never forget it because, aside from Hope being taken, it was the worst day of my life.

But it seemed like your best.

You were so excited to move. Why, Les? I wish I had thought to ask you while you were alive. I want to know what it was you hated about living there so much, because I really don't want to go back to Austin. I don't want to have to leave Mom. I don't want to have to stay with Dad and pretend that I'm okay with him giving up on his family all those years ago. I don't want to go back to a town where every time I turn a corner, I'm looking for Hope.

I miss you so damn much, Les, but it's different from the way I miss Hope. With you, I know it's not a possibility that I'll ever see you again. I know you're gone and you're not suffering anymore. But I don't have that sense of closure with Hope. Because I don't know that she's not suffering anymore. I don't know if she's dead or alive. My mind does this awful thing where it imagines the worst possible scenarios for her, and I hate it.

What are the chances that the only two girls in my life I've ever loved... I've lost? It's killing me piece by piece every single day. I know I should probably find a way to try to get over it... to let go of the blame. But to be honest, I don't want to get over it. I don't want to forget that my inability to protect either of you is why I'm the only one of us left. I deserve to be reminded every second that I'm alive that I let both of you down, so that I can be conscious not to let myself ever do this again to anyone else.

Yeah, I definitely need a reminder. Maybe I should get a tattoo.

Chapter Five-and-a-half

Les,

What a year. I almost forgot about this notebook. Must have left it behind in my haste to pack last September. It was still sitting on my dresser, and judging by the layer of dust on it, I'm guessing Mom hasn't been snooping in it. If Mom reacted to my moving in with Dad for the past year in the same way she reacted to your death, I'm sure she hasn't set foot in my bedroom since the day I left. It seems easier for her to just close the doors and not think about the stillness of the rooms behind them.

I'm pretty sure the plan was for me to stay in Austin until I graduated, but I thwarted that plan with my magical ability to turn eighteen. Dad couldn't really hold me there against my will anymore. And speaking of turning eighteen... it was weird not having to share a birthday with you. But it was nice because Dad bought me a new car. I'm pretty sure if you were alive he would have made us share the car, but you aren't alive so I get to keep it all to myself. And he didn't make me leave it in Austin when I came back home a few days ago, so that's a plus.

I missed Mom, which is the primary reason I came back. And as much as I hate to admit it, I've missed

Daniel. In fact, I'm about to leave with him in a few minutes. Got to go catch up with the old crowd. It's Saturday night, so I'm sure we'll find somewhere for me to show up and give people something else to talk about.

Daniel says there have been some pretty far-out rumors related to where I've been for the past year. He said he didn't waste time dispelling any of them. He's the only one who knows where I really took off to, so I appreciate that he didn't feel the need to set anyone straight. I think he likes the fact that he's the only one who knows the truth.

One more tiny thing could be responsible for my coming back. My huge fight with Dad. Remind me to tell you all about it later.

Oh, wait. I guess you can't remind me. Fine, I'll remind myself.

Holder, don't forget to tell Les about your fight with Dad.

H

Chapter Six

I can't believe he talked me into any form of social gathering my first week back. I swore I wouldn't be around these people again, but it has been a whole year. I've had a while to adjust, so maybe they have, too.

I walk up to the unfamiliar house a few feet ahead of Daniel, but stop just short of passing through the front door. Of all the people from school I haven't seen for the past year, the last person I expect to run into is Grayson. But of course the last thing I expect is always the first to happen.

I haven't seen him since the night before Les died, when I left him bleeding on the living room floor of his best friend's house. He's walking out as I'm walking in and for a few seconds, we're face to face, staring each other down. I haven't really thought about him much since I left, but seeing him now brings every ounce of hatred I had for him right back to the surface like it never even left.

I can tell by the look in his eyes that he has absolutely no idea what to say to me. I'm blocking his exit and he's blocking my entrance and neither of us seems to want to be the one to step aside. Both of my hands are clenched into defensive fists, preparing for whatever he has to say. He could yell at me, he could spit at me, he could even apologize to me. Whatever words come out of his mouth, it won't matter. The urge I'm having right now isn't to listen to him speak; it's to shut him up.

Daniel walks in shortly after me and notices the silent standoff occurring between us. He slips around me, then stands facing me, blocking my view of Grayson. He slaps my cheeks with both hands until my eyes meet his. "No time for jerk-offs!" He yells over the music. "We have beer that needs consuming!" He grabs my shoulders, still blocking my view from Grayson, and pulls me to the right. I continue to resist, not wanting to be the first to back down from our visual standoff.

Jaxon walks up and places his hand on Grayson's arm, pulling him in the opposite direction. "Let's go see what Six and Sky are up to!" he yells to him.

Grayson nods, watching me sternly as he backs away. "Yeah," he answers Jaxon. "This party just got lame."

If this were last year, he'd be on the floor with my knee resting comfortably on his throat. But this isn't last year, and his throat isn't worth it. I simply smile at him while I continue to allow Daniel to pull me away and toward the kitchen. Once Jaxon and Grayson have exited the front door, I release a pent-up breath. I'm relieved at their decision to leave the party in search of whatever girls are pathetic enough to entertain them.

I grimace with that last thought, knowing I inadvertently lumped Les into that category of girls. But fortunately, I don't have to worry about the chicks Grayson hooks up with anymore. Les isn't here to be deceived by him, so as far as I'm concerned, Grayson can hook up with whoever is desperate enough to have him.

"Press mouth to rim, tilt head back, down your shot, and get happy," Daniel says, handing me a shot of something. I don't ask what it is, I just do what he says and down it.

One more shot, two beers, and half an hour later, Daniel and I have made our way into the living room. I'm on the couch with my feet propped up on the coffee table and Daniel is next to me, running through the list of people we're friends with and telling me all about what they've been up to for the past year. I forgot how talkative alcohol makes him and I'm finding it hard to keep up. I bring my fingers to the bridge of my nose, squeezing the headache away. I don't really know anyone at this party. Daniel says most of them are friends of the kid who lives here, but I don't even know who lives here. I ask Daniel why we're even here if he doesn't know anyone and the question miraculously shuts him up. He looks past me into the kitchen and nods in that direction. "Her," he says.

I look behind me at a couple of girls leaning against the bar. One of them is staring straight at Daniel, stirring her drink flirtatiously.

"If she's the reason we're here, why aren't you over there?"

Daniel turns around and faces forward, folding his arms across his chest. "No fucking way, man. We haven't talked since we broke up two weeks ago. If she wants to apologize to me she can walk her pretty little ass over here."

I glance back at the girl again and notice that maybe she's not looking at him flirtatiously like I first thought. Because flirtatious grins and evil grins are divided by a very faint line and I'm not sure which side of the line she's standing on, now that I'm witnessing her glare.

"How long did you date her?"

"A few months. Long enough to find out she's fucking crazy," he says with a huge roll of his eyes. "And long enough to realize that the *reason* why I love her is because she's fucking crazy." He sees me staring at her and he narrows his eyes. "Stop looking at her, man. She'll know we're talking about her."

I laugh and look away, but not fast enough to avoid witnessing the duo making their way back through the front door. Grayson is following behind Jaxon and they're both headed toward the kitchen. I rest my head into the couch and wish I had downed a few more shots. I really don't want to be preoccupied with Grayson for the rest of the night.

Daniel begins talking incessantly again. I tune him out after he tells me about his new tires for the second time tonight, and I'm doing a pretty good job of staying inside my own head until Jaxon and Grayson move closer to the living room. They have no idea I'm seated on the couch and I'd really like to keep it that way. Now if Daniel would just shut up long enough for me to tell him I'm ready to leave.

"I'm so fucking sick of it," I overhear Grayson saying. "Every Saturday night it's the same thing. I swear to God if she doesn't give it up next weekend I'm done."

Jaxon laughs. "I'm pretty sure all Sky needs is a good dose of rejection. Girls like rejection."

I'm not sure who Sky is, but I like that she's refusing to give it up to Grayson. Smart girl.

"I doubt that would work with her," Grayson says, laughing. "She's pretty damn stubborn."

"Yeah she is," Jaxon agrees. "You would think with everything we've heard about her that she'd be a little less difficult. That girl has got to be the sluttiest *virgin* I've ever met."

Grayson laughs at Jaxon's comment, and I have to try extra hard in my attempt to tune them out. Hearing the way they're talking about this girl infuriates me, because I know Grayson more than likely talked about Les this same way when he dated her.

Grayson continues talking shit about her, and the more I sit here and listen to it, the more I have to hear that pathetic laugh come out of his mouth. All it makes me want to do is shut him up.

I pull my feet off the coffee table and begin to turn around in order to tell them to fuck off, but Daniel puts a hand on my shoulder and shakes his head. "Allow me," he says with a mischievous grin. He pulls his legs up onto the couch and spins around, facing Grayson and Jaxon.

"Excuse me," he says, holding his hand up in the air like he's in class. He's always so animated, even when he knows he's about to get his ass kicked. I may be able to hold my own against Grayson, but Daniel knows he can't, yet that doesn't seem to stop him.

Both Grayson and Jaxon turn to him, but Grayson's eyes stop short once they collide with mine. I hold his obnoxious stare while Daniel hugs the pillow on the back of the couch and continues speaking to them. "I couldn't help but overhear your conversation just now. As much as I'd like to agree that Sky is the sluttiest virgin either of you have ever met, I feel the need to point out that this observation is completely inaccurate. You see, after I spent last night with her, she can't really be considered a virgin anymore. So, maybe it's not her *virginity* she's attempting to hold on to by refusing to sleep with you, Grayson. It's more than likely her dignity."

Grayson is over the back of the couch and has Daniel pinned to the floor in a matter of seconds. I, being of somewhat sound mind, give Daniel the ten seconds he needs to reverse the situation before I interrupt. However, I'm disappointed in my lack of faith in Daniel because he has Grayson flipped over and on his back in less than five. He must have been working out while I was away.

I slowly stand up when I see Jaxon make his way to the front of the couch to assist Grayson. He grabs Daniel by the shoulder to pull him off Grayson, but I grab the back of Jaxon's shirt and yank him until he's seated on the couch. I step closer, just as Grayson delivers a punch to Daniel's jaw. Daniel is about to return the swing, but I grab his arm and pull him up before he has the chance.

Over the years this has become a game to Daniel. He urges people on and counts on me to step in and put a stop to his fights before he gets fucked up. Unfortunately, since I always seem to be in the background during these incidents, my name has become associated with all of the fights and his quick temper. In reality, I've only actually ever hit three people.

1) *The asshole who talked shit about Les.*
2) *Grayson.*
3) *My father.*

And I only regret the last one.

People are rushing through the front door to get a glimpse of the action, but they'll be disappointed, because I'm pushing Daniel out of the house before he can do or say anything else. The last thing I need right now is an excuse to fight Grayson. I've been back less than a week. I sure as hell don't want to give my mother another reason to force me back to Austin.

Daniel is wiping blood from his lip and I've still got hold of his arm when we reach his car. He yanks his arm free and grabs the bottom of his shirt, pulling it up to his mouth. "Dammit," he says, pulling back the shirt to look at the blood. "Why do I keep instigating shit that risks fucking up this beautiful face of mine?" He grins and wipes the blood from his mouth for a second time.

"I wouldn't worry about it," I say, laughing at how worried he always is about his looks. "You're still prettier than me."

Daniel grins. "Thanks, babe," he says teasingly.

Someone is walking up behind Daniel and for a second my fists clench, thinking it might be Grayson. I relax when I see it's just the girl Daniel was referring to who was staring at him from the kitchen earlier. I don't know why I relax, though, because this girl has a definite murderous look about her. Daniel is still wiping the blood from his mouth when she walks up beside him.

"Who the hell is *Sky*?"

Daniel snaps his head in her direction and his eyes grow wide with surprise. "*Who?* What the hell are you talking about, Val?"

She rolls her eyes and lifts her hand, pointing toward the house. "I heard you in there telling Grayson you screwed her last night!"

Daniel glances at the house, then back to Val, and it suddenly hits him. "No, Val!" Daniel says, walking forward and grabbing her hands. "No, no, no! He was talking shit and I was just trying to piss him off. I don't even know the girl he was talking about. I swear—"

She's walking away from him and he's following after her, pleading with her to listen to him. I decide now is a good time to head home. I caught a ride here with Daniel, but it looks like he'll be preoccupied for a while. I'm only four miles from my house so I text him and tell him I'm headed home, then start in that direction.

This entire night has reminded me of all the things I don't want to be around. Drama. Testosterone. Grayson. Everything about high school in general, really. I'm supposed to fill out my transfer paperwork on Monday, but I honestly don't know that I really want to go back. I know there are ways I can test out. There's just no way in hell my mother would allow that to happen.

Chapter Six-and-a-half

Les,

Okay, so here goes.

Last week, our dear stepmother Pamela walked in on me and a girl. She wasn't just any girl. Her name was Makenna and I'd been out with her a few times. She was cool but it was nothing serious and that's all I'm going to say about that. But anyway, Pamela got home early and Makenna and I were sort of in a compromising position on the living room sofa. You remember the sofa that Pamela kept the plastic on for three years because she was too scared anyone would get stains on it?

Yeah. It wasn't pretty.

Especially since Makenna and I had made our way into the living room after leaving a trail of clothing from the pool, down the hallway, and to the couch. So, not only were we both completely naked, but I had to walk down the hall and back outside to find my shorts and Makenna's clothes. Pamela was screaming at me the entire way outside and the entire way back into the house and the entire way to Makenna's car.

It embarrassed the hell out of Makenna and she kind of called things off with me after that. But that's fine, because I have this cool tattoo now that says *Hopeless* (remember the nickname I gave you and Hope?) and it reminds me not to get too close to anyone, so I hadn't allowed myself to develop any real feelings for her yet. It was really just about the sex.

I can't believe I just said that to my own sister. Sorry.

Anyway, as you can guess, Dad was furious when he got home. He has one rule and one rule only in his house.

Don't piss off Pamela.

I broke the rule. I broke it hard.

He actually tried to ground me, and I might have laughed a tiny bit when he said it. I wasn't trying to be disrespectful, because you know that, as much as he disappointed me throughout the years, I still wouldn't do something to outright disrespect him. But the fact that he tried to ground me four days after I turned eighteen just really struck a funny chord and dammit... I laughed.

He didn't find it amusing at all and he was pissed. He started yelling at me, calling me disrespectful and ungrateful, and it pissed me off because I mean shit, Les. I'm eighteen! I'm a guy! Guys do shit like have sex with girls in their parents' houses when they're eighteen. But Christ if he didn't act like I'd murdered someone! So, yeah. He pissed me off and I might have lost my temper.

But that's not the bad part. The bad part happened after I yelled at him in return and he bowed up to me. He actually had the balls to bow up to me. Not that he's bigger than me, but still. I'm his son and he bowed up to me like he wanted to fight me.

So what did I do?

I hit him.

I didn't hit him very hard, but it was hard enough that it hurt him in the most sensitive spot possible. His pride.

He didn't hit me back. He didn't even yell at me. He just pulled his hand up to his jaw and he looked at me like he was disappointed, then he turned around and walked away. I left an hour later and drove back home. We haven't spoken since.

I know I should probably call him and apologize, but didn't he start it by bowing up to me? Just a little bit? What kind of dad does that to his own son?

But then again, what kind of son hits his own dad?

God, Les. I feel like shit. I never should have done it. I know I need to call him, but... I don't know. Shit.

To my knowledge, he never even told Mom what happened because she hasn't mentioned it at all. She was surprised to see me back when I walked through the front door a few days ago. Happy, but surprised. She didn't ask what prompted my return, so I didn't volunteer the information. She seems different now. I can still see the heartache in her eyes, but it's not as prominent as it was when I left last year. She actually smiles now, which is good.

Her happiness will be short-lived, though. It's Monday and school started today. The first day of senior year. She left for work before I woke up. I actually had my alarm set and everything ready. I made it to school and did my morning workout, but all I could think about while I was running the track was how much I didn't want to be there.

I don't want to be there without you. I don't want to face everything I hate about that school and the majority of the people in it.

So what did I do when I finished my run? I walked back to the parking lot, got into my car, drove home, and went back to sleep. Now it's almost three o'clock in the afternoon and Mom will be home in a couple of hours. I'm about to head to the grocery store for a few things because I'll be cooking her dinner tonight. I plan to break the news to her about my dropping out of school. I know she won't be happy about my testing out, rather than getting a traditional diploma, so I put cookies on the grocery list, too. Women love cookies, right?

I can't believe I'm not going back to school. I just never thought it would come to that. I'm blaming you for that one, too.

H

Chapter Seven

"Will that be all for you today?" the cashier asks.

I mentally run through the items on my list, ending with cookies. "Yep," I say as I pull my wallet from my pocket to pay the cashier. I'm just relieved I got in and out without seeing anyone I know.

"Hey, Holder."

Spoke too soon.

I glance up to see the cashier operating the line next to me, staring me down. She's practically offering herself up on a platter with the way she's looking at me. Whoever this girl is, her expression is begging for attention. I feel sort of bad for her, especially with the way her voice climbed into that annoying, high-pitched, *why-do-girls-think-baby-talk-is-sexy* range. I glance down at her nametag, because I honestly can't place her face for the life of me.

"Hey . . . *Shayla*." I give her a quick nod, then look back at my cashier, hoping my guarded response is enough to let her know that I'm not in the mood to feed her ego.

"It's *Shayna*," she snaps.

Oops.

I glance at her nametag again, disappointed that I'm giving her even more reason to keep talking. However, her nametag clearly reads *Shayla*. I want to laugh, but feel even more sympathy for her now. "Sorry. But you do realize your nametag says Shayla, right?"

She immediately flips the nametag up on her smock and frowns. I'm hoping this is embarrassing enough that she doesn't look up at me again, but it doesn't even faze her.

"When did you get back?" she asks.

I have no idea who this chick is, but she somehow knows me. Not only does she know me, but she knows I had to *leave* in order to come *back*. I sigh, disappointed that I still underestimate everyone's penchant for gossip.

"Last week," I say, offering up no further explanation.

"So are they gonna let you come back to school?" she asks.

What's with the "*let you*" part of her question? Since when was I not allowed back at school? That has to be attached to some sort of rumor.

"Doesn't matter. Not going back."

I haven't really decided whether or not I'll be enrolling tomorrow, since I failed to do it today. It really all depends on my conversation with my mother tonight, but it seems easier just to give the people what they want, which is more fuel for their gossip. Besides, if I dispel every single thing everyone has said about me for the past year, I'll be leaving everyone with no one to spread rumors about.

"You suck, man," my cashier says quietly as he removes the debit card from my hand. "We had bets on how long it would take her to realize her nametag was misspelled. She's been wearing it for two months now and I had dibs on three. You just lost me twenty bucks."

I laugh. He hands me back the debit card and I place it in my wallet. "My bad," I say. I pull out a twenty-dollar bill and hold it out to him. "Take this, because I'm pretty sure you would have won."

He shakes his head, refusing to take the twenty.

I'm placing the money back into my wallet when I notice out of the corner of my eye someone in the next checkout line. The girl has completely turned around and is staring at me, more than likely trying to get my attention in the same way that Shayna/Shayla tried. I just hope this chick doesn't start up with that same baby-talk voice.

I glance up at her to get a quick look. I really wanted to avoid glancing at her, but when people are staring you down it's hard not to make eye contact, if even for a second. But the second I actually do make eye contact with her, I freeze.

I can't look away now, even though I'm trying like hell to shake the image standing in front of me.

My heart stops.

Time stops.

The whole *world* stops.

My quick glance turns into a full-on, unintentional stare.

I recognize those eyes.

Those are *Hope's* eyes.

It's her nose, her mouth, her lips, her hair. Everything about this girl is Hope. Out of all the times in the past I thought I'd spotted her when glancing at girls my age, I've never been more sure than I am right now. I'm so sure about it that it completely inhibits my ability to speak. I don't think I could say her name even if she begged me to.

So many emotions are coursing through me right now and I can't tell if I'm angry or elated or freaked the hell out.

Does she recognize me, too?

We're still staring at each other and I can't stop wondering if I look familiar to her. She doesn't smile. I wish she would smile because I would recognize Hope's smile anywhere.

She tucks in her chin, darts her eyes away, and quickly turns around to face her cashier again. She's obviously flustered and it's not in the same way that I tend to leave girls like Shayna/Shayla flustered. It's a completely different reaction, which only makes me all the more curious if she just remembered me.

"Hey." The word rushes loudly out of my mouth involuntarily and I notice her flinch when I speak. She's hurrying her cashier at this point, grabbing her sacks in a frenzy. It's almost as if she's trying to get away from me.

Why is she trying to run from me? If she didn't just recognize me . . . why would she be this disturbed? And if she *did* recognize me, why wouldn't she be happy?

She exits the store in a rush, so I grab my sacks and leave the receipt with the cashier. I have to get outside before she drives away. I can't just let her go again. I head directly through the exit and scroll over the parking lot until I spot her. Luckily, she's still loading her groceries into her backseat. I pause before walking up behind her, hoping I don't come off as crazy, because that's exactly how I feel right now.

She's about to shut her door, so I take a few steps closer.

I don't think I've ever been this scared to speak.

What do I say? What the hell do I say?

I've imagined this moment for thirteen years and I have no fucking idea how to approach her.

"Hey."

Hey? Jesus, Holder. Nice. Real nice.

She freezes midmovement. I can tell by the way her shoulders rise and fall that she's taking a calming breath. Does she need calming because of me? My heart is racing at warp speed and thirteen years' worth of pent-up adrenaline is making its way through my body.

Thirteen years. I've been looking for her for thirteen years and I very well may have just found her. *Alive.* And in the same *town* as me. I should be elated, but I can't stop thinking about Les and how I know she prayed every single day for this moment. Les spent her whole life wishing we would find Hope and now I've found her and Les is dead. If this girl really is Hope, I'll be devastated that she showed up thirteen months too late.

Well, maybe not *devastated.* I forgot that word is on reserve. But I'll be pretty damn pissed.

She's facing me now. She's looking right at me and it's killing me because I want to grab her and hug her and tell her how sorry I am for ruining her life, but I can't do any of these things because she's looking at me like she has no clue who I am. I just want to scream, "Hope! It's me! It's Dean!"

I grip the back of my neck and try to process this whole situation. This isn't how I pictured finding her. Maybe I fictionalized it and played it up all these years but I thought her recovery would be way more climactic. I thought she would have way more tears and way more emotion and not appear to be nearly as . . . *inconvenienced*?

The look on her face right now doesn't register as recognition in the least. She looks terrified. Maybe she *doesn't* recognize me. Maybe she appeared flustered inside because of the idiotic way I was staring at her. Maybe she appears terrified now because I practically chased her down and I'm giving her absolutely no explanation. I'm just standing here like a creepy stalker and I have no idea how to even ask her if she's the girl I lost all those years ago.

She eyes me warily up and down. I hold out my hand, hoping to ease some of her fear with an introduction. "I'm Holder."

She drops her gaze to my extended hand and, rather than accept the handshake, she actually takes a step away from me.

"What do you want?" she says sharply, cautiously peering back up to my face.

Definitely not the reaction I expected.

"Um," I say, not really meaning to appear taken aback. But honestly, this isn't going in the direction I was hoping it would go. I don't even know what direction that was at this point. I'm starting to doubt my own sanity. I glance across the parking lot at my car and wish I had just kept walking, but I know if I did, I'd regret not confronting her.

"This might sound lame," I warn, looking back at her, "but you look really familiar. Do you mind if I ask what your name is?"

She releases a breath and rolls her eyes, then reaches behind her to grab the doorknob of her car. "I've got a boyfriend," she says. She turns and opens the door, then quickly climbs into the car. She starts to pull the door shut, but I catch it with my hand.

I can't let her leave until I'm positive she's not Hope. I've never been so sure about anything in my life and I'm not about to let thirteen years of guilt and obsessing and analyzing her disappearance go to waste just because I'm afraid I might piss her off.

"Your name. That's all I want."

She stares at my hand holding open her door. "Do you mind?" she says through clenched teeth. Her eyes fall to the tattoo on my arm and my adrenaline kicks up a notch when she reads it, hoping it'll spark some recognition on her part. If she can't remember my face, I'm almost positive she'll remember the nickname I gave her and Les.

Not even the slightest jar of emotion flashes in her eyes.

She attempts to pull the door shut again but I refuse to release it until I get what I need from her.

"Your name. *Please*."

When I say *please* this time, her expression eases slightly and she looks back up at me. It isn't until she looks at me this way, without all the anger, that I realize why I'm so flustered. It's because I care more for this girl than any other girl in the world who isn't Les. I loved Hope like a sister when we were kids and seeing her again has brought back all those same feelings. It's causing my hands to shake and my heart to pound and my chest to ache because all I want to do is wrap my arms around her and hold her and thank God we finally found each other.

But all those feelings come to a screeching halt when the wrong answer comes out of her mouth. "Sky," she says quietly.

"Sky," I say aloud, trying to make sense of it. Because she's *not* Sky. She's Hope. She can't not be my Hope

Sky.

Sky, Sky, Sky.

She's not saying she's Hope, but the name *Sky* is still eerily familiar. What's so significant about that name?

Then it hits me.

Sky.

This is the girl Grayson was referring to Saturday night.

"Are you sure?" I ask her, hoping for a miracle that she's as dense as Shayna and just gave me the wrong name. If she really isn't Hope, then I completely understand her reaction to my seemingly erratic behavior.

She sighs and pulls her ID from her back pocket. "Pretty sure I know my own name," she says, flashing her driver's license in front of me.

I take it from her.

Linden Sky Davis.

A wave of disappointment crashes around me, swallowing me up. *Drowning* me. I feel like I'm losing her all over again.

"Sorry," I say, backing away from her car. "My mistake."

She watches me as I back up even farther so she can shut her door. In a way, she looks disappointed. I don't even want to think about what kind of expression she's seeing on my face right now. I'm sure it's a mixture of anger, disappointment, embarrassment . . . but most of all, *fear.* I watch as she drives away and I feel like I just let Hope go all over again.

I know she's not Hope. She proved she wasn't Hope.

So why is my gut instinct telling me to stop her?

"Shit," I groan, threading my hand through my hair. I'm seriously messed up. I can't get over Hope. I can't get over Les. It's getting so bad it's to the point that I'm chasing random girls down in the damn grocery store parking lot?

I turn away and slam my fist down on the hood of the car next to me, pissed at myself for thinking I finally had it all together. I don't have it together. Not in the least.

I'm not even completely out of my car before I have Facebook pulled up on my phone. I enter Sky's name and no results come up. I swing open the front door and head straight up the stairs to get my laptop.

I can't let this rest. If I don't convince myself that she isn't Hope, I'll drive myself crazy. I open my laptop and enter her information again but come up empty. I search every site I can think of for over half an hour, but her name doesn't return any results. I try searching by her birthday, but come up empty again.

I type in Hope's information and immediately have a screen full of news articles and returns. But I don't need to look at them. I've spent the last several years reading every article and every lead that's reported about Hope's disappearance. I know them by heart. I slam the computer shut.

I need to run.

Chapter Eight

She has no distinct features that I can remember. No birthmarks. The fact that I saw a girl with brown hair and brown eyes and felt she was the same brown-haired, brown-eyed girl from thirteen years ago is quite possibly borderline obsessive.

Am I obsessed? Do I somehow feel as though I won't be able to move past Les's death if I don't rectify at least one of the things I've fucked up in my life?

I'm being ridiculous. I've got to let it go. I've got to let go of the fact that I'll never have Les back and I'll never find Hope.

I have these same thoughts for the entire two miles of my run. The weight in my chest lightens little by little with each step I take. I remind myself with each step that Sky is Sky and Hope is Hope and Les is dead and I'm the only one left and I've got to get my shit together.

The run begins to help ease some of the tension built up from the incident at the grocery store. I've convinced myself that Sky isn't Hope, but for some reason even though I'm almost positive she's not Hope, I still find myself thinking about Sky. I can't get the thought of her out of my head and I wonder if that's Grayson's fault. If I hadn't heard him talking about her at the party the other night, I probably would have moved on from the grocery store incident fairly quickly and I wouldn't be thinking about her at all.

But I can't stop this growing urge to protect her. I know how Grayson is and somehow, just seeing this girl for even a few minutes, I know she doesn't deserve what he's likely going to put her through.

There isn't a single girl in this world who deserves the type of guy Grayson is.

Sky said she had a boyfriend at the store and the possibility that she might consider Grayson her boyfriend gets under my skin. I don't know why, but it does. Just thinking she was Hope for even a few minutes already has me feeling extremely territorial about her.

Especially now as I round the corner and see her standing in front of my house.

She's here. *Why the hell is she here?*

I stop running and drop my hands to my knees, keeping my eyes trained on her back while I catch my breath. *Why the hell is she standing in front of my house?*

She's at the edge of my driveway, propped up against my mailbox. She's drained the last of her water bottle and she's shaking it above her mouth, attempting to get more water out of it, but it's completely empty. When she realizes this, her shoulders slump and she tilts her face toward the sky.

It's obvious she's a runner with those legs.

Holy shit, I can't breathe.

I try to recall everything on her driver's license and what all Grayson said about her Saturday night because I suddenly want to know everything there is to know about her. And not because I thought she was Hope, but because whoever she is . . . she's fucking beautiful. I don't know that I even noticed how attractive she was at the store, because my mind wasn't going there. But right now, seeing her in front of me? My mind is *all over* that.

She takes a deep breath, then begins walking. I immediately kick into gear and ease up behind her.

"Hey, you."

She pauses at the sound of my voice and her shoulders immedi-

68 | **Colleen Hoover**

ately tense. She turns around slowly and I can't help but smile at the wary expression strewn across her face.

"Hey," she says back, shocked to see me standing in front of her. She actually seems more at ease this time. Not as terrified of me as she was in the parking lot, which is good. Her eyes slowly drop down to my chest, then to my shorts. She looks back up at me momentarily, then diverts her gaze to her feet.

I casually lean against the mailbox and pretend to ignore the fact that she totally just checked me out. I'll ignore it to save her embarrassment, but I'm definitely not going to forget it. In fact, I'll probably be thinking about the way her eyes scrolled down my body for the rest of the damn day.

"You run?" I ask. It's probably the most obvious question in the world right now, but I'm completely out of material.

She nods, still breathing heavily from the effect of her workout. "Usually in the mornings," she confirms. "I forgot how hot it is in the afternoons." She lifts her hand to her eyes to shield them from the sun while she looks at me. Her skin is flush and her lips are dry. I hold out my water bottle and she flinches again. I try not to laugh, but I feel pretty damn pathetic that I freaked her out so much at the store that she's afraid I might actually do something to *harm* her.

"Drink this." I nudge my water bottle toward her. "You look exhausted."

She grabs the water without hesitation and presses her lips to the rim, downing several gulps. "Thanks," she says, handing it back to me. She wipes the water off her top lip with the back of her hand and glances behind her. "Well, I've got another mile and a half return, so I better get started."

"Closer to two and a half," I say. I'm trying not to stare, but it's so hard when she's wearing next to nothing and every single curve of her mouth and neck and shoulders and chest and stomach seems like it was made just for me. If I could preorder the perfect girl, I wouldn't even come close to the version standing in front of me right now.

I press the bottle of water to my mouth, knowing it's more than likely the closest I'll ever get to her lips. I can't even take my eyes off her long enough to take a drink.

"Huh?" she says, shaking her head. She seems flustered. God, *please* let her be flustered.

"I said it's more like two and a half. You live over on Conroe, that's over two miles away. That's almost a five-mile run round trip." I don't know many girls who run, let alone a five-mile stretch. Impressive."

Her eyes narrow and she pulls her arms up, folding them across her stomach. "You know what street I live on?"

"Yeah."

Her gaze remains tepid and focused on mine and she's quiet. Her eyes eventually narrow slightly and it looks like she's growing annoyed with my continued silence.

"Linden Sky Davis, born September 29; 1455 Conroe Street. Five feet three inches. Donor."

As soon as the word "donor" leaves my mouth, she immediately steps back, her look of annoyance turning into a mixture of shock and horror. "Your ID," I say quickly, explaining why I know so much about her. "You showed me your ID earlier. At the store."

"You looked at it for two seconds," she says defensively.

I shrug. "I have a good memory."

"You stalk."

I laugh. "*I* stalk? You're the one standing in front of my house." I point to my house behind me, then tap my fingers against the mailbox to show her that she's the one encroaching. Not me.

Her eyes grow wide in embarrassment as she takes in the house behind me. Her face grows redder with the realization of how it must look for her to be randomly hanging out in front of my house. "Well, thanks for the water," she says quickly. She waves at me and turns around, breaking into a stride.

"Wait a sec," I yell after her. I run past her and turn around, trying to think up an excuse for her not to leave just yet. "Let me refill your water." I reach down and grab her water bottle. "I'll be right back." I take off toward the house, hoping to buy myself some more time with her. I've obviously got a lot to make up for in the first-impressions department.

"Who's the girl?" my mother asks once I reach the kitchen. I run Sky's bottle of water under the tap until it's full, then I turn around to face her. "Her name is Sky," I say, smiling. "Met her at the grocery store earlier."

My mother glances out the window at her, then looks back at me and cocks her head. "And you already brought her to our house? Moving a little quickly, don't you think?"

I hold up the water bottle. "She just happened to be running by and now she's out of water." I walk toward the door and turn back to my mother and wink. "Lucky for me, we just happen to have water."

She laughs. The smile on my mother's face is nice because they've been so few and far between. "Well, good luck, Casanova," she calls after me.

I run the water back out to Sky and she immediately takes another drink. I attempt to find a way to rectify her first impression of me.

"So . . . earlier?" I say hesitantly. "At the store? If I made you uneasy, I'm sorry."

She looks me straight in the eyes. "You didn't make me uneasy."

She's lying. I *absolutely* made her uneasy. Terrified her, even. But she's looking at me now with such confidence.

She's confusing. *Really* confusing.

I watch her for a minute, trying my best to read her, but I have no clue. If I was to hit on her right now, I don't know if she'd punch me or kiss me. At this point, I'm pretty sure I'd be more than okay with either.

"I wasn't trying to hit on you, either," I say, wanting to get some sort of reaction from her. "I just thought you were someone else."

"It's fine," she says softly. Her smile is tight-lipped and the disappointment in her voice is clear. It makes me smile, knowing that disappointed her a little bit.

"Not that I *wouldn't* hit on you," I clarify. "I just wasn't doing it at that particular moment."

She smiles. It's the first time I actually get a genuine smile from her and it feels like I just won a triathlon.

"Want me to run with you?" I ask, pointing toward her path home.

"No, it's fine."

I nod, but don't like her answer. "Well, I was going that way anyway. I run twice a day and I've still got a couple . . ."

I take a step closer to her when I notice the fresh, prominent bruise under her eye. I grab her chin and tilt her head back to get a better look at it. My previous thoughts are sidetracked and I'm suddenly overwhelmed with a need to kick the ass of whoever touched her.

"Who did this to you? Your eye wasn't like this earlier."

She backs away from my grasp. "It was an accident. Never interrupt a teenage girl's nap." She tries to laugh it off, but I know better. I've seen enough unexplained bruises on Les in the past to know that girls can hide this kind of shit better than anyone wants to admit.

I run my thumb over her bruise, calming the anger coursing through me. "You would tell someone, right? If someone did this to you?"

She just stares up at me. No response. No, "*Yes, of course I would tell.*" Not even a, "*Maybe.*" Her lack of acknowledgment takes me right back to these situations with Les. She never admitted to Grayson physically hurting her, but the bruises I saw on her arm the week before I made him break up with her almost ended in murder. If I find out he's the one who did this to Sky, he'll no longer have a hand left to lay on her.

"I'm running with you," I say. I place my hands firmly on her shoulders and turn her around without giving her the opportunity to object.

She doesn't even try to object, though. She begins running, so I fall into a steady stride with her. I'm fuming the entire run back to the house. Pissed that I never got to the bottom of what happened with Les and pissed that Sky might be dealing with the same shit.

We don't speak the entire run back to her house until she turns and waves good-bye at the edge of her driveway. "I guess I'll see you later?" she says, walking backward toward her house.

"Absolutely," I say, knowing full well I'll be seeing her again. Especially now that I know where she lives.

She smiles and turns toward her house and it isn't until she's halfway up her driveway that I realize I don't even have a way to contact her. She doesn't have a Facebook, so I can't contact her that way. I don't know her phone number. I can't really just show up at her house unannounced.

I don't want her to walk away until I know for sure I'll talk to her again.

I immediately twist the lid off my water bottle and pour the contents of it onto the grass. I put the lid back on it.

"Sky, wait," I yell. She pauses and turns back around. "Do me a favor?"

"Yeah?"

I toss her the conveniently empty bottle of water. She catches it, then nods and runs inside to refill it. I pull my cell phone from my pocket and immediately text Daniel.

Sky Davis. Girl Grayson was talking about Saturday night? Does she have a boyfriend?

Sky opens her front door and begins to make her way back outside when he responds.

She has several from what I hear.

I'm still staring at the text when she reaches me with the water. I take it from her and down a drink, not sure why it's hard for me to find truth in Daniel's text. As much as she's still an enigma to me, I can tell by the way she's so guarded that she doesn't let people in that easily. Based on my interaction with her, she just doesn't fit the description that's being painted of her by everyone else.

I put the lid back on the water bottle and do my best to keep my eyes focused on hers, but dammit if that sports bra isn't a magnet right now. "Do you run track?" I ask her, attempting to stay focused.

She covers her stomach with her arms and her movement makes me want to punch myself for being so obvious about checking her out. The last thing I want to do is make her uncomfortable.

"No," she says. "I'm thinking about trying out, though."

"You should. You're barely out of breath and you just ran close to five miles. Are you a senior?"

She smiles. That's twice she's smiled at me like that, and it's really beginning to mess with my head.

"Shouldn't you already know if I'm a senior?" she says, still grinning. "You're slacking on your stalking skills."

I laugh. "Well, you make it sort of difficult to stalk you. I couldn't even find you on Facebook."

She smiles again. I hate that I'm keeping count. *Three.*

"I'm not on Facebook," she says. "I don't have internet access."

I can't tell if she's lying to let me off easily, or if she's actually being honest about not having internet access. I don't know which one is harder to believe. "What about your phone? You can't get internet on your phone?"

She lifts her arms to tighten her ponytail and I feel like *I'm* the one out of breath right now. "No phone. My mother isn't a fan of modern technology. No TV, either."

I wait for her to laugh, but it's obvious in just a few short seconds that she's completely serious. This isn't good. How the hell am I supposed to get in touch with her? Not that I need to. I just have a pretty good feeling I'll *want* to. "Shit." I laugh. "You're serious? What do you do for fun?"

She shrugs. "I run."

Yes, she certainly does. And if I have anything to do with it, she won't be running alone, anymore.

"Well in that case," I say, leaning toward her, "you wouldn't happen to know what time a certain someone gets up for her morning runs, would you?"

She sucks in a quick breath, then attempts to control it with a smile. *Three and a half.*

"I don't know if you'd want to get up that early," she says.

If she only knew I would go so far as to never sleep *again* if she would just agree to run with me. I lean in a little closer and lower my voice. "You have no *idea* how bad I want to get up that early."

As soon as her fourth smile appears, she *disappears*. It happens so fast, I don't even have time to react. The sound she makes when she smacks the pavement makes me wince. I immediately kneel down and roll her over.

"Sky?" I say, shaking her. She's out cold. I look toward her house, then scoop her up and rush her to the door. I don't bother knocking, since I have no extra hands. I lift my foot and kick at the front door, hoping someone is home to let me in.

Within seconds, the front door swings open and a woman appears. She looks at me in utter confusion until she recognizes Sky in my arms.

"Oh, my God!" She immediately opens the door to let me in.

"She passed out in the driveway," I say. "I think she's dehydrated."

The woman immediately runs to the kitchen while I lower Sky onto the living room sofa. As soon as her head meets the arm of the couch, she moans and her eyelids flutter open. I breathe a sigh of relief, then step aside when her mother reappears.

"Sky, drink some water," she says. She helps her take a sip, then she sets the glass of water down. "I'll get you a cold rag," she says, walking toward the hallway.

Sky looks up at me and winces. I kneel next to her, feeling awful that I just let her fall like that. It happened so fast, though. One second she was standing in front of me; the next second she wasn't. "You sure you're okay?" I ask after her mother has left the room. "That was a pretty nasty fall."

There's gravel and dirt stuck to her cheek, so I wipe most of it away. She squeezes her eyes shut and throws her arm over her face.

"Oh, God," she groans. "I'm so sorry. This is so embarrassing."

I take her wrist and pull it away from her face. The last thing I want her to feel is embarrassed. I'm just thankful she's okay. And even more thankful it gave me an excuse to carry her inside. Now I'm inside her house with an excuse to come back and check on her this week. Things couldn't have worked out better for me.

"Shh," I whisper. "I'm sort of enjoying it."

Her mouth curls up into a smile. *Five.*

"Here's a rag, sweetie. Do you want something for the pain? Are you nauseous?" Her mother hands me the rag and walks to the kitchen. "I might have some calendula or burdock root."

Sky rolls her eyes. "I'm fine, Mom. Nothing hurts."

I wipe the rest of the dirt off her cheek with the rag. "You might not be sore now, but you will be," I say quietly. She didn't see how hard she hit the ground. She'll definitely feel it tomorrow. "You should take something, just in case."

She nods and attempts to sit up, so I assist her. Her mother walks back into the room with a small glass of juice and hands it to Sky.

"I'm sorry," she says, extending her hand out to me. "I'm Karen Davis."

I stand up and return the handshake. "Dean Holder," I say, taking a quick glance at Sky. "My friends call me Holder."

Karen smiles. "How do you and Sky know each other?"

"We don't, actually," I say. "Just in the right place at the right time, I guess."

"Well, thank you for helping her. I don't know why she fainted. She's never fainted." She turns her attention to Sky. "Did you eat anything today?"

"A bite of chicken for lunch," Sky says. "Cafeteria food sucks ass."

Cafeteria food. So she goes to public school. I might just be rethinking my educational decision after all.

Karen rolls her eyes and throws her hands up in the air. "Why were you running without eating first?"

"I forgot," Sky says defensively. "I don't usually run in the evenings."

Karen walks back to the kitchen with the glass and sighs heavily. "I don't want you running anymore, Sky. What would have happened if you had been by yourself? You run too much, anyway."

The look on Sky's face is priceless. Apparently running is as vital to her as breathing.

"Listen," I say, finding an opportunity to appease all parties involved, especially myself. "I live right over on Ricker and I run by here every day on my afternoon runs. If you'd feel more comfortable, I'd be happy to run with her for the next week or so in the mornings. I usually run the track at school, but it's not a big deal. You know, just to make sure this doesn't happen again."

Karen returns to the living room and eyes both of us. "I'm okay with that," she says. She turns her attention to Sky. "If Sky thinks it's a good idea."

Please think it's a good idea.

"It's fine," Sky says with a shrug.

I was hoping for a "*Hell yes,*" but "*fine*" will suffice.

She attempts to stand up again, but she sways to the left. I immediately reach out and grab her arm to ease her back down onto the sofa.

"Easy," I say to her. I look at Karen. "Do you have any crackers she can eat? That might help."

Karen walks away to the kitchen and I give Sky my full attention again. "You sure you're okay?" I run my thumb over her cheek for no reason at all other than the simple fact that I wanted to touch her cheek again. As soon as my fingers graze her skin, chills rush down her arms. She tightens her arms over her chest and rubs the chills away. I can't help but grin, knowing it was my hand on her skin that did that to her. Best. Feeling. Ever.

I glance at Karen to make sure she's not making her way back into the living room, then I lean in toward Sky. "What time should I come stalk you tomorrow?"

"Six-thirty?" she says breathlessly.

"Six-thirty sounds good." *Six-thirty is my new favorite time of day.*

"Holder, you don't have to do this." She looks me directly in the eyes as if she wants to give me the opportunity to back out. Why the hell would I want to back out?

"I know I don't have to do this, Sky. I do what I want." I lean even closer, hoping to see the chills run down her arms again. "And I want to run with you."

I pull away just as Karen is walking back into the living room. Sky keeps her eyes focused hard on mine and it makes me wish more than anything that it was tomorrow morning already.

"Eat," Karen says, placing crackers in Sky's hand.

I stand up and tell Karen good-bye. "Take care of yourself," I say to Sky as I back my way toward the front door. "I'll see you in the morning?"

She nods and it's all the confirmation I need. I pull the door shut behind me as I leave, pleased that I somehow managed to redeem myself. As soon as I'm out of her driveway and back on the sidewalk, I pull my phone from my pocket and call Daniel.

"Hey, Hopeless," he says when he answers.

"I said stop calling me that, Jackass."

"Shoulda thought about that before you got the tattoo," he quips back. "What's up?"

"Sky Davis," I say quickly. "Who is she, where's she from, does she go to school here, and is she dating Grayson?"

Daniel laughs. "Whoa, buddy. Slow down. First of all, I've never met her. Second of all, if that's the same Sky that I claimed to have deflowered in front of Val at that party the other night, there's no way I'm asking around about her. I'm still trying to convince Val I never really slept with the chick. Asking people about her will only make it worse for me, man."

I groan. "Daniel, please. I need to know and you're better with this shit than I am."

There's a long pause on his end. "Fine," he says. "But on one condition."

I knew there'd be a condition. There's always a condition when it comes to Daniel. "What condition?"

"You come to school tomorrow. Just one day. Enroll tomorrow and try it for one day and if you absolutely hate it you can officially drop out with my blessing."

"Deal," I say immediately. I can do one day. Especially if Sky will be there.

Chapter Eight-and-a-half

Les,

Holy shit, Les. HOLY. SHIT.

It feels like forever since I wrote to you but it was just this morning. So much has happened, my hands are shaking and I can barely write.

I still haven't talked to Mom about dropping out yet, but only because I'm not so sure I want to drop out anymore. We'll see after tomorrow.

Are you sitting down for this? Sit your ass down, Les.

I.

Found.

Hope.

But I didn't.

Well, I'm still not so sure I didn't, but I'm more sure that she isn't Hope than sure that she is. Does that even make sense? I mean, the second I saw her I was positive it was her. But when I realized she didn't recognize me, I thought maybe I was wrong or she was pretending or... I don't know. I just started doubting myself. Then I acted sort of stalkerish and crazy so she showed me her ID, which was really dumb of her if you consider how stalkerish I was acting. But her ID proved she wasn't Hope, which crushed me, but only for a couple of hours. Because when I went running I ran into her again thanks to fate or coincidence or divine intervention or maybe you had something to do with it. Whatever or whoever made it happen, she was there, standing in front of our house, looking all beautiful and shit. Jesus, she looked good, Les.

I'm sure you want to hear that, right?

Anyway, so I'm convinced now that if she really is Hope, she would have remembered me. Especially after I told her mother that my name was Dean Holder. I glanced down at Sky to see if my first name rang a bell but based on her lack of reaction, it didn't ring a bell at all, so there's no way she could be the same girl.

Do you want to know the strangest part, Les? The part of this entire day that has thrown me for the biggest loop?

I don't even want her to be Hope.

If she's Hope, all of the drama and the stress and the media attention would surround us again and I don't want that for her. This girl seems happy and healthy and not at all how I expected our Hope to be if we ever found her. So I'm glad Sky isn't Hope and Hope isn't Sky.

I had Daniel do some investigating and I learned a little bit about her. She's lived in this area for years and has been homeschooled by her mom, who seems really nice, by the way.

Daniel also said she's not officially dating Grayson, so that's a plus. I'm still not sure how she's connected to him, because according to Daniel she's definitely connected to him in some way. I'm hoping to stop that before it becomes anything significant, though.

Sorry I'm rambling. It's just been the type of day you don't expect at all when you wake up for it. I'll let you know how tomorrow goes. I owe Daniel a day of school.

P.S. Sky had a black eye today. She never said what actually happened, but you know how paranoid I am about anything remotely connected to Grayson. I'll never forget that day you came home with those bruises on your arm, Les. You begged me not to kill him because I swear to you, I would have if you hadn't sworn that he didn't do it.

I don't know if you were telling the truth when you said it happened during your athletics class. I don't know if Grayson is capable of doing something like that. But seeing Sky with that bruise under her eye had me just as worked up as when I thought Grayson had hurt you. And you aren't here for me to protect anymore, so I feel this unrelenting need to protect Sky and I don't even know her.

Don't tell Daniel this, not that you could, but I would have shown up to school tomorrow whether he made it a condition or not. I need to see how Sky and Grayson interact with my own two eyes so I can determine whether I actually need to kill him this time.

H

Chapter Nine

I'm ten minutes early when I reach her house, so I take a seat on the curb and stretch. After leaving here yesterday, I felt like me offering to run with her might have been a little forward. It is out of my way and I don't usually run this much in a day, but I didn't know how else I would see her again.

I hear her walking up behind me, so I spin around and stand up. "Hey, you."

I expect her to smile or return a greeting of some sort, but instead she eyes me up and down with an uncomfortable frown. I shrug it off, hoping she's just not a morning person.

"You need to stretch first?" I ask her.

She shakes her head. "Already did."

I'm curious if the solemn attitude is because she's sore from her fall yesterday. Her black eye is still prominently displayed, but her cheek doesn't look as bad as I thought it would. I reach out and run my thumb over the scrape on her face. "Doesn't look so bad. You sore?" She shakes her head no. "Good. You ready?"

She nods. "Yeah."

Three words is all the conversation I get from her? She turns and we both begin running in silence. I've never run with a girl before but I expected there to be a little more back and forth. I can't tell from the guarded greeting we just had in her front yard if she's uncomfortable around me, or if the quietness is actually a *sign* of comfort. It could go either way.

The tension lessens once I fall into step behind her. It's easier to get away with not speaking when I'm not running side by side with her. I just have no idea what to say. I'm not much of a talker to begin with, but being in her presence suppresses the conversational side of me even more. I guess if I really want to get anywhere with her, I need to suck it up. I speed up and step back into stride with her.

"You better try out for track," I say. "You've got more stamina than most of the guys from the team last year."

She shakes her head and continues to focus on the sidewalk in front of us. "I don't know if I want to," she says. "I don't really know anyone at school. I planned on trying out, but so far most of the people at school are sort of . . . mean. I don't really want to be subjected to them for longer periods of time under the guise of a team."

I hate that she's been in school for a day and she already knows how mean everyone is. I wonder what the hell they did to make her first day so bad?

"You've only been in public school for a day. Give it time. You can't expect to be homeschooled your whole life, then walk in the first day with a ton of new friends."

I feel bad telling her the exact opposite of what I really feel. If I was being completely honest, I'd tell her to go back to homeschooling, because she had it made before she entered public school. I turn to look at her but she's not running next to me. I spin around and she is stopped several feet behind me with her hands on her hips. I rush to her.

"Are you okay? Are you dizzy?" I hold her shoulders in case she feels faint again. I'd feel like the ultimate jackass if I just let her bust the pavement like I did yesterday.

She shakes her head no, then pushes my hands off her shoulders. "I'm fine," she says.

She's pissed about something. I try to think of what I might have said, but nothing seemed offensive. "Did I say something wrong?"

She drops her eyes to the pavement and starts walking again, so I follow her. "A little," she says with a miffed tone. "I was halfway joking about the stalking yesterday, but you admitted to looking me up on Facebook right after meeting me. Then you insist on running with me, even though it's out of your way. Now you somehow know how long I've been in public school? And that I was homeschooled? I'm not gonna lie, it's a little unnerving."

Shit. What the hell is wrong with me? How do I admit that I learned most of what I know about her based on overhearing Grayson at a party and through speculative rumors from Daniel? She doesn't need to know that. I don't *want* her to know that.

I sigh and continue walking toward her house with her. "I asked around," I say. "I've lived here since I was ten, so I have a lot of friends. I was curious about you."

She focuses on me as if she's trying to figure out how I know so much about her. I'm not about to admit the things I overheard Grayson say, because I don't want to hurt her. But I also don't want to admit that I begged Daniel for more information, because I don't want to scare her off. But based on the skeptical look spread across her face, she's already formed a good amount of distrust in me.

I take her by the elbow and she stops walking. I turn her so that she's facing me.

"Sky. I think we got off on the wrong foot at the store yesterday. And the talk about stalking, I swear, it was a joke. I don't want you to feel uncomfortable around me. Would it make you feel better if you knew more about me? Ask me something and I'll tell you. Anything."

"If I ask you something, will you be honest?"

I look her hard in the eyes. "That's all I'll ever be," I say. And I intend to be completely honest with her, unless I think it'll hurt her.

"Why did you drop out of school?"

I sigh, wishing she had asked me something a little less complicated. I should have known things wouldn't be simple with her, though.

I start walking again. "Technically, I haven't dropped out yet."

"Well you obviously haven't been in over a year. I'd say that's dropping out."

That comment makes me curious if she's heard the rumors about *me*. Of course I've been to school in the past year, it just wasn't *this* one. But she didn't ask about the rumored stint in juvi, so I'm not going to offer up unnecessary information.

"I just moved back home a few days ago," I say. "My mother and I had a pretty shitty year last year, so I moved in with my dad in Austin for a while. I've been going to school there, but felt like it was time to come back home. So here I am."

She squints like she's trying to scowl at me, but the expression she makes is too adorable to find intimidating. I keep my smile in check, though, because I can tell she's taking this school thing seriously. "None of that explains why you decided to drop out, rather than just transfer back."

She's right, but only because I really don't know the answer to her question.

"I don't know. To be honest, I'm still trying to decide what I want to do. It's been a pretty fucked-up year. Not to mention I hate this school. I'm tired of the bullshit and sometimes I think it would be easier to just test out."

She stops dead in her tracks again and glares at me. "That's a crap excuse."

"It's crap that I hate high school?"

"No. It's crap that you're letting one bad year determine your fate for the rest of your life. You're nine months away from graduation, so you drop out? It's just . . . it's stupid."

She's really taking this seriously. I laugh, even though I'm trying really hard not to. "Well, when you put it so eloquently."

She crosses her arms and huffs. "Laugh all you want. You quitting school is just giving in. You're proving everyone that's ever doubted you right."

Her eyes drop to the tattoo on my arm. I've never wanted to hide it until this moment, but something about her reading it seems like an invasion of privacy in a way. Maybe because I was so certain yesterday that she was half the reason for the tattoo on my arm. But now that I know she's not, I really don't want her asking about it. "You're gonna drop out and show the world just how hopeless you really are? Way to stick it to 'em."

I look down at the tattoo. She has no idea what the meaning is behind it and I realize that. But her assumption that it means anything other than what it means sort of pisses me off. I don't want to explain it to her and I certainly don't want to be judged by someone who seems to be receiving her own fair share of judgments. Rather than stick around and allow her to decipher me even more, I nudge my head toward her house. "You're here," I say flatly. I turn around and head toward home without looking back at her. No need to get too detailed with her, anyway, until I find out more about her relationship with Grayson. And in order to do that, I need to hurry up and get back to my house so I can shower and change in time for my first and possibly *only* day of senior year.

This is a large school, which is why I didn't expect to actually have a class with her, much less the first one. And with Mr. Mulligan, to top it off.

She didn't seem too happy to see me, either. And the fact that she just practically ran past me to get out of the classroom doesn't seem to bode well. I pick up my textbook and make my way out of the classroom. Rather than search for my next class, I head straight to find her, instead.

She's facing her locker, switching books. I walk up behind her but pause for a moment before speaking to her. I want to give her a chance to get what she needs from her locker, because I'm hoping I'll be walking her to her next class.

"Hey, you," I say optimistically. There's a pause.

"You came," she says, her voice cool and composed. She turns around to face me and just seeing her eyes again makes me smile. I lean against the locker next to hers and tilt my head against the cold metal. I eye her outfit for a second, taking in the fact that she some-how looks even better after a shower.

"You clean up nice. Although, the sweaty version of you isn't so bad, either," I say, smiling at her. I'm trying to ease some of the ten-sion rolling off her, but nothing seems to be working in my favor.

"Are you here stalking me or did you actually re-enroll?" she asks.

A joke. She made a joke.

"Both," I say, tapping my fingers against the metal. I'm still smil-ing at her but she won't maintain eye contact with me for more than two seconds. She shifts her feet and looks nervously around us.

"Well, I need to get to class," she says, her voice monotone. "Welcome back."

She's being weird. "You're being weird."

She rolls her eyes and turns back to her locker. "I'm just sur-prised to see you here," she says unconvincingly.

"Nope," I say. "It's something else. What's wrong?"

My persistence seems to be paying off because she sighs and presses her back against the locker and looks up at me. "You want me to be honest?"

"That's all I ever want you to be."

She purses her lips together. "Fine," she says. "I don't want to give you the wrong idea. You flirt and say things like you have intentions with me that I'm not willing to reciprocate. And you're . . ."

She doesn't want to give me the wrong idea? Who is this and what the hell did she do with the girl who was blatantly flirting with me last night? I narrow my eyes at her. "I'm *what*?" I say, challenging her to finish her thought.

"You're . . . *intense*. Too intense. And moody. And a little bit scary. And there's the other thing . . . I just don't want you getting the wrong idea."

And *there it is*. She's been fed the lies and now I'm left to have to defend myself to the one person I incorrectly assumed might empathize with me.

"*What* other thing?"

"You know," she says, darting her eyes to the floor.

I take a step toward her and place my hand against the locker beside her head. "I *don't* know, because you're skirting around whatever issue it is you have with me like you're too afraid to say it. Just say it."

Her eyes grow wide and I immediately feel guilty for being so harsh with her. It just frustrates me no end that she would feed into their bullshit. The *same* bullshit that surrounds *her*.

"I heard about what you did," she blurts out. "I know about the guy you beat up. I know about you being sent to juvi. I know that in the two days I've known you, you've scared the shit out of me at least three times. And since we're being honest, I also know that if you've been asking around about me, then you've probably heard about my reputation, which is more than likely the only reason you're even making an effort with me. I hate to disappoint you, but I'm not screwing you. I don't want you thinking anything will happen between us besides what's already happening. We run together. That's it."

Wow.

I was expecting her to hear the rumors about me, but I wasn't expecting her to think I believe the rumors about her. So that's why her guard is up? Because she thinks I heard the rumors and now I'm just trying to *screw* her?

I mean, don't get me wrong. I'm not saying the thought hasn't crossed my mind. But *Jesus*, not like *that*. The fact that she even feels this way only makes me want to hug her. The thought of anyone intentionally trying to get close to her for that sole reason pisses me off. It doesn't help matters that Grayson is standing next to her now.

Where the hell did he come from? And why the hell does he have his arm around her like he owns her?

"Holder," Grayson says. "Didn't know you were coming back."

They're the first words he's spoken directly to me since the night before Les died. I'm afraid if I look at him I'll lose it, so I keep my eyes trained hard on Sky's. Unfortunately, my eyes can't seem to stop looking at the hand that's still gripping her waist. The hand that Sky hasn't slapped away. The hand that has obviously been around that same waist before. The same hand that used to be around Les.

This entire situation is too ironic. So much so, I crack a smile. *Just my luck.*

I straighten up and keep my eyes locked on the hand around Sky's waist. "Well, I'm back," I say. I can't watch this for another second. That familiar feeling of wanting to rip his fucking hand off has returned tenfold.

I walk away and make it a few feet down the hall before I turn around and face Sky again. "Track tryouts are Thursday after school. Go."

I don't wait for her response. I walk to my locker and exchange books, then head to my next class. I don't know why, though. I'm pretty sure I won't be coming back tomorrow.

*   *   *

"Hey, dickweed. What's this sudden infatuation with Sky?" Daniel asks as we make our way toward the cafeteria.

"It's nothing," I say, attempting to brush it off. "I met her yesterday and was just curious about her. But apparently she's with Grayson, so . . . whatever."

Daniel raises an eyebrow, but says nothing about the Grayson comment. He pushes through the cafeteria doors and we walk to our table. I take a seat and scan the crowd, searching for her.

"You gonna eat today?" he asks.

I shake my head. "Nah. I don't really feel like it." I lost my appetite this morning as soon as Grayson's arm went around Sky's waist.

Daniel shrugs and walks away to get himself food. I search the cafeteria a while longer and finally spot her a few tables down, sitting with a guy. He's not Grayson, though. I scan the crowd for Grayson and find him seated at a table on the opposite end of the cafeteria. They're not sitting together. Why wouldn't they sit together if they're dating? And if they're not dating, why would he be touching her like he was?

"I got you a water," Daniel says, sliding it across the table to me. "Thanks."

He sets his tray down and takes a seat across from me. "Why are you being such a cunt nugget?"

Water spews out of my mouth and I drop my arms onto the table and laugh, wiping my mouth. "*Cunt nugget?*"

He nods and pops the lid on his soda. "Something's off with you. You stared at that girl the entire time I was in line for food. You won't tell me anything about her. You've been on edge since you got here this morning and it has nothing to do with the fact that it's your first day back at school since . . . well . . . since your *last* day at school. And you haven't even commented about how no one seems to give a shit that you're even here today. Aren't you a little excited everyone has stopped with the gossip?"

I would be excited if I was convinced the gossip had stopped. But it hasn't stopped, it's just been shifted in a different direction. I heard Sky's name mentioned in every single class I've had today. Not to mention the shit I've seen slapped on her locker in the form of sticky-notes.

"They didn't stop with the gossip, Daniel. They just found someone new to target."

Daniel starts to reply, but he's cut off by several trays dropping down onto the table. Guys slide into seats and several of them welcome me back, going on about how I made it right in time for football season. That leads into a conversation about practices and Coach Riley, but none of it can hold my attention like she does. I ignore everyone around me and watch her, still trying to figure her out.

I honestly don't want to impede if she's dating Grayson. If she's happy with him, then fine. Good for them. But I'll be damned if I don't get to the bottom of what happened to her eye. I need a straight explanation from her before I can let it go. Otherwise, I'll be going to Grayson to find out what happened to her eye, and I know how that'll end.

The guy she's sitting with nods in my direction when he sees me staring at them. I make it a point not to turn away, because I actually want to get her attention. When she looks at me, I nudge my head toward the cafeteria doors, then stand up and walk toward them.

I walk out into the hallway, hoping she'll follow me. I know it's not my business, but if I expect to make it through the rest of the day without murdering Grayson, I have to know the truth. I walk around the corner for more privacy and lean back against the row of lockers. She walks around the corner and spots me, then comes to a stop.

"Are you dating Grayson?" I ask. I keep it short and sweet. She doesn't seem to like having conversations with me, so I don't want to force her to do something she doesn't want to do. I just want the truth so I can justify my next move.

She rolls her eyes and walks to the lockers across from me, leaning against them to face me. "Does it matter?"

Hmm. It shouldn't matter, but it does. I have no idea what kind of person she is, but Grayson doesn't deserve her. So yes, it does matter.

"He's an asshole," I say.

"Sometimes you are, too," she bites back.

"He's not good for you."

She laughs and rolls her eyes toward the ceiling, shaking her head. "And you *are*?"

I groan. She's missing my point completely. I turn around to face the lockers and hit one of them with an open palm, releasing some of the frustration she's causing me with her stubbornness. When the sound echoes through the hallway I cringe. That came off a little harsher than I meant for it to.

But I am angry and I hate that I'm angry because I shouldn't even give a shit. Les isn't around for Grayson to fuck over, so why *do* I care?

Because I don't want her with him. That's why.

I turn around and face her again. "Don't factor me into this. I'm talking about Grayson, not me. You shouldn't be with him. You have no idea what kind of person he is."

She rolls her head back against the locker, fed up with me. "Two days, Holder. I've known you all of two days," she says. She kicks off the lockers and walks toward me, eyeing me angrily. "In those two days, I've seen five different sides of you, and only one of them has been appealing. The fact that you think you have any right to even voice an opinion about me or my decisions is absurd. It's ridiculous."

I inhale through my nose and exhale through my clenched teeth, because I'm pissed. Pissed that she's *right*. She's seen me go from hot to cold more than once over these past two days and I haven't given her a single explanation. She deserves an explanation for my oddly overprotective behavior, so I attempt to give her one.

I take a step toward her. "I don't like him. And when I see things like this?" I bring my fingers up to trace the bruise underneath her eye. "And then see him with his arm around you? Forgive me if I get a little *ridiculous*."

The moment my fingers finish tracing the bruise, I fail to remove them from her cheek. Her breath hitches and her eyes grow wider and I can't help but notice the obvious reaction she has to my touch. I have an overwhelming urge to run my hand through her hair and pull her mouth to mine, but she pulls away from me and takes a step back.

"You think I should stay away from Grayson because you're afraid he has a temper?" She narrows her eyes and tilts her head. "A bit hypocritical, don't you think?"

I keep my eyes locked on hers as I process her comment. She's comparing me to *Grayson*?

I have to turn away from her so she doesn't see the disappointment on my face. I grip the back of my neck with both hands, then slowly turn back around to face her, but I keep my eyes trained on the floor.

"Did he hit you," I say with a defeated sigh. I look back up at her and directly into her eyes. "Has he *ever* hit you?"

She doesn't flinch or look away. She just shakes her head. "No," she says softly. "And no. I told you . . . it was an accident."

I can tell by her reaction that she's telling the truth. He didn't hit her. He never hit her, and I'm more than relieved. But still confused. If she's not dating him and he really didn't hit her, then what's her connection to him? Does she *want* to date him? Because I sure as hell don't want her to.

The bell rings right when I open my mouth to ask her what her relationship is with Grayson. The hallway fills with students and she breaks eye contact with me, then walks back toward the cafeteria.

I haven't seen Daniel again. I also didn't have another class with Sky, which disappoints me. I don't know why, though. We can't seem to have a conversation without it ending in an argument, but that doesn't stop me from wanting to have another conversation with her.

I leave my books in my locker, still not sure if I'll be back tomorrow. I grab my keys and walk toward the parking lot. I'm several feet from my car when I look up and see Grayson leaning against it. I stop and assess the situation. He's eyeing me coldly, but he's alone. Not sure what he wants or why he's touching my car.

"Grayson, whatever it is, I'm not interested. Just let it go." I'm not in the mood for him right now and he really needs to get the hell off my car.

"You know," he says, pushing off the car with his foot. He folds his arms across his chest and walks toward me. "I really wish I *could* just let it go, Holder. But for some reason you seem so focused on my business, you really make it impossible for me to let it go."

He's within reach of my fist now, which isn't very smart of him. I keep my eyes locked on his, but watch his hands out of my peripheral vision.

"You've been back less than a day and you're already at it again," he says, stupidly walking even closer to me. "Sky is off-limits to you, Holder. Don't talk to her. Don't look at her." *I can't believe I'm still allowing him to speak.* "Don't go fucking *near* her. The last thing I need is for another one of my girlfriends to kill herself because of you."

I'm in that moment.

The moment when rational thought is drowned out by anger.

The moment when a person's conscience is stifled by rage.

The moment when the vision of releasing every pent-up feeling I've had for thirteen months surfaces, and it actually feels *good*. His face would feel so good against my fist right now and the thought of it makes me smile as I clench my fists and inhale a breath.

But Grayson quickly becomes an afterthought when I look over his shoulder and see Sky across the parking lot, climbing into her car. She doesn't even glance around the parking lot to look for Grayson. She just climbs into her car, shuts her door, and leaves.

It's in that moment that I realize he's full of shit.

They weren't sitting together at lunch.

She wasn't at the party with him Saturday night.

She's not waiting for him after school.

She's not even looking for him in the parking lot right now.

Everything falls into place as Grayson takes a step back, gauging my reaction, waiting for me to take his bait. Sky doesn't care about him. That's why he's so pissed that I was talking to her in the hallway. She doesn't give a shit about him and he doesn't want me to know that.

He's not worth it, I repeat to myself.

I watch as Sky pulls out of the parking lot, then I slowly refocus my gaze on Grayson. I'm oddly calm after coming to this new realization, but his jaw is clenched tighter than his fists. He wants me to fight him. He wants me to get kicked out of school.

He doesn't deserve to get a single damn thing he wants.

I raise my arm. His eyes dart to my hand and he puts his own hands up in defense. I point the clicker toward my car and press the button, unlocking my doors. I silently walk around him and climb into my car, then pull out of the parking lot without giving him the reaction he was hoping for.

Fuck him. He's not worth it.

Chapter Ten

I open the refrigerator door because I'm starving, but I haven't had anything to eat in over thirteen months. I haven't taken a single bite of food since Les died and it's weird that I'm still alive after all this time.

It takes the refrigerator light a second to kick on, even after I have the door open. As soon as the contents of the refrigerator are illuminated, I'm immediately disappointed. Every single shelf is stuffed with Les's jeans. They're all folded neatly on the shelves of the refrigerator and it pisses me off because this is where the food should be and I'm fucking hungry.

I open one of the crisper drawers, hoping the food is hidden in there, but there's no food. Just another pair of neatly folded jeans. I shut it and open the other crisper drawer and her jeans are in there, too.

How many fucking pairs of jeans does she *need*? And why are they in the refrigerator where the food is supposed to be?

I close the refrigerator door and open the freezer, but I'm met with the same thing, only this time the jeans are frozen. They're all in freezer bags labeled "Les's jeans." I slam the freezer door shut, irritated, and turn toward the pantry, hoping to find something to eat in there.

I walk around the kitchen island and look down.

I see her.

I squeeze my eyes shut and open them again, but she's still there.

Les is huddled in a fetal position on the kitchen floor, her back pressed up against the pantry door.

This makes no sense.

How is she here?

She's been dead for thirteen months.

I'm hungry.

"Dean," she whispers.

Her eyes flick open and I immediately have to reach my hand out in order to steady myself against the island. My body suddenly becomes too heavy to hold up and I take a small step back, right before my legs give out and I fall to my knees in front of her.

Her eyes are open wide now and they're completely gray. No pupil, no irises. Just glossed-over gray eyes that are searching for me, unable to find me.

"Dean," she says again in a hoarse whisper. She blindly reaches her arm out toward me and her fingers feel around in front of her.

I want to help her. I want to reach out and grab her hand but I'm too weak to move. Or my body weighs too much. I don't know what it is that's stopping me, but I'm only two feet in front of her and I'm doing everything I can to lift my arm and take her hand but it won't fucking move. The more I struggle to regain control over my movements, the harder it becomes to breathe. She's crying now, saying my name. My chest tightens and my throat begins to close up and now I can't even calm her down with words because nothing will come out. I work the muscles in my jaw, but my teeth are clenched tight and my mouth won't open.

She's pulling herself up on her elbow, slowly scooting closer to me. She's trying to reach out for me but her lifeless eyes can't find me. She's crying even harder now.

"Help me, Dean," she says.

She hasn't called me Dean since we were kids and I don't know why she's calling me Dean now. I don't like it.

I squeeze my eyes shut and try to focus on getting my voice to work or my arms to move, but all the concentration in the world can't help me right now.

"Dean, *please*," she cries, only this time it's not her voice. It's the voice of a child. "Don't go," the child begs.

I open my eyes and Les is no longer there, but someone else has taken her place. A little girl is sitting with her back pressed against the pantry door and her head is buried in her arms that are wrapped tightly around her legs.

Hope.

I still can't move or speak or breathe and my chest is growing tighter and tighter with each sob that racks the little girl's body. All I can do is sit and watch her cry, because I'm physically unable to even turn my head or close my eyes.

"Dean," she says, her voice muffled by her arms and her tears. It's the first time I've heard her say my name since the day she was taken and it knocks out what little breath I had left in me. She slowly lifts her head away from her arms and widens her eyes. They're solid gray, identical to Les's. She leans her head back against the pantry door and wipes away a tear with the back of her hand.

"You found me," she whispers.

Only this time, it's not the voice of the little girl anymore. It's not even Les's voice.

It's Sky's.

Chapter Eleven

I open my eyes and I'm no longer on the kitchen floor.

I'm in my bed.

I'm covered in sweat.

I'm gasping for air.

Chapter Twelve

I couldn't go back to sleep last night after the nightmare. I've been awake since two in the morning and it's now after six.

I drop down onto the sidewalk when I reach her house. I stretch my legs out in front of me and lean forward, grabbing my shoes while I stretch the muscles in my back. I've been tense for days and nothing I do seems to help.

Before I went to sleep last night I had no intention of running with her again today. But I've been sitting alone for over four hours, wide awake, and the only thing that even remotely appealed to me was the thought of seeing Sky again.

I also had no intention of going back to school today but it seems way more appealing than staying home all day. It's like I've been living minute to minute since the moment I got back from Austin last week. I'm not sure from one moment to the next what I'm doing or where I'll be or even what frame of mind I'll be in.

I don't like this instability.

I also don't like that I'm at her house again today, waiting on her to come outside for her morning run. I don't like that I still feel the need to be around her. I don't like the fact that I don't want her to believe the rumors about me. I don't give a shit when anyone else believes them. Why do I give a shit if *she* believes them?

I shouldn't. I should just go back home and leave her to believe whatever she wants to believe.

I stand up in an attempt to talk myself into leaving, but I just stand here, waiting on her. I know I need to leave and I know I don't want to be involved with anyone even remotely interested in Grayson, but I can't do it. I can't leave because I want to see her again a whole lot more than I want to leave.

A noise comes from the side of her house, so I take a few steps to get a look. She's climbing headfirst out of her window.

Just seeing her again, even from a distance, reminds me of why I crave to be around her so much. It's only been a few days, but since the moment I met her, no matter where I am, I'm constantly wondering about her. My attention is constantly homed in on her like I'm a compass and she's my North.

Once she's outside, she pauses and looks up toward the sky, inhaling a deep breath. I take a few hesitant steps toward her. "Do you always climb out your window or were you just hoping to avoid me?"

She spins around, wide-eyed. I try not to let my eyes dip below her neck, but the things I've seen her run in are hard not to stare at.

Keep looking at her face, Holder. You can do it.

She glances at me, but doesn't make eye contact. Her eyes lock on my stomach and I'm curious if it's because she likes that I'm not wearing a shirt or if it's because she can't stand me to the point that it's hard for her to look me in the eyes. "If I was trying to avoid you I would have just stayed in bed." She walks past me and lowers herself onto the sidewalk.

I hate that her voice does things to my body that no other voice could ever do. But I also love it and want her to keep talking, even if she *is* rude most of the time.

I watch as she pushes her legs out in front of her and begins to stretch. She seems fairly calm today, despite the fact that I showed up. I sort of expected her to tell me to go the hell away after how we left things in the hallway yesterday.

"I wasn't sure if you'd show up," I say, taking a seat on the sidewalk in front of her.

She lifts her head and looks me in the eyes this time. "Why

wouldn't I? I'm not the one with the issues. Besides, neither of us owns the road."

Issues?

She thinks I have *issues?*

I'm not the one feeding into the rumors like she is. I'm also not the one leaving notes on her locker, nor am I one of the many people at school who have treated her like shit. If anything, I've been one of the few people to be nice to her.

But she thinks *I'm* the one with the issues?

"Give me your hands," I say, mirroring her position. "I need to stretch, too."

She shoots me a curious look, but takes my hands and leans back, pulling me forward.

"For the record," I say, "I wasn't the one with the issue yesterday."

I can feel her lean back farther, tightening her grip on my wrists. "Are you insinuating *I'm* the one with the issue?" she asks.

"Aren't you?"

"Clarify," she says. "I don't like vague."

She doesn't like vague.

Funny, because I don't either. I like truth and that's exactly the point I'm trying to make to this girl. "Sky, if there's one thing you should know about me, it's that I don't do vague. I told you I'll only ever be honest with you, and to me, vague is the same thing as dishonesty." I switch positions and pull her forward as I lean back.

"That's a pretty vague answer you just gave me," she says.

"I was never asked a question. I've told you before, if you want to know something, just ask. You seem to think you know me, yet you've never actually asked me anything yourself."

"I *don't* know you," she snaps.

I laugh, because she's absolutely right. She doesn't know me at all, but it certainly seems like she's a quick one to judge.

I don't know why I'm even bothering with her. She obviously doesn't *want* me to bother with her. I should just leave and let her think whatever the hell she wants to think.

I drop her hands and stand up. "Forget it," I mutter, turning to walk away. As much as I like being around her, there's only so much I'm willing to put up with.

"Wait," she says, following after me.

I honestly expected her to just let me walk away. Hearing the word "wait" come out of her mouth and knowing she's following behind me does this thing to my chest that makes it feel alive again and it pisses me off because I don't want her to have that effect on me. "What did I say?" she asks, catching up to me. "I *don't* know you. Why are you getting all pissy with me again?"

Pissy?

Her word-choice makes me want to smile, but the fact that she doesn't recognize that she's the one who has been *pissy* for two days irritates the hell out of me. I stop walking and turn to face her, taking two steps toward her.

"I guess after spending time with you over the last few days, I thought I'd get a slightly different reaction from you at school. I've given you plenty of opportunity to ask me whatever you want to ask me, but for some reason you want to believe everything you hear, despite the fact that you never heard any of it from *me*. And coming from someone with her own share of rumors, I figured you'd be a little less judgmental."

Her eyes narrow and she puts her hands on her hips. "So that's what this is about? You thought the slutty new girl would be sympathetic to the gay-bashing asshole?"

I groan out of frustration. I hate hearing her refer to herself like that. "Don't do that, Sky."

She takes a step toward me. "Don't do what? Call you a gay-bashing asshole? Okay. Let's practice this honesty policy of yours. Did you or did you not beat up that student last year so badly that you spent a year in juvenile detention?"

I want to grab her by the shoulders and shake her out of sheer frustration. Why can't she see that she's behaving just like everyone else? I know she's not like them, so I don't understand her attitude at all. Anyone that can brush off rumors about themselves isn't the type of person who would spread them. So why the hell is she *believing* them?

I look her hard in the eyes. "When I said *don't do that*, I wasn't referring to you insulting me. I was referring to you insulting *yourself*." I close the gap between us and when I do, she takes in a small rush of air and closes her mouth. I lower my voice and confirm the only part of the rumors that are true. "And yes. I beat his ass to within an inch of his life, and if the bastard was standing in front of me right now, I'd do it again."

We stare at each other in silence. She's looking at me with a mixture of anger and fear, and I hate that she's feeling either of those things. She takes a slow step back, putting space between us, but doesn't break her firm stare.

"I don't want to run with you today," she says flatly.

"I don't really feel like running with you, either."

I turn around at the same time she does and immediately feel nothing but regret. I didn't accomplish anything by coming here today. If anything, I just made things worse with her. I shouldn't have to come out and tell her that the majority of what she thinks she knows about me is false. I shouldn't have to explain myself to anyone and neither should she.

But I regret that I *didn't* explain myself, because I need her to know that I'm not that guy.

I just don't know why I need her to know that.

Chapter Twelve-and-a-half

Les,

Remember when we were fourteen and I had a crush on Ava? You hardly knew her but I forced you to become friends with her so she could come to the house and spend the night with you. She was the first girl I ever kissed and we lasted all of two weeks before she started to get on my everlasting nerve. Unfortunately, by the time we broke up, you really did like her. Then I was forced to see her on a recurring basis for an entire year after that until she moved.

I know you were sad when she moved, but I was so relieved. It was way too awkward having to interact with her on a regular basis after that.

I also know it was cruel of me to force you to be her friend just so she would come stay the night at our house. I thought I learned my lesson and I never asked you to do it again.

Well, I didn't learn my lesson. Today I've been wishing you were still here, purely for selfish reasons, because I would give anything for you to be friends with Sky. After running with her this morning, I can see clearly that she's irritating and irrational and stubborn and gorgeous as hell and I want so bad to stop thinking about her, but I can't. If you were here,

I could ask you to be her friend so she would have a reason to come over to our house, even though we're eighteen now and not fourteen. But I want an excuse to talk to her again. I want to give her one more chance to hear me out, but I don't know how to go about doing that. I don't want to do it at school and we aren't running together anymore. Short of walking up to her house and knocking on her front door, I can't figure out a way to get her to talk to me.

Wait. That's actually not a bad idea.

Thanks, Les.

H

Chapter Thirteen

"We going out tonight?" I ask Daniel as we make our way toward the parking lot. We usually do something on Friday nights, but tonight I'm actually hoping he says no. I decided a few days ago that I wanted to go to Sky's house tonight to try to talk to her. I don't know if it's a good idea, but I know if I don't at least try, I'll drive myself crazy wondering if it would have made a difference.

"Can't," Daniel says. "I'm taking Val out. We could do something tomorrow night, though. I'll call you."

I nod and he turns to head toward his car. I open my door, but pause when I see Sky's car out of the corner of my eye. She's leaning against it, talking to Grayson.

From the looks of it, they might be doing more than just talking.

I'd be lying if I didn't admit that seeing his hands on her makes every muscle in my body clench tight. I prop my arm on my door and watch them for some stupid, self-torturous reason.

From here, she doesn't look happy. She pushes him away from her and takes a step away from him. She's watching him while he talks, then he moves in and wraps his arms around her again. I take a step away from my car, prepared to walk across the parking lot and pull his ignorant ass off her. She clearly doesn't want him touching her, but I stop and take a step back when it looks like she relents and gives in to him. As soon as he leans in to kiss her, I have to look away.

It's physically impossible to watch. I don't understand her. I don't understand what she sees in him and I really don't understand why she can't seem to stand me, when he's the actual asshole.

Maybe I'm wrong about her. Maybe she really *is* just like everyone else. Maybe I've just been hoping she was different for my own sake.

Or maybe *not*.

I'm looking at them again, seeing her reaction to what he's doing to her. His arms are still around her and it looks like he's still kissing her neck or shoulder or wherever the fuck his mouth is. But I could have sworn she just rolled her eyes.

Now she's looking at her watch, not responding to him at all. She drops her arm and rests her hands at her sides and she's just standing there, looking more inconvenienced by him than interested.

I continue to watch them and continue to grow more and more confused by her lack of interest. Her expression is almost lifeless, until the second she locks eyes with mine. Her whole body tenses and her eyes grow wide. She immediately looks away and pushes Grayson off her. She turns her back to him and gets into her car. I'm too far away to hear what she says to him, but the fact that she's driving away and he's flipping her off with both hands tells me that whatever she said to him wasn't at all what he wanted to hear.

I smile.

I'm still confused, I'm still angry, I'm still intrigued and I'm still planning on showing up on her doorstep tonight. Especially after witnessing whatever that was I just witnessed.

I ring the doorbell and wait.

I'm a ball of nerves right now, but only because I don't have a clue how she'll react to seeing me on her doorstep. I also don't know what the hell I'm going to say to her once she does finally open the door.

I ring the doorbell again after waiting several moments. I'm sure I'm the last person she'll expect to see here on a Friday night.

Shit. It's Friday night. She's probably not even home.

I hear footsteps making their way toward the door and it opens. She's standing in front of me a frazzled mess. Her hair is loosely pulled back, but strands have fallen all around her face. She's got white powder dusted across her nose and cheek and even has some in the loose strands of hair framing her face. She looks adorable. And shocked.

Several seconds pass with us just standing there and I realize that I should probably be the one speaking right now, since I'm the one who showed up at her house.

God, why does every single thing about her throw me off like this?

"Hey," she says.

Her calm voice is like a breath of fresh air. She doesn't seem pissed that I'm here unannounced. "Hi," I say, returning her greeting.

Another round of awkward silence ensues and she tilts her head to the side. "Um . . ." She squints and crinkles up her nose and I can tell she's not sure what to do or say next.

"You busy?" I ask her, knowing just by the disarray of her appearance that whatever she was doing, she was working hard at it.

She turns and glances back into her house, then faces me again. "Sort of."

Sort of.

I take her reply for what it is. She's obviously trying not to be rude, but I can see that this stupid idea of mine to just show up unannounced was just that . . . a stupid idea.

I glance at my car behind me, gauging how far the walk of shame I'm about to take will be. "Yeah," I say, pointing over my shoulder at my car. "I guess I'll . . . go." I take a step down and begin to turn toward my car, wishing I was anywhere but in this awkward predicament.

"No," she says quickly. She takes a step back and opens the door for me. "You can come in, but you might be put to work."

Instant relief overcomes me and I nod, walking inside. A quick glance around the living room makes it appear that she might be the only one home right now. I hope she is, because it would make things a lot easier if it were just the two of us.

She walks around me and into the kitchen. She picks up a measuring cup and resumes whatever it was she was doing before I showed up on her doorstep. Her back is to me and she's quiet. I slowly make my way into the kitchen and eye the baked goods lining her bar.

"You prepping for a bake sale?" I ask, making my way around the bar so that her back isn't completely to me.

"My mom's out of town for the weekend," she says, glancing up at me. "She's antisugar, so I kind of go crazy when she's not here."

Her mom's out of town, so she bakes? I really can't figure this girl out. I reach over to the plate of cookies between us on the bar and pick one up, looking to her for permission to try it.

"Help yourself," she says. "But be warned, just because I like to bake doesn't mean I'm good at it." She refocuses her attention to the bowl in front of her.

"So you get the house to yourself and you spend Friday night baking? Typical teenager," I tease. I take a bite of the cookie and *ohmygod*. She can bake. I like her even more.

"What can I say?" she says with a shrug. "I'm a rebel."

I smile, then eye the plate of cookies again. There have to be a dozen there and I plan on eating at least half of them before she kicks me out of her house. I'm gonna need milk.

She's still intensely focused on the bowl in front of her, so I take it upon myself to find my own glass. "Got any milk?" I ask, making my way to the refrigerator. She doesn't answer my question, so I open the refrigerator and remove the milk, then pour myself a glass. I finish the rest of the cookie, then take a drink. I wince, because whatever the hell this is, it's not real milk. Or it's rotten. I glance at the label before shutting the refrigerator and see that it's almond milk. I don't want to be rude, so I take another drink and turn around.

She's looking straight at me with an arched eyebrow. I smile. "You shouldn't offer cookies without milk, you know. You're a pretty pathetic hostess." I swipe another cookie and take a seat at the bar.

She grins right before she turns around to face the counter again. "I try to save my hospitality for *invited* guests."

I laugh. "Ouch."

The sarcasm in her voice is nice, though, because it helps ease my tension. She powers on the mixer and keeps her focus on the bowl in front of her. I love that she hasn't asked why I'm here. I know she's wondering what I'm doing here, but I also know from previous interaction with her that she's incredibly stubborn and more than likely won't ask what I'm doing here, no matter how much she wants to know.

She turns off the mixer and pulls the mixing blades loose, then brings one to her mouth and licks it.

Holy shit.

I gulp.

"Want one?" she says, holding one up for me to take. "It's German chocolate."

"How hospitable of you."

"Shut up and lick it or I'm keeping it for myself," she says teasingly. She smiles and walks to the cabinet, then fills a glass with water. "You want some water or do you want to continue pretending you can stomach that vegan shit?"

I laugh, then immediately push my cup toward her. "I was trying to be nice, but I can't take another sip of whatever the hell this is. Yes, water. *Please.*"

She laughs and fills my cup with water, then takes a seat across from me. She picks up a brownie and takes a bite, holding eye contact with me. She doesn't speak but I know she's curious why I'm here. The fact that she still hasn't asked, though, makes me admire her stubbornness.

I know I should offer up my reason for showing up out of the blue, but I'm a little stubborn myself and feel like dragging this thing out with her a little longer. I'm kind of enjoying it.

We silently watch each other until she's almost finished with her brownie. The way she's semismiling at me while she eats is making my pulse race and if I don't look away from her, I'm afraid I'll blurt out everything I want to say to her all at once.

In order to avoid that, I stand up and walk into the living room to take a look around. I can't watch her eat for another second and I need to refocus my attention on why I'm here, because *I'm* even starting to forget.

There are several pictures hanging on her walls, so I walk closer to them to take a look. There aren't any pictures of her that are more than a few years old, but the ones where she's younger than she is now are jarring to look at. She really does look just like Hope.

It's surreal, looking into those big brown eyes of the little girl in the picture. If it weren't for the fact that she's in several pictures with her mother, I'd be convinced she really was Hope.

But she can't be Hope, because Hope's mother passed away when she was just a little girl. Unless Karen isn't Sky's mom.

I hate that my mind is still going there. "Your mom seems really young," I say, noticing the noticeable small age difference between them.

"She *is* young."

"You don't look like her. Do you look like your dad?"

She shrugs. "I don't know. I don't remember what he looks like."

She looks sad when she says it, but I'm curious why she doesn't remember what he looks like.

"Is your dad dead?"

She sighs. I can tell she's uncomfortable talking about it. "I don't know. Haven't seen him since I was three." It's clear she doesn't feel like elaborating. I walk back to the kitchen and reclaim my seat.

"That's all I get? No story?"

"Oh, there's a story. I just don't want to tell it."

I can see I'm not getting any more information out of her right now, so I change the subject. "Your cookies were good. You shouldn't downplay your baking abilities."

She smiles, but her smile fades as soon as the phone on the counter between us sounds off, indicating a text. I look down at it just as she jumps up and rushes to the oven. She swings it open to eye the cake and I realize she thinks the sound came from the oven, rather than the phone.

I pick up the phone just as she shuts the oven and turns to face me. "You got a text." I laugh. "Your cake is fine."

She rolls her eyes and throws the oven mitt on the counter, then walks back to her seat. I'm curious about the cell phone, especially since she told me earlier this week that she didn't have one.

"I thought you weren't allowed to have a phone," I say, glancing at all the texts as I scroll my finger down the screen. "Or was that a really pathetic excuse to avoid giving me your number?"

"I'm *not* allowed," she says. "My best friend gave it to me the other day. It can't do anything but text."

I turn the phone around to face her. "What the hell kind of texts *are* these?" I read one out loud.

"*Sky, you are beautiful. You are possibly the most exquisite creature in the universe and if anyone tells you otherwise, I'll cut the bitch.*" I glance at her, the texts making me even more curious about her than I was before. "Oh, God," I say. "They're all like this. Please tell me you don't text these to yourself for daily motivation."

She laughs and snatches the phone out of my hand. "Stop. You're ruining the fun of it."

"Oh, my God, you do? Those are all from you?"

"No!" she says defensively. "They're from Six. She's my best friend and she's halfway around the world and she misses me. She wants me to not be sad, so she sends me nice texts every day. I think it's sweet."

"Oh, you do not," I say. "You think it's annoying and you probably don't even read them."

"She means well," she says, folding her arms defensively across her chest.

"They'll ruin you," I tease. "Those texts will inflate your ego so much, you'll explode." I scroll through the settings on her phone and punch the number into my phone. There's no way I'm leaving here without her number, and this is the perfect excuse to get it. "We need to rectify this situation before you start suffering from delusions of grandeur." I give her back her phone and text her.

Your cookies suck ass. And you're really not that pretty.

"Better?" I ask after she reads it. "Did the ego deflate enough?"

She laughs and places the phone facedown on the counter. "You know just the right things to say to a girl." She walks into the living room and spins around to face me. "Want a tour of the house?"

I don't hesitate. Of course I want a tour of her house. I follow her through the house and listen as she speaks. I pretend to be interested in everything she's pointing out, but in reality I can only concentrate on the sound of her voice. She could talk to me all night and I'd never get tired of listening to her.

"My room," she says, swinging open the door to her bedroom. "Feel free to look around, but being as though there aren't any people eighteen or older here, stay off the bed. I'm not allowed to get pregnant this weekend."

I pause as I'm passing through her door and eye her. "Only *this* weekend?" I ask, matching her wit. "You plan on getting knocked up next weekend, instead?"

She smiles and I continue making my way into her room. "Nah," she says. "I'll probably wait a few more weeks."

I shouldn't be here. Every minute I spend with her makes me like her more and more. Now I'm in her room and there's no one in the house other than her and me, not to mention the fact that there's this bed between us that she told me to stay off of.

I shouldn't be here.

I came here to show her I'm the good guy, not the bad guy. So why am I looking at her bed and not having good thoughts right now?

"I'm eighteen," I say, unable to stop imagining what she looks like when she lies in this bed.

"Yay for you?" she says, confused.

I smile at her, then nod toward her bed as explanation. "You said to stay off your bed because I'm not eighteen. I'm just pointing out that I am."

Her shoulders tense and she inhales a quick breath. "Oh," she says, slightly flustered. "Well then, I meant nineteen."

I like her reaction a little too much, so I try to refocus and concentrate on why I'm here.

Why *am* I here? Because all that's running through my mind right now is *bed, bed, bed.*

I'm here to make a point. A much-needed, valid point. I walk as far away from the bed as I can get and end up at the window.

The same window I've heard so much about over the course of the past week at school. It's amazing the things you can learn if you just shut up and listen.

I lean my head out of it and look around, then pull back inside. I don't like that she keeps it open. It's not safe.

"So this is the infamous window, huh?"

If that comment doesn't direct the conversation in the direction I'm hoping, I don't know what will.

"What do you want, Holder?" she snaps.

I turn to face her and she's eyeing me fiercely. "Did I say something wrong, Sky? Or untrue? Unfounded, maybe?"

She immediately walks to her door and holds it open. "You know exactly what you said and you got the reaction you wanted. Happy? You can go now."

I hate that I'm pissing her off, but I ignore her request for me to leave. I look away and walk to the side of her bed and pick up a book. I pretend to flip through it while I contemplate how to start the conversation.

"Holder, I'm asking you as nicely as I'm going to ask you. Please leave."

I set the book down and take a seat on her bed, despite the fact that she told me not to. She's already pissed at me. What's one more thing?

She stomps over to the bed and actually grabs my legs, attempting to physically pull me off the bed. She then reaches up and yanks on my wrists in an attempt to pull me up, but I pull her down to the bed and flip her onto her back, holding her arms to the mattress.

Now that I've got her good and riled up, it would be a good time to tell her what I came here to tell her. That I'm *not* that guy. That I wasn't in juvi for a year. That I didn't beat that kid up because he was gay.

But here I am holding her down to the mattress and I have no idea how we even got to this point, but I'll be damned if I can form a coherent thought. She's not struggling to get out from under me at all and we're both staring at each other like we're daring the other one to be the first to make a move.

My heart is pounding against my chest and if I don't back away from her right now I'll do something to those lips of hers that will for sure end up with me getting slapped.

Or kissed back.

The thought is tempting, but I don't risk it. I let go of her arms and wipe my thumb across the end of her nose. "Flour. It's been bugging me," I say. I back away and rest my back against her headboard.

She doesn't move. She's breathing heavily and staring up at the ceiling. I'm not sure what she's thinking, but she's not trying to kick me out of her room anymore, so that's good.

"I didn't know he was gay," I say.

She turns her head in my direction and she's still flat on her back. She doesn't say anything, so I use the opportunity to explain in more detail while I've got her full attention.

"I beat him up because he was an asshole. I had no idea he was gay."

She eyes me, expressionless, then slowly turns her head back toward the ceiling. I give her a moment to ponder what I just said. She'll either believe me and feel guilty or she *won't* believe me and she'll still be pissed. Either way, I don't want her to feel guilty *or* pissed. But we're not left with any other choices of emotions in this situation.

I remain quiet, wanting her to respond to me with *something*, at least.

A sound comes from the kitchen and it actually resembles an oven timer rather than her phone. "Cake!" she yells. She's off the bed and out the bedroom door and I find myself alone in her room on her bed. I close my eyes and lean my head against the headboard.

I want her to believe me. I want her to trust me and I want her to know the truth about my past. There's something about her that tells me she's not like all the other people I've encountered who disappoint me. I just hope I'm not wrong about her, because I like being around her. She actually makes me feel like I have a purpose. I haven't felt like I had a purpose in over thirteen months.

I glance up when she walks back into the room and she smiles sheepishly. She has a cookie in her mouth and another in her hand. She holds it out to me and drops down next to me on the bed. Her head lands against her pillow and she sighs.

"I guess the gay-bashing asshole remark was really judgmental on my part then, huh? You aren't really an ignorant homophobe who spent the last year in juvenile detention?"

Mission accomplished.

And it was so much easier than I thought it would be.

I smile and scoot down until I'm flat on the bed next to her. "Nope," I say, looking up at the stars plastered across her ceiling. "Not at all. I spent the entire last year living with my father in Austin. I don't even know where the story about me being sent to juvi came into the picture."

"Why don't you defend yourself against the rumors if they aren't true?"

What an odd question, coming from someone who hasn't defended herself at all this entire week. I glance in her direction. "Why don't *you*?"

She quietly nods. "Touché."

We both look back up to her ceiling. I like that she was so easy to come around. I like that she didn't argue about it, especially knowing how stubborn she is.

I like that I was right about her.

"The window comment from earlier?" she says. "You were just making a point about rumors? You really weren't trying to be mean?"

I hate that she actually thought I was just being cruel, even if it was only for a minute. I don't want her to ever think that about me. "I'm not mean, Sky."

"You're intense. I'm right about that, at least."

"I may be intense, but I'm not mean."

"Well, I'm not a slut."

"I'm not a gay-bashing asshole."

"So we're all clear?"

I laugh. "Yeah, I guess so."

It's quiet for another moment until she inhales a long, deep breath. "I'm sorry, Holder."

"I know, Sky," I say. I didn't come here for an apology. I don't want her to feel guilty about her misconception. "I know."

She doesn't say anything else and we both continue to look up at the stars. I'm conflicted right now because we're both on her bed and as much as I try to ignore my attraction for her, it's sort of hard when I'm inches from her.

I'm curious if she finds *me* attractive at all. I'm almost positive she does based on the tiny things she does when I'm around her that she tries to hide. Like the times I've caught her staring at my chest when I ran with her. Or the way she sucks in a breath when I lean in to speak to her. Or how she always seems to be struggling not to smile when she's trying so hard to be mad at me.

I'm not positive what she thinks about me or how she feels, but I know one thing . . . she definitely doesn't act indifferent toward me like she does toward Grayson.

Thinking about that incident and how just a few hours ago she was kissing him makes me grimace. It may not be appropriate to ask her about it, but I sure as hell can't stop thinking about how much I hate the thought of her kissing anyone, *especially* Grayson. And if there's ever a chance that I'll be the one kissing her, I need to know that she won't be kissing him again.

Ever.

"I need to ask you something," I say. I prepare myself to bring it up, knowing she more than likely doesn't want to talk about it. But I have to know how she feels about him. I inhale a deep breath and roll over to face her. "Why were you letting Grayson do what he was doing to you in the parking lot?"

She winces and shakes her head ever so slightly. "I already told you. He's not my boyfriend and he's not the one who gave me the black eye."

"I'm not asking because of any of that," I say, even though I really am. "I'm asking because I saw how you reacted. You were irritated with him. You even looked a little bored. I just want to know why you allow him to do those things if you clearly don't want him touching you."

She's quiet for a second. "My lack of interest was that obvious?"

"Yep. And from fifty yards away. I'm just surprised he didn't take the hint."

She immediately flips onto her side and props up on her elbow. "I know, right? I can't tell you how many times I've turned him down but he just doesn't stop. It's really pathetic. And unattractive."

I can't even describe how good it feels to hear her say that.

"Then why do you let him do it?"

She keeps her eyes locked on mine, but she doesn't answer me. We're inches apart. On her bed. Her mouth is right here.

So close.

We both flip onto our backs almost simultaneously.

"It's complicated," she says. Her voice sounds sad and I definitely didn't come here to make her feel sad.

"You don't have to explain. I was just curious. It's really not my business."

She pulls her arms up behind her head and rests her head on her hands. "Have you ever had a serious girlfriend?"

I have no idea where she's going with this, but at least she's talking, so I go with it. "Yep," I say. "But I hope you aren't about to ask for details, because I don't go there."

"That's not why I'm asking," she says, shaking her head. "When you kissed her, what did you feel?"

I *definitely* don't know where she's going with this. But still, I indulge her. It's the least I can do for showing up unannounced, then practically insulting her reputation before getting my point across.

"You want honesty, right?"

"That's all I ever want," she says, mimicking my own words.

I grin. "All right, then. I guess I felt . . . horny."

When I say the word horny, I swear she sucks in a breath. She's quick to recover, though. "So you get the butterflies and the sweaty palms and the rapid heartbeat and all that?" she asks.

"Yeah. Not with every girl I've been with, but most of them."

She tilts her head toward me and arches an eyebrow, which makes me grin. "There weren't *that* many," I say. At least I don't *think* there were that many. I'm not sure what number constitutes a lot at this point and even then, people measure things on different scales. "What's your point?" I ask, relieved she isn't asking me to clarify exactly how many there have been.

"My point is that I *don't*. I don't feel any of that. When I make out with guys, I don't feel anything at all. Just numbness. So sometimes I let Grayson do what he does to me, not because I enjoy it, but because I like not feeling anything at all."

I was absolutely not expecting that answer. I'm not sure that I *like* that answer. I mean, I like that she doesn't actually feel anything for

Grayson, but I hate that it hasn't stopped her from letting him try to get what he wants.

I also don't like that she admitted to never feeling anything, because I can honestly say when I'm around her, I've never felt so *much*.

"I know it doesn't make sense, and no, I'm not a lesbian," she says defensively. "I've just never been attracted to anyone before you and I don't know why."

I quickly turn and look at her, not sure that I heard her correctly. But based on her reaction and the way her arm comes up and immediately covers her face, I know for a fact I heard her correctly.

She's attracted to me.

And she didn't intend to admit that out loud.

And I'm pretty sure that accidental admission just made my entire year.

I reach over and slide my fingers around her wrist, pulling her arm away from her face. I know she's embarrassed right now, but there's no way in hell I'm letting this go.

"You're attracted to me?"

"Oh, God," she groans. "That's the last thing you need for your ego."

"That's probably true," I admit, laughing. "Better hurry up and insult me before my ego gets as big as yours."

"You need a haircut," she blurts out. "Really bad. It gets in your eyes and you squint and you're constantly moving it out of the way like you're Justin Bieber and it's really distracting."

I know she doesn't have access to technology, so I let it slide that Justin Bieber cut his hair off a long time ago. I'm disappointed that I even know that. I tug at my hair with my fingers and fall back against my pillow. "Man. That really hurt. It seems like you've thought that one out for a while."

"Just since Monday," she says.

"You *met* me on Monday. So technically, you've been thinking about how much you hate my hair since the moment we met?"

"Not *every* moment."

I laugh. I wonder if it's possible for people to fall in love with a person one characteristic at a time, or if you fall for the entire person at once. Because I think I just fell in love with her wit. And her bluntness. And maybe even her mouth, but I won't allow myself to stare at it long enough to confirm.

Shit. That's already three characteristics and I've only been here an hour.

"I can't believe you think I'm hot," I say, breaking the silence.

"Shut up."

"You probably faked passing out the other day, just so you could be carried in my hot, sweaty, manly arms."

"Shut up," she says again.

"I'll bet you fantasize about me at night, right here in this bed."

"Shut up, Holder."

"You probably even . . ."

She slaps her hand over my mouth. "You're way hotter when you aren't speaking."

I shut up, but only because I want to revel in the fact that this night has already turned out better than I ever anticipated. Every second I'm with her I like her more and more. I like her sense of humor and I like that she gets *my* sense of humor. She's the first girl besides Les to ever actually give me a run for my money and I can't seem to get enough of it.

"I'm bored," I say, hoping she'll suggest an interesting make-out session in lieu of staring at her ceiling. Although, if my options are limited to staring at her ceiling all night or going home, I'll gladly stare at her ceiling.

"So go home."

"I don't want to," I say resolutely. I'm having way too much fun to go home. "What do you do when you're bored? You don't have internet or TV. Do you just sit around all day and think about how hot I am?"

"I read," she says. "A lot. Sometimes I bake. Sometimes I run."

"Read, bake, and run. And fantasize about me. What a riveting life you lead."

"I like my life."

"I sort of like it, too," I say. And I *do* like it. We already have the running in common. And she may not realize it, but we also have the fantasizing in common. I don't bake, but I do like *her* baking.

That leaves reading. I read when I need to, which isn't a lot. But I suddenly want to know everything about everything that interests her and if reading interests her, it interests me too. I reach over and pick up the book from her nightstand. "Here, read this."

"You want me to read it out loud? You're that bored?"

"Pretty damn bored."

"It's a romance." She says it like it's a warning.

"Like I said. Pretty damn bored. Read."

She shrugs and adjusts her pillow, then begins reading.

"*I was almost three days old before the hospital forced them to decide. They agreed to take the first three letters of both names and compromised on Layken . . .*"

She continues to read and I continue to let her. After several chapters, I can't tell if my rapid-fire pulse is a result of listening to her voice for so long or if it's from the sexual tension in the book. Maybe both of them coupled together is what's doing it. Sky should really think about a career in voiceovers or audiobooks or some shit like that because her voice is . . .

"*He glides across the room . . .*"

Her voice is trailing off.

". . . and bends down, snatching up the . . ."

And . . . she's out. The book falls against her chest and I laugh quietly, but I don't get up. because the fact that she fell asleep doesn't mean I'm ready to leave.

I lie with her for about half an hour, confirming the fact that yes, I'm definitely in love with her mouth. I watch her sleep until my phone chimes. I scoot her away from me and onto her back, then pull my phone out of my pocket.

> **Dude. It's Daniel, me. Val is f'ng crazy n I think I'm at that Burker Ging and come get me I can't drive. I drank and I hate her.**

I text him back immediately.

> **Good idea. Stay put. Be there in thirty.**

I slide the phone back in my pocket, but it sounds off again with an incoming text.

> **Holder?**

I shake my head and shoot a text back that says, *Yeah?* He replies immediately.

> **Oh, good. Just mak'n sure it was u, man.**

Jeez. He's more than just *drunk*.

I stand up and take the book out of her hands, then set it on the nightstand and mark the page she stopped at so I'll have an excuse to come back over here tomorrow. I walk to the kitchen and spend the next ten minutes cleaning up her mess. I swear you would think she harbored resentment toward flour considering the amount I have to wipe up. After all the food is wrapped in Saran Wrap (minus the few cookies I might have swiped), I walk back to her bedroom, then sit down on the edge of her bed.

She's snoring.

I love it.

Shit. That's four things already.

I really need to leave.

Before standing up to leave, I slowly lean forward, hesitating, not wanting to wake her. But I can't leave here without a little preview. I continue inching toward her until my mouth grazes her lips, and I kiss her.

Chapter Thirteen-and-a-half

Les,

Sky, Sky, Sky, Sky, Sky, Sky, Sky, Sky, Sky.

There. Get used to it, because I have a feeling she's all I'm going to be talking about for a while. Oh, my God, Les. I can't even explain to you how perfect this girl is. And when I say perfect, I mean imperfect, because there's just so much wrong with her. But everything wrong with her is everything that draws me in and makes her perfect.

She's flat-out rude to me and I love it. She's stubborn and I love it. She's a smartass and she's sarcastic and every witty thing that comes out of her mouth is like music to my ears because that's exactly what I want. She's what I need and I don't want her to change at all. There's not a single thing about her I would change.

There is one thing about her that worries me, though, and that's the fact that she seems to be a little emotionally detached. And as noticeable as it was when I saw her with Grayson, I don't see that at all when she's with me. I'm almost convinced she feels different about me, but I would be lying if I said I wasn't worried that she wouldn't feel anything if I kissed her. Because dammit, Les, I want to kiss her so fucking bad but I'm too scared. I'm scared if I kiss her too soon, it'll feel like every other kiss she's ever received. She'll feel nothing.

I don't want her to feel nothing when I kiss her. I want her to feel everything.

H

Chapter Fourteen

What you want to do tonight?

I read Daniel's text and respond.

Sorry. Plans.

WTF, puss flap!? No! Me. You. Plans.

Can't. Pretty sure I have a date.

Sky?

Yep.

Can I come?

Nope.

Can I be your date next Saturday, then?

Sure, babe.

Can't wait, sugar.

I laugh at Daniel's text, then clear the screen and find Sky's number.

I haven't heard from her since she fell asleep on me last night, so I'm not even sure if she wants me at her house tonight.

What time can I come over? Not that I'm looking forward to it or anything. You're really, really boring.

After I hit send, I get another incoming text from a number I don't recognize.

If you're dating my girl, get your own prepaid minutes and quit wasting mine, Jackass.

The only person I know with prepaid minutes is Sky. And she said her best friend bought her the phone, so I'm seriously hoping this text is from her friend and not someone else. I immediately text back, hoping to find out more.

How do I get more minutes?

As soon as I hit send on that text, Sky's response comes through.

Be here at seven. And bring me something to eat. I'm not cooking for you.

Rude.

I love it.

She texted me again while I was at the grocery store, asking me to hurry. I really, seriously like that she wanted me here sooner. I like it a lot. I like *her* a lot. I like this whole *weekend* a lot.

Her front door swings open just moments after I ring the doorbell. She's smiling as soon as she sees me and I curse under my breath because that's just one more thing about her that I just fell in love with. She looks down at the sacks of groceries in my hands and arches an eyebrow.

I shrug. "One of us has to be the hospitable one." I walk up the steps and ease past her, then make my way into her kitchen. "I hope you like spaghetti and meatballs, because that's what you're getting."

"You're cooking dinner for me?" she asks skeptically from behind me.

"Actually, I'm cooking for *me*, but you're welcome to eat some if you want." I glance back at her and smile so she'll know I'm teasing.

"Are you always so sarcastic?"

I shrug. "Are *you*?"

"Do you always answer questions with questions?"

"Do *you*?"

She grabs a towel off the bar and throws it at me but I dodge it. "You want something to drink?" I ask her.

"You're offering to make me something to drink in my own house?"

I walk to the refrigerator and scan the shelves, but my options are limited. "Do you want milk that tastes like ass or do you want soda?"

"Do we even have soda?"

I peer around the refrigerator door and grin at her. "Can either of us say anything that isn't a question?"

"I don't know, can we?"

"How long do you think we can keep this up?" I ask, taking the last soda from the fridge. "You want ice?"

"Are *you* having ice?"

Dammit, she's cute. "Do you think I should have ice?"

"Do you *like* ice?"

She's quick. I'm impressed. "Is your ice any good?"

"Well, do you prefer crushed ice or cubed ice?"

I almost answer by saying cubed, but realize that wouldn't be a question. I narrow my eyes and glare at her. "No ice for you."

"Ha! I win," she gloats.

"I let you win because I feel sorry for you," I say, making my way back to the stove. "Anyone that snores as bad as you do deserves a break every now and then."

"You know, the insults are really only funny when they're in text form," she says.

She stands up and walks to the freezer at the same time I turn around to walk to the refrigerator for the minced garlic. Her back is to me and she's filling her cup with ice. She turns around when I reach the refrigerator. She looks up at me with those big brown eyes and those pouty lips and I take a step closer to her, hoping I make her flustered again. I love making her flustered.

I lift my arm and press my palm flat against the refrigerator and look her in the eyes. "You know I'm kidding, right?"

She immediately sucks in a rush of air and nods. I grin and move in even closer. "Good. Because you *don't* snore. In fact, you're pretty damn adorable when you sleep." I don't know why I told her she didn't snore. Maybe I don't want her to know just how long I actually stayed in her bed watching her after she fell asleep last night.

She tugs on her bottom lip, looking up at me hopefully. Her chest is heaving and her arms are dusted in chills and I wish more than anything I could just grab her face and kiss her. I want to kiss her more than I want air.

But I already told myself I wouldn't, so I'm not.

That doesn't mean I can't have a little fun with her, though. I move my lips until they're almost touching her ear. "Sky. I *need* you . . ." I pause for a second and wait for her to catch her breath. ". . . to move. I need in the fridge." I pull back and watch for her reaction. Her palms are flat against the refrigerator behind her like she's struggling to hold herself upright.

Seeing her physical reaction to my proximity makes me smile. When I smile and she sees I was purposely teasing her, she narrows her eyes and I laugh.

She pushes against my chest and shoves me back. "You're such an ass!" she says, walking to the bar.

"I'm sorry, but damn. You're so blatantly attracted to me, it's hard not to tease you." I'm still laughing when I walk back to the stove with the garlic. I pour some into the pan and glance at her. She's covering her face with her hands from embarrassment and I immediately feel guilty. I don't want her thinking I'm not into her, because I'm positive I'm into her way more than she's into me. I guess I haven't made that very clear to her, though, which is a little unfair.

"Want to know something?" I ask.

She looks up at me and shakes her head. "Probably not."

"It might make you feel better," I say.

"I doubt it."

I look at her and she's not smiling and I hate it. I meant for this to be lighthearted; I didn't mean to hurt her feelings. "I might be a little bit attracted to you, too," I admit, hoping it'll help her realize that I didn't mean to embarrass her.

"Just a little bit?" she asks, teasingly.

No. Not just a little bit. A whole helluva lot.

I continue to prepare the food and I'm doing everything I can to get it all started so I can sit and talk with her while it cooks. She just sits silently at the bar, watching me work my way around her kitchen. I love that she's not modest when it comes to the way she watches me. She stares at me like she doesn't want to look at anything else and I like it.

"What does *lol* mean?"

"Seriously?"

"Yes, seriously. You typed it in your text earlier."

"It means laugh out loud. You use it when you think something is funny."

"Huh," she says. "That's dumb."

"Yeah, it is pretty dumb. It's just habit, though, and the abbreviated texts make it a lot faster to type once you get the hang of it. Sort of like OMG and WTF and IDK and . . ."

"Oh, God, stop," she says quickly. "You speaking in abbreviated text form is really unattractive."

I wink at her. "I'll never do it again, then." I walk to the counter and pull the vegetables out of the sack. I run them under the water and move the cutting board to the bar in front of her. "Do you like chunky or smooth spaghetti sauce," I ask, placing the tomato in front of me. She's looking past me, lost in thought. I wait to see if she'll answer me when she catches back up, but she just keeps staring off into space.

"You okay?" I ask her, waving my hand once in front of her eyes. She finally snaps out of it and looks up at me. "Where'd you go? You checked out for a while there."

She shakes it off. "I'm fine."

I don't like her tone of voice. She doesn't seem fine.

"Where'd you go, Sky?" I ask her again. I want to know what she was thinking. Or maybe I don't want to know, because if she was thinking about how she wants me to leave then I hope she continues to pretend she's fine.

"Promise you won't laugh?" she asks.

Relief rushes through me because I don't think she'd ask me that if she was hoping I would leave. But I'm not about to promise her I won't laugh, so I shake my head in disagreement. "I told you that I'll only ever be honest with you, so no. I can't promise I won't laugh because you're kind of funny and that's only setting myself up for failure."

"Are you always so difficult?"

I grin, but don't respond. I love it when she gets irritated with me, so I don't give her a response on purpose.

She straightens up in her chair and says, "Okay, fine." She inhales a deep breath like she's preparing for a long speech.

I'm nervous.

"I'm really not any good at this whole dating thing, and I don't even know if this *is* a date, but I know that whatever it is, it's a little more than just two friends hanging out, and knowing that makes me think about later tonight when it's time for you to leave and whether or not you plan to kiss me and I'm the type of person who hates surprises so I can't stop feeling awkward about it because I *do* want you to kiss me and this may be presumptuous of me, but I sort of think you want to kiss me, too, and so I was thinking how much easier it would be if we just went ahead and kissed already so you can go back to cooking dinner and I can stop trying to mentally map out how our night's about to play out."

I'm pretty sure it's too soon to love her, but *shit*. She's got to stop doing and saying these unexpected things that make me want to fast-forward whatever's going on between us. Because I want to kiss her and make love to her and marry her and make her have my babies and I want it all to happen *tonight*.

But then we'll be out of firsts, and the firsts are the best part. Good thing I'm patient.

I set the knife down on the cutting board and look her in the eyes. "That," I say, "was the longest run-on sentence I've ever heard."

She doesn't like my comment. She huffs and falls back against her seat in a pout.

"Relax." I laugh. I take a second to finish the sauce and start the pasta and do everything I need to do to get to a point where I can actually talk to her while I'm not trying to cook at the same time. When I finally get the pasta going, I wipe my hands on the dishtowel and place it on the counter. I walk around the bar to where she's seated.

"Stand up," I tell her.

She slowly stands up and I place my hands on her shoulders, then look around the room for a good spot to break the news to her that I'm not going to kiss her tonight. As much as I want to and as much as I now know she wants me to, I still want to wait.

And I know I told her I'm not mean, but I never said I wasn't cruel. And I'm just having too much fun watching her when she's flustered and I really want to make her flustered again. "Hmm," I say, still pretending I'm looking for the perfect spot to kiss her. I glance into the kitchen, then take her by the wrists and pull her with me. "I sort of liked the fridge backdrop." I push her against the fridge and she lets me. She hasn't stopped watching me intently the whole time and I love it. I lift my arms to the sides of her head and begin to lean in toward her. She closes her eyes.

I keep mine open.

I look at her lips for a moment. Thanks to the peck I stole while she was sleeping last night, I kind of have an idea what they feel like. But now I can't help but wonder what they taste like. I'm so tempted to lean in a few more inches and see for myself, but I don't.

I've got this.

They're just lips.

I watch her for a few more seconds until her eyes flick open when I fail to kiss her. Her whole body jumps when she sees how close I am and it makes me laugh.

Why do I enjoy teasing her so much?

"Sky?" I say, looking down at her. "I'm not trying to torture you or anything, but I already made up my mind before I came over here. I'm not kissing you tonight."

The hope in her expression dwindles almost immediately.

"Why not?" she says. Her eyes are full of rejection and I absolutely hate it, but I'm still not kissing her. But I do want her to know how much I *want* to kiss her.

I bring my hand up to her face and trace a line down her cheek. The feel of her skin beneath my fingertips is like silk. I keep trailing down her jaw, then her neck. My whole body is tense because I'm not sure if she feels all of this the way I do. I can't imagine someone like Grayson could be lucky enough to touch her face or taste her mouth and that he wouldn't care if she was even enjoying it or not.

When my hand reaches her shoulder, I stop and look her in the eyes. "I want to kiss you," I say. "Believe me, I do."

So, so bad.

I remove my hand from her shoulder and bring it up to her cheek. She leans into my hand and looks up at me, her eyes full of disappointment. "But if you really want to, then why don't you?"

Ugh. I hate that look. If she keeps looking at me like that I'll lose every shred of willpower I have left. Which isn't much.

I tilt her face up to mine. "Because," I whisper. "I'm afraid you won't feel it."

The look on her face when I say it is a mixture of realization and regret. She knows I'm referring to her lack of response to other guys and I'm not sure she knows how to respond. She's silent, but I just want her to argue with me. I want her to tell me how wrong I am. I want her to tell me she already feels like I do, but instead she just nods and covers my hand with hers.

I close my eyes, wishing she had responded any other way. But the fact that she didn't just proves that not kissing her tonight is exactly what needs to happen. I don't understand why she's so closed off, but I'll wait however long I have to. There's no way I could walk away from this girl now.

I pull her away from the refrigerator and wrap my arms around her. She slowly returns the embrace by clasping her arms around my waist and conforming to my chest. She willingly leans into me and just feeling her want me to hold her is better than anything I've felt this entire year. All she did was hug me back, but little does she know she just knocked a whole lot of life back into me. I press my lips into her hair and inhale. I could stay like this all night.

But the damn oven timer dings, reminding me that I'm cooking her dinner. If it means having to let her go, I'd rather starve. But I promised to cook for her, so I release my hold from around her and take a step back.

The embarrassed and almost heartbroken look on her face is the last thing I expect to see. She drops her gaze down at the floor and I realize that I just disappointed her. A lot. All I'm trying to do is go at a pace that's best for her. I can't have her thinking that I'm going slow because it's my choice. Because if she didn't have whatever issue it is she has with guys, we wouldn't be standing in this kitchen right now. We'd be back on her bed just like we were last night, only this time she wouldn't be reading to me.

I grab both of her hands and interlock our fingers. "Look at me." She hesitantly lifts her face and looks at me. "Sky, I'm not kissing you tonight but believe me when I tell you, I've never wanted to kiss a girl more. So stop thinking I'm not attracted to you because you have no idea just how much I am. You can hold my hand, you can run your fingers through my hair, you can straddle me while I feed you spaghetti, but you are not getting kissed tonight. And probably not tomorrow, either. I need this. I need to know for sure that you're feeling every single thing that I'm feeling the moment my lips touch yours. Because I want your first kiss to be the best first kiss in the history of first kisses."

The sadness is gone from her eyes now and she's actually smiling at me. I lift her hand and kiss it. "Now stop sulking and help me finish the meatballs. Okay?" I ask, wanting reassurance from her that she believes me. "Is that enough to get you through a couple more dates?"

She nods, still smiling. "Yep. But you're wrong about one thing."

"What's that?"

"You said you want my first kiss to be the best first kiss, but this won't be my first kiss. You know that."

I don't know how to break it to her, but she hasn't been kissed before. Not like she deserves, anyway. I hate that she doesn't realize this, so I take it upon myself to show her exactly what a real kiss feels like.

I let go of her hands and cup her face, walking her back against the refrigerator. I lean in until I can feel her breath on my lips and she gasps. I love the helpless, hungry look in her eyes right now, but it doesn't compare to what it does to me when she bites her lip.

"Let me inform you of something," I say, lowering my voice. "The moment my lips touch yours, it *will* be your first kiss. Because if you've never felt anything when someone's kissed you, then no one's ever really kissed you. Not the way *I* plan on kissing you."

She exhales a pent-up breath and her arms are covered in chills again.

She felt *that*.

I grin victoriously and back away from her, then turn my attention to the stove. I can hear her sliding down the refrigerator. I turn around and she's sitting on the floor, looking up at me in shock. I laugh.

"You okay?" I say with a wink.

She smiles up at me from the floor and pulls her legs up to her chest with a shrug. "My legs stopped working." She laughs. "Must be because I'm *so* attracted to you," she says sarcastically.

I look around the kitchen. "You think your mother has a tincture for people who are too attracted to me?"

"My mother has a tincture for everything," she says.

I walk over and take her hand, then pull her up. I press my hand against the small of her back and pull her against me. She looks up at me with hooded eyes and a small gasp parts her lips. I lower my mouth to her ear and whisper, "Well, whatever you do . . . make sure you never take that tincture."

Her chest rises against mine and she's looking into my eyes like everything I've said tonight meant nothing. She wants me to kiss her and she doesn't care that I'm doing everything in my power *not* to.

I slide my hand down her back and slap her on the ass. "Focus, girl. We have food to cook."

"Okay, I have one," she says, placing her cup down on the table.

We're playing a game she suggested called Dinner Quest, where no question is off limits and eating and drinking isn't allowed until the question has been answered. I've never heard of it, but I like the thought of being able to ask her anything I want to ask her.

"Why did you follow me to my car at the grocery store?" she asks.

I shrug. "Like I said, I thought you were someone else."

"I know," she says. "But who?"

Maybe I don't want to play this game. I'm not ready to tell her about Hope. I'm definitely not ready to tell her about Les, but there's no way around it because my answer just dug me into a hole. I shift in my seat and reach for my drink, but she snatches it out of my hands.

"No drinks. Answer the question first." She sets my drink back down on the table and waits for my explanation. I really don't want to go into my screwed up past, so I try to keep my answer simple.

"I wasn't sure who you reminded me of," I lie. "You just reminded me of someone. I didn't realize until later that you reminded me of my sister."

She makes a face and says, "I remind you of your sister? That's kind of gross, Holder."

Oh, *shit*. That's not at *all* what I meant. "No, not like that. Not like that at all, you don't even look anything like she did. There was just something about seeing you that made me think of her. And I don't even know why I followed you. It was all so surreal. The whole situation was a little bizarre, and then running into you in front of my house later . . ."

Should I really tell her how that made me feel? How I thought for sure Les had something to do with it or that it was divine intervention or a freaking miracle? Because I honestly feel like it was too perfect to be chalked up to coincidence.

"It was like it was meant to happen," I finally say.

She inhales a deep breath and I look up at her, afraid of how forward that might have been. She smiles at me and points to my drink. "You can drink now," she says. "Your turn to ask me a question."

"Oh, this one's easy. I want to know whose toes I'm stepping on. I received a mysterious inbox message from someone today. All it said was, 'If you're dating my girl, get your own prepaid minutes and quit wasting mine, jackass.'"

"That would be Six," she says, smiling. "The bearer of my daily doses of positive affirmation."

Thank God.

"I was hoping you'd say that. Because I'm pretty competitive, and if it came from a guy, my response would not have been as nice."

"You responded? What'd you say?"

"Is that your question? Because if it isn't, I'm taking another bite."

"Hold your horses and answer the question," she says.

"Yes, I responded to her text. I said, 'How do I buy more minutes?'"

Her cheeks redden and she grins. "I was only joking, that wasn't my question. It's still my turn."

I drop my fork onto my plate and sigh at her stubbornness. "My food's getting cold."

She ignores my feigned irritation and she leans forward, looking me directly in the eyes. "I want to know about your sister. And why you referred to her in the past tense."

Ah, shit. Did I refer to her in the past tense? I look up at the ceiling and sigh. "Ugh. You really ask the deep questions, huh?"

"That's how the game is played. I didn't make up the rules."

I guess there's no getting out of this explanation. But honestly, I don't mind telling her. There are certain things about my past I'd rather not discuss, but Les doesn't really feel like my past. She still feels very much a part of my present.

"Remember when I told you my family had a pretty fucked-up year last year?"

She nods, and I hate that I'm about to put a damper on our conversation. But she doesn't like vague, so . . . "She died thirteen months ago. She killed herself, even though my mother would rather we use the term 'purposely overdosed.'"

I keep my eyes locked on hers, waiting for the "I'm so sorry," or the "It was meant to happen," to come out of her mouth like it comes out of everyone else's mouth.

"What was her name?" she asks. The fact that she even asks like she's genuinely interested is unexpected.

"Lesslie. I called her Les."

"Was she older than you?"

Only by three minutes. "We were twins," I say, right before I take a bite.

Her eyes widen slightly and she reaches for her drink. I intercept her this time.

"My turn," I say. Now that I know nothing is off limits, I ask her about the one thing she didn't really want to talk about yesterday. "I want to know the story about your dad."

She groans, but plays along. She knows she can't refuse to answer that question, because I just completely opened up to her about Les.

"Like I said, I haven't seen him since I was three. I don't have any memories of him. At least, I don't think I do. I don't even know what he looks like."

"Your mom doesn't have any pictures of him?"

She cocks her head slightly, then leans back in her seat. "You remember when you said my mom looked really young? Well, it's because she is. She adopted me."

I drop my fork.

Adopted.

The genuine possibility that she could be Hope bombards my thoughts. It wouldn't make sense that she was three when she was adopted, though, because Hope was five when she was taken. Unless she's been lied to.

But what are the chances? And what are the chances that someone like Karen would be capable of stealing a child?

"*What?*" she asks. "You've never met anyone who was adopted?"

I realize the shock I'm feeling in my head and my heart is also registering in my expression. I clear my throat and try to regroup, but a million more questions are forming in my mind. "You were adopted when you were three? By Karen?"

She shakes her head. "I was put into foster care when I was three, after my biological mother died. My dad couldn't raise me on his own. Or he didn't *want* to raise me on his own. Either way, I'm fine with it. I lucked out with Karen and I have no urge whatsoever to go figure it all out. If he wanted to know where I was, he'd come find me."

Her mother is dead? Hope's mother is dead.

But Hope was never put into foster care and Hope's dad didn't put her up for adoption. It all makes absolutely no sense, but at the same time I can't rule out the possibility. She's either been fed complete lies about her past, or I'm going insane.

The latter is more likely.

"What does your tattoo mean?" she asks, pointing at it with her fork.

I look down at my arm and touch the letters that make up Hope's name.

If she was Hope, she would remember the name. That's the only thing that stops me from believing in the possibility that she could be Hope.

Hope would remember.

"It's a reminder," I say. "I got it after Les died."

"A reminder for what?"

And this is the only answer she'll get that's vague, because I'm definitely not about to explain. "It's a reminder of the people I've let down in my life."

Her expression grows sympathetic. "This game's not very fun, is it?"

"It's really not." I laugh. "It sort of sucks ass. But we need to keep going because I still have questions. Do you remember anything from before you were adopted?"

"Not really. Bits and pieces, but it comes to a point that, when you don't have anyone to validate your memories, you just lose them all. The only thing I have from before Karen adopted me is some jewelry, and I have no idea who it came from. I can't distinguish now between what was reality, dreams, or what I saw on TV."

"Do you remember your mother?"

She pauses for a moment. "Karen is my mother," she says flatly. I can tell she doesn't want to talk about it and I don't want to push her. "My turn. Last question, then we eat dessert."

"Do you think we even have enough dessert?" I say, trying to lighten the mood.

"Why did you beat him up?" she says, darkening the mood completely.

I don't want to get into that one. I push my bowl away. I'll just let her win this round. "You don't want to know the answer to that, Sky. I'll take the punishment."

"But I do want to know."

Just thinking about that day already has me worked up again. I pop my jaw to ease the tension. "Like I told you before, I beat him up because he was an asshole."

"That's vague," she says, narrowing her eyes. "You don't do vague."

I know that I like her stubbornness, but I only like it when she's not pushing me to bring up the past. But I also have no clue what she's been told about the whole situation. I've made it a point to get her to open up to me and ask me questions so she can hear the truth from me. If I refuse to answer her, then she'll stop opening up.

"It was my first week back at school since Les died," I say. "She went to school there, too, so everyone knew what happened. I overheard the guy saying something about Les when I was passing him in the hallway. I disagreed with it, and I let him know. I took it too far and it came to a point when I was on top of him that I just didn't care.

I was hitting him, over and over, and I didn't even care. The really fucked-up part is that the kid will more than likely be deaf out of his left ear for the rest of his life, and I *still* don't care."

My fist is clenched on the table. Just thinking about the way everyone acted after she died has me pissed off all over again.

"What did he say about her?"

I lean back in my chair and my eyes drop to the table between us. I don't really feel like looking her in the eyes when I'm only thinking about stuff that infuriates me. "I heard him laughing, telling his friend that Les took the selfish, easy way out. He said if she wasn't such a coward, she would have toughed it out."

"Toughed what out?"

"Life."

"You don't think she took the easy way out." She doesn't say it like it's a question. She says it like she's truly trying to understand me. That's all I've wanted from her all week. I just want her to understand me. To believe *me* and not everyone else.

And no. I *don't* think she took the easy way out. I don't think that at all.

I reach across the table and pull her hand between both of mine. "Les was the bravest fucking person I've ever known," I say. "It takes a lot of guts to do what she did. To just end it, not knowing what's next? Not knowing if there's *anything* next? It's easier to go on living a life without any life left in it than it is to just say 'fuck it' and leave. She was one of the few that just said, 'fuck it.' And I'll commend her every day I'm still alive, too scared to do the same thing."

I look at her after I'm finished speaking and her eyes are wide. Her hand is shaking, so I clasp my hands around hers. We look at each other for several seconds and I can tell she has no idea what to say to me. I attempt to lighten the mood and change the subject. She said that was the last question, then we get dessert.

I lean forward and kiss the top of her head, then walk into the kitchen. "You want brownies or cookies?" I watch her from the kitchen as I grab the desserts and she's staring at me, wide-eyed.

I freaked her out.

I just completely freaked her out.

I walk back to where she's seated and I kneel down in front of her. "Hey. I didn't mean to scare you," I tell her, taking her face in my hands. "I'm not suicidal if that's what's freaking you out. I'm not fucked up in the head. I'm not deranged. I'm not suffering from post-traumatic stress disorder. I'm just a brother who loved his sister more than life itself, so I get a little intense when I think about her. And if I cope better by telling myself that what she did was noble, even though it wasn't, then that's all I'm doing. I'm just coping." I allow her time to let my words sink in, then finish my explanation. "I fucking loved that girl, Sky. I need to believe that what she did was the only answer she had left, because if I don't, then I'll never forgive myself for not helping her find a different one." I press my forehead to hers, looking her firmly in the eyes. "Okay?"

I need her to understand that I'm trying. I might not have it together and I might not know how to move past Les's death, but I'm trying.

She presses her lips together and nods, then pulls my hands away. "I need to use the bathroom," she says, quickly slipping around me. She rushes to the bathroom and shuts the door behind her.

Jesus Christ, why did I even go there? I walk to the hallway, prepared to knock on the door and apologize, but decide to give her a few minutes first. I know that was really heavy. Maybe she just needs a minute.

I wait across the hallway until the bathroom door opens up again. It doesn't look like she's been crying.

"We good?" I ask her, taking a step closer to her.

She smiles up at me and exhales a shaky breath. "I told you I think you're intense. This just proves my point."

She's already herself again. I love that about her.

I smile and wrap my arms around her, then rest my chin on top of her head while we make our way to her bedroom. "Are you allowed to get pregnant yet?"

She laughs. "Nope. Not this weekend. Besides, you have to kiss a girl before you can knock her up."

"Did someone not have sex education when she was home-schooled? Because I could totally knock you up without ever kissing you. Want me to show you?"

She falls onto the bed and picks up the book that she read to me last night. "I'll take your word for it," she says. "Besides, I'm hoping we're about to get a hefty dose of sex education before we make it to the last page."

I lie down beside her and pull her to me. She rests her head on my chest and begins reading to me.

I ball my hand up into a tight fist and keep it at my side, doing everything in my power not to touch her mouth. I've just never seen anything so perfect before.

She's been reading for well over half an hour now and I haven't heard a damn word she's said. Last night it was so much easier to pay attention to the actual story because I wasn't looking directly at her. Tonight it's taking every ounce of willpower I have not to claim her mouth with mine. She's propped against me with her head on my chest, using me as her pillow. I'm hoping she can't feel my heart pounding right now because every time she glances up at me when she flips a page, I squeeze my fists even tighter and try to keep my hands to myself but my resistance resonates in my pulse. And it's not that I don't *want* to touch her. I want to touch her and kiss her so bad it physically hurts.

I just don't want it to be insignificant to her. When I touch her . . . I want her to feel it. I want every single thing I say to her and every single thing I do to her to have significance.

Last night when she told me she's never felt anything when she was kissed, my heart did this crazy thing where it felt bound, like it was being constricted, just like the lungs in my chest. I've dated a lot of girls, even though I might have downplayed that to her. With every single girl I've been with, my heart has never reacted like it reacts to her. And I'm not referring to my heart's *feelings* for her, because let's be honest, I barely know her. I'm referring to my heart's literal, *physical* reaction to her. Every time she speaks or smiles or, God forbid, *laughs* . . . my heart reacts like it's been sucker-punched. I hate it and like it and somehow have become addicted to it. Every time she speaks, the sucker-punch in my chest reminds me that there's still something there.

A huge internal part of me was lost when I lost Hope, and I was convinced Les took the very last contents of my chest with her when she died last year. After being with Sky these last two days, I'm not so sure about that, anymore. I don't think my chest has been empty this whole time like I thought. Whatever is left inside me has just been asleep, and she's somehow slowly waking it up.

With every word she speaks and every glance she sends my way, she's unknowingly pulling me out of this thirteen-year-long nightmare I've been trapped in, and I want to continue to allow her to pull me.

Fuck it.

I unclench my fist and bring it up to her hair that's spilled across my chest. I pick up a loose strand and curl it around my finger, keeping my eyes trained on her mouth while she reads to me. I find myself still comparing her to Hope every now and then, despite my efforts not to. I'm trying to recall exactly what Hope's eyes looked like or if she had the same four freckles across the bridge of her nose that Sky has. Every time I start to compare them, I force myself to stop. It doesn't matter anymore and I need to let it go. Sky has proved that she can't be Hope and I have to accept it. The odds of the girl I lost being right here, pressed against my chest, her strand of hair between my fingertips . . . it's impossible. I need to separate the two of them in my head before I screw up and do something stupid, like refer to Sky by the wrong name.

That would suck.

I notice her lips are pressed into a tight, thin line and she isn't speaking anymore. It's a damn shame because her mouth is fucking hypnotizing.

"Why'd you stop talking?" I ask her, without looking at her eyes. I keep my gaze trained on her lips, hoping they start moving again.

"Talking?" she says, her top lip curling up in a grin. "Holder, I'm *reading*. There's a difference. And from the looks of it, you haven't been paying a lick of attention."

The feistiness in her reply makes me smile. "Oh, I've been paying attention," I say, lifting up onto my elbows. "To your mouth. Maybe not to the words coming out of it, but definitely to your mouth." I slide out from under her until she's on her back, then I scoot down until I'm beside her. I pull her against me and take her hair between my fingertips again. The fact that she doesn't resist in the slightest only means I'll be at war with myself the rest of the damn night. She's already made it clear she wants me to kiss her, and I'll be damned if backing away from having her pressed up against the refrigerator wasn't the hardest thing I've ever had to do.

Shit. Just thinking about it is almost as intense as when it was actually happening.

I drop the strand of hair and watch as my fingers fall straight to her lips. I don't know how the last five seconds just occurred, but I'm looking down at my hand as it grazes over her mouth like I have no control over my limbs anymore. My hand has a mind of its own but I really don't care . . . nor do I want to stop it.

I feel her breath against my fingertips and I have to bite the inside of my cheek to center my focus on something other than what I want. Because it's not my wants that are important right now—it's hers. And I highly doubt she wants to taste my mouth as much as I need to taste hers right now.

"You have a nice mouth," I say, still slowly tracing it with the tips of my fingers. "I can't stop looking at it."

"You should taste it," she says. "It's quite lovely."

Holy shit.

I squeeze my eyes shut and drop my head to her neck, forcing my focus away from those lips. "Stop it, you evil wench."

She laughs. "No way. This is your stupid rule; why should I be the one to enforce it?"

Oh, Jesus. It's a game to her. This whole *not kissing* thing is a game to her and she's going to tease the hell out of me. I can't do this. If I give in and kiss her before she's ready I know I won't be able to stop. And I don't know what the hell is going on inside my chest right now but I really like the way it feels when I'm around her. If I can drag whatever this is out to make sure she feels the same way, then that's exactly what I'll do. Even if it takes me weeks to ensure she gets to that point, then I guess I'll wait weeks. In the meantime, I'll do whatever I can to make sure her next first is anything but insignificant.

"Because you know I'm right," I say, explaining exactly why she needs to help me enforce this rule. "I can't kiss you tonight because kissing leads to the next thing, which leads to the next thing, and at the rate we're going we'll be all out of firsts by next weekend. Don't you want to drag our firsts out a little longer?" I pull away from her neck and look down at her, very aware that there is less space between our mouths right now than between our bodies.

"Firsts?" she says, looking up at me curiously. "How many firsts are there?"

"There aren't that many, which is why we need to drag them out. We've already passed too many since we met."

She tilts her head and her expression grows attractively serious. "What firsts have we already passed?"

"The easy ones," I say. "First hug, first date, first fight, first time we slept together, although I wasn't the one sleeping. Now we barely have any left. First kiss. First time to sleep together when we're both actually *awake*. First marriage. First kid. We're done after that. Our lives will become mundane and boring and I'll have to divorce you and marry a wife who's twenty years younger than me so I can have a lot more firsts and you'll be stuck raising the kids." I bring my hand to her cheek and smile at her. "So you see, babe? I'm only doing this for your benefit. The longer I wait to kiss you, the longer it'll be before I'm forced to leave you high and dry."

She laughs and the sound is so toxic I'm forced to swallow the huge lump in my throat so I can make room to breathe again.

"Your logic terrifies me," she says. "I sort of don't find you attractive anymore."

Challenge accepted.

I slowly slide on top of her, careful to hold my weight up with my hands. If my body were to touch any part of hers right now, we'd already be moving on to seconds and thirds. "You *sort of* don't find me attractive?" I say, staring straight down into her eyes. "That can also mean you sort of *do* find me attractive."

Her eyes grow dark and she shakes her head. I can see the dip in the base of her throat barely move as she gulps before speaking. "I don't find you attractive at all. You repulse me. In fact, you better not kiss me because I'm pretty sure I just threw up in my mouth."

I laugh, then drop onto my elbow so I can move closer to her ear, still careful not to touch any other part of her.

"You're a liar," I whisper. "You're a whole *lot* attracted to me and I'm about to prove it."

I had every intention of pulling away, but as soon as the scent of her hits me, I can't pull back. My lips are pressed against her neck before I even have a chance to weigh the decision. But right now it feels a hell of a lot more like a *necessity* to taste her rather than just a *decision*. She gasps when I pull back and I can't help but hope that her gasp was genuine. The thought of her actually feeling what I felt when my lips touched her neck makes me feel ridiculously victorious. It's too bad I like a challenge, because that gasp just made me want to up my game. I drop my mouth back to her ear and whisper, "Did you feel that?"

Her eyes are closed and she's shaking her head no, breathing heavily. I look down at her chest, heaving dangerously close to mine.

"You want me to do it again?" I whisper.

I want her to *beg* me to do it again, but she shakes her head no. She's breathing twice as fast as she was sixty seconds ago, so I know I'm getting to her. I laugh that she's so adamantly shaking her head no, while at the same time clenching the sheet next to her with her fist. I move closer to her mouth because I suddenly have an overwhelming need to take in some of the breaths she's wasting. It feels like I need them more than she does right now, so I inhale at the same time my lips meet her cheek. I don't stop there, though. I *can't* stop there. I continue to trail kisses from her cheek, down to her ear. I pause and catch my breath enough to speak in a steady voice. "How about that?"

Again, she stubbornly shakes her head, but tilts it back and slightly to the left, allowing me better access. I lift my hand from the bed and bring it to her waist, keeping my eyes trained on her as I slip my hand under her shirt, just far enough to graze her stomach with my thumb. I watch for any kind of reaction from her, but she's got a stern, tight-lipped expression on her face now, like she's trying to hold her breath. I don't want her to hold her breath. I need to hear her breathe.

When I drop my mouth and nose to her jawline, she releases her pent-up breaths just like I was hoping she would. I trail my nose across her jaw, inhaling the scent of her, then move down, listening intently to every single gasp that escapes her lips as if they're the last sounds I'll ever hear. When I reach her ear, four of my senses are in overdrive and one is seriously lacking—*taste*. I know I can't taste her mouth tonight, but I have got to taste at least one part of her. I press my lips to her ear and she immediately brings her hand up to my neck, pulling me in deeper. Feeling her need my mouth against her skin rips my chest wide open and I completely give in, wanting to feel that need from her even more. I immediately part my lips and glide my tongue across her skin, taking in the sweetness of her and locking it in my memory. I've never tasted anything that rivaled perfection like she does.

Then she moans and *holy hell*. Everything I thought I previously knew about my desires or wants or needs becomes lost in that sound. From this point forward, my new and only goal in life is to find a way to get her to make that exact same sound again.

I bring my hand to the side of her head and completely let loose, kissing and teasing every inch of her neck, trying to find that exact spot that got to her a few seconds ago. She drops her head against her pillow and I take the opportunity to explore more of her neck. As soon as my lips begin to trail toward the rise in her chest, I force myself north again, not wanting to push it to the point that she asks me to stop. Because I absolutely don't want to stop whatever this is we're doing.

Her eyes are still closed and I drop my mouth to her lips, kissing her softly near the corner of her mouth.

And there it is. The softest, most delicate sound escapes her throat again. I can't ignore the fact that another part of me wakes up with that sound. I continue kissing a full circle around the edges of her lips, impressed that I'm somehow able to find strength to pull back.

I have to stop for a moment because if I don't, I'll for sure break my one and only rule tonight—which is absolutely no mouth contact. I know if I kiss her right now it'll be great. But I don't want her to have great. I want her to have incredible. Looking at her lips right now, I know for a fact it'll be incredible for me.

"They're so perfect," I say. "Like hearts. I could literally stare at your lips for days and never get bored."

She opens her eyes and smiles. "No. Don't do that. If all you do is stare, then *I'll* be the bored one."

Damn that smile. It's painful having to watch that mouth smile and frown and pout and laugh and speak when all I want to watch it do is kiss me.

But then she licks her lips and everything I thought I just knew about pain actually starts to feel good compared to the way my heart is gouged out of my chest with that small tease. *Jesus Christ*, this girl.

I groan and press my forehead to hers. Having her mouth this close to mine sucks the self-control right out of me. I drop myself on top of her and it's as if a rush of warm air swarms the room and encircles us. We both feel everything simultaneously and we moan together, move together, and breathe together.

Then we completely give in together. All four of our hands are frantically pulling off my shirt as if two hands can't do it fast enough. As soon as it's off, her legs lock around my waist and she pulls me tightly against her. I drop my forehead back to hers and move against her, finding a new way to force those tiny sounds from her mouth that have quickly become my new favorite song. We continue to move together and the more she gasps and quietly moans, the closer my lips move to hers, wanting to experience those sounds first-hand. I just need a tiny sample of what her kiss will feel like. A little preview, that's all. I allow my lips to brush against hers and we both suck in a breath.

She feels it. She actually fucking feels this right now and I think I'm drowning in satisfaction. I don't want to speed things up and I definitely don't want to slow things down. I just want to keep things exactly as they are right now because it's perfect.

I bring my hand to the side of her head and keep my forehead pressed against hers, my lips resting against hers. I love the feel of our mouths sliding together, so I pull back and lick my lips to create smoother traction. I straighten my legs out, taking some of my weight off my knees, not expecting the small shift to do what it does to her. She arches her back and whispers, "*Oh, God.*"

I feel like I should answer her, because it sure as hell seems like she's referring to me right now with the way she throws her arms around my neck and tucks her head against me. Her arms are trembling and her legs are clenching my waist and I realize that not only is she *feeling* this right now, she's doing everything in her power to fight it.

"Holder," she whispers, clenching my back. I'm not sure if she's wanting me to answer her or not, but I forgot how to speak so it doesn't matter. I can barely even remember how to breathe right now.

"Holder."

She says my name with more urgency this time so I kiss the side of her head and slow my movements against her. She hasn't asked me to stop or slow down yet, but I'm pretty sure that's what she's about to do. I do whatever I can to intercept her plea because she feels incredible and I absolutely don't want to stop.

"Sky, if you're asking me to stop, I will. But I'm hoping you're not, because I really don't want to stop, so please." I lift up and look down at her, still barely moving against her. She still hasn't asked me to stop yet and honestly, I'm afraid to. I'm afraid if I stop, then whatever she's feeling right now will disappear. That scares me because I know that with me, I'll be feeling her for days after this. I love knowing that what I'm doing to her right now is having enough of an effect that she feels she needs me to stop before she passes an unexpected first tonight.

I reach to her cheek and stroke it with the back of my hand, wanting . . . no, *needing* for her to pass this first tonight. "We won't go any further than this, I promise," I say to her. "But please don't ask me to stop where we already are. I need to watch you and I need to hear you because the fact that I know you're actually feeling this right now is so fucking amazing. You feel incredible and this feels incredible and *please*. Just . . . *please*."

I drop my mouth to hers and kiss her softly, immediately pulling back before that amazing connection turns into more than just a peck. Her lips feel so inconceivably perfect; I have to lift off her completely in order to regain my bearings. Otherwise, I won't be able to hold myself at bay for another second. I look down at her and she's looking back up at me, searching my eyes for an answer to a question she can only answer for herself. I wait patiently for her to decide where we go from here.

Her head begins to shake back and forth and she places her hands on my chest.

"Don't. Whatever you do, don't stop."

I remain still for a few seconds, repeating what she just said in my head several times until I'm absolutely certain she just told me *not* to stop. I slip my hand behind her neck and pull her forehead to mine. "*Thank* you," I say breathlessly. I ease myself back down on top of her until we recapture our rhythm. She feels so incredible pressed against me, I don't know that I'll ever be the same again. This girl just raised the bar so far above all other girls' heads, no one could ever come close.

I kiss her everywhere my lips have already touched her tonight, picking up pace with the timing of her gasps and moans. When I feel her body tensing around mine I pull away from her neck and look down at her. She digs her nails deeper into my skin, then tilts her head back and closes her eyes. She looks absolutely beautiful like this, but I need her eyes on mine. I need to watch her feel this.

"Open your eyes," I tell her. She winces, but doesn't look up at me. "*Please.*"

Her eyes immediately open beneath me when I say please. Her eyebrows crease together and she loses all rhythm to her breathing pattern. She's fighting to breathe now as her body begins to tremble beneath me, all the while keeping our gaze locked together. All I can do is hold my breath and watch the most incredible thing I've ever seen unfold beneath me. When the loudest of her moans has escaped her lips, she can no longer keep her eyes open. As soon as she closes them, I drop my lips back to hers, needing to feel them against mine again. When she's finally calm, I move my lips down to her neck and kiss it like I wish I could be kissing her mouth right now.

But seeing how much she needs me to kiss her mouth right now is making the wait even more important for me. Considering what just happened between us, it almost seems absurd to keep up the assurance of not kissing her. But I'm stubborn and I like knowing that the next time we're together like this, we'll be able to experience another first that's likely to drive me even more insane than tonight has.

I press my lips to her shoulder and push up on my arm. I trail my fingers down her hairline and wipe away the loose strands from her face. She looks absolutely content and it's the most beautiful, satisfying thing I've ever felt.

"You're incredible," I say, knowing that word is a severe understatement for what she actually is. She smiles at me and inhales a deep breath at the same time I do. I collapse beside her on the bed, needing to get off her immediately. My chest is completely alive right now and the only thing that I know could satisfy me is to be pressed against her again with my mouth on hers. I force the image of it out of my mind and attempt to cool myself off by matching my breathing pattern with hers.

After silently finding a stable enough point to touch her again, I move my hand closer to hers on the bed and wrap my pinky around hers. The sensation of her pinky in mine feels way too familiar. Way too right. Way too long overdue. I squeeze my eyes shut and attempt to deny my conscience the satisfaction of being right.

She's Sky. That's who she is. I only doubt this because of how she feels so familiar. Familiarity is hardly enough to convince me otherwise.

I hope my instincts are wrong, because if I'm right, the truth will destroy her.

Please, just let her be Sky.

My fear of being right keeps pushing through and I sit up on the bed, needing to separate myself from her. I need to clear my head of all this craziness. "I have to go," I say, looking down at her. "I can't be on this bed with you for another second."

I'm being honest. I *can't* be on this bed with her for another second, although I'm sure she thinks it's for other reasons. Not for the reason I really need to separate myself from her—the fact that I'm terrified my intuition is finally right for once.

I stand and pull my shirt over my head and notice that she's looking at me like I'm rejecting her. I know she probably thought I'd end up kissing her tonight, but she's got a lot to learn when it comes to doubting my word.

I lean in close to her and smile reassuringly. "When I said you weren't getting kissed tonight, I meant it. But *dammit*, Sky. I had no idea how fucking difficult you would make it." I slip my hand behind her neck and lean in to kiss her cheek. When she gasps, it takes everything I have to release my hold and climb off the bed. I watch her as I walk toward the window and pull my phone from my pocket. I send her a quick text, then wink at her, right before I climb outside. I pull the window shut and back a few steps away. As soon as the window is shut, she jumps off her bed and runs out of her bedroom, more than likely to go grab her phone and check her text. Normally, her excitement would more than likely make me laugh. Instead I find myself staring blankly through her bedroom window. My heart feels heavy and my mind even heavier as the pieces of the puzzle slowly begin to fit together, right down to her name.

"The sky is always beautiful . . ."

The memory causes me to flinch. I brace my hand against the brick wall and inhale a deep breath. It's almost laughable, really—the fact that I can sit here and entertain the possibility that this could actually happen after thirteen years. If it were true . . . if she really were her . . . it would ruin her. Which is exactly why I refuse to accept it without tangible proof—something I can actually touch that would confirm it. Without tangible proof, she'll remain Sky to me.

I just want her to be Sky.

Chapter Fifteen

Les,

Remember when we were kids and I made everyone stop calling me Dean? I have never told anyone the truth about why I go by Holder, not even you.

We were eight years old and it was the first and only time we ever went to Disneyland. We were waiting in line for one of the roller-coasters and you and Dad were in front of me because you couldn't ride it by yourself. I was a few inches taller than you and it pissed you off that I was able to ride most of the rides alone and you weren't.

When we made it to the front of the line, they put you and Dad on first and I had to wait for the next car to pull in. I was standing there alone, patiently waiting. I turned around to find Mom and she was about a hundred yards away at the exit to the ride, waiting for all of us to finish. I waved at her and she waved back at me. I turned back around when the next car pulled up.

That's when I heard her.

I heard Hope yelling my name. I spun around and stood on my tiptoes, facing the sound of her voice.

"Dean!" she yelled. She sounded really far away, but I knew it was her because she said it with that accent of hers. She always dragged out the middle of my name and made it longer than one syllable. I always liked how she said my name, so hearing her yell it, I knew it was her. She must have spotted me and now she was trying to call for me to come help her.

"Dean," she yelled again, only this time she sounded farther away. I could hear the panic in her voice. I began to panic myself, because I knew I'd get in trouble if I lost my place in line. Mom and Dad spent the entire week before we left reminding us to stay by one of them at all times.

I glanced over at Mom but she wasn't looking at me, she was watching you and Dad on the ride. I didn't know what to do, because she wouldn't know where I was if I left the line. But as soon as Hope screamed my name again I didn't care. I had to find her.

I started running toward the back of the line—toward the sound of her voice. I was yelling her name, hoping she would hear me and walk toward the sound of my voice.

God, Les. I was so excited. I was terrified and excited and knew that all our prayers had been answered, but it was up to me to hurry up and find her and I was scared I wouldn't be able to. She was here and I couldn't get to her fast enough.

I had it all planned out in my head. As soon as I found her, I would hug the hell out of her first, then I was going to grab her hands and pull her back to where Mom was standing. We were going to wait by the exit to the ride so when you walked off, she would be the first thing you would see.

I knew how happy you were going to be when you saw her. Neither of us had been truly happy in the two years since she was taken and this was our chance. After all, Disneyland is the happiest place on earth, and for the first time, I was starting to believe it.

"Hope!" I yelled, cupping my hands around my mouth. I had been running for several minutes, still trying to listen for the sound of her voice. She would yell my name, then I would yell her name, and this went on for what felt like forever until someone grabbed my arm and yanked it, stopping me in my tracks. Mom threw her arms around me and hugged me, but I was trying to get out of her grasp.

"Dean, you can't run off like that!" she said. She was kneeling down, shaking my shoulders, looking me frantically in the eyes. "I thought I lost you."

I pulled away from her and tried to keep running toward Hope, but Mom wouldn't let go of my shoulders. "Stop it!" she said, confused why I was trying to get away from her.

I looked back at her in a panic and shook my head vigorously, trying to catch my breath and find the words. "It's..." I pointed toward the direction I wanted to run. "It's Hope, Mom! I found Hope! We have to go to her before I lose her again."

Sadness instantly reached her eyes and I knew she didn't believe me. "Dean," she whispered, shaking her head sympathetically. "Sweetie."

She felt sorry for me. She didn't believe me, because this wasn't the first time I thought I'd found her. But I knew I was right this time. I knew it.

"Dean!" Hope cried again. "Where are you?" She was much closer this time and I could tell by the sound of her voice that she was crying now. Mom's eyes darted toward the voice and I knew she heard her calling for me, too.

"We have to find her, Mom," I pleaded. "It's her. That's Hope."

Mom looked me in the eyes and I could see the fear in them. She nodded, then grabbed my hand.

"Hope?" she yelled, scanning over the crowd. We were both calling her name now and I remember looking up at Mom at one point, watching her while she helped me search. I loved her more than I ever had in that moment, because she actually believed me.

We heard my name called again and it was so much closer this time. Mom looked down at me and her eyes were wide. We both broke out into a run toward the sound of Hope's voice. We pushed through the crowd and... that's when I saw her. Her back was to us and she was standing all by herself.

"Dean!" she yelled again.

Mom and I were both frozen. We couldn't believe it. She was standing right in front of us, looking for me. After two years of not knowing who took her or where she was, we had finally found her. I started to walk forward, but I was suddenly shoved aside by a teenage boy rushing toward her. When he reached her, he grabbed her by the arm and spun her around.

"Ashley! Thank God!" he said, pulling her to him.

"Dean," she said to the boy, wrapping her arms around his neck. "I got lost."

He picked her up. "I know, sis. I'm so sorry. You're okay now."

She pulled her tear-streaked face away from his chest and she glanced in our direction.

She wasn't Hope.

She wasn't Hope at all.

And I wasn't the Dean she was looking for.

Mom squeezed my hand and knelt down in front of me. "I'm so sorry, Dean," she said. "I thought it was her, too."

A sob broke free from my chest and I cried. I cried so damn hard, Les. Mom wrapped her arms around me and she started crying, too, because I don't think she knew that an eight-year-old could have his heart crushed like that.

But I was crushed. My heart broke all over again that day.

And I never wanted to hear the name Dean again.

H

Chapter Sixteen

I practically skip down the stairs and into the kitchen. It's the second Monday of school and just thinking about my attitude when I woke up last week as opposed to this morning makes me laugh. I never in a million years imagined I'd be so consumed with the thought of a girl as I have been. Since the second I left her house Saturday night, I've done nothing but eat, breathe, and sleep with her on my mind.

"So how are you liking Sky?" my mom asks. She's seated at the kitchen table eating her breakfast and reading the paper. I'm surprised she remembers her name. I only mentioned her once. I shut the refrigerator door and walk to the bar.

"She's great," I say. "I like her a lot."

My mom puts down the paper and cocks her head. "*She?*" she says with an arched eyebrow. I don't understand her confusion. I just stare at her until she shakes her head and laughs. "Oh, Jesus," she says. "You've got it bad."

Still confused. "What do you mean? You asked how I liked Sky and I answered you."

She's laughing even harder now. "I said *school*, Holder. I asked how you were liking *school*."

Oh.

Maybe I *do* have it bad.

"Shut up." I laugh, embarrassed.

She stops laughing and picks the newspaper up, holding it out in front of her. I grab my drink and my backpack and head toward the door. "Well?" she asks. "How do you like *school*?"

I roll my eyes at her. "It's fine," I say, backing out of the kitchen. "But I like Sky more."

I walk to the car and shove my backpack inside. I wish I had thought to offer to pick her up today, but after spending most of Sunday texting back and forth, we agreed that we would take things slow. We decided not to run together in the mornings. She said it would be too much, too soon, and I definitely want to keep it at her pace, so I agreed. However, I can't deny the fact that I was a little disappointed that she wants to run alone. I want to be around her every second of the day, but I also know she's right. We spent one weekend together and it already feels like I've connected with her on a much deeper level than with any other girl I've dated. It's a good feeling, but it also scares the hell out of me.

Before I back out of the driveway, I pull my phone out and text her.

I don't know if your ego needs deflating today. I'll judge for myself when I finally get to see you in fifteen minutes.

I set my phone down and back out of the driveway. When I make it to the first stop sign, I pick my phone back up and text her again.

Fourteen minutes.

I keep the phone in my hand and text her again when another minute has passed.

Thirteen minutes.

I do this every minute until I pull into the school parking lot and all the minutes have passed.

When I reach the classroom I peek through the window of the door. She's seated in the back of the room next to a conveniently empty desk. My pulse kicks up a notch just from seeing her again. I open the door and walk inside and her face immediately lights up with a smile as soon as she sees me.

I reach the back of the room and begin to lay my backpack down on the empty desk at the same time some dude tries to set his drinks down. I look at him and he looks at me, then we both look at Sky, because I don't want to shove him away until she gives me permission.

"Looks like we have quite the predicament here, boys," she says with an adorable grin. She looks at the coffee being held in the hands of the guy standing next to me. "I see the Mormon brought the queen her offering of coffee. Very impressive." She looks at me and arches an eyebrow. "Do you wish to reveal your offering, hopeless boy, so that I may decide who shall accompany me at the classroom throne today?"

She's teasing me. I love it. And now that I think about it, this must be the guy she's been sitting with at lunch all week. One look at his hot pink shoes and matching pants relieves me of any worry that he's about to become my competition.

I pick up my backpack and let him have the seat. "Looks like someone's in need of an ego-shattering text today." I take an empty seat in the row in front of her.

"Congratulations, squire," she says to the guy with the coffee. "You are the queen's chosen one today. Sit. It's been quite the weekend."

He takes a seat, but he's eyeing her curiously. It's clear by the look on his face that he has no idea what happened between Sky and me this weekend. "Breckin, this is Holder," Sky says, introducing me to him. "Holder is not my boyfriend, but if I catch him trying to break the record for best first kiss with another girl, then he'll soon be my *not breathing* nonboyfriend."

Oh, don't worry, babe. I'm not about to try and break that record with anyone but you.

I smile at her. "Likewise."

"Holder, this is Breckin," she says, gesturing her hand toward him. "Breckin is my new very bestest friend ever in the whole wide world."

If he's Sky's best friend, then I'm pretty sure he's about to become my second-best friend. I reach my hand out to him. Breckin is cautious as he returns the handshake, then he turns to Sky and lowers his voice. "Does *not-your-boyfriend* realize I'm Mormon?"

Sky smiles and nods. "It turns out, Holder doesn't have an issue with Mormons at all. He just has an issue with assholes."

Breckin laughs and I'm still trying to process if Mormon really means Mormon in this case, because it sure sounds like code for something else entirely.

"Well, in that case, welcome to the alliance," Breckin says to me.

I look down at the coffee cup on his desk. If Mormon means Mormon, that better be decaf. "I thought Mormons weren't allowed to have caffeine," I say to him.

Breckin shrugs. "I decided to break that rule the morning I woke up gay."

I laugh. I think I like this Mormon.

Sky leans back in her seat and smiles at me. It feels good to get the approval from the only friend she seems to have here. Mr. Mulligan walks in so I lean toward Sky before he starts his lecture. "Wait for me after class?"

She smiles and nods.

When we reach her locker, it's lined with sticky notes again.

Assholes.

I wad them up and drop them on the floor, just as I always do when I pass her locker. She switches her books, then turns to face me. "You trimmed your hair," she says.

I'm not even about to admit how hard it is to find a barber open on Sunday.

"Yeah. This chick I know couldn't stop whining about it. It was really annoying."

"I like it," she says.

"Good."

She smiles at me and clutches her books to her chest. I can't stop thinking about Saturday night and how I'd give anything to be back in her room with her right now. Why the hell didn't I kiss her? I'm kissing her today, dammit. After school. Or *during* school if I can get away with it. Or right now.

"I guess we should get to class," she says, glancing past me.

"Yep," I agree. We really probably should get to class but she's not *in* my next class so I really have no urge to get to class.

She stares at me a little while longer. Long enough for me to mentally map out a plan. I know it's Monday, but I want to take her out tonight. That way I'll have to walk her to her door. Then once we get to her front door, I'm going to kiss her crazy for at least half an hour just like I should have done Saturday night.

She kicks off the locker and begins to walk away, but I grab her arm and pull her back. I push her up against the locker and she gasps while I block her in with my arms.

She's flustered again.

I reach my hand up to her face and slide it under her jaw, then run my thumb across her bottom lip. I can feel her chest heave against mine and her breaths come in quicker succession.

"I wish I had kissed you Saturday night," I whisper, staring down at her mouth. She parts her lips and I continue to run my thumb across them. "I can't stop imagining what you taste like." I press my thumb to the center of her lips and I quickly lean in and kiss her. I pull away just as fast, though, because that tease just about kills me. Her eyes are closed and I release her face and walk away.

I'm pretty sure I just became the master of willpower, because walking away from that mouth was one of the hardest things I've ever done.

"Hey, whisker biscuit," Daniel says, cutting in line to stand in front of me.

"Whisker biscuit?" I sigh and shake my head. I swear I don't know where he comes up with this shit.

"Well, you don't like it when I call you Hopeless. Or cunt nugget. Or piss flap. Or—"

"You could just call me Holder."

"Everyone else calls you Holder and I hate everyone else, so no. I can't." He takes two empty trays and hands me one. He nods in the direction of Sky's table. "So, I hope your ditching me Saturday night for cheese tits over there was worth it."

"Her name is Sky," I correct.

"Well I can't call her Sky. Everyone else calls her Sky and I hate everyone else, so . . ."

I laugh. "Well then why do you call Valerie by *her* name?"

He spins around. "Who's Valerie?" he asks, looking at me like I've lost my mind.

"*Val?* Your ex-girlfriend? Or current girlfriend. Whatever she is."

Daniel laughs. "No, man. Her name isn't Valerie, it's Tessa."
What the hell?

"I call her Val because it's short for Valium and I always tell her she needs to take that shit by the bucketful. I wasn't lying when I said she was fucking crazy."

"Do you call *anyone* by their actual name?"

He ponders my question for a second, then looks at me, confused. "Why would I want to do that?"

I give up. "I'm sitting with Sky today," I tell him. "You want to sit with us?"

Daniel shakes his head. "Nah. Val's having a good day so I better take advantage of it." He takes his change from the cafeteria cashier. "See you later, buttshark."

I'm kind of relieved he's sitting with Val. I don't know if I'm ready for Sky to get a dose of Daniel yet. I pay for my food and walk toward their table. When I reach them, it sounds like Sky is giving Breckin a recap of our weekend. Breckin sees me walk up behind her but he just winks and doesn't let her know I'm listening.

"He showed up at my house on Friday and after quite a few misunderstandings, we finally came to an understanding that we just misunderstood each other. Then we baked, I read him some smut, and he went home. He came back over Saturday night and cooked for me. Then we went to my room and . . ."

I drop my tray down beside hers and take a seat. "Keep going," I say. "I'd love to hear what we did next."

She shoots me a quick grin when she sees my tray beside hers, then she rolls her eyes and turns back to Breckin. "Then we broke the record for best first kiss in the history of first kisses without even kissing."

"Impressive," Breckin says.

"It was an excruciatingly boring weekend," I say.

Breckin shoots me a look like he wants to kick my ass for insulting Sky. He just scored major points for that one.

"Holder loves boring," Sky clarifies. "He means that in a nice way."

Breckin picks up his fork and looks back and forth between us. "Not much confuses me. But you two are an exception."

He's not the only one confused by us. I'm seriously confused by us. I've never felt this comfortable with a girl before and we aren't even dating. We haven't even kissed. Although I did give her one hell of a *non*kiss. Just thinking about it has me anxious. "You busy tonight?"

She wipes her mouth with her napkin. "Maybe," she says, smiling.

I wink at her, knowing that's her stubborn way of saying she's not busy.

"Was it the smut I let her borrow that she read to you?" Breckin asks.

"Smut?" I laugh. "I don't *think* it was smut, but I didn't catch most of the book because my mind was a little sidetracked."

Sky slaps me on the arm. "You let me read for three hours straight and you weren't even paying attention?"

I throw my arm over her shoulder and pull her to me, then kiss her on the side of the head. "I already told you I was paying attention," I whisper in her ear. "Just not to the words coming out of your mouth." I turn back to Breckin. "I did catch some of it, though. Not a bad book. I didn't think I'd ever be interested in a romance novel but I'm curious how that dude's gonna find a way out of that shit."

Breckin agrees and brings up a part of the plot. We begin talking about the book and I can't help but notice how quiet Sky is the whole time I'm talking with Breckin. I keep glancing at her but she's zoned out, just like when she zoned out in her kitchen Saturday night. After a while of her not talking or even taking a bite of her food, I become concerned that something is wrong.

"You okay?" I ask, turning my attention toward her. She doesn't even blink. I snap my fingers in front of her face. "Sky," I say a little louder. Her eyes finally jerk up to mine and she snaps out of it. "Where'd you go?" I ask, concerned.

She smiles, but looks embarrassed by the fact that she just zoned out. I reach up and cup her cheek, running my thumb reassuringly back and forth. "You have to quit checking out like that. It freaks me out a little bit."

She shrugs. "Sorry. I'm easily distracted." She smiles and pulls my hand away from her face, giving it a reassuring squeeze. "Really, I'm fine."

I look down at her hand that's now holding mine. I see the familiar half of a silver heart dangling from beneath her sleeve, so I immediately flip her hand over and twist her wrist back and forth.

She's wearing Les's bracelet.

Why the *hell* is she wearing Les's bracelet?

"Where'd you get that?" I ask her, still looking at the bracelet that sure as hell shouldn't be on her wrist right now.

She looks down at her hand and shrugs like it's not a big deal.

She just shrugs?

She shrugs like she doesn't give a shit that she just completely knocked the breath out of me. How can she be wearing this bracelet? It's Les's bracelet. The last time I saw this bracelet it was on Les's wrist.

"Where'd you get it?" I demand.

She's looking at me now like she's terrified of the person in front of her. I realize I'm holding on to her wrist with a tight grip so I release it, just as she pulls away from me.

"You think I got it from a guy?" she asks, confused.

No, I don't think it's from a *guy. Christ.* I don't think that at all. What I *think* is that she's wearing my dead sister's bracelet and she's refusing to tell me how she got it. She can't just shrug and sit here, acting like it's a coincidence, because that bracelet is handmade and there's only one other bracelet like it in the whole damn world. So unless she's Hope, then she's somehow wearing Les's bracelet and I want to know why the hell she's wearing it!

Unless she's Hope.

The truth hits me head-on and I think I'm about to be sick. *No, no, no.*

"Holder," Breckin says, shifting forward. "Ease up, man."

No, no, no. This can't be Hope's bracelet. How could she even still have it after all this time? Her words from Saturday night rush through my head.

"The only thing I have from before Karen adopted me is some jewelry, and I have no idea who it came from."

I lean forward, praying this bracelet isn't the jewelry she was referring to. "Who gave you the damn bracelet, Sky?"

She gasps, still unable to give me an answer. She can't answer me because she honestly has no idea. She's looking at me like I just crushed her and hell . . . I think I did.

I know she doesn't have a clue what's going through my mind right now, but how could I even begin to tell her? How in the hell do I explain to her that she may not know where the bracelet on her wrist came from, but I *do*? How do I tell her that bracelet came from Les? From the best friend she doesn't even remember? And how do I admit that she got that bracelet just minutes before I walked away from her? Minutes before her entire life was ripped out from under her?

I *can't* tell her. I can't tell her, because she honestly has no memory of me or Les or how she got this damn bracelet. From looking at her, I don't even think she remembers Hope. She doesn't even remember *herself*. She said Saturday night she has no memory of her life before Karen.

How can she not remember? How can anyone not remember being stolen from her own home? From her best friend?

How can she not remember *me?*

I squeeze my eyes shut and turn away from her. I press my palms against my forehead and inhale a deep breath. I have got to calm down. I'm terrifying her right now and that's the last thing I want to do. I grip the back of my neck in order to keep my hands busy so that I don't punch the table.

She's Hope. Sky is Hope and Hope is Sky and, "Shit!"

I don't mean to say it out loud, because I know I'm freaking her out. But this is as calm as I'm able to be right now. I have to get out of here. I have to figure out how the hell to explain this to her.

I stand up and rush toward the exit to the cafeteria before I do or say anything else. As soon as I'm through the doors and alone in the hallway, I collapse against the nearest locker, and pull my trembling hands to my face.

"Shit, shit, shit!"

Chapter Seventeen

Les,

I'm sorry I didn't find her sooner. I can't help but wonder if it would have made a difference. I'm so sorry.

H

Chapter Eighteen

Les,

She still has your bracelet, though. That has to mean something to you.

H

Chapter Nineteen

Les,

I don't know what to do. It's been over six hours now and I keep trying to figure out if I should go to her house and tell her everything or if I should give it more time.

    I think I'll give it more time. I need to process this.

    H

Chapter Twenty

Les,

What if I call Karen and explain everything to her? Sky seems to have a good relationship with her. Karen could figure out what to do.

H

Chapter Twenty-one

Les,

Shit. What if Karen is the one who did it?

H

Chapter Twenty-two

Les,

What if I tell Mom? I could tell Mom and she could figure out what we need to do or if we need to call the police. She's a lawyer. I'm sure she deals with this kind of stuff all the time.

   H

Chapter Twenty-three

Les,

I can't tell Mom. Mom's in intellectual property law.
She wouldn't know what to do any more than I do.

    H

Chapter Twenty-four

Les,

It's almost midnight. Twelve hours I've let this continue without giving her a single explanation for what happened at lunch today. God, I hope I didn't make her cry.

H

Chapter Twenty-five

Les,

She's probably asleep right now. I'll tell her in the morning. She runs every morning so I'll just show up and run with her, then I'll tell her. We'll figure out what to do after that.

H

Chapter Twenty-six

Les,

I can't sleep.
    I can't believe I actually found her.

    H

Chapter Twenty-seven

Les,

Why do you think she calls herself Sky?

There was this thing we used to do when we were little. We only did it a few times because she was taken shortly after that. But she used to cry all the time and I hated it, so we would lie in the driveway and watch the sky and I would hold on to her finger. I remember thinking it was gross to hold a girl's hand so I would always hold her pinky, instead. Because even though I was just a kid and it was gross to hold a girl's hand, I really did want to hold her hand.

I used to tell her to think about the sky when she got sad and she always promised me she would. Now here she is. And her name is Sky.

It's three in the morning. None of this makes any sense. I'm going to sleep now.

H

Chapter Twenty-eight

Les,

Well, I ran with her. Sort of. It was more like I chased her. I couldn't bring myself to speak to her once I showed up. Then after the run we were both so exhausted we just collapsed onto the grass.

I was hoping that the incident in the cafeteria yesterday would spark some sort of memory from her. I was hoping when I showed up today that she would know exactly what upset me so much yesterday. I wanted her to tell me she remembered so I wouldn't have to be the one to tell her.

How do you tell someone something like that, Les? How do I tell her that the mother who raised her could very well be the one who stole her from us?

If I said anything, her life would change forever. And she likes her life. She likes running and reading and baking and... holy shit.

Holy shit.

It didn't make sense until just now, but the whole internet thing? Her mom not wanting her to have a phone? Karen did it. Karen fucking took her and she's doing everything she can to make sure Sky doesn't find out.

I don't know what to do. I know I can't be around

her right now. There's no way I can be around her and pretend everything is fine when it's not. But there's no way I can tell her the truth, either, because it would turn her world upside down.

I don't know what will be more painful. Staying away from her so she doesn't find out, or telling her the truth and ruining her life all over again.

H

Chapter Twenty-eight-and-a-half

Les,

It's Thursday night. I haven't spoken to her since Monday. I can't even look at her because it hurts so much. I still don't know what to do and the longer I just let this go on, the more of an asshole it makes me look. But every time I work up the nerve to talk to her I have no idea what I'd even say. I told her I'd always be honest with her and this is just something I can't be honest with her about.

I've been trying to figure out why Karen would do something like this, but there isn't a single valid excuse in the whole world that could justify someone taking a child. I've even thought about the chance that maybe Hope's dad didn't really want her, so he just gave her away. But I know that's not true because he did everything he could to find her for months.

I just can't figure it out. I don't even know if I need to. Until I barged into her life two weeks ago, she was happy. If I don't walk away now, it'll ruin all that.

Ironic, isn't it? I walked away from her thirteen years ago and ruined her life. Now if I decide not to walk away from her, I'll ruin her life again.

Just goes to show that everything I do is hopeless. Fucking hopeless.

H

Chapter Twenty-nine

"Yo, flipdick. We on for tonight?" Daniel says, walking up to my locker.

The last thing I feel like doing tonight is going out. I know Daniel would probably get my mind off her with all the crazy shit that comes out of his mouth, but I don't really *want* to get my mind off her. I haven't spoken to her since Monday and the only thing that sounds appealing besides being with her is wallowing alone in self-pity.

"Maybe tomorrow. I don't really feel like doing anything tonight."

Daniel leans his elbow into the locker and he lowers his head, leaning toward me. "You're really being a mangina," he says. "You didn't even date the chick. Get the fuck over it and . . ." Daniel glances over my shoulder without finishing the sentence. "What the hell is your problem, powder puff?" He's speaking to someone now standing behind me. The way he says it can only mean it's Grayson. Fearing I'm about to get sucker-punched from behind, I spin around.

It's not Grayson.

Breckin is facing me and he doesn't look very pleased about it.

"Hey," I say.

"I need to talk to you," he says. I know he wants to talk about Sky and I really don't want to talk about Sky. Not to Breckin, not to Daniel, not even to Sky. No one understands anything about anything and frankly, it's nobody's business.

"Sorry, Breckin. I'm not really in the mood to talk about her."

Breckin takes a quick step forward and I take a quick step back because I wasn't expecting him to rush me like he just did. My back is against the locker and Daniel is laughing. Probably because Breckin is a good fifty pounds lighter than I am and several inches shorter and he's probably wondering why the hell I haven't laid Breckin on his ass yet. But that doesn't stop Breckin from moving in even closer and shoving his finger hard against my chest.

"I don't really give a shit what kind of mood you're in, because I'm in a pretty shitty mood myself, Holder. You aren't the one having to pick up all the shattered pieces of Sky this week. I don't know what the hell happened in the cafeteria Monday, but it was enough to show me that I don't like you. I don't like you one goddamn bit and I have no idea what Sky sees in you . . . because what you did to her? How you led her on for days and then just walked away like she was a waste of your time?" Breckin shakes his head, still fuming. He drops his eyes down to my arm. Down to the tattoo. "I feel sorry for you," he sighs. He inhales a calming breath and slowly looks back up at me. "I feel sorry for you, because people like her don't come along more than once. She deserves someone who realizes that. Someone who appreciates her. Someone who would never just . . ." he shakes his head, looking at me disappointedly. "Someone who would never crush her hope and then just walk away."

Breckin backs up a step when he's finished and Daniel gives me the look. The look that indicates he's ready to start one of his fights. Before I even have the chance to tell Daniel to refrain, he begins to lunge forward toward Breckin. I quickly step in between them and shove Daniel against the locker with my arm, keeping it pressed against his chest. "Don't," I say, holding Daniel back.

"Let him hit me," Breckin says loudly from behind me. "Or better yet, why don't you just do it, Holder? You proved to Sky on Monday what a badass you are. Have at it!"

I release Daniel and turn around to face Breckin. The last thing I want to do is hit him. Why would I hit him when everything he just said to me was the absolute truth? He's pissed at me because of how I treated Sky. He's pissed and he's protecting her and I have no idea how to tell him how much it means to me to know she has him.

I turn around and open my locker, then grab my backpack and car keys. Daniel is watching me closely, wondering why I'm not kicking Breckin's ass right now. I face Breckin again and he's eyeing me with just as much confusion as Daniel. I begin to walk away, but pause when I'm shoulder to shoulder with Breckin. "I'm glad she has you, Breckin."

He doesn't respond. I pull my backpack onto my shoulder and walk away.

Chapter Twenty-nine-and-a-half

Les,

I haven't spoken to her in two weeks. I'm still going to school, though, because I can't imagine the thought of not being able to see her every day. But I just watch her from a distance. I hate that she seems sad now.

I was hoping that my actions in the cafeteria last Monday would have left her pissed off, if even a little bit. But when I decided it was better not to allow myself back into her life, I was hoping her anger would help her get over me faster. But she doesn't seem angry. She just seems heartbroken and that crushes me.

I made a list over the weekend of the pros and cons of telling her the truth about who she is. I'll share it with you so you'll understand my decision better, because I know it doesn't make sense.

Pros to telling Sky the truth:

* Her family deserves to know what happened to her and that she's okay.
* She deserves to know what happened.

Cons to telling Sky the truth:

* The truth would ruin the life she has now.
* She never seemed happy to me when we were little, but she seems happy now. Forcing her back into a life she doesn't even remember doesn't seem like the right thing to do.
* If she found out I knew all along who she was, she would never forgive me for keeping it from her.
* I know she thinks her birthday is next week, but she still has months to go before she actually turns eighteen. If she finds out right now, the decision about what happens to her will be made for her by her father and the state. When she finds out the truth, I want her to be old enough to make her own decisions about what happens to her life.

As much as I don't want to believe Karen did this, what if she did? If the truth came out, Karen would be punished. And that probably should be listed in pros, but I just don't think her going to prison would in any way be a pro for Sky.

So you can see the cons won, which is why I've decided not to tell her the truth. Not yet, anyway. After I decided I wasn't going to tell her what happened to her as a child, I also thought about whether it was a good idea to at least try and apologize for what happened at lunch that day. I thought that somehow I could still keep the secret until she's out of high school and in the meantime, we could be together. I want to be with her again more than anything, but there are so many reasons why I shouldn't be.

Pros to being with Sky:

* I fucking miss her. I miss her rude comments, her laughter, her smile, her scowl, her cookies, her brownies, her kiss. (Even though I never really had that one. I know I'd miss it if I did.)
* She wouldn't be as heartbroken if I would just apologize. We could go back to whatever it was that we were doing and I could pretend she wasn't Hope. It would be cruel, but at least she'd be happy.

Cons to being with Sky:

* Being around her could trigger her memory. I'm not sure that I'm ready for her to remember me yet.
* Once she finds out the truth, she'll hate me for deceiving her. At least if I'm not with her, she'll be able to respect the fact that I didn't lie to her while I was allowing her to fall in love with me.
* If I spend any time with her, I know I'll slip up. I'll call her Hope or I'll say something about when we were kids or I'll talk too much about you and that could spark a memory.
* How could I ever introduce her to Mom? I'm pretty sure with as much time as Hope spent at our house, Mom would immediately recognize her.

* I'll do something to fuck it all up again. That's the only thing I seem to be consistent at in this life. Fucking things up for you and Hope.
* If I walk out of her life completely, she can go on living the contented life she's been living for the past thirteen years.
* If I stay, I'll inevitably have to tell her the truth. And no matter how much she probably needs to hear the truth; it'll turn her world upside down. I can't watch that, Les. I just can't.

So there you have it in big, bold ink. I'm not telling her the truth and I'm not letting her forgive me. She's better off without me. She's better off keeping the past in the past and keeping me at a distance.

H

Chapter Thirty

I grab the sack from the floorboard and walk to the front door, then ring the doorbell. I don't know if this is a good idea. In fact, I *know* it's not a good idea. But for whatever reason I trust him to do this for me.

The front door opens and a woman, more than likely his mother, is standing in the doorway.

"Is Breckin here?" I ask her.

She starts at the top of my head, then slowly scrolls down my entire body, stopping at my shoes. It's not the kind of scroll a guy gets from a woman who's checking him out. It's a scroll of disapproval. "Breckin isn't expecting company," she says coldly.

Okay. I didn't anticipate this obstacle.

"It's okay, Mom," I hear Breckin say as he opens the door further. "He's not here for my gay parts."

Breckin's mother scoffs, then rolls her eyes and walks away while I'm trying to hold back my laughter. Breckin is now standing in her place, scrolling over me disapprovingly just like she did. "What do you want?"

I shift my feet, feeling a little uncomfortable at how unwelcome I am at this house. "I want a couple of things," I say. "I'm here to apologize, for one. But I'm also here to ask you for a favor."

Breckin arches an eyebrow. "I told my mother you weren't here for my gay parts, Holder. So go ahead and apologize, but I'm not doing you any favors."

I laugh. I love that he can be so pissed, yet make fun of himself at the same time. That's such a Les thing to do. "Can I come in?" I ask. I feel pretty damn awkward on the porch right now and I don't really want to have this conversation standing in a doorway. Breckin steps back and opens the door farther.

"That better be an apology gift," he says, indicating the sack in my hand. He doesn't look back or invite me to follow him as he makes his way toward the hallway, so I shut the front door and glance around, then follow him. He opens the door to his bedroom and I walk in behind him. He points to a chair. "Sit there," he says firmly. He walks to his bed and takes a seat on the edge of it, facing me. I slowly take a seat in the chair and he rests his elbows on his knees and clasps his hands in front of him, looking me straight in the eyes. "I take it you'll be apologizing to Sky next? After you leave here? Because she's the one you really need to be apologizing to."

I set the sack down at my feet and lean back in the chair. "You're really protective of her, aren't you?"

Breckin shrugs indifferently. "Well, with all the assholes treating her like shit, *someone* has to watch out for her."

I purse my lips into a tight line and nod, but don't say anything right away. He stares at me for a while, more than likely attempting to figure out the motive behind my being here. I blow out a quick breath, then begin with what I came here to say.

"Listen, Breckin. I'm probably not going to make a whole lot of sense, but hear me out, okay?"

Breckin straightens up at the same time he rolls his eyes. "Please tell me you're about to explain what the hell happened in that cafeteria. We've tried to analyze your behavior no less than a dozen times, but you don't make any sense."

I shake my head. "I can't tell you what happened, Breckin. I can't. All I can tell you is that Sky means more to me than you could ever comprehend. I screwed up and it's too late to go back and make it right with her. I don't want her forgiveness because I don't deserve it. You and I both know she's better off without me. But I needed to come here and apologize to you because I know just from watching you how much you care about her. It kills me that I hurt her but I know that my hurting her indirectly hurt you, too. So, I'm sorry."

I keep my eyes trained on his. He tilts his head slightly and chews on his bottom lip while he studies me.

"Her birthday is next Saturday," I say, picking up the sack. "I got her this and I want you to give it to her. I don't want her to know it's from me. Just tell her you got it for her. I know she'll like it." I take the e-reader out of the sack and toss it to him. He catches it, then looks down at it.

He stares at it for a few minutes, then flips it over and looks at the back of it. He tosses it on the bed beside him, then clasps his hands together again, staring down at the floor. I wait for him to speak because I've said everything I came here to say.

"Can I just say one thing?" he says, lifting his gaze.

I nod. I figured he'd have way more than just *one* thing to say after all that.

"I think what pissed me off the most is the fact that I liked her with you," he says. "I liked seeing how happy she was that day. And even though it was just thirty minutes that I watched you with her at lunch before you went and flipped the fuck out," he says, waving his arm in the air, "it just seemed so *right*. You seemed right for her and she seemed right for you and . . . I don't know, Holder. You just don't make any sense. You didn't make sense when you walked away from her that day and you sure aren't making any sense right now. But I can tell you care about her. I just don't understand you. I don't understand you at all and it pisses me off because if there's one thing in the world I'm good at, it's understanding people."

I wasn't counting while he was talking, but I'm pretty sure that was more than just one thing. "Can you just trust that I really do care about her?" I say. "I want what's best for her and although it kills me that I'm not what's best for her, I want to see her happy."

Breckin smiles, then reaches beside him and picks up the e-reader. "Well, I think once I give her this awesome present I spent my life savings on, she'll forget all about Dean Holder. I'm pretty sure it'll be all about sawdust and sunshine once she dives into the books I'm about to load on here."

I smile, even though I have no idea what he means by sawdust and sunshine.

Chapter Thirty-and-a-half

Les,

Breckin is pretty cool. You would like him. I went to his house Friday night and gave him the gift I bought for Sky. We talked things out for a while and I don't think he wants to kick my ass anymore. Not that he could have. But that's what solidified my respect for him. The fact that he was so mad he wanted to fight me, even though he knew there wasn't a chance in hell he would win.

I wasn't sure how going over there would turn out, but I ended up staying until almost midnight. I've never really been into video games, but we played Modern Warfare and it was nice just letting my mind take a break for a while. Although I'm not sure how much of a break it took because Breckin made it a point to bring up how much I talked about Sky. He doesn't understand why I won't just apologize to her if I obviously like her as much as I do. Unfortunately, I can't explain it to him, so he'll never understand it. But he seems okay with that.

Neither of us thinks it's a good idea to let Sky know we hung out. I don't want her upset with Breckin, but now it feels like I'm somehow cheating on her by being friends with him. But I can assure you, Les. I wasn't there for his gay parts.

H

Chapter Thirty-one

"What do you want to do?" I ask.

"I don't care what we do," Daniel says.

"Me neither."

We're sitting in his driveway. I'm leaned back in my seat with my foot propped on his dash. He's in the same position in the driver's seat, only his hand is hanging loosely from the steering wheel and his head is resting against the headrest. He's staring out the window and he's being unusually distant.

"What's wrong with you?" I ask.

He continues to stare out the window and sighs a heavy, depressing sigh. "Broke up with Val again," he says disappointedly. "She's crazy. She's so fucking crazy."

"I thought that's why you loved her?"

"But that's also why I *don't*." He drops his leg to the floorboard and scoots his seat forward. "Let's get out of here." He cranks the car and begins backing out of the driveway.

I put my seatbelt on and slide my sunglasses off my head and over my eyes. "What do you want to do?"

"I don't care what we do," he says.

"Me neither."

"Is Breckin home?" I ask his mother, who's now eyeing Daniel from the doorway in the same way she was eyeing me last Friday night.

"Well, aren't you becoming a real regular," Breckin's mother says to me. There isn't any humor behind her voice and quite frankly, she's a little intimidating.

We stand silently for several awkward seconds and she still doesn't invite us in. Daniel leans his head toward mine. "Hold me. I'm scared."

The door widens and Breckin replaces his mother after she turns and walks away. He's now the one eyeing Daniel suspiciously. "I'm definitely not doing *you* any favors," Breckin says to him.

Daniel turns to face me, shooting me a quizzical look. "It's Friday night and you bring me to powder puff's house?" He shakes his head disappointedly. "What the hell has happened to us, man? What the hell have these bitches *done* to us?"

I look at Breckin and nudge my head sympathetically in Daniel's direction. "Girl trouble. I thought some Modern Warfare could help."

Breckin sighs, rolls his eyes, then steps aside to let us in. We make our way inside and Breckin closes the door behind us, then stops in front of Daniel. "You call me powder puff again and my new second-best friend ever in the whole wide world will kick your ass."

Daniel grins, then cuts his eyes to mine. We have one of our silent conversations where he tells me this kid isn't half bad. I smile, completely agreeing with him.

"Let me get this straight," Breckin says, trying to clarify the confession Daniel just made. "You don't even know what the girl *looked* like?"

Daniel smiles boastfully. "No clue."

"What was her name?" I ask.

He shrugs. "No clue."

Breckin sets down his game controller and turns to face Daniel. "How the hell did you end up in the maintenance closet with her?"

Daniel's face is still awash with a smug grin. He seems so proud of it, I'm shocked this is the first time he's mentioned it to me.

"Funny story, really," he says. "Last year I was never assigned a fifth-period class. It was a mistake on administration's part, but I didn't want them to know. Every day during fifth period while everyone else went to their scheduled classes, I would hide out in the janitor's closet and nap. They never cleaned that section of the hallway until after school, so no one ever went in there.

"I guess it was about six or seven months ago, right before the end of the school year, I was having one of my fifth-period naps and all of a sudden someone opens the door, slips inside, and trips over me. I couldn't see who she was because I always kept the lights out, but she landed right on top of me. We were in this really compromising position and she smelled really good and she didn't weigh very much, so I didn't mind her landing on me. I wrapped my arms around her and made no attempt to roll her off me because she felt so damn good. She was crying, though," he says, losing some of the excitement in his eyes. He leans back in his chair and continues. "I asked her what was wrong and all she said was, 'I hate them.' I asked her who she hated and she said, 'Everybody. I hate everybody.' The way she said it was just heartbreaking and I felt bad for her and her breath smelled so fucking good and I knew exactly what she meant because I hate everyone, too. So I kept my arms wrapped around her and I said, 'I hate everybody, too, Cinderella.' We were still in . . ."

"Wait, wait, wait," Breckin says, interrupting the story. "You called her Cinderella? What the hell for?"

Daniel shrugs. "We were in a janitor's closet. I didn't know her name and there were all these mops and brooms and shit and it reminded me of Cinderella, okay? Give me a break."

"But why would you even call her *anything*?" Breckin asks, not understanding Daniel's penchant for random nicknames.

Daniel rolls his eyes. "I didn't know her fucking *name*, Einstein! Now stop interrupting me, I'm just now getting to the good part." He leans forward again. "So I said to her, 'I hate everybody, too, Cinderella.' We were still in the same position and it was dark and to be honest, it was really kinda hot. You know, not knowing who she was or what she looked like. Sort of mysterious. Then she just laughs and leans forward and kisses me. Of course I kissed her back because I'd already finished my nap and we still had about fifteen minutes to kill. We kissed for the rest of the period. That's all we did. We never spoke another word and we never did more than just kiss. When the bell rang, she hopped up and walked out. I didn't even see what she looked like."

He's staring at the floor, smiling. I've honestly never seen him talk about a girl like this before. Not even Val.

"But I thought you said she was the best sex you ever had?" Breckin says, bringing us back to the point that started this whole conversation.

Daniel grins boastfully again. "She was. Turns out I wasn't hard to find after that. She showed up again a week later. The closet light was out like always and she walked in and shut the door behind her. She was crying again. She said, 'Are you in here, kid?' The way she called me kid made me think she might have been a teacher and I'd be lying if I said that didn't turn me on. Then one thing led to another and let's just say I became her Prince Charming for the rest of the hour. And *that* was the best sex I ever had."

Breckin and I both laugh.

"So who was she?" I ask.

Daniel shrugs. "I never found out. She never showed up again after that and school ended a few weeks later. Then I met Val and my life spiraled out of control." He exhales a deep rush of air, then turns to face Breckin. "Is it racist of me to not really want to hear about your gay sex?"

Breckin laughs and throws his game controller at Daniel. "Racist isn't the correct term, dipshit. Homophobic and discriminatory, yes. And understandable. I wouldn't tell you, anyway."

Daniel looks at me. "I don't even have to guess who you'll say was your best," he says. "The way Sky has you broken right now, I think it's pretty obvious."

I shake my head. "Well, you're wrong, because not only did I never have sex with her, but we never even kissed."

Daniel laughs but Breckin doesn't and neither do I, which quickly shuts Daniel up. "Please tell me you're kidding."

I shake my head.

Daniel stands up and tosses his controller onto the bed. "How the hell have you not kissed her?" he says, raising his voice. "Because the way you've been acting this month had me thinking she was the fucking love of your life."

I cock my head. "Why do you seem pissed off by this?"

He rolls his head. "Seriously?" He stalks toward me and bends forward, placing his hands on either side of my chair. "Because you're being a *pussy*. P-U-S-S-Y." He lets go of my chair and backs up. "*Jesus*, Holder. I was actually feeling sorry for you. Suck it up, man. Go to her house and fucking kiss her already and allow yourself to be happy for once."

He drops down onto the bed and grabs his controller. Breckin smiles a tight-lipped smile and shrugs. "I don't really like your friend, but he does make a good point. I still don't understand why you got so mad at her and walked away, but the only way to make it up to her is to not *stay* away." He turns back toward the TV and I'm staring at both of them, completely speechless.

They make it sound so simple. They make it sound so easy, like her whole life isn't hanging in the balance. They don't know what the fuck they're talking about.

"Take me home," I say to Daniel. I don't want to be here anymore. I walk out of Breckin's bedroom and make my way back to Daniel's car.

Chapter Thirty-two

Les,

Everyone likes to have an opinion, don't they? Daniel and Breckin have no clue what I've been through. What either of us has been through.
Fuck it. I don't even feel like telling you about it.

H

I close the notebook and stare at it. Why the hell do I even write in it? Why the hell do I bother when she's fucking *dead*? I throw the notebook across the room and it hits the wall and falls to the floor. I throw the pen at the notebook and then grab my pillow from behind my head and throw it, too.

"Dammit," I groan, frustrated. I'm pissed that Daniel thinks my life is so simple. I'm pissed that Breckin still thinks I should just apologize to her, like that would make it all okay. I'm pissed that I'm still writing to Les even though she's dead. She can't read it. She'll never read it. I'm just putting all the shit I'm living through down on paper for no reason other than the fact that there isn't a single god-damned person in the world right now that I can talk to.

I lie down, then get pissed again and punch my bed because my damn pillow is all the way across the room. I stand up and walk to the pillow, snatching it up. I look down at the notebook beneath it, spread open on the floor.

The pillow falls out of my hand.

My knees fall to the floor.

My hands clench the notebook that has flipped open to the very last page.

I frantically flip through the pages covered in Les's handwriting until I find where the words begin. As soon as I see the first words written on top of the page, my heart comes to a screeching halt.

Dear Holder,

If you're reading this, I'm so, so sor

I slam the notebook shut and throw it across the room.

She wrote me a letter?

A fucking *suicide* letter?

I can't breathe. Oh, God, I can't breathe. I pull myself up and jerk open my window, then stick my head out. I take a deep breath and it's not enough air. There isn't enough air and I can't breathe. I shut the window and run to my bedroom door. I swing it open and rush down the stairs, taking them several at a time. I pass by my mother and her eyes grow wide, seeing me in such a hurry.

"Holder, it's midnight! Where are—"

"Running!" I yell, then slam the front door behind me.

And that's what I do. I run. I run straight to Sky's house because she's the only thing in the world that can help me breathe again.

Chapter Thirty-three

These past few weeks of doing everything in my power to avoid her have taken every ounce of my strength and I can't do it anymore. I thought by staying away from her I was being strong, but not being near her is making me weaker than I've ever been. I know I shouldn't be here and I know she doesn't want me here but I have to see her. I have to hear her, I have to touch her, I have to feel her against me because that weekend I spent with her was the only time since I walked away from her thirteen years ago that I actually looked *forward*.

I've never looked forward before. I've always looked back. I think about the past way too much and I think about what I should have done and everything I did wrong and I've never once looked forward in my life. Being with her had me thinking about tomorrow and the day after that and the day after that and next year and forever. I need that right now because if I don't get to hold her one more time . . . I'm scared I'll look back again and the past will completely swallow me up.

I grab the windowsill and close my eyes. I inhale several times in an attempt to calm my pulse and the trembling going on with my hands right now.

I hate that she always leaves her window unlocked. I push it up and slide the curtains back, then climb inside. I contemplate saying something so she'll know I'm in her room, but I also don't want to scare her if she's asleep.

I turn and close the window and walk to her bed, then slowly ease myself down. She's facing the other way, so I lift the covers and scoot in beside her. Her posture immediately stiffens and she pulls her hands up to her face. I know she's awake and I know she knows it's me climbing into her bed, but the fact that it terrifies her completely breaks me.

She's scared of me. I didn't expect fear to be a reaction from her at all. Anger, yes. I'd so much rather her be angry at me right now than scared.

She's not telling me to leave yet and I don't think I could even if she asked me to. I have to feel her in my arms, so I move closer to her and slide my arm under her pillow. I wrap my other arm around her and slide my fingers into hers, then bury my face into her neck. Her scent and her skin and the feel of her heartbeat against our hands is exactly what I need, more tonight than ever before. I just need to know that I'm not alone, even if she doesn't have a clue how much allowing me to hold her is helping.

I kiss her softly on the side of her head and pull her closer. I don't deserve to be back in her bed or in her life after all I've put her through. In this moment, she's allowing me to be here. I'm not going to think about what might happen in the next few minutes. I'm not going to think about what happened in the past. I'm not looking forward *or* backward. I'm just holding her and thinking about this. Right now. Her.

She hasn't spoken in almost half an hour, but neither have I. I'm not apologizing to her, because I don't deserve her forgiveness and that's not why I'm here. I can't tell her what happened that day at lunch because I don't want her to know yet. I have no idea what to say, so I just hold her. I kiss her hair and I silently thank her for helping me breathe again.

I fold my arm up and hold her tighter. I'm trying not to fall apart right now. I'm trying so hard. She inhales a breath, then speaks to me for the first time in almost a month. "I'm so mad at you," she whispers.

I squeeze my eyes shut and press my lips desperately against her skin. "I know, Sky." I slip my hand around her to pull her closer. "I know."

Her fingers slide through mine and she squeezes my hand. All she did was squeeze my hand, but that one small gesture does more for me in this moment than I could ever give her in return. Knowing she's reassuring me, even in the slightest way, is more than I deserve from her.

I press my lips to her shoulder and kiss her softly. "I know," I whisper again as I continue kissing up her neck. She's responding to my touch and to my kiss and I want to stay here forever. I wish I could freeze time. I want to freeze the past and the future and just focus on being here in this moment with her forever.

She reaches up and runs her hand to the back of my head, pulling me against her neck even harder. She wants me here. She needs me here just as much as I need to be here and just knowing that is enough to freeze time for just a little while.

I raise up in the bed next to her and gently pull on her shoulder until she's flat on her back, looking up at me. I brush the hair away from her eyes and look down at her. I've missed her so much and I'm so scared she'll come to her senses and ask me to leave. God, I've missed her. How did I ever think walking away from her would be good for *either* of us?

"I know you're mad at me," I say, running my hand down to her neck. "I need you to be mad at me, Sky. But I think I need you to still want me here with you even more."

She continues to keep her eyes locked with mine and she nods her head slightly. I drop my forehead to hers and take her face in my hands, and she does the same to me.

"I *am* mad at you, Holder," she says. "But no matter how mad I've been, I never for one second stopped wanting you here with me."

Those words knock the breath out of me at the same time they completely fill my lungs back up with her air. She wants me here and it's the best fucking feeling in the world. "*Jesus*, Sky. I've missed you so bad." I feel like she's my lifeline and if I don't kiss her immediately, I'll die.

I dip my head and press my mouth to hers. We both inhale a deep breath the second our lips meet. She pulls me to her, welcoming me back into her life. Our mouths are pressed desperately together but our lips are completely still and we're both attempting to inhale another breath. I pull back slightly because the feel of her beneath me and having her mouth willingly pressed to mine is completely overwhelming me. In all my eighteen years, nothing has ever felt more perfect. As soon as my lips separate from hers, she looks up into my eyes and wraps her hands around my neck. She lifts up from the bed slightly, bringing her mouth back to mine. This time she kisses *me*, softly parting my lips with hers. When our tongues meet, she moans and I push her back against the mattress, kissing *her* this time.

For the next few minutes, we're completely lost in what feels like sheer perfection. Time has completely stopped, and all I'm thinking about while we kiss is how this is what saves people. Moments like these with people like her are what make all the suffering worth it. It's moments like these that keep people looking forward and I can't believe I've let them slip by for an entire month.

I know I told her that she's never really been kissed before, but until this moment I had no idea that *I* had never really been kissed before. Not like this. Every kiss, every movement, every moan, every touch of her hand against my skin. She's my saving grace. My Hope.

And I'm never walking away from her again.

*   *   *

I hear the door to her bedroom close, so I know she's about to walk in on me cooking breakfast for her. I still haven't explained what the hell I've done to her over the past month and I'm not sure that I can, but I'll do whatever it takes to get her to accept it without letting her forgive me. No matter what happened between us last night, I still don't deserve her forgiveness and honestly, she's not the type of girl who would put up with the shit I've put her through. If she forgave me, I feel like she would be compromising her strength. I don't want her compromising anything about herself for my sake.

I know she's standing behind me. Before everything I've done catches back up with her again, I try to explain away the fact that I've made myself at home in her kitchen again.

"I left early this morning," I say with my back still turned to her, "because I was afraid your mom would walk in and think I was trying to get you pregnant. Then when I went for my run, I passed by your house again and realized her car wasn't even home and remembered you said she does those trade days every month. So I decided to pick up some groceries because I wanted to cook you breakfast. I also almost bought groceries for lunch and dinner, but maybe we should take it one meal at a time today."

I turn around to face her and I don't know if it's because I've spent the last few weeks having to be so far away from her or what, but she's the most beautiful thing I've ever laid eyes on. I look her up and down, recognizing that this is the first time I've ever fallen in love with a piece of clothing before. What the hell is she trying to do to me?

"Happy birthday," I say casually, trying not to show her just how flustered I am looking at her in that outfit. "I really like that dress. I bought real milk, you want some?" I take a glass and pour her some milk, then slide it to her. She eyes the milk warily but I don't give her time to drink it. Seeing those lips and that mouth and . . . *shit*.

"I need to kiss you," I say, walking swiftly to her. I take her face in my hands. "Your mouth was so damn perfect last night, I'm scared I dreamt that whole thing." I expect her to resist, but she doesn't. Instead, I'm met with eager perfection when she grabs me by the shirt with both hands and kisses me back. Knowing that she still wants me after all I've put her through makes me appreciate her even more. And knowing I still have a chance with her?

That I'll still get to kiss her like this?

It's almost too much.

I separate from her and back away, smiling. "Nope. Didn't dream it."

I face the stove again so that I can stop concentrating on her mouth long enough to make her a plate of food. I have so much I need to say to her and I don't even know where or how to start. I fix our plates and walk them to the bar where she's seated.

"Are we allowed to play Dinner Quest, even though it's breakfast time?" I ask her.

She nods. "If I get the first question."

She isn't smiling. She hasn't smiled for me in over a month. I hate that I'm the reason she doesn't smile anymore.

I lay my fork down on my plate and bring my hands up, clasping them under my chin. "I was thinking about just letting you have *all* the questions," I say.

"I only need the answer to one," she says.

I sigh, knowing for a fact she needs more than just one answer. But the fact that she only wants the answer to one question leads me to believe she's about to ask me about the bracelet. And that's the one question I'm not willing to share the answer to just yet.

She leans forward in her chair and I brace myself for her question.

"How long have you been using drugs, Holder?"

I immediately look up at her, not expecting that to have been her question at all. It comes from so far out of left field that I keep my eyes locked with hers, but the randomness of the question makes me want to laugh. Maybe I should be disturbed by the fact that my behavior has given her such an absurd thought, but instead I feel nothing but relief.

I'm trying. I'm trying so hard not to laugh, but the anger in her eyes is adorable. It's adorable and beautiful and honest and I'm so *relieved*. I have to look away from her because I'm trying my damndest not to smile. She's being so serious and straightforward right now, but dammit. I can't.

My smile finally gives way and I laugh. Her eyes grow angrier, which only makes me laugh harder. "*Drugs?*" I'm trying to stop, but the more I think about how much this has affected us the entire last month, it just makes me laugh even harder. "You think I'm on *drugs*?"

Her expression doesn't change at all. She's pissed. I hold my breath in an attempt to stop the laughter until I'm able to keep a straight face. I lean forward and take her hand in mine, looking her directly in the eyes. "I'm not on drugs, Sky. I promise. I don't know why you would think that, but I swear."

"Then what the hell is wrong with you?" she snaps.

Shit. I hate the look on her face. She's hurt. Disappointed. Exhausted. I'm not sure which part of my unexplained, erratic behavior she's referring to, but I honestly have no idea how to answer that. What *is* wrong with me? What's *not* wrong with me?

"Can you be a little less vague?" I ask her.

She shrugs. "Sure. What happened to us and why are you acting like it never happened?"

Damn. That hurts. She thinks I just brushed everything that happened between us under the rug? I want to tell her everything. I want to tell her how much she means to me and how this has been one of the hardest months of my life. I want to tell her about Les and her and me, and how much it fucking hurts that she doesn't remember. How can she just forget such a significant part of her life?

Maybe Les and I weren't as significant to her as I thought. I look down at my arm. I trace the H and the O and the P and the E, wishing she remembered. But then again, if she remembered . . . she'd also know the meaning behind this tattoo. She'd know that I let her down. She'd remember that everything that's happened in her life for the last thirteen years is a direct result of me.

I look her in the eyes and answer her with the most honest answer I'll allow myself to give her. "I didn't want to let you down, Sky. I've let everyone down in my life that's ever loved me, and after that day at lunch I knew I let you down, too. So . . . I left you before you could start loving me. Otherwise, any effort to try not to disappoint you would be hopeless."

Her eyes cloud with disappointment. I know I'm being vague again, but I can't tell her. Not right now. Not until I know for sure that she'll be okay.

"Why couldn't you just say it, Holder? Why couldn't you just apologize?"

The hurt in her voice grips my heart. I look her directly in the eyes so she'll see how important it is to me that she never accepts how I treated her. "I'm not apologizing to you . . . because I don't want you to forgive me."

She immediately squeezes her eyes shut, trying to hold back tears. Nothing I can say could make her feel better about what happened between us. I release her hand and stand up, then walk to her and pick her up. I set her down on top of the bar so that we're at eye level. She may not believe the words that come out of my mouth, but I need her to feel me. I need her to see the sincerity in my eyes and the honesty in my voice so she'll know I didn't mean to hurt her. I only wanted to protect her from feeling this way, but I've only made it worse.

"Babe, I screwed up. I've screwed up more than once with you, I know that. But believe me, what happened at lunch that day wasn't jealousy or anger or anything that should ever scare you. I wish I could tell you what happened, but I can't. Someday I will, but I can't right now and I need you to accept that. Please. And I'm not apologizing to you, because I don't want you to forget what happened and you should never forgive me for it. Ever. Never make excuses for me, Sky."

She's taking in every word I'm saying and I love that about her. I lean in and kiss her, then pull back and continue saying what I need to say while she's still willing to hear me out.

"I told myself to just stay away from you and let you be mad at me, because I do have so many issues that I'm not ready to share with you yet. And I tried so hard to stay away, but I can't. I'm not strong enough to keep denying whatever this is we could have. And yesterday in the lunchroom when you were hugging Breckin and laughing with him? It felt so good to see you happy, Sky. But I wanted so bad to be the one who was making you laugh like that. It was tearing me up inside that you were thinking that I didn't care about us, or that spending that weekend with you wasn't the best weekend I've ever had in my life. Because I *do* care and it *was* the best. It was the best fucking weekend in the history of all weekends."

I run my hands down her hair to the base of her neck and brush her jawline with my thumbs. I have to take in a calming breath to say what I want to say next, because I don't want to scare her. I just need to be honest with her.

"It's killing me, Sky," I say quietly. "It's killing me because I don't want you to go another day without knowing how I feel about you.

And I'm not ready to tell you I'm in love with you, because I'm not. Not yet. But whatever this is I'm feeling—it's so much more than just *like*. It's so much more. And for the past few weeks I've been trying to figure it out. I've been trying to figure out why there isn't some other word to describe it. I want to tell you exactly how I feel but there isn't a single goddamned word in the entire dictionary that can describe this point between *liking* you and *loving* you, but I need that word. I need it because I need you to hear me say it."

I kiss her and pull back, but she's still looking at me in disbelief. I kiss her again and again, pausing after each kiss, hoping she'll respond with something. I don't care if she slaps me or kisses me back or tells me she loves me. I just want her to acknowledge everything I said. Instead, she's just staring at me and it's making me so damn nervous.

"Say something," I plead.

She continues to stare at me for a long time. I try to stay patient. She's always patient with me even though she's so quick-witted. What I wouldn't give for her to be a little more quick-witted in this moment. I need a reaction from her.

Something. Anything.

"Living," she finally whispers.

That's not what I expected to come out of her mouth, but at least it's something. I laugh and shake my head, confused about what she means. *"What?"*

"Live. If you mix the letters up in the words like and love, you get live. You can use that word."

Not only does she *get* me and not only is she smiling at me; but she just somehow gave me the one word I've been searching for since the moment I laid eyes on her in the grocery store.

I don't deserve her. I don't deserve her understanding and I sure as hell don't deserve the way she just made my heart feel. I laugh and take her in my arms, bringing my mouth to hers. "I live you, Sky," I say against her lips. "I live you so much."

And as perfect as that word sounds, as perfectly as it describes the point we're at, I know it's a lie.

I don't just live her. I *love* her. I've loved her since we were kids.

Chapter Thirty-four

Les,

I'm not reading that letter. I'm never reading it. Ever. And I'm done writing in this fucking notebook. So I guess that means I'm done writing to you, too.

H

Chapter Thirty-five

The phone rings and before I can even say hello, Daniel starts talking. "Do you and cheese tits want to come over and watch a movie with me and Val tonight?"

"I thought you broke up with Val."

"Not today," Daniel says.

"I don't know if that's a good idea." I've heard enough about Val to know that I'm not sure I feel comfortable taking Sky over there. We've only been dating two weeks.

"It *is* a good idea," Daniel argues. "My parents leave at eight. Be here at eight-oh-one."

He hangs up abruptly, so I text Sky.

Want to watch a movie with Daniel and Val tonight?

I hit send and toss my phone on the bed. I walk to my closet to inspect my shirt selection, but then I remember that I don't really have much of a shirt selection. I grab a random T-shirt and am pulling it on over my head when Sky's text sounds off.

Two conditions. (Per Karen.) I have to be home by midnight and you can't get me pregnant.

I laugh and text her back.

Considering how boring you are, I'm pretty sure you'll be home in less than an hour.

Does that mean you're still gonna try to get me pregnant, though?

Damn straight.

Laugh out loud.

She actually typed *laugh out loud*.

I really *do* lol, then I put my phone in my pocket and head to my car.

I've never really had a conversation with Val before and tonight is no exception. Sky and I are on the couch in front of the TV in Daniel's basement. Daniel and Val are in the chair and they're completely mauling each other, making me question why Daniel would even want us here in the first place if this is all they're gonna do.

Sky and I are watching them uncomfortably. It's hard to pay attention to the TV when there's actual slurping occurring.

The second Daniel's hand begins to slip up Val's shirt, I toss the remote at them, hitting Daniel in the knee. He jumps and lifts his hand to flip me off, but never breaks contact with Val's mouth. He does somehow glance at me, though, and I silently tell him to get the hell out of his basement, or get the hell out of her shirt.

He stands up and Val is now wrapped around him. They say nothing as he carries her up the stairs and to his bedroom.

"*Thank you,*" Sky says, breathing a sigh of relief. "I was about to hurl."

She's curled up beside me on the couch with her head resting on my shoulder. I ease myself down into the couch so that we're more comfortable, and we both look back at the TV. But I know we aren't really paying attention to it because the energy in the room completely shifted the second Daniel and Val left. We haven't had privacy like this since we officially started dating two weeks ago.

Her hand is in mine and they're clasped together, resting on her thigh. She's not wearing the dress that completely melted me the first time I saw her in it, but she *is* wearing a dress. And I love this dress just as much as the other dress.

I wish she were wearing jeans, though. I overheard Les talking with one of her friends once when we were sixteen. They were about to go on a double date and the friend was explaining to Les the rules of "make-out" clothes. She said if Les just wanted to kiss the guy, she needed to wear jeans because the guy would be less likely to slip his hand where he shouldn't. Then she told Les if she planned to move past first base, that a skirt or a dress was the way to go. *Easy access*, she said. I remember waiting in the living room after hearing that conversation to see which outfit Les chose. She walked down the stairs in a skirt and I marched her right back up to her room and forced her to change into a pair of jeans.

I wish Sky were wearing jeans right now because my hands are starting to sweat and I know she can feel my pulse through the palm of my hand. Her dress makes me think she wants to take things a step further tonight and I absolutely can't get that out of my head. I sure as hell *want* to take the next step, but what if Sky doesn't know the rules to "make-out" clothes? What if she's wearing this dress just for the hell of it? What if she's just wearing this dress because her washing machine broke and all her jeans were dirty? What if she's wearing this dress because she didn't have time to change into jeans before I showed up at her house? What if she's wearing this dress because she went to some sort of random church today that has service on Saturdays?

I wish I knew what was going through her head right now. I rest my head against the back of the couch and swallow the huge lump in my throat before I speak. "I like your dress," I say. It comes out in more of a raspy whisper because my throat is so weak right now just thinking about her. But I think she liked the way I said it, because she tilts her head and looks up at me, then slowly drops her eyes to my mouth. Thanks to the angle we're sitting, we wouldn't even have to shift positions to kiss. Her mouth is so incredibly close, it's practically on top of mine. But neither of us is taking advantage of that. *Yet.*

"Thank you," she whispers. The sweet breath from her words crashes against my mouth, warming me from the inside out.

The tension is so thick now, I can't even inhale.

"You're welcome," I whisper back, staring at her mouth the same way she's staring at mine. We're both quiet for a moment, just silently staring. She slides her lips together and moistens them and I'm pretty sure I mutter "*holy shit*" under my breath.

She likes that she just got me all flustered because she grins. "Wanna make out?" she whispers.

Oh, hell yes.

My lips are on hers before the sentence is even completely out of her mouth. I lower my hands to her waist and pull her until she's straddling me.

Straddling me *in. Her. Dress.*

I keep my hands locked tight on her hips while her hands slowly make their way up my neck and into my hair. The way her chest is pressed against mine makes my head spin, and it feels like the only thing that could set it straight again is if I pull her even closer and kiss her even harder. So that's what I do. I slide my hands away from her hips and reach behind her and pull her closer, pressing her into me so perfectly that she moans and tugs on my hair. I keep one hand on her ass, letting it flow with the rhythm of her movements while my other hand slides up her back and into her hair. I pull her mouth deeper into mine while I straighten my posture and lean forward so that my back is no longer touching the couch and my mouth is as meshed with hers as it's gonna get. Only that just makes my head spin even worse, so we're kissing faster now and she's moaning louder and I'm gripping her hips again and moving her against me so perfectly that I'm pretty sure she's about to have a repeat of what I did to her the first night we made out.

I don't want that yet because she's wearing this dress and it's absolutely amazing and I'm not even taking advantage of it. I grip her shoulders and push her away from me, letting myself fall back against the couch.

We're both gasping for breath. We're both smiling. We're both looking at each other like this is the best night ever because it's only ten o'clock and we've got a good two hours left of this. I release her shoulders and take her face in my hands, then slowly pull her back to my mouth. I change the position of my hands to support her weight and I stand up, then lower her onto the couch. I join her, pressing one knee between her legs and the other on the couch beside her.

I'm starting to get the impression that Daniel picked out this oversized couch in the same way that girls pick out their make-out clothes. Because it's the perfect couch for this sort of thing.

I begin to kiss down her chin, down her neck and down to the area where her dress stops and her cleavage begins. I slowly glide my hand over her dress and up the length of her body until I reach her breast. I stroke my hand over the material and she hardens beneath my fingertips.

Ohmygod I fucking *love* tonight.

I groan and grab her breast a little harder and she moans, arching her back, pressing more of herself against my hand. I claim her mouth with mine and continue kissing her until we have to break for air again. I press my cheek against hers.

My lips are right next to her ear.

"Sky?" I whisper.

She inhales a quick breath. "Yeah?"

I inhale a slow one. "I live you."

She exhales. "I live *you*, Dean Holder."

I exhale.

And inhale.

And exhale.

I repeat that sentence silently in my head. *I live* you, *Dean Holder.*

It's the first time I've heard her say Dean.

It's also the first time I've ever had my heart impaled by a word before.

I lift away from her cheek and look down at her. "Thank you."

She smiles. "For what?"

For being alive, I think to myself.

"For being you," I say out loud.

Her smile fades and I swear she looks right through my eyes and straight into my soul. "I'm good at being me," she says. "Especially when I'm with you."

I stare at her for several seconds, then I have to lower my cheek to hers again. I want to kiss her, but I keep my cheek pressed firmly against hers because I don't want her to see the tears in my eyes.

I don't want her to see how much it hurts to know she can be this close to me . . . and somehow not *remember* me.

Chapter Thirty-five-and-a-half

Dear all dead people who aren't Les, since I'm not writing letters to Les anymore,

I've loved Hope since we were kids.
  But tonight?
  Tonight I fell in love with Sky.

  H

Chapter Thirty-six

Les,

I know I said I wasn't writing to you anymore. Shut up. I'm still not writing in that notebook because I don't want to touch it, knowing that letter from you is in there. I can't read it, so I just bought a new notebook. Problem solved. Now I need to catch you up.

I've been dating Sky for a month now. She still hasn't had any recollection of me or you or all of us as kids. I keep catching myself almost slipping up, but luckily I haven't.

Remember that guy I got arrested for beating up last year? The one who was talking shit about you? Well, his brother finally said something to me today. I've been waiting for him... or anyone, really... to bring it up since the day I got back to school. It would have been fine had he just confronted me, but he didn't. He had to use Sky and Breckin and even you as a way to get back at me. He started talking shit about them to me at lunch and I swear to God, Les. I wanted to hurt him just as badly as I hurt his brother. Actually, I probably would have hurt him worse than I hurt his brother had Sky not been there.

She saw where my mind was going and she immediately pulled me out of the situation, forcing me out of the lunchroom. When we made it to my car in the parking lot I just completely broke down on her. It was like the entire past year of my life was repeatedly punching me in the gut and I just had to get it out. I told Sky everything I was feeling and for the first time since it happened... I admitted to myself and out loud that I was the one in the wrong. And I also admitted for the first time that you were in the wrong. I told Sky how pissed I was at you. How angry I've been since the second I walked in and found you lifeless in your bed. I've been so mad at you, Les, for so many things.

But the thing that pissed me off the most was the fact that you never once thought about what it would do to me when I found you. You knew I would be the one to find you and the fact that you knew that and you still killed yourself?

I hated that you did it anyway, knowing you wouldn't be the only one who died. I was so mad because you let me die, too.

Sky's right. I've got to let go of the blame. But until Sky knows the truth, I don't think I'll be able to forgive myself. I'm not even ready to forgive you.

H

Chapter Thirty-seven

I've never brought her to my house before, even though we've been dating for a month now. Hope spent a lot of time at our house when we were kids, so I'm worried my mother will recognize her and say something when she meets her. So until Sky knows the truth about her past, I don't want to risk her finding out from anyone other than me.

I don't want Sky to think I don't want her to be a part of my life by never allowing her to come to my house or meet my family, so I've taken the opportunity to bring her here tonight since I know my mother won't be home. And even though we're finally alone, kissing on my bed, I don't feel right about it. The night didn't start out well and the guilt from everything that has happened up to this point is in the forefront of my mind, even though I'd rather my mind be focused on the moment.

She's been distant all day and I should have known it was my fault somehow. After we left the art gallery where we went to support Breckin and his boyfriend, Max, she hardly spoke two words to me. I wondered if it had something to do with last night and sure enough, it had *everything* to do with last night.

After my mother's Halloween party at the law firm yesterday, where I may or may not have snuck too many drinks, I went to Sky's house and crawled through her window. Things were good and we fell asleep, only to wake up to her crying hysterically. She was crying and shaking and I've never seen anyone react to a nightmare like that.

Ever.

It scared the shit out of me. Mostly because I didn't know how to help her, but also because I really didn't know where the hell I was when I woke up next to her. I was still a little buzzed from the drinks and I had little recollection of even leaving my house and sneaking into her bedroom. It scared me to know that I was around her while I was incoherent. I was scared that I might have let something slip about her past. I held her until she stopped crying but then I left because I could still feel the effects of the alcohol and I really didn't want to say something to screw all this up.

But apparently I did, because earlier when we were downstairs, she said something about Hope. She said her name and it completely stunned me. Knocked the breath out of me. And if I wasn't trying my damndest to act like I didn't know what she was talking about, it would have knocked me to my knees.

But I let her explain herself and it turns out my fears were dead-on about being around her while I wasn't completely coherent. Apparently I mumbled Hope's name instead of Sky's, and for the entire past day she's been making herself sick about it. She's been thinking Hope was someone else entirely and the thought of her thinking I would want or need or even entertain the thought of another girl just completely breaks my heart.

So right now, I'm doing everything I can to show her that she's the only girl I think about.

Just her.

I'm kissing her, propped up on my hands and knees, attempting to avoid making her feel like I brought her here for anything other than to just spend time with her.

But she *is* wearing a dress again.

After those two hours in Daniel's basement I think we were both pretty impressed with how well my hands and her dress became acquainted. We were also pretty impressed with how well my hands and the clothing *under* her dress became acquainted.

But now, here she is, wearing a dress again. And we passed quite a few firsts on that couch two weeks ago. So much so that it pretty much only leaves one more first to pass tonight and the fact that she knows that and *I* know that and she's still wearing a dress has my mind jumbled and my heart racing.

It also didn't help matters that before we made it up here to the bedroom, we were making out on the stairs and she blurted out the fact that she was a virgin. I already knew she was a virgin, but just the fact that she was thinking about it while I was kissing her to the point that she actually blurted it out loud leads me to believe that she just wanted to warn me for when we got to that point.

And I'm thinking she's at that point, which is why she felt the need to clear the air downstairs, so she wouldn't have to say it when it actually came to that point.

To the point it's at right now.

The point at which I'm thanking the angels and the gods and the birds and the bees and sweet baby Jesus that she's wearing this dress. If there's one thing that can ease my guilt and allow me to focus solely on her for the time being, it's this dress.

"Holy shit, Sky," I say, kissing her madly. "God, you feel incredible. Thank you for wearing this dress. I really . . ." I kiss down her chin until my lips meet her neck. "I really like it. Your dress." I continue kissing her neck and she tilts her head back, allowing me easier access. I drop my hand to her thigh and run it up under her dress. When I reach the top of her thigh I desperately want to keep going. But the fact that she's allowed me there once before doesn't mean I'm allowed there right now.

But apparently I am, because she twists her body more toward mine, directing my hand to keep heading where it's heading. Her hands crawl up my back just as my hand greets the panties lining her hip. I slip my fingers underneath the lining and begin to tug at the same time she pulls on my shirt.

She begins to pull it over my head and I'm forced to move my hand away. I squeeze her thigh, not wanting to have to pull back, but I'm pretty sure I want my shirt off just as much as she wants it off.

As soon as I lift up onto my knees, away from her, she whimpers. The sound makes me smile and after my shirt is off, I bend forward and kiss the corner of her lips. I bring my hand to her face and gently stroke her hairline, watching her. I know we're about to pass the most significant first of all and I want to memorize everything about this moment. I want to remember exactly what she looks like lying beneath me. I want to remember exactly what she sounds like the moment I'm inside her. I want to remember what she tastes like and what she feels like and what she—

"Holder," she says, breathlessly.

"Sky," I say, mimicking her. I don't know what she's about to say but whatever it is, it can wait a few seconds, because I need to kiss her again. I dip my head and part her lips until our tongues meet. We kiss slowly while I memorize every inch of her mouth.

"Holder," she says again, pulling away from my mouth. She brings her hand to my cheek and looks up into my eyes. "I want to. Tonight. Right now."

Right now. She said *right now.* That's nice because I conveniently don't have any prior engagements right now. I can do right now.

"Sky . . ." I say, wanting to make sure she's not doing this just to benefit me. "We don't have to. I want you to be absolutely positive it's what you want. Okay? I don't want to rush you into anything."

She smiles and strokes her fingernails up and down my arms. "I know that. But I'm telling you I want this. I've never wanted it with anyone before, but I want it with you."

There's no doubt in my mind that I want her. I want her *right now* and she obviously wants me, too. But I can't help but feel guilty, knowing I'm still deceiving her. I haven't told her the truth about us and I feel like if she knew, she wouldn't be making this decision.

I'm about to pull away from her until she places her hand on my cheeks and lifts herself off the bed until her lips are touching mine. "This isn't me saying *yes*, Holder. This is me saying *please*."

What was it I was thinking just now? Something about waiting? *Fuck that.*

Our lips collide and I groan, pushing her back against the bed. "We're really doing this?" I ask, not really believing it myself.

"Yes." She laughs. "We're really doing this. I've never been more positive of anything in my life."

My hand resumes its position and I begin to pull down her panties.

"I just need you to promise me one thing first," she says.

I pull my hand away, thinking maybe she's about to tell me to go a little slower. "Anything."

She takes my hand and places it right back on her hip. "I want to do this," she says, firmly looking into my eyes. "But only if you promise we'll break the record for the best first time in the history of first times."

I smile. *Damn straight.* "When it's you and me, Sky . . . it'll never be anything less."

I slide my arm underneath her back and pull her up. I curl my fingers underneath the straps of her dress, then slowly slide them down her arms. She fists one of her hands through my hair, pressing her cheek to mine while my lips meet her shoulder. My fingers are still holding on to the straps of her dress.

"I'm taking it off."

She nods and I grab the loose material at her waist and begin to lift the dress over her head. Once it's completely off, I lower her back down onto the bed and she opens her eyes. I scroll over her body, running my hand down her arm and across her stomach, coming to rest on the curve of her hip. I let everything I'm seeing sink in because this is what I want to remember the most. I want to remember exactly what she looks like the second she hands over a piece of her heart.

"Holy shit, Sky," I whisper, running my hands across her skin. I bend down and kiss her softly on the stomach. "You're incredible."

I watch my hand as it glides across her body. I watch as it slides up her stomach and meets her breast. I watch my thumb disappear beneath her bra. As soon as my entire hand has slipped beneath her bra, she's locking her legs around my waist. I groan and wish at this point that I had more hands because they want to be everywhere, all at once. And I don't want there to be any material in the way of their journey.

I reach down and pull her underwear off, then remove her bra. I'm kissing her the whole time, even when I slide off the bed to remove the rest of my own clothes. I climb back onto the bed with her. Back on top of her.

As soon as I'm pressed against her I'm hit with the revelation that I've never experienced or felt anything like her in my life. This is how it should be when people pass this first. This is exactly how it should feel and it's incredible.

I reach across the bed and pull a condom out of my nightstand. We haven't stopped kissing for a single second, but I need to see her face. I need to see that she wants me to be inside her as much as I want to *be* inside her.

I grab the condom and lift up onto my knees. I open it, but before I put it on I look down at her. Her eyes are closed tightly and her eyebrows are drawn together.

"Sky?" I say. I want her to open her eyes. I just need one final look of reassurance from her, but she fails to open her eyes. I lower myself on top of her again, stroking her cheek. "Babe," I whisper. "Open your eyes."

Her lips begin to tremble and she pulls her arms up, crossing them over her eyes. "Get off me," she whispers.

My heart sinks, not knowing what I did wrong. I've done everything I could to make this right but it's obviously gone wrong somewhere and I have no idea where. I sit up on my knees and scoot away from her just as a violent sob breaks from her. She twists away from me and hugs her arms, covering herself. "*Please*," she cries.

"Sky, I stopped," I say, stroking her arm. She pushes my hand away with her own and her whole body starts to shake. Her lips are moving and she's speaking under her breath, but I can't hear what she's saying. I lean forward to try and hear what she's trying to tell me.

"Twenty-eight, twenty-nine, thirty, thirty-one . . ."

She's counting in rapid succession and crying hysterically, curling herself into a ball on my mattress.

"Sky!" I say louder, trying to get her to stop. I don't know what the hell is wrong or what I did but this isn't her and it's starting to freak me out. She's responding like I'm not even here. I try to pull her arm away from her eyes so she'll look at me, but she starts slapping my hand away, crying hysterically.

"Dammit, Sky!" I yell, frantic. I pull on her arm again but she's fighting it. I don't know what to do or why she won't snap out of this, so I scoop her up into my arms and pull her against my chest. She's still counting and crying and I think I might be on the verge of crying, too, because she's losing it and I have no idea how to help her. I rock her back and forth and brush the hair from her face, trying to get her to snap out of it, but she just continues to cry. I pull the sheet up and wrap it around us, then kiss her on the side of her head. "I'm sorry," I whisper, at a loss for what to do next.

Her eyes flick open and she looks up at me, her whole being consumed with fear. "I'm sorry, Sky," I say, still not knowing what went wrong or why she's terrified of me right now. "I'm so sorry."

I continue to rock her, still not understanding what's causing her reaction, but I've never seen eyes so terrified before and I have no fucking clue how to calm her down.

"What happened?" she cries, still looking at me with eyes full of fear.

She completely checked out and she doesn't even remember doing it?

"I don't know," I tell her, shaking my head. "You just started counting and crying and shaking and I kept trying to get you to stop, Sky. You wouldn't stop. You were terrified. What did I do? Tell me, because I'm so sorry. I am so, so sorry. What the fuck did I do?"

She shakes her head, unable to answer me. It kills me that I don't know if I did something wrong to force her so far into her own head that she lost her grasp on reality.

I squeeze my eyes shut and press my forehead to hers. "I'm so sorry. I never should have let it go that far. I don't know what the hell just happened, but you're not ready yet, okay?"

She nods, still holding on to me tightly. "So we didn't . . . we didn't have sex?" she asks timidly.

My heart sinks because I realize with those words that no matter what I try to do to protect her, there's something tearing her apart. She completely checked out like I've never experienced before and there was nothing in my power I could do to stop it. I bring my hands to her cheeks. "Where'd you go, Sky?"

She looks at me confused and shakes her head. "I'm right here. I'm listening."

"No, I mean earlier. Where'd you go? You weren't here with me because no, nothing happened. I could see on your face that something was wrong, so I didn't do it. But now you need to think long and hard about where you were inside that head of yours, because you were panicked. You were hysterical and I need to know what it was that took you there so I can make sure you never go back."

I squeeze her tight, then kiss her on the forehead. I know she probably needs to regain her bearings right now, so I stand up and pull on my jeans and T-shirt, then help her back into her dress. "I'll go get you some water. I'll be right back." I lean forward, not sure if she even wants me near her right now, but I kiss her on the lips to reassure her.

I walk out of my room and head straight down to the kitchen. As soon as my elbows meet the countertop, I bury my face in my arms and muster up every ounce of willpower in me to stop myself from breaking down. I inhale several deep breaths, exhaling even bigger ones, hoping I can stay strong for her. But seeing her that helpless and knowing there was nothing I could do to help her?

It's the most disappointed in myself I've ever been.

Chapter Thirty-eight

I'm still leaning on the counter with my head in my hands when I hear a door close upstairs. I've been down here for several minutes now and I don't want her to think I'm trying to avoid her, so I head back upstairs. I check the bedroom and bathroom, but she's not in either. I look at Les's bedroom door and pause before reaching down and turning the knob.

She's sitting on Les's bed, holding a picture. "What are you doing?" I ask her. I don't know why she's in here. I don't want to be in here and I want her to come back to my room with me.

"I was looking for the bathroom," she says quietly. "I'm sorry. I just needed a second."

I nod, since I apparently needed a second, too. I look around the room. I haven't set foot in here since the day I found the notebook. Her jeans are still in the middle of the floor, right where she left them.

"Has no one been in here? Since she . . ."

"No," I say, not wanting to hear her finish that sentence. "What would be the point of it? She's gone."

She nods, then places the picture back down on the nightstand. "Was she dating him?"

Her question throws me for a second, then I realize she must have seen a picture of Les and Grayson together. I never told her they dated. I should have told her.

I step into the bedroom for the first time in over a year. I walk to the bed and take a seat next to her. I slowly scan the room, wondering why my mom and I thought it would be a better idea to just close the door after she died, rather than get rid of her things. I guess neither of us is ready to let her go just yet.

I glance at Sky and she's still looking at the picture frame on Les's nightstand. I wrap my arm around her shoulders and pull her to me. She brings a hand to my chest and clenches my shirt in her fist.

"He broke up with her the night before she did it," I say, giving her an explanation. I don't really want to talk about it, but the only other thing left to talk about is what just happened in my bed and I know Sky more than likely needs a little more time before we bring that up.

"Do you think he's the reason why she did it? Is that why you hate him so much?"

I shake my head. "I hated him before he broke up with her. He put her through a lot of shit, Sky. And no, I don't think he's why she did it. I think maybe it was the deciding factor in a decision she had wanted to make for a long time. She had issues way before Grayson ever came into the picture. So no, I don't blame him. I never have." I grab her hand and stand up, because I honestly don't want to talk about it. I thought I could, but I can't. "Come on. I don't want to be in here anymore."

I take her hand and she stands up, then we walk toward the door. She yanks her hand free once I reach the door, so I turn around. She's staring at a picture of me and Les when we were kids.

She's smiling at the picture, but my pulse immediately quickens when I realize that she's seeing me and Les as children. She's seeing us in the exact way she used to know us. I don't want her to remember. If she were to have even the slightest recollection right now, she might start asking questions. The last thing she needs after the breakdown she just had is to find out the truth.

She squeezes her eyes shut for a few seconds and the look on her face kicks my pulse up a notch. "You okay?" I ask, attempting to pull the picture out of her hands. She immediately snatches it back and looks up at me.

It's the first sign of recognition I've seen on her face and it feels like my entire body is wilting.

I manage to take a step toward her, but she immediately takes a step back. She keeps looking at the picture, then back up to me and I just want to grab the frame and throw it across the fucking room and pull her out of here, but I have a feeling it's too late.

Her hand goes up to her mouth and she chokes back a sob. She looks up at me like she wants to say something, but she can't speak.

"Sky, no," I whisper.

"How?" she says achingly, looking back down at the picture. "There's a swing set. And a well. And . . . your cat. It got stuck in the well. Holder, I know that living room. The living room is green and the kitchen had a countertop that was way too tall for us and . . . your mother. Your mother's name is Beth." Her rush of words come to a pause and she darts her eyes back up to mine. "Holder?" she says, sucking in a breath. "Is Beth your mother's name?"

Not tonight, not tonight. God, she doesn't *need* this tonight. "Sky . . ."

She looks at me, heartbroken. She rushes past me and across the hall, into the bathroom, where she slams the door behind her. I follow after her and try to open the door but she's locked it.

"Sky, open the door. Please."

Nothing. She doesn't open the door and she says nothing.

"Baby, please. We need to talk and I can't do it from out here. Please, open the door."

Another moment passes without her opening the door. I grip the edges of the doorframe and wait. It's too late to backtrack now. All I can do is wait until she's ready to hear the truth.

The door swings open and she's looking at me, her eyes full of anger now rather than fear.

"Who's Hope?" she says, barely above a whisper.

How do I say it? How do I tell her the answer to that question, because as soon as I do I know I'll have to watch as her entire world collapses around her.

"Who the hell is Hope?" she says, much louder this time.

I can't. I can't tell her. She'll hate me and that would destroy me.

Her eyes fill with tears. "Is it me?" she asks, her voice barely audible. "Holder . . . am I Hope?"

A rush of breath escapes my lungs and I can feel the tears following. I look up to the ceiling to try to hold them back. I close my eyes and press my forehead against my arm, inhaling the breath that will encase the voice that will release the one word that will destroy her again.

"Yes."

Her eyes grow wide and she just stands there, slowly shaking her head. I can't even imagine what must be going through her head right now.

She suddenly shoves past me, out into the hallway. "Sky, wait," I yell as she descends the steps two at a time. I rush after her, trying to catch her before she leaves. As soon as she hits the bottom step, she collapses to the floor.

"Sky!" I drop to my knees and take her in my arms, but she's pushing against me. I can't let her run. She needs to know the rest of the truth before she leaves here.

"Outside," she breathes. "I just need outside. Please, Holder."

I know how it feels to need air this badly. I release my hold and look her in the eyes. "Don't run, Sky. Go outside, but please don't leave. We need to talk."

She nods and I help her stand up. She walks outside and into the front yard where she tilts her head back and stares up at the stars.

Up at the sky.

I watch her the whole time, wanting nothing more than to hold her. But I know that's the last thing she wants right now. She knows I've been lying to her and she has every right to hate me.

After a while, she finally turns and heads back inside. She brushes past me without making eye contact and she walks straight into the kitchen. She takes a bottle of water out of the fridge and opens it, downing several gulps before finally making eye contact with me.

"Take me home."

I'll get her out of the house, but I'm not taking her home.

We're at the airport now. I couldn't think of anywhere else quiet enough to take her and I refused to take her home until she asked me everything she needs to ask me. The only thing she asked me with any sincerity on the way here was why I got my tattoo. I told her the same thing I told her last time she asked me about it; only this time I think she actually understood.

"Are you ready for answers?" I ask her. We've been silently watching the stars for several minutes now. I'm just trying to give her a chance to calm down. To clear her head.

"I'm ready if you're actually planning on being honest this time," she says, anger lacing her voice.

I turn to face her and the hurt in her eyes is as prominent as the stars in the sky. I lift up onto my elbow and look down at her.

Just a while ago I was looking down at her this same way, memorizing everything about her. When we were in that moment on my bed I was looking at her with so much hope. I felt like she was mine and I was hers and that moment and feeling would last forever. But now, looking down at her . . . I feel like it's all about to end.

I lower my hand to her face and touch her. "I need to kiss you."

She shakes her head. "No," she says resolutely.

I feel like tonight is the end of us and if she doesn't let me kiss her one more time it'll kill me. "I need to kiss you," I say again. "Please, Sky. I'm scared that after I tell you what I'm about to tell you . . . I'll never get to kiss you again." I grasp her face harder and pull her closer. *"Please."*

Her eyes are desperately searching mine, possibly to see if there's any shred of truth behind my words. She doesn't say anything. She just barely nods, but it's enough. I lower my head and press my lips firmly against hers. She grasps my forearm with her hand and parts her lips, allowing me to kiss her more intimately.

We continue to kiss for several minutes, because I don't know that either of us wants to face the truth just yet. I lift up onto my knees without breaking away from her and I climb on top of her. She runs her hand through my hair and to the back of my head, where she pulls against me, urging me closer.

She begins to clench my shirt with her fists as a cry breaks free from her throat. I move my lips to her cheek and kiss her softly, then lower my mouth to her ear. "I'm so sorry," I whisper, holding on to her with my free hand. "I'm so sorry. I didn't want you to know."

She pushes me off her, then sits up. She pulls her knees to her chest and buries her face in them.

"I just want you to talk, Holder. I asked you everything I could ever ask you on the way here. I need you to answer me now so I can just go home," she says, sounding tired and exhausted. I stroke her hair and give her the answers she needs.

"I wasn't sure if you were Hope the first time I saw you. I was so used to seeing her in every single stranger our age, I had given up trying to find her a few years ago. But when I saw you at the store and looked into your eyes . . . I had a feeling you really were her. When you showed me your ID and I realized you weren't, I felt ridiculous.

It was like the wake-up call I needed to finally just let the memory of her go.

"We lived next door to you and your dad for a year. You and me and Les . . . we were all best friends. It's so hard to remember faces from that long ago, though. I thought you were Hope, but I also thought that if you really were her, I wouldn't be doubting it. I thought if I ever saw her again, I'd know for sure.

"When I left the grocery store that day, I immediately looked up the name you gave me online. I couldn't find anything about you, not even on Facebook. I searched for an hour straight and became so frustrated that I went for a run to cool down. When I rounded the corner and saw you standing in front of my house, I couldn't breathe. You were just standing there, worn out and exhausted from running and . . . *Jesus*, Sky. You were so beautiful. I still wasn't sure if you were Hope or not, but at that point it wasn't even going through my mind. I didn't care who you were; I just needed to know you.

"After spending time with you that week, I couldn't stop myself from going to your house that Friday night. I didn't show up with the intention of digging up your past or even in the hope that something would happen between us. I went to your house because I wanted you to know the real me, not the me you had heard about from everyone else. After spending more time with you that night, I couldn't think of anything else besides figuring out how I could spend more time with you. I had never met anyone who got me the way you did. I still wondered if it was possible . . . if you were her. I was especially curious after you told me you were adopted, but again, I thought maybe it was a coincidence.

"But then when I saw the bracelet . . ."

I need her to look me in the eyes for this, so I lift her chin and make her look at me.

"My heart broke, Sky. I didn't want you to be her. I wanted you to tell me you got the bracelet from your friend or that you found it or you bought it. After all the years I spent searching for you in every single face I ever looked at, I finally found you . . . and I was devastated." As soon as I say the word, I regret it. Because I know that isn't true. I was upset. I was overwhelmed. But I didn't even know the meaning of devastated. I sigh and finish my confession. "I didn't want you to be Hope. I just wanted you to be you."

She shakes her head. "But why didn't you just tell me? How hard would it have been to admit that we used to know each other? I don't understand why you've been lying about it."

God, this is so hard.

"What do you remember about your adoption?"

"Not a lot," she says, shaking her head. "I know I was in foster care after my father gave me up. I know Karen adopted me and we moved here from out of state when I was five. Other than that and a few odd memories, I don't know anything."

She's not getting it. That's not what *she* remembers at all. It's what she's been *told*. I move from my position beside her and sit directly in front of her, facing her. I grab her by the shoulders. "That's all stuff Karen told you. I want to know what *you* remember. What do *you* remember, Sky?"

She breaks eye contact with me, trying to think. When she comes up empty, she looks back up at me. "Nothing. The earliest memories I have are with Karen. The only thing I remember from before Karen was getting the bracelet, but that's only because I still have it and the memory stuck with me. I wasn't even sure who gave it to me."

I lower my lips to her forehead and kiss her, knowing the next words that come out of my mouth will be the words I know she doesn't want to hear. As if she can see how much this is hurting me, she wraps her arms around my neck and climbs onto my lap, holding me tightly. I wrap my arms around her, not quite understanding how she can even find it in herself to want to comfort me right now.

"Just say it," she whispers. "Tell me what you're wishing you didn't have to tell me."

I lower my head to hers, squeezing my eyes shut. She thinks she wants to know the truth, but she doesn't. If she could feel what it's about to do to her, she wouldn't want to know.

"Just tell me, Holder."

I sigh, then pull away from her. "The day Les gave you that bracelet, you were crying. I remember every single detail like it happened yesterday. You were sitting in your yard against your house. Les and I sat with you for a long time, but you never stopped crying. After she gave you your bracelet she walked back to our house but I couldn't. I felt bad leaving you there, because I thought you might be mad at your dad again. You were always crying because of him and it made me hate him. I don't remember anything about the guy, other than I hated his guts for making you feel like you did. I was just a kid, so I never knew what to say to you when you cried. I think that day I said something like, 'Don't worry . . .'"

"He won't live forever," she says, finishing my sentence. "I remember that day. Les giving me the bracelet and you saying he won't live forever. Those are the two things I've remembered all this time. I just didn't know it was you."

"Yeah, that's what I said to you." I take her face in my hands. "And then I did something I've regretted every single day of my life since."

"Holder," she says, shaking her head. "You didn't do anything. You just walked away."

I nod. "Exactly. I walked to my front yard even though I knew I should have sat back down in the grass beside you. I stood in my front yard and I watched you cry into your arms, when you should have been crying into mine. I just stood there . . . and I watched the car pull up to the curb. I watched the passenger window roll down and I heard someone call your name. I watched you look up at the car and wipe your eyes. You stood up and you dusted off your shorts, then you walked to the car. I watched you climb inside and I knew whatever was happening I shouldn't have just been standing there. But all I did was watch, when I should have been with you. It never would have happened if I had stayed right there with you."

She takes a deep breath. "*What* never would have happened?"

I brush my thumbs over her cheekbones and look at her with as much calmness and reassurance as I can muster, because I know she's about to need it.

"They took you. Whoever was in that car, they took you from your dad, from me, from Les. You've been missing for thirteen years, Hope."

Chapter Thirty-nine, Chapter Thirty-nine-and-a-half, Chapter Thirty-nine-and-three-quarters

She closes her eyes and lays her head on my shoulder. She tightens her grip around me, so I tighten mine in return. I wait. I wait for it to sink in. I wait for the tears. I wait for the heartbreak because I know for a fact it's coming.

We sit in silence for several minutes, but the tears never come. I begin to wonder if everything I just said to her is even registering. "Say something," I beg.

She doesn't make a sound. She doesn't even move. Her lack of reaction is starting to worry me, so I place my hand on the back of her head and lower my head closer to hers. "*Please*. Say something."

She slowly lifts her face away from my shoulder and she looks at me with dry eyes. "You called me Hope. Don't call me that. It's not my name."

I didn't even realize I did. "I'm sorry, Sky."

Her eyes grow cold and she slides off me, then stands up. "Don't call me that, either," she says.

I stand up and take both of her hands, but she pulls away and turns toward the car. I haven't really thought out what I would do or say after she finally found out the truth from me. I'm not at all prepared for whatever comes next.

"I need a chapter break," she says, continuing to walk away.

"I don't even know what that means," I say, following behind her. Whatever she needs, it's more than just a chapter break. She needs a chapter break within a chapter break within a chapter break. I can't imagine how confused she must be right now.

She continues to walk away so I grab her arm but she immediately jerks away from me. She spins around and her eyes are wide with fear and confusion. She begins to take deep breaths like she's attempting to hold off a panic attack. I don't know what to say to her and I know she doesn't want me to touch her right now.

She takes two quick steps forward and she reaches up and grabs my face, standing on the tips of her toes. She presses her lips firmly to mine and kisses me desperately, but I can't find it in me to kiss her back. I know she's just scared and confused right now and she's doing whatever she can to not think about it.

She pulls away from my mouth when she realizes I'm not kissing her back, then she reaches up and slaps me.

What she's experiencing right now is more than likely more traumatic and more emotional than anything someone can experience in life, short of death. I try to remember that when she reaches up and slaps me again, then pushes against my chest. Panic consumes her completely and she's screaming and hitting me and the only thing I can do is spin her around and pull her against my chest. I wrap my arms around her from behind and press my lips to her ear. "Breathe," I whisper. "Calm down, Sky. I know you're confused and scared, but I'm here. I'm right here. Just breathe."

I hold her for several minutes, allowing her time to gather her thoughts. I know she has questions. I just need her mind to the point that it can handle all the answers.

"Were you ever going to tell me who I was?" she asks after she pulls away from me. "What if I never remembered? Would you have ever told me? Were you scared I would leave you and you'd never get your chance to screw me? Is that why you've been lying to me this whole time?"

The questions she just asked have all been my biggest fears. I've been so scared she wouldn't understand my reasoning for not telling her. "No. That's not how it was. That's not how it *is*. I haven't told you because I'm scared of what will happen to you. If I report it, they'll take you from Karen. They'll more than likely arrest her and send you back to live with your father until you turn eighteen. Do you want that to happen? You love Karen and you're happy here. I didn't want to mess that up for you."

She shakes her head and laughs a disheartening laugh. "First of all," she says. "They wouldn't put Karen in jail because I can guarantee you she knows nothing about this. Second, I've been eighteen since September. If my age was the reason you weren't being honest, you would have told me by now."

I look down at the ground because it's too hard to look her in the eyes.

"Sky, there's so much I still need to explain to you," I say. "Your birthday wasn't in September. Your birthday is May 7. You don't even turn eighteen for six more months. And Karen?" I walk forward and take her hands. "She has to know, Sky. She *has* to. Think about it. Who else could have done this?"

As soon as I say it, she pulls her hands from mine and steps back like I've just insulted her.

"Take me home," she says, shaking her head in disbelief. "I don't want to hear anything else. I don't want to know anything else tonight."

I grab her by the hands again and she slaps them away. "TAKE ME HOME!"

We're parked in her driveway sitting silently in her car. I made her promise me she wouldn't say anything to Karen during the drive back to her house. She says she isn't going to say anything until we talk again tomorrow, but I still don't like the thought of leaving her here in the condition she's in.

She pulls open the door, but I grab her hand. "Wait," I say. She pauses. "Will you be okay tonight?"

She sighs and falls back against the passenger seat. *"How?"* she says with a defeated voice. "How can I possibly be okay after tonight?"

I push her hair behind her ear. I don't want to leave her. I want to reassure her that I'm not walking away from her this time. "It's killing me . . . letting you go like this," I say. "I don't want to leave you alone. Can I come back in an hour?"

She shakes her head no. "I can't," she says weakly. "It's too hard being around you right now. I just need to think. I'll see you tomorrow, okay?"

I nod, then pull my hand back and place it on the steering wheel. As much as it hurts, I need to give her what she wants right now. I know she needs time to process all the things going through her mind. To be honest, I think I need time to process it, too.

Chapter Forty

Les,

She knows.
And I can't believe I just dropped her off at her house and left. I don't care if she doesn't want to be around me right now. There's no way in hell I can just leave her alone. I wish you were here right now because I don't know what the hell I'm doing.

H

I shoot straight up when I hear her scream next to me on her bed. She's gasping for breath.

Another nightmare.

"What the hell are you doing here?" she says.

I glance down at my watch, then rub my eyes. I'm trying to sort out what all has been real in the past few hours and what all was a dream.

Unfortunately, it was *all* real.

I place my hand on her leg and scoot closer to her. Her eyes are terrified. "I couldn't leave you. I just needed to make sure you were okay." I slide my hand around her neck and her pulse is pounding against my palm. "Your heart. You're scared."

She's looking at me wide-eyed. Her chest is heaving and the fear rolling off her is breaking me. She brings her hand to mine and squeezes it. "Holder . . . I remember."

I immediately turn her to face me and I force her eyes up to mine. "What do you remember?" I ask, nervous for her answer.

She begins to shake her head, not wanting to say it. I need her to say it, though. I need to know what she remembers. I nod my head, silently coaxing her to continue. She takes a deep breath. "It was Karen in that car. She did it. She's the one who took me."

This is exactly what I didn't want her to feel. I hug her. "I know, babe. I know."

She clings to my shirt and I tighten my grip, but push her away as soon as her bedroom door swings open.

"Sky?" Karen says, watching us from the doorway.

Karen looks at me, trying to figure out why I'm here. She turns back to Sky. "Sky? What . . . what are you doing?"

Sky spins back around and looks me desperately in the eyes. "Get me out of here," she begs in a whisper. "Please."

I nod, then stand up and walk to her closet. I don't know where she wants to go, but I know she'll need clothes. I find a duffel bag on the top shelf, then walk it to her bed. "Throw some clothes in here. I'll get what you need out of the bathroom."

She nods and heads to her closet while I head into her bathroom to grab whatever else she might need. Karen is pleading with her not to leave. When my hands are full, I walk out of the bathroom and Karen has her hands on Sky's shoulders.

"What are you doing? What's wrong with you? You're not leaving with him."

I walk around Karen and try to remain as calm as possible for all of our sakes. "Karen, I suggest you let go of her."

Karen spins around, shocked at my words. "You are *not* taking her. If you so much as walk out of this house with her, I'm calling the police."

I don't say anything. I'm not sure if Sky wants her to know that she knows the truth, so I do my best to refrain from saying what I've wanted to say to Karen since the moment I realized she's the one responsible. I zip the duffel bag and reach for Sky's hand. "You ready?"

She nods.

"This isn't a joke!" Karen yells. "I'll call the police! You have no right to take her!"

Sky reaches into my pocket and pulls out my cell phone, then steps toward Karen. "Here," she says. "Call them."

She's testing Karen. Her wheels are churning as fast as mine and she's hoping she can prove that Karen is innocent in all of this. It makes my heart break for her, because I know Karen isn't innocent. This is only going to end badly.

Karen refuses to take the phone and Sky grabs her hand and shoves the phone into her palm. "Call them! Call the police, Mom! *Please*," she says. Sky's eyebrows draw apart and she pleads desperately, one last time. "Please," she whispers.

I can't watch Sky endure this for another second, so I grab her hand and lead her to the window, then help her climb out of it.

Chapter Forty-one

I lift my head off the pillow and immediately cover my eyes. The afternoon sun is so bright, it's painful. I pry my arm from around her and quietly lift off the bed.

I somehow managed the whole drive to Austin last night. I don't think I could have stayed awake another minute, so I pulled over at the first hotel we could find. It was daytime when we finally made it to our room, so we both took turns showering, then crashed. She's been asleep for over six hours now and I know how much she needs it.

I softly brush the hair away from her cheek and lean down and kiss it. She pulls her arm out from under the blanket and looks up at me with tired eyes. "Hey," she whispers, somehow smiling despite everything she's going through.

"Shh," I say, not wanting her to wake up just yet. "I'm about to leave for a little while to get us something to eat. I'll wake you when I get back, okay?"

She nods and closes her eyes, then rolls back over.

After we finish eating, she walks to the bed and slips on her shoes. "Where you headed?" I ask her.

She ties her shoes and stands up, wrapping her arms around my neck. "I want to go for a walk," she says. "And I want you to go with me. I'm ready to start asking questions."

I give her a quick kiss, then grab the key and head to the door. "Then let's go."

We eventually make our way to the hotel courtyard and take a seat in one of the cabanas. I pull her to me. "You want me to tell you what I remember? Or do you have specific questions?"

"Both," she says. "But I want to hear your story first."

I kiss her on the side of the head, then rest my head against hers while we stare out over the courtyard. "You have to understand how surreal this feels for me, Sky. I've thought about what happened to you every single day for the past thirteen years. And to think I've been living two miles away from you for seven of those years? I'm still having a hard time processing it myself. And now, finally having you here, telling you everything that happened . . ."

I sigh, remembering back to that day. "After the car pulled away, I went into the house and told Les that you left with someone. She kept asking me who, but I didn't know. My mother was in the kitchen, so I went and told her. She didn't really pay any attention to me. She was cooking supper and we were just kids. She had learned to tune us out. Besides, I still wasn't sure anything had happened that wasn't supposed to happen, so I didn't sound panicked or anything. She told me to just go outside and play with Les. The way she was so nonchalant about it made me think everything was okay. Being so young, I was positive adults knew everything, so I didn't say anything else about it. Les and I went outside to play and another couple of hours had passed by when your dad came outside, calling your name. As soon as I heard him call your name, I froze. I stopped in the middle of my yard and watched him standing on his porch, calling for you. It was that moment that I knew he had no idea you had left with someone. I knew I did something wrong."

"Holder," she interrupts. "You were just a little boy."

Yeah. A little boy who was old enough to know the difference between right and wrong. "Your dad walked over to our yard and asked me if I knew where you were." This is where it gets hard for me. This is the point I realized the awful mistake I had made. "Sky, you have to understand something," I say to her. "I was scared of your father. I was just a kid and knew I had just done something terribly wrong by leaving you alone. Now your police chief father is standing over me, his gun visible on his uniform. I panicked. I ran back into my house and ran straight to my bedroom and locked the door. He and my mother beat on the door for half an hour, but I was too scared to open it and admit to them that I knew what happened. My reaction worried both of them, so he immediately radioed for backup. When I heard the police cars pull up outside, I thought they were there for me. I still didn't understand what had happened to you. By the time my mother coaxed me out of the room, three hours had already passed since you left in the car."

She can feel how much this hurts me to talk about. She pulls one of her hands out of the sleeve of her shirt and places it in mine.

"I was taken to the station and questioned for hours. They wanted to know if I knew the license plate number, what kind of car took you, what the person looked like, what they said to you. Sky, I didn't know *anything*. I couldn't even remember the color of the car. All I could tell them was exactly what you were wearing, because you were the only thing I could picture in my head. Your dad was furious with me. I could hear him yelling in the hallway of the station that if I had just told someone right when it happened, they would have been able to find you. He blamed me. When a police officer blames you for losing his daughter, you tend to believe he knows what he's talking about. Les heard him yelling, too, so she thought it was all my fault. For days, she wouldn't even talk to me. Both of us were trying to understand what had happened. For almost six years we lived in this perfect world where adults are always right and bad things don't happen to good people. Then, in the span of a minute, you were taken and everything we thought we knew turned out to be this false image of life that our parents had built for us. We realized that day that even adults do horrible things. Children disappear. Best friends get taken from you and you have no idea if they're even alive anymore.

"We watched the news constantly, waiting for reports. For weeks they would show your picture on TV, asking for leads. The most recent picture they had of you was from right before your mother died, when you were only three. I remember that pissing me off, wondering how almost two years could have gone by without some-one having taken a more recent picture. They would show pictures of your house and would sometimes show our house, too. Every now and then, they would mention the boy next door who saw it happen, but couldn't remember any details. I remember one night . . . the last night my mother allowed us to watch the coverage on TV . . . one of the reporters showed a panned-out image of both our houses. They mentioned the only witness, but referred to me as '*The boy who lost Hope.*' It infuriated my mother so bad; she ran outside and began screaming at the reporters, yelling at them to leave us alone. To leave *me* alone. My dad had to drag her back inside the house.

"My parents did their best to try to make our life as normal as possible. After a couple of months, the reporters stopped showing up. The endless trips to the police station for more questioning finally stopped. Things began to slowly return to normal for everyone in the neighborhood. Everyone but Les and me. It was like all of our hope was taken right along with our Hope."

She sighs when I've finished and she's quiet for a while. "I've spent so many years hating my father for giving up on me," she says. "I can't believe she just took me from him. How could she do that? How could *anyone* do that?"

"I don't know, babe."

She sits up in the chair and looks me in the eyes. "I need to see the house," she says. "I want more memories, but I don't have any and right now it's hard. I can barely remember anything, much less him. I just want to drive by. I need to see it."

"Right now?"

"Yes. I want to go before it gets dark."

Chapter Forty-two

I should never have let her come here. As soon as we pulled up in front of the house, I could tell just looking at it wouldn't be enough for her. Sure enough, she got out of the car and demanded to see the inside of it. I tried to talk her out of it, but I can do only so much.

I'm standing outside her window, waiting. I don't want her to be in there right now, but I could clearly see that she's not having it any other way. I lean against the house and hope she hurries the hell up. It doesn't look like any of the neighbors are home, but that doesn't mean her father isn't going to drive up any second now.

I look down at the ground beneath my feet, then glance behind me at the house. This is the exact spot she was standing in when I walked away from her thirteen years ago. I close my eyes and rest my head against the house. I never expected I'd ever be back here with her again.

My eyes flash open and I stand up straight the second I hear the crash come from inside her bedroom, followed by screaming. I don't give myself time to question what the hell is going on in there. I just run.

I run through the back door and down the hall until I'm in her old bedroom with her. She's crying hysterically and throwing things across the room, so I immediately wrap my arms around her from behind to calm her down. I have no idea what the hell brought this on, but I'm at an even bigger loss how to stop it. She's frantically jerking against me, attempting to get out of my hold, but I just grip her even tighter. "Stop," I say against her ear. She's still frantic and I need her to calm down before someone hears her.

"Don't touch me!" she screams. She claws at my arms but I don't relent, even for a second. She eventually weakens and becomes defeated by whatever it is that has hold of her mind right now. She grows limp in my arms and I know I need to get her out of here, but I can't have her reacting like this once I get her outside.

I loosen my grip and turn her around to face me. She falls against my chest and sobs, grabbing fistfuls of my shirt while she tries to hold herself up. I lower my mouth to her ear.

"Sky. You need to leave. Now." I'm trying to be strong for her, but I also need her to know that being here is a very bad idea. Especially after she's just destroyed the entire room. He'll know someone was here for a fact now, so we need to leave.

I pick her up and carry her out of the bedroom. She keeps her face buried in my chest while I walk her outside and to the car. I reach into the backseat and hand her my jacket.

"Here, use that to wipe off the blood. I'm going back inside to straighten up what I can."

I watch her for a few seconds to make sure she's not about to panic again, then I shut the door and head back inside to her bedroom. I straighten up what I can, but the mirror is a hard one to cover up. I'm hoping that her father doesn't come into this room very often. If I can make it look like nothing outside this room was disturbed, it could be weeks before he even notices the mirror.

I put the blanket back on the bed and hang the curtains back up, then head back outside. When I reach the car, just the sight of her is enough to nearly bring me to my knees.

This isn't her.

She's scared. Broken. She's shaking and crying and I'm wondering for the first time if any of the decisions I've made over the last twenty-four hours have been smart ones.

I put the car in drive and pull away from the house, never wanting to see it or think about it again. I hope to hell she doesn't, either. I place my hand on the back of her head, which is tucked against her knees. I run my fingers through her hair and don't move my hand away from her the entire drive back to the hotel. I need her to know that I'm here. That no matter how she feels right now, she's not alone. If I've learned anything from losing her all those years ago or from what happened with Les, it's that I never want to let her feel alone again.

Once we're back inside the hotel room, I help her down onto the bed, then grab a wet rag and come back and inspect the cuts.

"It's just a few scratches," I say. "Nothing too deep."

I remove my shoes and climb onto the bed with her. I pull the blanket over us and rest her head against my chest while she cries.

The length of time she cries and the desperation with which she's holding on to me make me hate myself for allowing this to happen to her. I was careless last night and didn't think to keep her out of Les's room. She wouldn't be experiencing any of this now had she not seen that photo. Then she would never have gone back into that house.

She lifts her gaze to mine and her eyes are so sad. I wipe away her tears and lower my mouth to hers, kissing her softly. "I'm sorry. I should have never let you go inside."

"Holder, you didn't do anything wrong. Stop apologizing."

I shake my head. "I shouldn't have taken you there. It's too much for you to deal with after just finding everything out."

She lifts up onto her elbow. "It wasn't just being there that was too much. It was what I remembered that was too much. You have no control over the things my father did to me. Stop placing blame on yourself for everything bad that happens to the people around you."

The things he did to her? I slide my hand to the base of her neck. "What are you talking about? What things did he do to you?"

She squeezes her eyes shut and drops her head to my chest, then starts crying again. The answer she's refusing to give me right now completely rips apart my heart. "No, Sky," I whisper. "No."

I'm overcome with several different emotions at once. I've never wanted to hurt someone like I want to hurt her bastard of a father, and if she didn't need me here with her right now I'd be on my way back to his house.

I close my eyes and can't get the thought of her as a little girl out of my head. Even when I was a little boy, I could tell she was broken, and she was the first thing I ever felt the urge to protect. And now, curled up against me, crying . . . the only thing I want to do is protect her from him, but I can't. I can't protect her from all the memories that are flooding her mind right now and I'd give anything if I could.

She clenches my shirt in her fists and the sobs continue. I hold her as tightly as I can, knowing there's nothing I can do to make her pain go away, so I just hold her like I used to hold Les. I never want to let her go.

She continues to cry and I continue to hold her and I'm trying so hard to be strong for her right now but I'm breaking. Knowing what happened to her and all she's had to live through is completely unhinging me and I have no idea how she's even able to hold up at all.

After several minutes, her tears begin to soften but they never cease. She eventually lifts her face off my chest, then slides on top of me. She closes her eyes and brings her lips to mine, then she immediately tries to take off my shirt. I have no idea why she's doing this, so I flip her onto her back. "What are you doing?"

She slides her hand behind my neck and pulls my mouth back to hers. As much as I love kissing her, this just doesn't feel right. When her hands grab at my shirt again, I push them away. "Stop it," I tell her. "Why are you doing this?"

She looks at me with desperation. "Have sex with me."

What the fuck?

I immediately climb off the bed and pace the floor. I don't even know how the hell to respond to that, especially after what she just remembered about her father. "Sky, I can't do this," I say, pausing to look at her. "I don't know why you're even asking for this right now."

She crawls to the edge of the bed where I'm standing and she pulls up onto her knees, grasping at my shirt. "Please," she begs. "Please, Holder. I need this."

I step away from her, out of her grasp. "I'm not doing this, Sky. *We're* not doing this. You're in shock or something . . . I don't know. I don't even know what to say right now."

She falls back down onto the bed and begins to cry again.

Dammit. I don't know how to help her. I'm completely unprepared for this.

"*Please*," she says, looking me in the eyes. Her voice and the pain behind it is shattering me from the inside out. She drops her eyes to her hands, which are folded in her lap. "Holder . . . he's the only one that's ever done that to me." She lifts her eyes to mine again. "I need you to take that away from him. *Please*."

If I had a soul before those words, it just completely broke in half. Tears fill my eyes and I hurt for her. I hurt for her so much because I don't want her to ever have to think about that bastard again. "*Please*, Holder," she says again.

Fuck.

I don't know what to do or how to deal with all of this. If I tell her no, I'll hurt her even more. If I agree to help her by doing this; I don't know if I'll be able to forgive myself.

She's looking up at me from the bed, completely broken. Her pleading eyes are waiting for my decision. And even though neither option is one I want to choose, I just go with whatever she thinks she needs right now. If I could trade lives with her I would do it in a heartbeat, just so she'd never have to feel whatever it is she's feeling. I'll do whatever it takes to ease her pain.

Whatever it takes.

I walk back to her and sink to my knees on the floor. I scoot her to the edge of the bed, then I remove both our shirts. I pick her up and walk her to the head of the bed and lay her down gently. I lower myself on top of her, then wipe her tears away again.

"Okay," I say to her.

I know she more than likely just wants to get this over with. There's no way this moment can be what it should be. I reach to my wallet and remove a condom, then take off my pants, watching her diligently the entire time. I don't want her to panic during this like she did last night, so I watch for any signs that she's changed her mind. She's been through enough. I just want to do whatever I can to help her, and if this will help her, it's what I'll do.

I kiss her the whole time I'm taking off her clothes. I don't even try to make it romantic. I just try to think whatever thoughts about her I can think that will help me get this over with faster.

Once her clothes are off, I put on the condom and ease myself against her. "Sky," I say, praying she'll ask me to stop. I don't want it to be like this for her.

She opens her eyes and shakes her head. "No, don't think about it. Just do it, Holder."

Her voice is completely emotionless. I squeeze my eyes shut and bury my face in her neck. "I just don't know how to deal with all of this. I don't know if this is wrong or if it's what you really need. I'm scared if I do this, I'll make it even harder for you."

She wraps her arms tightly around my neck and she begins to cry again. Rather than release me, she just pulls me tighter and lifts her hips in a silent plea for me to keep going.

I kiss her on the side of her head and give her what she needs.

The moment I push into her, tears escape my eyes. She never makes a sound. She just keeps herself wrapped tightly around me and I go through the motions, trying desperately not to think about how different I wanted this to be.

I try not to think about how I feel like I'm taking advantage of her with every movement against her.

I try not to think about how doing this makes me feel like I'm no better than her father.

That thought freezes me. I'm still inside her, but I can't move. I can't do this to her for another second.

I pull away from her neck and look down at her, then roll off her completely. I sit on the edge of the bed and fist my hands in my hair.

"I can't do it," I say to her. "It feels wrong, Sky. It feels wrong because you feel so good but I'm regretting every single fucking second of it." I stand up and toss the empty condom into the trashcan, pull my clothes back on, then walk to the door, knowing I'm letting her down again.

I make my way outside and, as soon as I'm alone in the parking lot, I scream out of frustration. I pace the sidewalk for a while, trying to figure out what to do. I turn and hit the building, over and over, then fall against the brick wall and wonder how the hell I've let her end up here. How the hell did I allow it to ever get to this point? The last twenty-four hours of my life have been one huge, colossal fuck-up.

And here I am, walking away from her again. Doing what I do best. Leaving her completely alone.

Wanting to rectify at least one of my bad decisions, I immediately walk back into the hotel room. When I make it inside, she's in the bathroom, so I sit on the bed and pick up my shirt, then wrap it around my now-bleeding hand.

The bathroom door opens and she pauses midstep, just as I look up at her. Her eyes drop to my hand and she immediately rushes to me, unwrapping the shirt to inspect my hand.

"Holder, what'd you do?" she says, twisting my hand back and forth.

"I'm fine," I say, wrapping my hand back up. I stand up and look down at her, wondering how the hell she could possibly be worried about *me* right now.

"I'm so sorry," she says quietly. "I shouldn't have asked you to do that. I just needed . . ."

Jesus. *She's* apologizing to *me*? "Shut up," I say, taking her face in my hands. "You have absolutely nothing to apologize for. I didn't leave earlier because I was mad at you. I left because I was mad at myself."

She nods, then pulls away from me and walks to the bed. "It's okay," she says, lifting the covers. "I can't expect you to want me in that way right now. It was wrong and selfish and way out of line for me to ask you to do that and I'm really sorry. Let's just go to sleep, okay?" She climbs into the bed and pulls the covers over her.

I'm trying to process her words, but they aren't making any sense. I don't feel that way about what she asked me to do at all. How the hell did she ever get these crazy thoughts in her head to begin with?

"You think I'm having a hard time with this because I don't *want* you?" I walk to the bed and kneel next to her. "Sky, I'm having a hard time with this because everything that's happened to you is breaking my fucking heart and I have no idea how to help you." I climb onto the bed with her and pull her to a sitting position with me. "I want to be there for you and help you through this but every word that comes out of my mouth feels like the wrong one. Every time I touch you or kiss you, I'm afraid you don't want me to. Now you're asking me to have sex with you because you want to take that from him, and I get it. I absolutely get where you're coming from, but it doesn't make it easier to make love to you when you can't even look me in the eyes. It hurts so much because you don't deserve for it to be like this. You don't deserve this life and there isn't a fucking thing I can do to make it better for you. I want to make it better but I can't and I feel so helpless."

I take her in my arms and she wraps her legs around me, hanging on to every word I'm saying.

"And even though I stopped, I should have never even started without telling you first how much I love you. I love you so much. I don't deserve to touch you until you know for a fact that I'm touching you because I love you and for no other reason."

I press my lips to hers desperately, needing her to know that I'm speaking nothing but truth now. Every word I speak and every time I touch her, there's nothing there but honesty.

She pulls away and kisses my chin and my forehead and my cheek, then my lips again. "I love you, too," she says, proving to me that words are yet another characteristic someone can fall in love with. But I'm not falling in love with her piece by piece anymore. I'm in love with the whole girl. Every single piece of her.

"I don't know what I'd do right now if I didn't have you, Holder. I love you so much and I'm so sorry. I wanted you to be my first, and I'm sorry he took that from you."

"Don't you ever say that again," I tell her. "Don't you ever *think* that again. Your father took that first from you in an unthinkable way, but I can guarantee you that's all he took. Because you are so strong, Sky. You're amazing and funny and smart and beautiful and so full of strength and courage. What he did to you doesn't take away from any of the best parts of you. You survived him once and you'll survive him again. I know you will."

I place my palm over her heart, then pull her hand to my heart. I lower my eyes to her level, making sure she's completely in this moment with me. "Fuck all the firsts, Sky. The only thing that matters to me with you are the forevers."

She releases a breath of relief, then completely kisses the hell out of me. I grab her head and lower her back onto the bed, climbing on top of her. "I love you," I say against her lips. "I've loved you for so long but I just couldn't tell you. It didn't feel right letting you love me back when I was keeping so much from you."

She's crying again, but she's also smiling. "I don't think you could have picked a better time to tell me you loved me than tonight. I'm happy you waited."

I dip my head and kiss her. I kiss her like she deserves to be kissed. I hold her like she deserves to be held. And I'm about to make love to her like she deserves to be loved. I untie the robe she's wearing and slide my hand across her stomach. "*God*, I love you," I say to her. My hand moves from her waist, down her hip and to her thigh. I can feel her tense up, so I pull back and look down at her. "Remember . . . I'm touching you because I love you. No other reason."

She nods and closes her eyes and I recognize the nervousness seeping off her. I pull her robe closed and bring my hand to her face.

"Open your eyes," I say. She opens them and they're full of tears. "You're crying."

She just nods and smiles up at me. "It's okay. They're the good kind of tears."

I silently watch her, gauging if we should even be doing this right now. I want to show her how much I love her and I want to erase what happened between us an hour ago, because it never should have happened. I want to make it right for her. It's always been so ugly for her, but she deserves to see how beautiful it can be.

"I want to make love to you, Sky," I say, lacing our fingers together. "And I think you want it, too. But I need you to understand something first." I lower my mouth and kiss away a falling tear. "I know it's hard for you to allow yourself to feel this. You've gone so long training yourself to block the feelings and emotions out any time someone touches you. But I want you to know that what your father physically did to you isn't what hurt you as a little girl. It's what he did to your faith in him that broke your heart. You suffered through one of the worst things a child can go through at the hands of your hero . . . the person you idolized . . . and I can't even begin to imagine what that must have felt like. But remember that the things he did to you are in *no way* related to the two of us when we're together like this. When I touch you, I'm touching you because I want to make you happy. When I kiss you, I'm kissing you because you have the most incredible mouth I've ever seen and you know I can't not kiss it. And when I make love to you—I'm doing exactly that. I'm making love to you because I'm in love with you. The negative feeling you've been associating with physical touch your whole life doesn't apply to me. It doesn't apply to *us*. I'm touching you because I'm in love with you and for no other reason." I kiss her softly. "I love you."

She kisses me harder than she's ever kissed me, pulling me down to the bed with her. We continue to kiss and she continues to allow me to explore every single part of her with my mouth and my hands. When I ready myself against her after putting another condom on, I look down at her and she's finally looking up at me with a serene expression. The love in her eyes right now can't be mistaken, but I still want to hear her say it.

"Tell me you love me."

She tightens her grip around me, looking me hard in the eyes. "I love you, Holder. *So* much," she says firmly. "And just so you know . . . so did Hope."

As soon as the words leave her mouth, I'm completely consumed by a sense of peace. For the first time since the second she was taken from me, I finally know what forgiveness feels like. "I wish you could feel what that just did to me." I claim her mouth with mine at the same time she completely consumes my heart.

Chapter Forty-three

When I turn my phone on, I'm flooded with texts. Several from Breckin, several from my mother. There are missed calls from Sky's phone, so I can only assume they're from Karen. I don't listen to any of the voicemails, though. I know everyone's just worried about us, especially Karen. I'm still not sure how what she did fits into the picture, but I find it hard to believe that what she did was done from a place of evil.

Sky rustles in the bed, rolling over. I look down at her and lean forward to kiss her but she turns her face away and I kiss her cheek, instead.

"Morning breath," she mumbles, sliding off the bed. She heads for the shower and I check the time. Check-out is in an hour, so I decide to gather our things.

After I've got most of our things packed, she walks out of the bathroom. "What are you doing?" she asks.

I glance at her. "We can't stay here forever, Sky. We need to figure out what you want to do."

She rushes toward me. "But . . . but I don't know yet. I don't even have anywhere to go."

Her voice is full of panic, so I walk to her in order to ease her mind. "You have me, Sky. Calm down. We can go back to my house and figure this out. Besides, we're both still in school. We can't just stop going and we definitely can't live in a hotel forever."

"One more day," she says. "Please, let's just stay one more day, then we'll go. I need to try to figure this out and in order to do that, I need to go there one more time."

I don't know how she can possibly think going back to that house is in any way a good idea. There's absolutely nothing she needs from there. "No way. I'm not putting you through that again. You're not going back."

"I need to, Holder," she says pleadingly. "I swear I won't get out of the car this time. I swear. But I need to see the house again before we go. I remembered so much while I was there. I just want a few more memories before you take me back and I have to decide what to do."

Jesus, she's relentless. I pace the floor, not knowing how I can get it through her head that she can't do this.

"Please," she says again.

Ugh! I can't say no to that voice.

"Fine," I groan. "I told you I would do whatever it was you felt you needed to do. But I'm not hanging all of those clothes back up."

She laughs and rushes to me, throwing her arms around my neck. "You're the best, most understanding boyfriend in the whole wide world."

I hug her back and sigh. "No, I'm not. I'm the most *whipped* boyfriend in the whole wide world."

We're sitting in my car across the street from her old house and I'm gripping the steering wheel so hard I'm afraid I might break it. Her father just pulled up into his driveway, and as mad and outraged as I've been in the past, I've never had the urge to actually kill someone until now. Just seeing him makes my stomach turn and my blood boil. I lift my hand to the ignition, knowing nothing good can come of this if I don't drive away right now.

"Don't leave," she says, pulling my hand away from the ignition. "I need to see what he looks like."

I sigh and fall back against the seat. She needs to hurry up and get what she needs because this is bad. This is bad, bad, bad.

"Oh, my God," she whispers. I turn to her, wanting to know what made her just say that. "It's nothing," she says. "He just looks . . . familiar. I haven't had an image of him in my head at all but if I was to see him walking down the street, I would know him."

We watch as he ends a conversation on his cell phone and walks to the mailbox.

"Have you had enough?" I ask her. "Because I can't stay here another second without jumping out of this car and beating his ass."

"Almost," she says, leaning across the seat to get a better look. I don't understand why she would even want to see him. I don't understand how she's not jumping out of this car in order to rip his balls off, because that's the only urge I have right now.

After her father finally disappears inside his house, I turn and look at her.

"Now?"

She nods. "Yeah, we can go now."

I place my hand on the ignition and crank the car, then watch in horror as she swings open the door and rushes out of the car.

What the fuck?

I turn the car off and swing open my door, running after her. I chase her all the way across the front yard and halfway up the porch steps. I wrap my arms around her and lift her up, then turn back to the car. She's trying to fight me and kick me and I'm doing everything I can to get her as far away from the house as I can so he doesn't hear her.

"What the hell do you think you're *doing*?" I say through clenched teeth.

"Let go of me right now, Holder, or I'll scream! I swear to God, I'll scream!"

I let go of her and spin her around to face me. I grip her shoulders tightly and try to shake some goddamned sense into her.

"Don't *do* this, Sky. You don't need to face him again, not after what he's done. I want you to give yourself more time."

She looks at me and begins to shake her head. "I have to know if he's doing this to anyone else. I need to know if he has more kids. I can't just let it go, knowing what he's capable of. I have to see him. I have to talk to him. I need to know that he's not that man anymore before I can allow myself to get back in that car and just drive away."

I take her face in my hands and try to reason with her. "Don't do this. Not yet. We can make a few phone calls. We'll find out whatever we can online about him first. Please, Sky." I turn her toward the car and she sighs. She finally relents and begins walking toward the car with me.

"Is there a problem here?"

We both spin around at the sound of his voice. He's standing at the base of the porch steps, eyeing me carefully. If I wasn't having to physically prevent Sky from falling to the ground right now, I'd be rushing him.

"Young lady, is this man hurting you?"

She grows limp in my arms the second he speaks to her directly. I pull her against my chest. "Let's go," I whisper. I turn her toward the car. I need to get her away from him. I just need to get her to the car.

"Don't move!" he yells.

Sky freezes at the sound of his voice, but I'm still trying to urge her toward the car.

"Turn around!"

I can't force Sky forward at this point and there really isn't a way out of this situation. I begin to turn her around with me and keep my arm wrapped around her. She looks into my eyes and there's more terror in them than I ever imagined a single person could feel.

"Play it off," I whisper in her ear. "He might not recognize you."

She nods and we both face her father now. I'm not concerned with the fact that he may recognize me. Other than the day Hope went missing, he never spoke to me. I'm just hoping to hell he doesn't recognize her, but I know he will. A parent would recognize his own child, no matter how long it's been.

He's making his way toward us, and the closer he gets, the more I see the recognition in his eyes. He knows her.

Shit.

He pauses when he's several feet from us and tries to look her in the eyes, but she presses herself against me and looks down at the ground.

"Princess?" he says.

She begins to slide out of my arms and I look down at her. Her eyes have rolled back into her head and she's falling. I keep a tight grip on her and ease her to the ground completely so that I can get a better grip on her. I need to get her out of here right now.

I slide my hands under her arms and try to pull her up. Her father comes closer and grabs her hands to help me.

"Don't you fucking touch her!" I scream. He immediately backs away, looking at me in shock.

I look back down at her and grab her head, trying to bring her back to consciousness.

"Baby, open your eyes. Please."

Her eyelids flutter open and she looks up at me. "It's okay," I reassure her. "You just passed out. I need you to stand up. We need to leave." I pull her to her feet and steady her against me. I give her a second to regain her strength. Her father is right in front of her now.

"It *is* you," he says staring at her. He looks at me, then back to Sky. "Hope? Do you remember me?" His eyes are full of tears.

"Let's go," I say to her, attempting to pull her with me. She has to know how much I'm trying to refrain from attacking him right now. We. Need. To. Leave.

She resists my pull as her father takes another step toward her, so I pull her a step away from him.

"Do you?" he says again. "Hope, do you remember me?"

Sky's whole body grows tense. "How could I *forget* you?" she spits.

He sucks in a breath. "It's you," he says, fidgeting his hand down at his side. "You're alive. You're okay." He pulls out his radio, but I take a step forward and knock it out of his hand before he can report it.

"I wouldn't let anyone know she's here if I were you," I say. "I doubt you would want the fact that you're a fucking pervert to be front-page news."

The blood drains from his face. "*What?*" He looks back at Sky and shakes his head. "Hope, whoever took you . . . they lied to you. They told you things about me that weren't true." He takes another step forward and I have to pull her back again. "Who took you, Hope? Who was it?"

She begins to shake her head back and forth. "I remember everything you did to me," she says, taking a confident step toward him. "And if you just give me what I'm here for, I swear I'll walk away and you'll never hear from me again."

He's shaking his head, not wanting to believe that she remembers. He watches her for a minute. I know he's just as caught off guard as we are.

"What is it you want?" he asks her.

"Answers," Sky says. "And I want anything you have that belonged to my mother."

Sky reaches down to my hand, which is wrapped around her waist, and she squeezes it. She's scared.

Her father glances at me, then back to Sky. "We can talk inside," he says quietly. He looks around the neighborhood nervously, making sure there aren't any witnesses. The fact that he's even looking for witnesses lights up a huge caution sign. There's no telling what this man is capable of.

"Leave your gun," I demand.

He pauses, then removes his gun from his holster. He lays it on the porch.

"Both of them," I say.

He reaches down and removes the extra gun from his leg, laying it on the porch right before he walks into his house. I spin Sky around to face me before we walk through the door.

"I'm staying right here with the door open. I don't trust him. Don't go any farther than the living room."

She nods and I give her a quick kiss, then watch her turn and step into the living room. She walks to the couch and takes a seat, eyeing him guardedly the entire time.

He raises his eyes to hers. "Before you say anything," he says. "You need to know that I loved you and I've regretted what I did every second of my life."

"I want to know why you did it," she says.

He leans back in his seat and rubs his hands over his eyes. "I don't know," he says. "After your mother died, I started drinking heavily again. It wasn't until a year later that I got so drunk one night that I woke up the next morning and knew I had done something terrible. I was hoping it was just a horrible dream, but when I went to wake you up that morning you were . . . different. You weren't the same happy little girl you used to be. Overnight, you somehow became someone who was terrified of me. I hated myself. I'm not even sure what I did to you because I was too drunk to remember. But I knew it was something awful and I am so, so sorry. It never happened again and I did everything I could to make it up to you. I bought you presents all the time and gave you whatever you wanted. I didn't want you to remember that night."

She grips her knees and I can tell by the way she's struggling for breath that she's doing everything she can to remain calm.

"It was night . . . after night . . . after night," she says. I immediately rush to the couch and kneel next to her. I wrap my arm around her back and grip her arm so that she stays put. "I was scared to go to bed and scared to wake up and scared to take a bath and scared to speak to you. I wasn't a little girl afraid of monsters in her closet or under her bed. I was terrified of the monster that was supposed to love me! You were supposed to be *protecting* me from the people like you!"

The pain in her voice is heart-wrenching. I want her out of here. I don't want her to have to hear him speak.

"Do you have any other children?" she asks.

He drops his head and presses a palm to his forehead, but fails to answer her. "*Do* you?" she screams.

He shakes his head. "No. I never remarried after your mother."

"Am I the only one you did this to?"

He keeps his eyes trained to the floor, avoiding her question.

"You owe me the truth," she says, her voice quiet now. "Did you do this to anyone else before you did it to me?"

There's a long silence. He's staring at the floor, unable to admit the truth. She's staring at him, waiting for him to give her what she came here for.

After a long silence, she begins to stand up. I grasp her arm but she looks me in the eyes and shakes her head. "It's okay," she says. I don't want to let her go, but I have to allow her to handle this the way she wants to handle it.

She walks to him and kneels in front of him. "I was sick," she says. "My mother and I . . . we were in my bed and you came home from work. She had been up with me all night and she was tired, so you told her to go get some rest."

He's looking her in the eyes like a regretful father. I don't know how.

"You held me that night like a father is supposed to hold his daughter. And you sang to me. I remember you used to sing a song to me about your ray of hope. Before my mother died . . . before you had to deal with that heartache . . . you didn't always do those things to me, did you?"

He shakes his head and touches her face.

I have the urge to rip his hand off, just like all the urges I've had to rip Grayson's hand off. Only this time I don't want to stop at his hand. I want to rip his head off and his balls off and . . .

"No, Hope," he says to her. "I loved you so much. I still do. I loved you and your mother more than life itself, but when she died . . . the best parts of me died right along with her."

"I'm sorry you had to go through that," she says with little emotion. "I know you loved her. I remember. But knowing that doesn't make it any easier to find it in my heart to forgive you for what you did. I don't know why whatever is inside of you is so different from what's inside other people . . . to the point that you would allow yourself to do what you did to me. But despite the things you did to me, I know you love me. And as hard as it is to admit . . . I once loved you, too. I loved all the good parts of you."

She stands up and steps back. "I know you aren't all bad. I *know* that. But if you love me like you say you do . . . if you loved my mother at *all* . . . then you'll do whatever you can to help me heal. You owe me that much. All I want is for you to be honest so I can leave here with some semblance of peace. That's all I'm here for, okay? I just want peace."

Her father is crying now. She walks back to me and I can honestly say I'm amazed by her right now. I'm amazed by her resolve. Her strength. Her courage. I slide my hand down her arm until I find her pinky, and I hold it. She wraps her pinky tightly around mine in return.

Her father sighs heavily, then looks back up at her. "When I first started drinking . . . it was only once. I did something to my little sister . . . but it was only one time. It was years before I met your mother."

She exhales a breath. "What about *after* me? Have you done it to anyone else since I was taken?" It's obvious he has by the guilt that consumes his features. "Who?" she asks. "How many?"

He shakes his head slightly. "There was just one more. I stopped drinking a few years ago and haven't touched anyone since. I swear. There were only three and they were at the lowest points of my life. When I'm sober, I'm able to control my urges. That's why I don't drink anymore."

"Who was she?" Sky asks.

He nudges his head to the right, toward the house next door.

Toward the house I used to live in.

The house I lived in with Les.

I don't hear another word after that.

Chapter Forty-four

One would think that finding my sister's body was the worst thing that's ever happened to me.

It wasn't. The worst thing that ever happened to me came later that night, when I had to tell my mother her daughter was dead.

I remember pulling Les onto my lap, doing everything I could to make sense of what was happening. I tried to make sense of why she wasn't responding. Why she wasn't breathing or talking or laughing. It just didn't make sense that someone could be here one minute, then the very next minute they're not. They're just . . . *not*.

I don't know how long I held her. It could have been seconds. It could have been minutes. Hell, I was so out of it that it could have been hours. I just know that I was still holding her when the front door slammed shut downstairs.

I remember panicking, knowing what was about to happen. I was about to have to walk downstairs and look my mother in the eyes. I was about to have to tell her that her daughter was dead.

I don't know how I did it. I don't know how I let go of Les long enough to stand up. I don't know how I found the strength to even stand. When I made it to the top of the stairs, she and Brian were removing their jackets. He took hers and turned around to hang it on the coatrack. She glanced up at me and smiled, but then she stopped smiling.

I began to walk down the stairs toward her. My body was so weak, I was taking them slowly. One at a time. Watching her the whole way.

I don't know if she had mother's intuition or if she could just tell by the look on my face what had happened, but she started to shake her head and back away from me.

I started to cry and she started to panic and she continued to back away from me until her back met the front door. Brian was looking back and forth between us, not understanding at all what was going on.

She turned around and gripped the doorframe, pressing her cheek against the door while she squeezed her eyes shut. It was like she was trying to shut me out. If she shut me out, she wouldn't have to face the truth.

Her body was racked with grief and she was crying so hard, there wasn't even a sound coming out of her mouth. I remember reaching the bottom step, watching her from where I was standing. Watching as she gave the word devastated a whole new meaning. I truly believed, at that point, that the word devastated should be reserved for mothers.

I no longer believe that.

The word devastated should be reserved for brothers, too.

"Les," I whisper, turning away from Sky and her father. "Oh, God, no." I press my head against the doorframe and grip the back of my neck with both hands. I begin to cry so hard that I'm not even able to make a sound. My chest hurts and my throat hurts, but my heart has just been completely obliterated.

Sky comes up behind me. She wraps her arms around me and tries to comfort me in whatever way she can, but I can't feel it. I can't feel her and I can't feel the devastation anymore because all I feel is this overwhelming amount of hatred and rage. I'm trying to refrain from lunging at him but I don't think I have enough self-control. I wrap my arm around Sky and pull her against me, hoping her presence can help calm me, but it doesn't. The only thing that could calm me would be knowing the man behind me is no longer breathing.

He's the reason. He's the reason for *all* of it.

He's why Les isn't here anymore. He's what broke Hope. He's the reason my mother knows the meaning of devastation. This bastard is who stole my sister's strength away from her, and I want him dead. But I want to be the one to do it.

I remove my arm from around Sky and push her away from me. I turn to face her father, but she steps between us, facing me with pleading eyes, pushing against my chest. She knows what I want to do to him and she's trying to push me out the door. I shove her out of the way because I don't know what I'm capable of right now and I don't want her to get hurt.

I begin to step toward him, but he reaches behind the couch, then quickly turns and holds up a gun. I honestly wouldn't even care that he's holding a gun, but my protective instinct kicks in when I think about Sky, so I pause. He pulls the radio to his mouth with his free hand, keeping his gun trained on me the entire time he speaks into it.

"Officer down at thirty-five twenty-two Oak Street."

His words immediately register in my head and I realize what he's about to do.

No.

No, no, no.

Not in front of Sky.

He turns his gun on himself, then looks at her. "I'm so sorry, Princess," he whispers.

I close my eyes and reach for her the second he fires the gun at himself. I cover her eyes and she begins to scream hysterically. She pulls my hand from her eyes, right when he falls to the floor, causing her to scream even louder.

I clamp my hand over her mouth and immediately pull her out the front door. She's too hysterical to carry right now, so I just drag her behind me.

The only thing running through my head at this point is how we need to get into the car. We need to get the hell out of here before anyone finds out we were ever here. Because if anyone finds out we were here, Sky's world will never be the same.

When I reach the car I keep my hand clamped to her mouth and I press her back against her door, looking her hard in the eyes. "Stop," I tell her. "I need you to stop screaming. Right now."

She nods vigorously, wide-eyed. "Do you hear that?" I say, trying to get her to understand the ramifications of what could happen if we don't leave right now. "Those are sirens, Sky. They'll be here in less than a minute. I'm removing my hand and I need you to get in the car and be as calm as you can because we need to get out of here."

She nods again so I remove my hand and quickly shove her into the car. I rush around to the driver's side and climb in, then crank the car and pull away. She leans forward in the seat and drops her head between her knees. She keeps saying, "No, no, no" under her breath, all the way back to the hotel.

Chapter Forty-five

Once we're back inside our hotel room, I walk her to the bed. She's having one of her moments where she's completely zoned out and I don't do anything to bring her out of it. It's probably best if she stays like this for a while.

I pull off my shirt, which is now covered in blood. I remove my socks and shoes and jeans and toss them all aside. I walk to where Sky is still standing and I remove her jacket. There's blood all over her and I'm trying to hurry so I can get her in the shower and wash it off. She finally turns to face me with a blank expression. I lay her jacket across the chair next to us, then lift her shirt over her head.

I reach down to the button on her jeans and undo it, then begin to lower them. When I reach her feet, she just stands still. I look up at her. "I need you to step out of them, babe."

She looks down at me and places her hands on my shoulders while I pull the jeans off her, one foot at a time. I feel her reach to my hair and brush her fingers through it. I toss her jeans aside and look back up at her. She's shaking her head looking down at her hands, which are now moving frantically over her stomach. She's smearing her father's blood all over her stomach, attempting to wipe it off. She's gasping for breath, trying to scream, but nothing's coming out. I stand up and immediately pick her up, rushing her to the shower. I need to get this off her before she completely loses control.

I set her down in the shower and turn on the water. Once it's warm, I close the shower curtain and pull her wrists away from her stomach. I wrap her arms around me and pull her against my chest, then turn her to where she's standing under the stream of water.

As soon as the water splashes her face, she gasps and the clarity begins to return to her eyes.

I grab the soap and a washcloth, and rub them under the water, then turn and begin wiping the blood off her face.

"Shh," I whisper, staring her in the eyes. "I'm getting it off you, okay?"

She squeezes her eyes shut and I diligently wash away every speck of blood from her face. When she's finally clean, I reach behind her in order to remove her ponytail holder.

"Look at me, Sky," I say. She opens her eyes and I rest my hand reassuringly on her shoulder. "I'm going to take off your bra now, okay? I need to wash your hair and I don't want to get anything on it."

Her eyes grow wide with my words and she pulls her arms through the straps of her bra, then frantically rips it over her head.

"Get it out," she says quickly, referring to the blood in her hair. "Just get it *off* me."

I take her wrists again and wrap her arms around me. "I'll get it. Hold on to me and try to relax. I'll do it."

I pour the shampoo into my hands and bring it to her hair. I have to wash it several times before the water finally runs clean. Once I'm finished washing her, I begin to wash my own hair. I get what I can but without being able to see myself, I don't know if I've washed away everything. I don't want to ask her to help me do this, but I have to make sure it's all gone. "Sky, I need you to make sure I got it all, okay? I need you to wipe away anything I missed."

She nods and takes the washcloth out of my hands. She eyes my hair and my back and my shoulders, then finally rubs the washcloth over my ear.

She pulls the washcloth away from me and looks down at it, running it under the stream of water.

"It's all gone," she whispers.

I take the washcloth and toss it onto the edge of the tub.

It's all gone, I repeat in my head.

I wrap my arms around her and close my eyes. I can feel it building. The questions. The memories. All the times I held Les at night while she cried and I had no idea what he'd done to her. No idea what she'd been through.

I hate him. I fucking hate that he got away with it for so long. He got away with what he did to Sky, to his sister, to Les. And the worst part is, he's not alive anymore for me to even be able to kill him.

Sky looks up at me and her eyes are full of sympathy. For a second I don't understand it, but then I realize I'm crying . . . and that she's just as sad for me as I am for her. Her shoulders begin to shake and a sob breaks free. She slaps her hand over her mouth and squeezes her eyes shut.

I pull her against my chest and kiss the side of her head.

"Holder, I'm so sorry," she cries. "Oh, my God, I'm so sorry."

I tighten my grip around her and press my cheek to the top of her head. I close my eyes and I cry. I cry for her. I cry for Les. I cry for myself.

She curls her arms up behind my shoulders, gripping me tightly, then she presses her lips against my neck. "I'm so sorry," she says quietly. "He never would have touched her if I . . ."

I grab her by the arms and push her away from me so that I can look her in the eyes. "Don't you dare say that." I grab her face with both hands. "I don't ever want you to apologize for a single thing that man did. Do you hear me? It's not your fault, Sky. Swear to me you will never let a thought like that consume you ever again."

She nods. "I swear."

I continue to maintain eye contact with her, needing to know that she's telling me the truth. This girl has done nothing that warrants an apology and I never want her thinking like that again.

She throws her arms around my neck, tears falling from both of us now. We hold each other tightly. Desperately. She kisses my neck repeatedly, wanting to reassure me in the only way she knows how.

I lower my lips to her shoulder and kiss her in return. She holds me tighter and I let her. I let her hold me as tight as she possibly can. I continue to kiss her neck and she continues to kiss mine, both of us working our way toward each other's mouth. Before I reach her lips, I pull back and look into her eyes. She looks into mine and for once in my life, I can honestly say I've found the only other person in this world who understands my guilt. The only person who understands my pain. The only person who accepts that it's who I am.

I used to think the best part of me died with Les, but the best part of me is standing right here in front of me.

In one swift movement, I crash my lips to hers and grip her by the hair. I push her against the shower wall and kiss her with so much conviction, I know she could never for a second doubt how much I love her. I slide my hands down her thighs and lift her up until she wraps her legs around my waist.

I press myself against her and continue kissing her, wanting to feel *her*, rather than the pain that's trying to take over. I want nothing but to be a part of her right now and let everything else in our lives just fade away.

"Tell me this is okay," I say as I pull away from her mouth and search her eyes. "Tell me it's okay to want to be inside you right now . . . because after everything we've been through today, it feels wrong to need you like I do."

She throws her arms around my neck and grasps my hair, pulling my mouth back to hers, showing me that she needs this just as much as I do. I groan and pull her away from the shower wall, then walk her out of the bathroom and into the bedroom. I drop her down onto the bed, then grab her panties and pull them down her legs. I crash against her mouth and pull off my boxers, which are now soaking wet. All I can think about is how much I need to be inside her right now. I pull apart from her long enough to get a condom on, then I grab her hips and pull her to the edge of the bed. I lift her leg to my side and slide my other arm underneath her shoulder.

She looks up at me and I look down at her. I grip her leg and her shoulder and keep my eyes trained on hers, then push into her. The second I'm inside her, it doesn't feel like enough. I press my lips to hers and try to search for whatever it is that's missing from the moment. I move in and out of her, more and more frantic with each thrust, trying desperately to reach a feeling that I don't even know exists. She relaxes her body against mine, following my movements, allowing me to be in control.

But I don't want that right now.

That's what's wrong with me.

My mind is so exhausted and so tired and my heart hurts so much right now. I just need her to help me figure out how to stop trying to be the hero for once.

I pull away from her and she looks up at me, never questioning why I've drastically slowed against her. She just brings her hands to my face and gently runs her fingers over my eyes and my lips and cheeks. I turn my mouth toward the inside of her palm and I kiss it, then drop down on top of her, stopping completely. I keep my gaze locked with hers and I pull her to me, then lift her up as I stand. I'm still inside her and she's wrapped around me, so I turn my back to the bed and slide down to the floor. I lean forward and kiss her bottom lip softly, then her whole mouth.

I bring a hand to her cheek and drop the other to her hip. I begin to move beneath her, slowly guiding her with my hand, wanting her to just take control. I need her to want to comfort me the same way that I always want to comfort her.

"You know how I feel about you," I whisper, staring into her eyes. "You know how much I love you. You know I would do whatever I could to take away your pain, right?"

She nods, never pulling her gaze from mine, even for a second.

"I need that from you so fucking bad right now, Sky. I need to know you love me like that."

Her expression grows soft and her eyes fill with compassion. She laces our hands together and places them over our hearts. She strokes her thumb against my hand and lifts up slightly, then slowly glides back down me again.

The incredible sensation that rushes through my body causes my head to collapse against the mattress behind me. I groan, unable to keep my eyes open.

"Open your eyes," she whispers, still moving against me. "I want you to watch me."

I lift my head and watch her. It's the easiest thing I've ever been asked to do, because she's fucking beautiful right now.

"Don't look away again," she says, lifting herself up. When she slides back onto my lap, I can barely keep my head up. Especially when that moan escapes her lips and she squeezes my hands even harder.

"The first time you kissed me?" she says. "That moment when your lips touched mine? You stole a piece of my heart that night."

You stole a piece of mine, too.

"The first time you told me you lived me because you weren't ready to tell me you loved me yet? Those words stole another piece of my heart."

But I did love you. I loved you so much.

I open my hand and press it flat against her heart. "The night I found out I was Hope? I told you I wanted to be alone in my room. When I woke up and saw you in my bed I wanted to cry, Holder. I wanted to cry because I needed you there with me so bad. I knew in that moment that I was in love with you. I was in love with the way you loved me. When you wrapped your arms around me and held me, I knew that no matter what happened with my life, you were my home. You stole the biggest piece of my heart that night."

I didn't steal it. You gave it to me.

She lowers her mouth to mine and I drop my head back against the mattress and let her kiss me. "Keep them open," she whispers, pulling away from my lips. I do what she says and somehow open my eyes again, looking directly into hers. "I want you to keep them open . . . because I need you to watch me give you the very last piece of my heart."

This moment. Right now. It's almost worth every ounce of pain I've ever had to endure.

I tighten my grip on her hands and lean into her, but I don't kiss her. We get as close as we possibly can and we keep our eyes open until the very last second. Until she completely consumes me and I completely consume her and I have no idea where my love ends and hers begins.

As soon as I begin to tremble and moan beneath her, my head falls against the mattress and she allows me to close my eyes this time. She continues to move on top of me until I'm completely and utterly still.

I give my heart a second to calm down, then I lift my head and look at her. I remove my hands from hers and I slide them through her hair to the back of her head. My lips connect with hers and I kiss her, pushing her off me and onto the floor beneath me. I slide my hand between us and flatten my palm against her stomach, then slowly lower my hand until I find the exact spot that makes my favorite sound escape her mouth. I drink in every single moan and breath that passes her lips. And I let her keep her eyes closed, but I keep mine open and watch her steal the very last piece of *my* heart.

Chapter Forty-six

Les,

I have so much I want to say, but I don't even know how to begin.

Everything with Sky couldn't have turned out better. She's back home with Karen now where she belongs.

I knew Karen wouldn't have harmed Sky. I could tell just from the little time I spent with them that Karen loved her as much as I did. It turns out, I was right. Karen took Sky from her father because Karen knew what he was doing to her. Karen was his sister... Sky's aunt. And she had been through every single thing that Sky went through. She took her because she couldn't just sit back and allow it to continue to happen. Now that Sky knows the whole truth, she's decided to stay with Karen. Karen risked her entire life for that girl. She risked her entire future and I could never thank her enough.

I said this to Sky and I'll say it to you. The only thing I wish Karen would have done differently is, I wish she could have taken you, too.

I didn't know, Les. I had no idea what he was doing to you and I'm so sorry.

I'll tell you more tomorrow, but tonight I just
needed to tell you that I love you.

H

Chapter Forty-seven

Happy Halloween. Sure hope you decide to wear something sexy for once.

I hit send and set the phone on my nightstand, then climb out of bed. I didn't leave Sky's house until after four o'clock this morning, then I came home and wrote Les a note before I crawled into bed. It's been days of little sleep and high emotion.

I walk to the closet and grab a T-shirt, then pull it on over my head. My phone sounds off so I walk to it and pick it up to read her text.

Hi, Holder. It's Karen. Still haven't returned Sky's phone to her, but I'll relay the message. Or not.

Oh, shit. I laugh and text Karen back.

lol . . . sorry about that. But while I'm texting you, how is she today?

I wait for her response, which doesn't take long.

She's okay. She's been through a lot and I know it'll take time. But she's the bravest girl I know, so I have complete faith in her.

I smile and text her back.

Yeah. She kind of reminds me of her mother.

She texts back a heart. I set my phone on the bed and sit down beside it. I pick it back up and scroll through it, finding my father's number.

Hey, Dad. Miss you. I'm thinking about bringing my girlfriend to visit during Thanksgiving break. I want you to meet her. Tell Pamela I promise to stay off her couch.

I hit send, but I know the text wasn't enough, so I text him one more time.

And I'm sorry. I'm really sorry.

I set the phone down and look across the room to the notebook still lying on the floor where I threw it. The one that contains the majority of my notes to Les.

I still don't want to read it, but I feel like I owe it to her. I stand up and walk to it. I bend over and pick it up at the same time I lower myself to the floor. I lean against the wall and pull my knees up, then open the notebook and flip to the back of it.

Chapter Forty-seven-and-a-half

Dear Holder,

If you're reading this, I'm so, so sorry. Because if you're reading this, then I know what I did to you.

But I really hope you never find this letter. I'm hoping whoever finds this notebook doesn't see much use for it and throws it out, because I don't want to break your heart. But I have so much I need to say to you that I'll never be able to tell you face to face, so I'm doing it here, instead.

I'm going to start with what happened when we were kids. With Hope.

I know how much you blamed yourself for walking away from her. But you need to realize that you weren't the only one, Holder. I walked away from her, too. And you were doing what any other child in that situation would do. You were trusting that the adults in her life were doing what was right for her. How could you have anticipated what was going to happen when she walked to that car? You couldn't have, so just stop thinking you could have done something differently. You couldn't have and frankly, you shouldn't have. Hope climbing into that car was the best thing that ever happened to her.

A few weeks after she was taken, her father asked

me if I wanted to help him make some flyers. Of course I wanted to help him. I would have done anything that would have helped bring Hope back to us.

When I walked into his house, I could feel something wasn't right. He walked me to her bedroom. He told me the materials for the flyers were in Hope's room. Then he shut the door behind us and completely shattered my life.

It went on for years after that. It went on until the day I couldn't bear it anymore and finally told Mom.

She immediately went to the police. That same day I was interviewed by a therapist and my confession was documented. I was only nine or ten years old, so I don't remember a lot about it. I just remember that weeks went by and Mom and Dad had to go to the police station several times. The whole time all of this was going on, Hope's father never once returned home.

I found out later he had been arrested. An investigation was completed and it was even taken to court. I remember the day Mom came home and told me we were moving. Dad couldn't leave his job and she refused to keep us in Austin, so she moved us. I don't know if you know this, but they tried to work it out. Dad tried to find a job that could support us in our new town, but he never did. I think they eventually realized that it was easier being apart. Maybe they both blamed each other for what happened to me.

Now that I look back on all the therapy Mom had me undergo, I hate that she didn't see the need for her to see a therapist, too. I always wondered if their marriage could have been saved if they had talked to someone about it. But then again, I've been in therapy for years and it obviously didn't save me. I wish it did, and maybe it could have if I knew how to apply it. It did help me get through for several years, but it couldn't save me from myself every time I had to close my eyes at night. And as much as Mom tried to save me, she couldn't do it, either. I wasn't looking to be saved.

I just wanted to be let go.

I found out several years later that Hope's father never had to pay for what he did to me. For what he did to Hope. He was extremely manipulative and made it seem like I was blaming him for Hope's disappearance and this was my way of getting back at him. The entire community rallied behind him. They couldn't believe someone would accuse a man of such a cruel act after having his daughter ripped out from under him.

So he got away with it. He was free to do whatever he wanted and I felt like I was locked in hell for eternity.

Mom didn't want you to find out what happened to me. She was afraid of what it would do to you. We both saw how much you blamed yourself for what happened to Hope and she didn't want to see you hurt any more.

I didn't want to see that, either.

Now comes the most difficult part of this letter. This is so hard for me to say, because I've held so much guilt over it. Every day that I saw the pain in your eyes, I knew that if I just confessed to you what I'm about to tell you, it would have relieved you of so much agony.

But I couldn't. I couldn't find a way to tell you that Hope was alive. That she was okay and that Mom and I saw her once, about three years ago.

I was fourteen and we were eating at a restaurant, just Mom and me. I was taking a drink when I looked up and saw her walking through the door.

I turned to Mom and I know I had to be as pale as a ghost, because she reached across the table and grabbed my hand.

"Lesslie, what's wrong, sweetie?"

I couldn't talk. All I could do was stare at Hope. Mom turned around and the second she laid eyes on her, she knew it was her. We were both stunned silent.

The waitress led them to a table right next to ours. Mom and I were both just sitting there, staring at her. Hope glanced at me when she took her seat, then looked away like she didn't even recognize me. It broke my heart that she didn't recognize me. I think I started crying at that point. I was just so emotionally overwhelmed and I didn't know what to do. I fingered the bracelet on my wrist and whispered her name, just to see if she would hear me and turn around again.

She didn't hear me, but the woman who was with her did. She darted her head in our direction with sheer panic in her eyes. It confused me. It confused Mom.

The woman looked at Hope. "I think I left the stove on," she said, standing up. "We need to leave." Hope looked confused, but she stood up, too. Her mother ushered her toward the exit to the restaurant. That's when Mom stood up and rushed after them. I did, too.

When we were all outside, the woman rushed Hope

to the car, then immediately shut her door. Mom and I walked up behind her and as soon as the woman turned around and faced Mom, tears welled in her eyes.

"Please," the woman begged. She didn't say anything after that. Mom stared at her for a while without saying anything in return. I just stood there, trying to understand what was happening.

"Why did you take her?" Mom finally asked her.

The woman began to cry and she kept shaking her head. "Please," she cried. "She can't go back to him. Please don't do that to her. Please, please, please."

My mother nodded. She stepped forward and placed a reassuring hand on the woman's shoulder. "Don't worry," Mom said. "Don't worry." Mom glanced at me and tears filled her eyes, then she glanced back to the woman. "I would do whatever it took to keep my daughter safe, too."

The woman looked at Mom in confusion. I know she didn't understand exactly just how much Mom knew, but she understood Mom's honesty. She tilted her head and exhaled. "Thank you," she said, backing away from us. "Thank you." She opened her door and climbed into her car, then they drove away.

I don't know where she lives. We never found out the woman's name and we never found out the name Hope goes by now. I also stopped wearing the bracelet after that day because I knew in my heart that she didn't need to be found. But I needed you to know, Holder. I just need you to know that she's alive and she's okay and you walking away from her that day was the best thing you could have done for her.

As far as me, well... I'm a lost cause. I've spent the last eight or so years existing in this constant nightmare and I'm just tired. The therapy and medication help numb the pain, but it's the numbness I don't want to endure, Holder. That's why I plan to do what I need to do, and that's what led to your reading this letter. I'm tired and exhausted and sick of living a life that I don't really want to live anymore. I'm tired of pretending to be happy for you, because I'm not happy. Every single time I smile, I feel like I'm lying to you, but I don't know how to live any other way. And I know when I do it, it'll break your heart. I know it'll devastate Mom and Dad. And I know that you'll hate me.

But knowing all of that can't change my mind. I've lost the ability to care anymore, so it's hard to empathize with what you'll experience after I'm gone. I don't remember what it's like to care enough about life that the thought of death could destroy me. So I need you to know that I'm sorry, but I can't help it.

I've been let down by this life one too many times and quite frankly, I'm tired of losing hope.

I love you more than you know.

Les

P.S. I hope you never allow yourself to believe I went through with it because you failed me in some way. All those nights you held me and just let me cry... you have no idea how many times you've already saved me.

Chapter Forty-eight

I drop the notebook onto the floor.

And I cry.

Chapter Forty-nine

I walk into my mother's office and she's on the phone. She looks up as I shut her door behind me. I walk to her desk and pull the receiver from her ear and hang it up.

"You *know*?" I ask her. "You know about what that bastard did to Les?" I wipe my eyes with the back of my hand, just as she stands up and her own eyes fill with tears. "You know what he did to Hope? And you know that Hope is alive and that she's fine? You know everything?"

My mother is shaking her head and fear is filling her eyes. She can't tell if I'm mad or if I've lost it or if I'm about to flip out.

"Holder . . ." she says. "We couldn't tell you. I knew what it would do to you if you knew something like that happened to your sister."

I collapse into a chair, unable to stand up for another second. She walks around the desk and kneels in front of me. "I'm so sorry, Holder. Please don't hate me. I'm so sorry."

She's crying, looking at me with so much regret and apology. I immediately find the strength to stand back up and I pull her up with me. "God, no," I say to her, throwing my arms around her neck. "Mom, I'm so glad you know. I'm so relieved Les had you through all of that. And Hope?" I push her away from me and look her in the eyes. "She's *Sky*, Mom. Hope is Sky and Sky is okay and I love her. I love her so much and I had no idea how to tell you because I was so scared you would recognize her."

Her eyes grow wide and she backs away from me, falling back into her chair. "Your girlfriend? Your girlfriend is Hope?"

I nod, knowing none of this is making any sense to her. "Remember when I met Sky at the store a few months ago? I recognized her. I thought she was Hope, but then I thought maybe she wasn't. Then I fucking fell in love with her, Mom. I can't even begin to tell you the shit we've been through this week." I'm talking faster than she can probably comprehend. I sit in the chair across from her and pull it closer to her, then lean forward and take her by the hands. "She's okay. I'm okay. I'm *more* than okay. And I know you did your best for Les, Mom. I hope you know that, too. You did everything you could, but sometimes even all the love in the world from mothers and brothers isn't enough to help pull someone out of their nightmare. We just need to accept that things are what they are, and all the guilt and regret in the world can't change that."

She begins to sob. I wrap my arms around her and I hold her.

Chapter Forty-nine-and-a-half

Sky and I took the last two days of the week off school. We figured we already missed three days, what's two more? Besides, Karen wanted to keep a close eye on Sky all week. She's concerned about how everything is affecting her.

I agreed to give Sky space for a few days, but what Karen doesn't realize is that Sky's window still sees regular traffic in the middle of the night. All from me.

I've spent the last few days in deep discussions with Mom. She wanted to know everything I knew about Les and Hope and of course she wanted to know what happened last weekend in Austin. Then she wanted to know all about my relationship with Sky, so I brought her up to date. Then she said she wanted to meet her.

So here we are. Sky just walked through the front door and my mom has her arms around her. She started crying almost immediately, which in turn made Sky tear up a little. Now they're standing in the foyer and my mother won't let go of her.

"I don't want to interrupt this homecoming," I say. "But if you don't let her go, Mom, you might scare her away."

My mother laughs and sniffles, pulling away from Sky. "You're so beautiful," she says, smiling at Sky. She turns to me. "She's beautiful, Holder."

I shrug. "Yeah, she's okay."

Sky laughs and hits me on the arm. "Remember? The insults are only funny in text form."

I grab her and pull her to me. "You're not beautiful, Sky," I whisper in her ear. "You're incredible."

She wraps her arms around me in return. "You're not so bad, yourself," she says.

My mother takes her by the hand and pulls her away from me and into the living room, then she begins to bombard her with questions. I appreciate it, though, because she doesn't ask her questions about her situation or her past. She just asks normal questions about what she wants to major in when she goes to college and *where* she's planning to go to college. I leave them both in the living room to continue their conversation while I walk to the garage and grab a few boxes. Mom and I have talked about clearing out Les's room before. Now that I have Sky here, I think I'll actually be able to do it.

I walk back to the living room and hand them each a box. "Come on," I say, heading toward the stairs. "We've got a room to clean."

We spend the rest of the afternoon cleaning out Les's room. We box her pictures and anything that meant something to her in one box, then we put all her clothes in boxes to take to Goodwill. I take both notebooks and I wrap them in the pair of jeans that have been on the floor for over a year and I place it all in a box. A box I keep.

After the room is finished, my mother and Sky head downstairs. I stack the boxes in the hallway, then turn to shut the door. Before I close it completely, I look to her bed. I don't watch her die again. I watch her smile.

Chapter Forty-nine-and-three-quarters

"I thought she said she wasn't going this weekend," I say to Sky as we walk through her front door.

"I begged her to go. She's been stuck to me like glue for days now and I told her if she didn't go do her flea market thing, I'd run away."

We make our way to Sky's bedroom and I close the door behind us. "So does that mean I can get you pregnant tonight?"

She turns around and faces me, then shrugs. "I guess we could practice," she says, smiling.

And we do. We practice at least three different times before midnight.

We're lying on her bed, tangled together beneath her sheet. She's holding up our hands, which are clasped between us, and she's staring at them. "I remember, you know," she says softly.

I tilt my head until it meets hers on the pillow. "You remember what?"

She pulls her fingers away, then she wraps her pinky around mine. "This," she whispers. "I remember the first time you held my hand like this. And I remember everything you said to me that night."

I close my eyes and inhale a deep breath.

"Not long after Karen brought me here, she asked me to forget my old name and all the bad that went along with it. So I thought about you . . . and I told her I wanted to be called Sky."

She lifts up onto her elbow and looks down at me. "You were always there, you know. Even when I couldn't remember . . . you were always there."

I push her hair behind her ear and kiss her, then pull back. "I love you so much, Sky."

"I love you, too, Holder."

I pull my arm out from under her and roll her onto her back, looking down at her. "Will you do me a favor?"

She nods.

"From now on, I want you to call me Dean."

Final Chapter

Les,

It's been a while. I came across these letters today after needing boxes to pack for college. I also came across the pair of jeans that sat in your bedroom floor for over a year. I just threw them in the hamper for you. You're welcome.

So... yeah. College. Me. Me going to college. Pretty cool, huh?

It's still about a month away before I go, but Sky has already been there for a couple of months. She had all her credits from being homeschooled, so right after high school graduation she left to get a head start on me.

She's so competitive.

But I'm not worried, because I plan on surpassing her once I get there. I have this elaborate evil plan all mapped out. Every time I catch her studying or doing homework, I'll just whisper something sexy in her ear or flash my dimples. Then she'll get all flustered and sidetracked and she'll fall behind on her schoolwork and she'll fail her classes and I'll get my degree first and victory will be mine!

Or I'll just let her win. I sort of like letting her win sometimes.

I miss her like crazy, but we'll be in the same town again in less than a month.

A town with no parents.

A town with no curfews.

And if I have anything to do with it, she'll have a closetful of nothing but dresses.

Shit. Now that I look at it, I think we both might end up failing.

A lot has happened since I last wrote to you, but then again nothing has happened. Compared to the first few months following my return from living with Dad in Austin, the rest of the year has been pretty tame. Once Sky found out the truth, Karen eased up on the technology restrictions. I got her an iPhone for her real birthday and she has a laptop now, so we get to see each other every night through Skype.

I love Skype. A lot. Just sayin'.

Mom and Dad are good. Dad didn't put two and two together when he met Sky, which I didn't really think he would to begin with. He never really spent a lot of time around her when we were kids because he worked so much. He does love her, though. And Mom? Good lord, Les. Mom can't get enough of her. It kind of weirds me out how close they've become, but it's also good. It's good for Mom. I think having Sky as part of the family now has helped relieve some of the grief she still feels from your death.

And yes, we all still feel it. Everyone who loved you still feels it. And while I don't really relive your death anymore, I still miss you like hell. I miss you so much. Especially when something happens that I know you would think was funny. I catch myself laughing and then all of a sudden I realize I'm the only one laughing and it hits me that I was expecting you to laugh, too. I miss your laugh.

I could go on and on about all the things I miss about you to the point that I start to feel sorry for myself again. But I've learned over the past year what it really means to be able to miss someone. In order to miss someone, that means you were privileged enough to have them in your life to begin with.

And while seventeen years doesn't seem like near enough time to have spent with you over the course of a lifetime, it's still seventeen more years than the people that never knew you at all. So if I look at it that way... I'm pretty damn lucky.

I'm the luckiest brother ever in the whole wide world.

I'm gonna go live my life now, Les. A life I'm actually able to look forward to, and I honestly thought I'd never be able to say that. Then again, I honestly thought I'd always be hopeless, but I find hope every single day.

And sometimes I find her at night, too... on Skype.

I love you.

Dean

Acknowledgments

First and foremost, a huge thank-you to Griffin Peterson for gracing the cover of *Losing Hope*. Your kindness and humbleness are much appreciated by me, as well as the readers.

Also, I would once again like to acknowledge all bloggers for your endless support. Without you, these books would not be possible.

During the process of writing both *Hopeless* and *Losing Hope*, I never expected the type of support and feedback I have received from readers. So many of you have shared your stories with me and have taken the time to let me know how these books helped you overcome your own struggles and "chapter breaks." For that, I thank each and every one of you who have reached out to me. It's why I continue to write . . . because you continue to support me.

About the Author

Colleen Hoover is the *New York Times* bestselling author of four novels: *Slammed*, *Point of Retreat*, *Hopeless*, and *This Girl*. She lives in Texas with her husband and their three boys. To read more about this author, visit her website at www.colleenhoover.com.

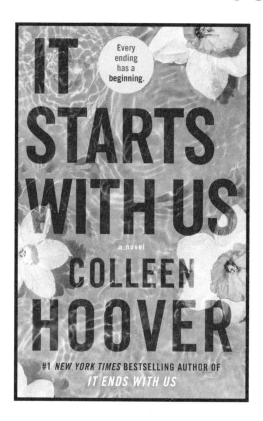

Hopeless

Hopeless

A Novel

Colleen Hoover

ATRIA PAPERBACK

NEW YORK   LONDON   TORONTO   SYDNEY   NEW DELHI

ATRIA PAPERBACK

A Division of Simon & Schuster, Inc.
1230 Avenue of the Americas
New York, NY 10020

First Atria Paperback edition May 2013

ATRIA PAPERBACK and colophon are trademarks of Simon & Schuster, Inc.

For information about special discounts for bulk purchases, please contact Simon & Schuster Special Sales at 1-866-506-1949 or business@simonandschuster.com.

The Simon & Schuster Speakers Bureau can bring authors to your live event. For more information or to book an event, contact the Simon & Schuster Speakers Bureau at 1-866-248-3049 or visit our website at www.simonspeakers.com.

Manufactured in China

30 29 28 27 26 25 24 23 22 21

Library of Congress Cataloging-in-Publication Data

Hoover, Colleen.
  Hopeless : a novel / by Colleen Hoover. — First ATRIA Books trade paperback edition.
      pages cm
1. Life change events—Fiction. I. Title.
  PS3608.O623H67 2013
  813'.6—dc23

                                                    2013006834

ISBN 978-1-4767-4355-4

For Vance.
Some fathers give you life. Some show you how to live it.
Thank you for showing me how.

Sunday, October 28, 2012
7:29 p.m.

I stand up and look down at the bed, holding my breath in fear of the sounds that are escalating from deep within my throat.

I will not cry.

I will not cry.

Slowly sinking to my knees, I place my hands on the edge of the bed and run my fingers over the yellow stars poured across the deep blue background of the comforter. I stare at the stars until they begin to blur from the tears that are clouding my vision.

I squeeze my eyes shut and bury my head into the bed, grabbing fistfuls of the blanket. My shoulders begin to shake as the sobs I've been trying to contain violently break out of me. With one swift movement, I stand up, scream, and rip the blanket off the bed, throwing it across the room.

I ball my fists and frantically look around for something else to throw. I grab the pillows off the bed and chuck them at the reflection in the mirror of the girl I no longer know. I watch as the girl in the mirror stares back at me, sobbing pathetically. The weakness in her tears infuriates me. We begin to run toward each other until our fists collide against the glass, smashing the mirror. I watch as she falls into a million shiny pieces onto the carpet.

I grip the edges of the dresser and push it sideways, letting out another scream that has been pent up for way too long. When the dresser comes to rest on its back, I rip open the drawers and throw the contents across the room, spinning and throwing and kicking at everything in my path. I grab at the sheer blue curtain panels and yank them until the rod snaps and the curtains fall around me. I reach over to the boxes piled high in the corner, and without even knowing what's inside, I take the top one and throw it against the wall with as much force as my five-foot, three-inch frame can muster.

"I hate you!" I cry. "I hate you, I hate you, I hate you!"

I'm throwing whatever I can find in front of me at whatever else I can find in front of me. Every time I open my mouth to scream, I taste the salt from the tears that are streaming down my cheeks.

Holder's arms suddenly engulf me from behind and grip me so tightly I become immobile. I jerk and toss and scream some more until my actions are no longer thought out. They're just reactions.

"Stop," he says calmly against my ear, unwilling to release me. I hear him, but I pretend not to. Or I just don't care. I continue to struggle against his grasp but he only tightens his grip.

"Don't touch me!" I yell at the top of my lungs, clawing at his arms. Again, it doesn't faze him.

Don't touch me. Please, please, please.

The small voice echoes in my mind and I immediately become limp in his arms. I become weaker as my tears grow stronger, consuming me. I become nothing more than a vessel for the tears that won't stop shedding.

I am weak, and I'm letting *him* win.

Holder loosens his grip around me and places his hands on my shoulders, then turns me around to face him. I can't even look at him. I melt against his chest from exhaustion and defeat, taking in fistfuls of his shirt as I sob, my cheek pressed against his heart. He places his hand on the back of my head and lowers his mouth to my ear.

"Sky." His voice is steady and unaffected. "You need to leave. Now."

Saturday, August 25, 2012
11:50 p.m.

Two months earlier . . .

I'd like to think most of the decisions I've made throughout my seventeen years have been smart ones. Hopefully
intelligence is measured by weight, and the few dumb decisions I've made will be outweighed by the intelligent ones.
If that's the case, I'll need to make a shitload of smart decisions tomorrow because sneaking Grayson into my bedroom window for the third time this month weighs pretty
heavily on the dumb side of the scale. However, the only
accurate measurement of a decision's level of stupidity is
time . . . so I guess I'll wait and see if I get caught before I
break out the gavel.

Despite what this may look like, I am *not* a slut. Unless, of
course, the definition of slut is based on the fact that I make
out with lots of people, regardless of my lack of attraction to
them. In that case, one might have grounds for debate.

"Hurry," Grayson mouths behind the closed window,
obviously irritated at my lack of urgency.

I unlock the latch and slide the window up as quietly
as possible. Karen may be an unconventional parent, but
when it comes to boys sneaking through bedroom windows
at midnight, she's your typical, disapproving mother.

"Quiet," I whisper. Grayson hoists himself up and throws one leg over the ledge, then climbs into my bedroom. It helps that the windows on this side of the house are barely three feet from the ground; it's almost like having my own door. In fact, Six and I have probably used our windows to go back and forth to each other's houses more than we've used actual doors. Karen has become so used to it, she doesn't even question my window being open the majority of the time.

Before I close the curtain, I glance to Six's bedroom window. She waves at me with one hand while pulling on Jaxon's arm with the other as he climbs into her bedroom. As soon as Jaxon is safely inside, he turns and sticks his head back out the window. "Meet me at your truck in an hour," he whispers loudly to Grayson. He closes Six's window and shuts her curtains.

Six and I have been joined at the hip since the day she moved in next door four years ago. Our bedroom windows are adjacent to each other, which has proven to be extremely convenient. Things started out innocently enough. When we were fourteen, I would sneak into her room at night and we would steal ice cream from the freezer and watch movies. When we were fifteen, we started sneaking boys in to eat ice cream and watch movies *with* us. By the time we were sixteen, the ice cream and movies took a backseat to the boys. Now, at seventeen, we don't even bother leaving our respective bedrooms until *after* the boys go home. That's when the ice cream and movies take precedence again.

Six goes through boyfriends like I go through flavors of ice cream. Right now her flavor of the month is Jaxon. Mine is Rocky Road. Grayson and Jaxon are best friends, which is how Grayson and I were initially thrown together. When Six's flavor of the month has a hot best friend, she eases him into my graces. Grayson is definitely hot. He's got an undeniably great body, perfectly sloppy hair, piercing dark eyes . . . the works. The majority of girls I know would feel privileged just to be in the same room as him.

It's too bad *I* don't.

I close the curtains and spin around to find Grayson inches from my face, ready to get the show started. He places his hands on my cheeks and flashes his panty-dropping grin. "Hey, beautiful." He doesn't give me a chance to respond before his lips greet mine in a sloppy introduction. He continues kissing me while slipping off his shoes. He slides them off effortlessly while we both walk toward my bed, mouths still meshed together. The ease with which he does both things simultaneously is impressive *and* disturbing. He slowly eases me back onto my bed. "Is your door locked?"

"Go double check," I say. He gives me a quick peck on the lips before he hops up to ensure the door is locked. I've made it thirteen years with Karen and have never been grounded; I don't want to give her any reason to start now. I'll be eighteen in a few weeks and even then, I doubt she'll change her parenting style as long as I'm under her roof.

Not that her parenting style is a negative one. It's just . . . very contradictory. She's been strict my whole life. We've never had access to the internet, cell phones, or even a television because she believes technology is the root of all evil in the world. Yet, she's extremely lenient in other regards. She allows me to go out with Six whenever I want, and as long as she knows where I am, I don't even really have a curfew. I've never pushed that one too far, though, so maybe I do have a curfew and I just don't realize it.

She doesn't care if I cuss, even though I rarely do. She even lets me have wine with dinner every now and then. She talks to me more like I'm her friend than her daughter (even though she adopted me thirteen years ago) and has somehow even warped me into being (almost) completely honest with her about everything that goes on in my life.

There is no middle ground with her. She's either extremely lenient or extremely strict. She's like a conservative liberal. Or a liberal conservative. Whatever she is, she's hard to figure out, which is why I stopped trying years ago.

The only thing we've ever really butted heads on was the issue of public school. She has homeschooled me my whole life (public school is another root of evil) and I've been begging to be enrolled since Six planted the idea in my head. I've been applying to colleges and feel like I'll have a better chance at getting into the schools that I want if I can add a few extracurricular activities to the applications. After months of incessant pleas from Six and me, Karen finally conceded and allowed me to enroll for my senior year. I could have enough credits to graduate from my home study program in just a couple of months, but a small part of me has always had a desire to experience life as a normal teenager.

Of course, if I had known then that Six would be leaving for a foreign exchange the same week as what was supposed to be our first day of senior year together, I never would have entertained the idea of public school. But I'm unforgivably stubborn and would rather stab myself in the meaty part of my hand with a fork than tell Karen I've changed my mind.

I've tried to avoid thinking about the fact that I won't have Six this year. I know how much she was hoping the exchange would work out, but the selfish part of me was really hoping it wouldn't. The idea of having to walk through those doors without her terrifies me. But I realize that our separation is inevitable and I can only go so long before I'm forced into the real world where other people besides Six and Karen live.

My lack of access to the real world has been replaced completely by books, and it can't be healthy to live in a land of happily-ever-afters. Reading has also introduced me to the (perhaps dramatized) horrors of high school and first days and cliques and mean girls. It doesn't help that, according to Six, I've already got a bit of a reputation just being associated with her. Six doesn't have the best track record for celibacy, and apparently some of the guys I've made out with don't have the best track record for secrecy. The combination should make for a pretty interesting first day of school.

Not that I care. I didn't enroll to make friends or impress anyone, so as long as my unwarranted reputation doesn't interfere with my ultimate goal, I'll get along just fine.

I hope.

Grayson walks back toward the bed after ensuring my door is locked, and he shoots me a seductive grin. "How about a little striptease?" He sways his hips and inches his shirt up, revealing his hard-earned set of abs. I'm beginning to notice he flashes them any chance he gets. He's pretty much your typical, self-absorbed bad boy.

I laugh when he twirls the shirt around his head and

throws it at me, then slides on top of me again. He slips his hand behind my neck, pulling my mouth back into position.

The first time Grayson snuck into my room was a little over a month ago, and he made it clear from the beginning that he wasn't looking for a relationship. I made it clear that I wasn't looking for *him*, so naturally we hit it off right away. Of course, he'll be one of the few people I know at school, so I'm worried it might mess up the good thing we've got going—which is absolutely nothing.

He's been here less than three minutes and he's already got his hand up my shirt. I think it's safe to say he's not here for my stimulating conversation. His lips move from my mouth in favor of my neck, so I use the moment of respite to inhale deeply and try again to feel something.

Anything.

I fix my eyes on the plastic glow-in-the-dark stars adhered to the ceiling above my bed, vaguely aware of the lips that have inched their way to my chest. There are seventy-six of them. Stars, that is. I know this because for the last few weeks I've had ample time to count them while I've been in this same predicament. Me, lying unnoticeably unresponsive, while Grayson explores my face and neck, and sometimes my chest, with his curious, overexcited lips.

Why, if I'm not into this, do I let him do it?

I've never had any emotional connection to the guys I make out with. Or rather, the guys that make out with *me*. It's unfortunately mostly one-sided. I've only had one guy come close to provoking a physical or emotional response from me once, and that turned out to be a self-induced delusion. His name was Matt and we ended up dating for less than a month before his idiosyncrasies got the best of me.

Like how he refused to drink bottled water unless it was through a straw. Or the way his nostrils flared right before he leaned in to kiss me. Or the way he said, "I love you," after only three weeks of declaring ourselves exclusive.

Yeah. That last one was the kicker. Buh-bye Matty boy.

Six and I have analyzed my lack of physical response to guys many times in the past. For a while she suspected I might be gay. After a very brief and awkward "theory-testing" kiss between us when we were sixteen, we both concluded that wasn't the case. It's not that I don't enjoy making out with guys. I do enjoy it—otherwise, I wouldn't do it. I just don't enjoy it for the same reasons as other girls. I've never been swept off my feet. I don't get butterflies. In fact, the whole idea of being swooned by anyone is foreign to me. The real reason I enjoy making out with guys is simply that it makes me feel completely and comfortably numb. It's situations like the one I'm in right now with Grayson when it's nice for my mind to shut down. It just completely stops, and I like that feeling.

My eyes are focused on the seventeen stars in the upper right quadrant of the cluster on my ceiling, when I suddenly snap back to reality. Grayson's hands have ventured further than I've allowed them to in the past and I quickly become aware of the fact that he has unbuttoned my jeans and his fingers are working their way around the cotton edge of my panties.

"No, Grayson," I whisper, pushing his hand away.

He pulls his hand back and groans, then presses his forehead into my pillow. "Come on, Sky." He's breathing heavily against my neck. He adjusts his weight to his right arm and looks down at me, attempting to play me with his smile.

Did I mention I'm immune to his panty-dropping grin?

"How much longer are you gonna keep this up?" He slides his hand over my stomach and inches his fingertips into my jeans again.

My skin crawls. "Keep *what* up?" I attempt to ease out from under him.

He pushes up on his hands and looks down at me like I'm clueless. "This 'good girl' act you've been trying to put on. I'm over it, Sky. Let's just do this already."

This brings me back to the fact that, contrary to popular belief, I am *not* a slut. I've never had sex with any of the boys I've made out with, including the currently pouting Grayson. I'm aware that my lack of sexual response would probably make it easier on an emotional level to have sex with random people. However, I'm also aware that it might be the very reason I *shouldn't* have sex. I know that once I cross that line, the rumors about me will no longer be rumors. They'll all be fact. The last thing I want is for the things people say about me to be validated. I guess I can chalk my almost eighteen years of virginity up to sheer stubbornness.

For the first time in the ten minutes he's been here, I notice the smell of alcohol reeking from him. "You're drunk." I push against his chest. "I told you not to come over here drunk again." He rolls off me and I stand up to button my pants and pull my shirt back into place. I'm relieved he's drunk. I'm beyond ready for him to leave.

He sits up on the edge of the bed and grabs my waist, pulling me toward him. He wraps his arms around me and rests his head against my stomach. "I'm sorry," he says. "It's just that I want you so bad I don't think I can take coming over here again if you don't let me have you." He lowers his hands and cups my butt, then presses his lips against the area of skin where my shirt meets my jeans.

"Then don't come over here." I roll my eyes and back away from him, then head to the window. When I pull the curtain back, Jaxon is already making his way out of Six's window. Somehow we both managed to condense this hour-long visit into ten minutes. I glance at Six and she gives me the all-knowing "time for a new flavor" look.

She follows Jaxon out of her window and walks over to me. "Is Grayson drunk, too?"

I nod. "Strike three." I turn and look at Grayson, who's lying back on the bed, ignorant of the fact that he's no longer welcome. I walk over to the bed and pick his shirt up, tossing it at his face. "Leave," I say. He looks up at me and cocks an eyebrow, then begrudgingly slides off the bed when he sees I'm not making a joke. He slips his shoes back on, pouting like a four-year-old. I step aside to let him out.

Six waits until Grayson has cleared the window, then she climbs inside when one of the guys mumbles the word "whores." Once inside, Six rolls her eyes and turns around to stick her head out.

"Funny how we're whores because you *didn't* get laid. Assholes." She shuts the window and walks over to the bed, plopping down on it and crossing her hands behind her head. "And another one bites the dust."

I laugh, but my laugh is cut short by a loud bang on my bedroom door. I immediately go unlock it, then step aside, preparing for Karen to barge in. Her motherly instincts don't let me down. She looks around the room frantically until she eyes Six on the bed.

"Dammit," she says, spinning around to face me. She puts her hands on her hips and frowns. "I could have sworn I heard boys in here."

I walk over to the bed and attempt to hide the sheer panic coursing throughout my body. "And you seem disappointed *because* . . ." I absolutely don't understand her reaction to things sometimes. Like I said before . . . *contradictory*.

"You turn eighteen in a month. I'm running out of time to ground you for the first time ever. You need to start screwing up a little more, kid."

I breathe a sigh of relief, seeing she's only kidding. I almost feel guilty that she doesn't actually suspect her daughter was being felt up five minutes earlier in this very room. My heart is pounding against my chest so incredibly loud, I'm afraid she might hear it.

"Karen?" Six says from behind us. "If it makes you feel better, two hotties just made out with us, but we kicked them out right before you walked in because they were drunk."

My jaw drops and I spin around to shoot Six a look that I'm hoping will let her know that sarcasm isn't at all funny when it's the *truth*.

Karen laughs. "Well, maybe tomorrow night you'll get some cute *sober* boys."

I don't think I have to worry about Karen hearing my heartbeat anymore, because it just completely stopped.

"Sober boys, huh? I think I can arrange that," Six says, winking at me.

"Are you staying the night?" Karen says to Six as she makes her way back to the bedroom door.

Six shrugs her shoulders. "I think we'll stay at my house

tonight. It's my last week in my own bed for six months. Plus, I've got Channing Tatum on the flat-screen."

I glance back at Karen and see it starting.

"Don't, Mom." I begin walking toward her, but I can see the mist forming in her eyes. "No, no, no." By the time I reach her, it's too late. She's bawling. If there's one thing I can't stand, it's crying. Not because it makes me emotional, but because it annoys the hell out of me. And it's awkward.

"Just one more," she says, rushing toward Six. She's already hugged her no less than ten times today. I almost think she's sadder than I am that Six is leaving in a few days. Six obliges her request for the eleventh hug and winks at me over Karen's shoulder. I practically have to pry them apart, just so Karen will get out of my room.

She walks back to the door and turns around one last time. "I hope you meet a hot Italian boy," she says to Six.

"I better meet more than just one," Six deadpans.

When the door closes behind Karen, I spin around and jump on the bed, then punch Six in the arm. "You're such a *bitch*," I say. "That wasn't funny. I thought I got caught."

She laughs and grabs my hand, then stands up. "Come. I've got Rocky Road."

She doesn't have to ask twice.

Monday, August 27, 2012
7:15 a.m.

I debated whether to run this morning but I ended up sleeping in, instead. I run every day except Sunday, but it seems wrong having to get up extra early today. Being the first day of school is enough torture in itself, so I decide to put off my run until after school.

Luckily, I've had my own car for about a year now, so I don't have to rely on anyone other than myself to get me to school on time. Not only do I get here on time, I get here forty-five minutes early. I'm the third car in the parking lot, so at least I get a good spot.

I use the extra time to check out the athletic facilities next to the parking lot. If I'm going to be trying out for the track team, I should at least know where to go. Besides, I can't just sit in my car for the next half hour and count down the minutes.

When I reach the track, there's a guy across the field running laps, so I cut right and walk up the bleachers. I take a seat at the very top and take in my new surroundings. From up here, I can see the whole school laid out in front of me. It doesn't look nearly as big or intimidating as I've been imagining. Six made me a hand-drawn map and even wrote a few pointers down, so I pull the paper out of my backpack and look at it for the first time. I think she's trying to overcompensate because she feels bad for abandoning me.

I look at the school grounds, then back at the map. It looks easy enough. Classrooms in the building to the right. Lunchroom on the left. Track and field behind the gym. There is a long list of her pointers, so I begin reading them.

—Never use the restroom next to the science lab. Ever. Not ever.

—Only wear your backpack across one shoulder. Never double-arm it, it's lame.

—Always check the date on the milk.

—Befriend Stewart, the maintenance guy. It's good to have him on your side.

—The cafeteria. Avoid it at all costs, but if the weather is bad, just pretend you know what you're doing when you walk inside. They can smell fear.

—If you get Mr. Declare for math, sit in the back and don't make eye contact. He loves high school girls, if you know what I mean. Or, better yet, sit in the front. It'll be an easy A.

The list goes on, but I can't read anymore right now. I'm still stuck on *"they can smell fear."* It's times like these that I wish I had a cell phone, because I would call Six right now and demand an explanation. I fold the paper up and put it back in my bag, then focus my attention on the lone runner. He's seated on the track with his back turned to me, stretching. I don't know if he's a student or a coach, but if Grayson saw this guy without a shirt, he'd probably become a lot more modest about being so quick to flash his own abs.

The guy stands up and walks toward the bleachers,

never looking up at me. He exits the gate and walks to one of the cars in the parking lot. He opens his door and grabs a shirt off the front seat, then pulls it on over his head. He hops in the car and pulls away, just as the parking lot begins to fill up. And it's filling up fast.

Oh, God.

I grab my backpack and purposefully pull both arms through it, then descend the stairs that lead straight to Hell.

Did I say Hell? Because that was putting it mildly. Public school is everything I was afraid it would be and worse. The classes aren't so bad, but I had to (out of pure necessity and unfamiliarity) use the restroom next to the science lab, and although I survived, I'll be scarred for life. A simple side note from Six informing me that it's used as more of a brothel than an actual restroom would have sufficed.

It's fourth period now and I've heard the words "slut" and "whore" whispered not so subtly by almost every girl I've passed in the hallways. And speaking of not-so-subtle, the heap of dollar bills that just fell out of my locker, along with a note, were a good indicator that I may not be very welcome. The note was signed by the principal, but I find that hard to believe based on the fact that "your" was spelled "you're," and the note said, *"Sorry you're locker didn't come with a pole, slut."*

I stare at the note in my hands with a tight-lipped smile, shamefully accepting my self-inflicted fate that will be the next two semesters. I seriously thought people only acted this way in books, but I'm witnessing firsthand that idiots actually exist. I'm also hoping most of the pranks being played at my expense are going to be just like the stripper-cash prank I'm experiencing right now. What idiot gives away money as an insult? I'm guessing a rich one. Or rich *ones*.

I'm sure the clique of giggling girls behind me that are scantily, yet expensively clad, are expecting my reaction to be to drop my things and run to the nearest restroom crying. There are only three issues with their expectations.

1. *I don't cry. Ever.*
2. *I've been to that restroom and I'll never go back.*
3. *I like money. Who would run from that?*

I set my backpack on the floor of the hallway and pick the money up. There are at least twenty one-dollar bills scattered on the floor, and more than ten still in my locker. I scoop those up as well and shove it all into my backpack. I switch books and shut my locker, then slide my backpack on both shoulders and smile.

"Tell your daddies I said thank you." I walk past the clique of girls (that are no longer giggling) and ignore their glares.

It's lunchtime, and looking at the amount of rain flooding the courtyard, it's obvious that Karma has retaliated with shitty weather. Who she's retaliating against is still up in the air.

I can do this.

I place my hands on the doors to the cafeteria and open them, half-expecting to be greeted by fire and brimstone.

I step through the doorway and it's not fire and brimstone that I'm met with. It's a decibel level of noise unlike anything my ears have ever been subjected to. It's almost as if every single person in this entire cafeteria is trying to talk louder than every other person in this entire cafeteria. I've just enrolled in a school of nothing but one-uppers.

I do my best to feign confidence, not wanting to attract unwanted attention from anyone. Guys, cliques, outcasts, *or* Grayson. I make it halfway to the food line unscathed, when someone slips his arm through mine and pulls me along behind him.

"I've been waiting for you," he says. I don't even get a good look at his face before he's guiding me across the cafeteria, weaving in and out of tables. I would object to this sudden disruption, but it's the most exciting thing that's happened to me all day. He slips his arm from mine and grabs my hand, pulling me faster along behind him. I stop resisting and go with the flow.

From the looks of the back of him, he's got style, as strange as that style may be. He's wearing a flannel shirt that's edged with the exact same shade of hot pink as his shoes. His pants are black and tight and very figure flattering . . . if he were a girl. Instead, the pants just accentuate the frailty of his frame. His dark brown hair is cropped short on the sides and is a little longer on top. His eyes are . . . staring at me. I realize we've come to a stop and he's no longer holding my hand.

"If it isn't the whore of Babylon." He grins at me. Despite the words that just came out of his mouth, his expression is contrastingly endearing. He takes a seat at the table and flicks his hand like he wants me to do the same. There are two trays in front of him, but only one *him*. He scoots one of the trays of food toward the empty spot in front of me. "Sit. We have an alliance to discuss."

I don't sit. I don't do anything for several seconds as I contemplate the situation before me. I have no idea who this kid is, yet he acts like he was expecting me. Let's not overlook the fact that he just called me a whore. And from the looks of it, he bought me . . . lunch? I glance at him sideways, attempting to figure him out, when the backpack in the seat next to him catches my eye.

"You like to read?" I ask, pointing at the book peering out of the top of his backpack. It's not a textbook. It's an actual book-book. Something I thought was lost on this generation of internet fiends. I reach over and pull the book out of his backpack and take a seat across from him. "What genre is it? And please don't say sci-fi."

He leans back in his seat and grins like he just won something. Hell, maybe he did. I'm sitting here, aren't I?

"Should it matter what genre it is if the book is good?" he says.

I flip through the pages, unable to tell if it's a romance or not. I'm a sucker for romances, and based on the look of the guy across from me, he might be, too.

"Is it?" I ask, flipping through it. "Good?"

"Yes. Keep it. I just finished it during computer lab."

I look up at him and he's still basking in his glow of victory. I put the book in my backpack, then lean forward and inspect my tray. The first thing I do is check the date on the milk. It's good.

"What if I was a vegetarian?" I ask, looking at the chicken breast in the salad.

"So eat around it," he retorts.

I grab my fork and stab a piece of the chicken, then bring it to my mouth. "Well you're lucky, because I'm not."

He smiles, then picks up his own fork and begins eating.

"Whom are we forming an alliance against?" I'm curious as to why I've been singled out.

He glances around him and raises his hand in the air, twirling it in all directions. "Idiots. Jocks. Bigots. Bitches." He brings his hand down and I notice that his nails are all painted black. He sees me observing his nails and he looks down at them and pouts. "I went with black because it best depicts my mood today. Maybe after you agree to join me on my quest, I'll switch to something a bit more cheerful. Perhaps yellow."

I shake my head. "I hate yellow. Stick with black, it matches your heart."

He laughs. It's a genuine, pure laugh that makes me smile. I like . . . this kid whose name I don't even know.

"What's your name?" I ask.

"Breckin. And you're Sky. At least I'm hoping you are. I guess I could have confirmed your identity before I spilled to you the details of my evil, sadistic plan to take over the school with our two-person alliance."

"I am Sky. And you really have nothing to worry about, seeing as how you really haven't shared any details about your evil plan yet. I am curious though, how you know who I am. I know four or five guys at this school and I've made out with every one of them. You aren't one of them, so what gives?"

For a split second, I see a flash of what looks like pity in his eyes. He's lucky it was just a flash, though.

Breckin shrugs. "I'm new here. And if you haven't deduced from my impeccable fashion sense, I think it's safe to say that I'm . . ." he leans forward and cups his hand to his mouth in secrecy. "Mormon," he whispers.

I laugh. "And here I was thinking you were about to say *gay*."

"That, too," he says with a flick of his wrist. He folds his hands under his chin and leans forward a couple of inches. "In all seriousness, Sky. I noticed you in class today and it's obvious you're new here, too. And after seeing the stripper money fall out of your locker before fourth period, then witnessing your nonreaction to it, I knew we were meant to be. Also, I figured if we teamed up, we might prevent at least two unnecessary teenage suicides this year. So, what do you say? Want to be my very bestest friend ever in the whole wide world?"

I laugh. How could I not laugh at that? "Sure. But if the book sucks, we're re-evaluating the friendship."

Monday, August 27, 2012
3:55 p.m.

Turns out, Breckin was my saving grace today . . . and he really *is* Mormon. We have a lot in common, and even more out of common, which makes him that much more appealing. He was adopted as well, but has a close relationship with his birth family. Breckin has two brothers who aren't adopted, and who also aren't gay, so his parents assume his gayness (his word, not mine) has to do with the fact that he doesn't share a bloodline with them. He says they're hoping it fades with more prayer and high school graduation, but he insists that it's only going to flourish.

His dream is to one day be a famous Broadway star, but he says he lacks the ability to sing or act, so he's scaling down his dream and applying to business school instead. I told him I wanted to major in creative writing and sit around in yoga pants and do nothing but write books and eat ice cream every day. He asked what genre I wanted to write and I replied, "It doesn't matter, so long as it's good, right?" I think that comment sealed our fate.

Now I'm on my way home, deciding whether or not to go fill Six in on the bittersweet happenings of day one, or go grocery shopping in order to get my caffeine fix before my daily run.

The caffeine wins, despite the fact that my affection for Six is slightly greater.

My minimal portion of familial contribution is the weekly grocery shopping. Everything in our house is sugar-free, carb-free, and *taste*-free, thanks to Karen's unconventional vegan way of life, so I actually prefer doing the grocery shopping. I grab a six-pack of soda and the biggest bag of bite-size Snickers I can find and throw them in the cart. I have a nice hiding spot for my secret stash in my bedroom. Most teenagers are stashing away cigarettes and weed—I stash away sugar.

When I reach the checkout, I recognize the girl ringing me up is in my second-period English class. I'm pretty sure her name is Shayna, but her nametag reads *Shayla*. Shayna/Shayla is everything I wish I were. Tall, voluptuous, and sun-kissed blonde. I can maybe pull off five-three on a good day and my flat brown hair could use a trim—maybe even some highlights. They would be a bitch to maintain considering the amount of hair that I have. It falls about six inches past my shoulders, but I keep it pulled up most of the time due to the southern humidity.

"Aren't you in my Science class?" Shayna/Shayla asks.

"English," I correct her.

She shoots me a condescending look. "I *did* speak English," she says defensively. "I said, 'aren't you in my Science class?'"

Oh, holy hell. Maybe I don't want to be *that* blonde.

"No," I say. "I meant English as in 'I'm not in your *Science* class, I'm in your *English* class.'"

She looks at me blankly for a second, then laughs. "Oh." Realization dawns on her face. She eyes the screen in front of her and reads out my total. I slip my hand in my back pocket and retrieve the credit card, hoping to hurry and excuse myself from what I fear is about to become a less than stellar conversation.

"Oh, dear *God*," she says quietly. "Look who's back."

I glance up at her and she's staring at someone behind me in the other checkout line.

No, let me correct that. She's *salivating* over someone behind me in the other checkout line.

"Hey, Holder," she says seductively toward him, flashing her full-lipped smile.

Did she just bat her eyelashes? Yep. I'm pretty sure she just batted her eyelashes. I honestly thought they only did that in cartoons.

I glance back to see who this *Holder* character is that has somehow managed to wash away any semblance of self-respect Shayna/Shayla might have had. The guy looks up at her and nods an acknowledgment, seemingly uninterested.

"Hey . . ." He squints his eyes at her nametag. "*Shayla*." He turns his attention back to his cashier.

Is he ignoring her? One of the prettiest girls in school practically gives him an open invitation and he acts like it's an inconvenience? Is he even *human*? This isn't how the guys I know are supposed to react.

She huffs. "It's *Shayna*," she says, annoyed that he didn't know her name. I turn back toward Shayna and swipe my credit card through the machine.

"Sorry," he says to her. "But you do realize your nametag says *Shayla*, right?"

She looks down at her chest and flips her nametag up so she can read it. "Huh," she says, narrowing her eyebrows as if she's deep in thought. I doubt it's that deep, though.

"When did you get back?" she asks Holder, ignoring me

completely. I just swiped my card and I'm almost positive she should be doing something on her end, but she's too busy planning her wedding with this guy to remember she has a customer.

"Last week." His response is curt.

"So are they gonna let you come back to school?" she asks.

I can hear him sigh from where I'm standing.

"Doesn't matter," he says flatly. "Not going back."

This last statement of his immediately gives Shayna/Shayla cold feet. She rolls her eyes and turns her attention back to me. "It's a shame when a body like that doesn't come with any brains," she whispers.

The irony in her statement isn't lost on me.

When she finally starts punching numbers on the register to complete the transaction, I use her distraction as an opportunity to glance behind me again. I'm curious to get another look at the guy who seemed to be irritated by the leggy blonde. He's looking down into his wallet, laughing at something his cashier said. As soon as I lay eyes on him, I immediately notice three things:

1. *His amazingly perfect white teeth hidden behind that seductively crooked grin.*

2. *The dimples that form in the crevices between the corners of his lips and cheeks when he smiles.*

3. *I'm pretty sure I'm having a hot flash.*

Or I have butterflies.

Or maybe I'm coming down with a stomach virus.

The feeling is so foreign; I'm not sure *what* it is. I can't say what is so different about him that would prompt my first-ever normal biological response to another person. However, I'm not sure I've ever seen anyone so incredibly like *him* before. He's beautiful. Not beautiful in the pretty-boy sense. Or even in the tough-guy sense. Just a perfect mixture of in-between. Not too big, but not at all small. Not too rough, not too perfect. He's wearing jeans and a white T-shirt, nothing special. His hair doesn't look like it's even been brushed today and could probably use a good trim, just like mine. It's just long enough in the front that he has to move it out of his eyes when he looks up and catches me full-on staring.

Shit.

I would normally pull my gaze away as soon as direct eye contact is made, but there's something odd about the way he reacts when he looks at me that keeps my focus glued to his. His smile immediately fades and he cocks his head. An inquisitive look enters his eyes and he slowly shakes his head, either in disbelief or . . . *disgust*? I can't put my finger on it, but it's certainly not a pleasant reaction. I glance around, hoping I'm not the recipient of his displeasure. When I turn back to look at him, he's still staring.

At *me*.

I'm disturbed, to say the least, so I quickly turn around and face Shayla again. Or Shayna. Whatever the hell her name is. I need to regain my bearings. Somehow, in the course of sixty seconds, this guy has managed to swoon me, then terrify the hell out of me. The mixed reaction is not good for my caffeine-deprived body. I'd much rather he regard me with the same indifference he showed toward

Shayna/Shayla, than to look at me like that again. I grab my receipt from what's-her-face and slip it into my pocket.

"Hey." His voice is deep and demanding and immediately causes my breathing to halt. I don't know if he's referring to what's-her-face or me, so I slip my hands through the handles of the grocery sacks, hoping to make it to my car before he finishes checking out.

"I think he's talking to you," she says. I grab the last of the sacks and ignore her, walking as fast as I can toward the exit.

Once I reach my car, I let out a huge breath as I open the back door to put the groceries inside. *What the hell is wrong with me?* A good-looking guy tries to get my attention and I *run?* I'm not uncomfortable around guys. I'm confident to a fault, even. The one time in my life I might actually feel what could possibly be an attraction for someone, and I run.

Six is going to kill me.

But that *look.* There was something so disturbing about the way he looked at me. It was uncomfortable, embarrassing, and somehow flattering all at once. I'm not used to having these sorts of reactions at all, much less more than one at a time.

"Hey."

I freeze. His voice is without a doubt directed at me now.

I still can't distinguish between butterflies or a stomach virus, but either way I'm not fond of the way that voice penetrates right to the pit of my stomach. I stiffen and slowly turn around, all of a sudden aware that I'm nowhere near as confident as my past would lead me to believe.

He's holding two sacks down at his side with one hand

while he rubs the back of his neck with his other hand. I'm really wishing the weather were still shitty and rainy so he wouldn't be standing here right now. He rests his eyes on mine and the look of contempt from inside the store is now replaced with a crooked grin that seems a bit forced in our current predicament. Now that I have a closer look at him, it's apparent the stomach virus isn't the root of the sudden stomach issues at all.

It's simply *him*.

Everything about him, from his tousled dark hair, to his stark blue eyes, to that . . . *dimple*, to his thick arms that I just want to reach out and touch.

Touch? Really, Sky? Get ahold of yourself!

Everything about him causes my lungs to fail and my heart to go into overdrive. I have a feeling if he smiles at me like Grayson tries to smile at me, my panties will be on the ground in record time.

As soon as my eyes leave his physique long enough for us to make eye contact again, he releases the tight grip he has on his neck and switches the sacks to his left hand.

"I'm Holder," he says, extending his hand out to me.

I look down at his hand, then take a step back without shaking it. This whole situation is entirely too awkward for me to trust him with this innocent introduction. Maybe if he hadn't pierced me with his intense glare in the store, I would be more susceptible to his physical perfection.

"What do you want?" I'm careful to look at him with suspicion rather than awe.

His dimple reappears with his hasty laugh and he shakes his head, then looks away again. "Um," he says with a nervous stutter that doesn't match his confident persona in the least. His eyes dart around the parking lot like he's look-ing for an escape, and he sighs before locking eyes with me again. His multitude of reactions confuses the hell out of me. He seems close to disgusted by my presence one minute, to practically running me down the next. I'm usually pretty good at reading people, but if I had to make an assumption about Holder based on the last two minutes alone, I'd have to say he suffers from split-personality disorder. His sudden shifts between flippant and intense are unnerving.

"This might sound lame," he says. "But you look really familiar. Do you mind if I ask what your name is?"

Disappointment sets in as soon as the pickup line es-capes his lips. He's one of *those* guys. You know. The in-credibly gorgeous guys who can have anyone, anytime, anywhere, and they know it? The guys that, all they have to do is flash a crooked smile or a dimple and ask a girl her name and she melts until she's on her knees in front of him? The guys who spend their Saturday nights climbing through windows?

I'm highly disappointed. I roll my eyes and reach be-hind me, pulling on the door handle to my car. "I've got a boyfriend," I lie. I spin around and open the door, then climb inside. When I reach to pull the door shut, I'm met with resistance when it refuses to budge. I look up to see his hand grasping the top of the car door, holding it open. There's a hard desperation in his eyes that sends chills down my arms.

He looks at me and I get *chills*? Who the hell *am* I?

"Your name. That's all I want."

I debate whether I should explain to him that my name isn't going to help him in his stalking endeavors. I'm more than likely the only seventeen-year-old left in America without an online presence. With my grip still on the door handle, I discharge a warning shot with my glare. "Do you mind?" I say sharply, my eyes darting to the hand that's preventing me from shutting my door. My eyes trail from his hand to the tattoo written in small script across his forearm.

Hopeless

I can't help but laugh internally. I am obviously the target of Karma's retaliation today. I'm finally introduced to the one guy that I find attractive, and he's a high school dropout with the word "hopeless" tattooed on himself.

Now I'm irritated. I pull on the door one more time, but he doesn't budge.

"Your name. *Please*."

The desperate look in his eyes when he says *please* prompts a surprisingly sympathetic reaction from me, way out of left field.

"Sky," I say abruptly, suddenly feeling compassion for the pain that is clearly masked behind those blue eyes of his. The ease with which I give in to his request based on one look leaves me disappointed in myself. I let go of the door and crank my car.

"Sky," he repeats to himself. He ponders this for a second, then shakes his head like I got the answer to his question wrong. "Are you sure?" He cocks his head at me.

Am I *sure*? Does he think I'm Shayna/Shayla and don't even know my own name? I roll my eyes and shift in my seat, pulling my ID from my pocket. I hold it up to his face.

"Pretty sure I know my own name." I begin to pull the

ID back when he releases my door and grabs the ID out of my hand, bringing it in closer for inspection. He eyes it for a few seconds, then flicks it over in his fingers and hands it back to me.

"Sorry." He takes a step away from my car. "My mistake."

His expression is glossed over with hardness now and he watches me as I put my ID back into my pocket. I stare at him for a second, waiting for something more, but he just works his jaw back and forth while I put my seatbelt on.

He's giving up on asking me out that easily? Seriously? I put my fingers on the door handle, expecting him to hold the door open again in order to spit out another lame pickup line. When that doesn't happen and he steps back even farther as I shut my door, eeriness consumes me. If he really didn't follow me out here to ask me out, what the hell was this all about?

He runs his hand through his hair and mutters to himself, but I can't hear what he says through the closed window. I throw the car in reverse and keep my eyes on him as I back out of the parking lot. He remains motionless, staring at me the entire time I pull away. When I'm heading in the opposite direction, I adjust the rearview mirror to get a last glance at him before exiting the parking lot. I watch as he turns to walk away, smashing his fist into the hood of a car.

Good call, Sky. He's got a temper.

Monday, August 27, 2012
4:47 p.m.

After the groceries are put away, I grab a handful of chocolate from my stash and shove it in my pocket, then crawl out my window. I push Six's window up and pull myself in. It's almost five o'clock in the afternoon and she's asleep, so I tiptoe to her side of the bed and kneel down. She's got her facemask on and her dirty blonde hair is matted to her cheek, thanks to the amount of drool she produces while she sleeps. I inch in as close as I can to her face and scream her name.

"SIX! WAKE UP!"

She jerks herself up with such force that I don't have time to move out of her way. Her flailing elbow crashes into my eye and I fall back. I immediately cover my throbbing eye with my hand and sprawl out on the floor of her bedroom. I look up at her out of my good eye, and she's sitting up in the bed holding on to her head, scowling at me. "You're such a bitch," she groans. She throws her covers off and gets out of bed, then heads straight for the bathroom.

"I think you gave me a black eye," I moan.

She leaves the bathroom door open and sits down on the toilet. "Good. You deserve it." She grabs the toilet paper and kicks the bathroom door shut with her foot. "You better have something good to tell me for waking me up. I was up all night packing."

Six has never been a morning person, and from the

looks of it, she's not an afternoon person, either. In all honesty, she's also not a night person. If I had to guess when her most pleasant time of day occurs, it's probably while she sleeps, which may be why she hates to wake up so much.

Six's sense of humor and straightforward personality are huge factors in why we get along so well. Peppy, fake girls annoy the hell out of me. I don't know that *pep* is even in Six's vocabulary. She's one black wardrobe away from being your typical, broody teenager. And fake? She's as straight shooting as they come, whether you want her to be or not. There isn't a fake thing about Six, other than her name.

When she was fourteen and her parents told her they were moving to Texas from Maine, she rebelled by refusing to respond to her name. Her real name is Seven Marie, so she would only answer to *Six* just to spite her parents for making her move. They still call her Seven, but everyone else calls her Six. Just goes to show she's as stubborn as I am, which is one of the many reasons we're best friends.

"I think you'll be happy I woke you up." I pull myself up from the floor and onto her bed. "Something monumental happened today."

Six opens the bathroom door and walks back to her bed. She lies down next to me and pulls the covers up over her head. She rolls away from me, fluffing her pillow with her hand until she gets comfortable. "Let me guess . . . Karen got cable?"

I roll onto my side and scoot closer to her, wrapping my arm around her. I put my head on her pillow and spoon her. "Guess again."

"You met someone at school today and now you're pregnant and getting married and I can't be a bridesmaid at your wedding because I'll be all the way across the damn world?"

"Close, but nope." I drum my fingers on her shoulder.

"Then *what*?" she says, irritated.

I roll over onto my back and let out a deep sigh. "I saw a guy at the store after school, and holy shit, Six. He was beautiful. Scary, but beautiful."

Six immediately rolls over, managing to send an elbow straight into the same eye that she assaulted a few minutes ago. "What?!" she says loudly, ignoring the fact that I'm holding my eye and groaning again. She sits up on the bed and pulls my hand away from my face. "What?!" she yells again. "Seriously?"

I stay on my back and attempt to force the pain from my throbbing eye into the back of my mind. "I know. As soon as I looked at him it was like my entire body just melted to the floor. He was . . . wow."

"Did you talk to him? Did you get his number? Did he ask you out?"

I've never seen Six so animated before. She's being a little too giddy, and I'm not sure that I like it.

"*Jesus*, Six. Simmer down."

She looks down at me and frowns. "Sky, I've been worried about you for four years, thinking this would never happen. I would be fine if you were gay. I would be fine if you only liked skinny, short, geeky guys. I would even be fine if you were only attracted to really old, wrinkly men with even wrinklier penises. What I haven't been fine with is the thought of you never being able to experience lust." She falls back onto the bed, smiling. "Lust is the best of all the deadly sins."

I laugh and shake my head. "I beg to differ. Lust sucks. I think you've played it up all these years. My vote is still with gluttony." With that, I pull a piece of chocolate out of my pocket and pop it into my mouth.

"I need details," she says.

I scoot up on the bed until my back meets the headboard. "I don't know how to describe it. When I looked at him, I never wanted to stop. I could have stared at him all day. But then when he looked back at me, it freaked me out. He looked at me like he was pissed off that I even noticed him. Then when he followed me to my car and demanded to know my name, it was like he was mad at me for it. Like I was inconveniencing him. I went from wanting to lick his dimples to wanting to get the hell *away* from him."

"He followed you? To your car?" she asks skeptically. I nod and give her every last detail of my trip to the grocery store, all the way up to the point where he smashed his fist into the car next to him.

"God, that's so bizarre," she says when I finish. She sits up and mirrors my position against her headboard. "Are you sure he wasn't flirting with you? Trying to get your number? I mean, I've seen you with guys, Sky. You put on a good act, even if you *don't* feel it with them. I know you know how to read guys, but I think maybe the fact that you were actually attracted to him might have muddied your intuition. You think?"

I shrug. She could be right. Maybe I just read him wrong and my own negative reaction prompted him to change his mind about asking me out. "Could be. But whatever it was, it was ruined just as fast. He's a dropout, he's moody, he's got a temper and . . . he's just . . . he's *hopeless*. I don't know what my type is, but I know I don't want it to be Holder."

Six grabs my cheeks, squeezing them together, and

turns my face to hers. "Did you just say *Holder*?" she asks, her exquisitely groomed eyebrow arched in curiosity.

My lips are squished together due to her hold on my cheeks, so I just nod rather than give her a verbal response.

"*Dean* Holder? Messy brown hair? Smoldering blue eyes? A temper straight out of Fight Club?"

I shrug. "Dowds sike dim," I say, my words barely audible thanks to the grip she still has on my face. She releases her hold and I repeat what I said. "Sounds like him." I bring my hand to my face and massage my cheeks. "You know him?"

She stands up and throws her hands up in the air. "*Why*, Sky? Of all the guys you could be attracted to, why the hell is it *Dean Holder*?"

She seems disappointed. Why does she seem so disappointed? I've never heard her mention Holder before, so it's not like she's ever dated him. Why the hell does it seem that this just went from sort of exciting . . . to very, very bad?

"I need details," I say.

She rolls her head and swings her legs off the bed. She walks to her closet and grabs a pair of jeans out of a box, then pulls them up over her underwear. "He's a jerk, Sky. He used to go to our school but he got sent to juvi right after school started last year. I don't know him that well, but I know enough about him to know he's not boyfriend material."

Her description of Holder doesn't surprise me. I wish I could say it didn't disappoint me, but I can't.

"Since when is *anyone* boyfriend material?" I don't think Six has ever had a boyfriend for more than one night in her life.

She looks at me, then shrugs. "Touché." She pulls a shirt on over her head and walks to her bathroom sink. She picks up a toothbrush and squeezes toothpaste onto it, then walks back into the bedroom brushing her teeth.

"Why was he sent to juvi?" I ask, not sure if I really want to know the answer.

Six pulls the toothbrush from her mouth. "They got him for a hate crime . . . beat up some gay kid from school. Pretty sure it was a strike three kind of thing." She puts the toothbrush back into her mouth and walks to the sink to spit.

A hate crime? Really? My stomach does a flip, but not in the good way this time.

Six walks back into the bedroom after pulling her hair into a ponytail. "This sucks," she says, perusing her jewelry. "What if this is the one time you get horny for a guy and you never feel it again?"

Her choice of words makes me grimace. "I wasn't horny for him, Six."

She waves her hand in the air. "Horny. Attracted. It's all the same," she says flippantly, walking back to the bed. She places an earring in her lap and brings the other one up to her ear. "I guess we should be relieved to know that you aren't completely broken." Six narrows her eyes and leans over me. She pinches my chin, turning my face to the left. "What in the hell happened to your eye?"

I laugh and roll off the bed, out of harm's way. "*You* happened." I make my way toward the window. "I need to clear my head. I'm gonna go for a run. Wanna come?"

Six crinkles up her nose. "Yeah . . . *no*. You have fun with that."

I have one leg over the windowsill when she calls back to me. "I want to know all about your first day at school later. And I have a present for you. I'm coming over tonight."

Monday, August 27, 2012
5:25 p.m.

My lungs are aching; my body went numb way back at Aspen Road. My breath has moved from controlled inhaling and exhaling to uncontrolled gasps and spurts. This is the point at which I usually love running the most. When every single ounce of my body is poured into propelling me forward, leaving me committedly focused on my next step and nothing else.

My next step.

Nothing else.

I've never run this far before. I usually stop when I know I hit my mile-and-a-half mark a few blocks back, but I didn't this time. Despite the familiar despair that my body is currently in, I still can't seem to shut my mind off. I keep running in hopes that I'll get to that point, but it's taking a lot longer than usual. The only thing that makes me decide to stop going is the fact that I still have to cover as much tread going home, and I'm almost out of water.

I stop at the edge of a driveway and lean against the mailbox, opening the lid to my water bottle. I wipe the sweat off my forehead with the back of my arm and bring the bottle to my lips, managing to get about four drops into my mouth before it runs dry. I've already downed an entire bottle of water in this Texas heat. I silently scold myself for deciding to skip my run this morning. I'm a wuss in the heat.

Fearing for my hydration, I decide to walk the rest of the way back, rather than run. I don't think pushing myself to the point of physical exertion would make Karen too happy. She gets nervous enough that I run by myself as it is.

I begin walking when I hear a familiar voice speak up from behind me.

"Hey, you."

As if my heart wasn't already beating fast enough, I slowly turn around and see Holder staring down at me, smiling, his dimples breaking out in the corners of his mouth. His hair is wet from sweat and it's obvious he's been running, too.

I blink twice, half believing this is a mirage brought on by my exhaustion. My instinct is telling me to run and scream, but my body wants to wrap itself around his glistening, sweaty arms.

My body is a damn traitor.

Luckily, I haven't recovered from the stretch I just completed, so he won't be able to tell that my erratic breathing pattern is mostly from just seeing him again.

"Hey," I say back, breathless. I do my best to keep looking at his face but I can't seem to stop my eyes from dipping below his neck. Instead, I just look down at my feet in order to avoid the fact that he isn't wearing anything but shorts and running shoes. The way his shorts are hanging off his hips is reason enough for me to forgive every single negative thing I've learned about him today. I have never, as long as I can remember, been the type of girl to swoon over a guy's looks. I feel shallow. Pathetic. Lame, even. And a little bit pissed at myself that I'm letting him get to me like this.

"You run?" he asks, leaning his elbow on the mailbox.

I nod. "Usually in the mornings. I forgot how hot it is in the afternoons." I attempt to look back up at him, lifting my hand over my eyes to shield the sun that's glowing over his head like a halo.

How ironic.

He reaches out and I flinch before I realize he's just handing me his bottle of water. The way his lips purse in an attempt not to smile makes it obvious he can see how nervous I am around him.

"Drink this." He nudges the half-empty bottle at me. "You look exhausted."

Normally I wouldn't take water from strangers. I would especially not take water from people I know are bad news, but I'm thirsty. *So* damn thirsty.

I grab the bottle out of his hands and tilt my head back, downing three huge gulps. I'm dying to drink the rest, but I can't deplete his supply, too. "Thanks," I say, handing it back to him. I wipe my hand over my mouth and look behind me at the sidewalk. "Well, I've got another mile and a half return, so I better get started."

"Closer to two and a half," he says, cutting his eyes to my stomach. He presses his lips to the bottle without wiping the rim off, keeping his eyes trained on me while he tilts his head back and gulps the rest of the water. I can't help but watch his lips as they cover the opening of the bottle that my lips were just touching. We're practically kissing.

I shake my head. "Huh?" I'm not sure if he said something out loud or not. I'm a little preoccupied watching the sweat drip down his chest.

"I said it's more like two and a half. You live over on

Conroe, that's over two miles away. That's almost a five-mile run round trip." He says it like he's impressed.

I eye him curiously. "You know what street I live on?"

"Yeah."

He doesn't elaborate. I keep my gaze fixed on his and remain silent, waiting for some sort of explanation.

He can see I'm not satisfied with his "yeah," so he sighs. "Linden Sky Davis, born September 29; 1455 Conroe Street. Five feet three inches. Donor."

I take a step back, suddenly seeing my near-future murder played out in front of my eyes at the hands of my dreamy stalker. I wonder if I should stop shielding my vision from the sun so I can get a better look at him in case I get away. I might need to recount his features to the sketch artist.

"Your ID," he explains when he sees the mixture of terror and confusion on my face. "You showed me your ID earlier. At the store."

Somehow, that explanation doesn't ease my apprehension. "You looked at it for two seconds."

He shrugs. "I have a good memory."

"You stalk," I deadpan.

He laughs. "*I* stalk? You're the one standing in front of my house." He points over his shoulder at the house behind him.

His house? What the hell are the chances?

He straightens up and taps his fingers against the letters on the front of the mailbox.

The Holders.

I can feel the blood rushing to my cheeks, but it doesn't matter. After a middle of the afternoon run in the Texas heat and a limited supply of water, I'm sure my entire body is flushed. I try not to glance back at his house, but curiosity is my weakness. It's a modest house, not too flashy. It fits in well with the midincome neighborhood we're in. As does the car that's in his driveway. I wonder if that's *his* car? I can deduce from his conversation with what's-her-face from the grocery store that he's my age, so I know he must live with his parents. But how have I not seen him before? How could I not know I lived less than three miles from the only boy in existence who can turn me into a ball of frustrated hot flashes?

I clear my throat. "Well, thanks for the water." I can think of nothing I want more than to escape this awkwardness. I give him a quick wave and break into a stride.

"Wait a sec," he yells from behind me. I don't slow down, so he passes me and turns around, jogging backward against the sun. "Let me refill your water." He reaches over and grabs my water bottle out of my left hand, brushing his hand against my stomach in the process. I freeze again.

"I'll be right back," he says, running off toward his house.

I'm stumped. That is a completely contradictory act of kindness. Another side effect of the split personality disorder, maybe? He's probably a mutation, like the Hulk. Or Jekyll and Hyde. I wonder if Dean is his nice persona and Holder is his scary one. Holder is definitely the one I saw at the grocery store earlier. I think I like Dean a lot better.

I feel awkward waiting, so I walk back toward his driveway, pausing every few seconds to look at the path that leads back to my home. I have no idea what to do. It feels like any decision I make at this point will be one for the dumb side of the scale.

Should I stay?

Should I run?

Should I hide in the bushes before he comes back outside with handcuffs and a knife?

Before I have a chance to run, his front door swings open and he comes back outside with a full bottle of water. This time the sun is behind me, so I don't have to struggle so hard to see him. That's not a good thing, either, since all I want to do is stare at him.

Ugh! I absolutely hate lust.

Hate. It.

Every fiber of my being knows he's not a good person, yet my body doesn't seem to give a shit at all.

He hands me the bottle and I quickly down another drink. I hate Texas heat as it is, but coupled with Dean Holder, it feels like I'm standing in the pits of Hell.

"So . . . earlier? At the store?" he says with a nervous pause. "If I made you uneasy, I'm sorry."

My lungs are begging me for air, but I somehow find a way to reply. "You didn't make me uneasy."

You sort of creeped me out.

Holder narrows his eyes at me for a few seconds, studying me. I've discovered today that I don't like being studied . . . I like going unnoticed. "I wasn't trying to hit on you, either," he says. "I just thought you were someone else."

"It's fine." I force a smile, but it's *not* fine. Why am I suddenly consumed with disappointment that he wasn't trying to hit on me? I should be happy.

"Not that I *wouldn't* hit on you," he adds with a grin. "I just wasn't doing it at that particular moment."

Oh, thank you, Jesus. His clarification makes me smile, despite all my efforts not to.

"Want me to run with you?" he asks, nudging his head toward the sidewalk behind me.

Yes, please.

"No, it's fine."

He nods. "Well, I was going that way anyway. I run twice a day and I've still got a couple . . ." He stops speaking midsentence and takes a quick step toward me. He grabs my chin and tilts my head back. "Who did this to you?" The same hardness I saw in his eyes at the grocery store returns behind his scowl. "Your eye wasn't like this earlier."

I pull my chin away and laugh it off. "It was an accident. Never interrupt a teenage girl's nap."

He doesn't smile. Instead, he takes a step closer and gives me a hard look, then brushes his thumb underneath my eye. "You would tell someone, right? If someone did this to you?"

I want to respond. Really, I do. I just *can't*. He's touching my face. His hand is on my cheek. I can't think, I can't speak, I can't *breathe*. The intensity that exudes from his whole existence sucks the air out of my lungs and the strength out of my knees. I nod unconvincingly and he frowns, then pulls his hand away.

"I'm running with you," he says, without question. He places his hands on my shoulders and turns me in the opposite direction, giving me a slight shove. He falls into stride next to me and we run in silence.

I want to talk to him. I want to ask him about his year in juvi, why he dropped out of school, why he has that tattoo . . . but I'm too scared to find out the answers. Not to mention I'm completely out of breath. So instead, we run in complete silence the entire way back to my house.

When we close in on my driveway, we both slow down to a walk. I have no idea how to end this. No one ever runs with me, so I'm not sure what the etiquette is when two runners part ways. I turn and give him a quick wave. "I guess I'll see you later?"

"Absolutely," he says, staring right at me.

I smile at him uncomfortably and turn away. *Absolutely?* I flip this word over in my mind as I head back up the driveway. What does he mean by that? He didn't try to get my number, despite not knowing I don't have one. He didn't ask if I wanted to run with him again. But he said *absolutely* like he was certain; and I sort of hope he *is*.

"Sky, wait." The way his voice wraps around my name makes me wish the only word in his entire vocabulary was *Sky*. I spin around and pray he's about to come up with another cheesy pickup line. I would totally fall for it now.

"Do me a favor?"

Anything. I'll do anything you ask me to, so long as you're shirtless.

"Yeah?"

He tosses me his bottle of water. I catch it and look down at the empty bottle, feeling guilty that I didn't think to offer him a refill myself. I shake it in the air and nod, then jog up the steps and into the house. Karen is loading the dishwasher when I run into the kitchen. As soon as the front door closes behind me, I gasp for the air my lungs have been begging for.

"My God, Sky. You look like you're about to pass out. Sit down." She takes the bottle from my hands and forces me into a chair. I let her refill it while I breathe in through my nose and out my mouth. She turns around and hands it to me and I put the lid on it, then stand up and run it back outside to him.

"Thanks," he says. I stand and watch as he presses those same full lips to the opening of the water bottle.

We're practically kissing again.

I can't distinguish between the effect my near-five-mile run has had on me and the effect Holder is having on me. Both of them make me feel like I'm about to pass out from lack of oxygen. Holder closes the lid on his water bottle and his eyes roam over my body, pausing at my bare midriff for a beat too long before he reaches my eyes. "Do you run track?"

I cover my stomach with my left arm and clasp my hands at my waist. "No. I'm thinking about trying out, though."

"You should. You're barely out of breath and you just ran close to five miles," he says. "Are you a senior?"

He has no idea how much effort it's taking on my part not to fall onto the pavement and wheeze from lack of air. I've never run this far in one shot before, and it's taking everything I have to come across like it's not a big deal. Apparently it's working.

"Shouldn't you already know if I'm a senior? You're slacking on your stalking skills."

When his dimples make a reappearance, I want to high-five myself.

"Well, you make it sort of difficult to stalk you," he says. "I couldn't even find you on Facebook."

He just admitted to looking me up on Facebook. I met him less than two hours ago, so the fact that he went straight home and looked me up on Facebook is a little bit flattering. An involuntary smile breaks out on my face, and

I want to punch this pathetic excuse for a girl that has taken over my normally indifferent self.

"I'm not on Facebook. I don't have internet access," I explain.

He cuts his eyes to me and smirks like he doesn't believe a thing I'm saying. He pushes the hair back from his forehead. "What about your phone? You can't get internet on your phone?"

"No phone. My mother isn't a fan of modern technology. No TV, either."

"Shit." He laughs. "You're serious? What do you do for fun?"

I smile back at him and shrug. "I run."

Holder studies me again, dropping his attention briefly to my stomach. I'll think twice from now on before I decide to wear a sports bra outside.

"Well in that case, you wouldn't happen to know what time a certain someone gets up for her morning runs, would you?" He looks back up at me and I don't see the person Six described to me in him at all. The only thing I see is a guy, flirting with a girl, with a seminervous, endearing gleam in his eye.

"I don't know if you'd want to get up that early," I say. The way he's looking at me coupled with the Texas heat is suddenly causing my vision to blur, so I inhale a deep breath, wanting to appear anything but exhausted and flustered right now.

He tilts his head toward mine and narrows his eyes. "You have no *idea* how bad I want to get up that early." He flashes me his dimple-laden grin, and I faint.

No . . . literally. I fainted.

And based on the ache in my shoulder and the dirt and gravel embedded in my cheek, it wasn't a beautiful, graceful fall. I blacked out and smacked the pavement before he even had a chance to catch me. *So* unlike the heroes in the books.

I'm flat on the couch, presumably where he laid me after carrying me inside. Karen is standing over me with a glass of water and Holder is behind her, watching the aftermath of the most embarrassing moment of my life.

"Sky, drink some water," Karen says, lifting the back of my neck, pressing me toward the cup. I take a sip, then lean back on the pillow and close my eyes, hoping more than anything that I black out again.

"I'll get you a cold rag," Karen says. I open my eyes, hoping Holder decided to sneak out once Karen left the room, but he's still here. And he's closer now. He kneels on the floor beside me and reaches his hand to my hair, pulling out what I assume is either dirt or gravel.

"You sure you're okay? That was a pretty nasty fall." His eyes are full of concern and he wipes something from my cheek with his thumb, then rests his hand on the couch beside me.

"Oh, God," I say, covering my eyes with my arm. "I'm so sorry. This is so embarrassing."

Holder grabs my wrist and pulls my arm away from my face. "Shh." The concern in his eyes eases and a playful grin takes over his features. "I'm sort of enjoying it."

Karen makes her way back into the living room. "Here's a rag, sweetie. Do you want something for the pain? Are you nauseous?" Rather than hand the rag to me, she hands it to Holder and walks back to the kitchen. "I might have some calendula or burdock root."

Great. If I wasn't already embarrassed enough, she's about to make it even worse by forcing me to down her homemade tinctures right in front of him.

"I'm fine, Mom. Nothing hurts."

Holder gently places the rag on my cheek and wipes at it. "You might not be sore now, but you will be," he says, too quiet for Karen to hear him. He looks away from examining my cheek and locks eyes with me. "You should take something, just in case."

I don't know why the suggestion sounds more appealing coming out of his mouth than Karen's, but I nod. And gulp. And hold my breath. And squeeze my thighs together. And attempt to sit up, because me lying on the couch with him hovering over me is about to make me faint again.

When he sees my effort to sit up, he takes my elbow and assists me. Karen walks back into the living room and hands me a small glass of orange juice. Her tinctures are so bitter, I have to down them with juice in order to avoid spitting them back out. I take this one from her hand and down it faster than I've ever downed one before, then immediately hand her back the glass. I just want her to go back to the kitchen.

"I'm sorry," she says, extending her hand to Holder. "I'm Karen Davis."

Holder stands up and shakes her hand in return. "Dean Holder. My friends call me Holder."

I'm jealous she's getting to touch his hand. I want to take a number and get in line. "How do you and Sky know each other?" she asks.

He looks down at me at the same time I look up at him. His lip barely curls up in a smile, but I notice. "We don't, actually," he says, looking back at her. "Just in the right place at the right time, I guess."

"Well, thank you for helping her. I don't know why she fainted. She's never fainted." She looks down at me. "Did you eat anything today?"

"A bite of chicken for lunch," I say, not admitting to the Snickers I had before my run. "Cafeteria food sucks ass."

She rolls her eyes and throws her hands up in the air. "Why were you running without eating first?"

I shrug. "I forgot. I don't usually run in the evenings."

She walks back to the kitchen with the glass and sighs heavily. "I don't want you running anymore, Sky. What would have happened if you had been by yourself? You run too much, anyway."

She's got to be kidding me. There is no way I can stop running.

"Listen," Holder says, watching as the rest of the color drains from my face. He looks back toward the kitchen at Karen. "I live right over on Ricker and I run by here every day on my afternoon runs." (He's lying. I would have noticed.) "If you'd feel more comfortable, I'd be happy to run with her for the next week or so in the mornings. I usually run the track at school, but it's not a big deal. You know, just to make sure this doesn't happen again."

Ah. Light bulb. No wonder those abs looked familiar.

Karen walks back to the living room and looks at me, then back at him. She knows how much I enjoy my solitary running breaks, but I can see in her eyes that she would feel more comfortable if I had a running partner.

"I'm okay with that," she says, looking back at me. "If Sky thinks it's a good idea."

Yes. Yes, I do. But only if my new running partner is shirtless.

"It's fine," I say. I stand up, and when I do, I get light-headed again. I guess my face goes pale, because Holder has his hand on my shoulder in less than a second, lowering me back to the couch.

"Easy," he says. He looks up at Karen. "Do you have any crackers she can eat? That might help."

Karen walks away to the kitchen and Holder looks back down at me, his eyes full of concern again. "You sure you're okay?" He brushes his thumb across my cheek.

I shiver.

A devilish grin creeps across his face when he sees me attempt to cover the chill bumps on my arms. He glances behind me at Karen in the kitchen, then refocuses his gaze to mine.

"What time should I come stalk you tomorrow?" he whispers.

"Six-thirty?" I breathe, looking up at him helplessly.

"Six-thirty sounds good."

"Holder, you don't have to do this."

His hypnotizing blue eyes study my face for several quiet seconds and I can't help but stare at his equally hypnotizing mouth while he speaks. "I know I don't have to do this, Sky. I do what I want." He leans in toward my ear and lowers his voice to a whisper. "And I want to run with you." He pulls back and studies me. Due to all the chaos parading through my head and stomach, I fail to muster a reply.

Karen is back with the crackers. "Eat," she says, placing them in my hand.

Holder stands up and says good-bye to Karen, then turns back to me. "Take care of yourself. I'll see you in the morning?"

I nod and watch him as he turns to leave. I can't tear my eyes away from the front door after it shuts behind him. I'm losing it. I've completely lost any form of self-control. So this is what Six loves? This is *lust*?

I hate it. I absolutely, positively *hate* this beautiful, magical feeling.

"He was so nice," Karen says. "And handsome." She turns to face me. "You don't know him?"

I shrug. "I know *of* him," I say. And that's *all* I say. If she only knew what kind of hopeless boy she just assigned as my "running partner," she'd have a conniption. The less she knows about Dean Holder, the better it'll be for both of us.

Monday, August 27, 2012
7:10 p.m.

"What the hell happened to your face?" Jack drops my chin and walks past me to the refrigerator.

Jack has been a fixture in Karen's life for about a year and a half now. He has dinner with us a few nights a week, and since tonight is Six's going away dinner, he's gracing us with his presence. As much as he likes to give Six a hard time, I know he'll miss her, too.

"I kicked the road's ass today," I reply.

He laughs. "So *that's* what happened to the road."

Six grabs a slice of bread and opens a jar of Nutella. I grab my plate and fill it with Karen's latest vegan concoction. Karen's cooking is an acquired taste, one that Six still hasn't acquired after four years. Jack, on the other hand, is Karen's twin incarnate, so he doesn't mind the cooking. Tonight's menu consists of something I can't even pronounce, but it's completely animal-product-free, like it always is. Karen doesn't force me to eat vegan, so unless I'm home, I usually eat what I want.

Everything Six eats is only eaten to complement her main course of Nutella. Tonight, she's having a cheese and Nutella sandwich. I don't know if I could ever acquire a taste for that.

"So, when are you moving in?" I ask Jack. He and Karen have been discussing the next step, but they can never seem to get past the hump of her strict antitechnology rule. Well, Jack can't get past it. It's not a hump that will ever be scaled by Karen.

"Whenever your mom caves and gets ESPN," Jack says.

They don't argue about it. I think their arrangement is fine with both of them, so neither of them is in a hurry to sacrifice their opposing views on modern technology.

"Sky passed out in the road today," Karen says, changing the subject. "Some adorable man-boy carried her inside."

I laugh. "*Guy*, Mom. Please just say guy."

Six glares at me from across the table and it occurs to me that I haven't filled her in on my afternoon run. I also haven't filled her in on my first day of school. It's been an active day today. I wonder who I'm going to fill in after she leaves tomorrow. Just the thought of her being on the other side of the world in two days fills me with dread. I hope Breckin can fill her shoes. Well, he would probably love to fill her shoes. Literally. But I'm hoping he does so in the figurative sense.

"You okay?" Jack asks. "It must have been a pretty good fall to get that shiner."

I reach up to my eye and grimace. I'd completely forgotten about the black eye. "That's not from fainting. Six elbowed me. Twice."

I expect one of them to at least ask Six why she attacked me, but they don't. This just goes to show how much they love her. They wouldn't even care if she beat me up, they'd tell me I probably deserved it.

"Doesn't that annoy you, having a number for a name?" Jack asks her. "I never understood that. It's like when a parent names their child after one of the days of the week." He pauses with his fork midair and looks at Karen. "When we have a baby, we aren't doing that to them. Anything you can find on a calendar is off-limits."

Karen stares at him with a stone-cold expression. If I had to guess by her reaction, this is the first time Jack has mentioned babies. If I had to guess based on the look on her face, babies aren't something she's anticipating in her future. Ever.

Jack refocuses his attention back to Six. "Isn't your real name like Seven or Thirteen or something like that? I don't get why you picked Six. It's possibly the worst number you could pick."

"I'm going to accept your insults for what they are," Six says. "Just your way of burying your devastation over my impending absence."

Jack laughs. "Bury my insults wherever you want. There'll be more to come when you get back in six months."

After Jack and Six leave, I help Karen in the kitchen with the dishes. Since the second Jack brought up babies, she's been unusually quiet.

"Why did that freak you out so bad?" I ask her, handing her the plate to rinse.

"What?"

"His comment about having a baby with you. You're in your thirties. People have babies at your age all the time."

"Was it that noticeable?"

"It was to me."

She grabs another plate from me to rinse, then lets out

a sigh. "I love Jack. I just love me and you, too. I like our arrangement and I don't know if I'm ready to change it, much less bring another baby into the picture. But Jack is so intent on moving forward."

I turn the water off and wipe my hands on the hand towel. "I'll be eighteen in a few weeks, Mom. As much as you want our arrangement to stay the same . . . it won't. I'll be off at college after next semester and you'll be living here alone. It might not hurt to entertain the idea of at least letting him move in."

She smiles at me, but it's a pained smile just like it always is when I bring up college. "I have been entertaining the idea, Sky. Believe me. It's just a huge step that can't be undone once it's taken."

"What if it's a step you don't *want* undone, though? What if it's a step that just makes you want to take another step, and another step, until you're full-on sprinting?"

She laughs. "That's exactly what I'm afraid of."

I wipe off the counter and rinse the rag in the sink. "I don't understand you, sometimes."

"And I don't understand you, either," she says, nudging my shoulder. "I'll never for the life of me understand why you wanted to go to public school so bad. I know you said it was fun, but tell me how you really feel."

I shrug. "It was good," I lie. My stubbornness wins every time. There's no way I'm telling her how much I hated school today, despite the fact that she would never say, *"I told you so."*

She dries her hands and smiles at me. "Happy to hear it. Now maybe when I ask you again tomorrow, you'll tell me the truth."

I grab the book Breckin gave me out of my backpack and plop down on my bed. I get through all of two pages when Six crawls through my window.

"School first, then present," she says. She scoots in on the bed next to me and I put the book down on my nightstand.

"School sucked ass. Thanks to you and your inability to just say no to guys, I've inherited your terrible reputation. But by divine intervention, I was rescued by Breckin, the adopted gay Mormon who can't sing or act but loves to read and is my new very bestest friend ever in the whole wide world."

Six pouts. "I'm not even out the door yet and you've already replaced me? Vicious. And for the record, I don't have an inability to say no to guys. I have an inability to grasp the moral ramifications of premarital sex. Lots and lots of premarital sex."

She places a box in my lap. An unwrapped box.

"I know what you're thinking," she says. "And you should know by now that my lack of wrapping doesn't reflect how I feel about you. I'm just lazy."

I pick the box up and shake it. "You're the one leaving, you know. I should be the one getting *you* a gift."

"Yes, you should be. But you suck at gift giving and I don't expect you to change on my account."

She's right. I'm a horrible gift giver, but mostly because I hate receiving gifts so much. It's almost as awkward as people crying. I turn the box and find the flap, then untuck it and open it. I pull out the tissue paper and a cell phone drops into my hand.

"Six," I say. "You know I can't . . ."

"Shut up. There is no way I'm going halfway across the world without a way to communicate with you. You don't even have an email address."

"I know, but I can't . . . I don't have a job. I can't pay for this. And Karen . . ."

"Relax. It's a prepaid phone. I put just enough minutes on it to where we can text each other once a day while I'm gone. I can't afford international phone calls, so you're out of luck there. And just to keep with your mother's cruel, twisted parental values, there isn't even internet on the damn thing. Just texting."

She grabs the phone and turns it on, then enters her contact info. "If you end up getting a hot boyfriend while I'm away, you can always add extra minutes. But if he uses up any of mine I'm cutting his balls off."

She hands me back the phone and I press the Home button. Her contact information pulls up as *Your very, VERY bestest friend ever in the whole wide world.*

I suck at receiving gifts and I *really* suck at good-byes. I set the phone back in the box and bend over to pick my backpack up. I pull the books out and set them on the floor, then turn around and dump my backpack over her and watch all the dollar bills fall in her lap.

"There's thirty-seven dollars here," I say. "It should hold you over until you get back. Happy foreign exchange day."

She picks up a handful of dollars and throws them up in the air, then falls back on the bed. "Only one day at public school and the bitches already made your locker rain?" she laughs. "Impressive."

I lay the good-bye card that I wrote to her on her chest, then lean my head into her shoulder. "You think *that's* impressive? You should have seen me work the pole in the cafeteria."

She picks the card up and brushes her fingers over it, smiling. She doesn't open it because she knows I don't like it when things get uncomfortably emotional. She tucks the card back to her chest and leans her head on my shoulder.

"You're such a slut," she says quietly, attempting to hold back tears that we're both too stubborn to cry.

"So I've heard."

Tuesday, August 28, 2012
6:15 a.m

The alarm sounds and I instantly debate skipping today's run until I remember who's waiting for me outside. I get dressed faster than I've ever dressed since the first day I started getting dressed, then head to the window. There's a card taped to the inside of my window with the word "slut" written on it in Six's handwriting. I smile and pull the card off the window, then throw it on my bed before heading outside.

He's sitting on the curb stretching his legs. His back is to me, which is good. Otherwise he would have caught my frown as soon as I noticed he was wearing a shirt. He hears me approaching and spins around to face me.

"Hey, you." He smiles and stands up. I notice when he does that his shirt is already soaked. He ran here. He ran over two miles here, he's about to run three more miles with me, then he'll be running over two miles home. I seriously don't understand why he's going to all this trouble. Or why I'm allowing it. "You need to stretch first?" he asks.

"Already did."

He reaches out and touches my cheek with his thumb. "Doesn't look so bad," he says. "You sore?"

I shake my head. Does he really expect me to vocalize a response when his fingers are touching my face? It's pretty hard to speak and hold your breath at the same time.

He pulls his hand back and smiles. "Good. You ready?"

I let out a breath. "Yeah."

And we run. We run side by side for a while until the path narrows, then he falls into step behind me, which makes me incredibly self-conscious. I normally lose myself when I run, but this time I'm acutely aware of every single thing, from my hair, to the length of my shorts, to each drop of sweat that trails down my back. I'm relieved once the path widens and he falls back into step beside me.

"You better try out for track." His voice is steady and it doesn't sound anything like he's already run four miles this morning. "You've got more stamina than most of the guys from the team last year."

"I don't know if I want to," I say, unattractively breathless. "I don't really know anyone at school. I planned on trying out, but so far most of the people at school are sort of . . . mean. I don't really want to be subjected to them for longer periods of time under the guise of a team."

"You've only been in public school for a day. Give it time. You can't expect to be homeschooled your whole life, then walk in the first day with a ton of new friends."

I stop dead in my tracks. He takes a few more steps before he notices I'm no longer beside him. When he turns around and sees me standing still on the pavement, he rushes toward me and grabs my shoulders. "Are you okay? Are you dizzy?"

I shake my head and push his arms off my shoulders. "I'm fine," I say with a very audible amount of annoyance in my response.

He cocks his head. "Did I say something wrong?"

I start walking in the direction of my house, so he follows suit. "A little," I say, cutting my eyes toward him. "I was halfway joking about the stalking yesterday, but you admitted to looking me up on Facebook right after meeting me. Then you insist on running with me, even though it's out of your way. Now you somehow know how long I've been in public school? And that I was homeschooled? I'm not gonna lie, it's a little unnerving."

I wait for the explanation, but instead he just narrows his eyes and watches me. We're both still walking forward, but he just silently watches me until we round the next corner. When he does finally speak, his words are preempted with a heavy sigh. "I asked around," he finally says. "I've lived here since I was ten, so I have a lot of friends. I was curious about you."

I eye him for a few steps, then drop my gaze down to the sidewalk. I suddenly can't look at him, wondering what else his "friends" have told him about me. I know the rumors have been going around since Six and I became best friends, but this is the first time I've ever felt remotely defensive or embarrassed by them. The fact that he's going out of his way to run with me can only mean one thing. He's heard the rumors, and he's probably hoping they're true.

He can tell I'm uncomfortable, so he grabs my elbow and stops me. "Sky." We turn and face each other, but I keep my eyes trained on the concrete. I'm actually wearing more than just a sports bra today but I fold my arms across my T-shirt anyway and hug myself. There's nothing showing that needs covering up, but I somehow feel really naked right now.

"I think we got off on the wrong foot at the store yesterday," he says. "And the talk about stalking, I swear, it was a joke. I don't want you to feel uncomfortable around me.

Would it make you feel better if you knew more about me? Ask me something and I'll tell you. Anything."

I'm really hoping he's being genuine because I can already tell he isn't the kind of guy a girl gets a simple crush on. He's the kind of guy you fall hard for, and the thought of that terrifies me. I don't really want to fall hard for anyone at all, especially someone who's only making an effort because he thinks I'm easy. I also don't want to fall for someone who has already branded himself hopeless. But I'm curious. So curious.

"If I ask you something, will you be honest?"

He tilts his head toward me. "That's all I'll ever be."

The way he lowers his voice when he speaks makes my head spin and for a second, I'm afraid if he keeps talking like that, I'll pass out again. Luckily, he takes a step back and waits on my question. I want to ask him about his past. I want to know why he was sent away and why he did what he did and why Six doesn't trust him. But again, I'm not sure I want to know the truth yet.

"Why did you drop out of school?"

He sighs like that's one of the questions he was hoping to be able to dodge. He begins walking forward again and I'm the one following him this time.

"Technically, I haven't dropped out yet."

"Well you obviously haven't been in over a year. I'd say that's dropping out."

He turns back to me and looks torn, like he wants to tell me something. He opens his mouth, then shuts it again after hesitating. I hate that I can't read him. Most people are easy to read. They're simple. Holder is all kinds of confusing and complicated.

"I just moved back home a few days ago," he says. "My mother and I had a pretty shitty year last year, so I moved in with my dad in Austin for a while. I've been going to school there, but felt like it was time to come back home. So here I am."

The fact that he failed to mention his stint in juvi makes me question his ability to be forthcoming. I understand it's probably not something he wants to talk about, but he shouldn't claim that he'll only ever be honest when he's being anything but.

"None of that explains why you decided to drop out, rather than just transfer back."

He shrugs his shoulders. "I don't know. To be honest, I'm still trying to decide what I want to do. It's been a pretty fucked-up year. Not to mention I hate this school. I'm tired of the bullshit and sometimes I think it would be easier to just test out."

I stop walking and turn to face him. "That's a crap excuse."

He cocks an eyebrow at me. "It's crap that I hate high school?"

"No. It's crap that you're letting one bad year determine your fate for the rest of your life. You're nine months away from graduation, so you drop out? It's just . . . it's stupid."

He laughs. "Well, when you put it so eloquently."

"Laugh all you want. You quitting school is just giving in. You're proving everyone that's ever doubted you right." I look down and eye the tattoo on his arm. "You're gonna drop out and show the world just how hopeless you really are? Way to stick it to 'em."

He follows my gaze down to his tattoo and he stares at it

for a moment, working his jaw back and forth. I really didn't mean to go off on a tangent, but skimping on an education is a touchy subject with me. I blame Karen for all those years of drilling it in my head that I'm the only one who can be held accountable for the way my life turns out.

Holder shifts his eyes away from the tattoo that we're both staring at, and he looks back up and nudges his head toward my house. "You're here," he says matter-of-factly. He turns away from me without so much as a smile or a wave good-bye.

I stand on the sidewalk and watch him as he disappears around the corner without once looking back in my direction.

And here I was, thinking I would actually have a conversation with just *one* of his personalities today. So much for that.

I walk into first period and Breckin is seated in the back of the room in all of his hot pink glory. How I didn't notice those hot pink shoes and the boy they're attached to before lunch yesterday boggles my mind.

"Hey, gorgeous," I say as I slide into an empty seat next to him. I take the cup of coffee out of his hands and take a sip. He lets me, because he doesn't know me well enough yet to object. Or maybe he lets me because he knows the ramifications of intercepting a self-proclaimed caffeine addict.

"I learned a lot about you last night," he says. "It's too bad your mother won't let you have internet. It's an amazing place to discover facts about yourself that you never even knew."

I laugh. "Do I even want to know?" I tilt my head back and finish off his coffee, then hand him back the cup. He looks down at the empty cup and places it back on my desk.

"Well," he says. "According to some probing on Facebook, you had someone named Daniel Wesley over on Friday night and that resulted in a pregnancy scare. Saturday you had sex with someone named Grayson and then kicked him out. Yesterday . . ." he drums his fingers on his chin. "Yesterday you were seen running with a guy named Dean Holder after school. That concerns me a bit because, rumor has it . . . he doesn't like *Mormons*."

Sometimes I'm thankful I don't have access to the internet like everyone else.

"Let's see," I say, running through the list of rumors. "I don't even know who Daniel Wesley is. Saturday, Grayson *did* come over, but he barely got to cop a feel before I kicked his drunk ass out. And yes, I was running with a guy named Holder yesterday, but I have no idea who he is. We just happened to be running at the same time and he doesn't live far from me, so . . ."

I immediately feel guilty for downplaying the run with Holder. I just haven't figured him out and I'm not sure I'm ready for someone to infiltrate mine and Breckin's twenty-hour-old alliance just yet.

"If it makes you feel better, I found out from some chick named Shayna that I'm a product of old money and I'm filthy rich," he says.

I laugh. "Good. Then you won't have a problem bringing me coffee every morning."

The classroom door opens and we both look up, just as Holder walks in dressed in a casual white T-shirt and dark denim jeans, his hair freshly washed since our run this morning. As soon as I see him, the stomach virus/hot flashes/butterflies return.

"Shit," I mutter. Holder walks to Mr. Mulligan's desk and lays a form on it, then walks toward the back of the room fiddling with his phone the whole time. He takes a seat at the desk directly in front of Breckin and never even notices me. He turns the volume down on his phone, then puts it in his pocket.

I'm too in shock that he showed up to even speak to him. Did I somehow change his mind about reenrolling?

Am I happy about the fact that I may have changed his mind? Because I sort of feel nothing but regret.

Mr. Mulligan walks in and sets his things on the desk, then turns toward the blackboard and writes his name, followed by the date. I'm not sure if he honestly thinks we forgot who he was since yesterday, or if he just wants to remind us that he thinks we're ignorant.

"Dean," he says, still facing the blackboard. He spins around and eyes Holder. "Welcome back, albeit a day late. I take it you won't be giving us any trouble this semester?"

My mouth drops at his condescending remark right off the bat. If this is the kind of shit Holder has to put up with when he's here, no wonder he didn't want to come back. At least I just get shit from other students. I don't care who the student is, teachers should never be condescending. That should be the first rule in the teacher handbook. The second rule should be that teachers aren't allowed to write their names on blackboards beyond third grade.

Holder shifts in his seat and replies to Mr. Mulligan's comment with just as much bite. "I take it you won't be saying anything that will incite me to *give* you trouble this semester, Mr. Mulligan?"

Okay, the "shit giving" is obviously a two-way street. Maybe my next lesson, beyond talking him into coming back to school, should be to teach him the meaning of respecting authority.

Mr. Mulligan tucks his chin in and glares at Holder over the rims of his glasses.

"Dean. Why don't you come to the front of the room and introduce yourself to your classmates. I'm sure there are some new faces since you left us last year."

Holder doesn't object, which I'm sure is exactly what Mr. Mulligan expected him to do. Instead, he practically leaps from his chair and walks swiftly to the front of the room. His sudden burst of energy causes Mr. Mulligan to take a quick step back. Holder spins around to face the class, not an ounce of self-doubt or insecurity about him.

"Gladly," Holder says, cutting his eyes toward Mr. Mulligan. "I'm Dean Holder. People call me Holder." He looks away from Mr. Mulligan and back toward the class. "I've been a student here since freshmen year with the exception of a one-and-a-half-semester sabbatical. And according to Mr. Mulligan, I like to incite trouble, so this class should be fun."

Several of the students laugh at this comment, but I fail to find the humor in it. I've already been doubting him based on everything I've heard; now he's showing his true colors by the way he's acting. Holder opens his mouth to continue with his introduction, but breaks out into a smile as soon as he spots me in the back of the room. He winks at me and I immediately want to crawl under my desk and hide. I give him a quick, tight-lipped smile, then look down at my desk as soon as other students begin turning around in their seats to see whom he's staring at.

An hour and a half ago, he walked away from me in a pissy mood. Now he's smiling at me like he's just seen his best friend for the first time in years.

Yep. He's got issues.

Breckin leans across his desk. "What the hell was that?" he whispers.

"I'll tell you at lunch," I say.

"Is that all the wisdom you wish to impart to us today?" Mr. Mulligan asks Holder.

Holder nods, then walks back to his seat, never pulling his gaze from mine. He sits and cranes his neck, facing me. Mr. Mulligan begins his lecture and everyone's focus returns to the front of the room. Everyone's but Holder's. I glance down to my book and flip it open to the current chapter, hoping he'll do the same. When I glance back up, he's still staring at me.

"*What?*" I mouth, tossing my palms up in the air.

He narrows his eyes and watches me silently for a moment. "Nothing," he finally says. He turns around in his seat and opens the book in front of him.

Breckin taps his pencil on my knuckles and looks at me inquisitively, then returns his attention to his book. If he's expecting an explanation of what just happened, he'll be disappointed when I'm unable to give him one. *I* don't even know what just happened.

I steal several glances in Holder's direction during the lecture, but he doesn't turn around again for the entire period. When the bell rings, Breckin jumps out of his seat and drums his fingers on my desk.

"Me. You. Lunch," he says, raising his eyebrow at me. He walks out of the classroom and I turn my gaze to Holder. He's watching the classroom door that Breckin just walked out of with a hard look in his eyes.

I grab my things and head out the door before Holder has a chance to strike up a conversation. I really am glad he decided to reenroll, but I'm disturbed at the way he looked at me like we were best friends. I really don't want Breckin, or anyone else for that matter, thinking I'm okay with the things Holder does. I'd rather just not associate myself with him, but I have a feeling that's going to be an issue for him.

I go to my locker and switch books, grabbing my English text. I wonder if Shayna/Shayla will actually acknowledge me in class today. Probably not, that was twenty-four hours ago. I doubt she has enough brain cells to recall information from that long ago.

"Hey, you."

I squeeze my eyes shut apprehensively, not wanting to turn around to see him standing there in all his beautiful glory.

"You came." I adjust the books in my locker, then turn around and face him. He smiles, then leans up against the locker next to mine.

"You clean up nice," he says, eyeing me up and down. "Although, the sweaty version of you isn't so bad, either."

He cleans up nice, too, but I'm not about to tell him that.

"Are you here stalking me or did you actually reenroll?"

He grins mischievously and drums his fingers against the locker. "Both."

I really need to cut it out with the stalking jokes. It would be funnier if I didn't think he was actually capable.

I look around at the hallway clearing out. "Well, I need to get to class," I say. "Welcome back."

He narrows his eyes at me, almost as if he can sense my discomfort. "You're being weird."

I roll my eyes at his assessment. How can he know how I'm being? He doesn't even know me. I look back into my locker and try to mask the real thoughts on why I'm being "weird." Thoughts like, why does his past not scare me more than it does? Why does he have a temper so bad that he would do what he did to that poor kid last year? Why does he want to go out of his way to run with me? Why was he asking around about me? Instead of verbally admitting to the questions inside my head, I just shrug and go with, "I'm just surprised to see you here."

He leans his shoulder against the locker next to mine and shakes his head. "Nope. It's something else. What's wrong?"

I sigh and lean against my locker. "You want me to be honest?"

"That's all I ever want you to be."

I pull my lips into a tight line and nod. "Fine," I say. I roll my shoulder against the locker and face him. "I don't want to give you the wrong idea. You flirt and say things like you have intentions with me that I'm not willing to reciprocate. And you're . . ." I pause, searching for the right word.

"I'm *what*?" he says, watching me intently.

"You're . . . *intense*. Too intense. And moody. And a little bit scary. And there's the other thing," I say, without saying it. "I just don't want you getting the wrong idea."

"What other thing?" He says it like he knows exactly what other thing I'm referring to, but he's daring me to say it.

I let out a breath and press my back against the locker, staring down at my feet. "You know," I say, not wanting to bring up his past any more than he probably does.

Holder steps in front of me and places his hand on the locker beside my head, then leans in toward me. I look up at him and he's staring down at me, less than six inches from my face.

"I *don't* know, because you're skirting around whatever issue it is you have with me like you're too afraid to say it. Just say it."

Looking up at him right now, feeling trapped like I'm

feeling, the same panic returns to my chest that he left there after our first encounter.

"I heard about what you did," I say abruptly. "I know about the guy you beat up. I know about you being sent to juvi. I know that in the two days I've known you, you've scared the shit out of me at least three times. And since we're being honest, I also know that if you've been asking around about me, then you've probably heard about my reputation, which is more than likely the only reason you're even making an effort with me. I hate to disappoint you, but I'm not screwing you. I don't want you thinking anything will happen between us besides what's already happening. We run together. That's it."

His jaw tightens, but his expression never changes. He lowers his arm and takes a step back, allowing me room to breathe again. I don't understand why anytime he steps within a foot of my personal space, it sucks the breath out of me. I especially don't understand why I like that feeling.

I tuck my books to my chest and begin to shove past him when an arm goes around my waist and I'm pulled away from Holder. I glance next to me to see Grayson eyeing Holder up and down, his grip tightening around my waist.

"Holder," Grayson says coldly. "Didn't know you were coming back."

Holder doesn't even acknowledge Grayson. He continues to stare at me for several seconds, only breaking his gaze from mine to look down at Grayson's hand that's gripping my waist. He nods slightly and smiles, as if he's come to some sort of realization, then brings his eyes back to mine.

"Well, I'm back," he says bluntly, without looking directly at Grayson.

What the hell is this? Where did Grayson come from, and why does he have his arm around me like he's staking claim?

Holder cuts his eyes away from mine and turns around to walk away, but stops abruptly. He spins back around and looks at me. "Track tryouts are Thursday after school," he says. "Go."

Then he's gone.

Too bad Grayson isn't.

"You busy this Saturday?" Grayson says in my ear, pulling me against him.

I push off his chest and pull my neck away from him. "Stop," I say, irritated. "I think I made myself pretty clear last weekend."

I slam my locker shut and walk away, wondering how in the hell I've escaped drama my entire life, yet I have enough for an entire book from the last two days alone.

Breckin takes his seat across from me and slides me a soda. "They didn't have coffee, but I found caffeine."

I smile. "Thank you, very bestest friend in the whole wide world."

"Don't thank me, I bought it with evil intentions. I'm using it to bribe you so I can get the dirt on your love life."

I laugh and open the soda. "Well, you'll be disappointed, because my love life is nonexistent."

He opens his own soda and grins. "Oh, I doubt that. Not from the way bad boy has been eyeing you from over there." He nudges his head to the right.

Holder is three tables down, staring at me. He's sitting with several guys from the football team who seem excited to have him back. They're patting him on the back and talking around him, never noticing that he's not even a part of their conversation. He takes a drink of his water, his eyes keeping their lock on mine. He sets his drink down on the table a little too forcefully, then nudges his head to the right as he stands up. I glance to the right and see the exit to the cafeteria. He's walking toward it, expecting me to follow him.

"Huh," I say, more to myself than to Breckin.

"Yeah. Huh. Go see what the hell he wants, then report back to me."

I take another drink of my soda, then set it on the table. "Yes, sir."

My body stands up to follow Holder, but I leave my heart at the table. I'm pretty sure it jumped out of my chest as soon as he indicated for me to follow him. I can put up a good front for Breckin all I want, but dammit if I can't have a little control over my own organs.

Holder is several feet in front of me and when he swings the doors open, they swing shut behind him. I place my hand on the swinging doors when I reach them and hesitate a moment before pushing out into the hallway. I think I'd rather be heading to detention right now than to talk to him. My stomach is tied up in so many knots it could make a Boy Scout envious.

I look both ways, but I don't see him. I take a few steps until I get to the edge of the lockers, then round the corner. His back is leaned up against one of them and his knee is bent, his foot propped against the locker behind him. His arms are folded across his chest and he's looking right at me. The baby-blue hue of his eyes isn't even kind enough to mask the anger behind them.

"Are you dating Grayson?"

I roll my eyes and walk to the lockers opposite him and lean against them. I'm really getting tired of his mood swings already, and I just met the guy. "Does it matter?" I'm curious how it's any of his business. He gives me that silent pause that I've noticed comes before almost everything he says.

"He's an asshole."

"Sometimes you are, too," I say quickly, not needing nearly as much time as he does to come up with a response.

"He's not good for you."

I let out an exasperated laugh. "And you *are*?" I ask, throwing his point right back at him. If we were keeping score, I'd say it's two and zero in my favor.

He drops his arms and turns around to face the lockers, hitting one of them with a flat palm. The sound of skin against metal reverberates in the hallway and straight into my stomach.

"Don't factor me into this," he says, turning back around. "I'm talking about Grayson, not me. You shouldn't be with him. You have no idea what kind of person he is."

I laugh. Not because he's funny . . . but because he's *serious*. This guy that I don't even know is seriously trying to tell me who I should and shouldn't date? I roll my head back against the locker in a wave of defeat.

"Two days, Holder. I've known you all of two days." I kick off the lockers behind me and walk toward him. "In those two days, I've seen five different sides of you, and only one of them has been appealing. The fact that you think you have any right to even voice an opinion about me or my decisions is absurd. It's ridiculous."

Holder works his jaw back and forth and stares down at me, arms tightly folded against his chest. He takes a challenging step toward me. His eyes are so hard and cold, I'm beginning to think this is a sixth side of him that I'm seeing. An even angrier, more possessive side.

"I don't like him. And when I see things like this?" He brings his hand to my face and gently runs his finger underneath the prominent bruise on my eye. "And then see him with his arm around you? Forgive me if I get a little *ridiculous.*"

His fingertips trailing across my cheekbone have left me breathless. It's a struggle to keep my eyes open and not lean in toward his palm, but I hold fast to my resolve. I'm building up an immunity to this boy. Or . . . at least I'm attempting to. That's my new goal, anyway.

I take a step away from him until his hand is no longer touching my face. He curls his fingers up into a fist and drops his hand to his side.

"You think I should stay away from Grayson because you're afraid he has a temper?" I tilt my head to the side and narrow my eyes at him. "A bit hypocritical, don't you think?"

After another few seconds of studying me, he lets out a short sigh with a barely noticeable roll of the eyes. He looks away and shakes his head, grabbing at the back of his neck. He stays in this position, facing opposite me for several seconds. When he slowly turns around, he doesn't look me in the eyes. He folds his arms across his chest once again and looks down at the floor.

"Did he hit you," he says without any inflection in his voice. He keeps his head trained to the floor, but looks up at me through his eyelashes. "Has he *ever* hit you?"

Here he goes again, inducing me into submission by a simple switch in demeanor. "No," I say, quietly. "And no. I told you . . . it was an accident."

We stare at each other in complete silence until the bell for second lunch rings and the hallway fills with students. I'm the first to break our gaze. I walk back to the cafeteria without looking back at him.

Wednesday, August 29, 2012
6:15 a.m.

I've been running for almost three years. I don't remember what started it or what made it so enjoyable that I became so disciplined at it. I think a lot of it has to do with how frustratingly sheltered I am. I try to stay positive about it, but it's hard seeing the interactions and relationships the other students have at school that I'm not a part of. Not having internet access wouldn't have been a big deal in high school a few years ago, but now it's pretty much social suicide. Not that I care what anyone thinks.

I won't deny it, I've had an overwhelming urge to look Holder up online. In the past when I had these urges to find out more about people, Six and I would just look them up at her house. But Six is on a transatlantic flight over the Atlantic ocean right now, so I can't ask her. Instead, I just sit on my bed and wonder. I wonder if he's really as bad as his reputation makes him out to be. I wonder if he has the same effect on other girls that he has on me. I wonder who his parents are, if he has siblings, if he's dating anyone. I wonder why he seems so intent on being angry with me all the time when we just met. Is he always this angry? Is he always so charming when he isn't busy being angry? I hate that he's either one way or the other and never in between. It would be nice to see a laid-back, calm side to him. I wonder if he even *has* an in between. I wonder . . . because that's all I can do. Silently wonder about the hopeless boy who somehow burrowed himself into the forefront of my thoughts and won't go the hell away.

I snap out of my trance and finish pulling my running shoes on. At least our tiff in the hallway yesterday was left unresolved. He won't be running with me today because of it, and I'm pretty relieved about that. I need the quiet time to myself today, more than anything. I don't know why, though. It'll just be spent wondering.

About him.

I open my bedroom window and crawl outside. It's darker than usual for this time of morning. I look up and see that the sky is overcast, a perfect indicator of my mood. I take in the direction of the clouds, then glance at the sky to the left, curious if I have enough time to run before the bottom falls out.

"Do you always climb out your window or were you just hoping to avoid me?"

I spin around at the sound of his voice. He's standing at the edge of the sidewalk, decked out in shorts and running shoes. No shirt today.

Dammit.

"If I was trying to avoid you I would have just stayed in bed." I walk toward him with confidence, hoping to hide the fact that the sight of him is causing my entire body to go haywire. A small part of me is disappointed he showed up today, but most of me is stupidly, pathetically happy. I walk past him and drop onto the sidewalk to stretch. I extend my legs out in front of me and lean forward, grabbing my shoes and burying my head against my knees—partly for the muscle stretch, but mostly to avoid having to look at him.

"I wasn't sure if you'd show up." He drops down and claims a spot on the sidewalk in front of me.

I raise up and look at him. "Why wouldn't I? I'm not the one with the issues. Besides, neither of us owns the road." I practically snap at him. I'm not even sure why.

He does that staring and thinking thing again where his intense gaze somehow renders me unresponsive. It's becoming such a habit of his I almost want to give it a name. It's like he holds me with his eyes while he silently thinks, purposefully giving no tells in his expression. I've never met anyone who puts so much thought into his own responses. The way he lets things soak in while he prepares his own response—it's like words are limited and he only wants to use the ones that are absolutely necessary.

I stop stretching and face him, unwilling to back down from this visual standoff. I'm not going to let him perform his little Jedi mind tricks on me, no matter how much I wish I could perform them on him. He's completely unreadable and even more unpredictable. It pisses me off.

He stretches his legs out in front of me. "Give me your hands. I need to stretch, too."

He's sitting with his hands out in front of me like we're about to play patty-cake. If anyone was to drive by right now I can just imagine the rumors. Just the thought of it makes me laugh. I place my hands in his outstretched palms and he pulls me forward toward him for several seconds. When he eases the tension, I pull back while he stretches forward, only he doesn't look down. He keeps his gaze locked on mine in his debilitating eye-hold while he stretches.

"For the record," he says, "I wasn't the one with the issue yesterday."

I pull him harder, more out of malice than a desire to help him stretch.

"Are you insinuating *I'm* the one with the issue?"

"Aren't you?"

"Clarify," I say. "I don't like vague."

He laughs, but it's an irritable laugh. "Sky, if there's one thing you should know about me, it's that I don't do vague. I told you I'll only ever be honest with you, and to me, vague is the same thing as dishonesty." He pulls my hands forward and leans back.

"That's a pretty vague answer you just gave me," I point out.

"I was never asked a question. I've told you before, if you want to know something, just ask. You seem to think you know me, yet you've never actually asked me anything yourself."

"I *don't* know you."

He laughs again and shakes his head, then releases my hands. "Forget it." He stands up and starts walking away.

"Wait." I pull myself up from the concrete and follow him. If anyone has the right to be angry here, it's me. "What did I say? I *don't* know you. Why are you getting all pissy with me again?"

He stops walking and turns around, then takes a couple of steps toward me. "I guess after spending time with you over the last few days, I thought I'd get a slightly different reaction from you at school. I've given you plenty of opportunity to ask me whatever you want to ask me, but for some reason you want to believe everything you hear, despite the fact that you never heard any of it from *me*. And coming from someone with her own share of rumors, I figured you'd be a little less judgmental."

My own share of rumors? If he thinks he's going to win points by having something in common with me, he's dead wrong.

"So that's what this is about? You thought the slutty new girl would be sympathetic to the gay-bashing asshole?"

He groans and runs his hands through his hair, frustrated. "Don't do that, Sky."

"Don't do what? Call you a gay-bashing asshole? Okay. Let's practice this honesty policy of yours. Did you or did you not beat up that student last year so badly that you spent a year in juvenile detention?"

He puts his hands on his hips and shakes his head, then looks at me with what seems like disappointment in his expression.

"When I said *don't do that*, I wasn't referring to you insulting me. I was referring to you insulting *yourself*." He takes a step forward, closing the gap between us. "And yes. I beat his ass to within an inch of his life, and if the bastard was standing in front of me right now, I'd do it again."

His eyes are filled with pure anger and I'm too scared to even ask him why or what it's about. He may have said he'd be honest about it . . . but his answers terrify me more than asking the questions. I take a step back at the same time he does. We're both quiet and I'm wondering how we even got to this point.

"I don't want to run with you today," I say.

"I don't really feel like running with you, either."

With that, we both turn in opposite directions. He toward his house, me toward my window. I don't even feel like running alone today.

I climb back in my window just as the rain starts pouring from the sky, and for a second, I feel sorry for him that he still has to run home. But only for a second, because Karma's a bitch, and Holder is definitely who she's retaliating against right now. I close the window and walk to my bed. My heart is racing as fast as if I had just run the three miles. Except right now it's racing because I'm so incredibly pissed.

I met the guy a couple of days ago, yet I've never argued more with anyone in my entire life. I could add up all the arguments Six and I have had over the last four years, and it wouldn't begin to compare to the last forty-eight hours with Holder. I don't know why he even bothers. I guess after this morning, he more than likely won't.

I pick the envelope up from my nightstand and tear it open. I pull Six's letter out and lean back on my pillow and read it, just hoping to escape from the chaos in my head.

Sky,

Hopefully by the time you're reading this (because I know you won't read it right away) I'll be madly in love with a hot Italian boyfriend and not thinking about you at all.

But I know that isn't the case, because I'll be thinking about you all the time.

I'll be thinking about all the nights we stayed up with our ice cream and our movies and our boys. But mostly, I'll be thinking about you, and all the reasons why I love you.

Just to name a few: I love how you suck at good-byes and feelings and emotions, because I do, too. I love how you always scoop from the strawberry and vanilla side of the ice cream because you know how much I love the chocolate, even though you love it, too. I love how you aren't weird and awkward, despite the fact that you've been severely cut off from socialization to the point where you make the Amish look trendy.

But most of all, I love that you don't judge me. I love that in the past four years, you've never once questioned me about my choices (as poor as they may be) or the guys I've been with or the fact that I don't believe in commitment. I would say that it's simple for you not to judge me, because you're a dirty slut, too. But we both know you're not. So thank you for being a nonjudgmental friend. Thank you for never being condescending or treating me like you're better than me (even though we both know you are). As much as I can laugh about the things people say about us behind our backs, it kills me that they say these things about you, too. For that, I'm sorry. But not too sorry, because I know if you were given the choice to either be my slutty best friend or be the girl with the good reputation, you'd screw every guy in the world. Because you love me that much. And I'd let you, because I love you that much.

And one more thing I love about you, then I'll shut up because I'm only six feet away writing this letter right now and it's really hard to not climb out my window and come squeeze you.

I love your indifference. I love how you really just don't give a shit what people think. I love how you are focused on your future and everyone else can kiss your ass. I love how, when I told you I was leaving for Italy after talking you into enrolling at my school, you *just smiled and shrugged your shoulders even though it would have torn most best friends apart. I left you hanging to follow my dream, and you didn't let it eat you up. You didn't even give me crap about it.*

I love how (last one, I swear) when we watched The Forces of Nature and Sandra Bullock walked away in the end and I was screaming at the TV for such an ugly ending, you just shrugged your shoulders and said, "It's real, Six. You can't get mad at a real ending. Some of them are ugly. It's the fake happily-ever-afters that should piss you off."

I'll never forget that, because you were right. And I know you weren't trying to teach me a lesson, but you did. Not everything is going to go my way and not everyone gets a happily-ever-after. Life is real and sometimes it's ugly and you just have to learn how to cope. I'm going to accept it with a dose of your indifference, and move on.

So, anyway. Enough about that. I just want you to know that I'll miss you and this new very best friend ever in the whole wide world at school better back off when I get home in six months. I hope you realize how amazing you are, but in case you don't, I'm going to text you every single day to remind you. Prepare to be bombarded for the next six months with endless annoying texts of nothing but positive affirmations about Sky.

I love you,
6

I fold the letter up and smile, but I don't cry. She wouldn't expect me to cry over it, no matter how much she might have just made me want to. I reach over to the nightstand and take the cell phone she gave me out of the drawer. I already have two missed text messages.

Have I told you lately how awesome you are? Missing you.

It's day two, you better text me back. I need to tell you about Lorenzo. Also, you're sickeningly smart.

I smile and text her back. It takes me about five tries before I figure it out. I'm almost eighteen and this is the first text I've ever sent? This has to be one for Guinness.

I can get used to these daily positive affirmations. Make sure to remind me of how beautiful I am, and how I have the most impeccable taste in music, and how I'm the fastest runner in the world. (Just a few ideas to get you started.) I miss you, too. And I can't wait to hear about Lorenzo, you slut.

Friday, August 31, 2012
11:20 a.m.

The next few days at school are the same as the first two. Full of drama. My locker seems to have become the hub for sticky notes and nasty letters, none of which I ever see actually being placed on or in my locker. I really don't get what people gain out of doing things like this if they don't even own up to it. Like the note that was stuck to my locker this morning. All it said was "Whore."

Really? Where's the creativity in that? They couldn't back it up with an interesting story? Maybe a few details of my indiscretion? If I have to read this shit every day, the least they could do is make it interesting. If I were going to stoop so low as to leave an unfounded note on someone's locker, I'd at least have the courtesy to entertain whoever read it in the process. I'd write something interesting like, *"I saw you in bed with my boyfriend last night. I really don't appreciate you getting massage oil on my cucumbers. Whore."*

I laugh and it feels odd, laughing out loud at my own thoughts. I look around and no one is left in the hallway but me. Rather than rip the sticky notes off my locker like I probably should, I take out my pen and make them a little more creative. You're welcome, passersby.

Breckin sets his tray down across from mine. We've been getting our own trays now, since he seems to think I want nothing but salad. He smiles at me like he's got a secret that he knows I want. If it's another rumor, I'll pass.

"How were track tryouts yesterday?" he asks.

I shrug. "I didn't go."

"Yeah, I know."

"Then why'd you ask?"

He laughs. "Because I like to clarify things with you before I believe them. Why didn't you go?"

I shrug again.

"What's with the shoulder shrugs? You have a nervous tic?"

I shrug. "I just don't feel like being part of a team with anyone here. It's lost its appeal."

He frowns. "First of all, track is one of the most individual sports you can join. Second, I thought you said extracurricular activities were the reason you were here."

"I don't *know* why I'm here," I say. "Maybe I feel like I need to witness a good dose of human nature at its worst before I enter the real world. It'll be less of a shock."

He points a celery stick at me and cocks his eyebrow. "This is true. A gradual introduction to the perils of society will help cushion the blow. We can't release you alone into the wild when you've been pampered in a zoo your whole life."

"Nice analogy."

He winks at me and bites his stick of celery. "Speaking of analogies. What's up with your locker? It was covered in sexual analogies and metaphors today."

I laugh. "You like that? Took me a while, but I was feeling creative."

He nods. "I especially liked the one that said '*You're such a slut, you screwed Breckin the Mormon.*'"

I shake my head. "Now that one I can't lay claim to. That was an original. But they're fun, aren't they? Now that they've been dirtied up?"

"Well," he says. "They *were* fun. They aren't there anymore. I saw Holder ripping them off your locker just now."

I snap my gaze back up to his and he's grinning mischievously again. I guess this is the secret he was having trouble holding in.

"That's strange." I'm curious why Holder would bother to do such a thing. We haven't been running together since we spoke last. In fact, we don't even interact at all. He sits across the room now in first period and I don't see him at all the rest of the day, aside from lunch. Even then, he sits on the other side of the cafeteria with his friends. I thought after coming to an impasse, we'd successfully moved on to mutual avoidance, but I guess I was wrong.

"Can I ask you something?" Breckin says.

I shrug again, mostly just to irritate him.

"Are the rumors about him true? About his temper? And his sister?"

I try not to appear taken aback by his comment, but it's the first I've heard anything about a sister. "I don't know. All I know is that I've spent enough time with him to know he scares me enough to not want to spend more time with him."

I really want to ask him about the sister comment, but I can't help which situations my stubbornness rears its ugly head in. For some reason, probing for information about Dean Holder is one of those situations.

"Hey," a voice from behind me says. I immediately know it isn't Holder's, because I'm indifferent to the voice. About the time I turn around, Grayson swings his leg over the seat bench next to me and sits. "You busy after school?"

I dip my celery stick into a blob of ranch dressing and take a bite. "Probably."

Grayson shakes his head. "That's not a good enough answer. I'll meet you at your car after last period."

He's up and gone before I can object. Breckin smirks at me.

I just shrug.

I have no idea what Grayson wants to talk about, but if he's thinking he's coming over tomorrow night, he needs a lobotomy. I'm so ready to just swear off guys for the rest of the year. Especially if it means not having Six to eat ice cream with after they go home. Ice cream was the only appealing part to making out with the guys.

At least he's true to form. He's waiting at my car, leaning up against my driver's-side door when I reach the parking lot. "Hey, Princess," he says. I don't know if it's the sound of his voice or the fact that he just gave me a nickname, but his words make me cringe. I walk up to him and lean against the car next to him.

"Don't call me Princess again. Ever."

He laughs and slides in front of me, gripping my waist in his hands. "Fine. How about beautiful?"

"How about you just call me Sky?"

"Why do you have to be so angry all the time?" He reaches up to my face and holds my cheeks in his hands, then kisses me. Sadly, I let him. Mostly because I feel like he's earned it for putting up with me for an entire month. He doesn't deserve a whole lot of return favors, though, so I pull my face away after just a few seconds.

"What do you want?"

He snakes his arms around my waist and pulls me against him. "You." He starts kissing my neck, so I push against him and he backs away. *"What?"*

"Can you not take a hint? I told you I'm not sleeping with you, Grayson. I'm not trying to play games or get you to chase me like other sick, twisted girls do. You want more and I don't, so I think we just need to accept that we're at an impasse and move on."

He stares at me, then sighs and pulls me against him, hugging me. "I don't need more, Sky. It's fine the way it is. I won't push it again. I just like coming to your house and I want to come over tomorrow night." He tries to flash me that panty-dropping grin. "Now stop being mad at me and come here." He pulls my face to his and kisses me again.

As irritated and as angry as I am, I can't help but be relieved that as soon as his lips meet mine, my irritation subsides, thanks to the numbness that takes over. For that reason alone, I continue to let him kiss me. He backs me against the car and runs his hands in my hair, then kisses down my jaw and to my neck. I lean my head against the car and bring my wrist up behind him to check the time on my watch. Karen's going out of town for work, so I need to go to the grocery store to get enough sugar to last me all weekend. I don't know how long he plans on feeling me up, but ice cream is really starting to sound tempting right about now. I roll my eyes and drop my arm. All at once, my heart rate triples and my stomach flips and I get all of the feelings a girl is supposed to get when a hot guy's lips are all over her. Only I'm not having the reaction to the hot guy whose lips are all over me. I'm having the reaction to the hot guy glaring at me from across the parking lot.

Holder is standing next to his car with his elbow on the top of his doorframe, watching us. I immediately shove Grayson off me and turn around to get in my car.

"So we're on for tomorrow night?" he asks.

I climb into the car and crank it, then look up at him. "No. We're done."

I pull the door shut and back out of the parking lot, not sure if I'm angry, embarrassed, or infatuated. How does he do that? How the hell does he incite these kinds of feelings from me from clear across a parking lot? I think I'm in need of an intervention.

Friday, August 31, 2012
4:50 p.m.

"Is Jack going with you?" I open the car door for Karen so she can throw the last of her luggage into the backseat.

"Yeah, he's coming. We'll be home . . . *I'll* be home on Sunday," she says, correcting herself. It pains her to count Jack as a "we." I hate that she feels that way because I really like Jack and I know he loves Karen, so I don't understand what her hang-up is at all. She's had a couple of boyfriends in the past twelve years, but as soon as it starts getting serious for the guy, she runs.

Karen shuts the back door and turns to me. "You know I trust you, but please . . ."

"Don't get pregnant," I interrupt. "I know, I know. You've been saying that every time you leave for the past two years. I'm not getting pregnant, Mom. Only terribly high and cracked out."

She laughs and hugs me. "Good girl. And wasted. Don't forget to get really wasted."

"I won't forget, I promise. And I'm renting a TV for the weekend so I can sit around and eat ice cream and watch trash on cable."

She pulls back and glares at me. "Now that's not funny."

I laugh and hug her again. "Have fun. I hope you sell lots of herbal thingies and soaps and tinctures and whatever else it is you do at these things."

"Love you. If you need me, you know you can use Six's house phone."

I roll my eyes at the same instructions she gives me every time she leaves. "See ya," I say. She gets in the car and pulls out of the driveway, leaving me parent-free for the weekend. To most teenagers, this would be the point at which they pull out their phones and post an invite to the most kick-ass party of the year. Not me. Nope. Instead, I go inside and decide to bake cookies, because that's the most rebellious thing I can come up with.

I love to bake, but I don't claim to be very good at it. I usually end up with more flour and chocolate on my face and hair than in the actual end product. Tonight's no exception. I've already made a batch of chocolate chip cookies, a batch of brownies, and something I'm not sure what it was supposed to be. I'm working on pouring the flour into the mixture for a homemade German chocolate cake when the doorbell rings.

I'm pretty sure I should know what to do in situations like this. Doorbells ring all the time, right? Not mine. I stare at the door, not sure what I'm expecting it to do. When it rings for a second time, I put down the measuring cup and wipe my hair out of my eyes, then walk to the front door. When I open it, I'm not even surprised to see Holder. Okay, I'm surprised. But not really.

"Hey," I say. I can't think of anything else to say. Even if I could think of something else to say, I probably wouldn't be able to say it since I can't freaking *breathe*! He's standing on the top step of my entryway, hands hanging loosely in the pockets of his jeans. His hair still needs a trim, but when he brings his hand up and pushes it out of his eyes, the thought of him trimming that hair is suddenly the worst idea in the world.

"Hi." He's smiling awkwardly and he looks nervous and it's terribly attractive. He's in a good mood. For now, anyway. Who knows when he'll get pissed off and feel like arguing again.

"Um," I say, uneasily. I know the next step is to invite him in, but that's only if I'm actually wanting him inside my house, and to be honest, the jury is still out on that one.

"You busy?" he asks.

I glance back into the kitchen at the inconceivable mess I've made. "Sort of." It's not a lie. I'm sort of incredibly busy.

He looks away and nods, then points behind him to his car. "Yeah. I guess I'll . . . go." He takes a step back off the top step.

"No," I say, much too quickly and a decibel too loudly. It's an almost desperate *no*, and I cringe from embarrassment. As much as I don't know why he's here or why he even keeps bothering, my curiosity gets the best of me. I step aside and open the door farther. "You can come in, but you might be put to work."

He hesitates, then ascends the step again. He walks inside and I shut the door behind us. Before it can get any more awkward, I walk into the kitchen and pick up the measuring cup and get right back to work like there isn't some random, temperamental, hot guy standing in my house.

"You prepping for a bake sale?" He makes his way around the bar and eyes the plethora of desserts covering my counter.

"My mom's out of town for the weekend. She's anti-sugar, so I kind of go crazy when she's not here."

He laughs and picks up a cookie, but looks at me first for permission.

"Help yourself," I say. "But be warned, just because I like to bake doesn't mean I'm good at it." I sift the last of the flour and pour it into the mixing bowl.

"So you get the house to yourself and you spend Friday night baking? Typical teenager," he says mockingly.

"What can I say?" I shrug. "I'm a rebel."

He turns around and opens a cabinet, eyeing the contents, then shuts it. He steps to the left and opens another cabinet, then takes out a glass. "Got any milk?" he asks while heading to the refrigerator. I pause from stirring and watch as he pulls the milk out and pours himself a glass like he's right at home. He takes a drink and turns around to catch me staring at him, then he grins. "You shouldn't offer cookies without milk, you know. You're a pretty pathetic hostess." He grabs another cookie and walks himself and the milk to the bar and takes a seat.

"I try to save my hospitality for *invited* guests," I say sarcastically, turning back to the counter.

"Ouch." He laughs.

I turn the mixer on, creating an excuse to not have to talk to him for three minutes on medium to high speed. I try to remember what I look like, without noticeably searching for a reflective surface. I'm pretty sure I've got flour everywhere. I know my hair is being held up with a pencil and my sweatpants are being worn for the fourth evening in a row. *Unwashed.* I try to nonchalantly wipe away any visible traces of flour, but I'm aware it's a lost cause. Oh, well, there's no way I could look any worse right now than when I was laid out on the couch with gravel embedded in my cheek.

I turn off the mixer and depress the button to free the mixing blades. I bring one to my mouth and lick it, and walk the other one to where he's seated. "Want one? It's German chocolate."

He takes it out of my hand and smiles. "How hospitable of you."

"Shut up and lick it or I'm keeping it for myself." I walk to the cabinet and grab my own cup, but pour myself a glass of water instead. "You want some water or do you want to continue pretending you can stomach that vegan shit?"

He laughs and crinkles up his nose, then pushes his cup across the bar toward me. "I was trying to be nice, but I can't take another sip of whatever the hell this is. Yes, water. *Please.*"

I laugh and rinse out his cup, then slide him the glass of water. I take a seat in the chair across from him and eye him while I bite into a brownie. I'm waiting for him to explain why he's here, but he doesn't. He just sits across from me and watches me eat. I don't ask him why he's here because I sort of like the quiet between us. It works better when we both shut up, since all of our conversations tend to end in arguments.

Holder stands up and walks into the living room without an explanation. He looks around curiously, his attention being stolen by the photographs on the walls. He walks closer to them and slowly scans each picture. I lean back in my chair and watch him be nosy.

He's never in much of a hurry and seems so assured in every movement he makes. It's like all of his thoughts and actions are meticulously planned out days in advance. I can just picture him in his bedroom, writing down the words he plans to use the following day, because he's so selective with them.

"Your mom seems really young," he says.

"She is young."

"You don't look like her. Do you look like your dad?" He turns and faces me.

I shrug. "I don't know. I don't remember what he looks like."

He turns back to the pictures and runs his finger across one of them.

"Is your dad dead?" He's so blunt about it, I'm almost certain he knows my dad isn't dead or he wouldn't have asked it like that. So carelessly.

"I don't know. Haven't seen him since I was three."

He walks back toward the kitchen and takes a seat in front of me again. "That's all I get? No story?"

"Oh, there's a story. I just don't want to tell it." I'm sure there is a story . . . I just don't *know* it. Karen doesn't know anything about my life before I was put into foster care and I've never seen the point of digging it up. What's a few forgotten years when I've had thirteen great ones?

He smiles at me again, but it's a wary smile when accompanied by the quizzical look in his eyes. "Your cookies were good," he says, skillfully changing the subject. "You shouldn't downplay your baking abilities."

Something beeps and I jump up from my seat and run to the oven. I open it, but the cake isn't even close to being done. When I turn around, Holder is holding up my cell phone. "You got a text." He laughs. "Your cake is fine."

I throw the oven mitt on the counter, then walk back to my seat. He's scrolling through the texts on my phone without a shred of respect for privacy. I really don't care, though, so I just let him.

"I thought you weren't allowed to have a phone," he says. "Or was that a really pathetic excuse to avoid giving me your number?"

"I'm *not* allowed. My best friend gave it to me the other day. It can't do anything but text."

He turns the screen around to face me. "What the hell kind of texts are these?" He turns the phone around and reads one.

"*Sky, you are beautiful. You are possibly the most exquisite creature in the universe and if anyone tells you otherwise, I'll cut the bitch.*" He arches an eyebrow and looks up at me, then back down to the phone. "Oh, God. They're all like this. Please tell me you don't text these to yourself for daily motivation."

I laugh and reach across the bar and snatch the phone out of his hand. "Stop. You're ruining the fun of it."

He leans his head back and laughs. "Oh, my God, you do? Those are all from you?"

"No!" I say, defensively. "They're from Six. She's my best friend and she's halfway around the world and she misses me. She wants me to not be sad, so she sends me nice texts every day. I think it's sweet."

"Oh, you do not. You think it's annoying and you probably don't even read them."

How does he know that?

I set the phone down and cross my arms over my chest. "She means well," I say, still not admitting that the texts are annoying the living hell out of me.

"They'll ruin you. Those texts will inflate your ego so much, you'll explode." He grabs the phone and pulls his own phone out of his pocket. He scrolls through the screens on both phones and punches some numbers on his phone. "We need to rectify this situation before you start suffering from delusions of grandeur." He hands me back my phone and types something into his own phone, then puts it in his pocket. My phone sounds off, indicating a new text message. I look down at the screen and laugh.

Your cookies suck ass. And you're really not that pretty.

"Better?" he says, teasingly. "Did the ego deflate enough?"

I laugh and set the phone down on the counter, then stand up. "You know just the right things to say to a girl." I walk to the living room and turn around. "Want a tour of the house?"

He stands up and follows me while I point out boring facts and knick-knacks and rooms and pictures, but of course he's slowly soaking it all in, never in a rush. He has to stop and inspect every tiny thing, never speaking a single word the whole time.

When we finally get to my bedroom, I swing open the door. "My room," I say, flashing my Vanna White pose. "Feel free to look around, but being as though there aren't any people eighteen or older here, stay off the bed. I'm not allowed to get pregnant this weekend."

He pauses as he's passing through the doorway and tilts his head toward me. "Only *this* weekend? You plan on getting knocked up next weekend, instead?"

I follow him into my bedroom. "Nah. I'll probably wait a few more weeks."

He inspects the room, slowly turning around until he's facing me again. "I'm eighteen."

I cock my head to the side, confused about why he pointed out that random fact. "Yay for you?"

He cuts his eyes to the bed, then back to me. "You said to stay off your bed because I'm not eighteen. I'm just pointing out that I am."

I don't like the way my lungs just constricted when he looked at my bed. "Oh. Well then, I meant nineteen."

He spins around, then walks slowly to the open window. He bends down and sticks his head out of it, then pulls back inside. "So this is the infamous window, huh?"

He doesn't look at me, which is probably a good thing because if looks could kill he'd be dead. Why the hell did he have to go and say something like that? I was actually enjoying his company for a change. He turns back to me and his playful expression is gone, replaced by a challenging one that I've seen too many times before.

I sigh. "What do you want, Holder?" He either needs to get his point across about why he's here, or he needs to leave. He folds his arms across his chest and narrows his eyes at me.

"Did I say something wrong, Sky? Or untrue? Unfounded, maybe?" It's obvious from his taunting remarks that he knows exactly what he was insinuating with the window comment. I'm not in the mood to play his games; I have cakes that need baking. And eating.

I walk to the door and hold it open. "You know exactly what you said and you got the reaction you wanted. Happy? You can go now."

He doesn't. He drops his arms and turns around, then walks to my nightstand. He picks up the book Breckin gave me and inspects it as though the last thirty seconds never even occurred.

"Holder, I'm asking you as nicely as I'm going to ask you. Please leave."

He lays the book down gently, then proceeds to lie down on the bed. He literally lies down on my bed. He's on my damn bed.

I roll my eyes and walk over to where he is, then reach down and pull his legs off my bed. If I have to physically remove him from the house, I'll do it. When I grab his wrists and lift upward, he pulls me to him in a move that happens faster than my mind can even comprehend. He flips me over until I'm on my back and he's holding my arms to the mattress. It happens so unexpectedly; I don't even have time to fight him. And looking up at him right now, half of me doesn't even *want* to fight him. I don't know if I should scream for help or rip off my clothes.

He releases my arms and brings one of his hands to my face. He brushes his thumb across my nose and laughs. "Flour," he says, wiping it away. "It's been bugging me." He sits up against my headboard and brings his feet back onto the bed. I'm still flat on the mattress, staring up at the stars, actually feeling something other than nothing for the first time ever while looking at them.

I can't even move, because I'm sort of afraid he's crazy. I mean literally, clinically insane. It's the only logical explanation for his personality. And the fact that I still find him so incredibly attractive can only mean one thing. I'm insane, too.

"I didn't know he was gay."

Yep, he's crazy.

I turn my head toward him, but say nothing. What the hell do you say to a crazy person who literally refuses to leave your house, then starts spouting off random shit?

"I beat him up because he was an asshole. I had no idea he was gay."

His elbows are resting on his knees and he's looking right at me, waiting for a reaction. Or a response. Neither of which he's getting for a few seconds, because I need to process this.

I look back up at the stars and give myself time to analyze the situation. If he's not crazy, then he's definitely trying to make a point. But what point? He comes over here, uninvited, to defend his reputation and insult mine? What would be the point of even making the effort? I'm just one person, what does my opinion matter?

Unless, of course, he likes me. The thought literally makes me smile and I feel dirty and wrong for hoping a lunatic likes me. I had it coming, though. I should have never let him in the house, knowing I'm alone. And now he knows I'll be home all weekend alone. If I had to weigh tonight's decisions, this would probably be so heavy it would break the dumb side of the scale. I foresee this ending in one of two ways. We'll either come to a mutual understanding of each other, or he's going to kill me and chop me up into tiny pieces and bake me into cookies. Either way, it makes me sad for all the dessert that isn't being eaten right now.

"Cake!" I yell, jumping up off the bed. I run to the kitchen just in time to smell my latest disaster. I grab the oven mitt and pull the cake out, then throw it on the counter in disappointment. It's not too badly burnt. I could probably salvage it by drowning it in icing.

I shut the oven and decide that I'm moving on to a new hobby. Maybe I'll make jewelry. How hard could that be? I grab two more cookies and walk back to my bedroom and hand one of the cookies to Holder, then lie down on the bed next to him.

"I guess the gay-bashing asshole remark was really judgmental on my part then, huh? You aren't really an ignorant homophobe who spent the last year in juvenile detention?"

He grins and scoots down on the bed next to me and looks up at the stars. "Nope. Not at all. I spent the entire last year living with my father in Austin. I don't even know where the story about me being sent to juvi came into the picture."

"Why don't you defend yourself against the rumors if they aren't true?"

He turns his head toward me on the pillow. "Why don't *you*?"

I purse my lips and nod. "Touché."

We both sit quietly on the bed eating our cookies. Some of the things he's said over the past few days are starting to make sense, and I begin to feel more and more like the people I despise. He told me outright that he would answer anything if I just asked, yet I chose to believe the rumors about him instead. No wonder he was so irritated with me. I was treating him just like everyone else treats me.

"The window comment from earlier?" I say. "You were just making a point about rumors? You really weren't trying to be mean?"

"I'm not mean, Sky."

"You're intense. I'm right about that, at least."

"I may be intense, but I'm not mean."

"Well, I'm not a slut."

"I'm not a gay-bashing asshole."

"So we're all clear?"

He laughs. "Yeah, I guess so."

I inhale a deep breath, then exhale, preparing to do something I don't do very often. Apologize. If I wasn't so stubborn, I might even admit that my judgmental behavior this week was completely mortifying and he had every right in the world to be angry with me for being so ignorant. Instead, I keep the apology short and sweet.

"I'm sorry, Holder," I say quietly.

He sighs heavily. "I know, Sky. I know."

And we sit like this in complete silence for what seems like forever but also doesn't feel like near long enough. It's getting late and I'm afraid he's about to say he needs to leave because there's nothing else to say, but I don't want him to. It feels right, being here with him now. I don't know why, but it just does.

"I need to ask you something," he says, finally breaking the silence. I don't respond, because it doesn't feel like his statement is waiting for a response. He's just taking one of his moments to prepare whatever it is he wants to ask me. He takes a breath, then rolls over onto his side to face me. He tucks his elbow under his head and I can feel him looking at me, but I keep staring at the stars. He's way too close for me to look at him right now, and by the way my heart is already pounding against my chest, I'm afraid moving any closer will physically kill me. It doesn't seem possible that lust can cause a heart to take this much of a beating. It's worse than running.

"Why were you letting Grayson do what he was doing to you in the parking lot?"

I want to crawl under my covers and hide. I was hoping this wouldn't come up. "I already told you. He's not my boyfriend and he's not the one who gave me the black eye."

"I'm not asking because of any of that. I'm asking because I saw how you reacted. You were irritated with him. You even looked a little bored. I just want to know why you allow him to do those things if you clearly don't want him touching you."

His words throw me for a loop and I'm suddenly feeling claustrophobic and sweaty. I don't feel comfortable talking about this. It makes me uneasy how he reads me so well, yet I can't read him for anything.

"My lack of interest was that obvious?" I ask.

"Yep. And from fifty yards away. I'm just surprised he didn't take the hint."

This time I turn to face him without thinking, and tuck my elbow under my head. "I know, right? I can't tell you how many times I've turned him down but he just doesn't stop. It's really pathetic. And unattractive."

"Then why do you let him do it?" he says, eyeing me sharply. We're in a compromising position right now, facing each other on the same bed. The way he's staring at me and dropping his eyes to my lips prompts me to roll onto my back again. I don't know if he feels the same, but he rolls onto his back, too.

"It's complicated."

"You don't have to explain," he says. "I was just curious. It's really not my business."

I tuck my hands behind my head and look up at the stars

that I've counted more times than I can count. I've been in this bed with Holder longer than I've probably been in this bed with *any* boy, and it occurs to me that I haven't felt the need to count a single star.

"Have you ever had a serious girlfriend?"

"Yep," he says. "But I hope you aren't about to ask for details, because I don't go there."

I shake my head. "That's not why I'm asking." I pause for a few seconds, wanting to word things the right way. "When you kissed her, what did you feel?"

He pauses for a moment, probably thinking this is a trick question. "You want honesty, right?" he asks.

"That's all I ever want."

I can see him smile out of the corner of my eyes. "All right then. I guess I felt . . . horny."

I try to appear unaffected, hearing that word come out of his mouth, but . . . *wow*. I cross my legs, hoping it'll help minimize the hot flashes racing through me. "So you get the butterflies and the sweaty palms and the rapid heartbeat and all that?"

He shrugs. "Yeah. Not with every girl I've been with, but most of them."

I angle my head in his direction, trying not to analyze the way that sentence came out. He turns his head toward me and grins.

"There weren't *that* many." He smiles and his dimple is even cuter close up. For a moment, I get lost in it. "What's your point?"

I bring my eyes back to his, briefly, then face the ceiling again. "My point is that I *don't*. I don't feel any of that. When I make out with guys, I don't feel anything at all.

Just numbness. So sometimes I let Grayson do what he does to me, not because I enjoy it, but because I like not feeling anything at all." He doesn't respond and his silence makes me uncomfortable. I can't help but wonder if he's mentally labeling *me* crazy. "I know it doesn't make sense, and no, I'm not a lesbian. I've just never been attracted to anyone before you and I don't know why."

As soon as I say it, he darts his head toward me at the same second I squeeze my eyes shut and throw my arm over my face. I can't believe I just admitted, out loud, that I'm attracted to him. I could die right now and it wouldn't be soon enough.

I feel the bed shift and he encompasses my wrist with his hand and removes my arm from over my eyes. I reluctantly open them and he's propped up on his hand, smiling at me. "You're attracted to me?"

"Oh, God," I groan. "That's the last thing you need for your ego."

"That's probably true." He laughs. "Better hurry up and insult me before my ego gets as big as yours."

"You need a haircut," I blurt out. "Really bad. It gets in your eyes and you squint and you're constantly moving it out of the way like you're Justin Bieber and it's really distracting."

He fingers his hair with his hand and frowns, then falls back onto the bed. "Man. That really hurt. It seems like you've thought that one out for a while."

"Just since Monday," I admit.

"You *met* me on Monday. So technically, you've been thinking about how much you hate my hair since the moment we met?"

"Not *every* moment."

He's quiet for a minute, then grins again. "I can't believe you think I'm hot."

"Shut up."

"You probably faked passing out the other day, just so you could be carried in my hot, sweaty, manly arms."

"Shut up."

"I'll bet you fantasize about me at night, right here in this bed."

"Shut up, Holder."

"You probably even . . ."

I reach over and clamp my hand over his mouth. "You're way hotter when you aren't speaking."

When he finally shuts his mouth, I remove my hand and put it back behind my head. Again, we both go a while without speaking. He's probably silently gloating at the fact that I admitted I'm attracted to him, while I'm silently cringing that he's now privy to that knowledge.

"I'm bored," he says.

"So go home."

"I don't want to. What do you do when you're bored? You don't have internet or TV. Do you just sit around all day and think about how hot I am?"

I roll my eyes. "I read," I say. "A lot. Sometimes I bake. Sometimes I run."

"Read, bake, and run. And fantasize about me. What a riveting life you lead."

"I like my life."

"I sort of like it, too," he says. He rolls over and grabs the book off my nightstand. "Here, read this."

I take the book out of his hands and open it to the

marker on page two. It's as far as I've gotten. "You want me to read it out loud? You're that bored?"

"Pretty damn bored."

"It's a romance," I warn.

"Like I said. Pretty damn bored. Read."

I scoot my pillow up toward the headboard and make myself comfortable, then start reading.

This morning if you had told me I'd be reading a romance novel to Dean Holder in my bed tonight, I'd tell you that you were crazy. But then again, I'm obviously not the best judge of crazy.

When I open my eyes, I immediately slide my hand to the other side of the bed, but it's empty. I sit up and look around. My light is off and my covers are on. The book is closed on the nightstand, so I pick it up. There's a bookmark almost three-quarters of the way through.

I read until I fell asleep? *Oh, no, I fell asleep.* I throw the covers off and walk to the kitchen, then flip on the light and look around in shock. The entire kitchen is clean and all the cookies and brownies are wrapped in Saran Wrap. I look down at my phone sitting on the counter and pick it up to find a new text message.

You fell asleep right when she was about to find out her mother's secret. How dare you. I'll be back tomorrow night so you can finish reading it to me. And by the way, you have really bad breath and you snore way too loud.

I laugh. I'm also grinning like an idiot, but luckily no

one is here to witness it. I glance at the clock on the stove and it's only just past two in the morning, so I go back to the bedroom and crawl into bed, hoping he really does show up tomorrow night. I don't know how this hopeless boy weaseled his way into my life this week, but I know I'm definitely not ready for him to leave.

Saturday, September 1, 2012
5:05 p.m.

I've learned an invaluable lesson about lust today. It causes double the work. I took two showers today, instead of just one. I changed clothes four times instead of the usual two. I've cleaned the house once (that's one more than I usually clean it) and I've checked the time on the clock no less than a thousand times. I may have checked my phone for incoming texts just as many.

Unfortunately, he didn't state in his text from last night what time he would be here, so by five o'clock I'm pretty much sitting and waiting. There isn't much else to do, since I've already baked enough sweets for an entire year and I've run no less than four miles today. I thought about cooking dinner for us, but I have no idea what time he's coming over, so I wouldn't know when to have it ready. I'm sitting on the couch, drumming my nails on the sofa, when I get a text from him.

What time can I come over? Not that I'm looking forward to it or anything. You're really, really boring.

He texted me. Why didn't I think of that? I should have texted him a few hours ago to ask what time he would be here. It would have saved me so much unnecessary, pathetic fretting.

Be here at seven. And bring me something to

eat. I'm not cooking for you.

I set the phone down and stare at it. An hour and forty-five minutes to go. Now what? I look around at my empty living room and, for the first time ever, the boredom starts to have a negative effect on me. Up until this week, I was pretty content with my lackluster life. I wonder if being exposed to the temptations of technology has left me wanting more, or if it's being exposed to the temptations of Holder. Probably both.

I stretch my legs out on the coffee table in front of me. I'm wearing jeans and a T-shirt today after finally deciding to give my sweatpants a break. I also have my hair down, but only because Holder has never seen me in anything other than a ponytail. Not that I'm trying to impress him.

I'm totally trying to impress him.

I pick up a magazine and flip through it, but my leg is shaking and I'm fidgeting to the point that I can't focus. I read the same page three times in a row, so I throw the magazine back on the coffee table and lean my head back into the couch. I stare at the ceiling. Then I stare at the wall. Then I stare at my toes and wonder if I should repaint them.

I'm going crazy.

I finally groan and reach for my phone, then text him again.

Now. Come right now. I'm bored out of my freaking mind and if you don't come right now I'll finish the book before you get here.

I hold the phone in my hands and watch the screen as it bounces up and down against my knee. He texts back right away.

Lol. I'm getting you food, bossy pants. Be there in twenty.

Lol? What the hell does that mean? Lots of love? Oh, God, that better not be it. He'll be out the door faster than Matty-boy. But really, what the hell does it mean?

I stop thinking about it and focus on the last word. Twenty. Twenty minutes. Oh, shit, that suddenly seems way too soon. I run to the bathroom and check my hair, my clothes, my breath. I make a quick run through the house, cleaning it for the second time today. When the doorbell finally rings, I actually know what to do this time. Open it.

He's standing with two armfuls of groceries, looking very domesticated. I eye the groceries suspiciously. He holds the sacks up and shrugs. "One of us has to be the hospitable one." He eases past me and walks straight to the kitchen and sets the sacks on the counter. "I hope you like spaghetti and meatballs, because that's what you're getting." He begins removing items from the sacks and pulling cookware out of cabinets.

I shut the front door and walk to the bar. "You're cooking dinner for me?"

"Actually, I'm cooking for *me*, but you're welcome to eat some if you want." He glances at me over his shoulder and smiles.

"Are you always so sarcastic?" I ask.

He shrugs. "Are *you*?"

"Do you always answer questions with questions?"

"Do *you*?"

I pick up a hand towel off the bar and throw it at him. He dodges it, then walks to the refrigerator. "You want something to drink?" he asks.

I put my elbows on the bar and rest my chin in my hands, watching him. "You're offering to make me something to drink in my own house?"

He searches through the refrigerator shelves. "Do you want milk that tastes like ass or do you want soda?"

"Do we even have soda?" I'm almost positive I already drank up the stash I bought yesterday.

He leans back out of the refrigerator and arches an eyebrow. "Can either of us say anything that isn't a question?"

I laugh. "I don't know, can we?"

"How long do you think we can keep this up?" He finds a soda and grabs two glasses. "You want ice?"

"Are *you* having ice?" I'm not stopping with the questions until he does. I'm highly competitive.

He walks closer to me and places our glasses on the counter. "Do you *think* I should have ice?" he says with a challenging grin.

"Do you *like* ice?" I challenge back.

He nods his head, impressed that I've kept up to speed with him. "Is your ice any good?"

"Well, do you prefer crushed ice or cubed ice?"

He narrows his eyes at me, aware that I just trapped him. He can't answer that one with a question. He pops the lid open and begins pouring the soda into my cup. "No ice for you."

"Ha!" I say. "I win."

He laughs and walks back to the stove. "I let you win because I feel sorry for you. Anyone that snores as bad as you do deserves a break every now and then."

I smirk at him. "You know, the insults are really only funny when they're in text form." I pick my glass up and take a drink. It definitely needs ice. I walk to the freezer and pull out a few ice cubes and drop them into my cup.

When I turn around, he's standing right in front of me, staring down at me. The look in his eyes is slightly mischievous, but just serious enough that it causes my heart to palpitate. He takes a step forward until my back meets the refrigerator behind me. He casually lifts his arm and places his hand on the refrigerator beside my head.

I don't know how I'm not sinking to the floor right now. My knees feel like they're about to give out.

"You know I'm kidding, right?" he says softly. His eyes are scrolling over my face and he's smiling just enough that his dimples are showing.

I nod and hope he backs the hell away from me, because I'm about to have an asthma attack and I don't even have asthma.

"Good," he says, moving in just a couple more inches. "Because you *don't* snore. In fact, you're pretty damn adorable when you sleep."

He really shouldn't say things like that. Especially when he's leaning in this close to me. His arm bends at the elbow and he's suddenly a whole lot closer. He leans in toward my ear and I inhale sharply.

"Sky," he whispers seductively into my ear. "I *need* you . . . to move. I need to get in the fridge." He slowly pulls back and keeps his eyes trained on mine, watching for my reaction. A smile pulls at the corners of his mouth and he tries to hold it in, but he breaks out in laughter.

I push against his chest and duck under his arm. "You're such an ass!"

He opens the refrigerator, still laughing. "I'm sorry, but

damn. You're so blatantly attracted to me, it's hard not to tease you."

I know he's joking, but it still embarrasses the hell out of me. I sit back down at the bar and drop my head into my hands. I'm beginning to hate the girl he's turning me into. It wouldn't be nearly as hard to be around him if I hadn't slipped and told him I was attracted to him. It also wouldn't be as hard if he weren't so funny. And sweet, when he wants to be. And hot. I guess that's what makes lust so bittersweet. The feeling is beautiful, but the effort it takes to deny it is way too hard.

"Want to know something?" he asks. I look up at him and he's looking down at the pan in front of him, stirring.

"Probably not."

He glances at me for a few seconds, then looks back down at the pan. "It might make you feel better."

"I doubt it."

He cuts his eyes to me again and the playful smile is gone from his lips. He reaches into a cabinet and pulls out a pan, then walks to the sink and fills it with water. He walks back to the stove and begins stirring again. "I might be a little bit attracted to you, too," he says.

I unnoticeably inhale, then let out a slow, controlled breath in an attempt not to appear blindsided by that comment.

"Just a little bit?" I ask, doing what I do best by infusing awkward moments with sarcasm.

He smiles again, but keeps his eyes trained on the pan in front of him. The room grows silent for several minutes. He's focused on cooking and I'm focused on him. I watch him as he moves effortlessly around the kitchen and I'm in awe at his level of comfort. This is my house and I'm more nervous than he is. I can't stop fidgeting and I wish he would start talking again. He doesn't seem as affected by the silence, but it's looming in the air around me and I need to get rid of it.

"What does *lol* mean?"

He laughs. "Seriously?"

"Yes, seriously. You typed it in your text earlier."

"It means laugh out loud. You use it when you think something is funny."

I can't deny the relief I feel that it wasn't *lots of love*.

"Huh," I say. "That's dumb."

"Yeah, it is pretty dumb. It's just habit, though, and the abbreviated texts make it a lot faster to type once you get the hang of it. Sort of like OMG and WTF and IDK and . . ."

"Oh, God, stop," I say, interrupting him before he spouts off more abbreviations. "You speaking in abbreviated text form is really unattractive."

He turns to me and winks, then walks to the oven. "I'll never do it again, then."

And it happens again . . . the silence. Yesterday the silence between us was fine, but for some reason, it's incredibly awkward tonight. It is for me, anyway. I'm beginning to think I'm just nervous for what the rest of the night holds. It's obvious with the chemistry between us that we'll end up kissing eventually. It's just really hard to focus on the here and now and be engaged in conversation when that's the only thing on my mind. I can't stand not knowing when he'll do it. Will he wait until after dinner when my breath smells like garlic and onions? Will he wait until it's time for him to leave? Will he just spring it on me when I'm least expecting it? I almost just want to get it over with right now. Cut to the chase so the inevitable can be put aside and we can get on with the night.

"You okay?" he asks. I snap my gaze back up to his and he's standing across the bar from me. "Where'd you go? You checked out for a while there."

I shake my head and pull myself back into the conversation. "I'm fine."

He picks up a knife and begins chopping a tomato. Even his tomato-chopping skills are effortless. Is there anything this boy is bad at? His knife stills on the cutting board and I look up at him. He's looking down at me with a serious expression.

"Where'd you go, Sky?" He watches me for a few seconds, waiting on my response. When I fail to give him one, he drops his eyes back to the cutting board.

"Promise you won't laugh?" I ask.

He squints and ponders my question, then shakes his head. "I told you that I'll only ever be honest with you, so no. I can't promise I won't laugh because you're kind of funny and that's only setting myself up for failure."

"Are you always so difficult?"

He grins at me, but doesn't respond. He keeps eyeing me like he's challenging me to say what's really on my mind. Unfortunately, I don't back down from challenges.

"Okay, fine." I sit up straight in my chair and take a deep breath, then let all my thoughts out at once. "I'm really not any good at this whole dating thing, and I don't even know if this *is* a date, but I know that whatever it is, it's a little more than just two friends hanging out, and knowing that makes me think about later tonight when it's time for you to leave and whether or not you plan to kiss me and I'm the type of person who hates surprises so I can't stop feeling awkward about it because I *do* want you to kiss me and this may be presumptuous of me, but I sort of think you want to kiss me, too, and so I was thinking how much easier it would be if we just went ahead and kissed already so you can go back to cooking dinner and I can stop trying to mentally map out how our night's about to play out." I inhale an incredibly huge breath, as though I have nothing left in my lungs.

He stopped chopping somewhere in the middle of that rant, but I'm not sure which part. He's looking at me with his mouth slightly agape. I take a deep breath and slowly exhale, thinking I may have just completely sent him out the front door. And sadly, I wouldn't blame him if he ran.

He lays the knife gently on the cutting board and places his palms on the counter in front of him, never breaking his gaze from mine. I fold my hands in my lap and wait for a reaction. It's all I can do.

"That," he says pointedly, "was the longest run-on sentence I've ever heard."

I roll my eyes and slouch back against my seat, then fold my arms across my chest. I just practically begged him to kiss me, and he's critiquing my grammar?

"Relax," he says with a grin. He slides the tomatoes off the cutting board and into the pan, then places it on the stove. He adjusts the temperature of one of the burners and pours the pasta into the boiling water. Once everything is set, he dries his hands on the hand towel, then walks around the bar to where I'm seated.

"Stand up," he directs.

I look up at him warily, but I do what he says. Slowly. When I'm standing up, facing him, he places his hands on my shoulders and looks around the room. "Hmm," he says, thinking audibly. He glances into the kitchen, then slides his hands down my shoulders and grabs my wrists. "I sort of liked the fridge backdrop." He pulls me into the kitchen, then positions me like a puppet with my back against the refrigerator. He places both of his hands against the refrigerator on either side of my head, and looks down at me.

It's not the most romantic way I've pictured him kissing me, but I guess it'll do. I just want to get it over with. Especially now that he's making such a big production out of it. He begins to lean in toward me, so I take a deep breath and close my eyes.

I wait.

And I wait.

Nothing happens.

I open my eyes and he's so close I actually flinch, which only makes him laugh. He doesn't back away, though, and his breath teases my lips like fingers. He smells like mint leaves and soda and I never thought the two would make a good combination, but they really do.

"Sky?" he says, quietly. "I'm not trying to torture you or anything, but I already made up my mind before I came over here. I'm not kissing you tonight."

His words cause my stomach to sink from the weight of my disappointment. My self-confidence has just gone out the window, and I really need an ego-building text from Six right now.

"Why not?"

He slowly drops one of his hands and brings it to my

face, then traces down my cheek with his fingers. I try not to shudder under his touch, but it's taking every ounce of my willpower not to appear completely flustered right now. His eyes follow his hand as it slowly moves down my jaw, then my neck, stopping at my shoulder. He brings his eyes back to mine and there's an undeniable amount of lust in them. Seeing the look in his eyes eases my disappointment by a tiny fraction.

"I want to kiss you," he says. "Believe me, I do." He drops his eyes to my lips and brings his hand back up to my cheek, cupping it. I willingly lean into his palm this time. I pretty much relinquished control to him the moment he walked through the front door. Now I'm nothing but putty in his hands.

"But if you really want to, then why don't you?" I'm terrified he's about to spout off an excuse that contains the word *girlfriend*.

He cases my face in both of his hands and tilts my face up toward his. He brushes his thumbs back and forth along my cheekbones and I can feel the rapid rise and fall of his chest against mine. "Because," he whispers. "I'm afraid you won't feel it."

I suck in a quick breath and hold it. The conversation we had on my bed last night replays in my head, and I realize that I never should have told him any of that. I never should have said I feel nothing but numbness when I kiss people, because he's the absolute exception to the rule. I bring my hand to his hand on my cheek, and I cover it with mine.

I'll feel it, Holder. I already do. I want to say those words out loud, but I can't. Instead, I just nod.

He closes his eyes and inhales, then pulls me away from the refrigerator and into his chest. He wraps one arm around my back and holds his other hand against my head. My arms are still awkwardly at my sides, so I tentatively bring them up and wrap them around his waist. When I do this, I quietly gasp at the peacefulness that consumes me, being wrapped up in him like this. We both simultaneously pull each other closer and he kisses me on top of the head. It's not the kiss I was expecting, but I'm pretty sure I love it just as much.

We're standing in the same position when the timer on the oven dings. He doesn't immediately release me, though, which makes me smile. When he does begin to drop his arms, I look down to the floor, unable to look at him. Somehow, my trying to rectify the awkwardness about kissing him has just made things even more awkward for me.

As if he can sense my embarrassment, he takes both of my hands in his and interlocks our fingers. "Look at me." I lift my eyes to his, trying to hide the disappointment from realizing our mutual attraction is on two different levels. "Sky, I'm not kissing you tonight but believe me when I tell you, I've never wanted to kiss a girl more. So stop thinking I'm not attracted to you because you have no idea just how much I am. You can hold my hand, you can run your fingers through my hair, you can straddle me while I feed you spaghetti, but you are not getting kissed tonight. And probably not tomorrow, either. I need this. I need to know for sure that you're feeling every single thing that I'm feeling the moment my lips touch yours. Because I want your first kiss to be the best first kiss in the history of first kisses." He pulls my hand up to his mouth and kisses it. "Now stop sulking and help me finish the meatballs."

I grin, because that was seriously the best excuse ever for being turned down. He could turn me down every day for the rest of my life, so long as it's followed up by that excuse.

He swings our hands between us, peering down at me. "Okay?" he says. "Is that enough to get you through a couple more dates?"

I nod. "Yep. But you're wrong about one thing."

"What's that?"

"You said you want my first kiss to be the best first kiss, but this won't be my first kiss. You know that."

He narrows his eyes and pulls his hands from mine, then cups my face again. He pushes me back against the refrigerator and brings his lips dangerously close to mine. The smile is gone from his eyes and is replaced by a very serious expression. An expression so intense, I stop breathing.

He leans in excruciatingly slowly until his lips just barely reach mine, and the anticipation of them alone is enough to paralyze me. He doesn't close his eyes, so neither do I. He holds me in this position for a moment, allowing our breath to blend between us. I've never felt so helpless and out of control of myself, and if he doesn't do something within the next three seconds, I'm more than likely going to pounce on him.

He looks at my lips and when he does, it prompts me to pull my bottom lip between my teeth. Otherwise, I just might bite him.

"Let me inform you of something," he says in a low voice. "The moment my lips touch yours, it *will* be your first kiss. Because if you've never felt anything when someone's kissed you, then no one's ever really kissed you. Not the way *I* plan on kissing you."

He drops his hands and keeps his eyes locked on mine while he backs up to the stove. He turns around to tend to the pasta like he didn't just ruin me for any other guy for the rest of my life.

I can't feel my legs, so I do the only thing I can. I slide down the refrigerator until my butt meets the floor, and I inhale.

"Your spaghetti sucks ass." I take another bite and close my eyes, savoring what is possibly the best pasta that's ever passed my lips.

"You love it and you know it," he says. He stands up from the table and grabs two napkins, then brings them back and hands me one. "Now wipe your chin, you've got sucky ass spaghetti sauce all over it."

After the incident against the refrigerator, the night pretty much went back to normal. He gave me a glass of water and helped me stand up, then slapped me on the ass and put me to work. It was all I needed to let go of the awkwardness. A good slap on the ass.

"Have you ever played Dinner Quest?" I ask him.

He slowly shakes his head. "Do I want to?"

I nod. "It's a good way to get to know each other. After our next date, we'll be spending most of our time making out, so we need to get all the questions out of the way now."

He laughs. "Fair enough. How do you play?"

"I ask you a really personal, uncomfortable question and you aren't allowed to take a drink or eat a bite of food until you answer it honestly. And vice versa."

"Sounds easy enough," he says. "What if I don't answer the question?"

"You starve to death."

He drums his fingers on the table, then lays his fork down. "I'm in."

I probably should have had questions prepared, but considering I just made this game up thirty seconds ago, that would have been sort of hard. I take a sip of what's left of my watered-down soda and think. I'm a little nervous about delving too deep, as it always seems to end badly with us.

"Okay, I have one." I set my cup down on the table and lean back in my chair. "Why did you follow me to my car at the grocery store?"

"Like I said, I thought you were someone else."

"I know, but who?"

He shifts uncomfortably in his seat and clears his throat. He naturally reaches for his glass, but I intercept it.

"No drinks. Answer the question first."

He sighs, but eventually relents. "I wasn't sure who you reminded me of, you just reminded me of someone. I didn't realize until later that you reminded me of my sister."

I crinkle my nose. "I remind you of your sister?" I wince. "That's kind of gross, Holder."

He laughs, then grimaces. "No, not like that. Not like that at all, you don't even look anything like she did. There was just something about seeing you that made me think of her. And I don't even know why I followed you. It was all so surreal. The whole situation was a little bizarre, and then running into you in front of my house later . . ." He stops midsentence and looks down at his hand as he traces the rim of his plate with his fingers. "It was like it was meant to happen," he says quietly.

I take a deep breath and absorb his answer, careful to tiptoe around that last sentence. He looks up at me with a nervous glance and I realize that he thinks his answer may have just scared me. I smile at him reassuringly and point to his drink. "You can drink now," I say. "Your turn to ask me a question."

"Oh, this one's easy," he says. "I want to know whose toes I'm stepping on. I received a mysterious inbox message from someone today. All it said was, 'If you're dating my girl, get your own prepaid minutes and quit wasting mine, jackass.'"

I laugh. "That would be Six. The bearer of my daily doses of positive affirmation."

He nods. "I was hoping you'd say that." He leans forward and narrows his eyes at me. "Because I'm pretty competitive, and if it came from a guy, my response would not have been as nice."

"You responded? What'd you say?"

"Is that your question? Because if it isn't, I'm taking another bite."

"Hold your horses and answer the question," I say.

"Yes, I responded to her text. I said, 'How do I buy more minutes?'"

My heart is a big puddle of mush right now, and I'm trying not to grin. It's really pathetic and sad. I shake my head. "I was only joking, that wasn't my question. It's still my turn."

He puts his fork back down and rolls his eyes. "My food's getting cold."

I place my elbows on the table and fold my hands under my chin. "I want to know about your sister. And why you referred to her in the past tense."

He tilts his head back and looks up, rubbing his hands down his face. "Ugh. You really ask the deep questions, huh?"

"That's how the game is played. I didn't make up the rules."

He sighs again and smiles at me, but there's a hint of sadness in his smile and it instantly makes me wish I could take the question back.

"Remember when I told you my family had a pretty fucked-up year last year?"

I nod.

He clears his throat and begins tracing the rim of his plate again. "She died thirteen months ago. She killed herself, even though my mother would rather we use the term, 'purposely overdosed.'"

He never stops looking at me when he speaks, so I show him the same respect, even though it's really difficult to look him in the eyes right now. I have no idea how to respond to that, but it's my own fault for bringing it up.

"What was her name?"

"Lesslie. I called her Les."

Hearing his nickname for her stirs up sadness within me and I suddenly don't feel like eating anymore. "Was she older than you?"

He leans forward and picks up his fork, then twirls it in his bowl. He brings the forkful of pasta to his mouth. "We were twins," he says flatly, right before taking the bite.

Jesus. I reach for my drink, but he takes it out of my hands and shakes his head. "My turn," he says with a mouthful. He finishes chewing and takes a sip, then wipes his mouth with a napkin. "I want to know the story about your dad."

I'm the one groaning this time. I fold my arms on the table in front of me and accept my payback. "Like I said, I haven't seen him since I was three. I don't have any memories of him. At least, I don't think I do. I don't even know what he looks like."

"Your mom doesn't have any pictures of him?"

It dawns on me when he asks this question that he doesn't even know I'm adopted. "You remember when you said my mom looked really young? Well, it's because she is. She adopted me."

Being adopted isn't really a stigma I've ever had to overcome. I've never been embarrassed by it, ashamed of it, or felt the need to hide the fact. But the way Holder is looking at me right now, you would think I just told him I was born with a penis. He's staring at me uncomfortably and it makes me fidget. "*What?* You've never met anyone who was adopted?"

It takes him a few more seconds to recover, but he puts away his puzzled expression and locks it up, replacing it with a smile. "You were adopted when you were three? By Karen?"

I nod my head. "I was put into foster care when I was three, after my biological mother died. My dad couldn't raise me on his own. Or he didn't *want* to raise me on his own. Either way, I'm fine with it. I lucked out with Karen and I have no urge whatsoever to go figure it all out. If he wanted to know where I was, he'd come find me."

I can tell he's not finished with the questions by the look in his eyes, but I really want to take a bite and get the ball back in my court.

I point to his arm with my fork. "What does your tattoo mean?"

He holds his arm out and traces his fingers over it. "It's a reminder. I got it after Les died."

"A reminder for what?"

He picks up his cup and diverts his eyes from mine. It's the only question he hasn't been able to answer with direct eye contact. "It's a reminder of the people I've let down in my life." He takes a drink and places his glass back on the table, still unable to make eye contact.

"This game's not very fun, is it?"

He laughs softly. "It's really not. It sort of sucks ass." He looks back up at me and smiles. "But we need to keep going because I still have questions. Do you remember anything from before you were adopted?"

I shake my head. "Not really. Bits and pieces, but it comes to a point that, when you don't have anyone to validate your memories, you just lose them all. The only thing I have from before Karen adopted me is some jewelry, and I have no idea who it came from. I can't distinguish now between what was reality, dreams, or what I saw on TV."

"Do you remember your mother?"

I pause for a moment and mull over his question. I don't remember my mother. At all. That's the only thing about my past that makes me sad. "Karen is my mother," I say point-blank. "My turn. Last question, then we eat dessert."

"Do you think we even have enough dessert?" he teases.

I glare at him, then ask my last question. "Why did you beat him up?"

I can tell by the shift in his expression that he doesn't need me to elaborate on the question. He shakes his head and pushes his bowl away from him. "You don't want to know the answer to that, Sky. I'll take the punishment."

"But I do want to know."

He tilts his head sideways and brings his hand to his

jaw, then pops his neck. He keeps his hand on his chin and rests his elbow on the table. "Like I told you before, I beat him up because he was an asshole."

I narrow my eyes at him. "That's vague. You don't do vague."

His expression doesn't change and he keeps his eyes locked on mine. "It was my first week back at school since Les died," he says. "She went to school there, too, so everyone knew what happened. I overheard the guy saying something about Les when I was passing him in the hallway. I disagreed with it, and I let him know. I took it too far and it came to a point when I was on top of him that I just didn't care. I was hitting him, over and over, and I didn't even care. The really fucked-up part is that the kid will more than likely be deaf out of his left ear for the rest of his life, and I *still* don't care."

He's staring at me, but not really looking at me. It's the hard, cold look that I've seen in his eyes before. I didn't like it then and I don't like it now . . . but at least now I can understand it more.

"What did he say about her?"

He slumps back in his chair and drops his eyes to an empty spot on the table between us. "I heard him laughing, telling his friend that Les took the selfish, easy way out. He said if she wasn't such a coward, she would have toughed it out."

"Toughed what out?"

He shrugs. "Life," he says indifferently.

"You don't think she took the easy way out," I say, dropping the end of the sentence as more of a statement than a question.

Holder leans forward and reaches across the table, taking my hand into both of his. He runs his thumbs across my palm and takes in a deep breath, then carefully releases it. "Les was the bravest fucking person I've ever known. It takes a lot of guts to do what she did. To just end it, not knowing what's next? Not knowing if there's *anything* next? It's easier to go on living a life without any life left in it than it is to just say 'fuck it' and leave. She was one of the few that just said, 'fuck it.' And I'll commend her every day I'm still alive, too scared to do the same thing."

He stills my hand between his, and it isn't until he does this that I realize I'm shaking. I look up at him and he's staring back at me. There are absolutely no words that can follow that up, so I don't even try. He stands up and leans over the table, then slides his hand behind my neck. He kisses me on top of the head, then releases his hold and walks to the kitchen. "You want brownies or cookies?" he asks over his shoulder, as if he didn't just absolutely stun me into silence.

He looks back at me and I'm still staring at him in shock. I don't even know what to say. Did he just admit that he's suicidal? Was he being metaphorical? Melodramatic? I have no idea what to do with the bomb he just placed in my lap.

He brings a plate of both cookies and brownies back to the table, then kneels down in front of me.

"Hey," he says soothingly, taking my face in his hands. His expression is serene. "I didn't mean to scare you. I'm not suicidal if that's what's freaking you out. I'm not fucked up in the head. I'm not deranged. I'm not suffering from post-traumatic stress disorder. I'm just a brother who loved his sister more than life itself, so I get a little intense when

I think about her. And if I cope better by telling myself that what she did was noble, even though it wasn't, then that's all I'm doing. I'm just coping." He's got a tight grip on my face and he's looking at me desperately, wanting me to understand where he's coming from. "I fucking loved that girl, Sky. I need to believe that what she did was the only answer she had left, because if I don't, then I'll never forgive myself for not helping her find a different one." He presses his forehead to mine. "Okay?"

I nod, then pull his hands from my face. I can't let him see me do this. "I need to use the bathroom." He backs up and I rush to the bathroom and shut the door behind me, then I do something I haven't done since I was five. I cry.

I don't ugly cry. I don't sob and I don't even make a noise. A single tear falls down my cheek and it's one tear too many, so I quickly wipe it away. I take a tissue and wipe at my eyes in an attempt to stop any other tears from forming.

I still don't know what to say to him, but I feel like he put a pretty tight lid on the subject, so I decide to let it go for now. I shake out my hands and take a deep breath, then open the door. He's standing across the hallway with his feet crossed at the ankles and his hands hanging loosely in his pockets. He straightens up and takes a step closer to me.

"We good?" he asks.

I smile my best smile and nod, then take a deep breath. "I told you I think you're intense. This just proves my point."

He smiles and nudges me toward the bedroom. He wraps his arms around me from behind and rests his chin on top of my head while we make our way toward my room. "Are you allowed to get pregnant yet?"

I laugh. "Nope. Not this weekend. Besides, you have to kiss a girl before you can knock her up."

"Did someone not have sex education when she was homeschooled?" he says. "Because I could totally knock you up without ever kissing you. Want me to show you?"

I hop on the bed and grab the book, opening it up to where we left off last night. "I'll take your word for it. Besides, I'm hoping we're about to get a hefty dose of sex education before we make it to the last page."

Holder drops down on the bed and I lie beside him. He puts his arm around me and pulls me toward him, so I rest my head on his chest and begin reading.

I know he's not doing it on purpose, but the entire time I'm reading I'm completely distracted by him. He's looking down at me, watching my mouth as I read, twirling my hair between his fingertips. Every time I flip a page, I glance up at him and he's got the same concentrated expression on his face each time. An expression so concentrated on my mouth, it tells me he's not paying a damn bit of attention to a single word I'm reading. I close the book and bring it to my stomach. I don't even think he notices I closed the book.

"Why'd you stop talking?" he says, never changing his expression or pulling his gaze from my mouth.

"Talking?" I ask curiously. "Holder, I'm *reading*. There's a difference. And from the looks of it, you haven't been paying a lick of attention."

He looks me in the eyes and grins. "Oh, I've been paying attention," he says. "To your mouth. Maybe not to the words coming out of it, but definitely to your mouth."

He scoots me off his chest and onto my back, then he slides down beside me and pulls me against him. Still, his expression hasn't changed and he's staring at me like he wants to eat me. I sort of wish he would.

He brings his fingers up to my lips and begins tracing them, slowly. It feels so incredible; I'm too scared to breathe for fear he might stop. I swear it's as though his fingers have a direct line to every sensitive spot on my entire body.

"You have a nice mouth," he says. "I can't stop looking at it."

"You should taste it," I say. "It's quite lovely."

He squeezes his eyes shut and groans, then leans in and presses his head into my neck. "Stop it, you evil wench."

I laugh and shake my head. "No way. This is your stupid rule, why should I be the one to enforce it?"

"Because you know I'm right. I can't kiss you tonight because kissing leads to the next thing, which leads to the next thing, and at the rate we're going we'll be all out of firsts by next weekend. Don't you want to drag our firsts out a little longer?" He pulls his head away from my neck and looks back down at me.

"Firsts?" I ask. "How many firsts are there?"

"There aren't that many, which is why we need to drag them out. We've already passed too many since we met."

I tilt my head sideways so I can look at him straight on. "What firsts have we already passed?"

"The easy ones. First hug, first date, first fight, first time we slept together, although I wasn't the one sleeping. Now we barely have any left. First kiss. First time to sleep together when we're both actually *awake*. First marriage. First kid. We're done after that. Our lives will become mundane and boring and I'll have to divorce you and marry a wife who's twenty years younger than me so I can have a lot more firsts and you'll be stuck raising the kids." He cups my cheek in his hand and smiles at me. "So you see, babe? I'm only doing this for your benefit. The longer I wait to kiss you, the longer it'll be before I'm forced to leave you high and dry."

I laugh. "Your logic terrifies me. I sort of don't find you attractive anymore."

He slides on top of me, holding up his weight on his hands. "You *sort of* don't find me attractive? That can also mean you sort of *do* find me attractive."

I shake my head. "I don't find you attractive at all. You repulse me. In fact, you better not kiss me because I'm pretty sure I just threw up in my mouth."

He laughs, then drops his weight onto one arm, still hovering over me. He lowers his mouth to the side of my head and presses his lips to my ear. "You're a liar," he whispers. "You're a whole *lot* attracted to me and I'm about to prove it."

I close my eyes and gasp the second his lips meet my neck. He kisses me lightly, right below the ear, and it feels like the whole room just turned into a Tilt-a-Whirl. He slowly moves his lips back to my ear and whispers, "Did you feel that?"

I shake my head no, but barely.

"You want me to do it again?"

I'm shaking my head no out of stubbornness, but I'm hoping he's telepathic and can hear what I'm really screaming inside my head, because hell yes, I liked it. Hell yes, I want him to do it again.

He laughs when I shake my head no, so he brings his lips closer to my mouth. He kisses me on the cheek, then continues trailing soft pecks down to my ear, where he stops and whispers again. "How about that?"

Oh, God, I've never been so *not* bored in my life. He's not even kissing me and it's already the best kiss I've ever had. I shake my head again and keep my eyes closed, because I like not knowing what's coming next. Like the hand that just planted itself on my outer thigh and is working its way up to my waist. He slides his hand under my T-shirt until his fingers barely graze the edge of my pants, and he leaves his hand there, slowly moving his thumb back and forth across my stomach. I'm so acutely aware of everything about him in this moment that I'm almost positive I could pick his thumbprint out of a lineup.

He runs his nose along my jawline and the fact that he's breathing just as heavily as I am assures me there's no way he can wait until after tonight to kiss me. At least that's what I'm desperately hoping.

When he reaches my ear again, he doesn't speak this time. Instead, he kisses it and there isn't a nerve ending in my body that doesn't feel it. From my head all the way down to my toes, my entire body is screaming for his mouth.

I place my hand on his neck and when I do, chills break out on his skin. Apparently, that one simple move momentarily melts his resolve and for a second, his tongue meets my neck. I moan and the sound completely sends him into a frenzy.

He moves his hand from my waist to the side of my head and he pulls my neck against his mouth, holding nothing back. I open my eyes, shocked at how quickly his demeanor changed. He kisses and licks and teases every inch of my neck, only gasping for air when it's absolutely necessary. As soon as I see the stars above my head, there isn't even enough time to count one of them before my eyes roll back in my head and I'm holding back sounds that I'm too embarrassed to utter.

He moves his lips farther from my neck and closer to my chest. If we didn't have such a limited supply of firsts, I'd tear my shirt off and make him keep going. Instead, he doesn't even give me this option. He kisses his way back up my neck, up my chin, and trails soft kisses around my entire mouth, careful not to once touch my lips. My eyes are closed, but I can feel his breath against my mouth, and I know he's struggling not to kiss me. I open my eyes and look at him and he's staring at my lips again.

"They're so perfect," he says, breathlessly. "Like hearts. I could literally stare at your lips for days and never get bored."

"No. Don't do that. If all you do is stare, then *I'll* be the bored one."

He grimaces, and it's obvious that he's having a really, really hard time not kissing me. I don't know what it is about him staring at my lips like he is, but it's definitely the hottest thing about this whole situation right now. I do something I probably shouldn't do. I lick them. Slowly.

He groans again and presses his forehead against mine. His arm gives way beneath him and he drops his weight on me, pressing himself against me. Everywhere. All of him. We moan simultaneously once our bodies find that perfect connection, and suddenly it's game on. I'm tearing off his shirt and he's on his knees, helping me pull it over his head. After it's completely off, I wrap my legs around his waist and lock him against me, because there could be nothing more detrimental than if he were to pull away right now.

He brings his forehead back to mine and our bodies reunite and fuse together like the last two pieces of a puzzle. He's slowly rocking against me and every time he does it, his lips come closer and closer, until they brush lightly against mine. He doesn't close the gap between our mouths, even though I absolutely need him to. Our lips are simply resting together, not kissing. Every time he moves against me, he lets out a breath that seeps into my mouth and I try to take them all in, because it feels like I need them if I want to survive this moment.

We remain in this rhythm for several minutes, neither of us wanting to be the first to initiate the kiss. It's obvious we both want to, but it's also obvious that I may have just met my match when it comes to stubbornness.

He holds the side of my head in place and keeps his forehead pressed against mine, but pulls his lips back far enough so he can lick them. When he lets them fall back into place, the wetness of his lips sliding against mine drags me completely under, and I doubt I'll ever be able to come up for air.

He shifts his weight, and I don't know what happens when he does this, but somehow it causes my head to roll back and the words, "*Oh, God,*" to come out of my mouth. I didn't mean to pull away from his mouth when I tilted my head back, because I really liked it being there, but I like where I'm going even more. I wrap my arms around his back and tuck my head against his neck for some semblance of stability, because it feels like the entire earth has been shifted off its axis and Holder is the core.

I realize what's about to happen and I begin to internally panic. Other than his shirt, we're completely clothed, not even kissing . . . yet the room is beginning to spin from the effect his rhythmic movements are having on my body. If he doesn't stop what he's doing, I'll fall apart and melt right here beneath him, and that would quite possibly mark the most embarrassing moment of my life. But if I ask him to stop, then he'll stop, and that would quite possibly mark the most *disappointing* moment of my life.

I try to calm my breaths and minimize the sounds escaping my lips, but I've lost any form of self-control. It's obvious my body is enjoying this nonkissing friction a little too much and I can't find it in me to stop. I'll try the next best thing. I'll ask *him* to stop.

"Holder," I say breathlessly, not really wanting him to stop, but hoping he'll get the hint and stop anyway. I need him to stop. Like two minutes ago.

He doesn't. He continues kissing my neck and moving his body against mine in a way that boys have done to me before, but this time it's different. It's so incredibly different and wonderful and it absolutely petrifies me.

"Holder." I attempt to say his name louder, but there isn't enough effort left in my body.

He kisses the side of my head and slows down, but he doesn't stop. "Sky, if you're asking me to stop, I will. But I'm hoping you're not, because I really don't want to stop, so please." He pulls back and looks down into my eyes, still barely moving his body against mine. His eyes are full of ache and worry and he's breathless when he speaks. "We won't go any further than this, I promise. But please don't ask me to stop where we already are. I need to watch you and I need to hear you because the fact that I know you're actually feeling this right now is so fucking amazing. You feel incredible and this feels incredible and *please*. Just . . . *please*."

He lowers his mouth to mine and gives me the softest peck imaginable. It's enough of a preview of what his real kiss will feel like and just the thought of it makes me shudder. He stops moving against me and pushes himself up on his hands, waiting for me to decide.

The moment he separates from me, my chest grows heavy with disappointment and I almost feel like crying. Not because he stopped or because I'm torn about what to do next . . . but because I never imagined that two people could connect on this sort of intimate level, and that it could feel so overwhelmingly right. Like the purpose of the entire human race revolves around this moment; around the two of us. Everything that's ever happened or will happen in this world is simply just a backdrop for what's occurring between us right now, and I don't want it to stop. I don't. I'm shaking my head, looking into his pleading eyes, and all I can do is whisper, "Don't. Whatever you do, don't stop."

He slides his hand behind my neck and lowers his head, pressing his forehead to mine. "*Thank* you," he breathes, gently easing himself onto me again, recreating the connection between us. He kisses the edges of my mouth several times, trailing close to my lips and down my chin and across my neck. The faster he breathes, the faster *I* breathe. The faster *I* breathe, the faster he plants kisses all over my neck. The faster he plants kisses all over my neck, the faster we move together—creating a tantalizing rhythm between us that, according to my pulse, isn't going to last much longer.

I dig my heels into the bed and my nails into his back.

He stops kissing my neck and looks down at me with heated eyes, watching me. He focuses on my mouth again, and as much as I want to watch him stare at me like he does, I can't keep my eyes open. They close involuntarily as soon as the first wave of chills washes over my body like a warning shot of what's about to come.

"Open your eyes," he says firmly.

I would if I could, but I'm completely helpless.

"Please."

That one word is all I need to hear and my eyes flick open beneath him. He's staring down at me with such an intense need, it's almost more intimate than if he were actually kissing me right now. As hard as it is to do in this moment, I keep my eyes locked on his as I drop my arms, clench the sheets with both fists and thank Karma for bringing this hopeless boy into my life. Because until this moment—until the first waves of pure and utter enlightenment wash over me—I had no idea that he was even missing.

I begin to shudder beneath him and he never once breaks our stare. I can no longer keep my eyes open no matter how hard I try, so I let them fall shut. I feel his lips slide delicately back to mine, but he still doesn't kiss me. Our mouths are stubbornly resting together as he holds his rhythm, allowing the last of my moans and a rush of my breaths and maybe even part of my heart to slip out of me and into him. I slowly and blissfully slide back down to earth and he eventually holds still, allowing me to recover from an experience that he somehow made not at all embarrassing for me.

When I'm completely spent and emotionally drained and my whole body is shaking, he continues to kiss my neck and shoulders and everywhere else in the vicinity of the one place I want kissed the most—my mouth.

But he would obviously rather hold his resolve than give in to his stubbornness, because he pulls his lips from my shoulder and brings his face closer to mine, but still refuses to make the connection. He reaches up and runs his hand along my hairline, smoothing away a stray strand from my forehead.

"You're incredible," he whispers, looking only at my eyes this time and not at all at my mouth. His words make up for his stubbornness and I can't help but smile back. He collapses to the bed beside me, still panting, while he makes a cognizant effort to contain the desire that I know is still coursing through him.

I close my eyes and listen to the silence that builds between us as our gasps for breath subside into soft, gentle rhythms. It's quiet and calm and quite possibly the most peaceful moment my mind has ever experienced.

Holder moves his hand closer to me on the bed between us and he wraps his pinky around mine as if he doesn't have the strength to hold my entire hand. But it's nice, because we've held hands before, but never pinkies . . . and I realize that this is another first we passed. And realizing this doesn't disappoint me, because I know that firsts don't matter with him. He could kiss me for the first time, or the twentieth time, or the millionth time and I wouldn't care if it was a first or not, because I'm pretty sure we just broke the record for the best first kiss in the history of first kisses—without even kissing.

After a long stretch of perfect silence, he takes a deep breath, then sits up on the bed and looks down at me. "I have to go. I can't be on this bed with you for another second."

I tilt my head toward his and look at him dejectedly as he stands up and pulls his shirt back on. He grins at me when he sees me pouting, then he bends forward until his face is hovering over mine, dangerously close. "When I said you weren't getting kissed tonight, I meant it. But *dammit*, Sky. I had no idea how fucking difficult you would make it." He slips his hand behind my neck and I gasp quietly, willing my heart to remain within the walls of my chest. He kisses my cheek and I can feel his hesitation when he reluctantly pulls away.

He walks backward toward the window, watching me the whole time. Before he slips outside, he pulls his phone out and runs his fingers swiftly over the screen for a few seconds, then slips it back into his pocket. He smiles at me, then climbs out the window and pulls it shut behind him.

I somehow find the strength to jump up and run to the kitchen. I grab my phone and, sure enough, there's a missed text from him. It's only one word, though.

Incredible.

I smile, because it was. It absolutely was.

Thirteen years earlier

"Hey."

I keep my head buried in my arms. I don't want him to see me crying again. I know he won't laugh at me—neither of them would ever laugh at me. But I really don't even know why I'm crying and I wish it would just stop but it won't and I can't and I hate it, hate it, hate it.

He sits down on the sidewalk next to me and she sits down on the other side of me. I still don't look up and I'm still sad, but I don't want them to leave because it feels nice with them here.

"This might make you feel better," she says. "I made us both one at school today." She doesn't ask me to look up so I don't, but I can feel her put something on my knee.

I don't move. I don't like getting presents and I don't want her to see me look at it.

I keep my head down and keep crying and wish that I knew what was wrong with me. Something's wrong with me or I wouldn't feel like this every time it happens. Because it's supposed to happen. That's what Daddy tells me, anyway. It's supposed to happen and I have to stop crying because it makes him so, so sad when I cry.

They sit by me for a long, long time but I don't know how long because I don't know if hours are longer than minutes. He leans over and whispers in my ear. "Don't forget what I told you. Remember what you need to do when you're sad?"

I nod into my arm, but I don't look up at him. I have been doing what he said I should do when I get sad, but sometimes I'm still sad, anyway.

They stay for a few more hours or minutes, but then she stands up. I wish they would stay for one more minute or two more hours. They never ask me what's wrong and that's why I like them so much and wish they would stay.

I lift my elbow and peek out from underneath it and see her feet walking away from me. I grab her present off my knee and run it through my fingers. She made me a bracelet. It's stretchy and purple and has half of a heart on it. I slide it on my wrist and smile, even though I'm still crying. I lift up my head and he's still here, looking at me. He looks sad and I feel bad because I feel like I'm making him sad.

He stands up and faces my house. He looks at it for a long time without saying anything. He always thinks a lot and it makes me wonder what he's always thinking about. He stops looking at the house and looks back down at me. "Don't worry," he says, trying to smile for me. "He won't live forever." He turns around and walks back to his house, so I close my eyes and lay my head on my arms again.

I don't know why he would say that. I don't want my daddy to die . . . I just want him to stop calling me Princess.

Monday, September 3, 2012
7:20 a.m.

I don't pull it out very often, but for some reason I want to look at it today. I guess talking about the past with Holder Saturday has left me feeling a little nostalgic. I know I told Holder I'd never look for my father, but sometimes I'm still curious. I can't help but wonder how a parent can raise a child for several years, then just give that child away. I'll never understand it, and maybe I don't need to. That's why I never push it. I never ask Karen questions. I never try to separate the memories from the dreams and I don't like bringing it up . . . because I just don't need to.

I take the bracelet out of the box and slide it onto my wrist. I don't know who gave it to me, and I don't even really care. I'm sure with two years in foster care, I received lots of things from friends. What's different about this gift, though, is that it's attached to the only memory I have of that life. The bracelet validates that my memory is a real one. And knowing that the memory is real somehow validates that I was someone else before I was me. A girl I don't remember. A girl who cried a lot. A girl that isn't anything like who I am today.

Someday I'll throw the bracelet away because I need to. But today, I just feel like wearing it.

Holder and I decided to take a breather from each other yesterday. And I say breather, because after Saturday night, we went quite a while on my bed without breathing at all. Besides, Karen was coming home and the last thing I wanted to do was reintroduce her to my new . . . whatever he is. We never got far enough to label what's going on between us. It feels like I haven't known him near long enough to refer to him as my boyfriend, considering we haven't even kissed yet. But dammit if it doesn't piss me off to think of his lips being on anyone else. So whether or not we're dating, I'm declaring us exclusive. Can you even be exclusive without actually kissing first? Are exclusive and dating mutually exclusive?

I make myself laugh out loud. Or *lol*.

When I woke up yesterday morning, I had two texts. I'm really getting into this whole texting thing. I get really giddy when I have one and I can't imagine how addictive email and Facebook and everything else technology-related must be. One of the texts was from Six, going on and on about my impeccable baking abilities, followed up with strict instructions to call her Sunday night from her house phone to catch her up on everything. I did. We talked for an hour and she's just as floored as I am that Holder isn't at all how we expected him to be. I asked her about Lorenzo and she didn't even know who I was referring to, so I laughed and dropped it. I miss her and hate that she's gone, but she's loving it and that makes me happy.

The second text I had was from Holder. All it said was, *"I'm dreading seeing you at school on Monday. So bad."*

Running used to be the highlight of my day, but now it's receiving insulting texts from Holder. And speaking of running and Holder, we aren't doing that anymore. To-gether, anyway. After texting back and forth yesterday, we decided it was probably best if we didn't run together on a daily basis because that might be too much, too soon. I told him I didn't want things to get weird between us. Besides, I'm really self-conscious when I'm sweaty and snotty and wheezing and smelly and I would just rather run alone.

Now I'm staring into my locker in a daze, sort of stall-ing because I really don't want to go to class. It's first period and the only class I have with Holder, so I'm really nervous about how it'll play out. I take Breckin's book out of my backpack and the other two books I brought him, then put the rest of my things in my locker. I walk into the classroom and to my seat, but Breckin isn't here yet, and neither is Holder. I sit down and stare at the door, not really sure why I'm so nervous. It's just different, seeing him here rather than on home turf. Public school is just way too . . . *public*.

The door opens and Holder walks in, followed closely by Breckin. They both start toward the back of the room. Holder smiles at me, walking down one aisle. Breckin smiles at me, walking down the other aisle, holding two cups of coffee. Holder reaches the seat next to me and starts to lay his backpack on it at the same time Breckin reaches it and begins to set the coffee cups down. They look up at each other, then they both look back at me.

Awkward.

I do the only thing I know how to do in awkward situa-tions—infuse them with sarcasm.

"Looks like we have quite the predicament here, boys." I smile at both of them, then eye the coffee in Breckin's hands. "I see the Mormon brought the queen her offering of coffee. Very impressive." I look at Holder and cock my eyebrow. "Do you wish to reveal your offering, hopeless boy, so that I may decide who shall accompany me at the classroom throne today?"

Breckin looks at me like I've lost my mind. Holder laughs and picks his backpack up off the desk. "Looks like someone's in need of an ego-shattering text today." He moves his backpack to the empty seat in front of Breckin and claims his spot.

Breckin is still standing, holding both coffees with an incredibly confused look on his face. I reach out and grab one of the cups. "Congratulations, squire. You are the queen's chosen one today. Sit. It's been quite the weekend."

Breckin slowly takes his seat and sets his coffee on his desk, then pulls his backpack off his shoulder, eyeing me suspiciously the whole time. Holder is seated sideways at his desk, staring at me. I gesture with my hand toward Holder. "Breckin, this is Holder. Holder is not my boyfriend, but if I catch him trying to break the record for best first kiss with another girl, then he'll soon be my *not breathing* non-boyfriend."

Holder arches an eyebrow at me and a hint of a smile plays in the corner of his mouth. "Likewise." His dimples are taunting me and I have to force myself to look directly into his eyes or I might be compelled to do something that would be grounds for suspension.

I gesture toward Breckin. "Holder, this is Breckin. Breckin is my new very bestest friend ever in the whole wide world."

Breckin eyes Holder and Holder smiles at him, then reaches out to shake his hand. Breckin tentatively shakes

Holder's hand in return, then pulls it back and turns to me, narrowing his eyes. "Does *not-your-boyfriend* realize I'm Mormon?"

I nod. "It turns out, Holder doesn't have an issue with Mormons at all. He just has an issue with assholes."

Breckin laughs and turns back to Holder. "Well, in that case, welcome to the alliance."

Holder gives him a half smile, but he's staring at the coffee cup on Breckin's desk. "I thought Mormons weren't allowed to have caffeine."

Breckin shrugs. "I decided to break that rule the morning I woke up gay."

Holder laughs and Breckin smiles and everything is right with the world. Or at least in the world of first period. I lean back in my chair and smile. This won't be hard at all. In fact, I think I just started loving public school.

Holder follows me to my locker after class. We don't speak. I switch my books while he rips more insults off my locker. There were only two sticky notes after class today, which makes me a little sad. They're giving up so easily and it's only the second week of school.

He wads the notes up and flicks them on the floor and I shut my locker, then turn toward him. We're both leaning against the lockers, facing each other.

"You trimmed your hair," I say, noticing it for the first time.

He runs his hand through it and grins. "Yeah. This chick I know couldn't stop whining about it. It was really annoying."

"I like it."

He smiles. "Good."

I purse my lips and rock back and forth on my heels. He's grinning at me and he looks adorable. If we weren't in a hallway right now full of people, I'd grab his shirt and pull him to me so I could show him just how adorable I think he looks. Instead, I push the images away and smile back at him. "I guess we should get to class."

He nods slowly. "Yep," he says, without walking away.

We stand there for another thirty seconds or so before I laugh and kick off the locker, then start to walk away. He grabs my arm and pulls me back so quickly, I gasp. Before I know it, my back is against the locker and he's standing in front of me, blocking me in with his arms. He shoots me a devilish grin, then tilts my face up to his. He brings his right hand to my cheek and slides it under my jaw, cupping my face. He delicately strokes both of my lips with his thumb and I have to remind myself again that we're in public and I can't act on my impulses right now. I press myself against the lockers behind me, trying to use the sturdiness of them to make up for the support my knees are no longer providing.

"I wish I had kissed you Saturday night," he says. He drops his eyes to my lips where his thumb is still stroking them. "I can't stop imagining what you taste like." He presses his thumb firmly against the center of my lips, then very briefly connects his mouth to mine without moving his thumb out of the way. His lips are gone and his thumb is gone and it happens so fast, I don't even realize *he's* gone until the hallway stops spinning and I'm able to stand up straight.

I don't know how much longer I can take this. I'm

reminded of my nervous rant on Saturday night, when I wanted him to just get it over with and kiss me in the kitchen. I had absolutely no idea what I would be in for.

"How?"

It's just one word, but as soon as I lay my tray down across from Breckin, I know exactly what all that word encompasses. I laugh and decide to spill all the details before Holder shows up at our table. *If* he shows up at our table. Not only have we not discussed relationship labels, we also haven't discussed lunchroom seating arrangements.

"He showed up at my house on Friday and after quite a few misunderstandings, we finally came to an understanding that we just misunderstood each other. Then we baked, I read him some smut, and he went home. He came back over Saturday night and cooked for me. Then we went to my room and . . ."

I stop talking when Holder takes a seat beside me.

"Keep going," Holder says. "I'd love to hear what we did next."

I roll my eyes and turn back to Breckin. "Then we broke the record for best first kiss in the history of first kisses without even kissing."

Breckin nods carefully, still looking at me with eyes full of skepticism. Or curiosity. "Impressive."

"It was an excruciatingly boring weekend," Holder says to Breckin.

I laugh, but Breckin looks at me like I'm crazy again. "Holder loves boring," I assure him. "He means that in a nice way."

Breckin looks back and forth between the two of us, then shakes his head and leans forward, picking up his fork. "Not much confuses me," he says, pointing his fork at us. "But you two are an exception."

I nod in complete agreement.

We continue with lunch and have somewhat normal, decent interaction among the three of us. Holder and Breckin start talking about the book he let me borrow and the fact that Holder is even discussing a romance novel at all is entertaining in itself, but the fact that he's arguing about the plot with Breckin is sickeningly adorable. Every now and then he places his hand on my leg or rubs my back or kisses the side of my head, and he's going through these motions like they're second nature, but to me not a single one of them goes unnoticed.

I'm trying to process the shift from last week to this week and I can't get past the notion that we might just be too good. Whatever this is and whatever we're doing seems too good and too right and too perfect and it makes me think of all the books I've read and how, when things get too good and too right and too perfect, it's only because the ugly twist hasn't yet infiltrated the goodness of it all and I suddenly—

"Sky," Holder says, snapping his fingers in front of my face. I look at him and he's eyeing me cautiously. "Where'd you go?"

I shake my head and smile, not knowing what just set off that mini internal panic attack. He slides his hand just below my ear and runs his thumb across my cheekbone. "You have to quit checking out like that. It freaks me out a little bit."

"Sorry," I say with a shrug. "I'm easily distracted." I bring my hand up and pull his hand away from my neck, squeezing his fingers reassuringly. "Really, I'm fine."

His gaze drops to my hand. He flips it over and slides my sleeve up, then twists my wrist back and forth.

"Where'd you get that?" he says, looking down at my wrist.

I look down to see what he's referring to and realize I'm still wearing the bracelet I put on this morning. He looks back up at me and I shrug. I'm not really in the mood to explain it. It's complicated and he'll ask questions and lunch is almost over.

"Where'd you get it?" he says again, this time a little more demanding. His grip tightens around my wrist and he's staring at me coldly, expecting an explanation. I pull my wrist away, not liking where this is going.

"You think I got it from a guy?" I ask, puzzled by his reaction. I hadn't really pegged him for the jealous type, but this doesn't really seem like jealousy. It seems like crazy.

He doesn't answer my question. He keeps glaring at me like I've got some sort of huge confession that I'm refusing to reveal. I don't know what he expects, but his attitude right now is more than likely going to end up with him getting slapped, rather than with me giving an explanation.

Breckin shifts uncomfortably in his seat and clears his throat. "Holder. Ease up, man."

Holder's expression doesn't change. If anything, it grows even colder. He leans forward a few inches and lowers his voice when he speaks. "Who gave you the damn bracelet, Sky?"

His words transform into an unbearable weight in my

chest and all the same warning signs that flashed in my head when I first met him are flashing again, only this time they're in big neon letters. I know my mouth is agape and my eyes are wide, but I'm relieved that hope isn't a tangible thing, because everyone around me would see mine crumbling.

He closes his eyes and faces forward, setting his elbows on the table. His palms press against his forehead and he inhales a long, deep breath. I'm not sure if the breath is more for a calming effect, or a distraction to keep him from yelling. He runs his hand through his hair and grips the back of his neck.

"Shit!" he says. His voice is harsh and it causes me to flinch. He stands up and walks away unexpectedly, leaving his tray on the table. My eyes follow him as he continues across the cafeteria without once looking back at me. He slaps the cafeteria doors with both palms and disappears through them. I don't even blink or breathe again until the doors finish swinging, coming to a complete standstill.

I turn back to Breckin and I can only imagine the shock on my face right now. I blink and shake my head, replaying the last two minutes of the scene in my head. Breckin reaches across the table and takes my hand in his, but doesn't say anything. There's nothing to say. We both lost all of our words the second Holder disappeared through those doors.

The bell rings and the cafeteria becomes a whirlwind of commotion, but I can't move. Everyone is moving around and emptying trays and clearing tables, but the world of our table is a stilled one. Breckin finally lets go of my hand and grabs our trays, then comes back for Holder's tray and clears off the table. He picks up my backpack and takes my hand again, pulling me up. He puts my backpack over his shoulder, then walks me out of the cafeteria. He doesn't walk me to my locker or walk me to my classroom. He holds my hand and pulls me along behind him until we're out the doors and across the parking lot and he's opening a door and pushing me inside an unfamiliar car. He slides into his seat and cranks the car, then turns in his seat and faces me.

"I'm not even going to tell you what I think about what just happened in there. But I know it sucked and I have no idea why you aren't crying right now, but I know your heart hurts, and maybe even your pride. So fuck school. We're going for ice cream." He puts his car in reverse, then pulls out of the parking spot.

I don't know how he does it because I was just about to burst into tears and sob and snot all over his car, but after those words come out of his mouth, I actually smile.

"I love ice cream."

The ice cream helped, but I don't think it helped that much because Breckin just dropped me off at my car and I'm sitting in my driver's seat, unable to move. I'm sad and I'm scared and I'm mad and I'm feeling all the things that I'm warranted to feel after what just happened, but I'm not crying.

And I won't cry.

When I get home I do the only thing that I know will help. I run. Only when I get back and climb in the shower I realize that, like the ice cream, the run really didn't help that much, either.

I go through the same motions that I go through any other night of the week. I help Karen with dinner, I eat with her and Jack, I work on schoolwork, I read a book. I try to act like it doesn't upset me at all, because I really wish it didn't, but the second I climb into bed and turn off my light, my mind begins wandering. Only this time it doesn't wander very far, because I'm stuck on just one thing and one thing only. Why the hell hasn't he apologized?

I half expected him to be waiting at my car when Breckin and I got back from ice cream, but he wasn't. When I pulled into my driveway, I expected him to be there, ready to grovel and beg and provide me with even the smallest bit of an explanation, but he wasn't here. I kept my phone hidden in my pocket (because Karen still doesn't know I have it) and I checked it every chance I got, but the only text I received was from Six and I still haven't even read it yet.

So now I'm in my bed, hugging my pillow, feeling incredibly guilty for not having the urge to egg his house and slash his tires and kick him in the balls. Because I know that's what I wish I was feeling. I wish I was pissed and angry and unforgiving, because it would feel so much better than feeling disappointed over the realization that the Holder I had this weekend . . . wasn't even Holder at all.

Tuesday, September 4, 2012
6:15 a.m.

I open my eyes and don't climb out of bed until the seventy-sixth star on my ceiling is counted. I throw the covers off and change into my running clothes. When I climb out of my bedroom window, I pause.

He's standing on the sidewalk with his back to me. His hands are clasped on top of his head and I can see the muscles in his back contracting from labored breaths. He's in the middle of a run and I'm not sure if he's waiting on me or just happens to be taking a breather, so I remain stilled outside my window and wait, hoping he keeps running.

But he doesn't.

After a couple of minutes, I finally work up the nerve to walk into the front yard. When he hears my footsteps, he turns around. I stop walking when we make eye contact and I stare back at him. I'm not glaring or frowning and I'm sure as hell not smiling. I'm just staring.

The look in his eyes is a new one and the only word I can use to describe it is regret. But he doesn't speak, which means he doesn't apologize, which means I don't have time to try to figure him out right now. I just need to run.

I walk past him and step onto the sidewalk, then start running. After a few steps, I hear him begin running behind me, but I keep my eyes focused forward. He never falls into step beside me and I make it a point not to slow down because I want him to stay behind me. At some point I begin running faster and faster until I'm sprinting, but he keeps in pace with me, always just a few steps behind. When we get to the marker that I use as a guide to turn around, I make it a point not to look at him. I turn around and pass him and head back toward my house, and the entire second half of the run is the exact same as the first. Quiet.

We're less than two blocks from reaching my house and I'm angry that he showed up at all today and even angrier that he still hasn't apologized. I begin running faster and faster, more than likely faster than I've ever run before, and he continues to match my speed step for step. This pisses me off even more, so when we turn on my street I somehow increase my speed and I'm running toward my house as fast as I possibly can and it's still not fast enough, because he's still there. My knees are buckling and I'm exerting myself so hard that I can't even catch a breath, but I only have twenty more feet until I reach my window.

I only make it ten.

As soon as my shoes meet the grass, I collapse onto my hands and knees and take several deep breaths. Never once, even in my four-mile runs, have I ever felt this drained. I roll onto my back on the grass and it's still wet with dew, but it feels good against my skin. My eyes are closed and I'm gasping so loud that I can barely hear Holder's breaths over my own. But I do hear them and they're close and I know he's on the grass next to me. We both lie still, panting for breath, and it reminds me of just a few nights ago when we were in the same position on my bed recovering from what he did to me. I think he's also reminded of this, because I barely feel his pinky when he reaches between us and wraps it around mine. Only this time when he does it, I don't smile. I wince.

I pull my hand away and roll over, then stand up. I walk the ten feet back to my house and I climb into my room, then close the window behind me.

Friday, September 28, 2012
12:05 p.m.

It's been almost four weeks now. He never showed up to run with me again and he never apologized. He doesn't sit by me in class or in the cafeteria. He doesn't send me insulting texts and he doesn't show up on weekends as a different person. The only thing he does, at least I think he's the one that does it, is remove the sticky notes from my locker. They're always crumpled in a wad on the hallway floor at my feet.

I continue to exist, and he continues to exist, but we don't exist together. Days continue to pass no matter who I exist with, though. And each additional day that plants itself between the present and that weekend with him just leaves me with more and more questions that I'm too stubborn to ask.

I want to know what set him off that day. I want to know why he didn't just let it go instead of storming off like he did. I want to know why he never apologized, because I'm almost positive I would have given him at least one more chance. What he did was crazy and strange and a little possessive, but if I weighed it on a scale against all the wonderful things about him, I know it wouldn't have weighed nearly as much.

Breckin doesn't even try to analyze it anymore so I pretend not to, either. But I do, and the thing that eats at me the most is the fact that everything that happened between us is starting to seem surreal, like it was all just a dream. I catch myself questioning whether that weekend even happened at all, or if it was just another invalidated memory of mine that may not even be real.

For this entire month, the one thing in the forefront of my mind more than anything (and I know this is really pathetic) is the fact that I never did get to kiss him. I wanted to kiss him so incredibly badly that knowing I won't get to experience it leaves me feeling like there's this huge gaping hole in my chest. The ease with which we interacted, the way he would touch me like it was what he was supposed to do, the kisses he would plant in my hair—they were all small pieces of something so much bigger. Something big enough that, even though we never kissed, deserves some sort of recognition from him. Some sort of respect. He treats whatever was about to develop between us like it was wrong, and it hurts. Because I know he felt it. I *know* he did. And if he felt it in the same way that I felt it, then I know he *still* feels it.

I'm not heartbroken and I still haven't shed a single tear over the entire situation. I can't be heartbroken because luckily, I had yet to give him that part of me. But I'm not too proud to admit that I am a little sad about it all, and I know it'll take time because I really, really liked him. So, I'm fine. I'm a little sad, and a whole lot confused, but I'm fine.

"What's this?" I ask Breckin, looking down at the table. He just placed a box in front of me. A very nicely wrapped box.

"Just a little reminder."

I look up at him questioningly. "For what?"

He laughs and pushes the box closer to me. "It's a reminder that tomorrow's your birthday. Now open it."

I sigh and roll my eyes, then push it to the side. "I was hoping you'd forget."

He grabs the gift and pushes it back in front of me. "Open the damn present, Sky. I know you hate getting gifts, but I love giving them, so stop being a depressing bitch and open it and love it and hug me and thank me."

I slump my shoulders and push my empty tray aside, then pull the box back in front of me. "You're a good gift wrapper," I say. I untie the bow and tear open one end of the box, then slide open the paper. I look down at the picture on the box and cock my eyebrow. "You got me a TV?"

Breckin laughs and shakes his head, then picks the box up. "It's not a TV, dummy. It's an e-reader."

"Oh," I say. I have no idea what an e-reader is, but I'm pretty sure I'm not supposed to have one. I would just accept it like I accepted Six's cell phone, but this thing is too big for me to hide in my pocket.

"You're kidding, right?" He leans toward me. "You don't know what an e-reader is?"

I shrug. "It still looks like a tiny TV to me."

He laughs even louder and opens the box, pulling the e-reader out. He turns it on and hands it back to me. "It's an electronic device that holds more books than you'll ever be able to read." He pushes a button and the screen lights up, then he runs his finger across the front, pressing it in places until the whole screen is lit up with dozens of small pictures of books. I touch one of the pictures and the screen changes, then the book cover fills the entire screen. He slides his finger across it and the page virtually turns and I'm staring at chapter one.

I immediately start scrolling my finger across the screen and watch as each page turns effortlessly, one right after the other. It's absolutely the most amazing thing I've ever seen. I hit more buttons and click on more books and scroll through more chapters and I honestly don't think I've ever seen a more magnificent, practical invention.

"Wow," I whisper. I keep staring at the e-reader, hoping he's not playing some cruel joke on me, because if he tries to pry this out of my hands I'll run.

"You like it?" he asks proudly. "I loaded about two hundred free books on there so you should be good for a while."

I look up at him and he's grinning from ear to ear. I set the e-reader down on the table, then lunge forward over the table and squeeze his neck. It's the best present I've ever received and I'm smiling and squeezing him so tight, I completely don't care that I'm supposed to be horrible at receiving gifts. Breckin returns my hug and kisses me on the cheek. When I let go of his neck and open my eyes, I involuntarily glance at the table that I've been trying to avoid glancing at for almost four weeks now.

Holder is turned around in his seat, watching us. He's smiling. It's not a crazy or seductive or creepy smile. It's an endearing smile, and as soon as I see it and the waves of sadness crash against my core, I look away from him and back to Breckin.

I take my seat and pick the e-reader back up. "You know, Breckin. You really are pretty damn great."

He smiles and winks at me. "It's the Mormon in me. We're a pretty awesome people."

Friday, September 28, 2012
11:50 p.m.

It's the last day I'll ever be seventeen. Karen is working out of town at her flea market again this weekend. She tried to cancel her trip because she felt bad for leaving during my birthday, but I wouldn't let her. Instead, we celebrated my birthday last night. Her gifts were good, but they're nothing like the e-reader. I've never been more excited to spend a weekend alone.

I didn't bake near as many things as the last time Karen was out of town. Not because I don't feel like eating them, but because I'm pretty sure my addiction to reading has just reached a whole new level. It's almost midnight and my eyes won't stay open, but I've read nearly two entire books and I absolutely need to get to the end of this one. I doze off, then awaken with a jerk, only to attempt to read another paragraph. Breckin has really great taste in books, and I'm sort of upset that it took him a whole month to tell me about this one. I know I'm not a big fan of happily-ever-afters, but if these two characters don't get theirs, I'll climb inside this e-reader and lock them inside that damn garage forever.

My eyelids slowly close and I keep trying to will them to stay open but the words are beginning to swim together on the screen and nothing is even making sense. I finally power off the e-reader and turn out my light and think about how my last day of being seventeen should have been so much better than it actually was.

My eyes flick open, but I don't move. It's still dark and I'm still in the same position I was in earlier, so I know I just fell asleep. I silence my breaths and listen for the same sound that pulled me out of my sleep—the sound of my window sliding open.

I can hear the curtains scraping against the rod and someone climbing inside. I know I should scream, or run for my door, or look around for some sort of object that can be used as a weapon. Instead, I remain frozen because whoever it is isn't trying to be at all quiet about the fact that he's climbing into my room, so I can only assume it's Holder. But still, my heart is racing and every muscle in my body stiffens when the bed shifts as he lowers himself onto it. The closer he gets, the more certain I am that it's him, because no one else can cause my body to react the way it's reacting right now. I squeeze my eyes shut and bring my hands to my face when I feel the covers lift up behind me. I'm absolutely terrified. I'm terrified, because I don't know *which* Holder is crawling into my bed right now.

His arm slides under my pillow and his other arm wraps tightly around my body when he finds my hands. He pulls me against his chest and laces his fingers into mine, then buries his head in my neck. I'm very conscious about the fact that I'm not wearing anything but a tank top and underwear, but I'm confident he's not here for that part of me. I'm still not positive *why* he's here, because he's not even talking, but he knows I'm awake. I know he knows I'm awake because the second his arms went around me, I gasped. He holds me as tight as he can and every now and then, he plants his lips into my hair and kisses me.

I'm angry with him for being here, but even angrier with myself for wanting him here. No matter how much I want to scream at him and make him leave, I find myself wishing he could squeeze me just a little bit tighter. I want him to lock his arms around me and throw away the key, because this is where he belongs and I'm scared he'll just let me go again.

I hate that there are so many sides to him that I don't understand, and I don't know if I even want to keep trying to understand them. There are parts of him I love, parts of him I hate, parts that terrify me, and parts that amaze me. But there's a part of him that does nothing but disappoint me . . . and that's the absolute hardest part of him to accept.

We lie here in complete silence for what could be half an hour, but I'm not sure. All I know is that he hasn't released his grip at all, nor has he made any attempt at explaining himself. But what's new? There isn't anything I'll ever get from him unless I ask the questions first. And right now, I just don't feel like asking any.

He releases my fingers from his and brings his hand to the top of my head. He presses his lips into my hair and he folds the arm up that's underneath my pillow and he's cradling me, burying his face in my hair. His arms begin to shake and he's holding me with such intensity and desperation that it becomes heartbreaking. My chest heaves and my cheeks burn and the only thing stopping the tears from flowing is the fact that my eyes are closed so tight, they can't escape.

I can't take the silence anymore, and if I don't get off my chest what I absolutely need to say, I might scream. I know my voice will be layered with heartbreak and sadness and I'll barely be able to speak while attempting to contain my tears, but I take a deep breath anyway and say the most honest thing I can say.

"I'm so mad at you."

As if it's possible, he somehow squeezes me even tighter. He moves his mouth to my ear and kisses it. "I know, Sky," he whispers. His hand slips underneath my shirt and he presses an open palm against my stomach, pulling me tighter against him. "I know."

It's amazing what the sound of a voice you've been longing to hear can do to your heart. He spoke five words just now, but in the time it took him to speak those five words, my heart was shredded and minced, then placed back inside my chest with the expectation that it should somehow know how to beat again.

I slip my fingers through the hand that's resting tightly against me and I squeeze it, not even knowing what it means, but every part of me wants to touch him and hold him and make sure he's really here. I need to know he's here and that this isn't just another vivid dream.

His mouth meets my shoulder and he parts his lips, kissing me softly. The feel of his tongue against my skin immediately sends a surge of heat through me and I can feel the flush rise from my stomach, straight up to my cheeks.

"I know," he whispers again, slowly exploring my collarbone and neck with his lips. I keep my eyes shut because the distress in his voice and the tenderness in his touch is making my head spin. I reach up behind me and run my hand through his hair, pressing him deeper into my neck. His warm breath against my skin becomes increasingly more frantic, along with his kisses. Our breathing picks up pace as he covers every inch of my neck twice over.

He lifts up on his arm and urges me flat onto my back, then brings his hand to my face and brushes the hair away from my eyes. Seeing him this close to me brings back every single feeling I've ever felt for this boy . . . the good *and* the bad. I don't understand how he can put me through what he's put me through when the sorrow in his eyes is so prominent. I don't know if it's the fact that I can't read him at all or if I read him too well, but looking up at him right now I know he feels what I'm feeling . . . which makes his actions that much more confusing.

"I know you're mad at me," he says, looking down at me. His eyes and his words are full of remorse, but the apology still doesn't come. "I need you to be mad at me, Sky. But I think I need you to still want me here with you even more."

My chest grows heavy with his words and it takes an extreme amount of effort to continue pulling breath into my lungs. I nod my head slightly, because I can completely agree to that. I'm pissed at him, but I want him here with me so much more than I *don't*. He drops his forehead to mine and we grab hold of each other's face, looking desperately into each other's eyes. I'm not sure if he's about to kiss me. I'm not even sure if he's about to get up and leave. The only thing I'm certain about right now is that after this moment, I will never be the same. I know, by the way his existence is like a magnetic pull on my heart, that if he ever hurts me again, I'll be far from just *fine*. I'll be broken.

Our chests are rising and falling as one as the silence and tension grow thicker. The firm grip he has on my face can be felt in every part of me, almost as if he's gripping me from the inside out. The intensity of the moment causes tears to sting at my eyes, and I'm completely taken aback by my unexpected emotions.

"I *am* mad at you, Holder," I say with an unsteady, but sure voice. "But no matter how mad I've been, I never for one second stopped wanting you here with me."

He somehow smiles and frowns in the same moment. "*Jesus*, Sky." His face contorts into an incredible amount of relief. "I've missed you so bad." He immediately drops his mouth and presses his lips to mine. The sensation has been so long overdue; neither of us has any patience left. I immediately respond by parting my lips and allowing him to fill me with the sweet taste of his mint leaves and soda. He's everything I've been imagining he would be and more. Gentle, rough, caring, selfish. In this one kiss I feel more of his emotions than in any words he's ever spoken. Our lips are finally intertwining for the first time, or the twentieth time, or the millionth time. It doesn't really matter because whichever time this is—it's absolutely perfect. It's incredible and flawless and almost worth everything we've been through in order to get to this moment.

Our lips move passionately together as we struggle to pull ourselves closer, wanting to find that perfect connection with our bodies that we've just found with our mouths. He works his mouth against mine delicately, yet fiercely, and I match him movement for movement. I release several moans and even more breaths and he drinks each one of them in with his mouth.

We kiss and kiss in every position possible, attempting to remain as restrained as our want will allow us. We kiss until I can no longer feel my lips and until I'm so exhausted and spent that I'm not even sure if we're still kissing when he presses his head to mine.

And that's exactly how we fall asleep—forehead to forehead, wrapped silently together. Because nothing else is spoken between us. Not even an apology.

Saturday, September 29, 2012
8:40 a.m.

I turn over to inspect the bed, half thinking what happened last night was a dream. Holder isn't here, but in his place is a small gift-wrapped box. I push myself up against my headboard and pick up the gift. I stare at it for a long time before I finally lift the lid and look inside. It's something that looks like a credit card, so I pick it up and read it.

He bought me a phone card with texting minutes. Lots of them.

I smile, because I know the significance of this card. It all lies within the message that Six sent him. He plans on stealing her girl, and he also plans on using a lot of her minutes. The gift makes me smile and I immediately reach to the nightstand and grab my phone. I have one missed text and it's from Holder.

You hungry?

The text is short and simple but it's his way of letting me know he's still here. Somewhere. Is he making me breakfast? I go to the bathroom before heading to the kitchen and brush my teeth. I change out of my tank top and pull on a simple sundress, then gather my hair up in a ponytail. I look at my reflection in the mirror and I see a girl who desperately wants to forgive a boy, but not without a hell of a lot of groveling first.

When I open the door to my bedroom, I'm met with the smell of bacon and the sound of grease sizzling from the kitchen. I walk down the hallway and around the corner, then pause. I stare at him for a while. His back is to me and he's working his way around the stove, humming to himself. He's shoeless, wearing jeans topped with a plain white sleeveless T-shirt. He already feels at home again, and I'm not sure how I feel about that.

"I left early this morning," he says, talking with his back still to me, "because I was afraid your mom would walk in and think I was trying to get you pregnant. Then when I went for my run, I passed by your house again and realized her car wasn't even home and remembered you said she does those weekend trade days every month. So I decided to pick up some groceries because I wanted to cook you breakfast. I also almost bought groceries for lunch and dinner, but maybe we should take it one meal at a time today." He turns around and faces me, slowly eyeing me up and down. "Happy birthday. I really like that dress. I bought real milk, you want some?"

I walk to the bar and keep my eyes trained on him, trying to process the plethora of words that just came out of his mouth. I scoot out a chair and take a seat. He pours me a glass of milk, even though I never said I wanted one, then slides it to me with a huge grin on his face. Before I can take a sip of the milk, he closes the gap between us and takes my chin in his hand.

"I need to kiss you. Your mouth was so damn perfect last night, I'm scared I dreamt that whole thing." He brings his mouth to mine and as soon as his tongue caresses mine, I can already tell this is going to be an issue.

His lips and his tongue and his hands are so incredibly perfect, I'll never be able to stay mad at him as long as he's able to use them against me like this. I grab his shirt and force my mouth against his even harder. He groans and fists his hands into my hair, then abruptly lets go and backs away. "Nope," he says, smiling. "Didn't dream it."

He walks back to the stove and turns off the burners, then transfers the bacon to a plate lined with eggs and toast. He walks it to the bar and begins filling the plate in front of me with food. He takes a seat and begins eating. He's smiling at me the whole time, and it suddenly hits me.

I *know*. I know what's wrong with him. I know why he's happy and angry and temperamental and all over the place and it finally makes so much sense.

"Are we allowed to play Dinner Quest, even though it's breakfast time?" he asks.

I take a sip of my milk and nod. "If I get the first question."

He lays his fork down on his plate and smiles. "I was thinking about just letting you have *all* the questions."

"I only need the answer to one."

He sighs and leans back against his seat, then looks down at his hands. I can tell by the way he's avoiding my gaze that he already knows I know. His reaction is one of guilt. I lean forward in my chair and glare at him.

"How long have you been using drugs, Holder?"

He shoots his eyes up to meet mine and his expression is stoic. He stares at me for a moment and I keep my stance, wanting him to know I'm not letting up until he tells me the truth. He purses his lips in a tight line, then looks down at his hands again. For a second I'm thinking he might be preparing to bolt out the front door in order to avoid talking about it, but then I see something on his face I wasn't expecting to see at all. A dimple.

He's grimacing, attempting to hold on to his expression, but the corners of his mouth give way and his smile breaks out into laughter.

He's laughing and he's laughing really hard and it's really pissing me off.

"*Drugs?*" he says between fits of laughter. "You think I'm on *drugs*?" He continues laughing until he realizes that I don't think it's the least bit funny at all. He eventually stops and sucks in a deep breath, then reaches across the table and takes my hand in his. "I'm not on drugs, Sky. I promise. I don't know why you would think that, but I swear."

"Then what the hell is wrong with you?"

His expression drops with that question, and he releases my hand from his. "Can you be a little less vague?" He falls back into his chair and folds his arms over his chest.

I shrug. "Sure. What happened to us and why are you acting like it never happened?"

His elbow is resting on the table and he looks down at his arm. He slowly traces each letter of his tattoo with his fingers, deep in thought. I know silence isn't considered a sound, but right now the silence between us is the loudest sound in the world. He pulls his arm off the table and looks up at me.

"I didn't want to let you down, Sky. I've let everyone down in my life that's ever loved me, and after that day at lunch I knew I let you down, too. So . . . I left you before you could start loving me. Otherwise, any effort to try not to disappoint you would be hopeless."

His words are full of apology and sadness and regret,

but he still can't just say them. He overreacted and jealousy got the best of him, but if he had just said those two words we would have been spared an entire month of emotional agony. I'm shaking my head, because I just don't get it. I don't understand why he couldn't just say *I'm sorry.*

"Why couldn't you just say it, Holder? Why couldn't you just apologize?"

He leans forward across the table and takes my hand, looking me hard in the eyes. "I'm not apologizing to you . . . because I don't want you to forgive me."

The sadness in his eyes must mirror mine and I don't want him seeing it. I don't want him seeing me sad, so I squeeze my eyes shut. He lets go of my hand and I hear him walk around the table until his arms are around me and he's picking me up. He sets me down on the bar so that we're at eye level and he brushes the hair from my face and makes me open my eyes again. His eyebrows are pulled together and the pain on his face is raw and real and heartbreaking.

"Babe, I screwed up. I've screwed up more than once with you, I know that. But believe me, what happened at lunch that day wasn't jealousy or anger or anything that should ever scare you. I wish I could tell you what happened, but I can't. Someday I will, but I can't right now and I need you to accept that. Please. And I'm not apologizing to you, because I don't want you to forget what happened and you should never forgive me for it. *Ever.* Never make excuses for me, Sky."

He leans in and kisses me briefly, then pulls back and continues. "I told myself to just stay away from you and let you be mad at me, because I do have so many issues that I'm not ready to share with you yet. And I tried so hard to stay away, but I can't. I'm not strong enough to keep denying whatever this is we could have. And yesterday in the lunchroom when you were hugging Breckin and laughing with him? It felt so good to see you happy, Sky. But I wanted so bad to be the one who was making you laugh like that. It was tearing me up inside that you were thinking that I didn't care about us, or that spending that weekend with you wasn't the best weekend I've ever had in my life. Because I *do* care and it *was* the best. It was the best fucking weekend in the history of all weekends."

My heart is beating wildly, almost as fast as the words are pouring out of him. He releases his firm hold on my face and strokes his hands over my hair, dropping them to the nape of my neck. He keeps them there and calms himself with a deep breath, then continues.

"It's killing me, Sky," he says, his voice much more calm and quiet. "It's killing me because I don't want you to go another day without knowing how I feel about you. And I'm not ready to tell you I'm in love with you, because I'm not. Not yet. But whatever this is I'm feeling—it's so much more than just *like*. It's *so* much more. And for the past few weeks I've been trying to figure it out. I've been trying to figure out why there isn't some other word to describe it. I want to tell you exactly how I feel but there isn't a single goddamned word in the entire dictionary that can describe this point between *liking* you and *loving* you, but I need that word. I need it because I need you to hear me say it."

He pulls my face to his and he kisses me. They're short kisses, mostly pecks, but he kisses me over and over, pulling back after each kiss, waiting for me to respond.

"Say something," he pleads.

I'm looking into his terrified eyes and for the first time since we met . . . I think I actually understand him. *All* of him. He doesn't react the way he does because there are five different sides to his personality. He reacts the way he does because there's only *one* side to Dean Holder.

Passionate.

He's passionate about life, about love, about his words, about Les. And I'll be damned if I wasn't just added to his list. The intensity he conveys isn't unnerving . . . it's *beautiful.* I've gone so long trying to find ways to feel numb any chance I get, but seeing the enthusiasm behind his eyes right now . . . it makes me want to feel every single thing about life. The good, the bad, the beautiful, the ugly, the pleasure, the pain. I *want* that. I want to start feeling life the same way he does. And my first step to doing so starts with this hopeless boy in front of me who's pouring his heart out, searching for that perfect word, wanting desperately to help me add feeling back into living.

Back into living.

The word comes to me like it's always been there, tucked away between like and love in the dictionary, right where it belongs. "Living," I say.

The desperation in his eyes eases slightly, and he lets out a short, confused laugh. "*What?*" He shakes his head, trying to understand my response.

"Live. If you mix the letters up in the words like and love, you get live. You can use that word."

He laughs again, but this time it's a laugh of relief. He wraps his arms around me and he kisses me with nothing but a hell of a lot of relief. "I live you, Sky," he says against my lips. "I live you so much."

Saturday, September 29, 2012
9:20 a.m.

I have no idea how he does it, but I've completely forgiven him, have become infatuated with him, and now I can't stop kissing him, all in the span of fifteen minutes. He definitely has a way with words. I'm starting to not mind that it takes him so long to think of them. He pulls away from my mouth and smiles, grabbing my waist with his hands.

"So what do you want to do for your birthday?" he asks, pulling me down off the bar. He gives me another quick peck on the mouth and walks to the living room where his wallet and keys are on the end table.

"We don't have to do anything. I don't expect you to entertain me just because it's my birthday."

He slips his keys into the pocket of his pants and looks up at me. His mouth hints at a wicked smile and he won't stop staring at me.

"What?" I ask. "You look guilty."

He laughs and shrugs. "I was just thinking of all the ways I could entertain you if we stayed here today. Which is exactly why we need to leave."

Which is exactly why I want to stay here.

"We could go see my mom," I suggest.

"Your mom?" He looks at me warily.

"Yeah. She runs an herbal booth at the flea market. It's the place she goes some weekends. I never go because she's there fourteen hours a day and I get bored. But it's one of the biggest flea markets in the world and I've always wanted to go walk around. It's only an hour-and-a-half drive. They have funnel cake," I add, trying to make it sound enticing.

Holder walks back to me and wraps his arms around me. "If you want to go to the flea market, then we're going to the flea market. I'm gonna run home and change and I have something I need to do. Pick you up in an hour?"

I nod. I know it's just a flea market, but I'm excited. I don't know how Karen will feel with me showing up unannounced with Holder. I haven't really told her anything about him, so I feel bad sort of springing him on her like this. It's her own fault, though. If she didn't ban technology I could call her and give her a heads up.

Holder gives me another quick peck and walks to the front door.

"Hey," I say, just as he's about to walk out. He spins around and looks at me. "It's my birthday and the last two kisses you've given me have been pretty damn pathetic. If you expect me to spend the day with you, I suggest you start kissing me like a boyfriend kisses his—"

The word slips from my mouth and I immediately cut the rest of the sentence off. We still haven't discussed labels yet and the fact that we just made up within the past half hour makes my lackadaisical use of the word *boyfriend* feel like something Matty-boy would have said to me. "I mean . . ." I stutter, then I just give up and clamp my mouth shut. I can't recover from that.

He's turned around facing me, still standing by the front door. He's not smiling. He's looking at me with that look again, holding my gaze with his, not speaking. He tilts his head toward me and raises both of his eyebrows curiously. "Did you just refer to me as your boyfriend?"

He's not smiling about the fact that I just referred to him as my boyfriend and that realization makes me wince. God, this seems so childish.

"No," I say stubbornly, folding my arms across my chest. "Only cheesy fourteen-year-olds do that."

He takes a few steps toward me, never changing his expression. He stops two feet in front of me and mirrors my stance. "That's too bad. Because when I thought you referred to me as your boyfriend just now, it made me want to kiss the living hell out of you." He narrows his eyes and there's a playful look about him that immediately relieves the knot in my stomach. He turns around and heads back to the door. "I'll see you in an hour." He opens the door and turns around before he leaves, slowly easing his way outside, teasing me with his playful grin and lickable dimples.

I sigh and roll my eyes. "Holder, wait."

He pauses and proudly leans against the doorframe.

"You better come kiss your girlfriend good-bye," I say, feeling every bit as cheesy as I sound. His face washes with victory and he walks back into the living room. He slips his hand to the small of my back and pulls me against him. It's our first freestanding kiss and I love the way he's securing me protectively with his arm around my lower back. He traces his fingers along my cheek and runs them through my hair, bringing his lips closer to mine. He's not staring at my lips, though. He's looking straight into my eyes and his are full of something I can't place. It's not lust this time; it's more like a look of appreciation.

He continues to stare at me without closing the gap

between our lips. He's not teasing me or trying to get me to kiss him first. He's just looking at me with appreciation and affection, and it turns my heart to butter. My hands are on his shoulders, so I slowly run them up his neck and through his hair, enjoying whatever this silent moment is that's occurring between us. His chest rises and falls against the rhythm of mine and his eyes begin searching my face, scrolling over every feature. The way he's looking at me is causing my entire body to grow weak, and I'm thankful his arm is still locked around my waist.

He lowers his forehead to mine and lets out a long sigh, looking at me with a look that's quickly turned into something resembling pain. It prompts me to slide my hands down to his cheeks and softly stroke them with my fingers, wanting to take away whatever it is that's behind those eyes right now.

"Sky," he says, focusing on me intently. He says it like he's about to follow it up with something profound, but instead, my name is the only thing he says. He slowly brings his mouth to mine and our lips meet. He inhales a deep breath as he presses his closed lips against mine, breathing me into him. He pulls away and looks back down into my eyes for several more seconds, stroking my cheek. I've never been savored like this before, and it's absolutely beautiful.

He dips his head again and rests his lips against mine, my top lip between both of his. He kisses me as softly as possible, treating my mouth as though it's breakable. I part my lips and allow him to deepen his kiss, which he does, but even then it's still soft. It's appreciative and gentle and he keeps one hand on the back of my head and one on my hip as he slowly tastes and teases every part of my mouth. This kiss is just like he is—studied and never in a hurry.

Just when my mind has succumbed to every part of being wrapped up in him, his lips come to a standstill and he slowly pulls back. My eyes flutter open and I let out a breath that may have been mixed with the words, "*Oh, my.*"

Seeing my breathless reaction causes him to break out with a smug grin. "That was our first official kiss as a couple."

I wait for the panic to set in, but it doesn't. "A couple," I repeat, quietly.

"Damn straight." He still has his hand on my lower back and I'm pressed against him, looking up at his eyes as they focus down on me. "And don't worry," he adds. "I'll be informing Grayson myself. I ever see him trying to touch you like he does and he'll be reintroduced to my fist."

His hand moves from my lower back and up to my cheek. "I'm really leaving now. I'll see you in an hour. I live you." He gives me a quick peck on the lips and backs away, then turns toward the door.

"Holder?" I say as soon as I suck enough breath back into my lungs to speak. "What do you mean by *reintroduced*? Have you and Grayson been in a fight before?"

Holder's expression turns into a tight-lipped blank one and he nods, but barely. "I told you before. He's not a good person." The door closes behind him and he leaves me with even more questions. But what's new?

I decide to forgo my own shower and call Six, instead. I've got a lot to catch her up on. I run to my room and crawl out the window, then slide hers up and pull myself inside. I pick up the phone by her bed and take out my cell phone to find the text that she sent with her international number. When I start dialing, my cell phone receives an incoming message from Holder.

I'm really dreading spending all day with you. This doesn't sound like fun at all. Also, your sundress is really unflattering and way too summery, but you should definitely keep it on.

I grin. Dammit, I really do live this hopeless boy.

I dial the number to reach Six and lie back on her bed. She answers groggily on the third ring.

"Hey," I say. "You sleeping?"

I can hear her yawn. "Obviously not. But you really need to start taking time differences into consideration."

I laugh. "Six? It's afternoon there. Even if I *did* take time differences into consideration, it wouldn't matter with you."

"I had a rough morning," she says defensively. "I miss your face. What's up?"

"Not much."

"You lie. You sound annoyingly happy. I'm guessing you and Holder finally worked out whatever the hell happened at school that day?"

"Yep. And you are the first to know that I, Linden Sky Davis, am now a taken woman."

She groans. "Why anyone would subject themselves to that sort of misery is beyond me. But I'm happy for you."

"Tha—" I was about to say thanks, but my words are cut off by a very loud "*Oh, my God!*" from Six's end.

"*What?*"

"I forgot. It's your freaking birthday and I forgot! Happy birthday Sky and holy crap I'm the worst best friend ever."

"It's okay," I laugh. "I'm sort of glad you forgot. You know how I hate presents and surprises and everything else that comes with birthdays."

"Oh, wait. I just remembered how incredibly awesome I am. Check behind your dresser today."

I roll my eyes. "Figures."

"And tell your new boyfriend to get him some damn minutes."

"Will do. I gotta go, your mom's gonna shit when she sees this phone bill."

"Yeah, well . . . she should be more in tune with the earth like your mom."

I laugh. "Love you, Six. Be safe, okay?"

"Love you, too. And Sky?"

"Yeah?"

"You sound happy. I'm happy you're happy."

I smile and the line disconnects. I head back to my room and, as much as I hate presents, I'm still human and naturally curious. I immediately walk to my dresser and look behind it. On the floor is a wrapped box, so I bend down and pick it up. I walk to my bed and sit, then slide the lid off it. It's a box full of Snickers.

Dammit, I love her.

Saturday, September 29, 2012
10:25 a.m.

I'm standing at my window impatiently waiting when Holder finally pulls up into the driveway. I walk out my front door and lock it behind me, then turn toward the car and freeze. He's not alone. The passenger door opens and a guy steps out. When he turns around, I'm positive my facial expression is stuck between an OMG and a WTF. *I'm learning.*

Breckin is holding the passenger door open with a huge grin on his face. "Hope you don't mind a third wheel today. My second best friend in the whole wide world invited me to come."

I reach the passenger door, confused as hell. Breckin waits until I climb inside, then he opens the back door and climbs into the backseat. I lean forward and tilt my head toward Holder, who's laughing like he just revealed the punch line to a really funny joke. A joke I'm not a part of.

"Would one of you like to explain what the hell is going on?" I say.

Holder grabs my hand and pulls it to his mouth, giving my knuckles a kiss. "I'll let Breckin explain. He talks faster, anyway."

I spin around in my seat as Holder begins backing out of the driveway. I arch an eyebrow at Breckin.

He shoots me a clear look of guilt. "I've sort of had a

double alliance going on for about two weeks now," he says sheepishly.

I shake my head, attempting to wrap this confession around my mind. I glance back and forth between them. "Two weeks? You guys have been talking for *two weeks?* Without me? Why didn't you tell me?"

"I was sworn to secrecy," Breckin says.

"But . . ."

"Turn around and put your seatbelt on," Holder says to me.

I glare at him. "In a minute. I'm trying to figure out why you made up with Breckin two weeks ago, but it took you until today to make up with me."

He glances at me, then looks back at the road in front of him. "Breckin deserved an apology. I acted like an asshole that day."

"And I *didn't* deserve one?"

He looks at me dead on this time. "No," he says firmly, turning his gaze back to the road. "You don't deserve words, Sky. You deserve actions."

I stare at him, wondering how long he stayed up at night forming that perfect sentence. He glances back at me and lets go of my hand, then tickles the top of my thigh. "Quit being so serious. Your boyfriend and your very best friend in the whole wide world are taking you to a flea market."

I laugh and slap his hand away. "How can I feel happy when my alliance has been infiltrated? You two have a hell of a lot of kissing up to do today."

Breckin rests his chin on the top of my headrest and looks down at me. "I think I've been the one that suffered the most out of this ordeal. Your boyfriend has ruined my last two Friday nights in a row, moping and whining about how much he wants you but how he doesn't want to let you down and blah, blah, blah. It's been rough not complaining to you about him at lunch every day."

Holder darts his head back toward Breckin. "Well, now you two can complain about me all you want. Life is back to how it should be." He slides his fingers through mine and squeezes my hand. My skin tingles and I'm not sure if it's from his touch or his words.

"I still think I deserve an ass kissing today," I say to both of them. "I want you to buy me whatever I want at the flea market. I don't care how much it costs or how big and heavy it is."

"Damn straight," Breckin says.

I groan. "Oh, God, Holder's already rubbing off on you."

Breckin laughs and reaches over the seat to grab my hands, then pulls me toward him. "He must be, because I really want to cuddle you in the backseat right now," Breckin says.

"I'm not rubbing off on you that much if you think I'd only be *cuddling* her in a backseat," Holder says. He slaps me on the ass right before I fall into the back with Breckin.

"You can't be serious," Holder says, holding the saltshaker I just placed in his hands. We've been walking around the flea market for over an hour now and I'm sticking to my plan. They're buying me whatever the hell I want. I have a betrayal to overcome and it's going to take a lot of random purchases before I feel better.

I look at the figurine in his hands and nod. "You're right. I should get the matching set." I pick up the pep- pershaker and hand it to him. They aren't anything I would ever want. I'm not sure how they could be anything *anyone* would ever want. Who makes ceramic salt and peppershak- ers fashioned out of small and large intestines?

"I bet they belonged to a doctor," Breckin says, admir- ing them with me. I reach into Holder's pocket and pull out his wallet, then turn to the man behind the table. "How much?"

He shrugs. "I don't know," he says unenthusiastically. "A dollar each?"

"How about a dollar for both?" I ask. He takes the dol- lar out of my hands and nods us away.

"Way to bargain," Holder says, shaking his head. "These better be on your kitchen table next time I come over."

"Gross, no," I say. "Who'd want to stare at guts while they eat?"

We browse a few more pavilions until we reach the pa- vilion Karen and Jack are set up in. When we reach their booth, Karen does a double take, eyeing Breckin and Holder.

"Hey," I say, holding out my hands. "Surprise!"

Jack jumps up and walks around the booth, giving me a quick hug. Karen follows him and is eyeing me guardedly the entire time.

"Relax," I say, after seeing her eye both Holder and Breckin with concern. "Neither one of them is getting me pregnant this weekend."

She laughs and finally wraps her arms around me. "Happy birthday." She pulls back and her motherly instincts kick in about fifteen seconds too late. "Wait. Why are you here? Is everything okay? Are you okay? Is the house okay?"

"It's fine. I'm fine. I was just bored so I asked Holder to come shopping with me."

Holder is behind me introducing himself to Jack. Breckin slips past me and gives Karen a hug. "I'm Breckin," he says. "I'm in an alliance to take over the public school system and all its minions with your daughter."

"Was," I clarify, glaring at Breckin. "He *was* in an alliance with me."

"I like you already," Karen says, smiling at Breckin. She looks past me at Holder and shakes his hand. "Holder," she says politely. "How are you?"

"Good," he says, his response guarded. I look at him and he appears extremely uncomfortable. I don't know if it's the salt and peppershakers he's holding, or the fact that seeing Karen this time garners a different reaction from him now that he's dating her daughter. I try to deflect the mood by turning around and asking Karen if she has a sack we can use for our things. She reaches under the table and holds it out to Holder. He places the shakers inside and she looks down into the sack and back up at me questioningly.

"Don't ask," I say. I take the sack from her and open it up so Breckin can place the other purchase inside. It's a small, wood-framed picture of the word "melt," written in black ink on white paper. It was twenty-five cents and made absolutely no sense, so of course I had to have it.

A couple of customers walk to the table so both Jack and Karen walk around the booth and begin helping them. I turn around and Holder is eyeing both of them with a hard look in his eyes. I haven't seen him with an expression like this since that day in the cafeteria. It unnerves me a little, so I walk up to him and slide my arm around his back, desperately wanting that look to go away.

"Hey," I say, pulling his focus down to me. "You okay?"

He nods and kisses me on the forehead. "I'm good," he says. He wraps his arm around my waist and smiles down at me reassuringly. "You promised me funnel cake," he says, brushing my cheek with his hand.

I nod, relieved to see he's okay. I don't really want Holder having one of his intense moments right now in front of Karen. I don't know that she'll quite understand his passionate approach to life like I'm starting to.

"Funnel cake?" Breckin says. "Did you say funnel cake?"

I turn back around and Karen's customer is gone. She's standing frozen behind the table, eyeing the arm that's wrapped around my waist. She looks pale.

What's the deal with everyone and their weird looks today?

"You okay?" I ask her. It's not like she's never seen me with a boyfriend before. Matt practically lived at our house the entire month I dated him.

She looks up at me, then glances at Holder briefly. "I just didn't realize you two were dating."

"Yeah. About that," I say. "I would have told you, but we sort of just started dating about four hours ago."

"Oh," she says. "Well . . . you look cute together. Can I talk to you?" She nudges her head behind her, indicating she wants privacy. I slip my arm out of Holder's and follow her to a safe speaking distance. She spins around and shakes her head.

"I don't know how I feel about this," she says, talking in a low whisper.

"About what? I'm eighteen and I have a boyfriend. Big deal."

She sighs. "I know, it's just . . . what happens tonight? When I'm not there? How do I know he won't hang around all night?"

I shrug. "You don't. You just have to trust me," I say, instantly feeling guilty for the lie. If she knew he already spent last night with me, I think it's safe to say Holder would no longer be my *breathing* boyfriend.

"It's just weird, Sky. We've never really discussed guy rules for when I'm not home." She looks extremely nervous, so I do what I can to ease her mind.

"Mom? Trust me. We literally just agreed to start dating a few hours ago. There's no way anything will happen between us that you fear might happen. He'll be gone by midnight, I promise."

She nods unconvincingly. "It's just . . . I don't know. Seeing the two of you just now with your arms around each other? The way both of you were interacting? It's not the way new couples look at each other, Sky. It just threw me off because I thought maybe you've been seeing him for a while but you've been keeping it from me. I want you to be able to talk to me about anything."

I grab her hand and squeeze it. "I know, Mom. And believe me, if we hadn't come here together today I would have told you all about him tomorrow. I'd probably have talked your ear off. I'm not keeping anything hidden from you, okay?"

She smiles and gives me a quick squeeze. "I still expect you to talk my ear off about him tomorrow."

Saturday, September 29, 2012
10:15 p.m.

"Sky, wake up."

I lift my head off Breckin's arm and wipe drool off the side of my cheek. He looks down at his wet shirt and grimaces.

"Sorry." I laugh. "You shouldn't be so comfortable."

We've arrived back at his house after spending eight hours walking and perusing junk. Holder and Breckin finally gave in and we all got a little competitive, seeing who could find the most random object. I think I still won with the gut shakers, but Breckin came in a close second with a velvet painting of a puppy riding on the back of a unicorn.

"Don't forget your painting," I say when he steps out of the car. He leans in and grabs the painting from the floorboard, then kisses my cheek.

"See you Monday," he says to me. He looks up at Holder. "Don't think you're getting my seat first period now just because she's your girlfriend."

Holder laughs. "I'm not the one bringing her coffee every morning. I doubt she'd let me overthrow you."

Breckin shuts the door and Holder waits until he's inside his house before he leaves. "What do you think you're doing back there?" he says, smiling at me in the rearview mirror. "Get up here."

I shake my head and remain put. "I sort of like having a chauffeur."

He puts the car in park and unbuckles his seatbelt, then turns around in his seat. "Come here," he says, reaching for my arms. He grabs my wrists and pulls me forward until our faces are just inches apart. He lifts his hands to my face and smashes my cheeks together like I'm a little kid. He gives me a loud peck on my squished-together lips. "I had fun today," he says. "You're kind of weird."

I cock my eyebrow, not sure if he just complimented me or not. *"Thanks?"*

"I like weird. Now get your ass in the front seat with me before I climb in the backseat and not cuddle you." He pulls my arm forward and I climb into the front seat, then put my seatbelt on.

"What are we doing now? Your house?" I ask.

He shakes his head. "Nope. One more stop."

"My house?"

He shakes his head again. "You'll see."

We drive until we're on the outskirts of town. I recognize we're at the local airport when he pulls the car over to the side of the road. He gets out without saying anything and comes around to open my door. "We're here," he says, waving his hand at the runway spread out in a field across from us.

"Holder, this is the smallest airport within a two-hundred-mile radius. If you're expecting to watch a plane land, we'll be here for two days."

He pulls on my hand and leads me down a small hill. "We're not here to watch the planes." He continues walking until he gets to a fence that edges the airport grounds. He shakes it to test for sturdiness, then takes my hand in his again. "Take off your shoes, it'll be easier," he says. I look at the fence, then look back at him.

"You expect me to climb that thing?"

"Well," he says, looking at it. "I could pick you up and throw you over, but it might hurt a little more."

"I'm in a dress! You didn't tell me we were climbing fences tonight. Besides, it's illegal."

He rolls his head and pushes me toward the fence. "It's not illegal when my stepdad manages the airport. And no, I didn't tell you we'd be climbing fences because I was scared you would change out of this dress."

I grab the fence and begin to test it when, in one swift movement, his hands are on my waist and I'm up in the air, already scaling over it.

"Jesus, Holder!" I yell, jumping down the other side.

"I know. That went a little too fast. I forgot to cop a feel." He pulls up on the fence and swings his leg over, then jumps down. "Come on," he says, grabbing my hand and pulling me forward.

We walk until we reach the runway. I pause and peer out over the massive length of it. I've never been on an airplane before and the thought of it sort of terrifies me. Especially seeing that there's a huge lake edging the far end of the runway.

"Have any planes ever landed in that lake?"

"Just one," he says, pulling me down with him. "But it was a small Cessna and the pilot was lit. He was okay, but the plane is still at the bottom of the lake." He lowers himself onto the runway and tugs at my hand, wanting me to do the same.

"What are we doing?" I ask, adjusting my dress and slipping off my shoes.

"Shush," he says. "Lie down and look up."

I lay my head back and look up, then suck in a sharp breath. Laid out before me in every direction is a blanket of stars brighter than I've ever seen them.

"Wow," I whisper. "They don't look like this from my backyard."

"I know. That's why I brought you." He reaches down between us and wraps his pinky around mine.

We sit for a long time without speaking, but it's a peaceful silence. Every now and then he lifts his pinky and grazes the side of my hand, but that's all he does. We're side by side and I'm in a dress with fairly easy access, but he never even so much as tries to kiss me. It's evident he didn't bring me out here in the middle of nowhere just to make out with me. He brought me out here to share this experience with me. Something else he's passionate about.

There is so much about Holder that surprises me, especially within the last twenty-four hours. I'm still not clear on what made him so upset in the cafeteria that day, but he seems confident that he knows exactly what it was and that it'll never happen again. And right now, all I can do is take his word. All I can do is take my trust and place it back into his hands. I just hope he knows that it's all the trust I have left to give him. I know for a fact that if he hurts me like he's hurt me before, it'll be the last time he ever hurts me.

I tilt my head toward his and watch him as he stares up to the sky. His brows are furrowed together and he's clearly got something on his mind. It seems like he always has something on his mind and I'm curious if I'll ever break through that. There are so many things I still want to know about his past and his sister and his family. But bringing it all up, when he's so deep in thought, would take him out of wherever his mind is right now. I don't want to do that. I know exactly where he is and what he's doing, staring off into space like he is. I know, because it's exactly what I do when I stare at the stars on my ceiling.

I watch him for a long time, then turn my gaze back up to the sky and begin to escape my own thoughts, when he breaks the silence with a question that comes out of nowhere.

"Have you had a good life?" he asks quietly.

I ponder his question, but mostly because I want to know what he was thinking about that made him ask it. Was he really thinking about my life or was he thinking about his own?

"Yeah," I reply honestly. "Yeah, I have."

He sighs heavily, then takes my hand completely in his. "Good."

Nothing else is spoken until half an hour later when he says he's ready to leave.

We pull up to my house at a few minutes before midnight. We both get out of the car and he grabs my sacks of random stuff and follows me to the front door. He stands in the doorway and sets them down. "I'm not coming in any further," he says, putting his hands in his pockets.

"Why not? Are you a vampire? Do you need permission to enter?"

He smiles. "I just don't think I should stay."

I walk to him and put my arms around him, then kiss him on the chin. "Why not? Are you tired? We can lie down, I know you barely got any sleep last night." I really don't want him to leave. I slept better last night in his arms than any other night before it.

He responds to my embrace by wrapping his arms around my shoulders and pulling me against his chest. "I can't," he says. "It's a combination of things, really. The fact that my mom will inundate me with questions about where I've been since last night. The fact that I heard you promise your mom I would leave by midnight. The fact that the entire time you were walking around today I couldn't stop thinking about what's underneath this dress."

He brings his hands to my face and stares down at my mouth. His eyelids become heavy and he drops his voice to a whisper. "Not to mention these lips," he says. "You have no idea how difficult it was trying to listen to a single word you said today when all I could think about was how soft they are. How incredible they taste. How perfect they fit between mine." He leans in and kisses me softly, then pulls away just as I begin to melt into him. "And this dress," he says, running his hand down my back and gently gliding it over my hip and to the top of my thigh. I shiver under his fingertips. "This dress is the main reason I'm not walking any further into this house."

With the way my body is responding to him, I quickly agree with his decision to leave. As much as I love being with him and love kissing him, I can already tell that I would have absolutely zero restraint, and I don't think I'm ready to pass that first yet.

I sigh, but I feel like groaning. As much as I can agree

with what he's saying, my body is still completely pissed off that I'm not begging him to stay. It's odd how just being around him today has somehow deepened the need I have to constantly want to be around him.

"Is this normal?" I ask, looking up into his eyes, which hold more desire than I've ever seen in them before. I know why he's leaving now, because it's clear that he wants to pass this first, too.

"Is *what* normal?"

I press my head into his chest to avoid having to look at him while I speak. Sometimes I say things that are embarrassing, but I just have to say them regardless. "Is the way we feel about each other normal? We haven't really known each other for very long. Most of that time was spent avoiding each other. But I don't know, it just seems different with you. I assume when most people date, the first few months are spent trying to build a connection." I lift my head off his chest and look up at him. "I feel like I had that with you the moment we met. Everything about us is so natural. It feels like we're already there, and we're trying to go backward now. Like we're trying to *re*-get to know each other by slowing it down. Is that weird?"

He brushes the hair out of my face and looks down at me with a completely different look in his eyes this time. The lust and desire has been replaced by anguish, and it makes my heart heavy seeing it in his eyes.

"Whatever this is, I don't want to analyze it. I don't want you analyzing it either, okay? Let's just be grateful I finally found you."

I laugh at his last sentence. "You say that like you've been looking for me."

He furrows his brows and places his hands on the sides of my head, tilting my face up to his. "I've been looking for you my whole damn life." His expression is solid and determined and he meshes our mouths together as soon as the sentence leaves his lips. He kisses me hard and with more passion than he's kissed me all day. I'm about to pull him inside with me but he lets go and backs away as soon as my hands fist in his hair.

"I live you," he says, forcing himself off the steps. "I'll see you on Monday."

"I live you, too."

I don't ask him why I'm not seeing him tomorrow, because I think the time will be good for us in order to process the last twenty-four hours. It'll be good for Karen as well, since I really need to fill her in on my new love life. Or, my new *live* life, rather.

Monday, October 22, 2012
12:05 p.m.

It's been almost a month since Holder and I declared ourselves a couple. So far, I haven't found any idiosyncrasies of his that drive me crazy. If anything, the small habits he has just make me adore him even more. Like the way he still stares at me like he's studying me, and the way he pops his jaw when he's irritated, and the way he licks his lips every time he laughs. It's actually sort of hot. And don't get me started on the dimples.

Luckily, I've had the same Holder since the night he crawled through my window and into my bed. I haven't seen any snippets of the moody and temperamental Holder at all since then. In fact, we somehow become more and more in tune with each other the more time we spend together, and I feel like I can read him now almost as well as he reads me.

With Karen being home every weekend, we haven't had a lot of alone time. Most of our time together is spent at school or on dates over the weekends. For some reason, he doesn't feel right coming to my bedroom when Karen is home and he always makes excuses when I suggest we go to his house. So instead, we've seen a lot of movies. We've also been out a few times with Breckin and his new boyfriend, Max.

Holder and I have been having a lot of fun together, but we haven't had a lot of *fun* together. We're both beginning to get a little frustrated at our lack of a decent place to make out. His car is kind of small, but we've made do. I think we're both counting down the hours until Karen is out of town again next weekend.

I sit down at the table with Breckin and Max, waiting for Holder to bring both our trays. Max and Breckin met at a local art gallery about two weeks ago, not even realizing they attended the same school. I'm happy for Breckin, because I started to get the feeling he felt like a third wheel, when it wasn't like that at all. I love his company, but seeing him pour his attention into his own relationship has made things a lot easier.

"Are you and Holder busy this Saturday?" Max asks when I take a seat.

"I don't think so. Why?"

"There's an art gallery downtown that's displaying one of my pieces in their local art show. I want you guys there."

"Sounds cool," Holder says, taking his seat next to me. "Which piece are you displaying?"

Max shrugs. "I don't know yet. I'm still trying to decide between two."

Breckin rolls his eyes. "You know which one you need to enter and it isn't either of those two."

Max cuts his eyes to Breckin. "We live in East Texas. I doubt the gay-themed painting will go over very well around here."

Holder looks back and forth between them. "Who gives a shit what people around here think?"

Max's smile fades and he picks up his fork. "My parents," he says.

"Do your parents know you're gay?" I ask.

He nods. "Yeah. They're pretty supportive for the most part, but they're still hoping none of their friends at church find out. They don't want to be pitied for having the child who's damned to Hell."

I shake my head. "If God's the type of guy that would damn you to Hell just for loving someone, then I wouldn't want to spend eternity with Him, anyway."

Breckin laughs. "I bet they have funnel cake in Hell."

"What time is it over Saturday?" Holder asks. "We'll be there, but Sky and I have plans later that night."

"It's over at nine," Breckin says.

I glance at Holder. "We have plans? What are we doing?"

He grins at me and wraps his arm around my shoulder, then whispers in my ear. "My mom will be gone Saturday night. I want to show you my bedroom."

My arms break out in chills and I suddenly have visions that are entirely too inappropriate for a high school cafeteria.

"I don't even want to know what he said to make you blush like that," Breckin says, laughing.

Holder pulls his arm away and rests his hand on my leg. I take a bite, then look back up at Max. "What's the dress code for this showing on Saturday? I have a sundress I was thinking about wearing that night, but it's not very formal." Holder squeezes my thigh and I grin, knowing exactly what kind of thoughts I just put into his head.

Max begins to answer me when a guy from the table behind us says something to Holder that I fail to catch. Whatever he said, it immediately gets Holder's attention and he turns completely around, facing the guy. "Could you repeat that?" Holder says, glaring at him.

I don't turn around. I don't even want to see who the guy is that's responsible for bringing back the temperamental Holder in less than two seconds flat.

"Maybe I need to speak more clearly," the guy says, raising his voice. "I said if you can't beat them *completely* to death, you might as well join them."

Holder doesn't move right away, which is good. It gives me time to grab his face and pull his focus to mine. "Holder," I say firmly. "Ignore it. *Please.*"

"Yeah, ignore it," Breckin says. "He's just trying to piss you off. Max and I get that shit all the time, we're used to it."

Holder works his jaw back and forth, breathing in slowly through his nose. The expression in his eyes slowly softens and he takes my hand, then slowly turns back around without looking at the guy again. "I'm good," he says, convincing himself more than the rest of us. "I'm good."

As soon as Holder faces forward, the laughter at the table behind us bellows throughout the lunchroom. Holder's shoulders tense, so I place my hand on his leg and squeeze, willing him to stay calm.

"That's nice," the guy says from behind us. "Let the slut talk you down from defending your new friends. I guess they don't mean as much to you as Lesslie did, otherwise I'd be in as bad a shape as Jake was last year after you laid into him."

It takes all I have not to jump up and kick the guy's ass myself, so I know Holder has absolutely no restraint left in him. He begins to turn around and his face is expressionless. I've never seen him so rigid—it's terrifying. I know something terrible is about to happen and I have no clue how to prevent it. Before he can leap across the table and beat the shit out of the guy, I do something that shocks even myself. I slap Holder as hard as I can across the face. He immediately pulls his hand to his cheek and looks at me, completely taken aback. But he's looking at me, which is good.

"Hallway," I say determinedly as soon as I have his attention. I push him until he's off the bench and I keep my hands on his back, then push him until he's walking toward the exit to the cafeteria. When we walk out into the hallway, he slams his fist into the nearest locker, causing a loud gasp to escape from my lips. The force behind his fist leaves a huge dent, and I'm relieved the guy in the cafeteria wasn't the recipient of that force.

He's seething. His face is red and I've never seen him this upset before. He begins pacing the hallway, pausing to stare at the cafeteria doors. I'm not convinced he isn't about to walk back through them, so I decide to get him even farther away.

"Let's go to your car." I push him toward the exit and he lets me. We walk all the way to the car and he's silently fuming the entire time. He climbs into the driver's seat and I climb into the passenger seat and we both shut our doors. I don't know if he's still on the verge of running back into the school and finishing the fight that asshole was trying to start, but I'll do everything I can to keep him out of there until he isn't angry anymore.

What happens next isn't what I'm expecting to happen at all. He reaches across the seat and pulls me tightly against him and begins to shake uncontrollably. His shoulders are trembling and he's squeezing me, burying his head in my neck.

He's crying.

I wrap my arms around him and let him hold on to me while he lets out whatever it is that's been pent up inside him. He slides me onto his lap and squeezes me tightly against him. I adjust my legs until they're on either side of him and I kiss him lightly on the side of his head over and over. He's barely making any sound and what little sound he is making is muffled into my shoulder. I have no idea what made him break just now, but it's the absolute most heartbreaking thing I've ever seen. I continue to kiss the side of his head and run my hands up and down his back. I do this for several minutes until he's finally quiet, but he still has a death grip around me.

"You want to talk about it?" I whisper, stroking his hair. I pull back and he leans his head into the headrest and looks at me. His eyes are red and full of so much hurt, I have to kiss them. I kiss each eyelid softly, then pull back again and wait for him to speak.

"I lied," he says. His words stab at my heart and I'm terrified of what he's about to say. "I told you I'd do it again. I told you I'd beat Jake's ass again if I had the chance." He takes my cheeks in his palms and looks at me desperately. "I wouldn't. He didn't deserve what I did to him, Sky. And that kid in there just now? He's Jake's little brother. He hates me for what I did and he has every right to hate me. He has every right to say whatever the fuck he wants to say to me, because I deserve it. I do. That's the only reason I didn't want to come back to this school, because I knew whatever anyone was going to say to me was deserved. But I can't let him talk about you and Breckin like that. He can say whatever the fuck he wants to say about me or Les because we deserve it, but you don't." His eyes are glossing over again and he's in absolute agony, holding my face in his hands.

"It's okay, Holder. You don't have to defend everyone. And you *don't* deserve it. Jake shouldn't have said what he did about your sister last year and his brother shouldn't have said what he did today."

He shakes his head in disagreement. "Jake was right. I know he shouldn't have said it and I definitely know I shouldn't have laid a finger on him, but he was right. What Les did wasn't brave or noble or courageous. What she did was selfish. She didn't even *try* to tough it out. She wasn't thinking about me, she wasn't thinking about my parents. She was thinking about herself and she didn't give a shit about the rest of us. And I hate her for it. I fucking hate her for it and I'm tired of hating her, Sky. I'm so tired of hating her because it's tearing me down and making me this person I don't want to be. She doesn't deserve to be hated. It's my fault she did what she did. I should have helped her, but I didn't. I didn't know. I loved that girl more than I've ever loved anyone and I had no idea how bad it was for her."

I wipe away his tear with my thumb and I do the only thing I can think to do because I have no idea what to say. I kiss him. I kiss him desperately and try to take away his pain the only way I know how to do. I've never experienced death like this, so I don't even try to understand where he's coming from. He wraps his hands in my hair and kisses me back with such strength, it's almost painful. We kiss for several minutes until the tension in him slowly begins to subside.

I pull my lips from his and look directly into his eyes. "Holder, you have every right to hate her for what she did. But you also have every right to still love her in spite of it. The only thing you don't have a right to do is to keep blaming yourself. You'll never understand why she did it, so you need to stop beating yourself up for not having all the answers. She made the choice she thought was best for her, even though it was the wrong one. But that's what you have to remember . . . *she* made that choice. Not you. And you can't blame yourself for not knowing what she failed to tell you." I kiss him on the forehead, then bring my eyes back to his. "You have to let it go. You can hold on to the hate and the love and even the bitterness, but you *have* to let go of the blame. The blame is what's tearing you down."

He closes his eyes and pulls my head to his shoulder, breathing out a shaky breath. I can feel him nodding and I can sense his whole demeanor coming to a quiet calm. He kisses me on the side of the head and we hold each other in silence. Whatever connection we thought we had before this . . . it doesn't compare to this moment. No matter what happens between us in this life, this moment has just merged pieces of our souls together. We'll always have that, and in a way it's comforting to know.

Holder looks at me and cocks his eyebrow. "Why the hell did you slap me?"

I laugh and kiss the cheek that I slapped. My fingerprints are barely visible now, but they're still there. "Sorry. I just needed to get you out of there and I couldn't think of any other way to do it."

He smiles. "It worked. I don't know if anyone else could have said or done anything that would have pulled me out of that. Thank you for knowing exactly how to handle me, because sometimes I'm not even sure how to handle myself."

I kiss him softly. "Believe me. I have no idea how to handle you, Holder. I just take you one scene at a time."

Friday, October 26, 2012
3:40 p.m.

"What time do you think you'll get back?" I ask. Holder has his arms around me and we're leaning up against my car. We haven't been able to spend much time together since what happened in his car at lunch on Monday. Fortunately, the guy who tried to start shit with Holder hasn't said anything else. It's been a rather peaceful week considering the dramatic start of it.

"We won't be back until pretty late. Their company Halloween parties usually last a few hours. But you'll see me tomorrow. I can pick you up for lunch if you want and we'll just stay together all day until the gallery showing."

I shake my head. "Can't. It's Jack's birthday and we're taking him out to lunch because he has to work tomorrow night. Just come pick me up at six."

"Yes, ma'am," he says. He kisses me, then opens my door so I can climb inside. I wave good-bye to him as he walks away, then I pull my phone out of my backpack. There's a text from Six, which makes me happy. I haven't been receiving my daily promised texts like she said I would. I didn't think I'd miss them, but now that I only get one every third day or so, it bums me out a little.

Tell your boyfriend thank you for finally adding minutes to your phone. Have you had sex with

him yet? Miss you.

I laugh at her candidness and text her back.

No, we haven't had sex yet. We've done almost everything else, though, so I'm sure his patience will wear out soon. Ask me again after tomorrow night, I might have a different answer. Miss you more.

I hit Send and stare at the phone. I haven't really thought about whether I'm ready to pass that first yet, but I guess I just admitted to myself that I am. I wonder if inviting me to his house is his way of finding out if I'm ready, too.

I put the car into reverse and my phone sounds off. I pick it up and it's a text from Holder.

Don't leave. I'm walking back to your car.

I put the car in park again and roll down my window, just as he approaches. "Hey," he says, leaning into my window. He darts his eyes away from mine and he looks around the car nervously. I hate this uncomfortable look about him, it always means he's about to say something I might not want to hear.

"Um . . ." He looks back at me and the sun is shining straight on him, highlighting every beautiful feature about him. His eyes are bright and they're looking into mine like they would never want to look anywhere else. "You uh . . . you just sent me a text that I'm pretty sure you meant to send to Six."

Oh, God, no. I immediately grab my phone and check to see if he's telling the truth. Unfortunately, he is. I throw the phone on the passenger seat and fold my arms across the steering wheel, burying my face into my elbow. "Oh, my, God," I groan.

"Look at me, Sky," he directs. I ignore him and wait for a magic wormhole to come and suck me away from all the embarrassing situations I get myself into. I feel his hand touch my cheek and he pulls my face in his direction. He's looking at me, full of sincerity.

"Whether it's tomorrow night or next year, I can promise you it'll be the best damn night of my life. You just make sure you're making that decision for yourself and no one else, okay? I'll always want you, but I'm not going to let myself have you until you're one hundred percent sure you want me just as much. And don't say anything right now. I'm turning around and walking back to my car and we can pretend this conversation never happened. Otherwise, you may never stop blushing." He leans in the window and gives me a quick kiss. "You're cute as hell, you know that? But you really need to figure out how to work your phone." He winks at me and walks away. I lean my head against the headrest and silently curse myself.

I hate technology.

I spend the rest of the night doing my best to push the embarrassing text out of my head. I help Karen package things up for her next flea market, then eventually crawl into bed with my e-reader. As soon as I power it on, my cell phone lights up on the nightstand.

I'm walking to your house right now. I know it's late and your mom is home, but I can't wait

until tomorrow night to kiss you again. Make sure your window is unlocked.

After I read the text I jump out of bed and lock my bedroom door, thankful Karen called it an early night two hours ago. I immediately go to the bathroom and brush my teeth and hair, then turn out the lights and crawl back into bed. It's after midnight and he's never snuck in while Karen was home before. I'm nervous, but it's an exciting nervous. The fact that I don't feel the least bit guilty that he's on his way over is proof that I'm going to Hell. I'm the worst daughter ever.

Several minutes later, my window slides up and I hear him making his way inside. I'm so excited to see him that I run to meet him at the window and wrap my arms around his neck, then jump up and make him hold me while I kiss him. His hands have a firm grip on my ass and he walks to the bed, dropping me down gently.

"Well, hello to you, too," he says, smiling widely. He stumbles slightly, then falls on top of me and brings his lips to mine again. He's trying to kick off his shoes but he struggles, then starts laughing.

"Are you drunk?" I ask.

He presses his fingers to my lips and tries to stop laughing, but he can't. "No. Yes."

"How drunk?"

He moves his head to my neck and runs his mouth lightly along my collarbone, sending a surge of heat through me. "Drunk enough to want to do bad things to you, but not drunk enough that I would do them drunk," he says. "But just drunk enough to still remember them tomorrow if I *did* do them."

I laugh, completely confused by his answer, yet completely turned on by it at the same time. "Is that why you walked here? Because you've been drinking?"

He shakes his head. "I walked here because I wanted a good-night kiss and fortunately, I couldn't find my keys. But I wanted one so bad, babe. I missed you so bad tonight." He kisses me and his mouth tastes like lemonade.

"Why do you taste like lemonade?"

He laughs. "All they had were these fruity froufrou drinks. I'm drunk off fruity froufrou girl drinks. It's really sad and unattractive, I know."

"Well, you taste really good," I say, pulling his mouth back to mine. He moans and presses himself against me, dipping his tongue farther into my mouth. As soon as our bodies connect on the bed, he pulls away and stands up, leaving me breathless and alone on the mattress.

"Time to go," he says. "I already see this heading somewhere I'm too drunk to go right now. I'll see you tomorrow night."

I jump up and run and block the window before he can leave. He stops in front of me and folds his arms over his chest. "Stay," I say. "Please. Just lie in bed with me. We can put pillows between us and I promise not to seduce you since you're drunk. Just stay for an hour, I don't want you to go yet."

He immediately turns and heads back to the bed. "Okay," he says simply. He throws himself onto my bed and pulls the covers out from beneath him.

That was easy.

I walk back to the bed and lie down beside him. Neither

of us places a pillow between us. Instead, I throw my arm over his chest and entwine my legs with his.

"Good night," he says, brushing my hair back. He kisses my forehead and closes his eyes. I tuck my head against his chest and listen to the rhythm of his heart. After several minutes, his breathing and heart rate have both regulated and he's sound asleep. I can't feel my arm anymore, so I gently lift it off him and quietly roll over. As soon as I get situated on my pillow, he slides his arm over my waist and his legs over mine. "I love you, Hope," he mutters.

Um . . .

Breathe, Sky.

Just breathe.

It's not that hard.

Take a breath.

I squeeze my eyes shut and try to tell myself I did not just hear what I thought I heard. But he said it clear as day. And I honestly don't know what breaks my heart more—the fact that he called me by someone else's name, or the fact that he actually said *love* this time instead of *live*.

I attempt to talk myself down from rolling over and punching him in his damn face. He's been drinking and he was half asleep when he said it. I can't assume she really means something to him when it could have just been a dream. But . . . who the hell is Hope? And why does he love her?

Thirteen years earlier

I'm sweating because it's hot under these covers, but I don't want to take them off my head. I know if the door opens, it won't matter if I have covers on or not, but I feel safer with them on anyway. I poke my fingers out and lift the piece of cover up that's in front of my eyes. I look at the doorknob like I do every night.

Don't turn. Don't turn. Please, don't turn.

It's always so quiet in my room and I hate it. Sometimes I hear things that I think might be the doorknob turning and it makes my heart beat really hard and really fast. Right now, just staring at the doorknob is making my heart beat really hard and really fast, but I can't stop staring at it. I don't want it to turn. I don't want that door to open, I don't.

Everything is so quiet.

So quiet.

The doorknob doesn't turn.

My heart stops beating so fast, because the doorknob never turns.

My eyes get really heavy and I finally close them.

I'm so glad that tonight's not one of the nights that the doorknob turns.

It's so quiet.

So quiet.

And then it's not, because the doorknob turns.

Saturday, October 27, 2012
Sometime in the middle of the night

"Sky."

I'm so heavy. Everything is so heavy. I don't like this feeling. There isn't anything physically on my chest, but I feel a pressure unlike anything I've ever felt. And sadness. An overwhelming sadness is consuming me, and I have no idea why. My shoulders are shaking and there are sobs coming from somewhere in the room. Who's crying?

Am *I* crying?

"Sky, wake up."

I feel his arm around me. His cheek is pressed against mine and he's behind me, holding me tightly against his chest. I grab his wrist and lift his arm off me. I sit up on the bed and look around. It's dark outside. I don't get it. I'm crying.

He sits up beside me and turns me toward him, brushing at my eyes with his thumbs.

"You're scaring me, babe." He's looking at me and he's worried. I squeeze my eyes shut and try to regain control, because I have no idea what the hell is happening and I can't breathe. I can hear myself crying and I can't inhale a breath because of it.

I look at the clock on the nightstand and it says three. Things are starting to come back into focus now, but . . . why am I crying?

"Why are you crying?" Holder asks. He pulls me to him and I let him. He feels safe. He feels like home when I'm wrapped up in him. He holds me and rubs my back, kissing the side of my head every now and then. He keeps saying, "Don't worry," over and over and he holds me for what feels like forever.

The weight gradually lifts off my chest, the sadness dissipates, and I'm eventually no longer crying.

I'm scared, though, because nothing like this has ever happened to me before. Never in my life have I felt sadness this unbearable, so how could it feel so real from a dream?

"You okay?" he whispers.

I nod against his chest.

"What happened?"

I shake my head. "I don't know. I guess it was a bad dream."

"Want to talk about it?" He soothes my hair with his hands.

I shake my head. "No. I don't want to remember it."

He hugs me for a long time, then kisses me on the forehead. "I don't want to leave you, but I need to go. I don't want you to get in trouble."

I nod, but I don't release my grip. I want to beg him not to leave me alone, but I don't want to sound desperate and terrified. People have bad dreams all the time; I don't understand why I'm responding like this.

"Go back to sleep, Sky. Everything's okay, you just had a bad dream."

I lie back down on the bed and close my eyes. I feel his lips brush against my forehead, and then he's gone.

Saturday, October 27, 2012
8:20 p.m.

I give both Breckin and Max a hug in the parking lot of the gallery. The gallery showing has ended and Holder and I are going back to his place. I know I should be nervous about what might happen between us tonight, but I'm not nervous at all. Everything with him feels right. Well, everything except the phrase that keeps repeating over and over in my head.

I love you, Hope.

I want to ask him about it, but I can't find the right moment. The gallery showing certainly wasn't the place to bring it up. Now seems like a good time, but every time I open my mouth to do it, I clamp it shut again. I think I'm more afraid of who she is and what she means to him than I am of actually working up the nerve to bring it up. The longer I put off asking him about it, the longer I have before I'm forced to learn the truth.

"You want to grab something to eat?" he asks, pulling out of the parking lot.

"Yeah," I say quickly, relieved that he interrupted my thoughts. "A cheeseburger sounds good. And cheese fries. And I want a chocolate milkshake."

He laughs and takes my hand in his. "A little demanding are we, Princess?"

I let go of his hand and turn to face him. "Don't call me that," I snap.

He glances at me and can more than likely see the anger on my face, even in the dark.

"Hey," he says soothingly, picking up my hand again. "I don't think you're demanding, Sky. It was a joke."

I shake my head. "Not demanding. Don't call me Princess. I hate that word."

He gives me a sidelong glance, then shifts his eyes back to the road. "Okay."

I turn my gaze out the window, trying to get the word out of my head. I don't know why I hate nicknames so much, but I do. And I know I overreacted just now, but he can never call me that again. He also shouldn't call me by the name of any of his ex-girlfriends either. He should just stick to Sky . . . it's much safer.

We drive in complete silence and I become increasingly more regretful for reacting like I did. If anything, I should be more upset by the fact that he called me by another girl's name than by his referring to me as Princess. It's almost like I'm displacing my anger because I'm too afraid to bring up what's really bothering me. Honestly, I just want a drama-free night with him tonight. There'll be plenty of time to ask him about Hope another day.

"I'm sorry, Holder."

He squeezes my hand and pulls it onto his lap, but doesn't say anything else.

When we pull into his driveway, I get out of the car. We never did stop for food, but I don't even feel like bringing it up now. He meets me at the passenger door and wraps his arms around me and I hug him back. He walks me until my back is against the car and I press my head to his shoulder, breathing in the scent of him. The awkwardness from the drive here still lingers, so I attempt to ease myself against him in a relaxing way to let him know I'm not thinking about it. He's lightly stroking his fingers up and down my arms, covering me in chills.

"Can I ask you something?" he says.

"Always."

He sighs, then pulls back and looks at me. "Did I freak you out Monday? In my car? If I did, I'm sorry. I don't know what got into me. I'm not a pussy, I swear. I haven't cried since Les died, and I sure as hell didn't mean to do it in front of you."

I lean my head into his chest again and hug him tighter. "You know last night when I woke up after that dream?"

"Yeah."

"That's the second time I've cried since I was five. The only other time I cried was when you told me about what happened to your sister. I cried when I was in the bathroom. It was just one tear, but it counts. I think when we're together, maybe our emotions become a little overwhelming and it turns us *both* into pussies."

He laughs and kisses me on top of the head. "I have a feeling I won't be living you for much longer." He gives me another quick kiss, then takes my hand. "Ready for the grand tour?"

I follow him toward his house, but I'm still stuck on the fact that he just told me he's about to stop living me. If he stops living me, that means he'll be loving me. He just confessed that he's falling in love with me without actually saying it. The most shocking thing about his confession is that I really liked it.

We walk inside and the house is nothing like I expected.

It doesn't seem very big from the outside, but there's a foyer. Normal houses don't have foyers. There's an archway to the right that leads to a living room. The walls are covered in nothing but books, and I feel like I've just died and gone to heaven. "Wow," I say, eyeing the bookshelves in the living room. Books are stacked on shelves from floor to ceiling on every single wall.

"Yeah," he says. "Mom was pretty pissed when they invented the e-reader."

I laugh. "I think I already like your mom. When do I get to meet her?"

He shakes his head. "I don't introduce girls to my mother." His voice is as detached as his words, and as soon as he says it, his expression drops and he knows he's just hurt my feelings. He walks swiftly to me and takes my face in his hands. "No, no. That's not what I meant. I'm not saying you're anything like the other girls I've dated. I didn't mean for it to come out like that."

I hear what he's saying, but we've been dating as long as we have and he still isn't convinced it's real enough for me to meet his mother? I wonder if we'll *ever* be real enough to him for me to meet his mother.

"Did Hope get to meet her?" I know I shouldn't have said it, but I couldn't keep it in any longer. Especially now, hearing him say "other girls." I'm not delusional; I know he dated other people before he met me. I just don't like hearing him say it. Much less calling me by their names.

"*What?*" he asks, dropping his hands. He's backing away from me. "Why did you say that?" The color is draining from his face and I immediately regret saying it.

"Never mind. It's nothing. I don't have to meet your

mom." I just want whatever this is to pass. I knew I wouldn't feel like talking about it tonight. I want to get back to the house tour and forget this conversation ever happened.

He grabs my hands and says it again. "Why would you say that, Sky? Why did you say that name?"

I shake my head. "It's not that big of a deal. You were drunk."

He narrows his eyes at me and it's clear I'm not escaping this conversation. I sigh and reluctantly give in, clearing my throat before I speak.

"Last night when you were falling asleep . . . you told me you loved me. But you called me Hope, so you weren't really talking to *me*. You'd been drinking and you were half asleep, so I don't need an explanation. I don't know if I really even want to know why you said it."

He brings his hands to his hair and groans. "Sky." He steps forward, taking me in his arms. "I'm so sorry. It must have been a stupid dream. I don't even know anyone named Hope and I've definitely never had an ex-girlfriend by that name if that's what you were thinking. I'm so sorry that happened. I should have never gone to your house drunk." He looks down at me and as much as my instincts are telling me he's lying, his eyes are completely sincere. "You have to believe me. It'll kill me if you think for a second that I feel anything at all for someone else. I've never felt this way about anyone."

Every word coming from his mouth is dripping with sincerity and honesty. Considering I can't even remember why I woke up crying, it's possible his sleep talking really was the result of a random dream. And hearing everything he just said to me puts into perspective just how serious things are becoming between us.

I look up at him, attempting to prepare some sort of response to everything he just said. I part my lips and wait for the words to come, but they don't. I'm suddenly the one needing more time to process my thoughts.

He's cupping my cheeks, waiting for me to break the silence between us. The proximity of his mouth to mine weathers his patience. "I need to kiss you," he says apologetically, pulling my face to his. We're still standing in the foyer, but he somehow picks me up effortlessly and sets me down on the stairs leading to the upstairs bedrooms. I lean back and he returns his lips to mine, his hands gripping the wooden steps on either side of my head.

Due to our position, he's forced to lower a knee between my thighs. It isn't that big a deal unless you take into consideration the dress that I have on. It would be so easy for him to take me right here on the stairs, but I'm hoping we at least make it to his room first before he tries. I wonder if he's expecting anything, especially after the text I accidentally sent him. He's a guy, of course he's expecting something. I wonder if he knows I'm a virgin. Should I even tell him I'm a virgin? I should. He'll probably be able to tell.

"I'm a virgin," I blurt against his mouth. I immediately wonder what the hell I'm doing even speaking aloud right now. I shouldn't be allowed to speak ever again. Someone should strip me of my voice, because I obviously have no filter when my sexual guard is down.

He immediately stops kissing me. He slowly backs his face away from mine and looks down into my eyes. "Sky," he says directly. "I'm kissing you because sometimes I can't *not* kiss you. You know what your mouth does to me. I'm not expecting anything else, okay? As long as I get to kiss you, the other stuff can wait." He's tucking my hair behind my ears now and looking down at me genuinely.

"I just thought you should know. I probably should have picked a better time to state that fact, but sometimes I just blurt things out without thinking. It's a really bad trait and I hate it because I do it at the most inopportune moments and it's embarrassing. Like right now."

He laughs and shakes his head. "No, don't stop doing that. I love it when you blurt things out without thinking. And I love it when you spout off long, nervous, ridiculous rants. It's kind of hot."

I blush. Being called hot is seriously . . . hot.

"You know what else is hot?" he says, leaning back in to me again.

The playfulness in his expression chips away at my embarrassment. "What?"

He grins. "Trying to keep our hands off each other while we watch a movie." He stands up and pulls me to my feet, then leads me up the stairs to his room.

He opens the door and walks in first, then turns around and tells me to close my eyes. I roll them, instead.

"I don't like surprises," I say.

"You also don't like presents and certain common terms of endearment. I'm learning. But this is just something cool I want to show you—it's not anything I bought you. So deal with it and shut your eyes."

I do what he says and he pulls me forward into the room. I already love it in here because it smells just like him. He walks me a few steps, then places his hands on my shoulders. "Sit," he says, pushing me down. I take a seat on what feels like a bed, then I'm suddenly flat on my back and he's lifting up my feet. "Keep your eyes closed."

I feel him pulling my feet onto the bed and propping me up against a pillow. His hand grabs the hem of my sundress and he pulls it down, making sure it stays in place. "Gotta keep you covered up. Can't be flashing me thigh when you're on your back like that."

I laugh, but I keep my eyes closed. He's suddenly crawling over me, careful not to knee me. I can feel him positioning himself next to me on his pillow. "Okay. Open your eyes and prepare to be wowed."

I'm scared. I slowly pry my eyes open. I hesitate to guess what I'm looking at, because I almost think it's a TV. But TVs don't usually take up eighty inches of wall space. This thing is ginormous. He points a remote at it and the screen lights up.

"Wow," I say, impressed. "It's huge."

"That's what *she* said."

I elbow him in the side and he laughs. He points the remote back up to the TV. "What's your favorite movie ever? I have Netflix."

I tilt my head in his direction. "Net *what*?"

He laughs and shakes his head in disappointment. "I keep forgetting you're technologically challenged. It's similar to an e-reader, only with movies and television shows instead of books. You can watch pretty much anything at the push of a button."

"Are there commercials?"

"Nope," he says proudly. "So what'll it be?"

"Do you have *The Jerk*? I love that movie."

His arm falls to his chest and he clicks the power button

and turns off the TV. He's silent for several long seconds, then he sighs forcefully. He leans over and sets the remote down on his nightstand, then rolls over and faces me. "I don't want to watch TV anymore."

He's pouting? What the hell did I say?

"Fine. We don't have to watch *The Jerk*. Pick something else out, you big baby." I laugh.

He doesn't respond for a few moments while he continues staring at me inexpressively. He lifts his hand and runs it across my stomach and around to my waist, then grips me tightly and pulls me against him. "You know," he says, narrowing his eyes as he meticulously rakes them down my body. He traces the pattern of my dress with a finger, delicately stroking over my stomach. "I can handle what this dress does to me." He lifts his eyes from my stomach, back up to my mouth. "I can even handle having to constantly stare at your lips, even when I don't get to kiss them. I can handle the sound of your laughter and how it makes me want to cover your mouth with mine and drink it all in."

His mouth is closing in on mine, and the way his voice has dropped into some sort of lyrical, godlike octave makes my heart pummel within my chest. He lowers his lips to my cheek and lightly kisses it, his warm breath colliding with my skin when he speaks. "I can even handle the millions of times I've replayed our first kiss over and over in my head this past month. The way you felt. The way you *sounded*. The way you looked up at me right before my lips met yours."

He rolls himself on top of me and brings my arms above my head, clasping them in his hands. I'm hanging on to every single word he's saying, not wanting to miss a single second of whatever it is he's doing right now. He straddles me, holding his weight up with his knees. "But what I can't handle, Sky? What drives me crazy and makes me want to put my hands and my mouth all over every single inch of you? It's the fact that you just said *The Jerk* is your favorite movie ever. Now *that*?" He drops his mouth to mine until our lips are touching. "That's incredibly fucking hot and I'm pretty sure we need to make out now."

His playfulness makes me laugh and I whisper seductively against his lips. "He hates these cans."

He groans and kisses me, then pulls away. "Do it again. Please. Hearing you talk in movie quotes is so much hotter than kissing you."

I laugh and give him another quote. "Stay away from the cans!"

He groans playfully in my ear. "That's my girl. One more. Do one more."

"That's all I need," I say teasingly. "The ashtray, this paddle game, and the remote control, and the lamp . . . and that's *all* I need. I don't need one other thing, not one."

He's laughing loudly now. As many times as Six and I stayed up watching this movie, he'll be surprised to know there's a lot more where those came from.

"That's *all* you need?" Holder quips. "Are you sure about that, Sky?" His voice is smooth and seductive and if I was standing up right now, my panties would without a doubt be on the floor.

I shake my head and my smile fades. "You," I whisper. "I need the lamp and the ashtray and the paddle game and the remote control . . . and *you*. That's all I need."

He laughs, but his laugh quickly fades once his eyes

drop to my mouth again. He scrutinizes it, more than likely mapping out just what he's about to do with it for the next hour. "I need to kiss you now." His mouth collides with mine and for this moment, he really *is* all I need.

He's propped up on his hands and knees, kissing me fiercely, but I need him to drop himself on top of me. My hands are still locked above my head and my mouth is useless to form words when he's teasing it like he is. The only thing I can do is lift my foot up and kick his knee out from under him, so that's what I do.

The second his body falls against mine, I gasp. Loudly. I hadn't taken into consideration that when I lifted my leg, it would also push the hem of my dress up. Way up. Couple that with the hard denim of his jeans and you have a pretty gasp-worthy combination.

"Holy shit, Sky," he says between breathless moments of completely ravishing my mouth with his. He's winded already and we haven't even been at it more than a minute. "God, you feel incredible. Thank you for wearing this dress." He's kissing me, sporadically muttering into my mouth. "I really . . ." He kisses my mouth, then runs his lips down my chin and halfway down my neck. "I really like it. Your dress." He's breathing so heavily now, I can barely make out the mumbling coming from him. He scoots slightly farther down on the bed until his lips are kissing the base of my throat. I tilt my head back to give him plenty of access, because his lips are more than welcome anywhere on me right now. He releases his grip on my hands so he can lower his mouth closer to my chest. One of his hands drops to my thigh, and he slowly runs it upward, pushing away what's left of the dress covering my legs. When he reaches the top of my thigh, he stills his hand and squeezes tightly, as if he's silently demanding his fingers not venture any further.

I twist my body beneath his, hoping he'll get the hint that I'm attempting to direct his hand to keep going wherever it wants to go. I don't want him to second-guess himself or think for a second that I'm hesitant to go any further. I just want him to do whatever it is he wants to do, because I need him to. I need him to conquer as many firsts as he can tonight, because I'm suddenly feeling greedy and I want us to pass them all.

He takes my physical cues and inches his hand closer to my inner thigh. The anticipation of him touching me alone is enough to cause every muscle from the waist down to clench. His lips have finally made their way past the base of my throat and down to the rise in my chest. I feel like the next step is for him to remove the dress completely so he can get to what's underneath it, but that would require his other hand, and I really like it where it is. I'd like it a little more if it were a few inches farther, but I absolutely don't want it farther away.

I bring my hands to his face and force him to kiss me harder, then drop my hands to his back.

He's still wearing a shirt.

This isn't good.

I reach around to his stomach and pull his shirt up over his head, but I don't realize that when I do, it also causes him to move his hand off my thigh. I may have whimpered a little, because he grins and kisses the corner of my mouth.

We keep our gaze locked and he gently strokes my face with his fingertips, trailing over every part of it. He never looks away and he keeps his eyes locked on mine, even when he dips his head to plant kisses around the edges of my lips. The way he looks at me makes me feel . . . I try to search for an adjective to follow up that thought, but I can't find one. He just makes me *feel*. He's the only boy that's ever cared whether I'm feeling anything at all, and for that alone, I let him steal another small piece of my heart. But it doesn't feel like enough, because I suddenly want to give it *all* to him.

"Holder," I breathe. He slides his hands up my waist and moves closer to me.

"Sky," he says, mimicking my tone. His mouth reaches my lips and he slips his tongue inside. It's sweet and warm and I know it hasn't been very long since I last tasted it, but I've missed it. His hands are on either side of my head and he's being careful not to touch me with any part of his hands or his body now. Only his mouth.

"Holder," I mumble, pulling away. I bring my hand to his cheek. "I want to. Tonight. Right now."

His expression doesn't change. He stares at me like he didn't hear me. Maybe he *didn't* hear me, because he certainly isn't taking me up on the offer.

"Sky . . ." His voice is full of hesitation. "We don't have to. I want you to be absolutely positive it's what you want. Okay?" He's caressing my cheek now. "I don't want to rush you into anything."

"I know that. But I'm telling you I want this. I've never wanted it with anyone before, but I want it with you."

His eyes are trained on mine and he's soaking in every single word I've said. He's either in denial or in shock, neither of which are helping my cause. I take both of my hands and place them on his cheeks, then pull his lips in close to mine. "This isn't me saying *yes*, Holder. This is me saying *please*."

With that, his lips crash to mine and he groans. Hearing that sound come from deep within his chest further solidifies my decision. I need him and I need him now.

"We're really doing this?" he says into my mouth, still kissing me frantically.

"Yes. We're really doing this. I've never been more positive of anything in my life."

His hand slides up my thigh and he slips his hand between my hip and my panties, then begins to slide them down.

"I just need you to promise me one thing first," I say.

He kisses me softly, then pulls his hand away from my underwear (dammit) and nods. "Anything."

I grab his hand and put it right back where it was on my hip. "I want to do this, but only if you promise we'll break the record for the best first time in the history of first times."

He grins down at me. "When it's you and me, Sky . . . it'll never be anything less."

He snakes his arm underneath my back and pulls me up with him. His hands move to my arms and he hooks his fingers underneath the thin straps of my dress, sliding them off my shoulders. I close my eyes tightly and press my cheek to his, fisting my hands in his hair. I can feel his breath meet my shoulder before his lips do. He barely kisses it, but it's as if he touches and ignites every part of me from the inside out with that one kiss.

"I'm taking it off," he says.

My eyes are still closed and I'm not sure if he's telling

me or asking my permission to remove the dress, but I nod anyway. He lifts my dress up and over my head—my bare skin prickling beneath his touch. He gently lays me back against my pillow and I open my eyes, looking up at him, admiring just how incredibly beautiful he really is. After regarding me intensely for several seconds, he drops his gaze to his hand that's curved around my waist.

He slowly moves his eyes up and down my body. "Holy shit, Sky." He runs his hand over my stomach, then leans down and kisses it softly. "You're incredible."

I've never been this exposed in front of someone before, but the way he's admiring me only makes me *want* to be this exposed. He slides his hand up to my bra and grazes his thumb just underneath it—causing my lips to part and my eyes to close again.

Oh, my God, I want him. Really, really bad.

I grab his face and pull it to mine, locking my legs around his hips. He groans and slips his hand away from my bra and down to my waist again. He slides my panties down my thighs, forcing me to unlock my legs and let him take them off completely. My bra is quick to follow and once all of my clothes have been removed, he scoots his legs off the bed and halfway stands up, leaning over me. I've still got hold of his face and we're still frantically kissing while he removes his pants, then climbs back onto the bed with me, lowering himself on top of me. We're skin to skin now for the first time, so close that air couldn't even pass between us, yet it still feels like we aren't near close enough. He reaches across the mattress and his hand fumbles over the nightstand. He removes a condom from the drawer, then lays it down on the bed, lowering himself on top of me again. The hardness and weight of him forces my legs farther apart. I wince when I realize the anticipation in my stomach is suddenly turning into dread.

And nausea.

And fear.

My heart is racing and my breaths begin to come in short gasps. Tears sting at my eyes as his hand moves around beside us on the bed, searching for the condom. He finds it and I hear him open it, but I'm squeezing my eyes shut. I can feel him pull back and lift up onto his knees. I know he's putting it on and I know what comes next. I know how it feels and I know how much it hurts and I know how it'll make me cry when it's over.

But how do I know? How do I know if I've never done this before?

My lips begin to tremble when he positions himself between my legs again. I try to think of something to take away the fear, so I visualize the sky and the stars and how beautiful it all is, attempting to ease my panic. If I remind myself that the sky is beautiful no matter what, I can think about that and forget how ugly *this* is. I don't want to open my eyes, so I just count silently inside my head. I visualize the stars above my bed and I start from the bottom of the cluster, working my way up.

One, two, three . . .

I count and I count and I count.

Twenty-two, twenty-three, twenty-four . . .

I hold my breath and focus, focus, focus on the stars.

Fifty-seven, fifty-eight, fifty-nine . . .

I want him to be done already. I just want him off me.

Seventy-one, seventy-two, seventy—

"Dammit, Sky!" Holder yells. He's pulling my arm away from my eyes. I don't want him to make me look, so I hold my arm tighter against my face so everything will stay dark and I can keep silently counting.

All of a sudden, my back is being lifted up in the air and I'm not against the pillow anymore. My arms are limp and his are wrapped tightly around me, but I can't move. My arms are too weak and I'm sobbing too hard. I'm crying so hard and he's moving me and I don't know why so I open my eyes. I'm going back and forth and back and forth and for a second, I panic and squeeze my eyes shut, thinking he's not finished. But I can feel the covers around me and his arm is squeezing my back and he's soothing my hair with his hand, whispering in my ear.

"Baby, it's okay." He's pressing his lips into my hair, rocking me back and forth with him. I open my eyes again and tears are clouding my vision. "I'm sorry, Sky. I'm so sorry."

He's kissing the side of my head over and over while he rocks me, telling me he's sorry. He's apologizing for something. Something he wants me to forgive him for this time.

He pulls back and sees that my eyes are open. His eyes are red but I don't see any tears. He's shaking, though. Or maybe it's me who's shaking. I think we're both shaking.

He's looking into my eyes, searching for something. Searching for *me*. I begin to relax in his arms, because when his arms are wrapped around me, I don't feel like I'm falling off the edge of the earth. "What happened?" I ask him. I don't understand where this is coming from.

He shakes his head, his eyes full of sorrow and fear and regret. "I don't know. You just started counting and crying and shaking and I kept trying to get you to stop, Sky. You wouldn't stop. You were terrified. What did I do? Tell me, because I'm so sorry. I am so, so sorry. What the fuck did I do?"

I just shake my head because I don't have an answer.

He grimaces and drops his forehead to mine. "I'm so sorry. I never should have let it go that far. I don't know what the hell just happened, but you're not ready yet, okay?"

I'm not ready yet?

"So we didn't . . . we didn't have sex?"

His hands loosen around me and I can feel his whole demeanor shift. The look in his eyes is nothing but loss and defeat. His eyebrows draw apart and he frowns, cupping my cheeks. "Where'd you go, Sky?"

I shake my head, confused. "I'm right here. I'm listening."

"No, I mean earlier. Where'd you go? You weren't here with me because no, nothing happened. I could see on your face that something was wrong, so I didn't do it. But now you need to think long and hard about where you were inside that head of yours, because you were panicked. You were hysterical and I need to know what it was that took you there so I can make sure you never go back."

He kisses me on the forehead and releases his hold from around my back. He stands up and pulls his jeans on, then picks up my dress. He shakes it out, then flips it over until it slides down his hands, then he walks toward me and puts it on over my head. He lifts my arms and helps me slide them into the dress, then he pulls it down over my waist, covering me. "I'll go get you some water. I'll be right back." He kisses me tentatively on the lips, almost as if he's scared to touch me again. After he walks out of the room, I lean my head against the wall and close my eyes.

I have no idea what just happened, but the fear of losing him because of it is a valid one. I just took one of the most intimate things imaginable, and I turned it into a disaster. I made him feel worthless, like he did something wrong, and now he feels bad for me because of it. He probably wants me to leave, and I don't blame him. I don't blame him a bit. I want to run away from me, too.

I throw the covers off and stand up, then pull my dress down. I don't even bother looking for my underwear. I need to find the bathroom and get myself together so he can take me home. This is twice this weekend that I've been reduced to tears and I don't even know why—and twice that he's had to save me. I'm not doing it to him again.

When I pass the stairs looking for the restroom, I glance down over the railing into the kitchen. He's leaning forward with his elbows on the bar and his face buried in his hands. He's just standing there, looking miserable and upset. I can't watch him anymore, so I open the first door to my right, assuming it's the bathroom.

It's not.

It's Lesslie's bedroom. I start to pull the door shut, but I don't. Instead, I open it wider and slip inside, then shut it behind me. I don't care if I'm in a bathroom, a bedroom, or a closet . . . I just need peace and quiet. Time to regroup from whatever the hell is going on with me. I'm beginning to think that maybe I *am* crazy. I've never spaced out that severely before and it terrifies me. My hands are still shaking, so I clasp them together in front of me and try to focus on something else in order to calm myself down.

I take in my surroundings and find the bedroom to be somewhat disturbing. The bed isn't made, which strikes me as odd. Holder's entire house is spotless, but Lesslie's bed isn't made. There's a pair of jeans in the middle of the floor and it looks like she just stepped out of them. I look around at the room and it seems typical of a teenage girl. Makeup on the dresser, an iPod on the nightstand. It looks like she still lives here. From the look of her room, it doesn't look like she's gone at all. It's obvious no one has touched this room since she died. Her pictures are all still hanging on the walls and stuck to her vanity mirror. All of her clothes are still in her closet, some piled on the closet floor. It's been over a year since he said she passed away, and I'm willing to bet that no one in his family has accepted it yet.

It feels eerie being in here, but it's keeping my mind off what's happening right now. I walk to the bed and look at the pictures hanging on the wall. Most of them are of Lesslie and her friends, with just a few of Holder and her together. She looks a lot like Holder with his intense, crystal-blue eyes and dark brown hair. What surprises me the most is how happy she looks. She looks so content and full of life in every single picture, it's hard to imagine what was really going on inside her head. No wonder Holder didn't have a clue about how desolate she really felt. She more than likely never let anyone know.

I pick up a picture from her nightstand that's turned facedown. When I flip it over and look at it, I gasp. It's a picture of her kissing Grayson on the cheek and they have their arms around each other. The picture stuns me and I have to take a seat on the bed to regain my bearings. This is why Holder hates him so much? This is why he didn't want him touching me? I wonder if he blames Grayson for what she did.

I'm holding the picture, still sitting on the bed, when the bedroom door opens. Holder peers around the door. "What are you doing?" He doesn't seem angry that I'm in here. He does seem uncomfortable, though, which is probably just a reaction from how I made him feel earlier.

"I was looking for the bathroom," I say, quietly. "I'm sorry. I just needed a second."

He leans against the doorway and crosses his arms over his chest while his eyes work their way around the room. He's taking in everything like I am. Like it's all new to him.

"Has no one been in here? Since she . . ."

"No," he says quickly. "What would be the point of it? She's gone."

I nod, then place the picture of Lesslie and Grayson back on the nightstand, facedown like she had left it. "Was she dating him?"

He takes a hesitant step into the bedroom, then walks over to the bed. He sits down beside me and rests his elbows on his knees, clasping his hands in front of him. He looks around the room slowly, not answering my question right away. He glances at me, then wraps his arm around my shoulders, pulling me to him. The fact that he's sitting here with me right now, still wanting to hold me, makes me want to burst into tears.

"He broke up with her the night before she did it," he says quietly.

I try not to gasp, but his words shock me. "Do you think he's the reason why she did it? Is that why you hate him so much?"

He shakes his head. "I hated him before he broke up with her. He put her through a lot of shit, Sky. And no, I don't think he's why she did it. I think maybe it was the deciding factor in a decision she had wanted to make for a long time. She had issues way before Grayson ever came into the picture. So no, I don't blame him. I never have." He stands up and takes my hand. "Come on. I don't want to be in here anymore."

I take one last glance around the room, then stand up to follow him. I stop before we reach the door, though. He turns around and watches me observe the pictures on her dresser. There's a framed picture of Holder and Lesslie when they were kids. I pick it up and bring it in closer for inspection. Something about seeing him that young makes me smile. Seeing both of them that young . . . it's refreshing. Like there's innocence about them before the ugly realities of life hit. They're standing in front of a white-framed house and Holder has his arm around her neck and he's squeezing her. She's got her arms wrapped around his waist and they're smiling at the camera.

My eyes move from their faces to the house behind them in the photo. It's a white-framed house with yellow trim, and if you were to see the inside of the house, the living room is painted two different shades of green.

I immediately close my eyes. *How do I know that? How do I know what color the living room is?*

My hands start shaking and I try to suck in a breath, but I can't. How do I know that house? I know that house like I somehow suddenly know the kids in the picture. How do I know there's a green-and-white swing set behind that house? And ten feet from the swing set is a dry well that has to stay covered because Lesslie's cat fell down it once.

"You okay?" Holder says. He tries to take the picture out of my hands, but I snatch it from him and look up at him. His eyes are concerned and he takes a step toward me. I take a step back.

How do I know him?

How do I know Lesslie?

Why do I feel like I *miss* them? I shake my head, looking down at the picture and back up at Holder, then down to the picture again. This time, Lesslie's wrist catches my eye. She's wearing a bracelet. A bracelet identical to mine.

I want to ask him about it but I can't. I try, but nothing comes out, so I just hold up the picture instead. He shakes his head and his face drops like his heart is breaking. "Sky, no," he says pleadingly.

"How?" My voice cracks and is barely audible. I look back down to the picture in my hands. "There's a swing set. And a well. And . . . your cat. It got stuck in the well." I dart my eyes up to his and the thoughts keep pouring out. "Holder, I know that living room. The living room is green and the kitchen had a countertop that was way too tall for us and . . . your mother. Your mother's name is Beth." I pause and try to take a breath, because the memories won't stop. They won't stop coming and I can't breathe. "Holder . . . is Beth your mother's name?"

Holder grimaces and runs his hands through his hair. "Sky . . ." he says. He can't even look at me. His expression is torn and confused and he's . . . he's been *lying* to me. He's holding something back and he's scared to tell me.

He *knows* me. How the hell does he know me and why hasn't he told me?

I suddenly feel sick. I rush past him and open the door across the hall, which happens to be a bathroom, thank God. I lock the door behind me and throw the framed picture on the counter, then fall straight to the floor.

The images and memories start inundating my mind like the floodgates have just been lifted. Memories of him, of her, of the three of us together. Memories of us playing, me eating dinner at their house, me and Les being inseparable. I loved her. I was so young and so small and I don't even know how I knew them, but I loved them. Both of them. The memory is coupled with the grief of now knowing the Lesslie I knew and loved as a little girl is gone. I suddenly feel sad and depressed that she's gone, but not for me. Not for Sky. I'm sad for the little girl I used to be, and somehow her grief over the loss of Lesslie is emerging through me.

How have I not known? How did I not remember him the first time I saw him?

"Sky, open the door. Please."

I fall back against the wall. It's too much. The memories and the emotions and the grief . . . it's too much to absorb all at once.

"Baby, please. We need to talk and I can't do it from out here. Please, open the door."

He *knew*. The first time he saw me at the grocery store, he knew. And when he saw my bracelet . . . he knew I got it from Lesslie. He saw me wearing it and he knew.

My grief and confusion soon turn to anger and I push myself up off the floor and walk swiftly to the bathroom door. I unlock it and swing it open. His hands are on either side of the doorframe and he's looking directly at me, but I feel like I don't even know who he is. I don't know what's real between us and what's fake anymore. I don't know what feelings of his are from his life with me or the life with that little girl I used to be.

I need to know. I need to know who she was. Who *I* was. I swallow my fear and release the question that I'm afraid I already know the answer to. "Who's Hope?"

His hardened expression doesn't change, so I ask him again, but louder this time.

"Who the hell is Hope?"

He keeps his eyes locked on mine and his hands placed firmly on the doorframe, but he can't answer me. For some reason he doesn't want me to know. He doesn't want me to remember who I was. I take a deep breath and try to fight back the tears. I'm too scared to say it, because I don't want to know the answer.

"Is it me?" I ask, my voice shaking and full of trepidation. "Holder . . . am I Hope?"

He lets out a quick breath at the same time he looks up at the ceiling, almost as if he's struggling not to cry. He closes his eyes and lays his forehead against his arm, then takes a long, deep breath before looking back at me. "Yes."

The air around me grows thick. Too thick to take in. I stand still, directly in front of him, unable to move. Everything grows quiet except for what's inside my head. There are so many thoughts and questions and memories and they're all trying to take over and I don't know if I need to cry or scream or sleep or run.

I need to go outside. I feel like Holder and the bathroom and the whole damn house are closing in on me and I need to go outside so there's room to get everything out of my head. I just want it all out.

I shove past him and he tries to grab my arm, but I yank it out of his grasp.

"Sky, wait," he yells after me. I keep running until I reach the stairs and I descend them as fast as I can, taking two at a time. I can hear him following me, so I speed up and my foot lands farther than I intend for it to. I lose my grip on the rail and fall forward, landing on the floor at the base of the stairs.

"Sky!" he yells. I try to pull myself up but he's on his knees with his arms around me before I even have the chance. I push against him, wanting him to let go of me so I can just go outside. He doesn't budge.

"Outside," I say, breathless and weak. "I just need outside. Please, Holder."

I can feel him struggling from within, not wanting to release me. He reluctantly pulls me away from his chest and looks down at me, searching my eyes. "Don't run, Sky. Go outside, but please don't leave. We need to talk."

I nod and he releases me, then helps me stand up. When I walk out the front door and onto the lawn, I clasp my hands together behind my head and inhale a huge, cold breath of air. I tilt my head back and look up at the stars, wishing more than anything that I was up there and not down here. I don't want the memories to keep coming, because with each confusing memory comes an even more confusing question. I don't understand how I know him. I don't understand why he kept it from me. I don't understand how my name could have been Hope, when all I've ever remembered being called was Sky. I don't understand why Karen would tell me that Sky was my birth name if it isn't. Everything I thought I understood after all these years is unraveling, revealing things that I don't want to know. I'm being lied to, and I'm terrified to know what it is that everyone's trying to keep from me.

I stand outside for what feels like forever, attempting to sort through this alone when I have no idea what it is I'm even trying to sort through. I need to talk to Holder and I need to know what he knows, but I'm hurt. I don't want to face him, knowing he's been hiding this secret all along. It makes everything that I thought was happening between us nothing but a façade.

I'm emotionally spent and have had all the revelations I can take for one night. I just want to go home and go to bed. I need to sleep on this before we go into the fact of why he didn't just tell me he knew me as a child. I don't understand why it was something he even thought he should keep from me.

I turn around and walk back toward the house. He's standing in the doorway, watching me. He steps aside to let me back in and I walk straight to the kitchen and open the refrigerator. I grab a bottle of water and open it, then take several gulps. My mouth is dry, as I never did get the water he said he was getting for me earlier.

I set the bottle down on the bar and look at him. "Take me home."

He doesn't object. He turns around and grabs his keys off the entryway table, then motions for me to follow him. I leave the water on the bar and silently follow him to the car. When I climb inside, he backs out of the driveway and pulls onto the road without speaking a word.

We pass my turnoff and it's apparent that he has no intention of taking me home. I glance over at him and his eyes are focused hard on the road in front of him. "Take me home," I say again.

He looks at me with a determined expression. "We need to talk, Sky. You have questions, I know you do."

I do. I have a million questions I need to ask, but I was hoping he would let me sleep on it so I could sort them out and try to answer as many of them as I could myself. But it's obvious he doesn't care what I prefer at this point. I reluctantly take off my seatbelt and turn in my seat, leaning with my back against the door to face him. If he doesn't want to give me time to let this soak in, I'll just lay all of my questions on him at once. But I'm making it fast because I want him to take me home.

"Fine," I say stubbornly. "Let's get this over with. Why have you been lying to me for two months? Why did my bracelet piss you off so much that you couldn't speak to me for weeks? Or why you didn't just say who you really thought I was the day we met at the grocery store? Because you knew, Holder. You knew who I was and for some reason you thought it would be funny to string me along until I figured it all out. Do you even *like* me? Was this game you've been playing worth hurting me more than I've ever been hurt in my life? Because that's what happened," I say, furious to the point that I'm shaking.

I finally give in to the tears because they're just one more thing that's trying to get out and I'm tired of fighting them. I wipe them away from my cheeks with the back of my hand and lower my voice. "You hurt me, Holder. So bad. You promised you would only ever be honest with me." I'm not raising my voice anymore. In fact, I'm talking so quietly that I'm not even sure he can hear me. He keeps staring at the road like the asshole that he is. I squeeze my eyes shut and fold my arms across my chest, then fall back into my seat. I stare out the passenger window and curse Karma. I curse Karma for bringing this hopeless boy into my life just so he could ruin it.

When he continues to drive without responding to a single word I've said, I can do nothing but let out a small, pathetic laugh. "You really are hopeless," I mutter.

Thirteen years earlier

"I need to pee," she giggles. We're crouched down under their porch, waiting for Dean to come find us. I like playing hide and seek, but I like to be the one hiding. I don't want them to know that I can't do the counting thing yet like they always ask me to do. Dean always tells me to count to twenty when they go hide, but I don't know how. So I just stand with my eyes closed and pretend I'm counting. Both of them are already in school and I can't go until next year, so I don't know how to count as good as they do.

"He's coming," she says, crawling backward a few feet. The dirt under the porch is cold, so I'm trying not to touch it with my hands like she is, but my legs are hurting.

"Les!" he yells. He walks closer to the porch and heads straight for the steps. We've been hiding a long time and he looks like he's tired of looking for us. He sits down on the steps, which are almost right in front of us. When I tilt my head, I can look right up at his face. "I'm tired of looking!"

I turn around and look at Lesslie to see if she's ready to run to base. She shakes her head no and holds her finger to her lips.

"Hope!" he yells, still sitting on the steps. "I give up!" He looks around the yard, then sighs quietly. He mumbles and kicks at the gravel under his foot and it makes me laugh. Lesslie punches me on the arm and tells me to be quiet.

He starts laughing, and at first I think it's because he hears us, but then I realize he's just talking to himself.

"Hope and Les," he says quietly. "Hopeless." He laughs again and stands up. "You hear that?" he yells, cupping his hands around his mouth. "The two of you are hopeless!"

Hearing him turn our names into a word makes Lesslie laugh and she crawls out from under the porch. I follow her and stand up as soon as Dean turns around and sees her. He smiles and looks at both of us, our knees covered in dirt, with cobwebs in our hair. He shakes his head and says it again. "Hopeless."

Saturday, October 27, 2012
11:20 p.m.

The memory is so vivid; I have no idea how it's just now coming to me. How I could see his tattoo day after day and hear him say Hope and how he talks about Les, yet still not remember. I reach over the seat and grab his arm, then pull his sleeve up. I know it's there. I know what it says. But this is the first time I'm looking at it, knowing what it actually means.

"Why did you get it?" He's told me before, but I want to know the real reason now. He pulls his gaze from the road and glances at me.

"I told you. It's a reminder of the people I've let down in my life."

I close my eyes and fall back into my seat, shaking my head. He said he doesn't do vague, but I can't think of an explanation more vague than the one he keeps giving me about his tattoo. How could he have let me down? The fact that he thinks he somehow let me down at that young an age doesn't even make sense. And the fact that he feels enough regret about it to turn it into some cryptic tattoo is really beyond any guesses I could fathom at this point. I don't know what else I can say or do to get him to take me back home. He didn't answer any of my questions and now he's playing his mind games again by giving me cryptic nonanswers. I just want to go home.

He pulls the car over and I'm hoping he's turning it around. Instead, he kills the ignition and opens his door. I look out the window and recognize that we're at the airport again. I'm annoyed. I don't want to come here and watch him stare at the stars again while he thinks. I want answers or I want to go home.

I swing open the door and reluctantly follow him to the fence, hoping if I appease him this one last time that I'll get a quick explanation from him. He helps me scale the fence again and we both walk back to our spots on the runway and lie down.

I look up in hopes of spotting a shooting star. I could really use a wish or two right now. I would wish I could go back to two months ago and never set foot in the grocery store that day.

"Are you ready for answers?" he says.

I turn my head toward his. "I'm ready if you're actually planning on being honest this time."

He faces me, then pulls up on his arm and rolls onto his side, looking down at me. He does his thing again, silently staring at me. It's darker than it was when we were out here the last time, so it's hard to make out the expression on his face. I can tell he's sad, though. His eyes have never been able to hide the sadness. He leans forward and lifts his hand, bringing it to my cheek. "I need to kiss you."

I almost break out into laughter, but I'm afraid if I do it will be the maniacal kind and that terrifies me, because I already assume I'm going crazy. I shake my head, shocked that he would even think I would let him kiss me right now. Not after finding out he's been lying to me for two solid months.

"No," I say forcefully. He keeps his face close to mine and his hand on my cheek. I hate that even though every ounce of anger in me is a result of his deceit, my body still responds to his touch. It's an odd internal battle when you can't decide if you want to punch the mouth sitting three inches in front of your face, or taste it.

"I need to kiss you," he says again, this time a desperate plea. "Please, Sky. I'm scared that after I tell you what I'm about to tell you . . . I'll never get to kiss you again." He pulls himself closer to me and strokes my cheek with his thumb, never taking his eyes off mine. *"Please."*

I nod slightly, unsure why my weakness is getting the best of me. He lowers his mouth to mine and kisses me. I close my eyes and allow him in, because a huge part of me is just as scared that this is the last time I'll feel his mouth against mine. I'm scared it's the last time I'll ever feel *anything*, because he's the only one I've ever wanted to feel anything with.

He adjusts himself until he's on his knees, holding on to my face with one hand and bracing his other hand on the concrete beside my head. I lift my hand and run it through his hair, pulling him to my mouth more urgently. Tasting him and feeling his breath as it mixes with mine momentarily takes everything about tonight and locks it away. In this moment, I'm focused on him and my heart and how it's swelling and breaking all at the same time. The thought that what I feel for him isn't even warranted or true is making me hurt. I hurt everywhere. In my head, in my gut, in my chest, in my heart, in my soul. Before, I felt like his kiss could cure me. Now his kiss feels like it's creating a terminal heartache deep within me.

He can sense my defeat taking over as the sobs start coming from my throat. He moves his lips to my cheek, then my ear. "I'm so sorry," he says, holding on to me. "I'm so sorry. I didn't want you to know."

I close my eyes and push him away from me, then sit up and take a deep breath. I wipe the tears away with the back of my hand and I pull my legs up, hugging them tightly. I bury my face in my knees so I don't have to look at him again.

"I just want you to talk, Holder. I asked you everything I could ever ask you on the way here. I need you to answer me now so I can just go home." My voice is defeated and done.

His hand moves to the back of my head and he drags his fingers through my hair, over and over again, while he works up a response. He clears his throat. "I wasn't sure if you were Hope the first time I saw you. I was so used to seeing her in every single stranger our age, I had given up trying to find her a few years ago. But when I saw you at the store and looked into your eyes . . . I had a feeling you really were her. When you showed me your ID and I realized you weren't, I felt ridiculous. It was like the wake-up call I needed to finally just let the memory of her go."

He stops talking and runs his hand slowly down my hair, resting it on my back, but tracing light circles with his finger. I want to push his hand away, but I want it right where it is even more.

"We lived next door to you and your dad for a year. You and me and Les . . . we were all best friends. It's so hard to remember faces from that long ago, though. I thought you were Hope, but I also thought that if you really were her, I wouldn't be doubting it. I thought if I ever saw her again, I'd know for sure.

"When I left the grocery store that day, I immediately looked up the name you gave me online. I couldn't find anything about you, not even on Facebook. I searched for an hour straight and became so frustrated that I went for a run to cool down. When I rounded the corner and saw you standing in front of my house, I couldn't breathe. You were just standing there, worn out and exhausted from running and . . . *Jesus*, Sky. You were so beautiful. I still wasn't sure if you were Hope or not, but at that point it wasn't even going through my mind. I didn't care *who* you were; I just needed to know you.

"After spending time with you that week, I couldn't stop myself from going to your house that Friday night. I didn't show up with the intention of digging up your past or even in the hope that something would happen between us. I went to your house because I wanted you to know the real me, not the me you had heard about from everyone else. After spending more time with you that night, I couldn't think of anything else besides figuring out how I could spend more time with you. I had never met anyone who got me the way you did. I still wondered if it was possible . . . if you were her. I was especially curious after you told me you were adopted, but again, I thought maybe it was a coincidence.

"But then when I saw the bracelet . . ." He stops talking and takes his hand off of my back. His fingers slide under my chin and he pulls my face away from my knees and makes me look him in the eyes. "My heart broke, Sky. I didn't want you to be her. I wanted you to tell me you got the bracelet from your friend or that you found it or you bought it. After all the years I spent searching for you in every single face I ever looked at, I finally found you . . . and I was devastated. I didn't want you to be Hope. I just wanted you to be you."

I shake my head, still just as confused as before. "But why didn't you just tell me? How hard would it have been to admit that we used to know each other? I don't understand why you've been lying about it."

He eyes me for a moment while he searches for a good enough response, then brushes hair away from my face. "What do you remember about your adoption?"

I shake my head. "Not a lot. I know I was in foster care after my father gave me up. I know Karen adopted me and we moved here from out of state when I was five. Other than that and a few odd memories, I don't know anything."

He squares his body up with mine and places both of his hands on my shoulders firmly, like he's getting frustrated. "That's all stuff Karen told you. I want to know what *you* remember. What do *you* remember, Sky?"

This time I shake my head slowly. "Nothing. The earliest memories I have are with Karen. The only thing I remember from before Karen was getting the bracelet, but that's only because I still have it and the memory stuck with me. I wasn't even sure who gave it to me."

Holder takes my face in his hands and lowers his lips to my forehead. He keeps his lips there, holding me against his mouth like he's afraid to pull away because he doesn't want to have to talk. He doesn't want to have to tell me whatever it is he knows.

"Just say it," I whisper. "Tell me what you're wishing you didn't have to tell me."

He pulls his mouth away and presses his forehead against

mine. His eyes are closed and he's got a firm grip on my face. He looks so sad and it makes me want to hold him despite my frustration with him. I reach my arms around him and I hug him. He hugs me back and pulls me onto his lap in the process. I wrap my legs around his waist and our foreheads are still meshed together. He's holding on to me, but this time it feels like he's holding on to me because his earth has been shifted off its axis, and I'm *his* core.

"Just tell me, Holder."

He runs his hand down to my lower back and he opens his eyes, pulling his forehead away from mine so he can look at me when he speaks.

"The day Les gave you that bracelet, you were crying. I remember every single detail like it happened yesterday. You were sitting in your yard against your house. Les and I sat with you for a long time, but you never stopped crying. After she gave you your bracelet she walked back to our house but I couldn't. I felt bad leaving you there, because I thought you might be mad at your dad again. You were always crying because of him and it made me hate him. I don't remember anything about the guy, other than I hated his guts for making you feel like you did. I was only six years old, so I never knew what to say to you when you cried. I think that day I said something like, 'Don't worry . . . '"

"He won't live forever," I say, finishing his sentence. "I remember that day. Les giving me the bracelet and you saying he won't live forever. Those are the two things I've remembered all this time. I just didn't know it was you."

"Yeah, that's what I said to you." He brings his hands to my cheeks and continues. "And then I did something I've regretted every single day of my life since."

I shake my head. "Holder, you didn't do anything. You just walked away."

"Exactly," he says. "I walked to my front yard even though I knew I should have sat back down in the grass beside you. I stood in my front yard and I watched you cry into your arms, when you should have been crying into mine. I just stood there . . . and I watched the car pull up to the curb. I watched the passenger window roll down and I heard someone call your name. I watched you look up at the car and wipe your eyes. You stood up and you dusted off your shorts, then you walked to the car. I watched you climb inside and I knew whatever was happening I shouldn't have just been standing there. But all I did was watch, when I should have been with you. It never would have happened if I had stayed right there with you."

The fear and regret in his voice is causing my heart to race against my chest. I somehow find strength to speak, despite the fear consuming me. "*What* never would have happened?"

He kisses me on the forehead again and his thumbs brush delicately over my cheekbones. He looks at me like he's scared he's about to break my heart.

"They took you. Whoever was in that car, they took you from your dad, from me, from Les. You've been missing for thirteen years, Hope."

Saturday, October 27, 2012
11:57 p.m.

One of the things I love about books is being able to define and condense certain portions of a character's life into chapters. It's intriguing, because you can't do this with real life. You can't just end a chapter, then skip the things you don't want to live through, only to open it up to a chapter that better suits your mood. Life can't be divided into chapters . . . only minutes. The events of your life are all crammed together one minute right after the other without any time lapses or blank pages or chapter breaks because no matter what happens life just keeps going and moving forward and words keep flowing and truths keep spewing whether you like it or not and life never lets you pause and just catch your fucking breath.

I need one of those chapter breaks. I just want to catch my breath, but I have no idea how.

"Say something," he says. I'm still sitting in his lap, wrapped around him. My head is pressed against his shoulder and my eyes are shut. He places his hand on the back of my head and lowers his mouth to my ear, holding me tighter. "*Please*. Say something."

I don't know what he wants me to say. Does he want me to act surprised? Shocked? Does he want me to cry? Does he want me to scream? I can't do any of those things because I'm still trying to wrap my mind around what he's saying.

"You've been missing for thirteen years, Hope."

His words repeat over and over in my mind like a broken record.

"Missing."

I'm hoping he means missing in a figurative sense, like maybe he's just missed me all these years. I doubt that's the case, though. I could see the look in his eyes when he said those words, and he didn't want to say them at all. He knew what it would do to me.

Maybe he really does mean missing in the literal sense, but he's just confused. We were both so young; he probably doesn't remember the sequence of events correctly. But the last two months flash before my eyes, and everything about him . . . all of his personalities and mood swings and cryptic words come into clear focus. Like the night he was standing in my doorway and said he'd been looking for me his whole damn life. He was being literal about that.

Or our first night sitting right here on this runway when he asked if I'd had a good life. He's worried for thirteen years about what happened to me. He was being very literal then, wanting to know if I was happy with where I ended up.

Or the day he refused to apologize for the way he acted in the cafeteria, explaining that he knew why it upset him but he just couldn't tell me yet. I didn't question it then, because he seemed sincere that he wanted to explain himself one day. Never in a million years could I have guessed why it upset him so much to see that bracelet on me. He didn't want me to be Hope because he knew the truth would break my heart.

He was right.

"You've been missing for thirteen years, Hope."

The last word of his sentence sends a shiver down my spine. I slowly lift my face away from his shoulder and look at him. "You called me Hope. Don't call me that. It's not my name."

He nods. "I'm sorry, Sky."

The last word of *that* sentence sends a shiver down my spine as well. I slide off of him and stand up. "Don't call me that, either," I say resolutely. I don't want to be called *Hope* or *Sky* or *Princess* or anything else that separates me from any other part of myself. I'm suddenly feeling like I'm completely different people, wrapped up into one. Someone who doesn't know who she is or where she belongs, and it's disturbing. I've never felt so isolated in my life; like there isn't a single person in this entire world I can trust. Not even myself. I can't even trust my own memories.

Holder stands up and takes my hands, looking down at me. He's watching me, waiting for me to react. He'll be disappointed because I'm not going to react. Not right here. Not right now. Part of me wants to cry while he wraps his arms around me and whispers, "Don't worry," into my ear. Part of me wants to scream and yell and hit him for deceiving me. Part of me wants to allow him to continue to blame himself for not stopping what he says happened thirteen years ago. Most of me just wants it all to go away, though. I want to go back to feeling nothing again. I miss the numbness.

I pull my hands from his and begin to walk toward the car. "I need a chapter break," I say, more to myself than to him.

He follows a step behind me. "I don't even know what that means." His voice sounds defeated and overwhelmed.

He grabs my arm to stop me, more than likely to ask how I'm feeling, but I jerk it away and spin around to face him again. I don't want him to ask me how I'm feeling, because I have no idea. I'm running through an entire gamut of feelings right now, some I've never even experienced before. Rage and fear and sadness and disbelief are building up inside me and I want it to stop. I just want to stop feeling everything that I'm feeling, so I reach up and grab his face and press my lips to his. I kiss him hard and fast, wanting him to react, but he doesn't. He doesn't kiss me back. He refuses to help make the pain go away like this, so my anger takes over and I separate my lips from his, then slap him.

He barely flinches and it infuriates me. I want him to hurt like I'm hurting. I want him to feel what his words just did to me. I slap him again and he allows it. When he still doesn't react, I push against his chest. I push him and shove him over and over—trying to give him back every ounce of pain he's just immersed into my soul. I ball my fists up and hit him in the chest and when that doesn't work, I start screaming and hitting him and trying to get out of his arms because they're wrapped around me now. He spins me around so that my back is against his chest and our arms are locked together, folded tightly across my stomach.

"Breathe," he whispers into my ear. "Calm down, Sky. I know you're confused and scared, but I'm here. I'm right here. Just breathe."

His voice is calm and comforting and I close my eyes and soak it in. He simulates a deep breath, moving his chest in rhythm with mine, forcing me to take a breath and follow his lead. I take several slow, deep breaths in time with his. When I've stopped struggling in his arms, he slowly turns me around and pulls me into his chest.

"I didn't want you to hurt like this," he whispers, cradling my head in his hands. "That's why I haven't told you."

I realize in this moment that I'm not even crying. I haven't cried at all since the truth passed his lips and I make it a point to refuse the tears that are demanding to be set free. Tears won't help me right now. They'll just make me weaker.

I place my palms on his chest and lightly push against him. I feel like I'm vulnerable to more tears when he holds me because he feels so comforting. I don't need anyone's comfort. I need to learn how to rely on myself to stay strong because I'm the only one I can trust—and I'm even skeptical about *my own* trustworthiness. Everything I thought I knew has been a lie. I don't know who's in on it or who knows the truth and I find myself without an ounce of trust left in my heart. Not for Holder, not for Karen . . . not even for myself, really.

I back a step away from him and look him in the eyes. "Were you ever going to tell me who I was?" I ask, glaring at him. "What if I never remembered? Would you have *ever* told me? Were you scared I would leave you and you'd never get your chance to screw me? Is that why you've been lying to me this whole time?"

His eyes are awash with offense the moment the words flow from my lips. "No. That's not how it was. That's not how it *is*. I haven't told you because I'm scared of what will happen to you. If I report it, they'll take you from Karen. They'll more than likely arrest her and send you back to live with your father until you turn eighteen. Do you want that to happen? You love Karen and you're happy here. I didn't want to mess that up for you."

I release a quick laugh and shake my head. His reasoning makes no sense. None of this makes any sense. "First of all," I say. "They wouldn't put Karen in jail because I can guarantee you she knows nothing about this. Second, I've been eighteen since September. If my age was the reason you weren't being honest, you would have told me by now."

He squeezes the back of his neck and looks down at the ground. I don't like the nervousness seeping from him right now. I can tell by the way he's reacting that he isn't finished with the confessions.

"Sky, there's so much I still need to explain to you." He brings his eyes back up to meet mine. "Your birthday wasn't in September. Your birthday is May 7. You don't even turn eighteen for six more months. And Karen?" He takes a step toward me, grabbing both of my hands. "She has to know, Sky. She *has* to. Think about it. Who else could have done this?"

I immediately pull my hands from his and back away. I know this has more than likely been torture for him, keeping this secret to himself. I can see in his eyes that it's agonizing for him having to tell me all of this. But I've been giving him the benefit of the doubt since the moment I met him, and any sorrow I felt for him has just been negated by the fact that he's now attempting to tell me that my own mother was somehow involved.

"Take me home," I demand. "I don't want to hear anything else. I don't want to know anything else tonight."

He tries to take my hands again, but I slap them away. "TAKE ME HOME!" I scream. I begin walking back to the car. I've heard enough. I need my mom. I just need to see her and hug her and know that I'm not completely alone in this, because that's exactly how I feel right now.

I reach the fence before Holder does and I try to pull myself up, but I can't. My hands and arms are trembling and weak. I'm still attempting it on my own when he quietly comes up behind me and hoists me up. I jump down over the other side and walk to the car.

He sits in the driver's seat and pulls his door shut, but doesn't start the car. He's staring at the steering wheel with his hand paused on the ignition. I watch his hands with mixed emotions, because I want them around me so bad. I want them holding me and rubbing my back and my hair while he tells me it'll all be okay. But I also look at his hands in disgust, thinking about all the intimate ways he's touched me and held me, knowing all along that he was deceiving me. How could he be with me, knowing what he knows, yet still allow me to believe the lies? I don't know how I can forgive him for that.

"I know it's a lot to take in," he says quietly. "I *know* it is. I'll take you home, but we need to talk about this tomorrow." He turns toward me, looking at me with hardened eyes. "Sky, you *cannot* talk to Karen about this. Do you understand? Not until the two of us figure it out."

I nod, just to appease him. He can't honestly expect me not to talk to her about this.

He turns his whole body toward mine in the seat and leans in, placing his hand on my headrest. "I'm serious, babe. I know you don't think she's capable of doing something like this, but until we find out more, you need to keep this to yourself. If you tell anyone, your entire life will change. Give yourself time to process everything. *Please.* Please promise me you'll wait until after tomorrow. After we talk again."

The terrified undertone in his words pierces my heart, and I nod again, but this time I actually mean it.

He watches me for several seconds, then slowly turns around and cranks the car, pulling onto the road. He drives me the four miles back to my home and nothing is spoken until he pulls into my driveway. My hand is on the door handle and I'm stepping out of the car when he takes my other hand.

"Wait," he says. I wait, but I don't turn back around. I keep one foot on the floorboard and one foot on the drive-way, facing the door. He moves his hand to the side of my head and brushes a strand of hair behind my ear. "Will you be okay tonight?"

I sigh at the simplicity of his question. *"How?"* I ease back against my seat and turn and face him. "How can I possibly be okay after tonight?"

He stares at me and continues to stroke the hair on the side of my head with his fingers. "It's killing me . . . letting you go like this. I don't want to leave you alone. Can I come back in an hour?"

I know he's asking if he can come through my window and lie with me, but I immediately shake my head no. "I can't," I say, my voice cracking. "It's too hard being around you right now. I just need to think. I'll see you tomorrow, okay?"

He nods and pulls his hand away from my cheek, then places it back on the steering wheel. He watches me as I step out of the car and walk away from him.

Sunday, October 28, 2012
12:37 a.m.

Stepping through the front door and into the living room, I'm hoping to be engulfed with a sense of comfort that I'm desperately in need of. The familiarity and sense of belonging in this house is something I need to calm me down so that I no longer feel like bursting into tears. This is my home where I live with Karen . . . a woman who loves me and would do anything for me, no matter what Holder may think.

I stand in the dark living room and wait for the feeling to envelop me, but it never does. I'm looking around with suspicion and doubt, and I hate that I'm observing my life from a completely different viewpoint right now.

I walk through the living room, pausing just outside Karen's bedroom door. I contemplate crawling into bed with her, but her light is out. I've never needed to be in her presence as much as I do in this moment, but I can't bring myself to open her bedroom door. Maybe I'm not ready to face her yet. Instead, I walk down the hallway to my bedroom.

The light in my room is peering out from the crack under the door. I put my hand on the doorknob and turn it, then slowly open the door. Karen is sitting on my bed. She looks up at me when she hears the door open and she immediately stands up.

"Where have you been?" She looks worried, but her voice has an edge of anger to it. Or maybe disappointment.

"With Holder. You never said what time I needed to be home."

She points to the bed. "Sit down. We need to talk."

Everything about her feels different now. I watch her guardedly. I feel like I'm going through false motions of being an obedient daughter while I nod. It's like I'm in a scene from a dramatic *Lifetime* movie. I walk over to the bed and sit, not sure what has her so riled up. I'm sort of hoping she found out everything that *I* found out tonight. It'll make it a hell of a lot easier when I tell her about it.

She takes a seat next to me and turns toward me. "You're not allowed to see him again," she says firmly.

I blink twice, mostly from shock at the subject matter. I wasn't expecting it to be about Holder. "What?" I say, confused. "Why?"

She reaches into her pocket and pulls out my cell phone. "What is this?" she says through gritted teeth.

I look at my phone being held tightly in her hands. She hits a button and holds up the screen to face me. "And what the hell kind of texts are these, Sky? They're awful. He says awful, vile things to you." She drops the phone onto the bed and reaches for my hands, grasping them. "Why would you allow yourself to be with someone who treats you this way? I raised you better than this."

She's no longer raising her voice. Now she's just playing the part of concerned mother.

I squeeze her hands in reassurance. I know I'll more than likely be in trouble for having the phone, but I need her to know that the texts aren't at all what she thinks they are. I actually feel a little silly that we're even having this conversation. When I compare this issue to the new issues I'm facing, it seems a little juvenile.

"Mom, he's not being serious. He sends me those texts as a joke."

She lets out a disheartened laugh and shakes her head in disagreement. "There's something off about him, Sky. I don't like how he looks at you. I don't like how he looks at *me*. And the fact that he bought you a phone without having any respect for my rules just goes to show you what kind of respect he holds for other people. Regardless of whether the texts are a joke, I don't trust him. I don't think you should trust him, either."

I stare at her. She's still talking, but the thoughts inside my head are becoming louder and louder, blocking out whatever words she's trying to drill into my brain. My palms instantly begin sweating and I can feel my heart pounding in my eardrums. All of her beliefs and choices and rules are flashing in my mind and I'm trying to separate them and put them into their own chapters, but they're all running together. I pull the first thought out of the pile of questions and just flat out ask her.

"Why can't I have a phone?" I whisper. I'm not even sure that I ask the question loud enough for her to hear me, but she stops moving her mouth so I'm pretty sure she heard me.

"And internet," I add. "Why don't you want me accessing the internet?"

The questions are becoming poison in my head and I feel like I have to get them out. It's all beginning to piece together and I'm hoping it's all coincidence. I'm hoping she's sheltered me my whole life because she loves me and wants to protect me. But deep down, it's quickly becoming apparent that I've been sheltered my whole life because she was *hiding* me.

"Why did you homeschool me?" I ask, my voice much louder this time.

Her eyes are wide and it's obvious she has no idea what is spurring these questions right now. She stands up and looks down at me. "You aren't turning this around on me, Sky. You live under my roof and you'll follow my rules." She grabs my phone off the bed and walks toward the door. "You're grounded. No more cell phones. No more boy-friend. We'll talk about this tomorrow."

She slams my door shut behind her and I immediately fall back onto the bed, feeling even more hopeless than before I walked through my front door.

I can't be right. It's just a coincidence, I *can't* be right. She wouldn't do something like this. I squeeze the tears back and refuse to believe it. There has to be some other explanation. Maybe Holder is confused. Maybe *Karen* is confused.

I know I'm confused.

I take off my dress and throw on a T-shirt, then turn out the light and crawl under the covers. I'm hoping I wake up tomorrow to realize this whole night was just a bad dream. If it's not, I don't know how much more I can take before my strength is completely diminished. I stare up at the stars, glowing above my head, and I begin counting them. I push everyone and everything else away and focus, focus, focus on the stars.

Thirteen years earlier

Dean walks back to his yard and he turns around and looks at me. I bury my head back into my arm and try to stop crying. I know they probably want to play hide and seek again before I have to go back inside, so I need to stop being sad so we can play.

"Hope!"

I look up at Dean and he isn't looking at me anymore. I thought he called my name, but he's looking at a car. It's parked in front of my house and the window is rolled down.

"Come here, Hope," the lady says. She's smiling and asking me to come to her window. I feel like I know her, but I can't remember her name. I stand up so I can go see what she wants. I wipe the dirt off my shorts and walk to the car. She's still smiling and she looks really nice. When I walk up to the car, she hits the button that unlocks the doors.

"Are you ready to go, sweetie? Your daddy wants us to hurry."

I didn't know I was supposed to go anywhere. Daddy didn't say we were going anywhere today.

"Where are we going?" I ask her.

She smiles and reaches over to the handle, then opens the door for me. "I'll tell you when we're on our way. Get in and put your seatbelt on, we can't be late."

She really doesn't want to be late to where we're going. I don't want her to be late, so I climb into the front seat and shut my door. She rolls up the window and starts driving away from my house.

She looks at me and smiles, then reaches into the backseat. She hands me a juice box, so I take it out of her hand and open the straw.

"I'm Karen," she says. "And you get to stay with me for a little while. I'll tell you all about it when we get there."

I take a sip from my juice. It's apple juice. I love apple juice.

"But what about my daddy? Is he coming, too?"

Karen shakes her head. "No, sweetie. It'll just be you and me when we get there."

I put the straw back in my mouth because I don't want her to see me smile. I don't want her to know that I'm happy my daddy isn't coming with us.

Sunday, October 28, 2012
2:45 a.m.

I sit up.

It was a dream.

It was just a dream.

I can feel my heart beating wildly in every facet of my body. It's beating so hard I can hear it. I'm panting for breath and covered in sweat.

It was just a dream.

I attempt to convince myself of just that. I want to believe with all my heart that the memory I just had wasn't a real one. It *can't* be.

But it was. I remember it clearly, like it happened yesterday. With every single memory I've recalled over the last few days, a new one pops up after it. Things I've either been repressing or was just too young to recall are coming back to me full force. Things I don't want to remember. Things I wish I never knew.

I throw the covers off me and reach over to the lamp, flipping the switch. The room fills with light and I scream at the realization that someone else is in my bed. As soon as the scream escapes my mouth, he wakes up and shoots straight up on the bed.

"What the hell are you doing here?" I whisper loudly.

Holder glances at his watch, then rubs his eyes with his palms. When he wakes up enough to respond, he places his hand on my knee. "I couldn't leave you. I just needed to make sure you were okay." He puts his hand on my neck, right below my ear, and brushes along my jaw with his thumb. "Your heart," he says, feeling my pulse beating against his fingertips. "You're scared."

Seeing him in my bed, caring for me like he is . . . I can't be mad at him. I can't blame him. Despite the fact that I want to be mad at him, I just can't. If he wasn't here right now to comfort me after the realization I just had, I don't know what I would do. He's done nothing but place blame on himself for every single thing that's ever happened to me. I'm beginning to accept the fact that maybe he needs comforting just as much as I do. For that, I allow him to steal another piece of my heart. I grab his hand that's touching my neck and I squeeze it.

"Holder . . . I remember." My voice shakes when I speak and I feel the tears wanting to come out. I swallow and push them back with everything that I have. He scoots closer to me on the bed and turns me to face him completely. He places both of his hands on my face and looks into my eyes.

"What do you remember?"

I shake my head, not wanting to say it. He doesn't let go of me. He coaxes me with his eyes, nodding his head slightly, assuring me that it's okay to say it. I whisper as quietly as possible, afraid to say it out loud. "It was Karen in that car. She did it. She's the one who took me."

Pain and recognition consume his features and he pulls me to his chest, wrapping his arms around me. "I know, babe," he says into my hair. "I know."

I cling to his shirt and hold on to him, wanting to swim in the comfort that his arms provide. I close my eyes, but only for a second. He's pushing me away as soon as Karen opens the door to my bedroom.

"Sky?"

I spin around on the bed and she's standing in the doorway, glaring at Holder. She cuts her eyes to me. "Sky? What . . . what are you doing?" Confusion and disappointment cloud her face.

I snap my gaze back to Holder. "Get me out of here," I say under my breath. "Please."

He nods, then walks to my closet. He opens the door as I stand up and grab a pair of jeans from my dresser and pull them on.

"Sky?" Karen says, watching both of us from the doorway. I don't look at her. I *can't* look at her. She takes a few steps into the bedroom just as Holder opens a duffel bag and lays it on the bed.

"Throw some clothes in here. I'll get what you need out of the bathroom." His tone of voice is calm and collected, which slightly eases the panic coursing through me. I walk to my closet and begin pulling shirts off of hangers.

"You aren't going anywhere with him. Are you insane?" Karen's voice is near panic, but I still don't look at her. I continue throwing clothes into my bag. I walk to the dresser and pull open the top drawer, taking a handful of socks and underwear. I walk to the bed and Karen cuts me off, placing her hands on my shoulders and forcing me to look at her.

"Sky," she says, dumbfounded. "What are you doing? What's wrong with you? You're not leaving with him."

Holder walks back into the bedroom with a handful

of toiletries and walks directly around Karen, piling them into the bag. "Karen, I suggest you let go of her," he says as calmly as a threat can possibly sound.

Karen scoffs and spins around to face him. "You are *not* taking her. If you so much as walk out of this house with her, I'm calling the police."

Holder doesn't respond. He looks at me and reaches out for the items in my hands, then turns and places them into the duffel bag, zipping it shut. "You ready?" he says, taking my hand.

I nod.

"This isn't a joke!" Karen yells. Tears are beginning to roll down her cheeks and she's frantic, looking back and forth between us. Seeing the pain on her face breaks my heart because she's my mother and I love her, but I can't ignore the anger and betrayal I feel over the last thirteen years of my life.

"I'll call the police," she yells. "You have no right to take her!"

I reach into Holder's pocket, then pull out his cell phone and take a step toward Karen. I look directly at her and as calmly as I can, I hold the phone out to her. "Here," I say. "Call them."

She looks down at the phone in my hands, then back up to me. "Why are you doing this, Sky?" She's overcome with tears now.

I grab her hand and shove the phone into it, but she refuses to grasp it. "Call them! Call the police, Mom! *Please*." I'm begging now. I'm begging her to call them—to prove me wrong. To prove that she has nothing to hide. To prove that *I'm* not what she's hiding. "Please," I say again quietly. Everything in my heart and soul wants her to take the phone and call them so I'll know I'm wrong.

She takes a step back at the same time she sucks in a breath. She begins to shake her head, and I'm almost positive she knows I know, but I don't stick around to find out. Holder grabs my hand and leads me to the open window. He lets me climb out first, then he climbs out behind me. I hear Karen crying my name, but I don't stop walking until I reach his car. We both climb inside and he drives away. Away from the only family I've ever really known.

Sunday, October 28, 2012
3:10 a.m.

"We can't stay here," he says, pulling up to his house. "Karen might come here looking for you. Let me run in and grab a few things and I'll be right back."

He leans across the seat and pulls my face toward his. He kisses me, then gets out of the car. The entire time he's inside his house, I'm leaning my head against the headrest, staring out the window. There isn't a single star in the sky to count tonight. Only lightning. It seems fitting for the night I've had.

Holder returns to the car several minutes later and throws his own bag into the backseat. His mother is standing in the entryway, watching him. He walks back to her and takes her face in his hands, just like he does mine. He says something to her, but I don't know what he's saying. She nods and hugs him. He walks back to the car and climbs inside.

"What did you tell her?"

He grabs my hand. "I told her you and your mother got into a fight, so I was taking you to one of your relatives' houses in Austin. I told her I'd stay with my dad for a few days and that I'd be back soon." He looks at me and smiles. "It's okay, she's used to me leaving, unfortunately. She's not worried."

I turn and look out my window when he pulls out of the

driveway, just as the rain begins to slap the windshield. "Are we really going to stay with your dad?"

"We'll go wherever you want to go. I doubt you want to go to Austin, though."

I look over at him. "Why wouldn't I want to go to Austin?"

He purses his lips and flips on the windshield wipers. He places his hand on my knee and brushes it with his thumb. "That's where you're from," he says quietly.

I look back out the window and sigh. There is so much I don't know. So much. I press my forehead against the cool glass and close my eyes, allowing the questions I've been suppressing all night to re-emerge.

"Is my dad still alive?" I ask.

"Yes, he is."

"What about my mom? Did she really die when I was three?"

He clears his throat. "Yes. She died in a car wreck a few months before we moved in next door to you."

"Does he still live in the same house?"

"Yes."

"I want to see it. I want to go there."

He doesn't immediately respond to this statement. Instead, he slowly inhales a breath and releases it. "I don't think that's a good idea."

I turn to him. "Why not? I probably belong there more than I do anywhere else. He needs to know I'm okay."

Holder pulls off to the side of the road and throws the car into park. He turns in his seat and looks at me dead-on. "Babe, it's not a good idea because you just found out about this a few hours ago. It's a lot to take in before you make any hasty decisions. If your dad sees you and recognizes you, Karen will go to prison. You need to think long and hard about that. Think about the media. Think about the reporters. Believe me, Sky. When you disappeared they camped out on our front lawn for months. The police interviewed me no less than twenty times over a two-month period. Your entire life is about to change, no matter what decision you make. But I want you to make the best decision for yourself. I'll answer any questions you have. I'll take you anywhere you want to go in a couple of days. If you want to see your dad, that's where we'll go. If you want to go to the police, that's where we'll go. If you want to just run away from everything, that's what we'll do. But for now, I just want you to let this soak in. This is your life. The rest of your *life*."

His words have tightened my chest like a vise. I don't know what I'm thinking. I don't know *if* I'm thinking. He's thought this through from so many angles and I have no clue what to do. I have no fucking clue.

I swing open the door and step out onto the shoulder of the highway, out into the rain. I pace back and forth, attempting to focus on something in order to hold the hyperventilating at bay. It's cold and the rain is no longer just falling; it's *pummeling*. Huge raindrops are stinging my skin and I can't keep my eyes open due to the force of them. As soon as Holder rounds the front of the car, I swiftly walk toward him and throw my arms around his neck, burying my face in his already soaked shirt. "I can't do this!" I yell over the sound of rain pounding the pavement. "I don't want this to be my life!"

He kisses the top of my head and bends down to talk

against my ear. "I don't want this to be your life, either," he says. "I'm so sorry. I'm so sorry I let this happen to you."

He slides a finger under my chin and pulls my gaze up to his. His height is shielding the rain from stinging my eyes, but the drops are sliding down his face, over his lips, and down his neck. His hair is soaked and matted to his forehead, so I wipe a strand out of his eyes. He already needs a trim again.

"Let's not let this be your life tonight," he says. "Let's get back in the car and pretend we're driving away because we *want* to . . . not because we *need* to. We can pretend I'm taking you somewhere amazing . . . somewhere you've always wanted to go. You can snuggle up to me and we can talk about how excited we are and we'll talk about everything we'll do when we get there. We can talk about the important stuff later. But tonight . . . let's not let this be your life."

I pull his mouth to mine and I kiss him. I kiss him for always having the perfect thing to say. I kiss him for always being there for me. I kiss him for supporting whatever decision I think I might need to make. I kiss him for being so patient with me while I figure everything out. I kiss him because I can't think of anything better than climbing back inside that car with him and talking about everything we'll do when we get to Hawaii.

I separate my mouth from his and somehow, in the midst of the worst day of my life, I find the strength to smile. "Thank you, Holder. *So* much. I couldn't do this without you."

He kisses me softly on the mouth again and smiles back at me. "Yes. You *could*."

Sunday, October 28, 2012
7:50 a.m.

His fingers have been slowly lacing through my hair. My head is resting in his lap and we've been driving for over four hours. He turned his phone off back in Waco after receiving pleading texts from Karen, using my phone, wanting him to bring me back home. The problem with that is, I don't even know where home is anymore.

As much as I love Karen I have no idea how to grasp what she did. There isn't a situation in the world that could ever make stealing a child okay, so I don't know that I'll ever want to go back to her. I plan on finding out as much information as I can about what happened before I make any decisions about how I need to handle this. I know the right thing to do would be to immediately call the police, but sometimes the right thing to do isn't always the best answer.

"I don't think we should stay at my father's house," Holder says. I assumed he thought I was sleeping, but it's obvious he knows I'm wide awake since he's talking to me. "We'll get a hotel for tonight and figure out what we need to do tomorrow. I didn't move out of his house on the best terms this summer, and we've got enough drama to deal with as it is."

I nod my head against his lap. "Whatever you want to do. I just know I need a bed, I'm exhausted. I have no idea how you're still awake." I sit up and stretch my arms out in front of me, just as Holder pulls his car into the parking lot of a hotel.

After he checks us in, he gives me the key to the room and leaves to go park the car and get our things. I slide the key card into the door and open it, then walk into the hotel room. There's only one bed, which I assumed he would request. We've slept in the same bed several times before so it would have been a lot more awkward had he requested separate beds.

He returns to the room several minutes later and sets our bags down. I rifle through mine, looking for something to sleep in. Unfortunately, I didn't bring any pajamas, so I grab a long T-shirt and some underwear.

"I need to take a shower." I grab the few toiletries I brought and carry them into the bathroom with me and take an extremely long shower. When I'm finished, I attempt to blow dry my hair but I'm too exhausted. I pull my hair up in a wet ponytail instead and brush my teeth. When I walk out of the bathroom, Holder is unpacking both of our bags and hanging our shirts in the closet. He glances at me and does a double take when he sees I'm only wearing a T-shirt and underwear. He eyes me, but only for a second before he glances away uncomfortably. He's trying to be respectful, considering the day I've had. I don't want him treating me like I'm fragile. If this were any other day, he'd be commenting on what I was wearing and his hands would be on my ass in two seconds flat. Instead, he turns his back to me and takes the last of his items out of his duffel bag.

"I'm going to take a quick shower," he says. "I filled up the ice bucket and grabbed a few drinks. I wasn't sure if you wanted soda or water, so I got both." He grabs a pair of boxer shorts and walks around me toward the bathroom, careful not to look at me. As he passes me, I grab his wrist. He stops and turns around, carefully looking me in the eyes and nowhere else.

"Can you do me a favor?"

"Of course, babe," he says sincerely.

I slide my hand through his, then bring it up to my mouth. I lightly kiss his palm, then rest it against my cheek. "I know you're worried about me. But if what's happening in my life is causing you to feel uncomfortable about being attracted to me to the point that you can't even look at me when I'm half-naked, it'll break my heart. You're the only person I have left, Holder. Please don't treat me differently."

He looks at me knowingly, then pulls his hand away from my cheek. His eyes drop to my lips, and a small grin plays at the corner of his mouth. "You're giving me the go-ahead to admit that I still want you, even though your life has turned to shit?"

I nod. "Knowing you still want me is more of a necessity now than it was *before* my life turned to shit."

He smiles, then drops his lips to mine, sweeping his hand across my waist and around to my lower back. His other hand is planted firmly on the back of my head, guiding it as he kisses me deeply. His kiss is exactly what I need right now. It's the only thing that could possibly feel good in a world full of nothing but bad.

"I really need to shower," he says between kisses. "But now that I have the go-ahead to still treat you the same?"

He grabs my ass and pulls me against him. "Don't fall asleep while I'm in there, because when I get out, I want to show you just how incredible I think you look right now."

"Good," I whisper against his mouth. He releases me, then walks to the bathroom. I lie down on the bed just as the water kicks on.

I attempt to watch TV for a while since I never have the opportunity, but nothing can hold my attention. It's been such a grueling twenty-four hours, the sun is already up and we haven't even gone to bed yet. I shut the blinds and curtains, then crawl back into bed and throw a pillow over my eyes. As soon as I begin to welcome sleep, I feel Holder crawl into bed behind me. He slides one arm under my pillow and one over my side. I can feel his warm chest pressed against my back and the strength of his arms around me. He slides his hands through mine and kisses me lightly on the back of the head.

"I live you," I whisper to him.

He kisses my head again and sighs into my hair. "I don't think I live you back anymore. I'm pretty sure I've moved beyond that. Actually, I'm positive I've moved beyond that, but I'm still not ready to say it to you. When I say it, I want it to be separate from this day. I don't want you to remember it like this."

I pull his hand to my mouth and kiss it softly. "Me, too."

And once again in my new world full of heartache and lies, this hopeless boy somehow finds a way to make me smile.

Sunday, October 28, 2012
5:15 p.m.

We sleep through breakfast and lunch. By the time afternoon hits and Holder walks in with food, I'm starving. It's
been over twenty-four hours since I've eaten anything. He
pulls two chairs up to the desk and takes the items and
drinks out of the sacks. He brought me the same thing I
requested after the art showing last night, but that we never
actually got around to ordering. I remove the lid from the
chocolate shake and down a huge drink, then take the wrapper off my burger. When I do, a small square piece of paper
falls out and lands on the table. I pick it up and read it.

*Just because you don't have a phone anymore and your
life is crazy dramatic, I still don't want your ego explod-
ing. You looked really homely in your T-shirt and panties. I really hope you buy yourself some footed pajamas
today so I don't have to look at your chicken legs again
all night.*

When I set the note down and look at him, he's grinning
at me. His dimples are so adorable; I actually lean over and
lick one this time.

"What was that?" he asks, laughing.

I take a bite of my burger and shrug. "I've been wanting
to do that since the day I saw you in the grocery store."

His smile turns smug and he leans back in his chair. "You wanted to lick my face the first time you saw me? Is that usually what you do when you're attracted to guys?"

I shake my head. "Not your face, your dimple. And no. You're the only guy I've ever had the urge to lick."

He smiles at me confidently. "Good. Because you're the only girl I've ever had the urge to love."

Holy shit. He didn't directly say he loves me, but hearing that word come out of his mouth makes my heart swell in my chest. I take a bite of my burger to hide my smile and let his sentence linger in the air. I'm not ready for it to leave just yet.

We both quietly finish our food. I stand up and clear off the table, then walk to the bed and slip my shoes on.

"Where you headed?" He's watching me tighten the laces on my shoes. I don't answer him right away because I'm not sure where it is I'm going. I just want to get out of this hotel room. When my shoelaces are tied, I stand up and walk to him, then wrap my arms around him.

"I want to go for a walk," I say. "And I want you to go with me. I'm ready to start asking questions."

He kisses my forehead, then reaches to the table and grabs the room key. "Then let's go." He reaches down and laces my fingers through his.

Our hotel isn't near any parks or walking trails, so instead we just head to the courtyard. There are several cabanas lining the pool, all of them empty. He leads me to one of them. We sit and I lean my head against his shoulder, looking out over the pool. It's October, but the weather is pretty mild. I pull my arms through the sleeves of my shirt and hug myself, snuggling against him.

"You want me to tell you what I remember?" he asks. "Or do you have specific questions?"

"Both. But I want to hear your story first."

His arm is draped over my shoulders. His fingers are stroking my upper arm and he kisses the side of my head. I don't care how many times he kisses me on the head; it always feels like a first.

"You have to understand how surreal this feels for me, Sky. I've thought about what happened to you every single day for the past thirteen years. And to think I've been living two miles away from you for seven of those years? I'm still having a hard time processing it myself. And now, finally having you here, telling you everything that happened . . ."

He sighs and I feel his head lean against the back of the chair. He pauses briefly, then continues. "After the car pulled away, I went into the house and told Les that you left with someone. She kept asking me who, but I didn't know. My mother was in the kitchen, so I went and told her. She didn't really pay any attention to me. She was cooking supper and we were just kids. She had learned to tune us out. Besides, I still wasn't sure anything had happened that wasn't supposed to happen, so I didn't sound panicked or anything. She told me to just go outside and play with Les. The way she was so nonchalant about it made me think everything was okay. Being six years old, I was positive adults knew everything, so I didn't say anything else about it. Les and I went outside to play and another couple of hours had passed by when your dad came outside, calling your name. As soon as I heard him call your name, I froze. I stopped in the middle of my yard and watched him standing on his porch, calling for you. It was that moment that I knew he had no idea you had left with someone. I knew I did something wrong."

"Holder," I interrupt. "You were just a little boy."

He ignores my comment and continues. "Your dad walked over to our yard and asked me if I knew where you were." He pauses and clears his throat. I wait patiently for him to continue, but it seems like he needs to gather his thoughts. Hearing him tell me what happened that day feels like he's telling me a story. It feels nothing like what he's saying is directly related to my life or to me.

"Sky, you have to understand something. I was scared of your father. I was barely six years old and knew I had just done something terribly wrong by leaving you alone. Now your police chief father is standing over me, his gun visible on his uniform. I panicked. I ran back into my house and ran straight to my bedroom and locked the door. He and my mother beat on the door for half an hour, but I was too scared to open it and admit to them that I knew what happened. My reaction worried both of them, so he immediately radioed for backup. When I heard the police cars pull up outside, I thought they were there for me. I still didn't understand what had happened to you. By the time my mother coaxed me out of the room, three hours had already passed since you left in the car."

He's still rubbing my shoulder, but his grip is tighter on me now. I push my arms through the sleeves of my shirt so I can take his hand and hold it.

"I was taken to the station and questioned for hours. They wanted to know if I knew the license plate number, what kind of car took you, what the person looked like, what they said to you. Sky, I didn't know *anything*. I couldn't even remember the color of the car. All I could tell them was exactly what you were wearing, because you were the only thing I could picture in my head. Your dad was furious with me. I could hear him yelling in the hallway of the station that if I had just told someone right when it happened, they would have been able to find you. He blamed me. When a police officer blames you for losing his daughter, you tend to believe he knows what he's talking about. Les heard him yelling, too, so she thought it was all my fault. For days, she wouldn't even talk to me. Both of us were trying to understand what had happened. For six years we lived in this perfect world where adults are always right and bad things don't happen to good people. Then, in the span of a minute, you were taken and everything we thought we knew turned out to be this false image of life that our parents had built for us. We realized that day that even adults do horrible things. Children disappear. Best friends get taken from you and you have no idea if they're even alive anymore.

"We watched the news constantly, waiting for reports. For weeks they would show your picture on TV, asking for leads. The most recent picture they had of you was from right before your mother died, when you were only three. I remember that pissing me off, wondering how almost two years could have gone by without someone having taken a more recent picture. They would show pictures of your house and would sometimes show our house, too. Every now and then, they would mention the boy next door who saw it happen, but couldn't remember any details. I remember one night . . . the last night my mother allowed us to watch the coverage on TV . . . one of the reporters showed a panned-out image of both our houses. They mentioned the only witness, but referred to me as '*The boy who lost Hope.*' It infuriated my mother so bad; she ran outside and began screaming at the reporters, yelling at them to leave us alone. To leave *me* alone. My dad had to drag her back into the house.

"My parents did their best to try to make our life as normal as possible. After a couple of months, the reporters stopped showing up. The endless trips to the police station for more questioning finally stopped. Things began to slowly return to normal for everyone in the neighborhood. Everyone but Les and me. It was like all of our hope was taken right along with our Hope."

Hearing his words and the desolation in his voice causes me nothing but guilt. One would think what happened to me would have been so traumatic that it would have affected me more than the people around me. However, I can barely even remember it. It was such an uneventful occurrence in my life, yet it practically ruined him and Lesslie. Karen was so calm and pleasant, and filled my head with lies about a life of adoption and foster care, that I never thought to even question it. Like Holder said, at such a young age you believe that adults are all so honest and truthful, you never even think to question them.

"I've spent so many years hating my father for giving up on me," I say quietly. "I can't believe she just took me from him. How could she do that? How could *anyone* do that?"

"I don't know, babe."

I sit up straight, then turn around to look him in the eyes. "I need to see the house," I say. "I want more memories, but I don't have any and right now it's hard. I can barely remember anything, much less him. I just want to drive by. I need to see it."

He rubs my arm and nods. "Right now?"

"Yes. I want to go before it gets dark."

The entire drive, I'm absolutely silent. My throat is dry and my stomach is in knots. I'm scared. I'm scared to see the house. I'm scared he might be home and I'm scared I might see him. I don't really want to see him yet; I just want to see the place that was my first home. I don't know if it will help me remember but I know it's something I have to do.

He slows the car down and pulls over to the curb. I'm looking at the row of houses across the street, scared to pull my gaze from my window because it's so hard to turn and look.

"We're here," he says quietly. "It doesn't look like anyone's home."

I slowly turn my head and look out his window at the first home I ever lived in. It's late and the day is being swallowed by night, but the sky is still bright enough that I can clearly make out the house. It looks familiar, but seeing it doesn't immediately bring back any memories. The house is tan with a dark brown trim, but the colors don't look familiar at all. As if Holder can read my mind, he says, "It used to be white."

I turn in my seat and face the house, trying to remember something. I try to visualize walking through the front door and seeing the living room, but I can't. It's like everything about that house and that life has been erased from my mind somehow.

"How can I remember what your living room and kitchen look like, but I can't remember my own?"

He doesn't answer me, because he more than likely knows I'm not really looking for an answer. He just places his hand on top of mine and holds it there while we stare at the houses that changed the paths of our lives forever.

Thirteen years earlier

"Is your daddy giving you a birthday party?" Lesslie asks.

I shake my head. "I don't have birthday parties."

Lesslie frowns, then sits down on my bed and picks up the unwrapped box lying on my pillow. "Is this your birthday present?" she asks.

I take the box out of her hands and set it back on my pillow. "No. My daddy buys me presents all the time."

"Are you going to open it?" she asks.

I shake my head again. "No. I don't want to."

She folds her hands in her lap and sighs, then looks around the room. "You have a lot of toys. Why don't we ever come here and play? We always go to my house and it's boring there."

I sit on the floor and grab my shoes to put them on. I don't tell her I hate my room. I don't tell her I hate my house. I don't tell her we always go to her house because I feel safer over there. I take my shoelaces between my fingers and scoot closer to her on the bed. "Can you tie these?"

She grabs my foot and puts it on her knee. "Hope, you need to learn how to tie your own shoes. Me and Dean knew how to tie our shoes when we were five." She scoots down on the floor and sits in front of me.

"Watch me," she says. "You see this string? Hold it out like this." She puts the strings in my hands and shows me how to wrap it and pull it until it ties like it's supposed to.

When she helps me tie both of them two times, she unties them and tells me to do it again by myself. I try to remember how she showed me to tie them. She stands up and walks to my dresser while I do my very best to loop the shoestring.

"Was this your mom?" she says, holding up a picture. I look at the picture in her hands, then look down at my shoes again.

"Yeah."

"Do you miss her?" she asks.

I nod and keep trying to tie my shoelaces and not think about how much I miss her. I miss her so much.

"Hope, you did it!" Lesslie squeals. She sits back down on the floor in front of me and hugs me. "You did it all by yourself. You know how to tie your shoes now."

I look down at my shoes and smile.

Sunday, October 28, 2012
7:10 p.m.

"Lesslie taught me how to tie my shoelaces," I say quietly, still staring at the house.

Holder looks at me and smiles. "You remember her teaching you that?"

"Yeah."

"She was so proud of that," he says, turning his gaze back across the street.

I place my hand on the door handle and open it, then step out. The air is growing colder now, so I reach back into the front seat and grab my hoodie, then slip it on over my head.

"What are you doing?" Holder says.

I know he won't understand and I really don't want him to try to talk me out of it, so I shut the door and cross the street without answering him. He's right behind me, calling my name when I step onto the grass. "I need to see my room, Holder." I continue walking, somehow knowing exactly which side of the house to walk to without having any actual concrete memories of the layout of the house.

"Sky, you can't. No one's here. It's too risky."

I speed up until I'm running. I'm doing this whether he gives me his approval or not. When I reach the window that I'm somehow certain leads to what used to be my bedroom, I turn and look at him. "I need to do this. There are things of my mother's that I want in there, Holder. I know you don't want me to do this, but I need to."

He places his hands on my shoulders and his eyes are concerned. "You can't just break in, Sky. He's a cop. What are you gonna do, bust out the damn window?"

"This house is technically still my home. It's not really breaking in," I reply. He does raise a good point, though. How am I supposed to get inside? I purse my lips and think, then snap my fingers. "The birdhouse! There's a birdhouse on the back porch with a key in it."

I turn and run to the backyard; shocked when I see there actually is a birdhouse. I reach my fingers inside and sure enough, there's a key. The mind is a crazy thing.

"Sky, don't." He's practically begging me not to go through with this.

"I'm going in alone," I say. "You know where my bedroom is. Wait outside the window and let me know if you see anyone pull up."

He sighs heavily, then grabs my arm as soon as I insert the key into the back door. "Please don't make it obvious you were here. And hurry," he says. He pulls me in for a hug, then waits for me to walk inside. I turn the key and check to see if it unlocks the door.

The doorknob turns.

I walk inside and shut the door behind me. The house is dark and sort of eerie. I turn left and walk through the kitchen, somehow knowing exactly where the door to my bedroom is. I'm holding my breath and trying not to think about the seriousness or implications of what I'm doing. The thought of getting caught is terrifying, because I'm still not sure if I even want to be found. I do what Holder says and walk carefully, not wanting to leave any evidence behind that I was here. When I reach my door, I take a deep breath and place my hand on the doorknob, then slowly turn it. When the door opens and the room becomes visible, I flip on the light to get a better look at it.

Other than a few boxes piled into the corner, everything looks familiar. It still looks like a small child's room, untouched for thirteen years. It makes me think of seeing Lesslie's room and how no one has touched it since she died. It must be hard to move past the physical reminders of people you love.

I run my fingers across the dresser and leave a line in the dust. Seeing the trace of my finger quickly reminds me that I'm not wanting to leave evidence of my being here, so I lift my hand and bring it down to my side, then wipe away the trail with my shirt.

The picture of my biological mother isn't on the dresser where I remember it being. I look around the room, hoping to find something of hers that I can take with me. I have no memories of her, so a picture is more than I could ever ask for. I just want something to tie me to her. I need to see what she looks like and hope it will give me any memories at all that I can hold on to.

I walk over to the bed and sit down. The theme in the room is the sky, which is ironic, considering the name Karen gave me. There are clouds and moons on the curtains and walls, and the comforter is covered in stars. There are stars everywhere. The big plastic kind that stick to walls and ceilings and glow in the dark. The room is covered in them, just like the stars that are on my ceiling back at Karen's house. I remember begging Karen for them when I saw them at the store a few years ago. She thought they were childish, but I had to have them. I wasn't even sure why I wanted them so bad, but now it's becoming clear. I must have loved stars when I was Hope.

The nervousness already planted in my stomach intensifies when I lie back on the pillow and look up at the ceiling. A familiar wave of fear washes over me, and I turn to look at the bedroom door. It's the exact same doorknob I was praying wouldn't turn in the nightmare I had the other night.

I suck in a breath and squeeze my eyes shut, wanting the memory to go away. I've somehow locked it away for thirteen years, but being here on this bed . . . I can't lock it away anymore. The memory grabs hold of me like a web, and I can't break out of it. A warm tear trickles down my face and I wish I had listened to Holder. I should never have come back here. If I had never come back, I never would have remembered.

Thirteen years earlier

I used to hold my breath and hope he would think I was sleeping. It doesn't work, because he doesn't care if I'm sleeping or not. One time I tried to hold my breath and hoped he would think I was dead. That didn't work either, because he never even noticed I was holding my breath.

The doorknob turns and I'm all out of tricks right now and I try to think of another one really fast but I can't. He closes the door behind him and I hear his footsteps coming closer. He sits down beside me on my bed and I hold my breath anyway. Not because I think it'll work this time, but because it helps me not feel how scared I am.

"Hey, Princess," he says, tucking my hair behind my ear. "I got you a present."

I squeeze my eyes shut because I do want a present. I love presents and he always buys me the best presents because he loves me. But I hate it when he brings the presents to me at nighttime, because I never get them right away. He always makes me tell him thank you first.

I don't want this present. I don't.

"Princess?"

My daddy's voice always makes my tummy hurt. He always talks to me so sweet and it makes me miss my mommy. I don't remember what her voice sounded like, but daddy said it sounded like mine. Daddy also says that mommy would be sad if I stopped taking his presents because she's not here to take his presents anymore. This makes me sad and I feel really bad, so I roll over and look up at him.

"Can I have my present tomorrow, Daddy?" I don't want to make him sad, but I don't want that box tonight. I don't.

Daddy smiles at me and brushes my hair back. "Sure you can have it tomorrow. But don't you want to thank Daddy for buying it for you?"

My heart starts to beat really loud and I hate it when my heart does that. I don't like the way my heart feels and I don't like the scary feeling in my stomach. I stop looking at my daddy and I look up at the stars instead, hoping I can think about how pretty they are. If I keep thinking about the stars and the sky, maybe it will help my heart to stop beating so fast and my tummy to stop hurting so much.

I try to count them, but I keep stopping at number five. I can't remember what number comes after five, so I have to start over. I have to count the stars over and over and only five at a time because I don't want to feel my daddy right now. I don't want to feel him or smell him or hear him and I have to count them and count them and count them and count them until I don't feel him or hear him or smell him anymore.

Then when my daddy finally stops making me thank him, he pulls my nightgown back down and whispers, "Goodnight, Princess." I roll over and pull the covers over my head and squeeze my eyes shut and I try not to cry again but I do. I cry like I do every time Daddy brings me a present at night.

I hate getting presents.

I stand up and look down at the bed, holding my breath in fear of the sounds that are escalating from deep within my throat.

I will not cry.

I will not cry.

Slowly sinking to my knees, I place my hands on the edge of the bed and run my fingers over the yellow stars poured across the deep blue background of the comforter. I stare at the stars until they begin to blur from the tears that are clouding my vision.

I squeeze my eyes shut and bury my head into the bed, grabbing fistfuls of the blanket. My shoulders begin to shake as the sobs I've been trying to contain violently break out of me. With one swift movement, I stand up, scream, and rip the blanket off the bed, throwing it across the room.

I ball my fists and frantically look around for something else to throw. I grab the pillows off the bed and chuck them at the reflection in the mirror of the girl I no longer know. I watch as the girl in the mirror stares back at me, sobbing pathetically. The weakness in her tears infuriates me. We begin to run toward each other until our fists collide against the glass, smashing the mirror. I watch as she falls into a million shiny pieces onto the carpet.

I grip the edges of the dresser and push it sideways, letting out another scream that has been pent up for way too long. When the dresser comes to rest on its back, I rip open the drawers and throw the contents across the room, spinning and throwing and kicking at everything in my path. I grab at the sheer blue curtain panels and yank them until the rod snaps and the curtains fall around me. I reach over to the boxes piled high in the corner and, without even knowing what's inside, I take the top one and throw it against the wall with as much force as my five-foot, three-inch frame can muster.

"I hate you!" I cry. "I hate you, I hate you, I hate you!"

I'm throwing whatever I can find in front of me at whatever else I can find in front of me. Every time I open my mouth to scream, I taste the salt from the tears that are streaming down my cheeks.

Holder's arms suddenly engulf me from behind and grip me so tightly I become immobile. I jerk and toss and scream some more until my actions are no longer thought out. They're just reactions.

"Stop," he says calmly against my ear, unwilling to release me. I hear him, but I pretend not to. Or I just don't care. I continue to struggle against his grasp but he only tightens his grip.

"Don't touch me!" I yell at the top of my lungs, clawing at his arms. Again, it doesn't faze him.

Don't touch me. Please, please, please.

The small voice echoes in my mind, and I immediately become limp in his arms. I become weaker, as my tears grow stronger, consuming me. I become nothing more than a vessel for the tears that won't stop shedding.

I am weak, and I'm letting *him* win.

Holder loosens his grip around me and places his hands on my shoulders, then turns me around to face him. I can't even look at him. I melt against his chest from exhaustion and defeat, taking in fistfuls of his shirt as I sob, my cheek pressed against his heart. He places his hand on the back of my head and lowers his mouth to my ear.

"Sky." His voice is steady and unaffected. "You need to leave. Now."

I can't move. My body is shaking so hard, I'm afraid my legs won't move, even if I will them to. As if he knows this, he scoops me up in his arms and walks me out of the bedroom. He carries me across the street and places me in the passenger seat. He takes my hand and looks at it, then grabs his jacket out of the backseat. "Here, use that to wipe off the blood. I'm going back inside to straighten up what I can." The door shuts and he sprints back across the street. I look down at my hand, surprised that I'm cut. I can't even feel it. I wrap my hand up in the sleeve of his jacket, then pull my knees up into the seat and hug them while I cry.

I don't look at him when he gets back into the car. My whole body is shaking from the sobs that are still pouring out of me. He cranks the car and pulls away, then reaches across the seat and places his hand on the back of my head, stroking my hair in silence the entire way back to the hotel.

He helps me out of the car and walks me back to the hotel room, never once asking me if I'm okay. He knows I'm not; there's really no point in even asking. When the hotel room door closes behind us, he walks me to the bed and I sit. He pushes my shoulders back until I'm flat on the bed and he slips off my shoes. He walks to the bathroom, then comes back with a wet rag and picks up my hand, wiping it clean. He checks it for shards of glass, then gently lifts my hand to his mouth and kisses it.

"It's just a few scratches," he says. "Nothing too deep." He adjusts me onto the pillow and slips his own shoes off, then climbs onto the bed beside me. He pulls the blanket over us and pulls me to him, tucking my head against his chest. He holds me and never once asks me why I'm crying. Just like he used to do when we were kids.

I try to get the images out of my head of what I remember happening to me at night in my room, but they won't go away. How any father could do that to his little girl . . . it's beyond my comprehension. I tell myself that it never happened, that I'm imagining it, but every part of me knows it did happen. Every part of me that remembers why I was happy to get into that car with Karen. Every part of me that remembers all the nights I've made out with guys in my bed, never feeling a single thing while looking up at the stars. Every part of me that broke out into a full-blown panic attack the night Holder and I almost had sex. Every single part of me remembers, and I would do anything just to forget. I don't want to remember how my father sounded or felt at night, but with each passing second the memories become more and more vivid, only making it harder for me to stop crying.

Holder is kissing me on the side of my head, telling me again how it'll be okay, that I shouldn't worry. But he has no idea. He has no idea how much I remember and what it's doing to my heart and my soul and my mind and to my faith in humanity as a whole.

To know that those things were done to me at the hands of the only adult I had in my life—it's no wonder I've blocked everything out. I hold barely any memories of the day I was taken by Karen, and now I know why. It didn't feel like I was in the middle of a calamitous event the moment she stole me away from my life. To a little girl who was terrified of her life, I'm sure it felt more like Karen was rescuing me.

I lift my gaze to Holder's and he's looking down at me. He's hurting for me; I can see it in his eyes. He wipes away my tears with his finger and kisses me softly on the lips. "I'm sorry. I should have never let you go inside."

He's blaming himself again. He always feels like he's done something terrible, when I feel like he's been nothing short of my hero. He's been with me through all of this, steadily carrying me through my panic attacks and freak-outs until I'm calm. He's done nothing but be there for me, yet he still feels like this is somehow his fault.

"Holder, you didn't do anything wrong. Stop apologizing," I say through my tears. He shakes his head and tucks a loose strand of hair behind my ear.

"I shouldn't have taken you there. It's too much for you to deal with after just finding everything out."

I lift up on my elbow and look at him. "It wasn't just being there that was too much. It was what I remembered that was too much. You have no control over the things my father did to me. Stop placing blame on yourself for everything bad that happens to the people around you."

He slides his hand up and through my hair with a worried look on his face. "What are you talking about? What things did he do to you?" The words are so hesitant to come out of his mouth because he more than likely knows. I think we've both known what happened to me as a child, we've just been in denial.

I drop my arm and rest my head on his chest and don't answer him. My tears come back full force and he wraps one arm tightly around my back and grips the back of my head with his other. He presses his cheek to the top of my head. "No, Sky," he whispers. "No," he says again, not wanting to believe what I'm not even saying. I grab fistfuls of his shirt and just cry while he holds me with such conviction that it makes me love him for hating my father just as much as I do.

He kisses the top of my head and continues to hold me. He doesn't tell me he's sorry or ask how he can fix it because we both know we're at a loss. Neither of us knows what to do next. All I know at this point is that I have nowhere to go. I can't go back to the father who has rightful custody over me. I can't go back to the woman who wrongfully took me. And with light shed on my past it turns out I'm still underage, so I can't even rely on myself. Holder is the only thing about my life that hasn't left me completely hopeless.

And even though I feel protected wrapped up in his arms, the images and memories won't escape my head and no matter what I do or how hard I try, I can't stop crying. He's quietly holding me and I can't stop thinking about the fact that I need it to stop. I need Holder to take all of these emotions and feelings away for a little while because I can't take it. I don't like remembering what happened all those nights my father came into my room. I hate him. With every ounce of my being, I hate that man for stealing that first away from me.

I lift up and scoot my face closer to Holder, leaning over him. He places his hand on the side of my head and his eyes search mine, wanting to know if I'm okay.

I'm not.

I slide my body on top of his and kiss him, wanting him to take away the feelings. I'd rather feel nothing at all than the hatred and sadness consuming me right now. I grab Holder's shirt and try to lift it over his head, but he pushes me off him and onto my back. He lifts up on his arm and looks down at me.

"What are you doing?" he asks.

I slide my hand behind his neck and pull his face to mine, pressing my lips back to his. If I just kiss him enough, he'll relent and kiss me back. Then it'll all go away.

He places his hand on my cheek and kisses me back momentarily. I let go of his head and start to pull off my shirt, but he pulls my hands away and brings my shirt back down. "Stop it. Why are you doing this?"

His eyes are full of confusion and concern. I can't answer his question about why I'm doing this, because I'm not even sure. I know I just want the feeling to go away, but it's more than that. It's so much more than that, because I know if he doesn't take away what that man did to me right now, I feel like I'll never be able to laugh or smile or breathe again.

I just need Holder to take it away.

I inhale a deep breath and look him directly in the eyes. "Have sex with me."

His expression is unyielding and he's staring at me hard now. He pushes up from the bed and stands up, then paces the floor. He runs his hands through his hair nervously and walks back toward the bed, standing at the edge of it.

"Sky, I can't do this. I don't know why you're even asking for this right now."

I sit up in the bed, suddenly scared that he won't go through with it. I scoot to the edge of the bed where he's standing and I sit up on my knees, grasping his shirt. "Please," I beg. "Please, Holder. I need this."

He pulls my hands from his shirt and takes two steps back. He shakes his head, still completely confused. "I'm not doing this, Sky. *We're* not doing this. You're in shock or something . . . I don't know. I don't even know what to say right now."

I sink back down onto the bed in defeat. The tears start flowing again and I look up at him in complete desperation.

"*Please.*" I drop my gaze to my hands and fold them together in my lap, unable to look him in the eyes when I speak. "Holder . . . he's the only one that's ever done that to me." I slowly raise my eyes back up to meet his. "I need you to take that away from him. *Please.*"

If words could break souls, my words just broke his in two. His face drops and tears fill his eyes. I know what I'm asking him to do and I hate that I'm asking him for this, but I need it. I need to do whatever I can to minimize the pain and the hatred in me. "*Please*, Holder."

He doesn't want our first time to be this way. I wish it wasn't, but sometimes factors other than love make these decisions *for* you. Factors like hate. Sometimes in order to get rid of the hate, you become desperate. He knows hate and he knows pain and right now he knows how much I need this, whether he agrees with it or not.

He walks back to the bed and sinks to his knees on the floor in front of me, bringing himself to my eye level. He grabs my waist and scoots me to the edge of the bed, then slides his hands behind my knees and wraps my legs around him. He pulls my shirt over my head, never once looking away from my eyes. When my shirt is off, he pulls his own shirt off. He wraps his arms around me and stands up, picking me up with him and walking to the side of the bed. He lays me down gently and lowers himself on top of me, then places his palms against the mattress on either side of my head, looking down at me with uncertainty. His finger brushes a tear away that's sliding down my temple. "Okay," he says assuredly, despite his contrasting eyes.

He lifts up onto his knees and reaches to his wallet on the nightstand. He takes a condom out, then removes his pants, never once taking his eyes off mine. He's watching me like he's waiting for any signs that I've changed my mind. Or maybe he's watching me like he is because he's afraid I'm about to have another panic attack. I'm not even sure that I won't, but I have to do this. I can't let my father own this part of me for one more second.

Holder's fingers grasp the button on my jeans and he unbuttons them, then slides them off me. I shift my gaze to the ceiling, feeling myself slip further and further away with every step closer he gets.

I wonder if I'm ruined. I wonder if I'll ever be able to find pleasure in being with him in this way.

He doesn't ask if I'm sure this is what I want. He knows I'm sure, so the question remains unspoken. He lowers his lips to mine and kisses me while he removes my bra and underwear. I'm glad he's kissing me, because it gives me an excuse to close my eyes. I don't like the way he's looking at me . . . like he wishes he were anywhere else right now than here with me. I keep my eyes closed when his lips separate from mine in order for him to put on the condom. When he's back on top of me, I pull him against me, wanting him to do this before he changes his mind.

"Sky."

I open my eyes and see doubt in his expression, so I shake my head. "No, don't think about it. Just do it, Holder."

He closes his eyes and buries his head in my neck, unable to look at me. "I just don't know how to deal with all of this. I don't know if this is wrong or if it's what you really need. I'm scared if I do this, I'll make it even harder for you."

His words cut to my heart, because I know exactly what he means. I don't know if this is what I need. I don't know if it'll ruin things between us. But right now I'm so desperate to take this one thing away from my father—I'd risk it all. My arms that are wrapped tightly around him begin to shake, and I cry. He keeps his head buried in my neck and cradles my face in his hand, but as soon as he hears my tears, I can feel him attempting to hold back his own. The fact that this is causing him just as much distress lets me know that he understands. I tuck my head into his neck and lift myself against him, silently pleading with him to just do what I'm asking.

He does. He positions himself against me, kisses me on the side of the head, then slowly enters me.

I don't make a sound, despite the pain.

I don't even breathe, despite my need for air.

I don't even think about what's going on between us right now, because I'm not thinking at all. I'm picturing the stars on my ceiling and I'm wondering if I just tear the damn things off the ceiling if I'll never have to count them again.

I'm successfully able to keep myself separated from what he's doing until he abruptly stills himself on top of me, his head still buried tightly against my neck. He's breathing heavily and, after a moment, he sighs and separates himself from me completely. He looks down at me and closes his eyes, then rolls away from me, sitting up on the edge of the bed with his back to me.

"I can't do it," he says. "It feels wrong, Sky. It feels wrong because you feel so good but I'm regretting every single fucking second of it." He stands up and pulls his pants on, then grabs his shirt and the room key from the dresser. He never looks back at me as he exits the hotel room without another word.

I immediately crawl off the bed and get in the shower because I feel dirty. I feel guilty for having him do what he just did and I'm hoping the shower will somehow wash away that guilt. I scrub every inch of my body with soap until my skin hurts, but it doesn't help. I've successfully taken another intimate moment and ruined it for him. I could see the shame in his face when he left. When he walked out the door, refusing to look at me.

I turn off the water and step out of the shower. After I dry off, I grab the robe from the back of the bathroom door and put it on. I brush out my hair and place my toiletries back into my cosmetic bag. I don't want to leave without telling Holder, but I can't stay here. I also don't want him to feel like he has to face me again after what just happened. I can call a cab to take me to the bus station and be gone before he comes back.

If he's planning on even coming back.

I open the bathroom door and step out into the hotel

room, not expecting him to be sitting on the bed with his hands clasped between his knees. He darts his eyes up to mine as soon as he sees the bathroom door open. I pause midstep and stare back at him. His eyes are red and he's got a makeshift bandage made out of his T-shirt wrapped around his hand and covered in blood. I rush to him and take his hand, unwrapping the shirt to inspect it.

"Holder, what'd you do?" I twist his hand back and forth and take in the gash across his knuckles. He pulls his hand away and rewraps it with the piece of T-shirt.

"I'm fine," he says, brushing it off. He stands up and I take a step back, expecting him to walk out the door again. Instead, he stays directly in front of me, looking down at me.

"I'm so sorry," I whisper, looking up at him. "I shouldn't have asked you to do that. I just needed—"

He grabs my face and presses his lips to mine, cutting me off midapology. "Shut up," he says, looking into my eyes. "You have absolutely nothing to apologize for. I didn't leave earlier because I was mad at you. I left because I was mad at myself."

I back out of his grasp and turn to the bed, not wanting to watch as he places even more blame on himself. "It's okay." I walk back to the bed and lift the covers. "I can't expect you to want me in that way right now. It was wrong and selfish and way out of line for me to ask you to do that and I'm really sorry." I lie down on the bed and roll away from him so he can't see my tears. "Let's just go to sleep, okay?"

My voice is much calmer than I expected it to be. I really don't want him to feel bad. He's done nothing but be here for me throughout all of this, and I've done nothing for him in return. The best thing I could do for him at this point is to just break it off so he doesn't feel obligated to stand by me through this. He doesn't owe me a thing.

"You think I'm having a hard time with this because I don't *want* you?" He walks around to the side of the bed that I'm facing and he kneels down. "Sky, I'm having a hard time with this because everything that's happened to you is breaking my fucking heart and I have no idea how to help you. I want to be there for you and help you through this but every word that comes out of my mouth feels like the wrong one. Every time I touch you or kiss you, I'm afraid you don't want me to. Now you're asking me to have sex with you because you want to take that from him, and I get it. I absolutely get where you're coming from, but it doesn't make it easier to make love to you when you can't even look me in the eyes. It hurts so much because you don't deserve for it to be like this. You don't deserve this life and there isn't a fucking thing I can do to make it better for you. I want to make it better but I can't and I feel so helpless."

He has somehow sat up on the bed and pulled me to him during all of that, but I was so caught up in his words I didn't even notice. He wraps his arms around me and pulls me onto his lap, then wraps my legs around him. He takes my face in his hands and looks me directly in the eyes.

"And even though I stopped, I should have never even started without telling you first how much I love you. I love you so much. I don't deserve to touch you until you know for a fact that I'm touching you because I love you and for no other reason."

He presses his lips to mine and doesn't even give me a chance to tell him I love him in return. I love him so much it physically hurts. I'm not thinking about anything else right now but how much I love this boy and how much he loves me and how despite what's going on in my life, I wouldn't want to be anywhere else than in this moment with him.

I try to convey everything I'm feeling through my kiss, but it's not enough. I pull away and kiss his chin, then his nose, then his forehead, then I kiss the tear that's rolling down his cheek. "I love you, too. I don't know what I'd do right now if I didn't have you, Holder. I love you so much and I'm so sorry. I wanted you to be my first, and I'm sorry he took that from you."

Holder adamantly shakes his head and shushes me with a quick kiss. "Don't you ever say that again. Don't you ever *think* that again. Your father took that first from you in an unthinkable way, but I can guarantee you that's all he took. Because you are so strong, Sky. You're amazing and funny and smart and beautiful and so full of strength and courage. What he did to you doesn't take away from any of the best parts of you. You survived him once and you'll survive him again. I know you will."

He places his palm over my heart, then pulls my hand to his chest over his own heart. He lowers his eyes to my level, ensuring I'm here with him, giving him my complete attention. "Fuck all the firsts, Sky. The only thing that matters to me with you are the forevers."

I kiss him. Holy *shit*, do I kiss him. I kiss him with every ounce of emotion that's coursing through me. He cradles my head with his hand and lowers me back to the bed, climbing on top of me. "I love you," he says. "I've loved you for so long but I just couldn't tell you. It didn't feel right letting you love me back when I was keeping so much from you."

Tears are streaming down my cheeks again, and even though they're the exact same tears that come from the exact same eyes, they're completely new to me. They aren't tears from heartache or anger . . . they're tears from the incredible feeling overcoming me right now, hearing him say how much he loves me.

"I don't think you could have picked a better time to tell me you loved me than tonight. I'm happy you waited."

He smiles, looking down at me with fascination. He dips his head and kisses me, infusing my mouth with the taste of him. He kisses me softly and gently, delicately sliding his mouth over mine as he unties my robe. I gasp when his hand eases inside, stroking my stomach with his fingertips. The feel of his touch on me right now is a completely different sensation than just fifteen minutes ago. It's a sensation I *want* to feel.

"*God*, I love you," he says, moving his hand from my stomach and across my waist. He slowly trails his fingers down to my thigh and I moan into his mouth, resulting in an even more determined kiss. He places a flat palm on the inside of my leg and puts slight pressure against it, wanting to ease himself against me, but I flinch and become tense. He can feel my involuntary moment of hesitation, so he pulls his lips from mine and looks down at me. "Remember . . . I'm touching you because I love you. No other reason."

I nod and close my eyes, still afraid that the same numbness and fear is about to wash over me again. Holder kisses my cheek and pulls my robe closed.

"Open your eyes," he says gently. When I do, he reaches up and traces a tear with his finger. "You're crying."

I smile up at him reassuringly. "It's okay. They're the good kind of tears."

He nods, but doesn't smile. He studies me for a moment, then takes my hand in his and laces our fingers together. "I want to make love to you, Sky. And I think you want it, too. But I need you to understand something first." He squeezes my hand and bends down, kissing another escaping tear. "I know it's hard for you to allow yourself to feel this. You've gone so long training yourself to block the feelings and emotions out anytime someone touches you. But I want you to know that what your father physically did to you isn't what hurt you as a little girl. It's what he did to your faith in him that broke your heart. You suffered through one of the worst things a child can go through at the hands of your hero . . . the person you idolized . . . and I can't even begin to imagine what that must have felt like. But remember that the things he did to you are in *no way* related to the two of us when we're together like this. When I touch you, I'm touching you because I want to make you happy. When I kiss you, I'm kissing you because you have the most incredible mouth I've ever seen and you know I can't not kiss it. And when I make love to you—I'm doing exactly that. I'm making love to you because I'm in love with you. The negative feeling you've been associating with physical touch your whole life doesn't apply to me. It doesn't apply to *us*. I'm touching you because I'm in love with you and for no other reason."

His gentle words flood my heart and ease my nerves. He kisses me softly and I relax beneath his hand—a hand that's touching me out of nothing but love. I respond by completely dissolving into him, allowing my lips to follow his, my hands to intertwine with his, my rhythm to match his. I quickly become invested, ready to experience him because I *want* to and for no other reason.

"I love you," he whispers.

The entire time he's touching me, exploring me with his hands and his lips and his eyes, he continues to tell me over and over how much he loves me. And for once, I remain completely in the moment, wanting to feel every single thing he's doing and saying to me. When he finally tosses the wrapper aside and readies himself against me, he looks down at me and smiles, then strokes the side of my face with his fingertips.

"Tell me you love me," he says.

I hold his gaze with unwavering confidence, wanting him to feel the honesty in my words. "I love you, Holder. *So* much. And just so you know . . . so did Hope."

His eyebrows draw apart and he lets out a quick rush of air as if he's been holding it in for thirteen years, waiting for those exact words. "I wish you could feel what that just did to me." He immediately covers my mouth with his and the familiar, sweet mixture of him seeps into my mouth at the same moment he pushes inside me, filling me with so much more than just himself. He fills me with his honesty, his love for me, and for a moment . . . he fills me with a piece of our forevers. I grasp his shoulders and move with him, feeling everything. Every single beautiful thing.

Monday, October 29, 2012
9:50 a.m.

I roll over and Holder is sitting up next to me on the bed, looking down at his phone. He shifts his focus to me when I stretch, then bends down to kiss me, but I immediately turn my head.

"Morning breath," I mumble, crawling out of bed. Holder laughs, then returns his attention to his phone. I somehow made it back into my T-shirt overnight, but I'm not even sure when that happened. I take it off and slip into the bathroom to shower. When I'm finished, I walk back into the room and he's packing up our things.

"What are you doing?" I ask, watching him fold my shirt and place it back into the bag. He looks up at me briefly, then back down to the clothes spread out on the bed.

"We can't stay here forever, Sky. We need to figure out what you want to do."

I take a few steps toward him, my heart speeding up in my chest. "But . . . but I don't know yet. I don't even have anywhere to go."

He hears the panic in my voice and walks around the bed, slipping his arms around me. "You have me, Sky. Calm down. We can go back to my house and figure this out. Besides, we're both still in school. We can't just stop going and we definitely can't live in a hotel forever."

The thought of going back to that town, just two miles

from Karen, makes me uneasy. I'm afraid being so close to her will incite me to confront her, and I'm not ready to do that yet. I just want one more day. I want to see my old house again for one last time in hopes that it will spark more memories. I don't want to rely on Karen to have to tell me the truth. I want to figure out as much as I can on my own.

"One more day," I say. "Please, let's just stay one more day, then we'll go. I need to try to figure this out and in order to do that, I need to go there one more time."

Holder puts space between us and he eyes me, shaking his head. "No way," he says firmly. "I'm not putting you through that again. You're not going back."

I place my hands on his cheeks reassuringly. "I need to, Holder. I swear I won't get out of the car this time. I swear. But I need to see the house again before we go. I remembered so much while I was there. I just want a few more memories before you take me back and I have to decide what to do."

He sighs and paces the floor, not wanting to agree to my desperate plea.

"Please," I say, knowing he won't be able to say no if I continue to beg. He slowly turns to the bed and picks the bags of clothes up, tossing them toward the closet.

"Fine. I told you I would do whatever it was you felt you needed to do. But I'm not hanging all of those clothes back up," he says, pointing to the bags by the closet.

I laugh and rush to him, throwing my arms around his neck. "You're the best, most understanding boyfriend in the whole wide world."

He sighs and returns my hug. "No, I'm not," he says, pressing his lips to the side of my head. "I'm the most *whipped* boyfriend in the whole wide world."

Monday, October 29, 2012
4:15 p.m.

Out of all the minutes in the day, we *would* pick the same ten minutes to sit across the street from my house that my father picks to pull up into the driveway. As soon as my father's car comes to a stop in front of the garage, Holder lifts his hand to his ignition.

I reach over and place my trembling hand on his. "Don't leave," I say. "I need to see what he looks like."

Holder sighs and forces his head into the back of his seat, knowing full well that we should leave, but also knowing there's no way I'll let him.

I quit looking at Holder and look back at the police cruiser parked in the driveway across the street from us. The door opens and a man steps out, decked out in a uniform. His back is to us and he's holding a cell phone up to his ear. He's in the middle of a conversation, so he pauses in the yard and continues talking into the phone without heading inside. Looking at him, I don't have any reaction at all. I don't feel a single thing until the moment he turns around and I see his face.

"Oh, my God," I whisper aloud. Holder looks at me questioningly and I just shake my head. "It's nothing," I say. "He just looks . . . familiar. I haven't had an image of him in my head at all but if I was to see him walking down the street, I would know him."

We both continue to watch him. Holder's hands are

gripping the steering wheel and his knuckles are white. I look down at my own hands and realize I'm gripping the seatbelt in the same fashion.

My father finally pulls the phone from his ear and places it into his pocket. He begins walking in our direction and Holder's hands immediately fall back to the ignition. I gasp quietly, hoping he doesn't somehow know we're watching him. We both realize at the same time that my father is just headed to the mailbox at the end of the driveway, and we immediately relax.

"Have you had enough?" Holder says through gritted teeth. "Because I can't stay here another second without jumping out of this car and beating his ass."

"Almost," I say, not wanting him to do anything stupid, but also not wanting to leave just yet. I watch as my father sorts through the mail, walking back toward the house, and for the first time it hits me.

What if he remarried?

What if he has other children?

What if he's doing this to someone else?

My palms begin to sweat against the slick material of the seatbelt, so I release it and wipe them across my jeans. My hands begin to tremble even more than before. I suddenly can't think of anything other than the fact that I can't let him get away with this. I can't let him walk away, knowing he might be doing this to someone else. I need to know. I owe it to myself and to every single child my father comes in contact with to ensure he's not the evil monster that's painted in my memories. In order to know for sure, I know I need to see him. I need to speak to him. I need to know why he did what he did to me.

When my father unlocks the front door and disappears inside, Holder lets out a huge breath.

"Now?" he says, turning toward me.

I know beyond a doubt he would tackle me right now if he expected me to do what I'm about to do. Just so I don't give off any clues, I force a smile and nod. "Yeah, we can go now."

He places his hand back on the ignition. At the same time he turns his wrist to crank it, I release my seatbelt, swing open the door, and run. I run across the street and across my father's front yard, all the way to the porch. I never even hear Holder coming up behind me. He doesn't make a noise as he wraps his arms around me and physically lifts me off my feet, carrying me back down the steps. He's still carrying me and I'm kicking him, trying to pry his arms from around my stomach.

"What the hell do you think you're *doing*?" He doesn't put me down, he just continues to dominate my strength while he carries me across the yard.

"Let go of me right now, Holder, or I'll scream! I swear to God, I'll scream!"

With that threat, he spins me around to face him and he shakes my shoulders, glaring at me with utter disappointment. "Don't *do* this, Sky. You don't need to face him again, not after what he's done. I want you to give yourself more time."

I look up at him with an ache in my heart that I'm sure is clearly seen in my eyes. "I have to know if he's doing this to anyone else. I need to know if he has more kids. I can't just let it go, knowing what he's capable of. I have to see him. I have to talk to him. I need to know that he's not that man anymore before I can allow myself to get back in that car and just drive away."

He shakes his head. "Don't do this. Not yet. We can make a few phone calls. We'll find out whatever we can online about him first. Please, Sky." He slides his hands from my shoulders to my arms and urges me toward his car. I hesitate, still adamant that I need to see him face to face. Nothing I find out about him online will tell me what I can gain from just hearing his voice or looking him in the eyes.

"Is there a problem here?"

Holder and I both snap our heads in the direction of the voice. My father is standing at the base of the porch steps. He's eyeing Holder, who still has a firm grip on my arms. "Young lady, is this man hurting you?"

The sound of his voice alone makes my knees buckle. Holder can feel me weakening, so he pulls me against his chest. "Let's go," he whispers, wrapping his arm around me and ushering me forward, back toward his car.

"Don't move!"

I freeze, but Holder continues to try to push me forward with more urgency.

"Turn around!" My father's voice is more demanding this time. Holder pauses right along with me now, both of us knowing the ramifications of ignoring the directions of a cop.

"Play it off," Holder says into my ear. "He might not recognize you."

I nod and inhale a deep breath, then we both turn around slowly. My father is several feet away from the house now, closing in on us. He's eyeing me hard, walking toward me with his hand on his holster. I dart my eyes to the ground, because his face is full of recognition and it terrifies me. He stops several feet from us and pauses. Holder tightens his grip around me and I continue to stare at the ground, too scared to even breathe.

"*Princess?*"

"Don't you fucking touch her!"

Holder is yelling and there's pressure under my arms.
His voice is close, so I know he's holding me. I drop my
hands to my sides and feel grass between my fingers.

"Baby, open your eyes. Please." Holder's hand is caressing the side of my face. I slowly open my eyes and look up.
He's looking down at me, my father hovering right behind
him. "It's okay, you just passed out. I need you to stand up.
We need to leave."

He pulls me to my feet and keeps his arm around my
waist, practically doing the standing for me.

My father is right in front of me now, staring. "It *is* you,"
he says. He glances at Holder, then back to me. "Hope? Do
you remember me?" His eyes are full of tears.

Mine aren't.

"Let's go," Holder says again. I resist his pull and step
out of his grasp. I look back at my father . . . at a man who is
somehow exhibiting emotions as if he once must have loved
me. He's full of shit.

"Do you?" he says again, taking another step closer.
Holder inches me back with each step closer my father gets.
"Hope, do you remember me?"

"How could I *forget* you?"

The irony is, I *did* forget him. Completely. I forgot all

about him and the things he did to me and the life I had here. But I don't want him to know that. I want him to know that I remember him, and every single thing he ever did to me.

"It's you," he says, fidgeting his hand down at his side. "You're alive. You're okay." He pulls out his radio, I'm assuming in an attempt to call in the report. Before his finger can even press the button, Holder reaches out and knocks the radio out of his hand. It falls to the ground and my father bends down and grabs it, then takes a defensive step back, his hand resting on his holster again.

"I wouldn't let anyone know she's here if I were you," Holder says. "I doubt you would want the fact that you're a fucking pervert to be front-page news."

All the color immediately washes from my father's face and he looks back at me with fear in his eyes. *"What?"* He's looking at me in disbelief. "Hope, whoever took you . . . they lied to you. They told you things about me that weren't true." He's closer now and his eyes are desperate and pleading. "Who took you, Hope? Who was it?"

I take a confident step toward him. "I remember everything you did to me. And if you just give me what I'm here for, I swear I'll walk away and you'll never hear from me again."

He continues to shake his head, disbelieving the fact that his daughter is standing right in front of him. I'm sure he's also trying to process the fact that his whole life is now in jeopardy. His career, his reputation, his freedom. If it were possible, his face grows even paler when he realizes that he can't deny it any longer. He knows I know.

"What is it you want?"

I look toward the house, then back to him again. "Answers," I say. "And I want anything you have that belonged to my mother."

Holder has a death grip on my waist again. I reach down and grip his hand with mine, just needing the reassurance that I'm not alone right now. My confidence is quickly fading with each moment spent in my father's presence. Everything about him, from his voice to his facial expressions to his movements, makes my stomach ache.

My father glances at Holder briefly, then turns to look at me again. "We can talk inside," he says quietly, his eyes darting around to the houses surrounding us. The fact that he appears nervous now only proves that he's weighed his options and he doesn't have very many to choose from. He nudges his head toward the front door and begins making his way up the steps.

"Leave your gun," Holder says.

My father pauses, but doesn't turn around. He slowly reaches to his side and removes his gun. He places it gently on the steps of the porch, then begins to ascend the stairs.

"Both of them," Holder says.

My father pauses again before reaching the door. He bends down to his ankle and lifts his pant leg, then removes that gun as well. Once both guns are out of his reach, he walks inside, leaving the door open for us. Before I step inside, Holder spins me around to face him.

"I'm staying right here with the door open. I don't trust him. Don't go any farther than the living room."

I nod and he kisses me quick and hard, then releases me. I step into the living room and my father is sitting on his couch, his hands clasped in front of him. He's staring down at the floor. I walk to the seat nearest me and sit on the edge of it, refusing to relax into it. Being in this house and in his presence is causing my mind to clutter and my chest to tighten. I take several slow breaths, attempting to calm my fear.

I use the moment of silence between us to find something in his features that resembles mine. The color of his hair, maybe? He's much taller than me and his eyes, when he's able to look at me, are dark green, unlike mine. Other than the caramel color of his hair, I look nothing like him. I smile at the fact that I look nothing like him.

My father lifts his eyes to mine and he sighs, shifting uncomfortably. "Before you say anything," he says. "You need to know that I loved you and I've regretted what I did every second of my life."

I don't verbally respond to that statement, but I have to physically restrain myself from reacting to his bullshit. He could spend the rest of his life apologizing and it would never be enough to erase even one of the nights my doorknob turned.

"I want to know why you did it," I say with a shaky voice. I hate that I sound so pathetically weak right now. I sound like the little girl who used to beg him to stop. I'm not that little girl anymore and I sure as hell don't want to appear weak in front of him.

He leans back in his seat and rubs his hands over his eyes. "I don't know," he says, exasperated. "After your mother died, I started drinking heavily again. It wasn't until a year later that I got so drunk one night that I woke up the next morning and knew I had done something terrible. I was hoping it was just a horrible dream, but when I went to wake you up that morning you were . . . different. You weren't the same happy little girl you used to be. Overnight, you somehow became someone who was terrified of me. I hated myself. I'm not even sure what I did to you because I was too drunk to remember. But I knew it was something awful and I am so, so sorry. It never happened again and I did everything I could to make it up to you. I bought you presents all the time and gave you whatever you wanted. I didn't want you to remember that night."

I grip my knees in an attempt not to leap across the living room and strangle him. The fact that he's trying to play it off as happening one time makes me hate him even more than before, if that's even possible. He's treating it like it was an accident. Like he broke a coffee mug or had a fucking fender bender.

"It was night . . . after night . . . after night," I say. I'm having to muster up every ounce of control I can find to not scream at the top of my lungs. "I was scared to go to bed and scared to wake up and scared to take a bath and scared to speak to you. I wasn't a little girl afraid of monsters in her closet or under her bed. I was terrified of the monster that was supposed to love me! You were supposed to be *protecting* me from the people like you!"

Holder is kneeling at my side now, gripping my arm as I scream at the man across the room. My whole body is shaking and I lean into Holder, needing to feel his calmness. He rubs my arm and kisses my shoulder, letting me get out the things I need to say without once trying to stop me.

My father sinks back into his seat and tears begin flowing from his eyes. He doesn't defend himself, because he knows I'm right. He has nothing at all to say to me. He just cries into his hands, feeling sorry that he's finally being confronted, and not at all sorry for what he actually did.

"Do you have any other children?" I ask, glaring at the eyes so full of shame that they can't even make contact with mine. He drops his head and presses a palm to his forehead, but fails to answer me. "*Do* you?" I yell. I need to know that he hasn't done this to anyone else. That he's not *still* doing it.

He shakes his head. "No. I never remarried after your mother." His voice is defeated and from the looks of him, so is he.

"Am I the only one you did this to?"

He keeps his eyes trained to the floor, continuing to avoid my line of questions with long pauses. "You owe me the truth," I say, steadily. "Did you do this to anyone else before you did it to me?"

I can sense him closing up. The hardness in his eyes makes it evident that he has no intention of revealing any more truths. I drop my head into my hands, not knowing what to do next. It feels so wrong leaving him to live his life like he is, but I'm also terrified of what might happen if I report him. I'm scared of how much my life will change. I'm scared that no one will believe me, since it was so many years ago. But what terrifies me more than any of that is the fear that I love him too much to want to ruin the rest of his life. Being in his presence not only reminds me of all the horrible things he did to me, it also reminds me of the father he once was underneath all of that. Being inside this house is causing a hurricane of emotions to build within me. I look at the table in the kitchen and begin to recall good memories of conversations we had sitting there. I look at the back door and remember us running outside to go watch the train pass by in the field behind our house. Everything about my surroundings is filling me with conflicting memories, and I don't like loving him just as much as I hate him.

I wipe tears from my eyes and look back at him. He's staring silently down at the floor and as much as I try not to, I see glimpses of my daddy. I see the man who loved me like he used to love me . . . long before I became terrified of the doorknob turning.

Fourteen years earlier

"Shh," she says, brushing the hair behind my ears. We're both lying on my bed and she's behind me, snuggling me against her chest. I've been up sick all night. I don't like being sick, but I love the way my mommy takes care of me when I am.

I close my eyes and try to fall asleep so I'll feel better. I'm almost asleep when I hear my doorknob turn, so I open my eyes. My daddy walks in and smiles down at my mommy and me. He stops smiling when he sees me, though, because he can tell I don't feel good. My daddy doesn't like it when I feel sick because he loves me and it makes him sad.

He sits down on his knees next to me and touches my face with his hand. "How's my baby girl feeling?" he says.

"I don't feel good, Daddy," I whisper. He frowns when I say that. I should have just told him I felt good so he wouldn't frown.

He looks up at my mommy, lying in bed behind me, and he smiles at her. He touches her face just like he touched mine. "How's my other girl?"

I can feel her touch his hand when he talks to her. "Tired," she says. "I've been up all night with her."

He stands up and pulls her hand until she stands up, too. I watch him wrap his arms around her and hug her, then he kisses her on the cheek. "I'll take it from here," he says, running his hand down her hair. "You go get some rest, okay?"

My mommy nods and kisses him again, then walks out of the room. My daddy walks around the bed and he lies in the same spot my mommy was in. He wraps his arms around me just like she did, and he starts singing me his favorite song. He says it's his favorite song, because it's about me.

"I've lost a lot in my long life.
Yes, I've seen pain and I've seen strife.
But I'll never give up; I'll never let go.
Because I'll always have my ray of hope."

I smile, even though I don't feel good. My daddy keeps singing to me until I close my eyes and fall asleep.

Monday, October 29, 2012
4:57 p.m.

It's the first memory I've had before all of the bad stuff took over. My only memory from before my mother died. I still don't remember what she looked like because the memory was more of a blur, but I remember how I felt. I loved them. *Both* of them.

My father looks up at me now, his face completely awash in sorrow. I have no sympathy for him whatsoever because . . . where was *my* sympathy? I do know that he's in a vulnerable position right now and if I can use that to my advantage in order to pull the truth from him, then that's what I'm going to do.

I stand up and Holder tries to take my arm, so I look down at him and shake my head. "It's okay," I assure him. He nods and reluctantly releases me, allowing me to walk toward my father. When I reach him, I kneel down on the floor in front of him, looking up into eyes full of regret. Being this close to him is causing my body to tense and the anger in my heart to build, but I know I have to do this if I want him to give me the answers I need. He needs to believe I'm sympathizing with him.

"I was sick," I say, calmly. "My mother and I . . . we were in my bed and you came home from work. She had been up with me all night and she was tired, so you told her to go get some rest."

A tear rolls down my father's cheek and he nods, but barely.

"You held me that night like a father is supposed to hold his daughter. And you sang to me. I remember you used to sing a song to me about your ray of hope." I wipe the tears out of my eyes and keep looking up at him. "Before my mother died . . . before you had to deal with that heart-ache . . . you didn't always do those things to me, did you?"

He shakes his head and touches my face with his hand. "No, Hope. I loved you so much. I still do. I loved you and your mother more than life itself, but when she died . . . the best parts of me died right along with her."

I fist my hands, recoiling slightly at the feel of his fin-gertips on my cheek. I push through, though, and somehow keep myself calm. "I'm sorry you had to go through that," I say firmly. And I *am* sorry for him. I remember how much he loved my mother, and regardless of how he dealt with his grief, I can find it in me to wish he never had to experience her loss.

"I know you loved her. I remember. But knowing that doesn't make it any easier to find it in my heart to forgive you for what you did. I don't know why whatever is inside of you is so different from what's inside other people . . . to the point that you would allow yourself to do what you did to me. But despite the things you did to me, I know you love me. And as hard as it is to admit . . . I once loved you, too. I loved all the good parts of you."

I stand up and take a step back, still looking into his eyes. "I know you aren't all bad. I *know* that. But if you love me like you say you do . . . if you loved my mother at *all* . . . then you'll do whatever you can to help me heal. You owe me that much. All I want is for you to be honest so I can leave here with some semblance of peace. That's all I'm here for, okay? I just want peace."

He's sobbing now, nodding his head into his hands. I walk back to the couch and Holder wraps his arm tightly around me, still kneeling next to me. Tremors are still wracking my body, so I wrap my arms around myself. Holder can feel what this is doing to me, so he slides his fingers down my arm until he finds my pinky, then wraps his around it. It's an extremely small gesture, but he couldn't have done anything more perfect to fill me with the sense of security that I need from him right now.

My father sighs heavily, then drops his hands. "When I first started drinking . . . it was only once. I did something to my little sister . . . but it was only one time." He looks back up at me and his eyes are still full of shame. "It was years before I met your mother."

My heart breaks at his brutal honesty, but it breaks even more that he somehow thinks it's okay that it only happened once. I swallow the lump in my throat and continue my questions. "What about *after* me? Have you done it to anyone else since I was taken?"

His eyes dart back to the floor and the guilt in his demeanor is like a punch straight to my gut. I gasp, holding back the tears. "Who? How many?"

He shakes his head slightly. "There was just one more. I stopped drinking a few years ago and haven't touched anyone since." He looks back up at me, his eyes desperate and hopeful. "I swear. There were only three and they were at the lowest points of my life. When I'm sober, I'm able to control my urges. That's why I don't drink anymore."

"Who was she?" I ask, wanting him to have to face the truth for just a few more minutes before I walk out of his life forever.

He nudges his head to the right. "She lived in the house next door. They moved when she was around ten, so I don't know what happened to her. It was years ago, Hope. I haven't done it in years and that's the truth. I swear."

My heart suddenly weighs a thousand pounds. The grip around my arm is gone and I look up to see Holder falling apart right before my eyes.

His face contorts into an unbearable amount of agony and he turns away from me, pulling his hands through his hair. "Les," he whispers painfully. "Oh, God, no." He presses his head into the doorframe, tightly gripping the back of his neck with both hands. I immediately stand and walk to him, placing my hands on his shoulders, fearing that he's about to explode. He begins to shake and he's crying, not even making a sound. I don't know what to say or what to do. He just keeps saying "no" over and over, shaking his head. My heart is breaking for him, but I have no clue how to help him right now. I understand what he means by thinking everything he says to me is the wrong thing, because there's absolutely nothing I could say to him right now that could help. Instead, I press my head against him and he turns slightly, cradling me in his arm.

The way his chest is heaving, I can feel him trying to keep his anger at bay. His breaths begin to come in sharp spurts as he attempts to calm himself. I grip him tighter, hoping to be able to keep him from unleashing his anger. As much as I want him to . . . as much as I want him to physically retaliate against my father for what he did to Les and me, I fear that in this moment, Holder is full of too much hate to find it in himself to stop.

He releases his hold and brings his hands up to my

shoulders, pushing me away from him. The look in his eyes is so dark; it immediately sends me into defense mode. I step between him and my father, not knowing what else I can do to keep him from attacking, but it's as though I'm not even here. When Holder looks at me, he looks straight through me. I can hear my father stand up behind me and I watch as Holder's eyes follow him. I spin around, prepared to tell my father to get the hell out of the living room, when Holder grips my arms and shoves me out of the way.

I trip and fall to the floor, watching in slow motion as my father reaches behind the couch and spins around, holding a gun in his hand, pointing it directly at Holder. I can't speak. I can't scream. I can't move. I can't even close my eyes. I'm forced to watch.

My father pulls his radio to his mouth, holding the gun firmly in his hand with a lifeless expression. He presses the button and never takes his eyes off Holder while he speaks into it. "Officer down at thirty-five twenty-two Oak Street."

My eyes immediately dart to Holder, then back to my father. The radio drops from his hands and onto the floor in front of me. I pull myself up, still unable to scream. My father's defeated eyes fall on mine as he slowly turns the gun and points it at himself. "I'm so sorry, Princess."

The sound explodes, filling the entire room. It's so loud. I squeeze my eyes shut and cover my ears, not sure where the sound is even coming from. It's a high-pitched noise, like a scream. It sounds like a girl screaming.

It's me.

I'm screaming.

I open my eyes and see my father's lifeless body just feet in front of me. Holder's hand clamps over my mouth and he lifts me up, pulling me out the front door. He's not even trying to carry me. My heels are dragging in the grass and he's holding on to my mouth with one hand and my waist with his other arm. When we reach the car, he keeps his hand clamped tight, muffling my scream. He's looking around frantically, making sure no one is witnessing whatever chaos this is going on right now. My eyes are wide and I'm shaking my head out of denial, expecting the last minute of my life to just go away if I refuse to believe it.

"Stop. I need you to stop screaming. Right now."

I nod vigorously, somehow silencing the involuntary sound coming from my mouth. I'm trying to breathe and I can hear the air being sucked in and out of my nose in quick spurts. My chest is heaving and when I notice the blood splattered across the side of Holder's face, I try not to scream again.

"Do you hear that?" Holder says. "Those are sirens, Sky. They'll be here in less than a minute. I'm removing my hand and I need you to get in the car and be as calm as you can because we need to get out of here."

I nod again and he removes his hand from my mouth, then shoves me into the car. He runs around to his side and quickly climbs in, then cranks the car and pulls onto the road. We round the corner just as two police cars turn the corner at the opposite end of the road behind us. We drive away and I drop my head between my knees, attempting to catch a breath. I don't even think about what just happened. I can't. It didn't happen. It couldn't have. I focus on the fact that this is all a horrible nightmare, and I just breathe. I breathe just to make sure I'm still alive, because this sure as hell doesn't feel like life.

Monday, October 29, 2012
5:29 p.m.

We both move through the hotel room door like zombies. I don't even remember getting from the car into the hotel. When he reaches the bed, Holder sits and removes his shoes. I've only made it a few feet, paused where the entry-way meets the room. My hands are at my sides and my head is tilted. I'm staring at the window across the room. The curtain panels are open, revealing nothing but a gloomy view of the brick building just feet away from the hotel. Just a solid wall of brick with no visible windows or doors. Just brick.

Looking out the window at the brick wall is how I feel when I view my own life. I try to look to the future, but I can't see past this moment. I have no idea what's going to happen, who I'll live with, what will happen to Karen, if I'll report what just happened. I can't even venture a guess. It's nothing but a solid wall between this moment and the next, without so much as a clue sprawled across it in spray paint.

For the past thirteen years, my life has been nothing but a brick wall separating the first few years from the rest. A solid block, separating my life as Sky from my life as Hope. I've heard about people somehow blocking out traumatic memories, but I always thought that maybe it was more of a choice. I literally, for the past thirteen years, have not had a single clue who I used to be. I know I was young when I was taken from that life, but even then I would assume I would have a few memories. I guess the moment I pulled away with Karen, I somehow made a conscious decision, at that young age, to never recall those memories. Once Karen began telling me stories of my "adoption," it must have been easier for my mind to grasp the harmless lies than to remember my ugly truth.

I know I couldn't explain at the time what my father was doing to me, because I wasn't sure. All I knew was that I hated it. When you aren't sure what it is you hate or why you even hate it, it's hard to hold on to the details . . . you just hold on to the feelings. I know I've never really been all that curious to delve up information about my past. I've never really been that curious to find out who my father was or why he "put me up for adoption." Now I know it's because somewhere in my mind, I still harbored hatred and fear for that man, so it was just easier to erect the brick wall and never look back.

I still do harbor hatred and fear for him, and he can't even touch me anymore. I still hate him, and I'm still scared to death of him, and I'm still devastated that he's dead. I hate him for instilling awful things in my memory and somehow making me grieve for him in the midst of all the awful. I don't want to grieve over his loss. I want to rejoice in it, but it's just not in me.

My jacket is being removed. I look away from the brick wall taunting me from outside the window and turn my head around to see Holder standing behind me. He lays my jacket across a chair, then takes off my blood-splattered shirt. A raw sadness consumes me, realizing I'm genetically linked to the lifeless blood now covering my clothes and face. Holder walks around to my front and reaches down to the button on my jeans and unbuttons them.

He's in his boxer shorts. I never even noticed he took off his clothes. My eyes travel up to his face and he's got specks of blood on his right cheek, the one that was exposed to the cowardliness of my father. His eyes are heavy, keeping them focused on my pants as he slides them down my legs.

"I need you to step out of them, babe," he says softly when he reaches my feet. I grasp his shoulders with my hands and take one foot out of my jeans, then the other. I keep my hands on his shoulders and my eyes trained on the blood splattered in his hair. I mechanically reach over and slip my fingers over a strand of his hair, then pull my hand up to inspect it. I slide the blood around between my fingertips, but it's thick. It's thicker than blood should be.

That's because it's not only my father's *blood* that's all over us.

I begin wiping my fingers across my stomach, frantically trying to get it off me, but I'm just smearing it everywhere. My throat closes up and I can't scream. It's like the dreams I've had where something is so terrifying, I lose any ability to make a sound. Holder looks up and I want to scream and yell and cry, but the only thing I can do is widen my eyes and shake my head and continue to wipe my hands across my body. When he sees me panicking, he stands straight up and lifts me into his arms, then swiftly carries me to the shower. He sets me down at the opposite end from the showerhead, then steps in with me and turns the water on. He closes the shower curtain once the water is warm, then he turns to face me and grabs my wrists that are still attempting to wipe the redness away. He pulls me to him and turns us both to where I'm standing under the warm stream of water. When the water splashes me in the eyes, I gasp and suck in a huge breath of air.

He reaches down to the side of the tub and grabs the bar of soap, tearing off the soaked paper packaging. He leans out of the shower and pulls back in, holding a washcloth. My whole body is shaking now, even though the water is warm. He rubs soap and water into the washcloth, then presses it to my cheek.

"Shh," he whispers, staring into my panic-stricken eyes. "I'm getting it off you, okay?"

He begins gently wiping my face and I squeeze my eyes shut and nod. I keep my eyes closed because I don't want to see the blood-tinted washcloth when he pulls it away from my face. I wrap my arms around myself and remain as still as possible under his hand, aside from the tremors still wracking my body. It takes him several minutes of wiping the blood away from my face and arms and stomach. Once he finishes that task, he reaches behind my head and removes my ponytail holder.

"Look at me, Sky." I open my eyes and he places his fingers lightly on my shoulder. "I'm going to take off your bra now, okay? I need to wash your hair and I don't want to get anything on it."

Get anything on it?

When I realize he's referring to what's more than likely embedded throughout my hair, I begin to panic again and pull the straps of my bra down, then just pull the bra over my head.

"Get it out," I say quietly and quickly, leaning my head back into the water, attempting to saturate my hair by running my fingers through it under the stream. "Just get it *off* me." My voice is more panicky now.

He grabs my wrists again and pulls them away from my hair, then wraps them around his waist.

"I'll get it. Hold on to me and try to relax. I'll do it."

I press my head against his chest and tighten my hold around him. I can smell the shampoo as he pours it into his hands and brings the liquid to my hair, spreading it around with his fingertips. He scoots us a step closer until the water touches my head, which is pressed into his shoulder. He massages and scrubs my hair, rinsing it repeatedly. I don't even ask why he keeps rinsing it; I just let him rinse it as many times as he needs to.

Once he's finished, he turns us around in the shower until he's under the stream of water and he runs the shampoo through his own hair. I release my hold from around his waist and back away from him, not wanting to feel like there's anything getting on me again. I look down at my stomach and hands and don't see any traces of my father left on me. I look back up at Holder and he's scrubbing his face and neck with a fresh washcloth. I stand there, watching him calmly wash away what happened to us no less than an hour ago.

When he's finished, he opens his eyes and looks down at me with regret. "Sky, I need you to make sure I got it all, okay? I need you to wipe away anything I missed."

He's talking to me so calmly, like he's trying not to break me. It's his voice that makes me realize that's exactly what he's trying to avoid. He's afraid I'm about to break, or crack, or flip out.

I'm scared he might be right, so I take the washcloth

out of his hands and force myself to be strong and inspect him. There's still a small area of blood over his right ear, so I reach the washcloth up and wipe it away. I pull the washcloth back and look down at the last speck of blood left on the two of us, then I run it under the stream of water and watch as it washes away.

"It's all gone," I whisper. I'm not even sure I'm referring to the blood.

Holder takes the washcloth out of my hand and tosses it onto the edge of the tub. I look up at him, and his eyes are redder than before and I can't tell if he's crying, because the water is running down his face in the same pattern that tears would be if they were even there. It's then, when all of the physical remnants of my past are washed away, that I'm reminded of Lesslie.

My heart breaks all over again, this time for Holder. A sob breaks out of me and I slap my hand over my mouth, but my shoulders continue to shake. He pulls me to his chest and presses his lips to my hair.

"Holder, I'm so sorry. Oh, my God, I'm so sorry." I'm crying and holding on to him, wishing his hopelessness were as easy to wash away as the blood. He's holding me so tightly, I can barely breathe. But he needs this. He needs me to feel his pain right now, just like I need for him to feel mine.

I take every single word my father said today and attempt to cry them out of me. I don't want to remember his face. I don't want to remember his voice. I don't want to remember how much I hate him and I especially don't want to remember how much I loved him. There's nothing like the guilt you feel when there's room in your heart to love evil.

Holder moves one of his hands to the back of my head

and pulls my face against his shoulder. His cheek presses against the top of my head and I can hear him crying now. It's quiet and he's trying so hard to hold it in. He's in so much pain because of what my father did to Lesslie, and I can't help but place some of that blame on myself. If I had been around, he never would have touched Lesslie and she never would have suffered. If I had never climbed into that car with Karen, Lesslie might still be alive today.

I curl my hands up behind Holder's arms and grip his shoulders. I lift my cheek and turn my mouth toward his neck, kissing him softly. "I'm so sorry. He never would have touched her if I . . ."

Holder grips my arms and pushes me away from him with such force, my eyes widen and I flinch when he speaks. "Don't you dare say that." He releases his hold and swiftly brings his hands to my face, gripping me tightly. "I don't ever want you to apologize for a single thing that man did. Do you hear me? It's not your fault, Sky. Swear to me you will never let a thought like that consume you ever again." His eyes are desperate and full of tears.

I nod. "I swear," I say weakly.

He never looks away, searching my eyes for truth. His reaction has left my heart pounding, shocked at how quick he was to dismiss any fault I may have had. I wish he was just as quick to dismiss his own faults, but he isn't.

I can't take the look in his eyes, so I throw my arms around his neck and hug him. He tightens his grip around me and holds me with pained desperation. The truth about Lesslie and the reality of what we just witnessed hits us both, and we cling to each other with everything we have. He's finished trying to be strong for me. The love he had for Lesslie and the anger he's feeling over what happened to her are pouring out of him.

I know Lesslie would need him to feel her heartache, so I don't even try to comfort him with words. We both cry for her now, because she had no one to cry for her then. I kiss the side of his head, my hands gripping his neck. Each time my lips touch him, he holds me just a little bit tighter. His mouth grazes my shoulder and soon we're both attempting to kiss away every ounce of the heartache that neither one of us deserves. His lips become adamant as he kisses my neck harder and faster, desperately trying to find an escape. He pulls back and looks into my eyes, his shoulders rising and falling with every breath he's struggling to find.

In one swift movement, he crashes his lips to mine with an intense urgency, gripping my hair and my back with his trembling hands. He pushes my back against the shower wall as he slides his hands down behind my thighs. I can feel the despair pouring out of him as he lifts me up and wraps my legs around his waist. He wants his pain to go away, and he needs me to help him. Just like I needed him last night.

I wrap my arms around his neck, pulling him against me, allowing him to consume me for a break from his heartache. I let him, because I need a break just as badly as he does right now. I want to forget about everything else.

I don't want this to be our life tonight.

With his body pressing me into the wall of the shower, he uses his hands to grip the sides of my face, holding me still as our mouths anxiously search each other's for any semblance of relief from our reality. I'm grasping his upper back with my arms as his mouth moves frenziedly down my neck.

"Tell me this is okay," he says breathlessly against my skin. He lifts his face back to mine, nervously searching my eyes as he speaks. "Tell me it's okay to want to be inside you right now . . . because after everything we've been through today, it feels wrong to need you like I do."

I grip his hair and pull him closer, covering his mouth with mine, kissing him with such conviction that my words aren't even needed. He groans and separates me from the shower wall, then walks out of the bathroom to the bed with me still wrapped around him. He's not being gentle at all with the way he rips off the last two items of clothing between us and ravishes my mouth with his, but I honestly don't know if my heart could take gentle right now.

He's standing at the edge of the bed leaning over me, his mouth meshed to mine. He breaks apart momentarily to put on a condom, then he grabs my waist and pulls me to the edge of the bed with him. He lifts my leg behind the knee and brings it up to his side, then slides his hand underneath my arm and grips my shoulder. The moment his eyes fall back to mine, he pushes himself into me without hesitation. I gasp from the sudden force of him, shocked by the intense pleasure that takes over the momentary flash of pain. I wrap my arms around him and move with him as he grips my leg tighter, then covers my mouth with his. I close my eyes and let my head sink deeper into the mattress as we use our love to temporarily ease the anguish.

His hands move to my waist and he pulls me against him, digging his fingers deeper into my hips with each frantic, rhythmic movement against me. I grab hold of his arms and relax my body, allowing him to guide me in whatever way can help him right now. His mouth breaks away and he opens his eyes at the same time I open mine. His eyes are still fresh with tears, so I let go of him and bring my hands to his face, attempting to soothe his pained features with my touch. He continues looking at me, but he turns his head and kisses the inside of my palm, then drops himself on top of me, stopping suddenly.

We're both panting for air and I can feel him inside me, still needing me. He keeps his eyes locked with mine as he slides his arms underneath my back and pulls me to him, lifting us both up. We never separate as he turns us around and slides himself down to the floor with his back against the bed, me straddling his lap. He slowly pulls me in for a kiss. A gentle kiss this time.

The way he's holding me against him protectively now, trailing kisses along my lips and jaw—it's almost as if he's a different Holder than the one I had just thirty seconds ago, yet still wholly passionate. One minute he's frantic and heated . . . the next minute he's gentle and coaxing. I'm beginning to appreciate and love the unexpectedness in him.

I can feel him wanting me to take control now, but I'm nervous. I'm not sure that I even know how. He senses my unease and he moves his hands to my waist, slowly guiding me, barely moving me on top of him. He's watching me earnestly, making sure I'm still here with him.

I *am*. I'm so completely here with him right now I can think of nothing else.

He brings one of his hands to my face, still guiding me with his other hand on my waist. "You know how I feel about you," he says. "You know how much I love you. You know I would do whatever I could to take away your pain, right?"

I nod, because I do know. And looking into his eyes

right now, seeing the raw honesty in them, I know he's felt this way about me long before this moment.

"I need that from you so fucking bad right now, Sky. I need to know you love me like that."

Everything about him, from his voice to the look on his face, becomes tortured. I would do whatever it took to take that away from him. I lace our fingers together and cover both our hearts with our hands, working up the courage to show him how incredibly much I love him. I stare him straight in the eyes as I lift up slightly, then slowly lower myself back down on top of him.

He groans heavily, then closes his eyes and leans his head back, letting it fall against the mattress behind him.

"Open your eyes," I whisper. "I want you to watch me."

He raises his head, looking at me through hooded eyes. I continue to slowly take control, wanting nothing more than for him to hear and feel and see just how much he means to me. Being in control is a completely different sensation, but it's a good one. The way he's watching me makes me feel needed like no one's ever been able to make me feel. In a way, he makes me feel *necessary*. Like my existence alone is necessary for his survival.

"Don't look away again," I say, easing myself up. When I lower myself back onto him, his head sways slightly from the intensity of the sensation and a moan escapes my throat, but he keeps his tortured eyes locked firmly on mine. I'm no longer in need of his guidance, and my body becomes a rhythmic reflection of his.

"The first time you kissed me?" I say. "That moment when your lips touched mine? You stole a piece of my heart that night." I continue my rhythm as he watches me fervently. "The first time you told me you lived me because you weren't ready to tell me you loved me yet?" I press my hand harder against his chest and move myself in closer to him, wanting him to feel every part of me. "Those words stole another piece of my heart."

He opens his hand that I have pressed over my heart until his palm is flat against my skin. I do the same to him. "The night I found out I was Hope? I told you I wanted to be alone in my room. When I woke up and saw you in my bed I wanted to cry, Holder. I wanted to cry because I needed you there with me so bad. I knew in that moment that I was in love with you. I was in love with the way you loved me. When you wrapped your arms around me and held me, I knew that no matter what happened with my life, you were my home. You stole the biggest piece of my heart that night."

I lower my mouth to his and kiss him softly. He closes his eyes and begins to ease his head against the bed again. "Keep them open," I whisper, pulling away from his lips. He opens them, regarding me with an intensity that penetrates straight to my core. "I want you to keep them open . . . because I need you to watch me give you the very last piece of my heart."

He releases a vast breath and it's almost as if I can see the pain literally escaping him. His hands tighten around mine as the look in his eyes instantly changes from an intense hopelessness to a fiery need. He begins moving with me as we hold each other's gaze. The two of us gradually become one as we silently express with our bodies and our hands and our eyes what our words are unable to convey.

We remain in a connected cadence until the very last

moment, when his eyes grow heavy. He drops his head back, consumed by the shudders that are taking over his release. When his heart rate begins to calm against my palm and he's able to connect with my eyes again, he pulls his hands from mine and grips the back of my head, kissing me with an unforgiving passion. He leans forward as he lowers my back to the floor, trading dominance with me, kissing me with abandon.

We spend the rest of the night taking turns expressing how we feel without uttering a single word. By the time we finally reach the point of exhaustion, wrapped up in each other's arms, I begin to fall asleep in a wave of disbelief. We have just wholly fallen into each other, heart and soul. I never thought I would ever be able to trust a man enough to share my heart, much less hand it over completely.

Monday, October 29, 2012
11:35 p.m.

Holder isn't next to me when I roll over and feel for him. I sit up on the bed and it's dark outside, so I reach over and turn on the lamp. His shoes aren't where they were when he took them off, so I pull on my clothes and make my way outside to find him.

I walk past the courtyard, not spotting him sitting in any of the cabanas. Just as I'm about to turn around and head back, I see him lying on the concrete next to the pool with his hands locked behind his head, looking up at the stars. He looks incredibly peaceful right now, so I choose to walk back to one of the cabanas and leave him undisturbed.

I curl up into the seat and pull my arms into my sweater, leaning my head back as I watch him. There's a full moon out, so everything about him is illuminated in a soft bask of light, making him appear almost angelic. He's lost in the sky with a look of serenity across his face, making me grateful that he's able to find enough peace within himself to get through today. I know how much Lesslie meant to him and I know what his heart is going through today. I know exactly what he's feeling, because our pain is shared now. Whatever he goes through, I feel. Whatever I go through, he feels. It's what happens when two people become one: they no longer share only love. They also share all of the pain, heartache, sorrow, and grief.

Despite the calamity that is my life right now, there's a warm sense of comfort surrounding me after being with him tonight. No matter what happens, I know for a fact that Holder will see me through every second of it, maybe even carrying me through at times. He's proven to me that I'll never feel completely hopeless again, so long as he's in my life.

"Come lie with me," he says, never taking his eyes off the sky above him. I smile and ease out of my seat, then walk toward him. When I reach him, he removes his jacket and places it over me as I ease down onto the cold concrete and curl up against his chest. He strokes my hair as we both stare up at the sky, silently regarding the stars.

Pieces of a memory begin to flash in my mind and I close my eyes, actually wanting to recall it this time. It feels like a happy one, and I'll take as many of those as I can get. I hug him tightly and allow myself to fall openly into the memory.

Thirteen years earlier

"Why don't you have a TV?" I ask her. I've been with her for lots of days now. She's really nice and I like it here, but I miss watching TV. Not as bad as I miss Dean and Lesslie, though.

"I don't have a TV because people have become dependent on technology and it makes them lazy," Karen says. I don't know what she means, but I pretend I do. I really like it at her house and I don't want to say anything that will make her want to take me back home to my daddy yet. I'm not ready to go back.

"Hope, do you remember a few days ago I told you I had something really important to talk to you about?"

I don't really remember, but I nod my head and pretend I do. She scoots her chair closer to mine at the table to get closer to me. "I want you to pay attention to me, okay? This is very important."

I nod my head. I hope she's not telling me she's taking me home now. I'm not ready to go home. I do miss Dean and Lesslie, but I really don't want to go back home with my daddy.

"Do you know what adoption means?" she asks.

I shake my head because I've never heard of that word.

"Adoption is when someone loves a child so much, that they want them to be their son or daughter. So they adopt them in order to become their mommy or daddy." She takes

my hand and squeezes it. "I love you so much that I'm going to adopt you so you can be my daughter."

I smile at her, but I really don't understand what she means. "Are you coming to live with me and my daddy?"

She shakes her head. "No, sweetie. Your daddy loves you very, very much, but he can't take care of you anymore. He needs for me to take care of you now, because he wants to make sure you're happy. So now, instead of living with your daddy, you're going to live with me and I'll get to be your mommy."

It feels like I want to cry, but I don't know why. I like Karen a lot, but I love my daddy, too. I like her house and I like her cooking and I like my room. I really want to stay here really bad, but I can't smile because my tummy hurts. It started hurting when she said my daddy couldn't take care of me anymore. I wonder if I made him mad. I don't ask if I made him mad, though. I'm scared if she thinks I still want to live with my daddy, that she'll take me back to live with him. I do love him, but I'm too scared to go back and live with him.

"Are you excited about me adopting you? Do you want to live with me?"

I do want to live with her but I feel sad because it took us lots of minutes or hours to drive here. That means we're far away from Dean and Lesslie.

"What about my friends? Will I get to see my friends again?"

Karen moves her head to the side and smiles at me, then tucks my hair behind my ear. "Sweetie, you're going to make a lot of new friends."

I smile back at her, but my tummy hurts. I don't want

new friends. I want Dean and Lesslie. I miss them. I can feel my eyes burning and I try not to cry. I don't want her to think I'm not happy about her adopting me, because I am.

Karen reaches down and hugs me. "Sweetie, don't worry. You'll see your friends again someday. But right now we can't go back, so we'll make new friends here, okay?"

I nod and she kisses me on top of the head while I look down at the bracelet on my hand. I touch the heart on it with my fingers and hope that Lesslie knows where I am. I hope they know I'm okay, because I don't want them to worry about me.

"There's one more thing," she says. "You're going to love it."

Karen leans back in her seat and pulls a piece of paper and a pencil to the spot in front of her. "The best part of being adopted is that you get to pick your very own name. Did you know that?"

I shake my head. I didn't know people got to pick their own names.

"Before we pick your name, we need to know what names we can't use. We can't use the name you had before, and we can't use nicknames. Do you have any nicknames? Anything your daddy calls you?"

I nod my head, but I don't say it.

"What does he call you?"

I look down at my hands and clear my throat. "Princess," I say quietly. "But I don't like that nickname."

She looks sad when I say that. "Well then, we will never call you Princess again, okay?"

I nod. I'm happy she doesn't like that name, either.

"I want you to tell me some things that make you happy.

Beautiful things and things you love. Maybe we can pick you a name from those."

I don't even need her to write them down, because there's only one thing I feel that way about. "I love the sky," I say, thinking about what Dean told me to remember forever.

"Sky," she says, smiling. "I love that name. I think it's perfect. Now let's think of one more name, because everyone needs two names. What else do you love?"

I close my eyes and try to think of something else, but I can't. The sky is the only thing I love that's beautiful and makes me happy when I think about it. I open my eyes back up and look at her. "What do you love, Karen?"

She smiles and puts her chin in her hand, resting her elbow on the table. "I love lots of things. I love pizza the most. Can we call you Sky Pizza?"

I giggle and shake my head. "That's a silly name."

"Okay, let me think," she says. "What about teddy bears? Can we call you Teddy Bear Sky?"

I laugh and shake my head again.

She pulls her chin out of her hand and leans toward me. "Do you want to know what I really love?"

"Yeah," I say.

"I love herbs. Herbs are healing plants and I love growing them to find ways to help people feel better. Someday I want to own my own herbal business. Maybe for good luck, we could pick out the name of an herb. There are hundreds of them and some of them are really pretty names." She stands up and walks to the living room and grabs a book, then brings it back to the table. She opens it up and points to one of the pages. "What about thyme?" she says with a wink.

I laugh and shake my head.

"How about . . . calendula?"

I shake my head again. "I can't even say that word."

She crinkles up her nose. "Good point. I guess you need to be able to say your own name." She looks down at the page again and reads a few more out loud, but I don't like them. She turns the page one more time and says, "What about Linden? It's more of a tree than an herb, but its leaves are shaped like a heart. Do you like hearts?"

I nod. "Linden," I say. "I like that name."

She smiles and closes the book, then leans down closer to me. "Well then, Linden Sky Davis it is. And just so you know, you now have the most beautiful name in the world. Let's not think about your old names ever again, okay? Promise me from now on we'll only think about your beautiful new name and your beautiful new life."

"I promise," I say. And I do promise. I don't want to think about my old names or my old room or all the things that my daddy did to me when I was his princess. I love my new name. I love my new room where I don't have to worry if the doorknob is going to turn.

I reach up and hug her and she hugs me back. It makes me smile, because it feels just like the way I thought it would feel every time I wished my mommy was alive to hug me.

Tuesday, October 30, 2012
12:10 a.m.

I reach my hand up to my face and wipe away a tear. I'm not even sure why my tears are falling right now; the memory wasn't really a sad one. I think it's the fact that it's one of the first moments I ever started to love Karen. Thinking about how much I love her makes me hurt because of what she did. It hurts because I feel like I don't even know her. I feel like there's a side to her that I never even knew existed.

That's not what scares me the most, though. What scares me the most is that I'm afraid the only side of her I *do* know . . . doesn't really exist at *all*.

"Can I ask you something?" Holder says, breaking the silence.

I nod against his chest, wiping the last tear from my cheek. He wraps both of his arms around me in an attempt to keep me warm when he feels me shiver against his chest. He rubs my shoulder with his hand and kisses my head.

"Do you think you'll be okay, Sky?"

It's not an uncommon question. It's a very simple, straightforward question, yet it's the hardest question I think I've ever had to answer.

I shrug. "I don't know," I reply honestly. I want to think I'll be okay, especially knowing Holder will be by my side. But to be honest, I really don't know if I will be.

"What scares you?"

"Everything," I reply quickly. "I'm terrified of my past. I'm terrified of the memories that flood my mind every time I close my eyes. I'm terrified of what I saw happen today and how it'll affect me the nights that you aren't there to divert my thoughts. I'm terrified that I don't have the emotional capacity to deal with what may happen to Karen. I'm scared of the thought that I have no idea who she even is anymore." I lift my head off his chest and look him in the eyes. "But do you know what scares me the most?"

He runs his hand over my hair and keeps his eyes on mine; wanting me to know that he's listening. "What?" he asks, his voice full of genuine concern.

"I'm scared of how disconnected I feel from Hope. I know we're the same person, but I feel like what happened to her didn't really happen to me. I feel like I abandoned her. Like I left her there, crying against that house, terrified for all of eternity, while I just got into that car and rode away. Now I'm two completely separate people. I'm this little girl, eternally scared to death . . . but I'm also the girl who abandoned her. I feel so guilty for putting up this wall between both lives and I'm scared neither of those lives or those girls will ever feel whole again."

I bury my head in his chest, knowing I'm more than likely not making any sense. He kisses the top of my head and I look back up at the sky, wondering if I'll ever be able to feel normal again. It was so much easier not knowing the truth.

"After my parents divorced," he says, "my mother was worried about us, so she put me and Les in therapy. It only lasted for about six months . . . but I remember always being so hard on myself, thinking I was the reason for their divorce. I felt like what I failed to do the day you were taken put a lot of stress on them. I know now that most of what I blamed myself for back then was out of my control. But there was something my therapist did once that sort of helped me. It felt really awkward at the time, but every now and then I catch myself still doing it in certain situations. He had me visualize myself in the past, and he would have me talk to the younger version of myself and say everything I needed to say." He pulls my face up so that I'm looking at him. "I think you should try that. I know it sounds lame, but really. It might help you. I think you need to go back and tell Hope everything you wish you could have told her the day you left her."

I rest my chin on his chest. "What do you mean? Like I should visualize myself talking to her?"

"Exactly," he says. "Just try it. Close your eyes."

I close them. I'm not sure what it is I'm doing, but I do it anyway.

"Are they closed?"

"Yes." I lay my hand over his heart and press the side of my head into his chest. "I'm not sure what to do, though."

"Just envision yourself as you are now. Envision yourself driving up to your father's house and parking across the street. But visualize the house how it was back then," he says. "Picture it how it was when you were Hope. Can you remember the house being white?"

I squeeze my eyes shut even harder, vaguely recalling the white house from somewhere deep within my mind. "Yes."

"Good. Now you need to go find her. Talk to her. Tell her how strong she is. Tell her how beautiful she is. Tell her everything she needs to hear from you, Sky. Everything you wish you could have told *yourself* that day."

I clear my mind and go with his suggestion. I envision myself as I am now and what would be happening if I actually drove up to that house. I would more than likely be wearing my sundress with my hair pulled back into a ponytail since it's so hot. It's almost as if I can feel the sun beating down through the windshield, warming my skin again.

I make myself step out of my car and walk across the street, even though I'm reluctant to head toward that house. My heart immediately speeds up. I'm not sure that I *want* to see her, but I do what Holder suggests and I keep walking forward. As soon as the side of the house is in view, she's there. Hope is sitting in the grass with her arms folded over her knees. She's crying into them and it completely shatters my heart.

I slowly walk up to her and pause, then tentatively lower myself to the ground, unable to take my eyes off this fragile little girl. When I'm situated on the grass directly in front of her, she lifts her head from her folded arms and looks up at me. When she does, my soul crumbles because the look in her dark brown eyes is lifeless. There's no happiness there at all. I try to smile at her, though, because I don't want her to see how much her pain is hurting me.

I stretch my hand out to her, but stop a few inches before I reach her. Her sad brown eyes drop to my fingers and she stares at them. My hands are shaking now and she can see that. Maybe the fact that she can see that I'm also scared helps me gain her trust, because she lifts her head even higher, then unfolds her arms and places her tiny hand in mine.

I'm looking down at the hand of my childhood, holding on to the hand of my present, but all I want to do is hold more than just her hand. I want to grab all of her pain and fear, too, and take it from her.

Remembering the things Holder said I should tell her, I look down at her and clear my throat, squeezing her hand tightly in mine.

"Hope." She continues to look at me patiently while I dig deep for the courage to speak to her . . . to tell her everything she needs to know. "Do you know that you're one of the bravest little girls I've ever met?"

She shakes her head and looks down at the grass. "No, I'm not," she says quietly, convinced in her belief.

I reach out and take her other hand in mine and look her directly in the eyes. "Yes, you are. You're *incredibly* brave. And you're going to make it through this because you have a very strong heart. A heart that is capable of loving so much about life and people in a way you never dreamt a heart could love. And you're beautiful." I press my hand to her heart. "In here. Your heart is so beautiful and someday someone is going to love that heart like it deserves to be loved."

She pulls one of her hands back and wipes her eyes with it. "How do you know all that?"

I lean forward and wrap my arms around her completely. She returns my embrace by putting her arms around me and letting me hold her. I lean my head down and whisper in her ear. "I know, because I've been through exactly what you're going through. I know how bad it hurts your heart that your daddy does this to you, because he did it to me, too. I know how much you hate him for it, but I also know how much you love him because he's your daddy. And it's okay, Hope. It's okay to love the good parts of him, because he's not all bad. It's also okay to hate those bad parts of him that make you so sad. It's okay to feel *whatever* you need to feel. Just promise me that you will never, ever feel guilty. Promise me that you will never blame yourself. It's not your fault. You're just a little girl and it's not your fault that your life is so much harder than it should be. And as much as you'll want to forget these things ever happened to you and as much as you'll want to forget this part of your life existed, I need for you to remember."

I can feel her arms trembling against me now and she's quietly crying against my chest. Her tears force the release of my own tears. "I want you to remember who you are, despite the bad things that are happening to you. Because those bad things aren't *you*. They are just things that *happen* to you. You need to accept that who you are, and the things that happen to you, are not one and the same."

I gently lift her head off my chest and look into her brown, tearful eyes. "Promise me that no matter what, you will never be ashamed of who you are, no matter how bad you want to be. And this might not make sense to you right now, but I want you to promise me that you will never let the things your daddy does to you define and separate you from who you are. Promise me that you will never lose Hope."

She nods her head as I wipe her tears away with my thumbs. "I promise," she says. She smiles up at me and for the first time since seeing her big brown eyes, there's a trace of life in them. I pull her onto my lap and she wraps her arms around my neck as I hold her and rock her, both of us crying in each other's arms.

"Hope, I promise that from this point forward, I will never, ever let you go. I'm going to hold you and carry you with me in my heart forever. You'll never have to be alone again."

I'm crying into Hope's hair, but when I open my eyes I'm crying into Holder's arms. "Did you talk to her?" he asks.

I nod my head. "Yes." I'm not even trying to choke back the tears. "I told her everything."

Holder begins to sit up, so I move up with him. He turns toward me and takes my face in his hands. "No, Sky. You didn't tell *her* everything . . . you told *you* everything. Those things happened to *you*, not to someone else. They happened to Hope. They happened to Sky. They happened to the best friend that I loved all those years ago, and they happened to the best friend I love who's looking back at me right now." He presses his lips to mine and kisses me, then pulls away. It's not until I look back at him that I notice he's crying with me. "You need to be proud of the fact that you survived everything you went through as a child. Don't separate yourself from that life. Embrace it, because I'm so fucking proud of you. Every smile I see on your face just blows me away, because I know the courage and strength it took when you were just a little girl to ensure that part of you remained. And your laugh? My *God*, Sky. Think about how much courage it took you to laugh again after everything that happened to you. And your heart . . ." he says, shaking his head disbelievingly. "How your heart can possibly find a way to love and trust a man again proves that I've fallen in love with the bravest woman I've ever known. I know how much courage it took for you to allow me in after what your father did to you. And I swear I will spend every last breath thanking you for allowing yourself to love me. Thank you *so* much for loving me, Linden Sky Hope."

He pronounces each of my names slowly, not even attempting to wipe away my tears because there are too many. I throw my arms around his neck and let him hold me. All seventeen years of me.

Tuesday, October 30, 2012
9:05 a.m.

The sun is so bright; it's beaming through the blanket I've pulled over my eyes. It's not the sun that woke me up, though. It was the sound of Holder's voice.

"Look, you have no idea what she's been through the past two days," Holder says. He's trying to speak softly, either in an attempt not to wake me, or in an attempt for me not to hear his conversation. I don't hear anyone speak in return, so he must be on the phone. Who the hell is he talking to, though?

"I understand your need to defend her. Believe me, I do. But you both need to know that she's not walking into that house alone."

There's a long pause before he sighs heavily into the phone. "I need to make sure she eats something, so give us some time. Yes, I promise. I'm waking her up as soon as I hang up. We'll leave within the hour."

He doesn't say good-bye, but I hear the phone drop onto the table. Within seconds, the bed dips and he's sliding an arm around me. "Wake up," he says into my ear.

I don't move. "I am awake," I say from underneath the covers. I feel his head press into my shoulder.

"So you heard that?" he asks, his voice low.

"Who was it?"

He shifts on the bed and pulls the covers off of my head.

"Jack. He claims Karen confessed everything to him last night. He's worried about her. He needs you to talk to her."

My heart stops midbeat. "She confessed?" I ask warily, sitting up in the bed.

He nods. "We didn't go into details, but he seems to know what's going on. I did tell him about your father, though . . . only because Karen wanted to know if you saw him. When I woke up today it was on the news. They ruled it a suicide, based on the fact that he called it in himself. They aren't even opening it for investigation." He holds my hand and caresses it with his thumb. "Sky, Jack sounds desperate for you to come back. I think he's right . . . we need to go back and finish this. You won't be alone. I'll be there and Jack will be there. And from the sound of it, Karen is cooperating. I know it's hard but we don't have a choice."

He's talking to me like I need to be convinced, when really I'm ready. I need to see her face to face in order to get the last of my questions answered. I throw the covers off me completely and scoot off the bed, then stand up and stretch. "I need to brush my teeth and change first. Then we can go." I walk to the bathroom and don't turn around, but I can feel the pride rolling off him. He's proud of me.

Holder hands me his cell phone once we're on the road. "Here. Breckin and Six are both worried about you. Karen got their numbers out of your cell phone and has been calling them all weekend, trying to find you."

"Did you talk to either of them?"

He nods. "I spoke with Breckin this morning, right before Jack called. I told him you and your mother got into a fight and you just wanted to get away for a few days. He's fine with that explanation."

"What about Six?"

He glances at me and gives me a half smile. "Six you might need to contact. I've been talking to her through email. I tried to appease her with the same story I told Breckin, but she wasn't buying it. She said you and Karen don't fight and I need to tell her the truth before she flies back to Texas and kicks my ass."

I wince, knowing Six must be worried sick about me. I haven't texted her in days, so I decide to put off calling Breckin and shoot Six an email, instead.

"How do you email someone?" I ask. Holder laughs and takes his phone, pressing a few buttons. He hands it back to me and points to the screen.

"Just type what you need to say in there, then hand it back to me and I'll send it."

I type out a short email, telling her that I found out a few things about my past and I needed to get away for a few days. I assure her that I'll call her to explain everything in the next few days, but I'm really not sure that I'll actually tell her the truth. At this point, I'm not sure I want anyone to know about my situation. Not until I have all the answers.

Holder sends the email, then takes my hand and laces his fingers through mine. I focus my gaze out the window and stare up at the sky.

"You hungry?" he asks, after driving in complete silence for over an hour. I shake my head. I'm too nervous to eat anything, knowing I'm about to face Karen. I'm too nervous to even hold a normal conversation. I'm too nervous to do anything but stare out the window and wonder where I'll be when I wake up tomorrow.

"You need to eat, Sky. You've barely eaten anything in three days and with your tendency to pass out, I don't think food would be a bad idea right now."

He won't give up until I eat, so I just relent. "Fine," I mumble.

He ends up choosing a roadside Mexican restaurant after I fail to make a choice about where to eat. I order something off the lunch menu, just to appease him. I more than likely won't be able to eat anything.

"You want to play Dinner Quest?" he says, dipping a tortilla chip into his salsa.

I shrug. I really don't want to face what I'll be doing in five hours, so maybe this will help get my mind off things. "I guess. On one condition, though. I don't want to talk about anything that has anything to do with the first few years of my life, the last three days, or the next twenty-four hours."

He smiles, seemingly relieved. Maybe he doesn't want to think about any of it, either.

"Ladies first," he says.

"Then put down that chip," I say, eyeing the food he's about to put in his mouth.

His eyes drop to the chip and he frowns playfully. "Make it a quick question then, because I'm starving."

I take advantage of my turn by downing a drink of my soda, then taking a bite of the chip that I just took out of his hands. "Why do you love running so much?" I ask.

"I'm not sure," he says, sinking back into his seat. "I started running when I was thirteen. It started out as a way to get away from Les and her annoying friends. Sometimes I would just need out of the house. The squealing and cackling of thirteen-year-old girls can be extremely painful. I liked the silence that came with running. If you haven't noticed, I'm sort of a thinker, so it helps me to clear my head."

I laugh. "I've noticed," I say. "Have you always been like that?"

He grins and shakes his head. "That's two questions. My turn." He takes the chip that I was about to eat out of my hand and he pops it into his mouth, then takes a drink of his soda. "Why didn't you ever show up for track tryouts?"

I cock my eyebrow and laugh. "That's an odd question to ask now. That was two months ago."

He shakes his head and points a chip at me. "No judging when it comes to my choice in questions."

"Fine." I laugh. "I don't know, really. School just wasn't what I thought it would be. I didn't expect the other girls to be so mean. None of them even spoke to me unless it was to inform me of what a slut I was. Breckin was the only person in that whole school who made any effort."

"That's not true," Holder says. "You're forgetting about Shayla."

I laugh. "You mean Shayna?"

"Whatever," he says, shaking his head. "Your go." He quickly shoves another chip in his mouth and grins at me.

"Why did your parents divorce?"

He gives me a tight-lipped smile and drums his fingers lightly on the table, then shrugs his shoulders. "I guess it was time for them to," he says indifferently.

"It was time?" I ask, confused by his vague answer. "Is there an expiration date on marriages nowadays?"

He shrugs. "For some people, yes."

I'm interested in his thought process now. I'm hoping he doesn't move on to his turn now that my question has been asked, because I really want to know his views on this. Not that I'm planning on getting married anytime soon. But he is the guy I'm in love with, so it wouldn't hurt to know his stance so I'm not as shocked years down the road.

"Why do you think their marriage had a time limit?" I ask.

"All marriages have a time limit if you enter them for the wrong reasons. Marriage doesn't get easier . . . it only gets harder. If you marry someone hoping it will improve things, you might as well set your timer the second you say, 'I do.'"

"What wrong reasons did they have to get married?"

"Me and Les," he says flatly. "They knew each other less than a month when my mother got pregnant. My dad married her, thinking it was the right thing to do, when maybe the right thing to do was to never knock her up in the first place."

"Accidents happen," I say.

"I know. Which is why they're now divorced."

I shake my head, sad that he's so casual about his parents' lack of love for each other. I guess it's been eight years, though. The ten-year-old Holder may not have been so casual about the divorce as it was actually occurring. "But you don't think divorce is inevitable for every marriage?"

He folds his arms across the table and leans forward, narrowing his eyes. "Sky, if you're wondering if I have commitment issues, the answer is no. Someday in the far, far, far away future . . . like postcollege future . . . when I propose to you . . . which I *will* be doing one day because you aren't getting rid of me . . . I won't be marrying you with the hope that our marriage will work out. When you become mine, it'll be a forever thing. I've told you before that the only thing that matters to me with you are the forevers, and I mean that."

I smile at him, somehow a little bit more in love with him than I was thirty seconds ago. "Wow. You didn't need much time to think *those* words out."

He shakes his head. "That's because I've been thinking about forever with you since the second I saw you in the grocery store."

Our food couldn't have arrived at a more perfect time, because I have no idea how to respond to that. I pick up my fork to take a bite but he reaches across the table and snatches it out of my hand.

"No cheating," he says. "We're not finished and I'm about to get really personal with my question." He takes a bite of his food and chews it slowly as I wait for him to ask me his "really personal" question. After he takes a drink, he takes another bite of food and grins at me, purposely dragging out his turn so he can eat.

"Ask me a damn question," I say with feigned irritation.

He laughs and wipes his mouth with his napkin, then leans forward. "Are you on birth control?" he asks in a hushed voice.

His question makes me laugh, because it really isn't all that personal when you're asking the girl you're having sex with. "No, I'm not," I admit. "I never really had a reason to be on it before you came barging into my life."

"Well, I want you on it," he says decisively. "Make an appointment this week."

I balk at his rudeness. "You could ask me a little more politely, you know."

He arches an eyebrow as he takes a sip of his drink, then places it calmly back down on the table in front of him. "My bad." He smiles and flashes his dimples at me. "Let me rephrase my words, then," he says, lowering his voice to a husky whisper. "I plan on making love to you, Sky. *A lot.* Pretty much any chance we get, because I rather enjoyed you this weekend, despite the circumstances surrounding it all. So in order for me to continue to make love to you, I would very much appreciate it if you would make alternative contraceptive arrangements so that we don't find ourselves in a pregnancy-induced marriage with an expiration date on it. Do you think you could do that for me? So that we can continue to have lots and lots and lots of sex?"

I keep my eyes locked on his as I slide my empty glass to the waitress, who is now staring at Holder with her jaw wide open. I keep a straight face when I reply.

"That's much better," I say. "And yes. I believe I can arrange that."

He nods once, then slides his glass next to mine, glancing up at the waitress. She finally snaps out of her trance and quickly refills our glasses, then walks away. As soon as she's gone, I glare at Holder and shake my head. "You're evil, Dean Holder." I laugh.

"*What?*" he says innocently.

"It should be illegal for the words 'make love' and 'sex' to flow past your lips when in the presence of any female besides the one who actually gets to experience you. I don't think you realize what you do to women."

He shakes his head and attempts to brush off my comment.

"I'm serious, Holder. Without trying to explode your ego, you should know that you're incredibly appealing to pretty much any female with a pulse. I mean, think about it. I can't even count the number of guys I've met in my life, yet somehow you're the only one I've ever been attracted to? Explain that one."

He laughs. "That's an easy one."

"How so?"

"Because," he says, looking at me pointedly. "You already loved me before you saw me in the grocery store that day. Just because you blocked the memory of me out of your mind doesn't mean you blocked the memory of me out of your heart." He brings a forkful of food to his mouth, but pauses before he takes a bite. "Maybe you're right, though. It could have just been the fact that you wanted to lick my dimples," he says, shoving the forkful into his mouth.

"It was definitely the dimples," I say, smiling. I can't count the number of times he's made me smile in the half hour we've been here, and I've somehow eaten half of the food on my plate. His presence alone works wonders for a wounded soul.

Tuesday, October 30, 2012
7:20 p.m.

We're a block from Karen's house when I ask him to pull over. The anticipation during the drive over here was torture enough, but actually arriving is absolutely terrifying. I have no idea what to say to her or how I'm supposed to react when I walk through the front door.

Holder pulls over to the side of the road and puts the car in park. He looks over at me with concern in his eyes. "You need a chapter break?" he asks.

I nod, inhaling a deep breath. He reaches across the seat and grabs my hand. "What is it that scares you the most about seeing her?"

I shift in my seat to face him. "I'm scared that no matter what she says to me today, I'll never be able to forgive her. I know that my life turned out better with her than it would have if I had stayed with my father, but she had no way of knowing that when she stole me from him. The fact that I know what she's capable of makes it impossible for me to forgive her. If I couldn't forgive my father for what he did to me . . . then I feel like I shouldn't forgive her, either."

He brushes his thumb across the top of my hand. "Maybe you'll never forgive her for what she did, but you *can* appreciate the life she gave you after she did it. She's been a good mom to you, Sky. Remember that when you talk to her today, okay?"

I expel a nervous breath. "That's the part I can't get over," I say. "The fact that she *has* been a good mom and I love her for it. I love her so much and I'm scared to death that after today, I won't have her anymore."

Holder pulls me to him and hugs me. "I'm scared for you, too, babe," he says, unwilling to pretend everything will be okay when it can't. It's the fear of the unknown that we're both wrapped up in. Neither of us has any idea what path my life will take after I walk through that front door, and if it's a path we'll even be able to take together.

I pull apart from him and place my hands on my knees, working up courage to get this over with. "I'm ready," I say. He nods, then pulls his car back onto the road and rounds the corner, coming to a stop in my driveway. Seeing my home causes my hands to tremble even more than they were before. Holder opens the driver's-side door when Jack walks outside and he turns to face me.

"Stay here," he says. "I want to talk to Jack first." Holder gets out of the car and shuts the door behind him. I stay put like he asked me to because I'm honestly in no hurry to get out of this car. I watch as Holder and Jack speak for several minutes. The fact that Jack is here, still supporting her, makes me wonder if Karen actually told him the truth about what she did. I doubt he would be here if he knew the truth.

Holder walks back to the car, this time to the passenger door where I'm seated. He opens the door and kneels down next to me. He brushes his hand across my cheek and strokes my face with the back of his fingertips. "Are you ready?" he asks.

I feel my head nodding, but I don't feel in control of

the movement. I see my feet stepping out of the car and my hand reaching into Holder's, but I don't know how I'm moving when I'm consciously trying to keep myself seated in the car. I'm not ready to go in, but I'm walking away from the car in Holder's arms toward the house, anyway. When I reach Jack, he reaches out to hug me. As soon as his familiar arms wrap around me, I catch back up to myself and take a deep breath.

"Thank you for coming back," he says. "She needs this chance to explain everything. Promise me you'll give that to her."

I pull away from him and look him in the eyes. "Do you know what she did, Jack? Did she tell you?"

He nods painfully. "I know and I know it's hard for you. But you need to let her tell you her side."

He turns toward the house and keeps his arm around my shoulders. Holder takes my hand and they both walk me to the front door like I'm a fragile child.

I'm *not* a fragile child.

I pause on the steps and turn to face them. "I need to talk to her alone."

I know I thought I wanted Holder with me, but I need to be strong for myself. I love the way he protects me, but this is the hardest thing I've ever had to do and I want to be able to say I did it myself. If I can face this on my own, I know I'll have the courage to face anything.

Neither of them objects, which fills me with appreciation for them, knowing they both have faith in me. Holder squeezes my hand and urges me forward with confidence in his eyes. "I'll be right here," he says.

I take a deep breath, then open the front door.

I step into the living room and Karen stops pacing the floor and spins around, taking in the sight of me. As soon as we make eye contact, she loses control and rushes toward me. I don't know what look I expected to see on her face when I walked through this door, but it certainly wasn't a look of relief.

"You're okay," she says, throwing her arms around my neck. She presses her hand to the back of my head and pulls me against her as she cries. "I'm so sorry, Sky. I'm so, so sorry you found out before I could tell you." She's trying hard to speak, but the sobs have taken over full force. Seeing her in this much pain tears at my heart. Knowing she's been lying to me doesn't immediately refute the thirteen years I've loved her, so seeing her in pain only causes me pain in return.

She takes my face in her hands and looks me in the eyes. "I swear to you I was going to tell you everything the moment you turned eighteen. I hate that you had to find it all out on your own. I did everything I could to prevent that from happening."

I grab her hands and remove them from my face, then step around her. "I have no idea how to respond to anything you're saying right now, Mom." I spin around and look her in the eyes. "I have so many questions but I'm too scared to ask them. If you answer them, how do I know you'll be telling me the truth? How do I know you won't lie to me like you've been lying to me for the last thirteen years?"

Karen walks to the kitchen and picks up a napkin to wipe her eyes. She inhales a few shaky breaths, attempting to regain control of herself. "Come sit with me, sweetie," she says, walking past me toward the couch. I remain standing while I watch her take a seat on the edge of the cushion. She glances up at me, her entire face awash with heartache. "Please," she says. "I know you don't trust me and you have every right not to trust me for what I did. But if you can find it in your heart to recognize the fact that I love you more than life itself, you'll give me this chance to explain."

Her eyes speak nothing but truth. For that, I walk to the couch and take a seat across from her. She takes a deep breath, then exhales, controlling herself long enough to begin with her explanation.

"In order for me to explain the truth about what happened with you . . . I first need to explain the truth about what happened to me." She pauses for a few minutes, attempting not to break down again. I can see in her eyes that whatever she's about to say is almost unbearable for her. I want to go to her and hug her, but I can't. As much as I love her, I just can't console her.

"I had a wonderful mom, Sky. You would have loved her so much. Her name was Dawn and she loved my brother and me with everything she had. My brother, John, was ten years older than me, so we never had to experience the sibling rivalry growing up. My father passed away when I was nine, so John was like the father figure in my life rather than a sibling. He was my protector. He was such a good brother and she was such a good mother. Unfortunately, when I turned thirteen, the fact that John was like a father to me became his reality the day my mother died.

"John was only twenty-three and was fresh out of college at the time. I didn't have any other family willing to take me in, so he did what he had to do. At first, things were okay. I missed my mother more than I should have and, to be honest, John was having a hard time dealing with everything laid out in front of him. He had just started his new job, fresh out of college, and things were tough for him. For both of us. By the time I turned fourteen, the stressors of his new job were really getting to him at this point. He began drinking and I began rebelling, staying out later than I should have on several occasions.

"One night when I came home, he was so angry with me. Our argument soon turned into a physical fight and he hit me several times. He had never physically hurt me before and it terrified me. I ran to my room and he came in several minutes later to apologize. His behavior the previous few months as a result of his alcohol abuse already had me scared of him. Now, coupled with the fact that it had caused him to physically hurt me . . . I was terrified of him."

Karen shifts in her seat and reaches down to sip from a glass of water. I watch her hand as she brings the glass to her mouth and her fingers are trembling.

"He tried to apologize but I refused to listen. My stubbornness pissed him off even more, so he pushed me back on the bed and started screaming at me. He went on and on, telling me that I had ruined his life. He said I needed to be thanking him for everything he was doing for me . . . that I owed him for having to work so hard to take care of me."

Karen clears her throat and new tears form in her eyes as she struggles to continue with the painful truth of her past. She brings her eyes to meet mine and I can tell that the words on the tip of her tongue are almost too hard for her to release.

"Sky . . ." she says achingly. "My brother raped me that

night. Not only did he do it that night, but it continued almost every night after that for two solid years."

I bring my hands to my mouth and gasp. The blood rushes from my head, but it feels as though it rushes from the rest of my body as well. I feel completely empty hearing her words, because I'm terrified to hear what I think she's about to tell me. The look in her eyes is even emptier than how I'm feeling right now. Rather than wait for her to tell me, I just come out and ask her.

"Mom . . . is John . . . he was my father, wasn't he?"

She quickly nods her head as tears drop from her eyes. "Yes, sweetie. He was. I'm so sorry."

My whole body jerks with the sob that breaks free and Karen's arms are around me as soon as the first tears escape my eyes. I throw my arms around her and grasp her shirt. "I'm so sorry he did that to you," I cry. Karen sits next to me on the couch and we hold each other while we cry over the things that were done to us at the hands of a man we both loved with all of our heart.

"There's more," she says. "I want to tell you everything, okay?"

I nod as she pulls herself away from me and takes my hands in hers.

"When I turned sixteen, I told a friend of mine what he was doing to me. She told her mother, who then reported it. By that time, John had been in the police force for three years and was making a name for himself. When he was questioned about the report, he claimed I was making it up because he wouldn't allow me to see my boyfriend. He was eventually cleared and the case was dismissed, but I knew I could never go back to live with him. I lived with a few friends until I graduated high school two years later. I never spoke to him again.

"Six years had passed before I saw him again. I was twenty-one and in college by that time. I was at a grocery store and was on the next aisle when I heard his voice. I froze, unable to breathe as I listened to his conversation. I would have been able to recognize his voice anywhere. There's something about a voice that terrifies you that you'll never be able to forget, no matter what.

"But that day, it wasn't his voice that had me paralyzed . . . it was yours. I heard him talking to a little girl and I was immediately taken back to all those nights he hurt me. I was sick to my stomach, knowing what he was capable of. I followed at a distance, watching the two of you interact. He walked a few feet away from the shopping cart at one point and I caught your eye. You looked at me for a long time and you were the most beautiful little girl I'd ever seen. But you were also the most broken little girl I'd ever seen. I knew the second I looked into your eyes that he was doing to you exactly what he had done to me. I could see the hopelessness and fear in your eyes when you looked back at me.

"I spent the next several days attempting to find out everything I could about you and your relationship to him. I learned about what happened to your mother, and that he was raising you alone. I finally got the courage to phone in an anonymous report, hoping he would finally get what he deserved. I learned a week later that after interviewing you, the case was immediately dismissed by Child Protective Services. I'm not sure if the fact that he was high up in law enforcement had anything to do with the dismissal, but I'm almost positive it did. Regardless, that was twice that he had gotten away with it. I couldn't bear the thought of allowing you to stay with him, knowing what was happening to you. I'm sure there were other ways I could have handled it, but I was young and scared to death for you. I didn't know what else to do because the law had already failed us both.

"A few days later I had made up my mind. If no one else was going to help you get away from him . . . then I was. The day when I pulled up to your house I'll never forget that broken little girl crying into her arms, sitting alone in the grass. When I called your name and you came to me, then climbed into the car with me . . . we drove away and I never looked back."

Karen squeezes my hands between hers and looks at me hard. "Sky, I swear with all of my heart that all I ever wanted to do was protect you from him. I did everything I could to keep him from finding you. To keep you from finding *him*. We never spoke about him again and I did my best to help you move past what happened to you so you could have a normal life. I knew that I couldn't get away with hiding you forever. I knew there would come a day that I would have to face what I did . . . but none of that mattered to me. None of that matters to me still. I just wanted you safe until you were old enough, so that you would never be sent back to him.

"The day before I took you, I went to your house and no one was there. I went inside because I wanted to find some things that might comfort you once you were safe with me. Something like a favorite blanket or a teddy bear. Once I was actually inside your bedroom, I realized that anything in that house couldn't possibly bring you comfort. If you were anything like me, everything that had a connection to him reminded you of what he had done to you. So I didn't take anything, because I didn't want you to remember what he had done to you."

She stands up and quietly walks out of the room, then returns moments later with a small wooden box. She places it into my hands. "I couldn't leave without these. I knew that when the day came for me to tell you the truth, that you would want to know all about your mother, too. I couldn't find much, but what I did find I kept for you."

Tears fill my eyes as I run my fingers over the wooden box that holds the only memories of a woman I never thought I would have a chance to remember. I don't open it. I can't. I need to open it alone.

Karen tucks my hair behind my ear and I look back up at her. "I know what I did was wrong, but I don't regret it. If I had to do it again just to know you would be safe, I wouldn't think twice about it. I also know that you probably hate me for lying to you. I'm okay with that, Sky, because I love you enough for the both of us. Never feel guilty for how you feel about what I've done to you. I've had this conversation and this moment planned out for thirteen years, so I'm prepared for whatever you decide to do and whatever decision you make. I want you to do what's best for you. I'll call the police right now if that's what you want me to do. I'll be more than willing to tell them everything I just told you if it would help you find peace. If you need me to wait until your actual eighteenth birthday so you can continue to live in this house until then, I will. I'll turn myself in the second you're legally allowed to take care of yourself, and I'll never question your request. But whatever you choose,

Sky. Whatever you decide to do, don't worry about me. Knowing you're safe now is everything I could ever ask for. Whatever comes next for me is worth every second of the thirteen years I've had with you."

I look back down at the box and continue to cry, not having a clue what to do. I don't know what's right or what's wrong or if right *is* wrong in this situation. I know that I can't answer her right now. I feel like with everything she's just told me, all that I thought I knew about justice and fairness has just slapped me in the face.

I look back up at her and shake my head. "I don't know," I whisper. "I don't know what I want to happen." I *don't* know what I want, but I know what I need. I need a chapter break.

I stand up and she remains seated, watching me as I walk to the door. I can't look her in the eyes as I open the front door. "I need to think for a while," I say quietly, making my way outside. As soon as the front door closes behind me, Holder's arms wrap around me. I cradle the wooden box in one hand and wrap my other arm around his neck, burying my head into his shoulder. I cry into his shirt, not knowing how to begin processing everything I've just learned. "The sky," I say. "I need to look at the sky."

He doesn't ask any questions. He knows exactly what I'm referring to, so he grabs my hand and leads me to the car. Jack slips back into the house as Holder and I pull out of the driveway.

Tuesday, October 30, 2012
8:45 p.m.

Holder never asks me what Karen said while I was inside the house with her. He knows that I'll tell him when I can, but right now in this moment, I don't think I can. Not until I know what I want to do.

He pulls the car over when we get to the airport, but pulls up significantly farther than where we normally park. When we walk down to the fence, I'm surprised to see an unlocked gate. Holder lifts the latch and swings it open, motioning for me to walk through.

"There's a gate?" I ask, confused. "Why do we always climb the fence?"

He shoots me a sly grin. "You were in a dress the two times we've been here. Where's the fun in walking through a gate?"

Somehow, and I don't know how, I find it in me to laugh. I walk through the gate and he closes it behind me, but remains on the other side of it. I pause and reach my hand out to him. "I want you to come with me," I say.

"Are you sure? I figured you'd want to think alone tonight."

I shake my head. "I like being next to you out here. It wouldn't feel right if I was alone."

He opens the gate and takes my hand in his. We walk down to the runway and claim our usual spots under the stars. I lay the wooden box next to me, still not sure that I have the courage to open it. I'm not really sure of anything right now. I lie still for over half an hour, silently thinking about my life . . . about Karen's life . . . about Lesslie's life . . . and I feel like the decision I'm having to make needs to be one for all three of us.

"Karen is my aunt," I say aloud. "My biological aunt." I don't know if I'm saying it out loud for Holder's benefit or if I just want to say it out loud for myself.

Holder wraps his pinky around mine and turns his head to look at me. "Your dad's sister?" he asks, hesitantly. I nod and he closes his eyes, understanding what that means for Karen's past. "That's why she took you," he says knowingly. He says it like it makes complete sense. "She knew what he was doing to you."

I confirm his statement with a nod. "She wants me to decide, Holder. She wants me to choose what happens next. The problem is, I don't know what choice is the right one."

He takes my entire hand in his now, intertwining our fingers. "That's because none of them are the right choice," he says. "Sometimes you have to choose between a bunch of wrong choices and no right ones. You just have to choose which wrong choice feels the least wrong."

Making Karen pay for something she did out of complete selflessness is without a doubt the *worst* wrong choice. I know it in my heart, but it's still a struggle to accept that what she did is something that should have no consequences. I know she didn't know it at the time, but the fact that Karen took me away from my father only led to what happened to Lesslie. It's hard to ignore that Karen's taking me indirectly led to what happened to my best friend—to the only other girl in Holder's life whom he feels he let down.

"I need to ask you something," I say to him. He silently waits for me to speak, so I sit up and look down at him. "I don't want you to interrupt me, okay? Just let me get this out."

He touches my hand and nods, so I continue. "I know that Karen did what she did because she was only trying to save me. The decision she made was made out of love . . . not hate. But I'm scared that if I don't say anything . . . if we keep it to ourselves . . . that it will affect *you*. Because I know that what my father did to Les was only done because I wasn't there, taking her place. And I know there was no way Karen could have foreseen what he would do. I know she tried to do the right thing by reporting him before she became so desperate. But what happens to us? To you and me, when we try to go back to how things were before? I'm scared you'll hate Karen forever . . . or that you'll eventually begin to resent me for whatever choice I make tonight. And I'm not saying I don't want you to feel whatever it is you need to feel. If you need to hate Karen for what happened to Les, I understand. I guess I just need to know that whatever I choose . . . I need to know . . ."

I attempt to find the most eloquent way to say it, but I can't. Sometimes the simplest questions are the hardest to ask. I squeeze his hand and look him in the eyes. "Holder . . . will you be okay?"

His expression is unreadable as he watches me. He laces his fingers through mine and turns his attention back to the sky above us.

"All this time," he says quietly. "For the past year I've done nothing but hate and resent Les for what she did. I hated her because we led the exact same life. We had the exact same parents who went through the exact same divorce. We had the exact same best friend who was ripped from our lives. We shared the exact same grief over what happened to you, Sky. We moved to the same town in the same house with the same mom and the same school. The things that happened in her life were the exact same things that happened in mine. But she always took it so much harder. Sometimes at night I would hear her crying. I would always go lie with her and hold her, but there were so many times I just wanted to scream at her for being so much weaker than me.

"Then that night . . . when I found out what she did . . . I hated her. I hated her for giving up so easily. I hated that she thought her life was so much harder than mine, when they were the exact same."

He sits up and turns to face me, taking both of my hands in his. "I know the truth now. I know that her life was a *million* times harder than mine. And the fact that she still smiled and laughed every single day, but I never had a single clue what kind of shit she had been through . . . I finally see how brave she really was. And it wasn't her fault that she didn't know how to deal with it all. I wish that she had asked for help or told someone what happened, but everyone deals with these things differently, especially when you think you're all alone. You were able to block it out and that's how you coped. I think she tried to do that, but she was a lot older when it happened to her so it made it impossible. Instead of blocking it out and never thinking about it again, I know she did the exact opposite. I know that it consumed every part of her life until she just couldn't take it anymore.

"And you can't say that Karen's choice had any direct

link to what your father did to Les. If Karen had never taken you away from him, he more than likely would have still done those things to Les whether you were there or not. It's who he was. It's what he did. So if you're asking me if I blame Karen, the answer is no. The only thing I wish Karen would have done differently . . . is I wish she could have taken Les, too."

He wraps his arms around me and brings his mouth to my ear. "Whatever you decide. Whatever you feel will make your heart heal faster . . . that's what I want for you. That's what Les wants for you, too."

I hug him back and bury my head against his shoulder. "Thank you, Holder."

He holds me silently while I think about the decision that isn't even much of a decision anymore. After a while, I pull away from him and lift the box into my lap. I run my fingers across the top of it and hesitate before touching the latch. I press on it and slowly lift the lid as I close my eyes, hesitant to see what's inside it. I take a deep breath once the lid is lifted, then I open my eyes and peer down into the eyes of my mother. I pick the picture up between my trembling fingers, looking at a woman who could be no one else but the person who created me. From my mouth to my eyes to my cheekbones, I'm her. Every part of me is her.

I set the picture down and pick up the one beneath it. This one causes even more emotions to resurface, because it's a picture of both of us. I can't be older than two and I'm sitting in her lap with my arms wrapped around her neck. She's kissing me on the cheek and I'm staring at the camera with a smile bigger than life. Tears fall onto the picture in my hands, so I wipe them off and place the pictures in

Holder's hands. I need for him to see what I so desperately had to go back to my father's house for.

There's one more item in the box. I pick it up and lace the necklace through my fingers. It's a silver locket in the shape of a star. I snap it open and look at the picture of myself as an infant. Inscribed inside the locket on the side opposite the photo it says, "My ray of Hope."

I unclasp the necklace and bring it to the back of my neck. Holder reaches up and takes both clasps while I pull my hair up. He fastens it and I let my hair down, then he kisses the side of my head.

"She's beautiful. Just like her daughter." He hands the pictures back to me and kisses me gently. He looks down at my locket and opens it, then stares at it for several moments, smiling. He snaps it shut and looks back into my eyes. "Are you ready?"

I place the pictures back inside the box and shut the lid, then look back up at him confidently and nod. "I am."

Tuesday, October 30, 2012
10:15 p.m.

Holder walks inside with me this time. Karen and Jack are on the couch and he has his arm around her, holding her hand. She looks up at me when I walk through the door and Jack stands up, preparing to give us privacy once again. "It's okay," I say to him. "You don't have to leave. This won't take long."

My words concern him, but he doesn't say anything in response. He walks a few feet away from Karen so that I can sit next to her on the couch. I place the box on the table in front of her, then take my seat. I turn toward her, knowing that she has no idea what her future holds for her. Despite the fact that she has no idea what choice I've made and what's going to happen to her, she still smiles at me reassuringly. She wants me to know that she's okay with whatever I chose.

I take her hands in mine and I look her directly in the eyes. I want her to feel and believe what I'm about to say to her, because I don't want there to be anything but truth between us.

"Mom," I say, regarding her with as much confidence as I can. "When you took me from my father, you knew the potential consequences of your decision, but you did it anyway. You risked your entire life just to save mine, and I could never ask for you to suffer because of that choice.

Giving up your life for me is more than I could ever ask of you. I'm not about to judge you for what you did. The only appropriate thing for me to do at this point . . . is to thank you. So, thank you. Thank you so much for saving my life, Mom."

Her tears are now falling even harder than my own. We wrap our arms around each other and we cry. We cry mother to daughter. We cry aunt to niece. We cry victim to victim. We cry survivor to survivor.

I can't begin to imagine the life that Karen has led the past thirteen years. Every choice she made was for my benefit alone. She had assumed once I turned eighteen, that she would confess what she did and would turn herself in to face the consequences. Knowing that she loves me enough that she would be willing to give her whole life up for me almost makes me feel unworthy, now that I know that two people in this world love me in that way. It's almost too much to accept.

It turns out Karen really does want to take the next step with Jack, but she was hesitant because she knew she would break his heart once he found out the truth. What she wasn't expecting is that Jack loves her unconditionally . . . the same way she loves me. Hearing her confess her past and the choices she had to make only made him more certain about his love for her. I'm guessing that his things will be completely moved in by next weekend.

Karen spends the evening patiently answering all of my questions. My main question was that I didn't understand how I could have a legal name and the documents to back it up. Karen laughed at that question and explained that, with enough money and the right connections, I was conveniently "adopted" from out of the country and obtained my citizenship when I was seven. I don't even ask her for the details, because I'm scared to know.

Another question I needed the answer to was the most obvious one . . . could we get a TV now. Turns out she doesn't despise technology nearly as much as she had to let on over the years. I have a feeling we'll be doing some shopping in the electronics department tomorrow.

Holder and I explained to Karen how he came to find out who I was. At first, she couldn't understand how we could have had such a strong connection at that young an age . . . strong enough for him to remember me. But after seeing us interact for a while longer, I think she's convinced that our connection is real now. Unfortunately, I can also see the concern in her eyes every time he leans in to kiss me or puts his hand on my leg. She is, after all, my mother.

After several hours pass and we've all reached the most peaceful point we can possibly reach after the weekend we've had, we call it a night. Holder and Jack tell us both good-bye and Holder assures Karen that he'll never again send me another ego-deflating text. He winks at me over her shoulder when he says it, though.

Karen hugs me more than I've ever been hugged in a single day. After her final hug for the night, I go to my room and crawl into my bed. I pull the covers up over me and lock my hands together behind my head, looking up at the stars on my ceiling. I contemplated tearing them down, thinking they would only serve to bring about more negative memories. I didn't remove them, though. I'm leaving them because now when I look at them, they remind me of Hope. They remind me of *me*, and everything I've had to overcome to get to this point in my life. And while I could sit here and feel sorry for myself, wondering why all of this happened to me . . . I'm not going to do it. I'm not going to wish for a perfect life. The things that knock you down in life are tests, forcing you to make a choice between giving in and remaining on the ground or wiping the dirt off and standing up even taller than you did *before* you were knocked down. I'm choosing to stand up taller. I'll probably get knocked down a few more times before this life is through with me, but I can guarantee you I'll never stay on the ground.

There's a light tap on my bedroom window right before it rises. I smile and scoot over to my side of the bed, waiting for him to join me.

"I don't get a greeting at the window tonight?" he says in a hushed voice, lowering the window behind him. He walks to his side of my bed and lifts the covers, then scoots in beside me.

"You're freezing," I say, snuggling into his arms. "Did you walk here?"

He shakes his head and squeezes me, then kisses my forehead. "No, I ran here." He slides one of his hands down to my butt. "It's been over a week since either of us has exercised. Your ass is starting to get really huge."

I laugh and hit him on the arm. "Try to remember, the insults are only funny in text form."

"Speaking of . . . does this mean you get your phone back?"

I shrug. "I don't really want that phone back. I'm hoping my whipped boyfriend will get me an iPhone for Christmas."

He laughs and rolls on top of me, meshing his ice-cold lips with mine. The contrasting temperatures of our mouths are enough to make him groan. He kisses me until his entire body is well above room temperature again. "You know what?" He pulls up on his elbows and peers down at me with his adorable, dimpled grin.

"What?"

His voice drops into that lyrical, godlike octave again. "We've never had sex in your bed."

I contemplate his thought for half a second, then shake my head and roll him onto his back. "And it will remain that way as long my mother is down the hall."

He laughs and grabs me by the waist and pulls me on top of him. I lay my head on his chest and he wraps his arms tightly around me.

"Sky?"

"Holder?" I mimic.

"I want you to know something," he says. "And I'm not saying this as your boyfriend or even as your friend. I'm saying this because it needs to be said by someone." He stops stroking my arm and he stills his hand on the center of my back. "I'm so proud of you."

I squeeze my eyes shut and swallow his words, sending them straight to my heart. He moves his lips to my hair and kisses me for either the first time or the twentieth time or the millionth time, but who's counting?

I hug him tighter and exhale. "Thank you." I lift my head up and rest my chin on his chest, looking up at him while he smiles back at me. "And it's not what you just said that I'm thanking you for, Holder. I need to thank you for every-thing. Thank you for giving me the courage to always ask the questions, even when I didn't want the answers. Thank you for loving me like you love me. Thank you for showing me that we don't always have to be strong to be there for each other—that it's okay to be weak, so long as we're *there*. And thank you for finally finding me after all these years." I trail my fingers across his chest until they reach his arm. I run them across each letter of his tattoo, then lean forward and press my lips to it and kiss it. "But mostly, thank you for losing me all those years ago . . . because my life wouldn't be the same if you had never walked away."

My body rises and falls against his huge intake of breath. He cups my face in his hands and he attempts to smile, but it doesn't reach his pain-filled eyes. "Out of all the times I imagined what it would be like if I ever found you . . . I never thought it would end with you thanking me for losing you."

"End?" I ask, disliking the term he chose. I lift up and kiss him briefly on the lips and pull back. "I hope this isn't our end."

"Hell no, this isn't our end," he says. He tucks a stray lock of hair behind my ear and keeps his hand there. "And I wish I could say we were about to live happily ever after, but I can't. We both still have so much to work through. With everything that's happened between you, me, your mother, your dad, and what I know happened to Les . . . there will be days that I don't think we'll know how to survive. But we will. We will, because we have each other. So, I'm not worried about us, babe. I'm not worried about us at all."

I kiss him on his dimple and smile. "I'm not worried about us either. And for the record, I don't believe in happily-ever-afters."

He laughs. "Good, because you're not really getting one. All you're getting is me."

"That's all I need," I say. "Well . . . I need the lamp. And the ashtray. And the remote control. And the paddle-ball game. And you, Dean Holder. But that's *all* I need."

Thirteen years earlier

"What's he doing out there?" I ask Lesslie, looking out the living room window at Dean. He's on his back in their driveway, looking up at the sky.

"He's stargazing," she says. "He does it all the time."

I turn around and look at her. "What's stargazing?"

She shrugs her shoulders. "I dunno. That's just what he calls it when he stares at the sky for a long time."

I look out the window again and watch him for a little longer. I don't know what stargazing is, but it sounds like something I would like. I love the stars. I know my mom loved them, too, because she put them all over my room. "I want to do it," I say. "Can we go do it, too?" I look back at her but she's taking off her shoes.

"I don't want to go. You can go and I'll help my mom get our popcorn and movie ready."

I like the days I get to have sleepovers with Lesslie. I like any days I don't have to be at home. I slide off the couch and walk to the front door to slip my shoes on, then walk outside and go lie next to Dean in the driveway. He doesn't even look at me when I lie down next to him. He just keeps looking up at the sky, so I do the same thing.

The stars are really bright tonight. I've never looked up at them like this before. They're so much prettier than the stars on my ceiling. "Wow. It's so beautiful."

"I know, Hope," he says. "I know."

It's quiet for a long time. I don't know if we watch the stars for lots of minutes or hours, but we keep watching them and we don't talk. Dean doesn't really talk a whole bunch. He's a lot quieter than Lesslie.

"Hope? Will you promise me something?"

I turn my head and look at him, but he's still looking up at the stars. I've never promised anyone anything before except my daddy. I had to promise him I wouldn't tell anyone how he makes me thank him and I haven't broken his promise, even though sometimes I wish I could. If I ever did break my daddy's promise, I would tell Dean because I know he would never tell anyone.

"Yes," I say to him.

He turns his head and looks at me, but his eyes look sad. "You know sometimes when your daddy makes you cry?"

I nod my head and try not to cry just thinking about it. I don't know how Dean knows that my daddy is always the reason why I'm crying, but he does.

"Will you promise me that when he makes you sad, you'll think about the sky?"

I don't know why he wants me to promise him that but I nod anyway. "But why?"

"Because." He turns his face back up to the stars. "The sky is always beautiful. Even when it's dark or rainy or cloudy, it's still beautiful to look at. It's my favorite thing because I know if I ever get lost or lonely or scared, I just have to look up and it'll be there no matter what . . . and I know it'll always be beautiful. It's what you can think about when your daddy is making you sad, so you don't have to think about him."

I smile, even though what we're talking about is mak-

ing me sad. I just keep looking up at the sky like Dean is, thinking about what he said. It makes my heart feel happy to have somewhere to go now when I don't want to be where I am. Now when I'm scared, I'll just think about the sky and maybe it'll help me smile, because I know it'll always be beautiful no matter what.

"I promise," I whisper.

"Good," he says. He reaches his hand out and wraps his pinky around mine.

Acknowledgments

WHEN I WROTE MY first two novels, I didn't use beta readers or bloggers. (By ignorance, not choice.) I didn't even know what an ARC was.

Oh, how I wish I had.

Thank you to ALL bloggers who work so hard to share your love for reading. You are definitely the lifeline for authors, and we thank you for everything you do.

A very special thank you to Maryse, Tammara Webber, Jenny and Gitte with Totallybookedblog.com, Tina Reber, Tracey Garvis-Graves, Abbi Glines, Karly Blakemore-Mowle, Autumn with Autumnreview.com, Madison with Madisonsays.com, Molly Harper with Toughcriticbookreviews.com, Rebecca Donovan, Nichole Chase, Angie Stanton, Sarah Ross, Lisa Kane, Gloria Green, Cheri Lambert, Trisha Rai, Katy Perez, Stephanie Cohen, and Tonya Killian for taking the time to give me such detailed, incredibly helpful feedback. I know I annoyed the living hell out of most of you for the entire month of December, so thank you for putting up with my many, many, many "updated" files.

And ERMAGHERD! I can't thank you enough, Sarah Augustus Hansen. Not only for making me the most beautiful cover ever, but for granting my requests for millions of changes, only to end up going with your original suggestion. Your patience with me knows no bounds. For that, I'm declaring Holder yours. Okay.

For my husband, who insists he be listed in the acknowledgments of this book for suggesting that one word which helped me finish that one sentence in that one paragraph in that one scene. Without that word (it was *floodgates*, people) I don't think this book would have been completed. He requested I say that. But in a way he's right. Without the one word he suggested, the book more than likely would have moved along just fine. But without his support, enthusiasm, and encouragement, I could have never written a single word at all.

For my family (namely Lin, because she needs me more than anyone else). I don't really remember what everyone looks like and I'm having a hard time recalling most of your names, but now that this book is complete I vow to answer your phone calls, respond to your texts, look you in the eyes when you speak to me (rather than gazing off into the land of fiction), come to bed before four in the morning, and never, ever check an email while I'm on the phone with you again. Until I start writing my next book, anyway.

And for the three best children in the whole wide world. I miss the living hell out of y'all. And yes, boys . . . Mommy just cussed. *Again.*

About the Author

COLLEEN HOOVER is the *New York Times* bestselling author of three novels: *Slammed*, *Point of Retreat*, and *Hopeless*. She lives in Texas with her husband and their three boys. To read more about this author, visit her website at www.colleenhoover.com.

If you or someone you know needs assistance/information regarding sexual abuse, please contact www.rainn.org or call 1-800-656-HOPE.

For your local suicide hotline number, please visit www .suicidehotlines.com, http://www.suicidepreventionlifeline .com or call 800-273-TALK.

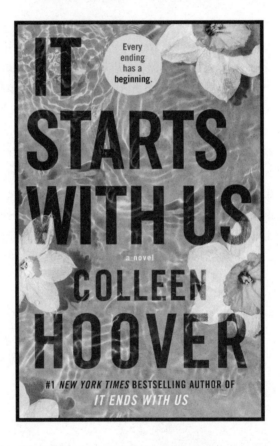